Understanding the

MYSTERIES

of

Daniel & Revelation

LOREN M.K. NELSON

Project Editor: Diane Kobor
Copy Editor: Irene Frase
Cover Designer: David Berthiaume
Text Designer: Greg Solie • AltamontGraphics.com

ISBN: 978-1-4507-1848-6

Acknowledgments

Originally I finished this work in 2005, but did not have the means to remunerate someone for editing this book until Irene Frase volunteered to do the first round of editing. A year after Irene completed her work, Pastor Bela Kobor visited my office and volunteered his wife Diane to help me get it done. With hundreds of hours editing and adding important data to this work, Diane spent the better part of a year to get this polished and ready for publishing.

People like Professor Edwin de Kock and Dr. C. Raymond Holmes encouraged me along the way. Elders Jay Gallimore, Daniel Scarone, and many others supported me and upheld this project in their prayers. Most of all, the Lord who inspired the books of Daniel and Revelation strengthened me to complete this book. The result is what you hold in your hand.

Contents

Preface

T his book provides a resource for those sharing the precious messages hidden in the chapters of Daniel and Revelation. May these pages be a ready source of information for individual and group studies as well as for those who preach from these prophetic books.

I have noticed over the years, along with many of my colleagues, a lack of this type of information. The volumes available often give no comment on verses that are key to a correct understanding of the text. Moreover, many books on Revelation give information from more than one school of interpretation. When an author picks and chooses from various schools of thought or holds all interpretations to be equal in value, this only adds to the uncertainty of interpretation and mystification of the books of prophecy.

The following paragraphs give a brief summary of the four schools of prophetic interpretation: preterism, futurism, idealism, and historicism.

Preterist School of Interpretation

Simply stated, preterism believes the book of Revelation was primarily addressed to the Christian church of the first century. The preterist views Revelation as encouragement to the church of that day to hold on to their faith through a time of terrible persecution. According to the preterist school, the main message of Revelation gives assurance that the Lord will overthrow Rome and His waiting people would be saved from Rome's tyranny.

This school of interpretation developed after the Reformers had identified the Roman Church as the Babylon of Revelation. The Jesuit Luis De Alcazar originated preterism in the early seventeenth century to counteract the Reformation's interpretation of Revelation. Preterism does not profess predictive prophecy, nor the inspiration of the book of Revelation. The writings of Scripture are simply historical documents that use the eschatological concepts of their own time.

Both preterism and futurism were part of the Counter-Reformation, the reaction within the Church of Rome to thwart the impact of the Reformation. The purpose was to divert the attention of Bible students and scholars from Rome's role in the historical sequence of events that fulfilled the prophecies of Daniel and Revelation.

Futurist School of Interpretation

Futurism believes that the prophecies of Revelation 4 and onward will take place in the future, just before the second coming of Jesus. Futurists and historicists hold the same position on the first three chapters of Revelation, believing that Revelation 1:9 to 3:22 represent the historical and successive periods of church history. Because futurists hold the position that the church will be removed from the world before Revelation 4, they feel that the rest of the prophecies of Revelation come near the end of time. In this view, the rest of Revelation only applies to the last generation of people living on the earth.

Like the preterist school, futurism was first proposed in 1585 by the Jesuit Francisco Ribera as part of the Counter-Reformation's scheme to turn aside the scriptural interpretation that pointed to the papacy as the fulfillment of the little horn of prophecy. For more than three hundred years, this was not a popular theory because Protestants still remembered their roots, both in history and the Bible. However, by the twentieth century, futurism grew popular, especially with the publication of the Scofield Bible and its futuristic footnotes. Made famous by the *Left Behind* series, this theory is now widely espoused by most Protestants who are ignorant of its Catholic origins.

Idealist School of Interpretation

As understood by the idealists, there is no historical purpose for any of the symbolic language of Revelation. They believe it is merely a description of the ongoing struggle between good and evil that has existed from time immemorial. This school does not apply the symbolic language to any actual time period or place. Idealism is heavily dependent upon preteristic ideas; consequently, many do not regard idealism as a separate school of interpretation.

Historicist School of Interpretation

Literal fulfillment of biblical prophecy marks the historicist position. This school interprets the symbols of Daniel and Revelation as representing the total history of the church till the end of time. For this school of interpretation, the books of Daniel and the Revelation are inseparable. White compares the two: "One is a prophecy, the other a revelation; one is a book sealed, the other a book opened."[1]

The strongest argument in favor of historicism is the exegesis of the biblical writers themselves. Some examples of their historicist viewpoint include Daniel in his interpretation of Jeremiah's prophecies, Isaiah's predictions on the

---

[1] Ellen G. White, Manuscript 59, 1900; quoted in *The Seventh-day Adventist Bible Commentary*, ed. F. D. Nichol, 2d ed. (Washington, DC: Review and Herald, 1980), 7:971.

fall of Babylon (Isaiah 13), and Paul's understanding of the "fullness of time" in Galatians 4:4.

The leaders of the Reformation joined the biblical authors in espousing the historicist position of interpreting prophecy. From my in-depth research of numerous historicist authors from the eighteenth to twentieth centuries, it appears that this school of interpretation has withstood the scrutiny of time. They are listed in the bibliography because of their contributions to the understanding of Daniel and Revelation.

Historicism is supported by the writers of the Bible, the Reformers, and modern scholars. In addition, the internal congruency of the Bible best fits the historicist view. This school puts all the parts of the biblical puzzle together in a logical order that matches successive historical events with precise fulfillments of prophecy. The progression of salvation's history is seen by the historicist as the prophetic fulfillment of the sanctuary's yearly service with its feasts and ceremonies. Based on the evidence, this writer takes the position that historicism comes with the strongest credentials, and thus he stays with this school of interpretation throughout the book.

Section One

Introduction to

Daniel

Daniel's Authorship

Based on internal and external evidence, this writer accepts Daniel's authorship. Why do humanist theologians argue against Daniel as the author, in spite of historical and archaeological evidence that supports his authorship? Since it is humanly impossible to declare the future with such great accuracy, skeptics think it must also be impossible for God. Because many of Daniel's prophecies have already been fulfilled, they claim the book must have been written after those historical events took place, and thus after the time of Daniel. They admit that Daniel was written many centuries ago, but parts of Daniel were still being fulfilled after the time they attribute to the writing of Daniel. No matter when they attribute its authorship, it stands as an accurate prophecy of both historical and current events. This has been their greatest embarrassment.

Some evidences of Daniel's authorship include his use of the phrase "Shushan, the citadel," his description of the Plain of Dura in Daniel 3, Daniel's relationship with Nebuchadnezzar which is linked to the chapter written by the king, the description of the final night of Belshazzar's reign, and the accuracy of stating that Daniel would be given a third part in the rule of Babylon since Belshazzar was co-regent with his father Nabonidus. In conclusion, internal evidence displays the book's accuracy and Daniel's authorship.

Major Emphases in Daniel

Judgment: Daniel means "God is judge." Thus Daniel's name gives an introduction to the theme of his book. The first chapter of Daniel describes God's judgment against Jerusalem which had been prophesied more than one hundred years earlier (2 Kings 20:16-18). Isaiah's prophetic warning came after King Hezekiah showed the glory of Israel's gold to the Babylonian ambassadors instead of giving glory to God for his healing and the miracle of the sundial going backwards ten degrees. Daniel begins with this judgment of God against Israel and concludes with His judgment "at the end of days."

Worship: Practically speaking, Daniel's book calls us to worship the Judge of the whole earth. The heavenly judgment scene portrays Him surrounded by millions of worshiping angels (Daniel 7:14). In the book of Daniel, God's people continually faced this issue. Whom will we worship, and how will we worship Him who made the heavens and the earth? Daniel and his friends considered their bodies to be the temple of God. Even though the temple in Jerusalem had been destroyed, they still had power over their own body temples, and they would not yield at any cost. God would remain on the throne of their hearts, and they would not bow down to any earthly power.

Daniel contrasts true worship with the subtlety of Babylon's system of false worship. Babylon applies cultural pressures (chapter 1) and relies on earthly wisdom and philosophy (chapter 2). Idols, worldly music, and flattery are external challenges to God's true worshippers (chapter 3), while internally they face temptations of self-worship and pride (chapter 4). Those who worship the God of heaven acknowledge His supremacy over every aspect of their lives. God's judgment brings deliverance to His people, but destruction upon all false worshippers and those who deify self (chapters 5–6).

The Time of the End: Daniel's special emphasis is the time of the end. Each group of prophecies builds on the dream given to Nebuchadnezzar in chapter 2, repeating and enlarging the prophecy with added details. Daniel ends with God's judgment and prophecies that pinpoint the time of the judgment. The last half of Daniel shows clearly that judgment comes before the earthly kingdoms are destroyed. Before Jesus comes back, He knows who will be rewarded with His kingdom. Deliverance came to Daniel and his friends because they obeyed God's will. In these last days, God's obedient worshipers will again be delivered as a result of His end-time judgment.

Sections of Daniel

The book of Daniel has two main sections. The first six chapters present real people facing life and death choices over the issue of worship, while chapters seven to twelve contain prophecies. The first half of Daniel sets the historical backdrop for the prophecies and provides divinely inspired examples of people who remained faithful when tested. More than mere historical background, these first six chapters introduce the spiritual tests and battles that relate to each prophetic scene in the second half of Daniel. Beyond the inner wrestling of each soul, every spiritual struggle has a profound effect on the lives of others. In Daniel's case, his witness transformed the lives of two kings, Nebuchadnezzar and Darius.

Through the prophecies in the second half of Daniel, God reaches out to a faithless world. Because He foretells the world's events with perfect accuracy, it is safe to trust in Him. These time prophecies provide sufficient evidence, even for the skeptics. This evidence not only pinpoints past and future events, but inspires faith in the God of heaven.

Daniel is historically and prophetically accurate. As God's love letter to you, it provides the fortification you need for the last moments of this world's history. Daniel, along with the book of Revelation, is the narrative of a loving God reaching out to His lost children. God prepares His faithful ones to stand firm until the end, like Daniel, with an uncompromising obedience.

Enjoy the book of Daniel as you never have before!

CHAPTER ONE

Daniel 1

Introduction

D aniel was born in Judah between 622 and 627 B.C. As a young man, he was taken captive to Babylon in approximately the year 605 B.C. Babylon was located on the River Euphrates, close to the site of the modern city of Baghdad in Iraq. Positioned in a flat valley between the Tigris and Euphrates Rivers, Babylon was known as "the land between the rivers."

Egypt, Lydia, and Babylon were the three divisions of the Assyrian Empire. In 626 B.C. Babylon rebelled against the Assyrian Empire and overthrew the Assyrian capital of Nineveh in 612 B.C. Babylon became the master of the Middle East when it defeated the Egyptian armies in 605 B.C. At this time, Nebuchadnezzar also subdued Jerusalem.

History records three attacks of Nebuchadnezzar against Jerusalem. In 605 B.C. he seized a selected group of captives, including Daniel and his three friends. Some of the sacred vessels of God's temple were also confiscated. During the second attack in 597 B.C., Nebuchadnezzar took more captives than before. The prophet Ezekiel was captured during this invasion, and Nebuchadnezzar seized a much larger portion of the temple's treasures. Finally, Nebuchadnezzar came for the last time in 586 B.C. Determined that rebellion would never rise again, he leveled the city and completely destroyed the temple after an extended siege. Most of the survivors went to Babylon to serve as slaves.

The first chapter gives more than an introduction and personal history of Daniel in Babylon. Far more reaching than what first meets the eye, Daniel 1 introduces the spiritual battle of this book. As Daniel began writing the comprehensive prophetic history of the world from his time to the return of Jesus, he realized the real issues in the great controversy between God and Satan. The real battle was not over the earthly city of Jerusalem with its temple, but rather the heavenly Jerusalem and our body temples. To whom will we yield our allegiance? Like Daniel and his three friends, we must keep the heavenly Jerusalem alive in our hearts and not yield our body temples to the enemy. Ultimately God will give us the heavenly Jerusalem as our inheritance.

One commentator in the *New Open Study Bible* notes that Daniel was "one of the few well-known Bible characters about whom nothing negative is ever written. His life was characterized by faith, prayer, courage, consistency, and lack of compromise. This 'greatly beloved' man (9:23; 10:11, 19) was mentioned three times by his sixth-century B.C. contemporary Ezekiel as an example of righteousness (Ezekiel 14:14, 20; 28:3)."[1]

Since chapter 1 was written as a testimony of Daniel's faithfulness to the God of Israel, it was written in Hebrew and with the Hebrews in mind, telling how God's people are pressured by culture to compromise their obedience.

Daniel 1:1: In the third year of the reign of Jehoiakim king of Judah came Nebuchadnezzar king of Babylon unto Jerusalem, and besieged it.

The third year of the reign of Jehoiakim was 606 B.C. Daniel must be understood within the contextual setting of Isaiah, Jeremiah, and Ezekiel. Jeremiah dates the conquest as the fourth year of Jehoiakim (Jeremiah 46:2). At first it appears that Daniel and Jeremiah contradict each other, when in reality they gave dates from a different perspective. Daniel dated the siege from the beginning of the campaign while Jeremiah gave the time of the final defeat. Thus Babylon's seige ended in the first part of 605 B.C. when Daniel and his friends were taken captive by Nebuchadnezzar.

Daniel 1:2: And the Lord gave Jehoiakim king of Judah into his hand, with part of the vessels of the house of God: which he carried into the land of Shinar to the house of his god; and he brought the vessels into the treasure house of his god.

Shinar and Babylon are synonymous terms because Babel or Babylon was built at Shinar (Genesis 11:2). The ancient kings did not have banks to deposit their treasures, so they used the temples of their personal gods for that purpose, believing these gods would protect their wealth. According to one archeological find, Nebuchadnezzar wrote, "Far-off lands, distant mountains, difficult roads I traversed, and the country overthrew. I bound as captives my enemies; both bad and good among the people I took under my care. Silver, gold, costly precious stones, palm-wood, cedar-wood, all kinds of precious things in rich abundance, the products of the mountains, the wealth of the seas, a heavy gift, a splendid present to my city Babylon, I brought."[2]

The Babylonians worshiped many gods of "gold and silver, bronze and iron, wood and stone" (Daniel 5:4). Before Nebuchadnezzar became a believer of the

---

[1]   *New Open Bible Study Edition of the New King James* (Nashville: Thomas Nelson Publishers, n.d.), 973.

[2]   Taylor G. Bunch, "The Book of Daniel," Typewritten manuscript, 1950, Department of Archives and Special Collections, Del Webb Memorial Library, Loma Linda University, Loma Linda, CA, 6.

true God, he entrusted himself to the care of the god Marduk or Bel Merodach and named his first-born son Evil Merodach. Bunch adds historical background: "In honor of this god Nebuchadnezzar built a great temple which together with its parks and gardens is estimated to have been not less than eight miles in circumference. In one of the king's inscriptions he calls it 'the house of heaven and earth.' He declared that he 'stored up inside it silver and gold and precious stones, and placed there the treasure-house of his kingdom.' He said that this temple of his god received 'within itself the abundant tribute of the kings of the nations, and of all people.'"[3]

Daniel 1:3-4: And the king spake unto Ashpenaz the master of his eunuchs, that he should bring certain of the children of Israel, and of the king's seed, and of the princes; [4] Children in whom was no blemish, but well favoured, and skilful in all wisdom, and cunning in knowledge, and understanding science, and such as had ability in them to stand in the king's palace, and whom they might teach the learning and the tongue of the Chaldeans.

The prophet Isaiah told Hezekiah that the king of Babylon would take all his treasures and some of his descendents, making them eunuchs in Babylon's palace (2 Kings 20:16-18). Little did Hezekiah realize that Daniel, one of his own descendents, would glorify the God of heaven where he had failed. Both Babylon and the succeeding kingdom of Medo-Persia would acknowledge the power of God to save His faithful servants.

Daniel 1:5: And the king appointed them a daily provision of the king's meat, and of the wine which he drank: so nourishing them three years, that at the end thereof they might stand before the king.

Daniel and his three friends were not only mentally outstanding, but they were also physically good looking and without blemish. The book of Daniel shows that their spiritual lives were extraordinary as well. White relates the story: "Seeing in these youth the promise of remarkable ability, Nebuchadnezzar determined that they should be trained to fill important positions in his kingdom. That they might be fully qualified for their lifework, he arranged for them to learn the language of the Chaldeans and for three years to be granted the unusual educational advantages afforded princes of the realm."[4]

This was not a regular college course, but rather what we would consider a post-graduate course in the University of Babylon since these men were to serve in the king's court. They were given the best opportunity to succeed; however, their required meals included items which God had instructed them not to eat.

---

[3]   Ibid.

[4]   Ellen G. White, *Prophets and Kings* (Mountain View, CA: Pacific Press, 1917), 480.

Daniel 1:6-7: Now among these were of the children of Judah, Daniel, Hananiah, Mishael, and Azariah: [7]Unto whom the prince of the eunuchs gave names: for he gave unto Daniel the name of Belteshazzar; and to Hananiah, of Shadrach; and to Mishael, of Meshach; and to Azariah, of Abednego.

These four names were only four among many, but they are singled out because of their faithfulness to the God of creation. Bunch explains the meaning of the new names given to Daniel and his friends:

> The kings and princes of Babylon and other pagan nations were given the names of their deities to assure them the protection and favor of their gods. Nebuchadnezzar means "Nebo protects the crown." *Nebu* represents the god Nebo; *Chad* means a vessel, and *Nezzar* is the one who watches. In other words the god Nebo cares for the vessel that contains and protects the crown. Nebo, meaning "the prophet," was the interpreter of the will of Bel-Merodach and to him was erected a shrine in the temple of Bel. Nebo was a solar deity and was supposed to be a symbol of the planet Mercury and was the celestial scribe and interpreter of the gods. He was therefore called "The god of writing and science." The dynastic titles of all pagan kings were the names of their chief gods. Pharaoh is the Hebrew for "Ph Ra," the sun, the chief God of the Egyptians. The names of all the Babylonian kings show their relation to Nebo, Bel or Baal, and Merodach.[5]

Daniel comes from two words: Dan (judge) and El (God), meaning "God is my judge." Nebuchadnezzar changed Daniel's name to Belteshazzar in honor of his god; it means "keeper of the hidden treasure of Bel" (Daniel 4:8).

Hananiah means "the Lord is gracious to me" or "to whom the Lord is gracious." This was changed to Shadrach which means "the servant of Sin" (moon god).

Mishael means "he who is like God." He was given the name Meshach, meaning "who is as Aku," the Sumerian moon god.

Azariah means "Jehovah helps." His name became Abednego, meaning "servant of Nebo" or "the servant of the shining fire."

All through Scripture, the name signified the character or characteristics of a particular person. Jacob's name meant supplanter until the night he wrestled with God. Jacob had repented and would not let go without His blessing. God granted his plea, changing his name to Israel which means "he who rules with God." **"And he said, Thy name shall be called no more Jacob, but Israel: for as a prince hast thou power with God and with men, and hast prevailed"** (Genesis 32:28).

Obviously the name changes did not affect the behavior of the four Hebrews, so the change in their names did not work as had been hoped. These four young

---

[5]   Bunch, "The Book of Daniel," 9.

men stood as proof that no matter where we are or whatever circumstances we face, we may "stand for the right though the heavens fall."[6] These young men proved that their Hebrew names were the right names. It would make sense to use their Hebrew names—Daniel, Hananiah, Mishael, and Azariah—instead of their Babylonian names—Belteshazzar, Shadrach, Meshach, and Abednego. Many today would call these young men narrow and rigid, but the world knows them as great men who changed their world.

Just think about the many worthies in the Scripture who went against popular culture. They are famous because they stood firm. It takes fortitude to be obedient to God when everyone else is unwilling. It takes courage to be a leader when everyone else follows the world's ways. It takes the power of God to stand up against ridicule and pressure to compromise. Daniel stands as a witness to those who wonder whether it is worth the cost. The answer is loud and clear, "Be faithful and God will bless!"

Daniel 1:8-17: But Daniel purposed in his heart that he would not defile himself with the portion of the king's meat, nor with the wine which he drank: therefore he requested of the prince of the eunuchs that he might not defile himself. [9]Now God had brought Daniel into favour and tender love with the prince of the eunuchs. [10]And the prince of the eunuchs said unto Daniel, I fear my lord the king, who hath appointed your meat and your drink: for why should he see your faces worse liking than the children which are of your sort? then shall ye make me endanger my head to the king. [11]Then said Daniel to Melzar, whom the prince of the eunuchs had set over Daniel, Hananiah, Mishael, and Azariah, [12]Prove thy servants, I beseech thee, ten days; and let them give us pulse to eat, and water to drink. [13]Then let our countenances be looked upon before thee, and the countenance of the children that eat of the portion of the king's meat: and as thou seest, deal with thy servants. [14]So he consented to them in this matter, and proved them ten days. [15]And at the end of ten days their countenances appeared fairer and fatter in flesh than all the children which did eat the portion of the king's meat. [16]Thus Melzar took away the portion of their meat, and the wine that they should drink; and gave them pulse. [17]As for these four children, God gave them knowledge and skill in all learning and wisdom: and Daniel had understanding in all visions and dreams.

Daniel's decision was made in his heart! Seiss pictures the scene: The temptation "was a most enticing appeal to the ambition of these young men. In the king's school, chosen for the king's service, and fed and feasted from the king's table with the food and drink of which the king himself partook, it would be difficult to imagine what could more stir and inflame the aspirations of their

---

[6]   Ellen G. White, *Education* (Mountain View, CA: Pacific Press, 1903), 57.

youthful hearts. What might they not hope when thus noticed and honored from the throne?"[7]

Bunch points out a lesson for us today: "These young men had in their characters that sterner stuff of which saints and prophets are made. The world may call them narrow and extreme but their stand was the foundation stone of their future greatness. The thing involved may seem little but principle is never small in its results in character building. He only who is faithful in the little things of life can be relied upon in the crises that make or break men's careers."[8]

The four young Hebrews took their stand in the area of diet, right where Adam and Eve failed. White brings home the importance of this seemingly small test: "What if Daniel and his companions had made a compromise with those heathen officers, and had yielded to the pressure of the occasion by eating and drinking as was customary with the Babylonians? That single instance of departure from principle would have weakened their sense of right and their abhorrence of wrong. Indulgence of appetite would have involved the sacrifice of physical vigor, clearness of intellect, and spiritual power. One wrong step would probably have led to others, until, their connection with Heaven being severed, they would have been swept away by temptation."[9]

Daniel was faithful to God and did not allow the Babylonian lifestyle to take control of his life. He would not turn over his physical sanctuary—his body, mind, and heart—to Babylonian influence. Unlike the temple in Jerusalem which the Babylonians had defiled, Daniel had control over the sanctuary of his body. He would not let them conquer his body temple, nor corrupt the sanctuary of his soul with the Babylonian lifestyle. Daniel and his friends determined to stand for God's truth no matter what the cost. By faith he went to Melzar and requested a diet of pulse. Like many people today, Melzar feared they would not fair well on such a simple diet, but granted them a ten-day test. The Babylonians were amazed when the four Hebrews faired better than their counterparts.

Verse 17 gives two important and noticeable results:

1. Increased understanding in learning.

2. Understanding of visions and dreams, which means an understanding of prophecy.

To understand prophecy as Daniel did, we must be faithful to the truths God has given us. This includes the area of diet. Had Daniel and his three friends not taken that simple stand, we no doubt would never have heard about them, nor would Daniel have been used by God to reach the highest echelons of society.

---

[7]   Joseph A. Seiss, *Voices from Babylon* (Philadelphia: Porter and Coates, 1879), 23-24.

[8]   Bunch, "The Book of Daniel," 11.

[9]   Ellen G. White, *Counsels on Health* (Mountain View, CA: Pacific Press, 1951), 66.

Daniel 1:18-20: Now at the end of the days that the king had said he should bring them in, then the prince of the eunuchs brought them in before Nebuchadnezzar. [19]And the king communed with them; and among them all was found none like Daniel, Hananiah, Mishael, and Azariah: therefore stood they before the king. [20]And in all matters of wisdom and understanding, that the king inquired of them, he found them ten times better than all the magicians and astrologers that were in all his realm.

These young men remained faithful during the ten-day test and throughout the rest of their training. At the end of the three-year time period, they were found ten times better or smarter than all the others. This was not only a tribute to the four Hebrews and their God, but also shows the understanding of King Nebuchadnezzar as he was the one who gave the examination.

This test is portrayed by White: "At the court of Babylon were gathered representatives from all lands, men of the highest talent, men the most richly endowed with natural gifts, and possessed of the broadest culture that the world could bestow; yet among them all, the Hebrew youth were without a peer. In physical strength and beauty, in mental vigor and literary attainment, they stood unrivaled. The erect form, the firm, elastic step, the fair countenance, the undimmed senses, the untainted breath—all were so many certificates of good habits, insignia of the nobility with which nature honors those who are obedient to her laws."[10]

White reasons from cause to effect: "A noble character is not the result of accident; it is not due to special favors or endowments of Providence. It is the result of self-discipline, of subjection of the lower to the higher nature, of the surrender of self to the service of God and man. . . . Intellectual power, physical stamina, and the length of life depend upon immutable laws. Through obedience to these laws, man may stand conqueror of himself, conqueror of his own inclinations, conqueror of principalities and powers, of 'the rulers of the darkness of this world,' and of 'spiritual wickedness in high places.' Ephesians 6:12."[11]

Daniel 1:21: And Daniel continued even unto the first year of king Cyrus.

What a statement of faithfulness! Daniel worked under many kings in Babylon: Nebuchadnezzar (605–561 B.C.), his son Evil Merodach (561–559 B.C.), Neriglissar (559–556 B.C.), Laborodoarchod (reigned nine months in 556 B.C.), and Nabonidis (556–539 B.C.) with whom Belshazzar co-reigned the last few years. After Babylon was defeated in 538 B.C., Daniel amazingly advanced during the reign of King Darius to become the highest political leader of the Medo-Persian Empire. Darius ruled for two years (539–537 B.C.), making the first year of Cyrus between 537 and 536 B.C., near the estimated time of Daniel's death (533 B.C.) Estimating Daniel's age to be sixteen to eighteen at the time of

[10]   White, *Prophets and Kings*, 485.

[11]   Ibid., 488-489.

the defeat of Jerusalem in 605 B.C., the date of his birth would be about 622 B.C. Thus Daniel died at approximately eighty-eight to ninety years of age. This would allow him to be a youth at the time of his capture rather than an older man. No matter which date you choose, Daniel was an old man at the time of his death, but one who had played an important role in two kingdoms as a trusted political leader under many kings.

Daniel's experience parallels that of God's people in the last days. If we remain faithful to God's word like Daniel and surrender our wills to God, we will be able to understand the prophecies more clearly than those around us!

When Nebuchadnezzar attacked God's holy city Jerusalem and the temple, he captured the temple's contents and took them to the temple of his god. He thereby changed the location of all the holy vessels and endeavored to change the character of the followers of the true God by giving them Babylonian names. Today, modern Babylon undermines true worship, attempting to transfer our loyalties from the God of heaven to a false system of worship (Revelation 13, 14, 17). Modern Babylon wishes to sit where only God should sit and rule that which only God should rule, claiming for herself the loyalty of the masses. This is the main issue in both Daniel and Revelation: whom will we worship?

Daniel 1:21 also clarifies when book of Daniel was written, and that time frame harmonizes with Daniel 10:1. In retrospect, chapter one was most likely penned around 536–537 B.C., the first year of Cyrus.

Summary

The first chapter of Daniel begins with historical facts surrounding the Babylonian attack on Jerusalem, the capture of some of the articles from the house of God (the sanctuary), and the abduction of the finest princes from the royal family. Chapter 1 gives the history of how Daniel and his three friends remained faithful to the God in heaven, the Creator of the universe, the real King of kings and Lord of lords. It tells how Nebuchadnezzar tried to undermine God's people, His truth, and His power. Nebuchadnezzar assaulted the holy city of Jerusalem and the sanctuary even as the antichrist would attack the heavenly sanctuary at a later date.

Daniel recorded how he and his friends, Hananiah, Mishael, and Azariah, remained true to God, not willing to defile their body sanctuaries, and how He blessed them with wisdom, understanding, visions, and dreams. The experience of the first chapter is given for our admonition, as an example for people living in the last days. When spiritual Babylon the great attacks the church and appears to have won, we too can remain faithful to God. When we, like Daniel, live in uncompromising obedience to the God of heaven, He unlocks of the prophecies of Daniel and Revelation for us so we can share them with others. As we live the truth and give the truth to all who will hear, we too will be strengthened by the power of God, just like Daniel and his friends.

CHAPTER TWO

Daniel 2

Introduction

Daniel 2 sends a message loud and clear: God loves man so much that He will go to extraordinary means to reach everyone. This chapter tells how the Lord of the universe reached a pagan earthly ruler, and it proclaims to every skeptic in the world that God exists. What sets the Creator apart from all other gods, is His ability to foretell the future with impeccable accuracy. In fact, God challenges anyone who is willing and honest to put Him to the test. This gauntlet is thrown down to all religions of the world. "World, can your supreme being foretell the future? Does your holy book predict the future with infallible accuracy? If not, how can you say your god is who he claims to be? How do we know he exists without proof?"

The second chapter of Daniel presents the history of the world from Nebuchadnezzar's time into the future. All may know that the Lord God of the Bible is like no other, foretelling the future with such great accuracy that all must stand in awe and ultimately believe that He is the only true God. Those who believe in the God of heaven can stand secure while other gods and religions fall short. No other religion has a deity like this! Only the Creator God of the Bible can foretell the future with unerring accuracy.

Although prophetic in nature, Daniel 2 tells how God gave evidence to an earthly king so that he might believe in the one and only God in heaven, the Potentate of the universe. Enjoy as Daniel 2 unfolds and challenges all other belief systems. Rejoice as God gives prophecy as one more reason to believe in Him!

The date for this dream would be approximately 601 B.C. Daniel and his friends were taken to Babylon in 605 B.C. and graduated from the University of Babylon in 602 B.C. Nebuchadnezzar's dream came one year later in 601 B.C.

Chapters 2 to 7 are written in Aramaic, the international language of the Middle East, because these messages describe religio-political events in Babylon and Medo-Persia as well as the future course of the Gentile powers.

Daniel 2:1-13: And in the second year of the reign of Nebuchadnezzar Nebuchadnezzar dreamed dreams, wherewith his spirit was troubled, and

his sleep brake from him. ²Then the king commanded to call the magicians, and the astrologers, and the sorcerers, and the Chaldeans, for to show the king his dreams. So they came and stood before the king. ³And the king said unto them, I have dreamed a dream, and my spirit was troubled to know the dream. ⁴Then spake the Chaldeans to the king in Syriack, O king, live for ever: tell thy servants the dream, and we will show the interpretation. ⁵The king answered and said to the Chaldeans, The thing is gone from me: if ye will not make known unto me the dream, with the interpretation thereof, ye shall be cut in pieces, and your houses shall be made a dunghill. ⁶But if ye show the dream, and the interpretation thereof, ye shall receive of me gifts and rewards and great honour: therefore show me the dream, and the interpretation thereof. ⁷They answered again and said, Let the king tell his servants the dream, and we will show the interpretation of it. ⁸The king answered and said, I know of certainty that ye would gain the time, because ye see the thing is gone from me. ⁹But if ye will not make known unto me the dream, there is but one decree for you: for ye have prepared lying and corrupt words to speak before me, till the time be changed: therefore tell me the dream, and I shall know that ye can show me the interpretation thereof. ¹⁰The Chaldeans answered before the king, and said, There is not a man upon the earth that can show the king's matter: therefore there is no king, lord, nor ruler, that asked such things at any magician, or astrologer, or Chaldean. ¹¹And it is a rare thing that the king requireth, and there is none other that can show it before the king, except the gods, whose dwelling is not with flesh. ¹²For this cause the king was angry and very furious, and commanded to destroy all the wise men of Babylon. ¹³And the decree went forth that the wise men should be slain; and they sought Daniel and his fellows to be slain.

The siege of Jerusalem occurred in the third year of the reign of Jehoiakim (Daniel 1:1). It appears to be the first year of the reign of Nebuchadnezzar as he is called king, but in reality, Nebuchadnezzar was not yet the sole ruler of Babylon. He co-reigned with his father Nabopolassar for two years before his father's death; then Nebuchadnezzar became the sole ruler of Babylon. This explains the apparent discrepancy in dates. Daniel 5 reveals another co-regency in Babylon.

The second year of Nebuchadnezzar was actually the fourth year of Daniel's captivity. He and his friends had been wise men for about a year. The king's dream would bring Daniel and his three friends into the limelight quickly and elevate these four young Jews to prominence, setting the framework for the salvation of King Nebuchadnezzar.

Troubled and sleepless, the king called for the magicians, astrologers, sorcerers, and Chaldeans to tell him what he had dreamed. However, they depended upon knowing the dream in order to give the king an explanation. Bunch mentions some of the methods of interpretation used by these wise men:

What an array of mighty men. They represent the wisdom and scholar-
ship of all nations. They were the priests and prophets of the gods of
Babylon which were considered the chief of all gods. There stood the
magicians, the cunning and crafty ancestors of the Magi. They pretend-
ed to be able to reveal the secrets of the gods through magic and divina-
tion. They believed in the presence of good and evil spirits with the latter
predominating. To these spirits they made offerings, intoned hymns and
made lamentations. They believed that all evil came as a result of the
ill-will of the spirits or at the instigation of human enemies. Like the
witch doctors of Africa they sought to discover the name of the enemy
by use of "charms," "spells," "omens" and "magic." Many clay tablets have
been found in the ruins of Babylonian palaces describing the magic of
the magicians.[1]

Nebuchadnezzar's wise men claimed to be in touch with the gods, with the
ability to interpret the gods' messages to the king, but their gods were not gods at
all. King Nebuchadnezzar was now keenly aware of this when they were unable
to deliver. His reasoned correctly that if they were in touch with the gods, then
the gods would make known to them not only the interpretation but also the
dream itself. Smith presents Nebuchadnezzar's point of view:

Some have severely censured Nebuchadnezzar in this matter, as act-
ing the part of a heartless, unreasonable tyrant. But what did these magicians profess to be able to do?—To reveal hidden things, to foretell
events, to make known mysteries entirely beyond human foresight and
penetration, and to do this by the aid of supernatural agencies. There
was nothing unjust in Nebuchadnezzar's demand that they should make
known his dream. When they declared that none but the gods whose
dwelling was not with flesh could make known the king's matter, it was
tacit acknowledgment that they had no communication with these gods,
and knew nothing beyond what human wisdom and discernment could
reveal. "For this cause the king was angry and very furious."[2]

Bunch relates the spiritualism of ancient Babylon to that of Rome: "The sorcerers claimed to hold communion with the spirits of the dead and were therefore spiritist mediums. Spiritism had its origin in Babylon. The Chaldeans were
the great philosophers and wise men of the Babylonians. They were the leaders
of all the groups. They were the professors who had taught Daniel and his fellows
the sciences and languages of their order. The fact that the king was a Chaldean
gave them special favor at court and a place next to the throne. All of those
groups combined to make up the 'College of Pontiffs' which was the ancestor of

[1]   Bunch, "The Book of Daniel," 15-16.

[2]   Uriah Smith, *The Prophecies of Daniel and the Revelation* (Nashville: Southern
Publishing Association, 1944), 31.

the 'College of Cardinals' in Roman Catholicism, which is almost an exact duplicate of the religious system of ancient Babylon and is therefore called 'Babylon the Great.'"[3]

The groundwork was set for God to make Himself known to Nebuchadnezzar. Before this, Nebuchadnezzar believed his gods were superior to the God of Israel because he had defeated His people in battle and conquered them. Now the Lord allowed him to see that his gods were no gods at all. The men who claimed to represent the gods of Babylon with philosophy and earthly wisdom were no challenge for Him. The God of heaven made Himself known as King of the universe, showing that Nebuchadnezzar and other kings ruled only at His will.

Daniel 2:14-23: Then Daniel answered with counsel and wisdom to Arioch the captain of the king's guard, which was gone forth to slay the wise men of Babylon: [15]He answered and said to Arioch the king's captain, Why is the decree so hasty from the king? Then Arioch made the thing known to Daniel. [16]Then Daniel went in, and desired of the king that he would give him time, and that he would show the king the interpretation. [17]Then Daniel went to his house, and made the thing known to Hananiah, Mishael, and Azariah, his companions: [18]That they would desire mercies of the God of heaven concerning this secret; that Daniel and his fellows should not perish with the rest of the wise men of Babylon. [19]Then was the secret revealed unto Daniel in a night vision. Then Daniel blessed the God of heaven. [20]Daniel answered and said, Blessed be the name of God for ever and ever: for wisdom and might are his: [21]And he changeth the times and the seasons: he removeth kings, and setteth up kings: he giveth wisdom unto the wise, and knowledge to them that know understanding: [22]He revealeth the deep and secret things: he knoweth what is in the darkness, and the light dwelleth with him. [23]I thank thee, and praise thee, O thou God of my fathers, who hast given me wisdom and might, and hast made known unto me now what we desired of thee: for thou hast now made known unto us the king's matter.

Why were Daniel and his three friends, recently pronounced ten times more intelligent than all the other wise men in the realm, left out of this counsel meeting? Divine intervention was leading. If the Hebrews were questioned initially, they would have taken it to God right away, and the magicians would not have been threatened. Their claims would have remained intact. By leaving out Daniel and his friends, it was only fair to give them time to commune with their God. The king granted their request, and the four friends immediately held a prayer meeting, knowing that only the God of heaven could reveal the dream. When Daniel was given the same dream, the young Hebrews held a praise service to God as their first priority.

---

[3]   Bunch, "The Book of Daniel," 16.

Daniel 2:24-49: Therefore Daniel went in unto Arioch, whom the king had ordained to destroy the wise men of Babylon: he went and said thus unto him; Destroy not the wise men of Babylon: bring me in before the king, and I will show unto the king the interpretation. [25]Then Arioch brought in Daniel before the king in haste, and said thus unto him, I have found a man of the captives of Judah, that will make known unto the king the interpretation. [26]The king answered and said to Daniel, whose name was Belteshazzar, Art thou able to make known unto me the dream which I have seen, and the interpretation thereof? [27]Daniel answered in the presence of the king, and said, The secret which the king hath demanded cannot the wise men, the astrologers, the magicians, the soothsayers, show unto the king; [28]But there is a God in heaven that revealeth secrets, and maketh known to the king Nebuchadnezzar what shall be in the latter days. Thy dream, and the visions of thy head upon thy bed, are these; [29]As for thee, O king, thy thoughts came into thy mind upon thy bed, what should come to pass hereafter: and he that revealeth secrets maketh known to thee what shall come to pass. [30]But as for me, this secret is not revealed to me for any wisdom that I have more than any living, but for their sakes that shall make known the interpretation to the king, and that thou mightest know the thoughts of thy heart. [31]Thou, O king, sawest, and behold a great image. This great image, whose brightness was excellent, stood before thee; and the form thereof was terrible. [32]This image's head was of fine gold, his breast and his arms of silver, his belly and his thighs of brass, [33]His legs of iron, his feet part of iron and part of clay. [34]Thou sawest till that a stone was cut out without hands, which smote the image upon his feet that were of iron and clay, and brake them to pieces. [35]Then was the iron, the clay, the brass, the silver, and the gold, broken to pieces together, and became like the chaff of the summer threshingfloors; and the wind carried them away, that no place was found for them: and the stone that smote the image became a great mountain, and filled the whole earth. [36]This is the dream; and we will tell the interpretation thereof before the king. [37]Thou, O king, art a king of kings: for the God of heaven hath given thee a kingdom, power, and strength, and glory. [38]And wheresoever the children of men dwell, the beasts of the field and the fowls of the heaven hath he given into thine hand, and hath made thee ruler over them all. Thou art this head of gold. [39]And after thee shall arise another kingdom inferior to thee, and another third kingdom of brass, which shall bear rule over all the earth. [40]And the fourth kingdom shall be strong as iron: forasmuch as iron breaketh in pieces and subdueth all things: and as iron that breaketh all these, shall it break in pieces and bruise. [41]And whereas thou sawest the feet and toes, part of potters' clay, and part of iron, the kingdom shall be divided; but there shall be in it of the strength of the iron, forasmuch as thou sawest the iron mixed with miry clay. [42]And as the toes of the feet were part of iron, and part of clay, so the kingdom shall be partly strong, and partly broken. [43]And whereas thou sawest iron mixed with miry clay, they shall mingle themselves with the seed of men: but they shall not cleave one to another, even as iron is not mixed with clay. ⁴⁴And in the days of these kings shall the God of heaven set up a kingdom, which shall never be destroyed: and the kingdom shall not be left to other people, but it shall break in pieces and consume all these kingdoms, and it shall stand for ever. ⁴⁵Forasmuch as thou sawest that the stone was cut out of the mountain without hands, and that it brake in pieces the iron, the brass, the clay, the silver, and the gold; the great God hath made known to the king what shall come to pass hereafter: and the dream is certain, and the interpretation thereof sure. ⁴⁶Then the king Nebuchadnezzar fell upon his face, and worshipped Daniel, and commanded that they should offer an oblation and sweet odours unto him. ⁴⁷The king answered unto Daniel, and said, Of a truth it is, that your God is a God of gods, and a Lord of kings, and a revealer of secrets, seeing thou couldest reveal this secret. ⁴⁸Then the king made Daniel a great man, and gave him many great gifts, and made him ruler over the whole province of Babylon, and chief of the governors over all the wise men of Babylon. ⁴⁹Then Daniel requested of the king, and he set Shadrach, Meshach, and Abednego, over the affairs of the province of Babylon: but Daniel sat in the gate of the king.

Ironically, Arioch claimed credit, saying "I have found" to the king (Dan 2:25). In contrast, Daniel gave all the glory to God and told the king about the One who reveals secrets. Daniel's answer challenged the Babylonian system that in all its pomp and circumstance could not deliver anything of real importance or substance. It was all outward form and adorning, yet this still draws people today toward Babylon and away from God. Make no mistake; Babylon's religion will be more popular than that of Daniel's God even in the last days. The following chapters tell more of Babylon's enticements.

God revealed to the king not only the dream but also the clear interpretation of the dream. He showed the king where he was in the stream of history. Nebuchadnezzar had been pondering the future. He had conquered the then-known world and wondered about the future of his kingdom. At this precise moment God intervened in his life with a dream. The God of the universe wanted Nebudchadnezzar to realize that there are tomorrows and consequences in our lives.

Daniel reminded Nebuchadnezzar of his dream. The great image was in living color! The head was gold, its chest and arms of silver, the belly and thighs of bronze, iron legs, and feet made of iron and clay. This strange image demanded an explanation, so the God of heaven also gave the meaning of the dream.

Daniel immediately began the interpretation before the king could distract him, declaring, "You are this head of gold." Babylon, the first kingdom in the dream, was the head of gold, but not the first kingdom to rule the world. Before Nebuchadnezzar's rule, Egypt and Assyria were the first kingdoms that controlled the world. This dream began with the current kingdom because God knew the arrogant heart of the king. Notwithstanding, God loved him and reached out to him. When man really knows his Creator, he realizes that God is in control. God used the most precious metal known to man, giving Nebuchadnezzar self worth in order to reach his heart. Babylon was the golden head, but the dream continued. Nebuchadnezzar was not just pondering the near future, but the destiny of the world. God told him what would happen in the "latter days."

Gold was followed by silver, bronze, iron, and the mixture of iron and clay, giving Nebuchadnezzar the history of the world before it happened. No doubt he had hoped that his kingdom would last forever, but God showed him the culmination of time, ending with the only everlasting kingdom in the universe.

The Head of Gold: God revealed the interpretation to Daniel—Babylon was the golden kingdom in this image. Bunch elaborates the glories of ancient Babylon:

> The city of Babylon has never been out rivaled. Located in the garden of the East it was 15 miles square and 60 miles in circumference. Fifty-six Philadelphias as laid out by William Penn could have been enclosed within its walls, and three of the modern Philadelphias with its parks and suburbs and rivers included could have been placed within the confines of Babylon. The wall around the city was not less than 150 feet high and enclosed not less than 230 square miles and embodied more solid masonry than the Great Chinese Wall. The walls were pierced by 100 gates of solid brass at the ends of the fifty streets, which were each 15 miles long and 150 feet wide. The city was filled with fields and gardens and parks and beautiful buildings. There were two great palaces "themselves very wildernesses of architectural magnificence and artistic adornment." (Seiss). The city was adorned with artificial mountains or "hanging gardens" reaching above the heights of the wall and with many mighty temples the very ruins of which have left piles of rubbish 140 feet in height.[4]

Using Nebuchadnezzar's own inscription, Bunch records the king's pride in this great city:

> The great double wall of Babylon I built. Buttresses for the embankment of its moat I completed. Two long embankments with cement and brick I made, and with the embankments which my father made I joined them. I strengthened the city. Across the river westward, I built the wall of Babylon with brick, the walls of the fortress of Babylon, its defense in war I raised. I caused to be put in order the double doors of bronze, and the railings and the gratings, in the great gateways. I enlarged the streets of Babylon so as to make them wonderful. I applied myself to the protection of Babylon and on the most elevated lands, close to the great gate of Ishtar, I constructed strong fortresses of bitumen and bricks, from the

---

4   Ibid., 24.

banks of the Euphrates down to the great gate, the whole extent of the streets. I established their foundations below the level of the waters. I fortified the walls with art. I surrounded the land with mighty streams; to cross them was as it were to cross the ocean. To render a flood from their midst impossible I heaped up masses of earth. I set up brick dams round about them."[5]

After the ravages of the Flood, ancient Babel became the first new city-state, founded before any other government in the world. The importance of Babylon as the progenitor of all false religion is defended by Bunch:

Babylon had been founded by Nimrod 1500 years before and it was at the very height of its glory during the reign of Nebuchadnezzar. It was the center of the world's wisdom and culture and later of its corruption. It had been the birthplace and incubator of idolatry and the breeding-place of every false and counterfeit religion. It was the "mother of all the abominations of the earth." It took courage for the young prophet to tell the haughty Nebuchadnezzar that only the head of the great image representing the history of the world signified Babylon, and that it would be superseded by another. God's decree for Babylon was far different from the meditations of the king as he retired the night of his dream. Nebuchadnezzar was sure that such a city and kingdom as that over which he ruled would stand forever. This belief was later manifested by the erection of a great image all of gold.[6]

The Babylonian kingdom ruled the world from 605 B.C. until they were conquered by Medo-Persia in 539 B.C.

Chest and arms of silver: These represented the kingdom that conquered Babylon: Medo-Persia. The Medo-Persian Empire lasted from 539 B.C. to 331 B.C. and was conquered by Alexander the Great.

From a human standpoint, Babylon seemed invincible. As silver is inferior to gold, the kingdom of the Medes and Persians was inferior to Babylon in its glory. Daniel 5:28 records the fall of Babylon and its overthrow by the Medes and Persians. As the chest and arms of the image had two shoulders and two arms, the kingdom that followed Babylon was a dual kingdom, two nations bound together by one ruler.

The Medes were the first to revolt against Babylon, and soon the Persians joined them. Bunch helps us to understand the complicated family relationships between Babylon, Media, and Persia: "The combined armies under the leadership of Cyrus, the Persian general, conquered the kingdom of Lydia and later the province and city of Babylon. Cyrus was the nephew of Darius the Median king. Darius was but one year older than Cyrus and the two were practically

---

[5]   Ibid., 24-25.

[6]   Ibid., 25.

joint-rulers until the death of Darius two years later left Cyrus the sole ruler of the new world empire. The father of Darius was Astyages whose sister was the wife of Nebuchadnezzar. Mandana, the daughter of Astyages and sister of Darius was the mother of Cyrus."[7] Mandana and Darius the Mede were brother and sister, and their aunt was Amytis, wife of Nebuchadnezzar.

Why would God call a heathen king His servant? Bunch explains: "Just as God chose Nebuchadnezzar as His *servant* in the punishment of the nations including the kingdom of Judah, so the Lord chose Cyrus as His servant in the punishing of wicked and corrupt Babylon. One hundred and fifty years before Cyrus was born, and 174 years before he conquered Babylon, the Lord had foretold his birth and career and declared of him: 'He is my shepherd, and shall perform all My pleasure.' See Isaiah 44:28; 45:1-5."[8]

The Persian religion was free of images and personal gods because its adherents worshiped the elements. Therefore the Lord said to Cyrus, "I am the LORD, and there is no other; there is no God besides Me. I will gird you, though you have not known Me, that they may know from the rising of the sun to its setting that there is none besides Me. I am the LORD, and there is no other; I form the light and create darkness, I make peace and create calamity; I, the LORD, do all these things" (Isaiah 54:5-7).

The Persians believed in two ruling principles: good and evil as represented by light and darkness respectively. Their chief god was Mithras; the religious system was founded by Zoroaster. Bunch suggests that these beliefs were closer to Judaism than idolatry: "The purity of the Zoroastrian religion doubtless made the hearts of Darius, Cyrus, and later Persian kings fertile ground for the religion of Jehovah and accounts for their warm friendship for Daniel, Zerubbabel, Ezra and Nehemiah, and the favors granted them and their people."[9]

Belly and thighs of bronze: This symbolized the kingdom of Greece that conquered Medo-Persia at the battles of Granicus, Issus, and Arbela. Greece conquered the Medo-Persian Empire with a relatively small Grecian army in just eight years.

The Battle of Granicus, fought May 22, 334 B.C., opened the whole area of Asia Minor for the Greeks. With the next major battle at Issus in November, 333 B.C., everything in Asia west of the Euphrates came under Alexander's authority. Finally, at the Battle of Arbela in 331 B.C., the remaining portion of the Medo-Persian Empire fell to Greece. From that point on, Alexander conquered all the way to India in the east, Egypt in the south, and Macedonia and Greece in the west. At thirty-two years of age, Alexander died on June 23, 323 B.C. His life was cut short due to his lifestyle.

---

[7]   Ibid., 27.

[8]   Ibid.

[9]   Ibid., 28.

Legs of iron: These symbolized the empire of Rome which was known as the iron monarchy. Later Rome was divided into the Eastern and Western Roman Empire, matching the two legs of iron. Rome took control of the then-known world in 168 B.C. and ruled until it broke apart from within, around A.D. 476.

Daniel 2:41-43 And whereas thou sawest the feet and toes, part of potters' clay, and part of iron, the kingdom shall be divided; but there shall be in it of the strength of the iron, forasmuch as thou sawest the iron mixed with miry clay. ⁴²And as the toes of the feet were part of iron, and part of clay, so the kingdom shall be partly strong, and partly broken. ⁴³And whereas thou sawest iron mixed with miry clay, they shall mingle themselves with the seed of men: but they shall not cleave one to another, even as iron is not mixed with clay.

Feet of iron and clay fitly represent what happened to the Roman Empire as it shattered apart, fully divided around A.D. 476. Like the symbols of iron and clay, some of the ten divisions were weak as clay and others as strong as iron.

They will not adhere to one another: These words have stood the test of time. Men such as Charlemagne, Charles V, Louis XIV, Napoleon, Kaiser Wilhelm, and Hitler have grappled against these words and failed. The Communist Soviet Union was destined for failure as it fought against God's word. In foretelling the future, the validity of the Bible has been vindicated. Time and again, monarchies sought to unite the world through marriages, fulfilling the prophecy, "They shall mingle themselves with the seed of men (Daniel 2:43). Bunch delineates the close family ties in Europe which played a role in the events that led to World War I:

> King Christian IX of Denmark had six children, three sons and three daughters. The eldest son became Frederick VIII of Denmark. The eldest daughter married Edward, the Prince of Wales, and became Queen Alexandria of England. The second son, Prince William, became the king of Greece and was known as George V. The second daughter married Czar Alexander of Russia. The two sons of Frederick VIII, king of Denmark, took the thrones of Denmark and Norway. A son of the Empress of Russia became Czar Nicholas, and a son of Queen Alexandria of England became George V, and a son of George V of Greece became Constantine X of Greece. Thus the kings of Norway, Denmark, Russia, England, and Greece were first cousins, all being grandsons of Christian IX of Denmark.[10]

During the nineteenth century, five major families dominated Europe: the **Hapsburgs** of Austria, **Hohenzollerns** of Germany and Prussia, **Romanovs** of Russia, **Bourbons** of France, and **Ottomans** of Turkey and the Middle East. The house of Bourbon was the first to fall, although they remained loyal to their

---

[10] Ibid., 30.

treaties with the Czar of Russia. The rest of the families lost power during World War I which began in June of 1914 when Austrian Prince Francis Ferdinand was assassinated by a Serbian terrorist during his visit to Sarajevo.

After the assassination the German Hohenzollerns made an alliance with the Hapsburgs of Austria. This brought Russia into the altercation and they called upon their alliance with France. Soon England and the United States were involved and thus began the World War that was supposed to end all wars. Again the Word of God was tested and proven to be accurate.

Daniel 2:44-45: And in the days of these kings shall the God of heaven set up a kingdom, which shall never be destroyed: and the kingdom shall not be left to other people, but it shall break in pieces and consume all these kingdoms, and it shall stand for ever. ⁴⁵Forasmuch as thou sawest that the stone was cut out of the mountain without hands, and that it brake in pieces the iron, the brass, the clay, the silver, and the gold; the great God hath made known to the king what shall come to pass hereafter: and the dream is certain, and the interpretation thereof sure.

In the days of these kings: For years, Europe has attempted to unite by marriage alliances and political treaties. All these imperfect kingdoms will be swept away when Jesus the Rock comes again. In contrast to these earthly kingdoms that were set up and taken down, the kingdom of the King of kings will last forever. This "dream is certain and its interpretation sure" (Daniel 2:45).

The stone cut out of the mountain without hands: Notice what this stone does. First, it is cut out of the mountain without hands, signifying this is not a human work. Next, it has power to destroy all the world's greatest kingdoms. In the end, this stone strikes the image and destroys it, becoming a mountain that fills the whole earth. This is God's kingdom and it will stand forever.

Daniel 2:46-49: Then the king Nebuchadnezzar fell upon his face, and worshipped Daniel, and commanded that they should offer an oblation and sweet odours unto him. ⁴⁷The king answered unto Daniel, and said, Of a truth it is, that your God is a God of gods, and a Lord of kings, and a revealer of secrets, seeing thou couldest reveal this secret. ⁴⁸Then the king made Daniel a great man, and gave him many great gifts, and made him ruler over the whole province of Babylon, and chief of the governors over all the wise men of Babylon. ⁴⁹Then Daniel requested of the king, and he set Shadrach, Meshach, and Abednego, over the affairs of the province of Babylon: but Daniel sat in the gate of the king.

Such respect from a heathen king! Like a preview of future chapters, this is but the beginning of Nebuchadnezzar's respect and reverence for the God of Daniel. May all earthly rulers show God this much respect and realize that all is overseen by the Potentate of the universe. May all rulers make God's representatives here on earth their counselors in the important issues of life. Unselfishly,

Daniel does not presume to take all the rewards from the king, but shares them with his three prayer partners.

Summary

Daniel 2 describes how God reached out to an earthly ruler and revealed Himself, using extraordinary means in order to reach this pagan ruler. The King of the universe gave Nebuchadnezzar an brief outline of future world events. This portion of prophecy gives all the evidence one would need as a basis for faith and challenges all who do not believe in the God of heaven. Daniel 2 reveals what will happen in the future, but more importantly, this message still draws men and women to believe in the "Lord of kings" and learn His plan for their lives (Daniel 2:47).

Nebuchadnezzar attacked and destroyed God's holy city of Jerusalem and the sanctuary. Daniel 2 reminds us that the God of heaven lives in a sanctuary made without hands, one that man cannot destroy. This prophecy sets itself in time, starting with the kingdoms of Daniel's day and moving to the time of the end. After the kings of the earth attempt to unite by marriages and alliances, Jesus will come again. In the place of the kings of this earth, God will set up His kingdom. The center of God's kingdom is the sanctuary in heaven where His throne resides, and His sanctuary and kingdom will never be destroyed. "The dream is certain and the interpretation thereof is sure" (Daniel 2:45).

CHAPTER THREE

Daniel 3

Introduction

A ccording to Daniel 3, worship remains the issue of the great controversy between God and Satan. Our great Redeemer who created and sustains mankind by His power commands all to worship Him. On the other hand, Satan, a created and fallen angel, also desires mankind's allegiance and worship. Herein lies the battleground of the controversy between Christ and Satan.

This battle pits the invisible against the visible. False worship deals only with the external or visible form with all kinds of music appealing to the tastes of the carnal heart. God wants our hearts, so the battle is over the hearts of men and women. True worship delineates what God deserves versus our own selfish desires; the unseen versus the seen.

In Daniel 2, God made His will known to Nebuchadnezzar. Daniel and his friends acknowledged the power of God and testified to others that He is in control, knowing the end from the beginning. In spite of this evidence, Nebuchadnezzar had already forgotten his confession of the God of gods and Lord of kings. Babylon of old parallels Babylon the great. The issue is the same for both. Whom shall we worship? What constitutes true worship?

Nebuchadnezzar rejected the fact that his kingdom would come to an end, replaced by a weaker kingdom. After the inferior kingdom of silver, each successive kingdom would be lower in value although stronger, but Nebuchadnezzar ignored this remarkable evidence from God. Like many today, he rejected God's predictions. Nebuchadnezzar foolishly believed he knew better than God, and he wanted to determine the future himself.

Nebuchadnezzar believed that if he made an image entirely of gold, it could revolutionize or change the future. He did not realize that outward forms do not change eternal truth and cannot replace true worship. In Nebuchadnezzar's day, men thought ceremonies and music were the essence of worship. The same was true in Jesus' day. When the woman of Samaria asked where should true worship be conducted, Jesus ably answered, **"The hour cometh, and now is, when the true worshippers shall worship the Father in spirit and in truth: for the**

Father seeketh such to worship him. God is a Spirit: and they that worship him must worship him in spirit and in truth" (John 4:23, 24). Worship must be based in God's truth and empowered by the Spirit, thereby yielding the fruit of uncompromising obedience.

Daniel 3:1-7: Nebuchadnezzar the king made an image of gold, whose height was threescore cubits, and the breadth thereof six cubits: he set it up in the plain of Dura, in the province of Babylon. ²Then Nebuchadnezzar the king sent to gather together the princes, the governors, and the captains, the judges, the treasurers, the counsellors, the sheriffs, and all the rulers of the provinces, to come to the dedication of the image which Nebuchadnezzar the king had set up. ³Then the princes, the governors, and captains, the judges, the treasurers, the counsellors, the sheriffs, and all the rulers of the provinces, were gathered together unto the dedication of the image that Nebuchadnezzar the king had set up; and they stood before the image that Nebuchadnezzar had set up. ⁴Then an herald cried aloud, To you it is commanded, O people, nations, and languages, ⁵That at what time ye hear the sound of the cornet, flute, harp, sackbut, psaltery, dulcimer, and all kinds of music, ye fall down and worship the golden image that Nebuchadnezzar the king hath set up: ⁶And whoso falleth not down and worshippeth shall the same hour be cast into the midst of a burning fiery furnace. ⁷Therefore at that time, when all the people heard the sound of the cornet, flute, harp, sackbut, psaltery, and all kinds of music, all the people, the nations, and the languages, fell down and worshipped the golden image that Nebuchadnezzar the king had set up.

In today's terms, the size of the image would be between nine and ten stories high. If you add a pedestal which supported most massive images of that day, it would have been more than ten stories high (over one hundred feet). Some believe this image was of Nebuchadnezzar, but the language does not lend itself to that. The only indication of the image's form is the context, the image of Nebuchadnezzar's dream. The image of Daniel 3, however, is not made of multiple metals; it is pure gold from head to foot. The dimensions are not in proportion to a man's form, but rather more in line with an obelisk, so common in the world at that time!

The image of jealousy in Ezekiel and Nebuchadnezzar's false image foreshadow the power revealed in Revelation 13, the beast power which is later identified in Revelation 17 as "Babylon the great." Although Nebuchadnezzar's Babylon was a golden kingdom, it ruled only a limited space in the Middle East. Babylon the great will be a world power with both civil and religious authority. Ancient Babylon's exercise of civil and religious authority in rebellion against God parallels Revelation's Babylon the great. In fact, all the rebellious features of Babylon, Medo-Persia, Greece, and Rome will be revived in Babylon the great. These similarities are further seen as Revelation 13 refers to Babylon the great with imagery from the book of Daniel.

All the important people of the kingdom of Babylon were invited to this event. The command was made to all and it was clear. The three Hebrew worthies had already made up their minds beforehand. They had time to decide and pray while those from all over the kingdom arrived on the specified day! The three Hebrews were from Babylon and not from a far place. The command was made plain; those who did not bow down and worship the image would be put to death. Like God's last-day people in the book of Revelation, they boldly faced a death decree.

Daniel 3:8-18: Wherefore at that time certain Chaldeans came near, and accused the Jews. ⁹They spake and said to the king Nebuchadnezzar, O king, live for ever. ¹⁰Thou, O king, hast made a decree, that every man that shall hear the sound of the cornet, flute, harp, sackbut, psaltery, and dulcimer, and all kinds of music, shall fall down and worship the golden image: ¹¹And whoso falleth not down and worshippeth, that he should be cast into the midst of a burning fiery furnace. ¹²There are certain Jews whom thou hast set over the affairs of the province of Babylon, Shadrach, Meshach, and Abednego; these men, O king, have not regarded thee: they serve not thy gods, nor worship the golden image which thou hast set up. ¹³Then Nebuchadnezzar in his rage and fury commanded to bring Shadrach, Meshach, and Abednego. Then they brought these men before the king. ¹⁴ Nebuchadnezzar spake and said unto them, Is it true, O Shadrach, Meshach, and Abednego, do not ye serve my gods, nor worship the golden image which I have set up? ¹⁵Now if ye be ready that at what time ye hear the sound of the cornet, flute, harp, sackbut, psaltery, and dulcimer, and all kinds of music, ye fall down and worship the image which I have made; well: but if ye worship not, ye shall be cast the same hour into the midst of a burning fiery furnace; and who is that God that shall deliver you out of my hands? ¹⁶Shadrach, Meshach, and Abednego, answered and said to the king, O Nebuchadnezzar, we are not careful to answer thee in this matter. ¹⁷If it be so, our God whom we serve is able to deliver us from the burning fiery furnace, and he will deliver us out of thine hand, O king. ¹⁸But if not, be it known unto thee, O king, that we will not serve thy gods, nor worship the golden image which thou hast set up.

The issue is worship. This is not just the public unveiling of a statue. All are commanded to fall down and worship. As believers of the invisible God, falling down and worshiping this image would be a denial of God. By doing so, they would exchange the invisible God for a visible image. They understood this challenge as it really was: to fall down and worship this image would be a denial of their faith. All forms of idolatry steal worship from the Creator who rightfully deserves it. One of the Ten Commandments, written by the finger of the God of heaven, explicitly states, "Thou shalt not bow down thyself to them [idols], nor serve them: for I the Lord thy God am a jealous God" (Exodus 20:5). As the young Hebrews refused to defile their body temples (Daniel 1), they now resist the popular and forced pressure to acknowledge a false god, made with hands of man who, in their understanding, was made by the hands of the invisible God.

Enemies are always ready and waiting to report on those who remain firm to the God of heaven. Immediately, the king heard about the three dissidents. If the disdain for Hebrews today in that part of the country is any indicator of their feelings, their enemies reported them with pleasure. The language indicates that Nebuchadnezzar was taken back by their perceived disloyalty. These Hebrews had proven their faithfulness to him in the past with their leadership, so this seemed out of place for them. He gave them another chance to worship his image. This showed his relationship with them. Nebuchadnezzar knew from experience their loyalty to his rulership, but they chose to worship and obey the King of kings rather than man.

Daniel 3:19-23: Then was Nebuchadnezzar full of fury, and the form of his visage was changed against Shadrach, Meshach, and Abednego: therefore he spake, and commanded that they should heat the furnace one seven times more than it was wont to be heated. [20]And he commanded the most mighty men that were in his army to bind Shadrach, Meshach, and Abednego, and to cast them into the burning fiery furnace. [21]Then these men were bound in their coats, their hosen, and their hats, and their other garments, and were cast into the midst of the burning fiery furnace. [22]Therefore because the king's commandment was urgent, and the furnace exceeding hot, the flame of the fire slew those men that took up Shadrach, Meshach, and Abednego. [23]And these three men, Shadrach, Meshach, and Abednego, fell down bound into the midst of the burning fiery furnace.

Nebuchadnezzar was angry before he offered the young men a second chance, but when he received their answer, it only added fuel to anger's fire. The Scripture says, "The expression on his face changed toward Shadrach, Meshach, and Abednego." He commanded his men to heat the furnace seven times hotter than normal. Seven is the perfect number. By heating it seven times hotter, the furnace was heated to its maximum capacity, the highest attainable temperature. The fact that seven is used in comparison to the sixty and six indicates that God might be involved in some miraculous way. The number seven is God's number whereas man's number is six.

That furnace was so hot it killed the men who attempted to execute the three Hebrews. The executioners bound and carried the young men, but burned to death as they threw them into the opening of the furnace.

The issue was worship: idolatry versus obedience to God. True worship is expressed in obedience. Would the Hebrews give the homage that only God had a right to ask of them, or would they yield to the false worship ordered by their earthly ruler? Throughout history, legislation has been used to force false worship. A false religion enforces its rules by policy and legislation, imposing itself upon its subjects. The empire that legislatively forces religion upon its citizens only produces hypocrisy. The same thing happens within the Christian church when man-made laws replace the perfect law of God's government. Rejecting the Ten Commandments written by the finger of God Himself, they worship and enforce the traditions of men.

Unless the heart is totally yielded to God, perfect and heartfelt obedience is not possible. The outward form of worship indicates the inward commitment and loyalties. Do we worship in the power of the Spirit and in truth, or are we worshiping form and fanfare? Does our worship produce hearty obedience, or is it tied only to outward ceremony? Is the drama of God's love in our heart, or does the drama of human theater intrigue and demand our worship? Does our religion depend upon self-gratification, or do we realize that we are always in the presence of the eternal and invisible King of the universe?

The loyalty of these Hebrews did not change with their circumstances. They had made a determined decision to remain obedient to God long before their Babylonian captivity.

Daniel 3:24-30: Then Nebuchadnezzar the king was astonied, and rose up in haste, and spake, and said unto his counsellors, Did not we cast three men bound into the midst of the fire? They answered and said unto the king, True, O king. ²⁵He answered and said, Lo, I see four men loose, walking in the midst of the fire, and they have no hurt; and the form of the fourth is like the Son of God. ²⁶Then Nebuchadnezzar came near to the mouth of the burning fiery furnace, and spake, and said, Shadrach, Meshach, and Abednego, ye servants of the most high God, come forth, and come hither. Then Shadrach, Meshach, and Abednego, came forth of the midst of the fire. ²⁷And the princes, governors, and captains, and the king's counsellors, being gathered together, saw these men, upon whose bodies the fire had no power, nor was an hair of their head singed, neither were their coats changed, nor the smell of fire had passed on them. ²⁸Then Nebuchadnezzar spake, and said, Blessed be the God of Shadrach, Meshach, and Abednego, who hath sent his angel, and delivered his servants that trusted in him, and have changed the king's word, and yielded their bodies, that they might not serve nor worship any god, except their own God. ²⁹Therefore I make a decree, That every people, nation, and language, which speak any thing amiss against the God of Shadrach, Meshach, and Abednego, shall be cut in pieces, and their houses shall be made a dunghill: because there is no other God that can deliver after this sort. ³⁰Then the king promoted Shadrach, Meshach, and Abednego, in the province of Babylon.

What a change in Nebuchadnezzar's focus! Man's heart plans, but God is really in charge of the agenda of life. This civil and religious dedication was taken over by the God of the universe. When the Hebrews were thrown into the furnace, the king thought he would see the terrible fiery death of three disloyal leaders. Instead, he witnessed the real issue at hand: whom should we worship? When he gazed upon four living beings in the furnace, he recognized the fourth One. The truth was forced from Nebuchadnezzar's lips, "This is the Son of God!"

Nebuchadnezzar had challenged the invisible God when he said: **"Who is that God that shall deliver you out of my hands?"** (Daniel 3:15). Now that God was walking in front of him! Again Nebuchadnezzar acknowledged the God of heaven, the One who delivered His obedient worshipers from death.

This experience parallels the test in the future when an image to the beast will be set up as foretold in Revelation 13. Just as God delivered the three Hebrews, He will deliver us in the end time. We must determine in our hearts to be loyal and obedient now. Then we will remain firm in our worship of the invisible God whose dwelling place is in the heavenly sanctuary made without hands.

White inspires us to stand faithful to God as did the three young Hebrews: "The greatest want of the world is the want of men—men who will not be bought or sold, men who in their inmost souls are true and honest, men who do not fear to call sin by its right name, men whose conscience is as true to duty as the needle to the pole, men who will stand for the right though the heavens fall."[1] These three Hebrews challenge us in these last days: be willing to stand alone for the sake of God's truth. Heaven's help is available when we are threatened by the false worship of Babylon. For those who have determined in their heart to remain obedient, compromise is not an option.

---

[1] White, *Education*, 57.

CHAPTER FOUR

Daniel 4

Introduction

Daniel 4 records Nebuchadnezzar's conversion experience. Historical records indicate Nebuchadnezzar went insane in 569 B.C. The dream warning him of his danger came in 570 B.C., one year before his insanity. Daniel had been in captivity thirty-five years at this time; the dream in Daniel 2 was given thirty-one years ago; and the events of Daniel 3 occurred eight years earlier. Daniel would have been in his fifties at this time.

The king had another dream, but this time he remembered it. Despite this fact, the wise men still could not interpret it. Then Daniel was called, and with God's help, he shared the dream's meaning. Again, God's foreknowledge cannot be overturned, and the king went into a state of insanity called lycanthropy. One characteristic of this mental illness is the complete negligence of personal hygiene.

Bunch fills in the details of the king's physical appearance: "Seven years of personal neglect caused the king's hair to grow long and become coarse and matted resembling eagle's feathers, and his finger and toe-nails became long and curved like the claws of a bird."[1]

Daniel 4:1-3: Nebuchadnezzar the king, unto all people, nations, and languages, that dwell in all the earth; Peace be multiplied unto you. ²I thought it good to show the signs and wonders that the high God hath wrought toward me. ³How great are his signs! and how mighty are his wonders! His kingdom is an everlasting kingdom, and his dominion is from generation to generation.

The remarkable features of this chapter in Daniel are expressed by Bunch: "This is the beginning of a regular royal decree and one of the most ancient on record. It is a complete state paper that has come down to us through 2,500 years of history. It is the epistle of Babylon's greatest monarch to the whole world relating the circumstances of his own conversion and calling upon all men to reverence and worship the true God. In the form of a royal decree Nebuchadnezzar

---

[1]   Bunch, "The Book of Daniel," 55.

sends an account of his own experience by imperial postmen to the inhabitants of the then known world."[2]

These words must have made it all worthwhile for Daniel and his three friends. By their faithful commitment to the God of heaven, the most powerful earthly king to rule on the throne of any kingdom was converted. According to historical accounts, Nebuchadnezzar went mad in 569 B.C. and became sane again in 562 B.C. Nebuchadnezzar died in 561 B.C., so he had about a year of knowing, acknowledging, and worshiping the true God of heaven.

Daniel 4:4-18: I Nebuchadnezzar was at rest in mine house, and flourishing in my palace: [5] I saw a dream which made me afraid, and the thoughts upon my bed and the visions of my head troubled me. [6]Therefore made I a decree to bring in all the wise men of Babylon before me, that they might make known unto me the interpretation of the dream. [7]Then came in the magicians, the astrologers, the Chaldeans, and the soothsayers: and I told the dream before them; but they did not make known unto me the interpretation thereof. [8]But at the last Daniel came in before me, whose name was Belteshazzar, according to the name of my god, and in whom is the spirit of the holy gods: and before him I told the dream, saying, [9]O Belteshazzar, master of the magicians, because I know that the spirit of the holy gods is in thee, and no secret troubleth thee, tell me the visions of my dream that I have seen, and the interpretation thereof. [10]Thus were the visions of mine head in my bed; I saw, and behold, a tree in the midst of the earth, and the height thereof was great. [11]The tree grew, and was strong, and the height thereof reached unto heaven, and the sight thereof to the end of all the earth: [12]The leaves thereof were fair, and the fruit thereof much, and in it was meat for all: the beasts of the field had shadow under it, and the fowls of the heaven dwelt in the boughs thereof, and all flesh was fed of it. [13]I saw in the visions of my head upon my bed, and, behold, a watcher and an holy one came down from heaven; [14]He cried aloud, and said thus, Hew down the tree, and cut off his branches, shake off his leaves, and scatter his fruit: let the beasts get away from under it, and the fowls from his branches: [15]Nevertheless leave the stump of his roots in the earth, even with a band of iron and brass, in the tender grass of the field; and let it be wet with the dew of heaven, and let his portion be with the beasts in the grass of the earth: [16]Let his heart be changed from man's, and let a beast's heart be given unto him: and let seven times pass over him. [17]This matter is by the decree of the watchers, and the demand by the word of the holy ones: to the intent that the living may know that the most High ruleth in the kingdom of men, and giveth it to whomsoever he will, and setteth up over it the basest of men. [18]This dream I king Nebuchadnezzar have seen. Now thou, O Belteshazzar, declare the interpretation thereof, forasmuch as all the wise men of my kingdom are

---

2   Ibid., 48.

not able to make known unto me the interpretation: but thou art able; for the spirit of the holy gods is in thee.

King Nebuchadnezzar never found peace in his life while rejecting the God of heaven. He came to know "the holy God," as he calls Him, whose works are so unlike the unholy actions of the gods he had always known (Daniel 4:8). Honest people will find that there is a difference between the holy God of the Bible and that of their own gods. If the God of the Scriptures were the same as the Allah of Islam, then King Nebuchadnezzar would never have been given such a prolonged opportunity to accept Him. Only the Creator would take thirty-five long years to lovingly draw Nebuchadnezzar rather than force an outward conversion upon him under duress. The king was compelled by the constant love and winning ways of the God of heaven. The goodness of God won his heart, not the fear factor. As he responded to this love, he found peace, true peace!

Daniel 4:18-33: This dream I king Nebuchadnezzar have seen. Now thou, O Belteshazzar, declare the interpretation thereof, forasmuch as all the wise men of my kingdom are not able to make known unto me the interpretation: but thou art able; for the spirit of the holy gods is in thee. [19]Then Daniel, whose name was Belteshazzar, was astonied for one hour, and his thoughts troubled him. The king spake, and said, Belteshazzar, let not the dream, or the interpretation thereof, trouble thee. Belteshazzar answered and said, My lord, the dream be to them that hate thee, and the interpretation thereof to thine enemies. [20]The tree that thou sawest, which grew, and was strong, whose height reached unto the heaven, and the sight thereof to all the earth; [21]Whose leaves were fair, and the fruit thereof much, and in it was meat for all; under which the beasts of the field dwelt, and upon whose branches the fowls of the heaven had their habitation: [22]It is thou, O king, that art grown and become strong: for thy greatness is grown, and reacheth unto heaven, and thy dominion to the end of the earth. [23]And whereas the king saw a watcher and an holy one coming down from heaven, and saying, Hew the tree down, and destroy it; yet leave the stump of the roots thereof in the earth, even with a band of iron and brass, in the tender grass of the field; and let it be wet with the dew of heaven, and let his portion be with the beasts of the field, till seven times pass over him; [24]This is the interpretation, O king, and this is the decree of the most High, which is come upon my lord the king: [25]That they shall drive thee from men, and thy dwelling shall be with the beasts of the field, and they shall make thee to eat grass as oxen, and they shall wet thee with the dew of heaven, and seven times shall pass over thee, till thou know that the most High ruleth in the kingdom of men, and giveth it to whomsoever he will. [26]And whereas they commanded to leave the stump of the tree roots; thy kingdom shall be sure unto thee, after that thou shalt have known that the heavens do rule. [27]Wherefore, O king, let my counsel be acceptable unto thee, and break off thy sins by righteousness, and thine iniquities by showing mercy to the poor;

if it may be a lengthening of thy tranquillity. ²⁸All this came upon the king Nebuchadnezzar. ²⁹At the end of twelve months he walked in the palace of the kingdom of Babylon. ³⁰The king spake, and said, Is not this great Babylon, that I have built for the house of the kingdom by the might of my power, and for the honour of my majesty? ³¹While the word was in the king's mouth, there fell a voice from heaven, saying, O king Nebuchadnezzar, to thee it is spoken; The kingdom is departed from thee. ³²And they shall drive thee from men, and thy dwelling shall be with the beasts of the field: they shall make thee to eat grass as oxen, and seven times shall pass over thee, until thou know that the most High ruleth in the kingdom of men, and giveth it to whomsoever he will. ³³The same hour was the thing fulfilled upon Nebuchadnezzar: and he was driven from men, and did eat grass as oxen, and his body was wet with the dew of heaven, till his hairs were grown like eagles' feathers, and his nails like birds' claws.

Nebuchadnezzar received his second dream from God, but he again went to the wise men instead of Daniel who was in touch with the holy God of heaven. When they were unable to answer his questions, he finally turned to Daniel. This time Nebuchadnezzar acknowledged that the answer would not come from Daniel himself, but because the "Spirit of the holy God" was in him (Daniel 4:8). Note the reason for this dream: "In order that the living may know that the Most High rules in the kingdom of men, gives it to whomever He will, and sets over it the lowest of men" (Daniel 4:17, NKJ). The dream announces that the holy God of heaven rules, and kings arise and fall at His will.

Daniel was astonished because he understood immediately the meaning of the dream. He had become Nebuchadnezzar's friend, and he really did not want to tell the king the meaning of the troubling dream. However, Daniel recognized that God was reaching out again to this earthly ruler. Who was he to question God? With tact and care Daniel slowly explained the dream.

Nebuchadnezzar, the great tree in the dream, would be cut down. His kingdom would taken from him for seven years until his pride was gone. He would be reduced to the level of a beast. Then, when he would acknowledge the ultimate rulership of the holy God, his kingdom would be returned to him. Daniel pleaded with Nebuchadnezzar to change his ways; perhaps God would change the verdict. In spite of this warning, Nebuchadnezzar continued his proud and wicked course of action, and the decree was fulfilled when the king lost his mind.

Daniel 4:34-37: And at the end of the days I Nebuchadnezzar lifted up mine eyes unto heaven, and mine understanding returned unto me, and I blessed the most High, and I praised and honoured him that liveth for ever, whose dominion is an everlasting dominion, and his kingdom is from generation to generation: ³⁵And all the inhabitants of the earth are reputed as nothing: and he doeth according to his will in the army of heaven, and among the inhabitants of the earth: and none can stay his hand, or say unto him, What doest

thou? [36]At the same time my reason returned unto me; and for the glory of my kingdom, mine honour and brightness returned unto me; and my counsellors and my lords sought unto me; and I was established in my kingdom, and excellent majesty was added unto me. [37]Now I Nebuchadnezzar praise and extol and honour the King of heaven, all whose works are truth, and his ways judgment: and those that walk in pride he is able to abase.

God gave Nebuchadnezzar a year to repent and change his ways, but he refused. Thus the sentence was executed because of his own decision. Lycanthropy is a rare form of insanity in which the individual believes himself to be some sort of wild animal. The termination of this disease may be just as rapid as its onset.

Pride is the sin most hateful to God (Proverbs 6:16; 8:13). Self-centered, proud thinking led to Lucifer's downfall (Isaiah 14:13-14); some call this affliction "I trouble." This sin affects Christians and worldlings alike, but often those who are proud are oblivious to their plight as were the Pharisees in Jesus' day. God humbled Nebuchadnezzar for seven long years, thus revealing the malignity of this soul-sickness. When the king gained true humility, praise and wisdom immediately came into his mind and mouth. Praise God, this disease is not hopeless. In Daniel 4:37 the good news has been given to us out of the mouth of Nebuchadnezzar, "Those that walk in pride He is able to abase!"

Summary

For thirty-nine years, God worked with Nebuchadnezzar to save him from sin, starting with the king's dream in Daniel 2 (602 B.C.) and ending with his conversion (562 B.C.) After his humbling experience cured his pride, Nebuchadnezzar glorified and magnified the King of heaven and honored the One who puts kings on their thrones and removes them at His will. Nebuchadnezzar was a believer for one year before he died.

Bunch relates Nebuchadnezzar's illness to examples from today's world: "Many are suffering with spiritual insanity and do not know it. Sin unbalances the mind so that men and women act more like animals than human beings. They renounce the duties and privileges of the higher spiritual nature and live as if there was nothing in them above the animal. They were created in the image of God but they live and act and die like brutes. Their spiritual faculties are completely deadened by uncontrolled animal passions."[3]

Think of your conversation. Is it dominated by expressions of your plans and your abilities? Don't let pride be your downfall. Those who truly worship God walk in humble, thankful obedience. Remember the experience of Nebuchadnezzar, and bow low before God of heaven, praising Him for His mighty acts and thanking Him for all His gifts.

---

[3]   Ibid., 56.

CHAPTER FIVE

Daniel 5

Introduction

D aniel 5 reveals part of the fulfillment of the prophetic dream in Daniel 2 as the Babylonian kingdom comes to an end. Babylon had only one great ruler, Nebuchadnezzar. When he passed from the scene, his son Evil Merodach ruled from 561 to 559 B.C. Then Neriglissar reigned from 559 to 556 B.C. followed by Laborodoarchod for only nine months (556 B.C.) Finally, Nabonidus came to the throne in 556 B.C. He shared the last three years of his reign with his son Belshazzar until the Medes and Persians overthrew Babylon in 539 B.C. At this time, Daniel was an old man about 83 years of age.

The story of Belshazzar's last night on earth reveals the tragic results of turning his back on the witness and heritage coming from his grandfather Nebuchadnezzar. He boldly led Babylon back into apostasy and refused to accept the light and truth God mercifully revealed to him. He lived his life for his own pleasure. When he blasphemed the God of heaven, he crossed the point of no return. At this point God rejected Belshazzar as king, and the fulfillment of Daniel 2 began in earnest.

Using archaeological and historical evidence, Bunch points out the danger of a skeptical attitude, one that refuses to believe the historical facts as recorded in the Bible:

> The name of Belshazzar was at one time one of the favorite battle grounds for skeptics. With an air of triumph they declared that his name was nowhere to be found in profane history and was not listed among the kings of Babylon. The list was complete without him and therefore he did not exist, and the Biblical account of him must be fiction. But the spade of the archeologist has caused these scoffers to beat an ignominious retreat. Discovered inscriptions show that Belshazzar was the son of Nabonidus and as crown prince was associated with his father in the rulership of the kingdom. The controversy was settled in 1854 when clay cylinders were discovered almost simultaneously by M. Oppert and Sir

Henry Rawlinson and are known as "The Mugheir Inscriptions." These inscriptions were written by Nabonidus himself.[1]

Belshazzar's supposed non-existence was still believed by atheist skeptics of the old Soviet Union when I made my first visit in January of 1992. It was difficult for them when they discovered that the controversy had been settled before the Bolshevik Revolution, yet they had been kept in ignorance for 138 years. Today in the United States, once the bastion of honesty and integrity, many skeptics still refuse to acknowledge the Bible's veracity although archaeology has confirmed its historicity over and over again.

Daniel 5 lifts the curtain on the final chapter of the Babylonian kingdom. Just as prophesied, Babylon was conquered by an inferior kingdom, the Medes and Persians.

Daniel 5:1-4: Belshazzar the king made a great feast to a thousand of his lords, and drank wine before the thousand. ²Belshazzar, whiles he tasted the wine, commanded to bring the golden and silver vessels which his father Nebuchadnezzar had taken out of the temple which was in Jerusalem; that the king, and his princes, his wives, and his concubines, might drink therein. ³Then they brought the golden vessels that were taken out of the temple of the house of God which was at Jerusalem; and the king, and his princes, his wives, and his concubines, drank in them. ⁴They drank wine, and praised the gods of gold, and of silver, of brass, of iron, of wood, and of stone.

At his great feast, Belshazzar was quite intoxicated when he made a drastic mistake, taking the sacred vessels of the sanctuary and using them in his drunken revelry. These vessels had always been handled with reverence by King Nebuchadnezzar, but this foolish king treated them sacrilegiously. These holy, golden vessels were dedicated to the God of heaven, the great I AM. God would not stand back because the cup of His wrath was full. Thus the curtain came down on the final act of the great Babylonian Empire. This imprudent young king did not take time to understand why King Nebuchadnezzar came to worship and reverence the God of heaven. Belshazzar's actions were typical of his time, but he had been given every opportunity to avail himself of the historical and sacred significance of these vessels. God held him accountable as He will many others today who, like Belshazzar, are unwilling to learn from history.

Daniel 5:5-9: In the same hour came forth fingers of a man's hand, and wrote over against the candlestick upon the plaster of the wall of the king's palace: and the king saw the part of the hand that wrote. ⁶Then the king's countenance was changed, and his thoughts troubled him, so that the joints of his loins were loosed, and his knees smote one against another. ⁷The king cried aloud to bring in the astrologers, the Chaldeans, and the soothsayers. And

[1]   Bunch, "The Book of Daniel," 58.

the king spake, and said to the wise men of Babylon, Whosoever shall read this writing, and show me the interpretation thereof, shall be clothed with scarlet, and have a chain of gold about his neck, and shall be the third ruler in the kingdom. [8]Then came in all the king's wise men: but they could not read the writing, nor make known to the king the interpretation thereof. [9]Then was king Belshazzar greatly troubled, and his countenance was changed in him, and his lords were astonied.**

There are limits to God's patience, Bunch declares: "The patience of a long-suffering God could endure the blasphemous scene no longer, and in that 'same hour' the command was given to the unseen watcher to inscribe on the palace wall a message of doom to the king and his kingdom."[2] White paints a word picture of that awful night of judgment:

Little did Belshazzar think that there was a heavenly Witness to his idol-atrous revelry; that a divine Watcher, unrecognized, looked upon the scene of profanation, heard the sacrilegious mirth, beheld the idolatry. But soon the uninvited Guest made His presence felt. When the revelry was at its height a bloodless hand came forth and traced upon the walls of the palace characters that gleamed like fire—words which, though unknown to the vast throng, were a portent of doom to the now con-science-stricken king and his guests.

Hushed was the boisterous mirth, while men and women, seized with nameless terror, watched the hand slowly tracing the mysterious char-acters. Before them passed, as in panoramic view, the deeds of their evil lives; they seemed to be arraigned before the judgment bar of the eternal God, whose power they had just defied. Where but a few moments be-fore had been hilarity and blasphemous witticism, were pallid faces and cries of fear. When God makes men fear, they cannot hide the intensity of their terror.

Belshazzar was the most terrified of them all. He it was who above all others had been responsible for the rebellion against God which that night had reached its height in the Babylonian realm. In the presence of the unseen Watcher, the representative of Him whose power had been challenged and whose name had been blasphemed, the king was para-lyzed with fear. Conscience was awakened.[3]

"The lampstand" indicates a definite lampstand, and the context speaks of all the vessels from the temple in Jerusalem (Daniel 5:5). Ford suggests this is the case: "It is possible that the lampstand here referred to was one taken from

[2]   Ibid., 61.

[3]   White, *Prophets and Kings*, 524.

Solomon's temple, which had ten lampstands (1 Ki 7:49). If so, the message of judgment was inscribed at a section of the banqueting chamber appropriate in more than one way. Thereby light was shed not only on the message of judgment but also on the reason for it."[4] How fitting for this illuminating message to be on the wall by the golden lampstand.

The king had defiled the vessels of the sanctuary just as Babylon the great will do in the last days. Even as this night became a night of terror for Belshazzar, so a terrible time will come for Babylon the great when the King of the universe sets up His everlasting kingdom.

Daniel 5:10-12: Now the queen by reason of the words of the king and his lords came into the banquet house: and the queen spake and said, O king, live for ever: let not thy thoughts trouble thee, nor let thy countenance be changed: ¹¹There is a man in thy kingdom, in whom is the spirit of the holy gods; and in the days of thy father light and understanding and wisdom, like the wisdom of the gods, was found in him; whom the king Nebuchadnezzar thy father, the king, I say, thy father, made master of the magicians, astrologers, Chaldeans, and soothsayers; ¹²Forasmuch as an excellent spirit, and knowledge, and understanding, interpreting of dreams, and showing of hard sentences, and dissolving of doubts, were found in the same Daniel, whom the king named Belteshazzar: now let Daniel be called, and he will show the interpretation.

The queen came into the banqueting room. Word of what had transpired spread from the palace to the city. Who is this queen? Scholars agree that she was the mother of Belshazzar and the daughter of King Nebuchadnezzar, thus her cousins were Darius the Mede and Mandana, Darius' sister. No matter who she was, the Queen realized that Daniel would be able to interpret the words because he was in touch with the King of the universe.

Daniel 5:13-16: Then was Daniel brought in before the king. And the king spake and said unto Daniel, Art thou that Daniel, which art of the children of the captivity of Judah, whom the king my father brought out of Jewry? ¹⁴I have even heard of thee, that the spirit of the gods is in thee, and that light and understanding and excellent wisdom is found in thee. ¹⁵And now the wise men, the astrologers, have been brought in before me, that they should read this writing, and make known unto me the interpretation thereof: but they could not show the interpretation of the thing: ¹⁶And I have heard of thee, that thou canst make interpretations, and dissolve doubts: now if thou canst read the writing, and make known to me the interpretation thereof, thou shalt be clothed with scarlet, and have a chain of gold about thy neck, and shalt be the third ruler in the kingdom.

---

4   Desmond Ford, *Daniel* (Nashville, TN: Southern Publishing Association, 1978), 126.

The question has been asked, "Was Daniel unknown to Belshazzar?" For sixty-six years Daniel had served the court of Babylon. How could the king ignore the illustrious life of this public servant? The same problem exists today. How can so many people in the world not know about Jesus? Even history books acknowledge the years before Christ (B.C.) and the era after our Lord (A.D.). Many choose not to acknowledge God's existence just like Belshazzar turned a deaf ear to Daniel's bold witness in Babylon. Thus Belshazzar ignored the God of heaven who delivered the three Hebrews from the furnace. Twice in his answer to Daniel, Belshazzar admits, "I have heard of you" (Daniel 5:14, 16). Everyone who knew Babylon's history knew about Daniel.

Daniel 5:17-24: Then Daniel answered and said before the king, Let thy gifts be to thyself, and give thy rewards to another; yet I will read the writing unto the king, and make known to him the interpretation. [18]O thou king, the most high God gave Nebuchadnezzar thy father a kingdom, and majesty, and glory, and honour: [19]And for the majesty that he gave him, all people, nations, and languages, trembled and feared before him: whom he would he slew; and whom he would he kept alive; and whom he would he set up; and whom he would he put down. [20]But when his heart was lifted up, and his mind hardened in pride, he was deposed from his kingly throne, and they took his glory from him: [21]And he was driven from the sons of men; and his heart was made like the beasts, and his dwelling was with the wild asses: they fed him with grass like oxen, and his body was wet with the dew of heaven; till he knew that the most high God ruled in the kingdom of men, and that he appointeth over it whomsoever he will. [22]And thou his son, O Belshazzar, hast not humbled thine heart, though thou knewest all this; [23]But hast lifted up thyself against the Lord of heaven; and they have brought the vessels of his house before thee, and thou, and thy lords, thy wives, and thy concubines, have drunk wine in them; and thou hast praised the gods of silver, and gold, of brass, iron, wood, and stone, which see not, nor hear, nor know: and the God in whose hand thy breath is, and whose are all thy ways, hast thou not glorified: [24]Then was the part of the hand sent from him; and this writing was written.

In Daniel's reply to Belshazzar, he did not excuse the king's ungodly behavior. Instead, he rebuked him and reminded Belshazzar of all that had happened in Daniel 4. Belshazzar had not sinned ignorantly, but in the clear light of God's power over the life of Nebuchadnezzar, the grandfather of Belshazzar. With no word for grandfather in the Hebrew and Chaldean languages, "father" was used to denote an ancestor. In the same way, the term "son of David" meant that David was the ancestor of Jesus.

Doukhan presents evidence of the king's guilt: "Belshazzar has not forgotten—he consciously and openly rebels against a God in whom he believes: 'Instead, you have set yourself up against the Lord of heaven' (verse 23). Indeed, the king is much more familiar with the Hebrew God than he cares to admit, a fact Daniel suggests at the end of his speech: 'But you did not honor the God who holds in his hand your breath and all your ways' (verse 23, literal translation)."[5]

Daniel 5:25-29: And this is the writing that was written, MENE, MENE, TEKEL, UPHARSIN. [26]This is the interpretation of the thing: MENE; God hath numbered thy kingdom, and finished it. [27]TEKEL; Thou art weighed in the balances, and art found wanting. [28]PERES; Thy kingdom is divided, and given to the Medes and Persians. [29]Then commanded Belshazzar, and they clothed Daniel with scarlet, and put a chain of gold about his neck, and made a proclamation concerning him, that he should be the third ruler in the kingdom.

Daniel interpreted the writing on the wall written by the fingers of a man's hand. He revealed to Belshazzar that his kingdom had come to an end as prophesied to Nebuchadnezzar in Daniel chapter 2. Since he was second to his father Nabonidus, King Belshazzar offered Daniel the third place of rulership in Babylon.

All of the words formed by the disembodied hand on the wall were written in Aramaic. God communicates in a language that can be understood by all. *Mene* means numbered, and like the English idiom "Your days are numbered," Belshazzar's days had come to an end. It was repeated twice, indicating a speedy fulfillment of this prophecy.

This doubling is analogous to the two visions God gave Pharaoh, hence Joseph's explanation, "The dream was doubled unto Pharaoh twice; it is because the thing is established by God, and God will shortly bring it to pass" (Genesis 41:32). The judgment of Belshazzar also came to pass quickly, that very night. *Tekel* (to weigh) implied that God had weighed Belshazzar in the moral balance of heaven. His blasphemous conduct with the holy vessels of the Lord exemplified his light, frivolous life. *Peres* (to divide) presents a bit of word play because *paras*, which is spelled with the same three consonants, means Persia. Hence Daniel's interpretation shows God's ingenuity in the use of the international language of the day: Your kingdom is divided (*peres*) and given to the Medes and Persians (*paras*).

Daniel 5:30-31: In that night was Belshazzar the king of the Chaldeans slain. [31]And Darius the Median took the kingdom, being about threescore and two years old.

The Medo-Persian armies led by Cyrus took Babylon in one night. Isaiah prophesied about this victory more than one hundred years before the birth of Cyrus: "Thus saith the Lord to His anointed, to Cyrus, whose right hand I have holden, to subdue nations before him; . . . to open before him the two leaved gates; and the gates shall not be shut; I will go before thee, and make the crooked

5   Jacques B. Doukhan, *Secrets of Daniel* (Hagerstown, MD: Review and Herald, 2000), 81.

places straight: I will break in pieces the gates of brass, and cut in sunder the bars of iron: and I will give thee the treasures of darkness, and hidden riches of secret places, that thou mayest know that I, the LORD, which call thee by thy name, am the God of Israel" (Isaiah 45:1-3). Cyrus and his men diverted the river that flowed through Babylon, ready to march in the dry riverbed into the city, but they still would not have gained entrance without divine aid. The inner gates were normally locked against invaders, but that night, in the midst of Belshazzar's drunken feast, the soldiers carelessly left those gates open, fulfilling God's words through Isaiah, "The gates shall not be shut" (Isaiah 45:1).

The fulfillment of this prophecy gave marvellous evidence of God's deliverance of His people from Babylon and His preparation to end their seventy years of captivity. When Cyrus took over the throne from Darius the Mede, he allowed the Jews to return to their homeland and gave them financial help in rebuilding Jerusalem and the temple (Isaiah 44:28; 45:13).

As the Babylon of Belshazzar's day and Babylon the great in Revelation are compared, they bear a striking resemblance to each other. Oxentenko lists fifteen similarities between ancient Babylon and spiritual Babylon of the last days as summarized below.[6]

As ancient Babylon encouraged drunkenness and drank from golden cups, so does Babylon the great. Immorality, blasphemy, and idolatry are fostered in both kingdoms, hence they could be called commandment-breaking kingdoms. They are religio-political entities. Both become mighty cities built over the River Euphrates that rule the world, and both quickly fall after the river is dried up. God's prophetic judgment was pronounced against both Babylons because both attack God's people and His sanctuary. In the end, both are defeated by kings from the east, according to God's prophetic word (Isaiah 44:27, 28; 45:1-5; Daniel 1:1; 4:29, 30; 5:1-4, 23-31; Revelation 16:12; 17:1-18; 18:1-20).

Summary

Within two chapters of Daniel, two very different men are portrayed. Chapter 4 gave the good news of Nebuchadnezzar's conversion from a proud monarch to a humble, thankful subject of the Kings of kings. God's patience and long-suffering is revealed in His dealings with this heathen king. In contrast with this happy ending, Daniel 5 presents a different picture. Again, God demonstrated endurance and mercy as He presented opportunities to Belshazzar, but this grandson of Nebuchadnezzar did not follow the same path. His life revealed the depths of sin and rebellion as he lived for himself and glorified idols instead of the living God.

Doukhan links the king's actions with his motives: "Belshazzar is not just reacting against his grandfather. Behind the person of Nebuchadnezzar, it is God,

---

[6]   Michael Oxentenko, "Daniel and Revelation," Typewritten manuscript, 1995, Center for Adventist Research, James White Library, Andrews University, Berrien Springs, MI, 42-45.

the God of Israel, that he is provoking. Belshazzar resents this disturbing God. Feeling threatened by Him, he seeks to destroy a truth that torments him. . . . Profaning the cult objects of the God of heaven is a way both to provoke God and to defy Him." [7]

Daniel 5 raises the question, "How will we apply God's light in our lives when He makes it available to us? Will we be like King Nebuchadnezzar or King Belshazzar?"

---

[7] Doukhan, *Secrets of Daniel*, 78.

CHAPTER SIX

Daniel 6

Introduction

C hapter 6 lifts the curtain on another kingdom, one inferior to that of Babylon in the height of its glory. Darius and Daniel had a relationship of mutual respect: the former a king and the latter recognized by the king as having special gifts. Darius probably realized that if the Babylonian king had listened to Daniel, Babylon would still be the great kingdom it once was, and he would not be ruling the world. So begins the battle between the faithful and those that are in the majority.

Daniel 6 gives a preview of life in the last days. The issue will be over worship and who is worshiped. The majority believe that strict obedience to the law of God is not that important. Most people are willing to make compromises that lead to false worship and creature worship as opposed to worshiping the Creator. In contrast, Daniel represents the faithful who will not yield to the pressures of the majority or culture or the times, but will remain steadfast and obedient no matter the cost.

Oxentenko points out parallels between Daniel 6 and Revelation:[2]

1. Daniel and God's people are persecuted for choosing to obey God's law (Daniel 6:5; Revelation 12:7).

2. King of Persia and the beast power make laws that require false worship (Daniel 6:6-9; Revelation 13:15).

3. Both the decree of Darius and the mark of the beast lead to the worship of a man (Daniel 6:7; Revelation 13:18).

4. The penalties for obeying God rather than man involve the death decree (Daniel 6:7; Revelation 13:15).

5. Daniel is found without fault before God and the king; in Revelation the people of God are found blameless and without fault (Daniel 6:22; Revelation 14:5).

---

[1] Oxentenko, 49.

6. God's faithful are saved by His miraculous intervention (Daniel 6:19-23; Revelation 19:11).

7. The wrath of the king gives the persecutors an unpleasant reward (Daniel 6:24; Revelation 16:6; 18:4).

Daniel 6:1-3: It pleased Darius to set over the kingdom an hundred and twenty princes, which should be over the whole kingdom; ²And over these three presidents; of whom Daniel was first: that the princes might give accounts unto them, and the king should have no damage. ³Then this Daniel was preferred above the presidents and princes, because an excellent spirit was in him; and the king thought to set him over the whole realm.

Daniel became one of the top three rulers rather quickly. Those around him who had aspirations for greatness realized that Daniel was different; he had an "excellent spirit in him" that distinguished him from the others (Daniel 6:3). Thus the king put him over the other rulers, next in command to the king himself. Darius and King Nebuchadnezzar were actually related by marriage. Bunch notes: "The father of Darius was Astyages whose sister was the wife of Nebuchadnezzar. Mandana, the daughter of Astyages and sister of Darius was the mother of Cyrus."[2] Nebuchadnezzar's Median wife, Amytis, was Darius' father's sister, or more simply, his aunt. Later, his nephew Cyrus would rule. These kings fully understood Daniel's position in the court of King Nebuchadnezzar. These connections, linked with God's providence, brought Daniel to the forefront and put him in leadership position. Little did the other governors and satraps realize the blessing of God in Daniel's connection to Darius the Mede and Cyrus the Persian.

Daniel 6:4-9: Then the presidents and princes sought to find occasion against Daniel concerning the kingdom; but they could find none occasion nor fault; forasmuch as he was faithful, neither was there any error or fault found in him. ⁵Then said these men, We shall not find any occasion against this Daniel, except we find it against him concerning the law of his God. ⁶Then these presidents and princes assembled together to the king, and said thus unto him, King Darius, live for ever. ⁷ All the presidents of the kingdom, the governors, and the princes, the counsellors, and the captains, have consulted together to establish a royal statute, and to make a firm decree, that whosoever shall ask a petition of any God or man for thirty days, save of thee, O king, he shall be cast into the den of lions. ⁸Now, O king, establish the decree, and sign the writing, that it be not changed, according to the law of the Medes and Persians, which altereth not. ⁹Wherefore king Darius signed the writing and the decree.

---

2   Bunch, "The Book of Daniel," 27.

Nothing could be found against Daniel other than his obedience to God. Jealous of Daniel's high position, the other governors studied to trap him. They knew Daniel would follow the law of God and worship Him alone. Going to Darius, they appealed to his vanity, leading him to believe that Daniel agreed with their decision. Obviously, Daniel would never have consented to their new law, but Darius believed their lie and made the new decree legal.

Daniel 6:10: Now when Daniel knew that the writing was signed, he went into his house; and his windows being open in his chamber toward Jerusalem, he kneeled upon his knees three times a day, and prayed, and gave thanks before his God, as he did aforetime.

Daniel did not play games with God. He continued his customary prayer and devotional life. Three times a day, Daniel prayed by his open window.

Daniel 6:11-15: Then these men assembled, and found Daniel praying and making supplication before his God. ¹²Then they came near, and spake before the king concerning the king's decree; Hast thou not signed a decree, that every man that shall ask a petition of any God or man within thirty days, save of thee, O king, shall be cast into the den of lions? The king answered and said, The thing is true, according to the law of the Medes and Persians, which altereth not. ¹³Then answered they and said before the king, That Daniel, which is of the children of the captivity of Judah, regardeth not thee, O king, nor the decree that thou hast signed, but maketh his petition three times a day. ¹⁴Then the king, when he heard these words, was sore displeased with himself, and set his heart on Daniel to deliver him: and he laboured till the going down of the sun to deliver him. ¹⁵Then these men assembled unto the king, and said unto the king, Know, O king, that the law of the Medes and Persians is, That no decree nor statute which the king establisheth may be changed.

Daniel's steadfast allegiance to the God of heaven was used against him by his enemies. The governors relied on the assumption that Daniel would continue his faithful worship of God. Immediately they accused him, reminding the king of his new decree. Note the contrast between King Nebuchadnezzar in chapter 3 and Darius. Nebuchadnezzar was furious with the three Hebrews, but Darius was furious with himself for falling into this trap. He remembered what happened to his Uncle Nebuchadnezzar when he foolishly challenged the God of heaven. All day King Darius tried everything within his power to free Daniel, but he was helpless.

Daniel 6:16-18: Then the king commanded, and they brought Daniel, and cast him into the den of lions. Now the king spake and said unto Daniel, Thy God whom thou servest continually, he will deliver thee. ¹⁷And a stone was brought, and laid upon the mouth of the den; and the king sealed it with his own signet, and with the signet of his lords; that the purpose might not be

changed concerning Daniel. [18]Then the king went to his palace, and passed
the night fasting: neither were instruments of music brought before him: and
his sleep went from him.

Unable to save Daniel, Darius cast his faith in Daniel's God as the only hope
for his friend. Then the king acted on that faith. He fasted and stayed up the
whole night, not leaving Daniel's destiny to chance. King Darius knew what God
had done for Daniel's three friends and believed the King of kings could do the
same for Daniel as he called upon Daniel's God.

**Daniel 6:19-22: Then the king arose very early in the morning, and went in
haste unto the den of lions. [20]And when he came to the den, he cried with
a lamentable voice unto Daniel: and the king spake and said to Daniel, O
Daniel, servant of the living God, is thy God, whom thou servest continually,
able to deliver thee from the lions? [21]Then said Daniel unto the king, O king,
live for ever. [22]My God hath sent his angel, and hath shut the lions' mouths,
that they have not hurt me: forasmuch as before him innocency was found in
me; and also before thee, O king, have I done no hurt.**

Very early in the morning, the king went to the den, fervently hoping that
Daniel would answer him when he called. Daniel's reply assured the king his
prayers were answered. Daniel testified that he was protected because he was
found innocent before God and the king.

Compare **Daniel 6:22** and **Revelation 14:5**. Daniel was found without fault
before God and the king, just as in Revelation the people of God are found blameless and without fault. Daniel is a figure of God's people at the end time, the ones
who will be characterized by their faithfulness to God. Like Daniel they will face
persecution and the threat of death, but they will remain loyal to the Creator.
They will not yield their allegiance nor their observance of religious duties in
worship. They never make compromises in their faith and will worship only the
God of heaven. The lions in the den with Daniel parallel Satan, the roaring lion,
but God's angels will keep His saints from being overcome.

**Daniel 6:23-28: Then was the king exceeding glad for him, and commanded
that they should take Daniel up out of the den. So Daniel was taken up out
of the den, and no manner of hurt was found upon him, because he believed
in his God. [24]And the king commanded, and they brought those men which
had accused Daniel, and they cast them into the den of lions, them, their children, and their wives; and the lions had the mastery of them, and brake all
their bones in pieces or ever they came at the bottom of the den. [25]Then king
Darius wrote unto all people, nations, and languages, that dwell in all the
earth; Peace be multiplied unto you. [26]I make a decree, That in every dominion of my kingdom men tremble and fear before the God of Daniel: for he is
the living God, and stedfast for ever, and his kingdom that which shall not be
destroyed, and his dominion shall be even unto the end. [27]He delivereth and**

rescueth, and he worketh signs and wonders in heaven and in earth, who hath delivered Daniel from the power of the lions. ²⁸So this Daniel prospered in the reign of Darius, and in the reign of Cyrus the Persian.

Like Nebuchadnezzar before him, Darius acknowledged the living God, the only One who could rescue Daniel. What a statement for the king to make! This sets the stage for God to be glorified in the life of the next king, Cyrus.

Summary

This ends the historical chapters found in the first half of Daniel. We have discovered how these experiences introduce the spiritual issues that will face God's people in the last days. With chapter 7, the prophetic section of the book of Daniel begins. Remember, the issues at stake are worship and obedience. The battle rages over who you will worship and how you worship. Remember how God reached out to heathen kings in order to save them. Remember the relationship of Babylon to the Assyrian Empire. Nebuchadnezzar's father was the general in charge of the Babylonian province of Assyria who then conquered the other two provinces of the empire. Darius the Mede and his nephew Cyrus the Persian were nephew and grand nephew of Nebuchadnezzar. God used these relationships to point the whole empire to Himself. Thus there is always more than meets the eye in the prophetic scheme of things!

CHAPTER SEVEN

Daniel 7

Introduction

God gave the dream of a multi-metal image, conveying to King Nebuchadnezzar what would happen in the future. Thus the dream in Daniel 2 covers a period of history that began in 605 B.C., reaches down to our own time, and extends into the future. More than 2,600 years of history are covered in one chapter. The head of gold represented Babylon, chest and arms of silver were Medo-Persia, the body and thighs of bronze symbolized Greece, the legs of iron were Rome, and the feet of iron and clay represented the division of Europe, partly strong and partly weak.

In Daniel 7, the same period of history is represented using the principal of repeat and enlarge. Four prophetic beasts are used to represent the history of the world as God adds more detail to this prophetic picture. With the metals in chapter 2, God represented the kingdoms of this world as man values them, whereas in Daniel 7 God portrayed the earthly kingdoms as He sees them, giving a spiritual viewpoint of these kingdoms. Babylon was not only glorious as gold, but bold as a lion and swift as an eagle. With chapter 7, the prophetic section of the book of Daniel begins in earnest. Historic particulars are inserted, giving the setting and laying a foundation for the historicist interpretation of the prophecies in Daniel and Revelation.

God uses symbols in prophecy; therefore the Bible itself must interpret these symbols rather than the fanciful ideas of man. Adapted from Oxentenko, the following symbols are listed with their biblical definitions:[1]

- Beasts = kingdoms (Daniel 7:17, 23)

- Sea/waters = multitudes of peoples (Revelation 17:1,15; Isaiah 57:20)

- Winds = war and strife (Jeremiah 49:36; Revelation 7:1)

- Horns = kings, power, authority (Daniel 7:24)

- Wings = great speed for conquest (Habakkuk 1:6-8; Jeremiah 4:13; Deuteronomy 48:29)

---

[1]   Oxentenko, 70.

- Day = a year (Numbers 14:34; Ezekiel 4:6

Daniel's Animal Dream

Daniel 7:1: In the first year of Belshazzar king of Babylon Daniel had a dream and visions of his head upon his bed: then he wrote the dream, and told the sum of the matters.

The chapter begins by setting the vision in its historical setting: the first year of Belshazzar. After ruling with his father Nabonidus for three years, Belshazzar died in 539 B.C. when Babylon was taken by the Medes and Persians. Calculating from these dates, Daniel's vision came in 541 B.C.

At this time, Daniel would have been eighty-one to eighty-six years of age since he was born between 622 and 627 B.C. The vision of Daniel 2 was sixty years earlier. Daniel must have wondered when the prophetic clock would run out for Babylon. He had observed five weak kings in succession since the death of Nebuchadnezzar, one of Daniel's dearest friends and a fellow believer. With his habit of devotion, Daniel had prayed that evening. As he slept, God gave him a dream that would, like Daniel 2, predict the future from Daniel's day until the end of the world. The setting is 541 B.C. and Babylon still ruled the world. Thus the vision would still include Babylon.

Daniel did not record every detail of his vision. The King James Version uses the word "sum" which means a summary of the dream. The significant elements were written down. Bunch uses Scripture to highlight the importance of Daniel's prophecies for the last days: "Why was this vision recorded by the prophet? Romans 15:4. For whose learning especially? 1 Corinthians 10:11. For no generation in human history do the Scriptures contain so many lessons as for the one in which we live. Daniel himself said that he was making known 'what shall be in the latter days.' Daniel 2:28; 10:14. He also declared that his prophecies would be studied and understood in 'the time of the end.' Daniel 12:4, 9. The accumulated light of all previous ages focuses in undimmed radiance upon our time. The vision now under consideration was recorded for our special benefit."[2]

Daniel 7:2-3: Daniel spake and said, I saw in my vision by night, and, behold, the four winds of the heaven strove upon the great sea. ³And four great beasts came up from the sea, diverse one from another.

God used a term familiar to Daniel—the great sea. Bunch gives historical background to help us understand this phrase:

This was doubtless the Mediterranean, which because of its size and importance was known to the ancients as "the great sea." See Numbers 34:6; Joshua 23:4. The Mediterranean Sea was the center around which the prophetic history of Daniel's visions unfolded. It was the center of the

---

2   Bunch, "The Book of Daniel," 86.

life and commerce of the old world as well as the great wars of human history. The Egyptians, Assyrians, and Babylonians fought on its eastern and southern shores, the Persians ruled it with their ships, and Alexander crossed part of it and traversed its eastern shores in his campaign of world conquest. The Romans fought all over and around it and called it "our own sea," and "a vast Roman lake." This great sea, the most important body of water on earth, witnessed most of the history unfolded from the days of Daniel to our own, and is destined to be the center of interest and importance to the end of time. The name, Mediterranean, means, "the middle of the earth."[3]

The Old Testament context explains the symbols of Daniel. Both Isaiah and Jeremiah use the imagery of water as John did in Revelation, describing waters as "peoples, multitudes, nations, and tongues" (Isaiah 8:7, 8; 28:2; Jeremiah 46:8; 47:2, 3; 51:12, 13; Revelation 17:15). The four great beasts come up from the sea of humanity which in Daniel's day was the area around the Mediterranean Sea. Bunch explains the meanings of these symbols:

The four beasts are also symbolic. Such beasts as those described in Daniel's vision do not live in the sea or have their origin there. They are beasts that live on the land. These symbolic beasts which came up out of the symbolic sea as the result of a symbolic storm were interpreted to Daniel by the angel of prophecy as representing universal rulerships or kingdoms. Verses 15-17. "Four kingdoms which shall arise out of the earth." Douay. "Four Empires which will be established on the earth."— Fenton. The fourth beast is declared to be the "fourth kingdom upon earth."—Verse 23. The ruler of a kingdom has always been identified with the kingdom itself. "The king is the state," declared Louis, the king of France.[4]

These four beasts are caricatures of four empires. Certain animals are used to symbolize nations to this day. For example, Russia is caricatured as a bear, the United States as an eagle, and China as a dragon. Like political cartoons today, the Bible uses beasts to symbolize nations. However, some have wrongly applied these modern caricatures in their interpretation of Scripture. Letting the Bible explain its own prophecies is the only safe path for us today.

The context of Daniel is cemented firmly in time to the first year of Belshazzar. Therefore the first kingdom must be Babylon and its three successors: Medo-Persia, Greece, and Rome. The angel told Daniel "the interpretation of these things: 'Those great beasts, which are four, are four kings which arise out of the earth'" (Daniel 7:15-17; NKJ).

[3] Ibid., 86-87.

[4] Ibid., 87.

The four beasts symbolize four successive kingdoms, each different from the other. This is corroborated by history according to Thomson: "If one were asked to name the world empires succeeding each other in history from the days of Nebuchadnezzar, without conscious reference to prophecy, the answer would be given unhesitatingly that there had been four: the Babylonian, the Medo-Persian, the Macedonian, and the Roman. There was no room for an intermediate rule which for a moment could be considered a power to rank with them in consequence. Each represented not only the domination of a distinct race and civilization, but each, in immediate succession, marked a particular and special epoch in historical development."[5]

Winged Lion Walks

Daniel 7:4: The first was like a lion, and had eagle's wings: I beheld till the wings thereof were plucked, and it was lifted up from the earth, and made stand upon the feet as a man, and a man's heart was given to it.

Using metals, Daniel 2 lists the nations, representing their value from man's viewpoint. In the prophetic section starting in Daniel 7, the Lord gives His view of their characters. God characterized Babylon as a lion with eagle's wings, and King Nebuchadnezzar used those same symbols. Visit the Pergammum Museum in Berlin, Germany and you will see a lion with eagle's wings and a man's head at the entrance of the Ishtar Gate exhibit. The first beast is unquestionably the kingdom of Babylon. Bunch gives additional evidences:

> Both Nebuchadnezzar and Babylon are compared in Scripture to a lion and an eagle. See Jeremiah 4:7,13; 48:40; 49:19, 22; Ezekiel 17:3; Habakkuk 1:6-8. Many figures of winged lions have been found in the ruins of Nineveh, Persepolis, Babylon, and other Assyrian and Babylonian cities. Babylon's war-god, Mars, was represented by a winged lion. It was doubtless the symbol of Babylon itself. Under Nebuchadnezzar, Babylon was as bold and dominant as a lion, the king of beasts, and as swift and far-reaching in her conquests as an eagle, the king of birds. In the image, Babylon was represented by gold, the king of metals. The noblest of metals in the form of the noblest part of man, and the noblest of beasts with the wings of the noblest of birds, are the prophetic symbols of Babylon, "the glory of kingdoms." Daniel asked no questions regarding this symbol and doubtless knew that it represented the same kingdom as the head of gold. He was very familiar with the many sculptured lions with eagles' wings at the entrances to the temples and palaces of the city of Babylon.[6]

---

5   W. H. Thomson, *The Great Argument* (London: Sampson Low, Marston, Searle, and Rivington: 1884), 294.

6   Bunch, "The Book of Daniel," 89.

"I watched till its wings were plucked off; and it was lifted up from the earth and made to stand on two feet like a man, and a man's heart was given to it" (Daniel 7:4; NKJ). The answer to this symbol come from Daniel 4. In his own words, Nebuchadnezzar shares the account of his conversion, seven years of lycanthropy, and his recovery. His testimony reveals that he was not healed until he ceased to be a heartless tyrant. His heart became like a man's when he gave honor to God in heaven. King Nebuchadnezzar became a subject of the King of kings. He realized his position as a created being in the care of his heavenly Father. Nebuchadnezzar was no longer a beast, but a new man with a heart toward his Creator. Soon after his death, Babylon declined and was overthrown by Medo-Persia.

Feasting Bear with Three Bones

Daniel 7:5: And behold another beast, a second, like to a bear, and it raised up itself on one side, and it had three ribs in the mouth of it between the teeth of it: and they said thus unto it, Arise, devour much flesh.

This is a fitting symbol for the Medo-Persian Empire. Like the bear, the armies of the Medes and Persians were large and slow. History records different figures for these large armies ranging from a conservative figure of 700,000 men in Darius' army to a high estimate of 2,500,000 men in the armies of Xerxes. Artaxerxes had an army of 900,000 men with a reserve of 300,000 more. An army this size would be large and ponderous to manage, moving more like a bear than a lion. These large Medo-Persian armies overthrew Babylon in 539 B.C.

Three ribs. The three ribs represent one of three scenarios. In the most popular view, the three ribs symbolize the three provinces of Babylon: Egypt, Lydia, and Babylon. Others say the ribs represent the triple alliance of Media, Lydia and Babylonia. The third view equates the ribs with the three powers that preceded Medo-Persia: Egypt, Assyria and Babylon. In the context of Isaiah, Jeremiah, and Ezekiel, it makes more sense that these three ribs symbolize the three broken kingdoms of Egypt, Assyria, and Babylon. This contextual understanding of the successive kingdoms of the world becomes necessary in placing the last-day events of Revelation in their proper order.

Daniel 7:6: After this I beheld, and lo another, like a leopard, which had upon the back of it four wings of a fowl; the beast had also four heads; and dominion was given to it.

This beast is like a leopard, swift and ferocious. The armies of Greece under Alexander the Great were tremendously swift. Bunch describes the rapidity of Alexander's conquests: "In two years he subdued the entire Balkan Peninsula and then crossed into Asia. His first great victory over the Persians was in the battle of Granicus on May 22, 334 B.C. This victory opened to him the whole of Asia Minor. The battle of Issus was fought in November of the next year and laid Egypt and all Asia west of the Euphrates at his feet. The Persian power completely crumbled as the result of the battle of Arbela in 331, leaving Alexander the undisputed ruler of the world. In this last battle Alexander had but 30,000 men compared with 1,000,000 Persians under Darius. It is said that in this battle elephants were used for the first time in warfare."[7]

The union of a leopard's speed and four wings symbolizes additional and incredible swiftness. As a bird covers large distances faster than a land animal, the wings symbolized the expeditious manner in which Alexander conquered the world. Maxwell summarizes: "Beginning almost from scratch Alexander united contentious Greece and conquered mighty Persia in twelve lightening years. He conquered Persia and *died* by the time he was only thirty-two!"[8]

Four-headed Leopard with Four Wings

The leopard's four heads symbolize the four divisions of the Greek Empire at the death of Alexander. Maxwell clearly delineates the four heads of the leopard-like kingdom of Greece:

> The *four heads* of the leopard will be identified in Daniel 8:22 as the **"four kingdoms"** that would divide up Alexander's Hellenistic Greek Empire after his death. Alexander died of a raging fever. As his strength ebbed, his military leaders filed past his bed in melancholy tribute. In response Alexander could only nod his head. He could not speak. He appointed no successor.
>
> Even before they buried him, his generals began to quarrel. Twenty-two bloody years later, after the landmark Battle of Ipsus in 301 B.C., four of the generals remained in control of four Hellenistic Greek kingdoms.[9]

Swain lists these four divisions of Greece: "[1] Cassander got Macedonia and Greece; [2] Lysimachus took Thrace and much of Asia Minor; [3] Ptolemy retained Egypt, Cyrenaica, and Palestine; and [4] the rest of Asia [that is, Syria and the lands Alexander had won in the east] went to Seleucus."[10]

Maxwell concludes: "The Battle of Ipsus was decisive. It marked the end of the vigorous attempt by Antigonus to form a single, reunited empire. The four-way division lasted until the death of Lysimachus in 281 B.C., after which there

---

[7]   Ibid., 93.

[8]   C. Mervyn Maxwell, *God Cares*, 2 vols. (Nampa, ID: Pacific Press, 1981), 1:109.

[9]   Ibid., 1:109-111.

[10] Joseph Ward Swain, *The Ancient World*, 2 vols. (New York: Harper & Row, 1950), 2:40-42; quoted in C. Mervyn Maxwell, *God Cares*, 2 vols. (Nampa, ID: Pacific Press, 1981), 1:111.

were for a while three main Hellenistic Greek kingdoms—Syria, Egypt, and Macedonia—along with a few minor ones."[11]

Daniel 7:7: After this I saw in the night visions, and behold a fourth beast, dreadful and terrible, and strong exceedingly; and it had great iron teeth: it devoured and brake in pieces, and stamped the residue with the feet of it: and it was diverse from all the beasts that were before it; and it had ten horns.

The fourth beast must be Rome because it followed the kingdom of Greece. Basing his statements on Scripture and history, Bunch lists important reasons for this conclusion:

> Most all ancient authorities including Josephus applied this symbol to Rome. Modern Biblical students are in almost universal agreement on this point. Indeed it would be very difficult to even imagine any other interpretation. Rome was "diverse" or different, not only from the other three universal empires, but "from all kingdoms." (Verse 23). Rome was the world's first republic with a representative form of government. Even under the emperors it was different, having a constitution and a Senate. It was so different from the others that no beast in nature could be found to adequately represent its character and career. It is therefore symbolized by a nondescript beast designated by the prophet as "dreadful and terrible, and strong exceedingly," and with "great iron teeth." Rome assumed world rulership in 168 B.C.[12]

Ten Horns on the Terrible Fourth Beast

With an understanding of biblical symbols, Smith describes the horns: "It had ten horns, which are explained in verse 24 to be ten kings, or kingdoms, which should arise out of this empire."[13] Notice the similarity to Daniel 2 as the two iron legs of the Roman Empire end in ten toes. Bunch recites Rome's decline: "Rome became so weakened by vice, luxury, wealth, idleness, and the intoxication of power, that during the fourth and fifth centuries the barbarians of the north broke through the barriers of Roman legions and established themselves within the empire. The mighty iron monarchy that had broken in pieces the nations of earth was herself broken into ten pieces by the northern invaders."[14]

With poetic prose, Ridpath paints the fall of pagan Rome: "At last the seals were loosed, and the barbaric tornado was poured out of the North. Through the Alpine passes came the rushing cohort of warriors each with the rage of Scythia

---

[11] Maxwell, 1:111.

[12] Bunch, "The Book of Daniel," 94.

[13] Smith, 110.

[14] Bunch, "The Book of Daniel," 96.

in his stomach and the icicles of the Baltic in his beard. The great hulk of Rome tottered, fell, and lay dead on the earth, like the stump of Dagon."[15]

Smith concludes: "The ten horns, beyond controversy, represent the ten kingdoms into which Rome was divided."[16] Taken from Oxentenko, these ten divisions show the partitioning of Rome. In time, the first seven formed the basis of modern Europe.[17]

1. Franks (French)

2. Visigoths (Spanish)

3. Lombards (Italians)

4. Suevi (Swiss)

5. Alemanni (Germans)

6. Anglo-Saxons (British)

7. Burgundians (Portuguese)

8. Heruli *

9. Vandals *

10. Ostrogoths *

*The Heruli, Vandals, and Ostrogoths were three kingdoms uprooted by the little horn power (Daniel 7:24). They no longer exist.

Daniel 7:8: I considered the horns, and, behold, there came up among them another little horn, before whom there were three of the first horns plucked up by the roots: and, behold, in this horn were eyes like the eyes of man, and a mouth speaking great things.

This scene envisions a developing power, a little horn that comes up among the ten horns. As it develops and grows, it takes up so much room that it uproots three of the powers. Evidently, these three horns get in the way of the growth and development of the little horn and must be uprooted in order to give it full freedom to develop.

One of the identifying characteristics of this little horn is its speech which is full of pompous words. The Psalmist writes of boasters: "How long will they mouth haughty speeches, go on boasting, all these evildoers?" (Psalm 94:4; NAB). "Until the pit be digged for the wicked. . . . The LORD our God shall cut them off" (Psalm 94:13, 23).

---

[15] John Clarke Ridpath, *History of the World* (Cincinnati, OH: The Jones Bros. Publishing Co., 1894), 3:29.

[16] Smith, 57.

[17] Oxentenko, 60.

The Greatest Boaster

The Aramaic word רַבְרְבָן (rab-rᵉ-ban) is made from the doubling of the root word רַב (rab). Rab is Aramaic for "great." The doubling of this root word in Daniel 7:8 strengthens the meaning, hence the little horn is speaking "very great things" about himself. This word is used when a chief captain speaks. This little horn does not consider himself to be a little horn, but rather greater than all to whom he speaks. He believes he has the authority to do so and has gone as far as to appropriate for himself that which belongs only to Jesus Christ. God proclaims him to be the opposite of what the little horn considers himself to be since He directs Daniel to call him a "little horn."

Who is the Little Horn?

Daniel was the first to ask this question: "Then I **desired to know the exact meaning of** the fourth beast, . . . and the meaning of the ten horns that were on its head and **the other horn which came up**, and before which three of them fell, namely, that horn which had eyes and a mouth uttering great boasts" (Daniel 7:19-20; NAU).

Nine important points from Scripture help us to clearly identify the little horn power. The following characteristics were adapted from Oxentenko.[18]

1. The little horn arises from the fourth beast (7:8, 20, 24). Out of the pagan Roman Empire, this new power would come forth. Since it grows out of Rome, in a sense it is a continuation of Rome. Daniel wanted to know the truth about this fourth beast, its ten horns, and the little horn that came up last, pulling up three of the ten horns (Daniel 7:19).

2. The little horn comes up after the ten horns (7:8, 24). "Another shall rise after them" (Daniel 7:24). Chronologically the little horn would come to power after the formation of ten kingdoms that grew from the crumbling ruins of Rome. Look for the little horn's rise to power after Rome's fall in A.D. 476.

3. The little horn was different than the ten kings (7:24, 25). Diverse means different. The ten horns were political kingdoms, but the little horn would say great words against God, claim great and god-like power for himself, and fight against God's law and His people. With these religious claims, this kingdom would have more than political rulership; hence it is a religio-political power.

4. The little horn pulls up three of the ten horns (7:8, 20, 24). "He shall subdue three kings" (Daniel 7:24). As this power rises, it pulls up and roots out three of the ten kingdoms that arose from the divided Roman Empire.

5. The little horn has eyes like a man (7:8, 20). In the Bible, eyes symbolize of divine intelligence, but this horn's eyes are the eyes of man, not the eyes of God. Thus the little horn rules by human intellect, preemptively seizing the authority of God in its fight against the Creator, His law, and His people.

---

[18] Ibid., 62-64.

6. The little horn speaks great things against the most High (7:8, 11, 20, 25). The little horn spoke great and pompous thing, even against God Himself. This is blasphemy.

7. The little horn rules for "a time, times, and the dividing of times" (7:25). This same time period is referred to seven times in the books of Daniel and Revelation: twice in Daniel (7:25; 12:7) and five times in Revelation (11:2, 3; 12:6, 14; 13:5). The last three uses of this time period in Revelation show that this power opposes the pure woman, God's symbol of His true church. Thus the religio-political power of the little horn usurps the role of God's church on earth.

What is a "time"? In Daniel 4:16, Nebuchadnezzar's dream stated that seven "times" would pass over him before the kingdom would be restored to him. History tells us that he was insane for seven years, and at the end of these "seven times," his sanity returned. Thus a "time" literally means one year. The Bible shows us that "time, times, and the dividing of times" is the same period as "forty-two months" and "one thousand two hundred sixty days" (Revelation 11:2, 3; 12:6, 14).

In apocalyptic prophecy, one prophetic day equals one literal year (Ezekiel 4:4-6; Daniel 11:13, 20). Months are based upon lunar reckoning (1 month = 29.56 days, rounded to 30 days). Therefore in apocalyptic prophecy one prophetic "time" (360 days) would equal 360 literal years. The following chart shows the relationship of the 1260 prophetic days and forty-two months to the phrase "time, times, and dividing of times."

Prophetic Time	in Years	in Months	in Days	Literal Years
Time	= 1 yr.	= 12 mo.	= 360 days	=360 literal yrs.
Times	= 2 yrs.	= 24 mo.	= 720 days	=720 literal yrs.
1/2 Time	= 1/2 yr.	= 6 mo.	= 180 days	=180 literal yrs.
A time, times, and half a time	= 3 1/2 yrs.	= 42 mo.	= 1260 days	= 1260 literal yrs.

Thus the little horn power would have political dominion for a long period of time. He would make his great religious boasts and persecute God's people for 1,260 years.

8. The little horn would "think to change times and laws" (7:25). This little horn power would be a religio-political power that attempts to change the "times and laws" of God, the Ten Commandments. The little horn tampered with the fourth commandment that deals with holy time (**Exodus 20:1-17; Deuteronomy 5:6-12**). It also removed the second commandment and split the tenth commandment into two pieces. Thus it thought to change God's times and His laws.

9. The little horn would war against God's people (7:21, 25). This little horn would be a persecuting power and "wear out the saints" for 1,260 literal years (Daniel 7:25). The long religious war described by Daniel 7:25 can also be found in Revelation 12:6, 14; 13:5. These last three references in Revelation to this long and unholy war show the opposition of the little horn power to God's true people as represented by a pure woman.

For an even more detailed listing of sixteen identifying marks of the little horn power, see the appendix. Bunch gives pages of historical facts with extensive documentation that make the prophecies of Daniel and Revelation plain.

The Little Horn's Identity

Only one power emerged out of the crumbling Roman Empire after A.D. 476 and rooted out three of the ten kingdoms with its rise to power. After the ten kingdoms of divided Rome came to power, papal Rome arose from the ashes of pagan Rome and established itself in the former capital of Rome, growing over the centuries to preeminence in Western Europe. This church-state kingdom became a persecuting power, the first "Christian" kingdom to wield a sword in the name of Christ. Rising up in Rome in place of the ancient emperors, papal Rome as symbolized by the little horn came into power exactly as specified by Daniel's prophecy. With unmistakable evidence, Daniel 7 pinpoints the identity of the little horn.

Smith discusses the characteristics of the little horn: "Now we have but to inquire if, since A.D. 476, any kingdom has risen among the ten division of the Roman Empire which was diverse from them all; and if so, what one? The answer is, Yes, the spiritual kingdom of the papacy. . . . Daniel beheld this power making war upon the saints. Has such a war been waged by the papacy? Millions of martyrs answer, Yes. Witness the cruel persecution of the Waldenses, the Albigenses, and Protestants in general by the papal power."[19]

Wright affirms this identification: "In all ages of the Church, from the days of Gregory the Great down to the present, men have pointed to the Papacy as the fulfillment of the prophecy. That interpretation is set forth in the Homilies of the Church of England and by all the Reformed churches. The interpretation, however, has been ignored or rejected by critics, for reasons, which need not be specified. It can, however, stand all the tests of criticism."[20]

As the papacy rose to power, it uprooted three Germanic tribes from among the ten horns: the Heruli, Vandals, and the Ostrogoths. The other seven kingdoms remain unto this day. This power reigned for 1,260 years from A.D. 538 to 1798. The long reign of papal rule came to an end when Napoleon's general, Berthier, took Pope Pius VI captive, giving the little horn power its deadly, but temporary, wound (Revelation 13:3).

---

[19] Smith, 117.

[20] C. H. H. Wright, *Daniel and His Prophecies* (London: Williams and Norgate, 1906), 168; quoted in Taylor G. Bunch, "The Book of Daniel," Typewritten manuscript, 1950, Department of Archives and Special Collections, Del Webb Memorial Library, Loma Linda University, Loma Linda, CA, 98.

Christian Apostasy

Daniel and Revelation are not the only sources of information on the little horn power. The New Testament gives parallel prophecies concerning the church, the coming apostasy, and the rise of the antichrist power.

Acts 20:29-31: For I know this, that after my departing shall grievous wolves enter in among you, not sparing the flock. ³⁰Also of your own selves shall men arise, speaking perverse things, to draw away disciples after them. ³¹Therefore watch, and remember, that by the space of three years I ceased not to warn every one night and day with tears.

Paul understood the prophecies in Daniel and warned God's people of the coming apostasy. During his farewell message in Miletus, Paul cautioned the Ephesian elders, giving them details about this apostasy. First "wolves" from without the church would become members: "grievous wolves shall enter in among you" (Acts 20:29). Then apostasy would also arise from the midst of the church: "Of your own selves shall men arise," Paul forewarned, "speaking perverse things, to draw away disciples after them" (Acts 20:30).

"Perverse" comes from the Greek word *diastrepho*, meaning "to distort, misinterpret, or morally corrupt." Like a cancer, the virus of false teachings from the outside would grow inside the church, within the body of Christ, so to speak.

Note that apostasy would begin quickly, within that generation of leaders. "Of your own selves" refers to the elders from Ephesus, so this "falling away" would start during their lifetime. Paul predicted that errors would creep into the church soon after his death (Acts 20:29-30).

The Little Horn: Man of Lawlessness

2 Thessalonians 2:1-4: Now we beseech you, brethren, by the coming of our Lord Jesus Christ, and by our gathering together unto him, ²That ye be not soon shaken in mind, or be troubled, neither by spirit, nor by word, nor by letter as from us, as that the day of Christ is at hand. ³Let no man deceive you by any means: for that day shall not come, except there come a falling away first, and that man of sin be revealed, the son of perdition; ⁴Who opposeth and exalteth himself above all that is called God, or that is worshipped; so that he as God sitteth in the temple of God, shewing himself that he is God.

As he explained last-day prophecies to the Christians, Paul referred to the predictions of Daniel 7 in his second letter to the church in Thessalonica. Scholars from many denominations have agreed that he is talking about the antichrist. "The man of sin" is also called "that Wicked" (2 Thessalonians 2:3, 8). "Wicked" comes from the Greek word *anomos* which means "lawless or not subject to the law of God." This lawless and disobedient power stands in opposition to the law of God. Therefore this man of lawlessness matches the little horn power of Daniel 7:25 who thinks that he can change God's times and laws.

Paul is clear: Before the coming of Christ, the church would fall into apostasy, and then the "man of sin" would be revealed (2 Thessalonians 2:3). "Falling away" is ἀποστασία (*apostasia*) in the Greek from whence the English word "apostasy" is derived (2 Thessalonians 2:3). *Apostasia* means "a falling away or defection," thus "an apostasy."

Since Paul emphasized this progression of events, we also should consider his list carefully: (1) apostasy comes from without and within the church, (2) then the man of lawlessness would come to power, and (3) lastly the second coming of Christ destroys the "man of sin." This chain of events shows Paul's reliance on Daniel 7.

The man of lawlessness is also called "the son of perdition" (2 Thessalonians 2:3). "Perdition" refers to the coming destruction of the little horn power. "Son of perdition" is used only one other time in the Bible—to describe Judas Iscariot. He was one of the twelve disciples, but fell away from his Lord and betrayed him. Judas took his own life, and in the resurrection of damnation he will face his final destruction. Like Judas, the man of lawlessness arises as a professed Christian. He would maintain the outward forms and profession of faithfulness, but he would be betray the pure faith of Jesus.

The Little Horn Rules the Church

The antichrist power exalts "himself above all that is called God, or that is worshipped; so that he" sits as God "in the temple of God," showing "himself that he is God" (2 Thessalonians 2:4). This is a blasphemous power, pretending to be God, and claiming God's authority in the church of God. By taking his "seat" of authority in the church, he claims for himself the prerogatives of God. The lawless one usurps the "temple of God," the symbol for the church (2 Thessalonians 2:4; Ephesians 2:19-22).

2 Thessalonians 2:7-10: For the mystery of iniquity doth already work: only he who now letteth will let, until he be taken out of the way. ⁸And then shall that Wicked be revealed, whom the Lord shall consume with the spirit of his mouth, and shall destroy with the brightness of his mouth, and shall destroy with the brightness of his coming: ⁹Even him, whose coming is after the working of Satan with all power and signs and lying wonders, ¹⁰And with all deceivableness of unrighteousness in them that perish; because they received not the love of the truth, that they might be saved.

Going into more detail, Paul predicts a clear revelation of this lawless one. The names Paul uses for the antichrist and the characteristics he gives match the description of the little horn. Following the outline of Daniel 7, Paul mentions that a power must be removed before the wicked man of lawlessness can be revealed. Since the power in Paul's day was pagan Rome, this also matches the timing of the little horn in Daniel 7 which arises after the fall of Rome.

As 2 Thessalonians 2:3 spoke of the apostasy of the church, so verses 4 to 10 show the rise of the little horn power. The falsehoods that entered the church during the apostasy prepared the way for the man of sin. Where does the man of lawlessness rule? He sits in the church of God, claiming to be God, and accepting worship that does not lawfully belong to him (2 Thessalonians 2:4).

The Little Horn as False Christ

The little horn's methods follow "after the working of Satan with all power and signs and lying wonders" (2 Thessalonians 2:9). Even as Satan desired the throne of God Himself, so also the little horn yearns for the worship that should only be given to Christ. Daniel 8:11-12 confirms the control taken in the fallen church by the little horn in matters of worship: **"Yea, he magnified himself even to the prince of the host, and by him the daily sacrifice was taken away, and the place of his sanctuary was cast down. . . . And it cast down the truth to the ground; and it practised, and prospered."**

The little horn power not only claims to be God, but he also takes the place of Christ in the church and casts away the truth of Christ's daily ministry in the heavenly sanctuary. Through his leadership in the fallen church, the man of sin tears down the work of Christ as our Intercessor, Sacrifice, and Mediator, and puts himself in Christ's position. The little horn throws down the truth of God, replacing it with false beliefs and "lying wonders" (Daniel 8:12; 2 Thessalonians 2:10). Thus worship of the little horn becomes the substitute for faith in the truths of God's word. The man of sin literally becomes the deceptive substitute for the only One who is the Truth (John 14:6).

God gave these serious prophecies to His people to protect them from the deceptive power of the little horn. Since "signs and wonders" are used by the lawless one through the power of Satan, miracles cannot be the test of truth. Jesus proclaimed: "Thy word is truth" (John 17:17). In this battle between the false Christ and God's people, "love of the truth" is our only protection from the "lying wonders" of that wicked one (2 Thessalonians 2:9-10). Just as Paul relied on Scripture to feed the early Christian church, God's word must remain our source of truth in these last days. Read, believe, and love the truths of the Holy Bible and put them into practice in your life.

The last great struggle in this world is between Satan and Christ, between those who uphold deception and the ones who follow "the Way, the Truth, and the Life" (John 14:6). The great controversy of the ages is within the church itself. Apostasy led to "wolves" in leadership positions, and falsehoods came in with them. As the little horn came into the church of God, the true worship of Christ was cast to the ground.

Sadly, most Christian churches are still waiting for the antichrist to come. As the Jews refused the real Messiah when He came, so the Christian church lost its spiritual vision. Most professed Christians do not realize that the antichrist is already here. After the fall of the Roman Empire, he ruled for 1,260 long years.

In the place of Christ, he made laws against the word of God and cast the truth of the Bible to the ground. Through this greatest of all apostasies, Christianity itself has been corrupted, slowly and nearly secretly from within.

This is Satan's greatest victory over the Christian church. When he saw that persecution from pagan Rome strengthened the church and purified it, the devil changed his battle plans. His ambassador, the little horn, has become the ruling power over all Christianity!

Judgment Against the Little Horn

Daniel 7:9-12: I beheld till the thrones were cast down, and the Ancient of days did sit, whose garment was white as snow, and the hair of his head like the pure wool: his throne was like the fiery flame, and his wheels as burning fire. [10]A fiery stream issued and came forth from before him: thousand thousands ministered unto him, and ten thousand times ten thousand stood before him: the judgment was set, and the books were opened. [11]I beheld then because of the voice of the great words which the horn spake: I beheld even till the beast was slain, and his body destroyed, and given to the burning flame. [12]As concerning the rest of the beasts, they had their dominion taken away: yet their lives were prolonged for a season and time.

The imagery of this judgment scene in heaven is similar to the sacred throne room scenes of Ezekiel 1 and Revelation 4. From His royal throne, God has kept exact records of this little horn's wicked actions, and it will be brought before the judgment seat of the Almighty. Then the little horn will meet its final demise in the fires of judgment. As for the other kingdoms, they remain, but not with the power they once had.

According to Daniel 7:11, the pompous and boastful words from the mouth of the little horn demand God's judgment. Coming out of the fourth beast of Daniel 7, the little horn had its origin in Rome. Truth never changes, but the little horn constantly adapts and modifies its rules to accommodate its purposes (2 Thessalonians 2:10).

White makes it clear: "The pope has been given the very titles of Deity. He has been styled 'Lord God the Pope,' and has been declared infallible. He demands the homage of all men. The same claim urged by Satan in the wilderness of temptation is still urged by him through the Church of Rome, and vast numbers are ready to yield him homage."[21]

God's judgment of death comes to the little horn because he is the man of sin and lawlessness. The Bible declares: "The wages of sin is death" (Romans 6:23).

[21] White, *The Great Controversy Between Christ and Satan* (Mountain View, CA: Pacific Press, 1911), 50.

Christ's Everlasting Kingdom

Daniel 7:13-14: I saw in the night visions, and, behold, one like the Son of man came with the clouds of heaven, and came to the Ancient of days, and they brought him near before him. ¹⁴And there was given him dominion, and glory, and a kingdom, that all people, nations, and languages, should serve him: his dominion is an everlasting dominion, which shall not pass away, and his kingdom that which shall not be destroyed.

The scene changes from the beast to the judgment and onward into the future. In the last judgment scene, Jesus comes to the Ancient of days to receive everlasting dominion and His kingdom, the only everlasting kingdom. This is in stark contrast to the transitory, temporary kingdom of the little horn.

The term "Son of man" appears 88 times in 84 verses of the New Testament. Jesus uses the term more often than anyone else as He refers to Himself as the "Son of man" 77 times. The little horn casts down the ministry of Christ, the Prince of the host, but in the judgment, Jesus receives honor from His Father before the entire universe. He became the "Son of man" to raise us up to reign with Him.

Jesus, the "Son of man" receives the kingdom purchased by His own blood which was shed on the cross at Mount Calvary. The little horn's dominion is declared to be the rightful possession of Christ. The fourth beast with its little horn is slain, but the glory of Christ's kingdom will never pass away. This parallels Revelation 11:15-17 when the kingdoms of this world become the kingdoms of Christ.

Help Me Understand Your Truth

Daniel 7:15-18: I Daniel was grieved in my spirit in the midst of my body, and the visions of my head troubled me. I came near unto one of them that stood by, and asked him the truth of all this. So he told me, and made me know the interpretation of the things. ¹⁷These great beasts, which are four, are four kings, which shall arise out of the earth. ¹⁸But the saints of the most High shall take the kingdom, and possess the kingdom for ever, even for ever and ever

Troubled by this vision, the prophet was anxious to understand the truth. The angel gave a brief, two-sentence explanation about the little horn, but this was not enough for Daniel.

Daniel 7:19-22: Then I would know the truth of the fourth beast, which was diverse from all the others, exceeding dreadful, whose teeth were of iron, and his nails of brass; which devoured, brake in pieces, and stamped the residue with his feet; ²⁰And of the ten horns that were in his head, and of the other which came up, and before whom three fell; even of that horn that had eyes, and a mouth that spake very great things, whose look was more stout than

his fellows. [21]I beheld, and the same horn made war with the saints, and prevailed against them; [22]Until the Ancient of days came, and judgment was given to the saints of the most High; and the time came that the saints possessed the kingdom.

Again, Daniel asks for a clearer understanding, but this time he is more specific in his request: "I want to know about the fourth beast, the ten horns, and the little horn" (Daniel 7:19-20). Like Jacob, he won't let go until he receives the blessing he needs from heaven. Now the angel sets the stage for understanding the little horn power in the context of the fourth kingdom.

Iron Teeth and Bronze Nails: What do the *iron* teeth and *bronze* nails in verse 19 symbolize? In Daniel 2, the third kingdom is bronze and the fourth is of iron, representing Greece and Rome respectively. These metals for the teeth and nails represent the doubled strength and brutality of Rome. More than this, de Kock explains, the Greek and Roman metals together evoke "a well-known concept, expressed in the word *Greco-Roman*."[22] Even though Rome was victorious over Greece in 168 B.C., *Koine* Greek continued to be the language of the people. The New Testament authors wrote in Greek more than two hundred years later. This is a good example of how the successive kingdoms kept alive certain aspects of the cultures they conquered.

Even as the iron portion of the kingdom had two legs, history shows two divisions of Rome which arose in A.D. 395: the Western Roman Empire with its capital in Rome and the Eastern Roman Empire with its capital in Constantinople. Out of these two divisions of the Roman Empire grew two branches of the Roman Church: the Roman Catholic and Greek Orthodox churches. Even though a schism between the two occurred more than a thousand years ago, there are only minor differences between the two in the eyes of Protestants. The Orthodox Church uses icons instead of images, their priests may marry, and their church is ruled by a group of patriarchs instead of a pope. Otherwise the theology and practice is virtually indistinguishable. Both churches have similar liturgy and beliefs, showing veneration for Mary and the saints.

Daniel 7:23-28: Thus he said, The fourth beast shall be the fourth kingdom upon earth, which shall be diverse from all kingdoms, and shall devour the whole earth, and shall tread it down, and break it in pieces. [24]And the ten horns out of this kingdom are ten kings that shall arise: and another shall rise after them; and he shall be diverse from the first, and he shall subdue three kings. [25]And he shall speak great words against the most High, and shall wear out the saints of the most High, and think to change times and laws: and they shall be given into his hand until a time and times and the dividing of time. [26]But the judgment shall sit, and they shall take away his dominion, to

---

[22] Edwin de Kock, *Christ and Antichrist in Prophecy and History* (Edinburg, TX: Diadone Enterprises, 2001), 81.

consume and to destroy it unto the end. [27]And the kingdom and dominion, and the greatness of the kingdom under the whole heaven, shall be given to the people of the saints of the most High, whose kingdom is an everlasting kingdom, and all dominions shall serve and obey him. [28]Hitherto is the end of the matter. As for me Daniel, my cogitations much troubled me, and my countenance changed in me: but I kept the matter in my heart.

The key to comprehending the little horn is an understanding of the fourth beast. This section of Daniel clearly interprets itself. The fourth beast is the fourth kingdom (Daniel 7:23). Rome, the fourth kingdom, is different from the kingdoms before it because it finds a way to stay alive and adapt to its times and circumstances. Rome never really dies. After its demise, it revives in a different form.

The fourth beast is the last animal kingdom in this vision. Daniel saw ten horns on the fourth beast and after that, another little horn appeared which uprooted three of the ten horns. All these horns and actions take place on the fourth beast, therefore it is still the kingdom of Rome. Thus when the little horn is destroyed after the judgment, the fourth beast out of which it grows is slain (Daniel 7:11).

Bunch enlarges on the longevity of Rome's power: "According to the vision of the fourth beast, Rome in its various aspects and phases was to dominate the world from the fall of Grecia till the saints of God are given the dominion of the earth. Whether it be Pagan Rome, divided Rome, or papal Rome, it is always Rome. Non-Catholic testimony is almost unanimous in applying the eleventh horn to the Papacy, or Ecclesiastical Rome."[23]

The fourth beast is pagan Rome in the context of Daniel 2 and 7, but in reality Rome was the sixth empire to rule the world. The next chapter demonstrates that when a kingdom is either nearing its end or has already met its demise, that kingdom is eliminated from the prophetic picture. In this vision, the lion of Babylon, the bear of Medo-Persia, and leopard kingdom of Greece were predecessors of Rome, the fourth kingdom. According to verse 24, the ten kingdoms, followed by the little horn, all arise out of pagan Rome.

The "eighth" horn: Daniel focuses on the fourth beast with its ten horns and the little horn. Sprouting in the midst of the first ten, the little horn appears to be an eleventh horn. It does not belong with the ten horns, but it stars as the eleventh horn for a short time. Then in its rise to power, the little horn uproots three of the ten horns. At this point, the fourth beast now has seven horns plus the little horn. In this sense, the little horn becomes the eighth horn. In Revelation 17, the number eight becomes important.

This eighth horn inherits the Roman Empire, and the saints are given into his hand for 1,260 prophetic days or three and one-half prophetic years (1,260 literal years). This little horn power claims the seat of Christ and pretends to

---

23   Bunch, "The Book of Daniel," 98.

exercise Christ's power in a prophetic time period that parallels the literal three and one-half years of Jesus' ministry here on earth. Thus the little horn masquerades as Christ and claims for himself Jesus' power and position of authority.

The Little Horn Versus the Most High

Backed up by other parallel prophecies in both the Old and New Testaments, Daniel 7:25 is packed with meaning: "And he shall speak great words against the most High, and shall wear out the saints of the most High, and think to change times and laws: and they shall be given into his hand until a time, and times and the dividing of time."

Little horn rises: "And another shall rise after them" (Daniel 7:24). The little horn arrives after the breakup of the Roman Empire into ten horns or kingdoms. Even as the little horn will attack the most High, so he also attacks three of the ten horns, pulling them up by the roots. Then the little horn becomes stronger and more powerful than the seven horns that remain of the first ten. Thus the long reign of the little horn power could not begin until after the fall of Rome.

Little horn attacks: By this time, the apostasy predicted by Paul has already come to pass (2 Thessalonians 2:3; Acts 20:29-30). As falsehoods and pagan practices began to replace the truths of God's word, the Christian church found a new leader in the little horn (2 Thessalonians 2:9-10). After his rise to power in this now paganized church, the little horn made his frontal attack against the law of the most High, against the saints of the most High, and against the most High Himself (Daniel 7:25).

The little horn's attack against God, His people, and His law lasted a very long time: 1,260 years during the Dark Ages. The papacy received its power, seat, and great authority from Rome through Justinian in A.D. 538. Adding 1,260 years to 538 gives 1798 as the end of that lengthy papal reign. This prophecy was fulfilled as the pope was taken captive in 1798 during the French Revolution, giving the little horn power its deadly wound.

"He shall wear out the saints of the most High" (Daniel 7:25). As the little horn continued to suppress truths from God's word, he attacked all those who followed the Bible. Those who kept the Ten Commandments were killed, and Bibles were burned along with their owners. As they refused to submit to the pagan teachings of papal Rome, multiplied millions died by burning, hanging, drowning, the rack, and other forms of torture. Those torture chambers still exist and tours can be taken in these dungeons of the Roman Church. Not only does the little horn become the greatest boaster, he also became the greatest murderer in human history.

"He shall think to change times and laws" (Daniel 7:25). In the sermon on the mount, Jesus warned against any attempt to change the law of God (Matthew 5:17-19). The little horn deleted the second commandment because it speaks against idol worship. Then he divided the tenth commandment into two parts so there would still be ten modified commandments.

Only the fourth commandment deals with holy time, yet the little horn power claims to have changed God's holy Sabbath. The only commandment that starts with the word "Remember" has been trampled in the dust, while the false sabbath of the papacy has been exalted by Catholics and Protestants alike.

Kept by God Himself, given in Eden to Adam and Eve, spoken with thunder by the voice of the Lord, and written with His own finger, the seventh-day Sabbath remains a precious gift from our Creator. As we remember that special sign, the Sabbath of the Lord, we exalt the One who made us and show our love and honor to Him by our submissive obedience.

The Fourth Commandment: Exodus 20:8-11: Remember the Sabbath day, to keep it holy. [9] Six days you shall labor and do all your work, [10] but the seventh day is the Sabbath of the LORD your God. In it you shall do no work: you, nor your son, nor your daughter, nor your male servant, nor your female servant, nor your cattle, nor your stranger who is within your gates. [11]For in six days the LORD made the heavens and the earth, the sea, and all that is in them, and rested the seventh day. Therefore the LORD blessed the Sabbath day and hallowed it.

Little horn destroyed: "They shall take away his dominion, to consume and to destroy it unto the end" (Daniel 7:26). "The beast was slain, and his body destroyed, and given to the burning flame" (Daniel 7:11). Then "the saints of the Most High shall receive the kingdom, and possess the kingdom forever, even forever and ever" (Daniel 7:18; NKJ). Christ's coming is sure, and His promises will soon be reality. His everlasting kingdom will come after the little horn's last war against God's people.

Look up to the heavenly sanctuary! Daniel saw the judgment of the little horn in heaven (Daniel 7:9-14). God's righteous judgment unravels the usurpation of Christ's authority by the little horn power. As the day of the judgment began, the downtrodden truths of God's word would be restored one by one to His people. The glory that belongs only to Jesus is magnified as His people share His restored word: "Fear God and give glory to Him, for the hour of His judgment has come!" (Revelation 14:7; NKJ). Like the light of dawn, the knowledge of the glory of the Creator Christ will be spread throughout the world.

In the judgment, God's people are given to Jesus as the citizens of His kingdom. Put your life fully on the side of the most High. Today let the King of kings and Lord of lords reign in your life, thoughts, and actions. Trust God's promise that His saints will possess the kingdom. Don't look to the little horn or the powers of this world. God's kingdom is not of this earth, but soon Jesus will come to receive His own and fulfill the precious promise of eternal life in His everlasting kingdom. What a glorious promise to the saints who have determined to be faithful even unto death!

Matthew 24:14-15; RSV: And this gospel of the kingdom will be preached throughout the whole world, a testimony to all nations; and then the end will come. So when you see the desolating sacrilege spoken of by the prophet Daniel, standing in the holy place (let the reader understand).

Jesus Himself preached from the book of Daniel. As He spoke of the last days, He reminded His listeners of the little horn power and its sacrilegious work. Jesus wants us to understand the prophecies of Daniel and how they relate to the gospel message in the last days. Pray for understanding, then put it into action, and share Christ's message with the world!

Summary

Like the second chapter of Daniel, the seventh chapter covers the rise and fall of the four world kingdoms of Babylon, Medo-Persia, Greece, and Rome. The universal message of Daniel 2 was given to an earthly ruler, but Daniel 7 contains more details because it is given to God's people. Like Daniel 2, chapter 7 begins with Babylon, but it also introduces a new detail: the little horn power which grows out of pagan Rome, the fourth beast of the vision. Coming up amid the ten divisions of Europe, the little horn uproots three kingdoms and fights against God, His law, and His people for 1,260 literal years. These characteristics and many others mark the little horn's identity as papal Rome.

CHAPTER EIGHT

Daniel 8

Introduction

C hapter 8 begins the section of Daniel written in Hebrew rather than Aramaic as in the previous chapters. Aramaic, the language of international commerce, was used for the prophecies in chapters 2 to 7, signifying that these messages were given for all peoples. Chapters 8 to 12, as well as chapter 1, were written specifically for God's people. The Jews felt that all was lost when the Babylonians took them into captivity. These last chapters of Daniel bring a message of hope for God's faithful throughout the ages until He returns according to His promise.

Daniel 8 begins with the second kingdom, Medo-Persia, because Babylon was already considered by God to be a past power. The message applies God's people in all ages. There is a God in heaven, and He has the future of all of us in His hands. The symbols are the same as those in chapter 7:

- Beasts = kingdoms (Daniel 7:17, 23)
- Sea/waters = multitudes of peoples (Revelation 17:1,15; Isaiah 57:20)
- Winds = war and strife (Jeremiah 49:36; Revelation 7:1)
- Horns = kings, power, authority (Daniel 7:24)
- Wings = great speed for conquest (Hab. 1:6-8; Jeremiah 4:13; Deuteronomy 48:29)
- Day = a year (Numbers 14:34; Ezekiel 4:6

Daniel 8 has three main divisions with Daniel's response at the end:

1. The Vision of the Ram, the Male Goat, and Little Horn
2. Identification of the Time and Length of the Vision
3. The Interpretation of the Vision
4. Daniel's Response

The Vision of the Ram

Daniel 8:1-4: In the third year of the reign of King Belshazzar a vision appeared unto me, even unto me Daniel, after that which appeared unto me at the first. ²And I saw in a vision; and it came to pass, when I saw, that I was at Shushan in the palace, which is in the province of Elam; and I saw in a vision, and I was by the river of Ulai. ³Then I lifted up mine eyes, and saw, and, behold, there stood before the river a ram which had two horns: and the two horns were high; but one was higher than the other, and the higher came up last. ⁴I saw the ram pushing westward, and northward, and southward; so that no beasts might stand before him, neither was there any that could deliver out of his hand; but he did according to his will, and became great.

Verse 1: The setting for chapter 8 is "the third year of the reign of King Belshazzar." Since first year of his reign was 541 B.C., this vision must be sometime early in the year 539 B.C. during the last months of Belshazzar's reign. Babylon was no longer the power it once was, so in the vision, God moved on into the future. Babylon's greatness was gone.

"In the third year of the reign of King Belshazzar **a vision appeared to me— to me, Daniel—after the one that appeared to me the first time**" (Daniel 8:1; NKJ). Daniel himself states the connection between this vision and the other one in chapter 7.

Verse 2: While in vision, Daniel found himself in Shushan, the royal city of the Persians which was in the province of Elam. This is supported by Scripture: "King Ahasuerus sat on the throne of his kingdom, which was in Shushan the citadel" (Esther 1:2). Daniel lived in Babylon, but God took him in vision to the capital of the Persian Empire. In his vision, Daniel stood by the Ulai River which connected the Kerkha and Abdizful Rivers just north of the main part of Susa, indicating that the palace was in the northern part of the city. Shushan or Susa, the ancient capital of Elam, was founded soon after the flood and occupied continuously until its abandonment in the thirteenth century A.D.

Verse 3: The ram had unequal horns; one was higher than the other, but the higher one came up last. Gabriel clearly states, "The ram which you saw, having *the two horns—they are the kings of Media and Persia*" (Daniel 8:20; NKJ). **The ram represents the Medo-Persian Empire.** Just as the bear in Daniel 7 had one side raised higher than the other, and one of the ram's horns is higher, the Persians became stronger than the Medes and absorbed their kingdom. Scripture provides a tailor-made description of this empire!

"Westward, and northward, and southward," verse 4: This accurately pictures the military conquests of the Medo-Persians. Comparing the northern, southern, and western boundaries of Babylon with the boundaries of the Medo-Persian Empire, one could readily see that they extended in only these three directions. Again the Scriptures are accurate in advance of the events. As the three ribs in chapter 7 represent the three provinces of Babylon (Babylon, Lydia, and Egypt) or the three kingdoms that had ruled the world until then (Babylon, Assyria, and Egypt), these three represent the three directions of the verse. Westward was Babylon, northward was Lydia or Assyria, and southward was Egypt. Why did the prophecy not say eastward? When God foretells the future, He does so with unerring accuracy. The three directions of the wind correlate to the three ribs in the bear's mouth in Daniel 7:5.

The Vision of the Male Goat

Daniel 8:5-8, 21-22: And as I was considering, behold, an he goat came from the west on the face of the whole earth, and touched not the ground: and the goat had a notable horn between his eyes. ⁶And he came to the ram that had two horns, which I had seen standing before the river, and ran unto him in the fury of his power. ⁷And I saw him come close unto the ram, and he was moved with choler against him, and smote the ram, and brake his two horns: and there was no power in the ram to stand before him, but he cast him down to the ground, and stamped upon him: and there was none that could deliver the ram out of his hand. ⁸Therefore the he goat waxed very great: and when he was strong, the great horn was broken; and for it came up four notable ones toward the four winds of heaven. . . . ²¹And the rough goat is the king of Grecia: and the great horn that is between his eyes is the first king. ²²Now that being broken, whereas four stood up for it, four kingdoms shall stand up out of the nation, but not in his power.

The Bible clearly identifies the male goat as Greece in verse 21, the kingdom that conquered Medo-Persia. Note that the male goat comes from the west just as Alexander the Great's armies came out of the west to conquer the Medes and the Persians. The Greek army was small in comparison to that of the Medo-Persian host, yet Alexander's army swiftly conquered and destroyed their enemy. The broken horn marked the early death of Alexander the Great, followed by the division of his empire among his four generals.

Cassander ruled Greece and Macedon in the west. Lysimachus governed Thrace, Bithynia, and the smaller provinces of Asia to the north. Ptolemy reigned over Egypt, Libya, Arabia, and Palestine in the south, and Seleucus ruled over the east from Syria to the Indus River. These locations are important in interpreting verse 9 which describes the rise of the little horn.

The Vision of the Little Horn

Daniel 8:9-12; NKJ: And out of one of them came a little horn which grew exceedingly great toward the south, toward the east, and toward the Glorious Land. ¹⁰And it grew up to the host of heaven; and it cast down some of the host and some of the stars to the ground, and trampled them. ¹¹He even exalted himself as high as the Prince of the host; and by him the daily sacrifices were taken away, and the place of His sanctuary was cast down. ¹²Because

of transgression, an army was given over to the horn to oppose the daily sacrifices; and he cast truth down to the ground. He did all this and prospered.

Verse 9: According to the grammatical construction of the original Hebrew, the little horn comes out of one of the "four winds of heaven," and not out of one of the four horns (Daniel 8:9; 11:4). In the phrase "out of one of them," one commentary points out, "the word for 'them,' *hem*, is masculine. This indicates that, grammatically, the antecedent is 'winds' (vs. 8) and not 'horns,' since 'winds' may be either masculine or feminine, but 'horns,' only feminine."[1]

The little horn grew **"toward the south, and toward the east, and toward the pleasant land"** (Daniel 8:9). The fourth kingdom has been identified as Rome based on its contextual setting, including chapters 2 and 7. Rome conquered Africa to the **south**; Greece, Asia Minor and India in the **east**; and Israel, known as the **pleasant land.**

Daniel 8:10-12: And it waxed great, even to the host of heaven; and it cast down some of the host and of the stars to the ground, and stamped upon them. ¹¹Yea, he magnified himself even to the prince of the host, and by him the daily sacrifice was taken away, and the place of his sanctuary was cast down. ¹²And an host was given him against the daily sacrifice by reason of transgression, and it cast down the truth to the ground; and it practiced, and prospered.

As both a religious and political power, the little horn makes war on these two fronts. Pagan Rome received its culture, architecture, laws, and much of its language from the Greeks. This same system was imposed on the conquered territories in order to bring the uniformity needed to form the great Roman Empire. The disintegrating empire of pagan Rome was given to Christian Rome. Through this granted authority, the little horn grew in civil power. As the political power of papal Rome increased, she intensified her religious attack on God's people, His truth, His sanctuary, and Christ Himself.

Attack against God's people: "It cast down some of the host and of the stars to the ground" (Daniel 8:10). In the Bible, stars represent God's people (cf. Daniel 12:3; Genesis 15:5; Deuteronomy 1:10). Daniel also speaks plainly: "He shall destroy the mighty and the holy people" (Daniel 8:24). How many? He "shall destroy many" (Daniel 8:25).

As the little horn grew in strength, he mounted a vicious attack on those who would not submit to his false doctrines. Smith comments on the ferocity of papal Rome's persecution: "Primitive Christians prayed for the continuance of [pagan] Rome, for they knew that when this form of government should cease, another far worse persecuting power would arise, which would literally 'wear out the saints of the Most High,' . . . Pagan Rome could slay the infants, but spare the

---

[1]   *The Seventh-day Adventist Bible Commentary*, ed. F. D. Nichol, 2d ed., 10 vols. (Washington, DC: Review and Herald, 1980), 4:840-841.

mothers; but papal Rome slew both the mothers and infants together. No age, no sex, no condition in life, was exempt from her relentless rage."[2]

Attack against God's Truth: "It cast down the truth to the ground" (Daniel 8:12). "Thy law is the truth" (Ps. 119:42). By his attempt to change God's law and substitute his own, the little horn cast the truth of God's word to the ground.

Jesus always relied on the truth as given in Scripture. When tempted by Satan, Jesus answered from God's holy word. Before His crucifixion, Jesus prayed for His disciples: "Sanctify them through Thy truth; Thy word is truth" (John 17:17). On the other hand, the little horn opposes the truth and tramples upon it. Paul warned that this power would cooperate with Satan "with all deceivableness of unrighteousness" and with "signs and lying wonders" (2 Thessalonians 2:10, 9). Because of the little horn's attack against the truth, his followers would believe lies instead of the truth (2 Thessalonians 2:11-12).

Attack against God's sanctuary: The little horn fights against the "daily," but note that the word "sacrifice" is not found in the Hebrew of Daniel 8:12. *Tamiyd*, the Hebrew word for "daily," means "continually, perpetual, always." All the references to *tamiyd* in the first five books of Moses relate to the sanctuary: the burnt offerings, the holy fire, the breastplate of judgment, the Urim and the Thummim on the breastplate, the engraved golden band of the mitre which read "Holiness to Yahweh," the bread of God's presence, the flames of the golden candlestick, the holy incense, the fiery cloud of God's presence, and God Himself. All of these aspects of God's sanctuary were perpetual, continual, daily, *tamiyd*. Therefore *tamiyd* represents Christ's continual ministry and mediation as our High Priest in the heavenly sanctuary and our continual dependence upon His merits.

When the little horn arose after the fall of pagan Rome, Jesus had already ascended into heaven itself as our Intercessor, Sacrifice, High Priest, and Mediator. Instead of pointing God's people to Jesus, the little horn cast down the place of Christ's sanctuary. In place of the continual holy work of Jesus, the little horn substituted his own ornate sanctuary, his own priests and clothing, his own sacrifices, his own mass, his own mediation, his own confessional, and his own judgments. Thus the little horn subverted the continual ministry of Christ. Ultimately, the little horn's earthly presence and ceremonies preemptively displaced the presence of God Himself in the church.

Attack against Christ Himself: In each of the last five chapters, Daniel emphasized the primacy of Christ and His special names: Messiah the Prince, Michael your Prince, the Prince of the covenant, Michael the great Prince (Daniel 9:25; 10:21; 11:22; 12:1).

The little horn gives Christ no such honor: "He magnified himself even to the Prince of the host" (Daniel 8:11). Daniel clearly states that the little horn works against Christ: "He shall also stand up against the Prince of princes" (Daniel 8:25).

---

[2]   Smith, 135.

He considers himself to be equal with Christ (Daniel 8:11). Interestingly, the papal church uses all the sanctuary colors in their clothing except for blue. Why? Because blue symbolized the obedience of Christ and His people to the Ten Commandments (Exodus 26:1, 31-32; Numbers 15:37-41).

The ministry of Christ in the heavenly sanctuary is a continual or daily ministry: "The former priests were many in number, because they were prevented by death from continuing in office; but He holds His priesthood **permanently**, because *He continues for ever*. Consequently he is able for all time to save those who draw near to God through Him, since He *always lives* to make intercession for them" (Hebrews 7:23-25; RSV). The Bible teaches that no one else may lawfully take over the intercessory work of Christ (cf. 1 Timothy 2:5; Hebrews 3:1; 4:14-16; 8:1-2).

What does God think of the little horn's claim to be equal with Christ? "He shall also stand up against the Prince of princes; but he shall be broken without hand" (Daniel 8:25). The blasphemous claims of the little horn power will bring the judgments of God upon his head.

How Long?

Daniel 8:13-14: Then I heard one saint speaking, and another saint said unto that certain saint which spake, How long shall be the vision concerning the daily sacrifice, and the transgression of desolation, to give both the sanctuary and the host to be trodden under foot? [14]And he said unto me, Unto two thousand and three hundred days; then shall the sanctuary be cleansed.

In vision Daniel hears that all-important question: How much longer will the little horn be allowed trample God's people, truth, sanctuary, and Son? The two heavenly beings ask the same question that troubles the mind of Daniel—How Long? This list of questions is adapted from Oxentenko:[3]

How long—*before God ends the persecution of His saints?*

How long—*before God restores truth to its rightful place?*

How long—*before Jesus is exalted as our High Priest in heaven?*

How long—*before God restores the true heavenly sanctuary to His people?*

How long—*before God restores His church to its original purity?*

The answer comes from heaven: "And he said unto me, 'For **two thousand three hundred days**; then the sanctuary shall be cleansed' (Dan 8:14; NKJ).

The language of Daniel 8:14 points to the day of judgment in the yearly ceremonies of ancient Israel: the **Day of Atonement**. In the heart of Leviticus, the whole sixteenth chapter is devoted to the Day of Atonement. This day, known as *Yom Kippur* to the Hebrews, falls on the tenth day of the seventh month of the religious calendar. *Yom Kippur* was and still is the highest holy day of the year for

---

[3]   Oxentenko, 77-78.

the Jewish people. This high holy day is followed by the grand celebration of the Feast of Tabernacles, the last feast in the Jewish ceremonial year. To learn more about the Feast of Tabernacles, see the chapter in this book on Revelation 8.

Leviticus 16:29-31, 33-34; NKJ: "This shall be a statute forever for you: In the seventh month, on the tenth day of the month, you shall afflict your souls, and do no work at all, whether a native of your own country or a stranger who dwells among you. For on that day the priest shall make atonement for you, to cleanse you, that you may be clean from all your sins before the LORD. It is a sabbath of solemn rest for you, and you shall afflict your souls. It is a statute forever. . . . Then he shall make atonement for the Holy Sanctuary, and he shall make atonement for the tabernacle of meeting and for the altar, and he shall make atonement for the priests and for all the people of the assembly. This shall be an everlasting statute for you, to *make atonement* for the children of Israel, for all their sins, once a year. And he did as the LORD commanded Moses."

In the daily ministry of the sanctuary, the priest carried the blood from the sin offerings and and sprinkled that blood before the veil in the holy place. Thus the sins of God's people necessitated the cleansing of the sanctuary.

The high priest went into the most holy place of the sanctuary only once a year on the Day of Atonement. Only on this day did the high priest bring blood from the sacrifices into the very presence of the Lord to sprinkle blood upon the mercy seat of the ark of the covenant (Leviticus 16:14-15). The high priest also applied blood to the horns of the altar of incense in front of the veil. The blood of the Lord's goat made "atonement for the holy place because of the uncleanness of the children of Israel, and because of their transgressions in all their sins" (Leviticus 16:16). Now the sanctuary was cleansed, or "set right" by the blood of the Lord's goat, the symbol of Christ.

The male goat in Daniel 8 is a symbol of Greece, but it also symbolizes the special sacrifice made on the great Day of Atonement. Of the two goats used on this holy day, the Lord's goat was sacrificed and the other was not. Therefore, the second goat was not a sacrifice and could not represent Jesus. "According to the law almost all things are purified with blood, and without shedding of blood there is no remission" (Hebrews 9:22; NKJ). The second goat was sent out into the wilderness, representing an entity that is far from God and His salvation. "Aaron shall cast lots for the two goats: one lot for the LORD and the other lot for the scapegoat. And Aaron shall bring the goat on which the LORD's lot fell, and offer it as a sin offering. But the goat on which the lot fell to be the scapegoat shall be presented alive before the LORD, to make atonement upon it, and to let it go as the scapegoat into the wilderness" (Leviticus 16:8-10; NKJ).

Evidently, the scapegoat or Azazel was a figure of Satan. Alberto Treiyer concludes the following: "A careful study of all the etymological propositions offered throughout the centuries to explain the term Azazel, shows that only one fits well with biblical and extrabiblical context, as much linguistically as themati-cally. This is: 'a fierce or furious god.'"[4]

Like the Lord's goat, every blood sacrifice in the Hebrew temple symbolized the death of Jesus Christ. Treiyer views the scapegoat as a symbol of Satan be-cause it is not sacrificed. Hence, Jesus cannot be represented by Azazel because the scapegoat was not sacrificed and did not cleanse anything. This scapegoat is contrasted with the sacrificial Lord's goat, as evil is contrasted with good.

After the high priest finished his atoning work in the holy and most holy places of the sanctuary, he confessed all the sins of Israel over the head of the scapegoat. Taken from the courtyard by "a fit man," this goat was banished from the camp (Leviticus 16:21). The scapegoat carried the blame of Israel's sins out into the wilderness, thus representing Satan, the originator of sin.

The cleansing of the sanctuary in Daniel 8:14 parallels the judgment scene in Daniel 7:13-14. On the Day of Atonement, God's people were to look by faith to the work of their high priest in the sanctuary. This heart-searching day was solemn as the people prayed, fasted, and confessed their sins (Leviticus 23:27). If anyone did not participate in the sacred and final proceedings of the Day of Atonement, they were to be "cut off" from among God's people (Leviticus 23:19). This emphasizes the work of decision and judgment during this day.

White shows how the Day of Atonement applies to us today: "The cleansing of the sanctuary therefore involves a work of investigation—a work of judgment. This work must be performed prior to the coming of Christ to redeem His peo-ple; for when He comes, His reward is with Him to give to every man according to his works."[5]

2300 Evenings and Mornings

A prophetic day equals one literal year in the apocalyptic prophecies of the Bible (Ezekiel 4:6). Thus "2300 evenings and mornings" would mean 2,300 literal years, making this the longest time prophecy in the Bible (Daniel 8:14). For an exhaustive study of the biblical evidence supporting the year-day principle, read chapter 3 in William Shea's *Selected Studies on Prophetic Interpretation.*[6]

In Daniel 8:15-16, the angel Gabriel was directed to make Daniel understand the vision. Significantly, in Daniel 8:17, 19, and 26, Gabriel declares three times that the vision of the 2300 days reaches to the time of the end, providing evidence within the book of Daniel for the year-day principle of apocalyptic prophecy.

4   Alberto Treiyer, *The Day of Atonement and the Heavenly Judgment: From the Pentateuch to Revelation* (Siloam Springs, AR: Creation Enterprises International, 1992), 257.

5   White, *The Great Controversy*, 422.

6   William H. Shea, "Year-Day Principle: Part 1," in *Selected Studies on Prophetic Interpretation*, Daniel and Revelation Committee Series, vol. 1 (Hagerstown, MD: Review and Herald, 1992), 67-104.

The book of Daniel is all about the time of the end! It was to be "closed up and sealed till the time of the end" according to Daniel 12:9. According to Daniel 9, the 2300 days of Daniel 8:14 began with the decree to rebuild the temple and the city of Jerusalem. These 2,300 literal years stretch from the time of the ram symbolizing Medo-Persia all the way to the nineteenth century. To be more exact, the 2300 prophetic days began in the fall of 457 B.C. and ended in the fall of 1844. When the 2300-day prophecy ended, this marked the beginning of the "time of the end."

The following chart is taken from Oxentenko.[7]

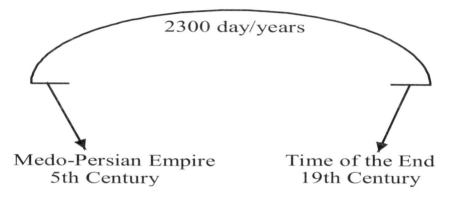

At the end of the 2300 literal years of Daniel 8:14, the message of Jesus' ministry in the heavenly sanctuary is restored, overturning the blasphemous work of the little horn power. As one of those who proclaimed the fulfillment of the 2300-day prophecy, White enlarges on these verses of Daniel:

> The coming of Christ as our high priest to the most holy place, for the cleansing of the sanctuary, brought to view in Daniel 8:14; the coming of the Son of man to the Ancient of Days, as presented in Daniel 7:13; and the coming of the Lord to His temple, foretold by Malachi, are descriptions of the same event; and this is also represented by the coming of the bridegroom to the marriage, described by Christ in the parable of the ten virgins, of Matthew 25.

> In the summer and autumn of 1844 the proclamation, "Behold, the Bridegroom cometh," was given. The two classes represented by the wise and foolish virgins were then developed—one class who looked with joy to the Lord's appearing, and who had been diligently preparing to meet Him; another class that, influenced by fear and acting from impulse, had been satisfied with a theory of the truth, but were destitute of the grace of God. In the parable, when the bridegroom came,

---

7   Oxentenko, 80.

"they that were ready went in with him to the marriage." The coming of the bridegroom, here brought to view, takes place before the marriage. The marriage represents the reception by Christ of His kingdom. The Holy City, the New Jerusalem, which is the capital and representative of the kingdom, is called "the bride, the Lamb's wife." Said the angel to John: "Come hither, I will show thee the bride, the Lamb's wife." "He carried me away in the spirit," says the prophet, "and showed me that great city, the holy Jerusalem, descending out of heaven from God." Revelation 21:9, 10. Clearly, then, the bride represents the Holy City, and the virgins that go out to meet the bridegroom are a symbol of the church. In the Revelation the people of God are said to be the guests at the marriage supper. Revelation 19:9. If *guests*, they cannot be represented also as the *bride*. Christ, as stated by the prophet Daniel, will receive from the Ancient of Days in heaven, "dominion, and glory, and a kingdom;" He will receive the New Jerusalem, the capital of His kingdom, "prepared as a bride adorned for her husband." Daniel 7:14; Revelation 21:2. Having received the kingdom, He will come in His glory, as King of kings and Lord of lords, for the redemption of His people, who are to "sit down with Abraham, and Isaac, and Jacob," at His table in His kingdom (Matthew 8:11; Luke 22:30), to partake of the marriage supper of the Lamb.

The proclamation, "Behold, the Bridegroom cometh," in the summer of 1844, led thousands to expect the immediate advent of the Lord. At the appointed time the Bridegroom came, not to the earth, as the people expected, but to the Ancient of Days in heaven, to the marriage, the reception of His kingdom. "They that were ready went in with Him to the marriage: and the door was shut." They were not to be present in person at the marriage; for it takes place in heaven, while they are upon the earth. The followers of Christ are to "wait for their Lord, when He will *return from* the wedding." Luke 12:36. But they are to understand His work, and to follow Him by faith as He goes in before God. It is in this sense that they are said to go in to the marriage.[8]

Interpretation of the Vision

Daniel 8:15-19: And it came to pass, when I, even I Daniel, had seen the vision, and sought for the meaning, then, behold, there stood before me as the appearance of a man. [16]And I heard a man's voice between the banks of Ulai, which called, and said, Gabriel, make this man to understand the vision. [17]So he came near where I stood: and when he came, I was afraid, and fell upon my face: but he said unto me, Understand, O son of man: for at the time of

---

8   White, *The Great Controversy*, 426-427.

the end shall be the vision. [18]Now as he was speaking with me, I was in a deep sleep on my face toward the ground: but he touched me, and set me upright. [19]And he said, Behold, I will make thee know what shall be in the last end of the indignation: for at the time appointed the end shall be.

"Understand, son of man, that the vision refers to the *time of the end*" (Daniel 8:17; NKJ). Shea summarizes the great power struggle between Christ and the little horn:

> The climax of this prophecy depicts, in essence, a struggle over the sanctuary between the little horn and the Prince of the host. Given the extent of this attack upon the Prince's sanctuary, the question naturally arises as to why the sanctuary assumes such importance in this prophecy. Clearly this is not a dispute over real estate or a building, whatever its actual physical makeup may be. What is of utmost importance here is what goes on in that sanctuary. . . . The heavenly High Priest as the Prince of the Host . . . is not only ruler over His host or people, He is also a heavenly Priest ministering in His sanctuary for them. It is this particular aspect of His work that is attacked by the little horn.[9]

Daniel 8:23-26: And in the latter time of their kingdom, when the transgressors are come to the full, a king of fierce countenance, and understanding dark sentences, shall stand up. [24]And his power shall be mighty, but not by his own power: and he shall destroy wonderfully, and shall prosper, and practice, and shall destroy the mighty and the holy people. [25]And through his policy also he shall cause craft to prosper in his hand; and he shall magnify himself in his heart, and by peace shall destroy many: he shall also stand up against the Prince of princes; but he shall be broken without hand. [26]And the vision of the evening and the morning which was told is true: wherefore shut thou up the vision; for it shall be for many days.

Verses 23-24: "In the latter time of their kingdom" refers to the beginning of the Roman Empire when the four divisions of the Greek Empire were coming to an end. This refers to the pagan phase of the Roman Empire. Both the pagan and papal phases of Rome rose up against the Prince of princes: pagan Rome crucified the Prince of peace on the cross, while papal Rome claimed to be Christ's substitute. Moving its capital to Constantinople, pagan Rome bequeathed the empire to the bishop at Rome. Truly Christian Rome has ruled the "holy Roman Empire" for "many days."

Kingdoms recognized in the Old Testament as enemies of God's people were religio-civil powers, undeniably connected with religion. Pagan Rome's weakness was its attempt to incorporate all the deities of the kingdoms before it. Rome's

9   William H. Shea, "Unity of Daniel," in *Symposium on Daniel*, Daniel and Revelation Committee Series, vol. 2 (Hagerstown, MD: Review and Herald, 1986), 199.

religion was inherited from the Greeks who had inherited theirs from the Medo-Persian culture, and the same goes for Babylon and Assyria whose religion was a modified copy of Egyptian worship. All of this came from the father of all lies, the devil, called Satan or Lucifer. This explains the phrase in verse 24: "*but not by his own power.*" Satan is the mastermind behind the false religions of the world.

The developing horn of Rome would became "exceedingly great" (Dan 8:9) with power over the masses of humanity. Rome has had immense influence over the affairs of this world. The disputes that embroiled the world in two World Wars advanced Rome's interests. At the death of Pope John Paul II, three presidents of the United States and leaders from all over the world attended his funeral. This was an unprecedented display of Rome's power. Revelation 13:3 says: "All the world wondered after the beast." Since the victor writes history, documents of the past have been bequeathed to us through the eyes of Christian Rome. This has also contributed to the power of Rome in the world.

Verse 25: Shea points out the other passages in Daniel that parallel the destruction of the little horn: "According to the prophecy, the little horn was to come to its end in a particular way, 'But, by no human hand, he shall be broken' (8:25). This phraseology sounds somewhat similar to the description of the fate for the king of the north in Daniel 11:45—'he shall come to his end, with none to help him.' The end to the little horn in Daniel 7 was to come about by a decision of God in the heavenly court. In Daniel 2 the image was brought to an end by a stone that smote the image on its feet, and that stone was cut out without the assistance of any human hand (Dan 2:45)."[10]

Verse 26: And the vision of the evening and the morning which was told is true: wherefore shut thou up the vision; for it shall be for many days. The vision of the evenings and mornings refers to the 2300 prophetic days of Daniel 8:14. In Daniel's day, the cleansing of the sanctuary lay in the distant future. That is why Daniel and the heavenly beings ask: "How long will the desolating power of the little horn continue?"

Daniel's Response

Daniel 8:27: And I Daniel fainted, and was sick certain days; afterward I rose up, and did the king's business; and I was astonished at the vision, but none understood it.

The vision overwhelms Daniel; it literally makes him sick. Doukhan writes his own translation of this verse: "Daniel is 'appalled by the vision' that he finds to be 'beyond understanding' (*eyn mebin*, verse 27)."[11] The key to understanding the 2300-day prophecy comes in the following chapters.

---

[10]   Shea, *Selected Studies on Prophetic Interpretation*, 49.

[11]   Doukhan, *Secrets of Daniel*, 132.

Summary

Greece reached the height of its power under Alexander, but the "notable horn" was broken when Alexander died. After his kingdom divided between his generals, a little horn comes out of one of the four winds of the compass.

In Daniel 8 the ram and goat symbols use sanctuary imagery to portray the severe defeat of Medo-Persia by Greece and the final kingdom of Rome in all its phases. Just as the Lord's goat and the scapegoat point us to the final events on the Day of Atonement, so the goat was used by God in Daniel 8 symbolizes God's final judgment which cleanses His sanctuary and ends the power of the little horn.

This little horn grew until it ruled the world as pagan Rome which later transformed into the Roman power of the papacy, more influential and powerful than any kingdom before it. Daniel 8 shows the attack of the little horn on the sanctuary in heaven, but it also reveals the solution: the cleansing and restoration of the sanctuary, the vindication of God's people, and the final destruction of the little horn.

Excursus on Antiochus Epiphanes

A pagan named Porphyry (A.D. 230-309) introduced the Antiochus Epiphanes theory in order to discredit the inspiration of the book of Daniel. He attempted unsuccessfully to prove that it was not written in Daniel's day.

There are many reasons why Antiochus Epiphanes cannot be the little horn power. This section shows why the preterist interpretation falls short of the Scriptural evidence.

First and foremost, Jesus did not identify Antiochus as the little horn power. When He was here on earth, Jesus warned His followers that the abomination of desolation was still a future event. This rules out Antiochus Epiphanes because he died in 164 B.C., long before Jesus was even born. Jesus said, **"Therefore when you see the 'abomination of desolation,' spoken of by Daniel the prophet, standing in the holy place (whoever reads, let him understand), then let those who are in Judea flee to the mountains"** (Matthew 24:15).

Daniel 7, which parallels chapter 8, points out that the little horn power arises out of the fourth beast (Daniel 7:8, 20, 24). Since Babylon was named by Daniel as the first kingdom (Daniel 2:37-38), and Gabriel designated Medo-Persia and Greece as the second and third kingdoms respectively (Daniel 8:20-21), the kingdom that conquered Greece is the fourth kingdom, Rome. This fits with the witness of Jesus because He lived during the time of the Roman Empire and pointed ahead to fulfillment of this prophecy during the days of Rome. Antiochus did not stand against the Prince of princes for Jesus was not yet born; instead, it was the government of Rome that allowed Him to be crucified. Thus the Grecian ruler Antiochus Epiphanes cannot be the little horn power.

Shea succinctly summarizes the progression of power in this prophecy: "In Daniel 8, the kingdoms are successively stronger: Medo-Persia, the ram, magnified himself; the goat of Greece magnified himself exceedingly; but the little horn magnified itself to heaven (Daniel 8:4, 8, 9-11)."[12] The little horn starts out small and ends up exceedingly great in comparison to all the kingdoms before it. History verifies that the conquests of Alexander the Great were greater than those of Medo-Persia, but the victories of the Roman Empire were even greater than those of Alexander the Great. Antiochus Epiphanes was not a great ruler, and therefore he does not fit the prophecy of a greater power than Alexander the Great! It would be inconsistent to interpret Antiochus as the little horn when each of the preceding horns does not represent a certain individual, but rather a phase of the kingdom. For example, the two horns on the ram represented Media and Persia. The single horn on the goat represented the kingdom of Greece under Alexander and how it was divided into four parts when he left no heirs to rule. No kingdom in Daniel's prophecies is represented by one king alone.

If Antiochus was so great, why did he yield over to the power of Rome? Antiochus attacked Egypt a second time in 168 B.C. Unfortunately for him, Egypt had become a protectorate of Rome in the meantime. As Antiochus entered Egypt, the Roman Consul Gaeus Popillius Laenas confronted him and demanded that he leave Egypt immediately. Antiochus told the governor that he would think about it. Gaeus Popillius Laenas supposedly took a cane and drew a circle around Antiochus in the sand, demanding an answer before Antiochus left the circle. Antiochus and the Syrians withdrew.

The Roman Empire grew from the area under Cassander and ruled the world from that very year 168 B.C. until A.D. 476. The Roman Empire ruled longer than any of its predecessors. Rome's conquests match the biblical description: "toward the south, toward the east, and toward the Glorious Land" (Daniel 8:9). Rome was victorious in Egypt, Greece, and the Holy Land. This was not fulfilled by Antiochus Epiphanes.

Most historians agree that Antiochus Epiphanes was one of the weakest of the Syrian kings. Monsignor Ronald Arbuthnot Knox, a Catholic theologian that lived in England (1888-1957), wrote these words in the footnotes of chapter 7 of his translation of the Bible from the Latin Vulgate. "The little horn is usually identified with Antiochus Epiphanes . . . the persecutor of the Macabees; but he was the eighth, not the tenth of his line, and the explanation given of the 'three horns' displaced by him seem curiously forced." In the footnotes for chapter 8, he writes: "The description of Antiochus Epiphanes is not particularly recognizable." In chapter 9, he states: "It must be admitted, however, that widely different views have been held about the application of the prophecy in detail. Modern commentators, who understand the whole passage as a reference to Antiochus

---

[12] William H. Shea, *Daniel: A Reader's Guide* (Nampa, ID: Pacific Press, 2005), 136.

Epiphanes, and the profanation of the Temple, . . . are driven to **very unconvincing explanations** of the time periods involved" (emphasis mine).[13]

Antiochus Epiphanes did not destroy the sanctuary or even cast it to the ground. None of the prophetic time periods in Daniel fit his actions. According to 1 Macabees 1:54, 59 and 4:52, Antiochus suppressed the Jewish sacrifices three years. This does not equal 1,260 prophetic days, but this is already a moot point.

The parallel vision in Daniel 11 shows that this prophecy took many years (Daniel 11:6, 8, 13). Gabriel emphasized twice that the vision was for the time of the end (Daniel 8:17, 19); this again excludes Antiochus Epiphanes. The prophetic period of 1,260 days would be 1,260 literal years, longer than a millennium. The little horn would war against the Prince of princes, His people, and His sanctuary for 1,260 years. This is why Daniel "fainted and was sick," for he knew that the time was long (Daniel 8:26; 10:1). In light of these Bible facts, the Antiochus Epiphanes theory fails to fulfill the required prophecies.

---

[13] Ronald Arbuthnot Knox, *The Holy Bible: A Translation from the Latin Vulgate in the Light of the Hebrew and Greek Originals* (New York: Sheed and Ward, Inc., 1950), 801.

CHAPTER NINE

Daniel 9

Introduction

The context for the ninth chapter is Daniel 8. This chapter resolves the unanswered questions about the 2,300 prophetic days and Daniel's vision in the previous chapter. With added light from heaven, Daniel 9 repeats and enlarges upon chapter 8. God would not leave Daniel without an answer.

According to Oxentenko, Daniel 9 has four main divisions:[1]

1. Jeremiah's prophecy (9:1, 2)

2. Daniel's prayer for understanding (9:3-19)

3. Gabriel sent to give him understanding (9:20-23)

4. Seventy-week prophecy given to contextualize the 2300-day prophecy (9:24-27)

Daniel 9:1, 2: In the first year of Darius the son of Ahasuerus, of the seed of the Medes, which was made king over the realm of the Chaldeans; ²In the first year of his reign I Daniel understood by books the number of the years, whereof the word of the LORD came to Jeremiah the prophet, that he would accomplish seventy years in the desolations of Jerusalem.

This was "the first year of Darius the son of Ahasuerus, of the seed of the Medes." Ahasuerus was also know as Astyages, the last king of the Medes and the brother of Amytis, Nebuchadnezzar's wife. Therefore Darius the Mede was the nephew of King Nebuchadnezzar. Darius was also the uncle of Cyrus because Mandana, Cyrus's mother, was sister to Darius. Daniel points out that Darius was ruler of the Chaldeans (Babylonians). This is an accurate picture because Cyrus was the real ruler of the Medo-Persian Empire while Darius controlled the old Babylonian part of the empire.

The first year of Darius' reign was 538 B.C. since he reigned from 538 to 536 B.C. Because the captivity spoken of by Jeremiah was to last 70 years, Daniel

---

[1]   Oxentenko, 81-82.

expected the Jewish exile to end soon. The exile began in 606/605 B.C., so it should end in 536 B.C.[2] Daniel expressed this heart-felt hope in his prayer.

The vision of chapter 8 sickened Daniel because he understood that it meant 2,300 literal years. After studying the seventy-year prophecy of Jeremiah, Daniel agonized in prayer for his people and the desolated temple. There was a discrepancy in his mind between the vision of Daniel 8 and Jeremiah's prophecy. In vision Daniel saw 23 centuries of the little horn's desolations and abominations. The very thought of waiting 2,300 years before the temple would be cleansed sickened Daniel. Thinking of the earthly sanctuary at Jerusalem, he feared that now their release from exile would be inexorably delayed.

Daniel 9 unlocks the mystery of the 2,300 days by revealing the Messianic prophecy, the seventy weeks. Gabriel, the same angel who would announce Messiah's birth, gave Daniel the beginning date for both prophecies and foretold with unerring accuracy the anointing of the Messiah, His death, the confirmation of God's great covenant with mankind, and the restoration of the heavenly sanctuary.

Daniel 9:3-19: And I set my face unto the Lord God, to seek by prayer and supplications, with fasting, and sackcloth, and ashes: ⁴And I prayed unto the LORD my God, and made my confession, and said, O Lord, the great and dreadful God, keeping the covenant and mercy to them that love him, and to them that keep his commandments; ⁵We have sinned, and have committed iniquity, and have done wickedly, and have rebelled, even by departing from thy precepts and from thy judgments: ⁶Neither have we hearkened unto thy servants the prophets, which spake in thy name to our kings, our princes, and our fathers, and to all the people of the land. ⁷O Lord, righteousness belongeth unto thee, but unto us confusion of faces, as at this day; to the men of Judah, and to the inhabitants of Jerusalem, and unto all Israel, that are near, and that are far off, through all the countries whither thou hast driven them, because of their trespass that they have trespassed against thee. ⁸O Lord, to us belongeth confusion of face, to our kings, to our princes, and to our fathers, because we have sinned against thee. ⁹To the Lord our God belong mercies and forgivenesses, though we have rebelled against him; ¹⁰Neither have we obeyed the voice of the LORD our God, to walk in his laws, which he set before us by his servants the prophets. ¹¹Yea, all Israel have transgressed thy law, even by departing, that they might not obey thy voice; therefore the curse is poured upon us, and the oath that is written in the law of Moses the servant of God, because we have sinned against him. ¹²And he hath confirmed his words, which he spake against us, and against our judges that judged us, by bringing upon us a great evil: for under the whole heaven hath not been done as hath been done upon Jerusalem. ¹³As it is written in the law of Moses,

---

[2] For a good explanation of this biblical chronology, see *The Seventh-day Adventist Bible Commentary*, 3:90-97.

all this evil is come upon us: yet made we not our prayer before the LORD our God, that we might turn from our iniquities, and understand thy truth. [14]Therefore hath the LORD watched upon the evil, and brought it upon us: for the LORD our God is righteous in all his works which he doeth: for we obeyed not his voice. [15]And now, O Lord our God, that hast brought thy people forth out of the land of Egypt with a mighty hand, and hast gotten thee renown, as at this day; we have sinned, we have done wickedly. [16]O Lord, according to all thy righteousness, I beseech thee, let thine anger and thy fury be turned away from thy city Jerusalem, thy holy mountain: because for our sins, and for the iniquities of our fathers, Jerusalem and thy people are become a re-proach to all that are about us. [17]Now therefore, O our God, hear the prayer of thy servant, and his supplications, and cause thy face to shine upon thy sanctuary that is desolate, for the Lord's sake. [18]O my God, incline thine ear, and hear; open thine eyes, and behold our desolations, and the city which is called by thy name: for we do not present our supplications before thee for our righteousnesses, but for thy great mercies. [19]O Lord, hear; O Lord, for-give; O Lord, hearken and do; defer not, for thine own sake, O my God: for thy city and thy people are called by thy name.

Daniel's Prayer

Daniel claimed the promise in Jeremiah 29:10-1: God's people would turn to Him with their entire heart, He would forgive them and return them to their land. No record in Scriptures exists of Daniel's rebellion against God, but he linked himself to his rebellious people and their sins. In this sense Daniel prefig-ures the Messiah later described in chapter nine.

Daniel prayed very earnestly with fasting, sackcloth, and ashes. He confessed the corporate sins of his people, their unfaithfulness, iniquities, and unwillingness to listen to the prophets, including himself with the transgressors. Disobedience to God's law looms high in Daniel's prayer. He knew that the curses were being visited upon the land and his people for their disobedience (Leviticus 27:16-25, 30-34; Deuteronomy 27:9–28:68). Daniel diligently confessed their public and private sins, corporate sins, and even their secret sins. This was not the prayer of a self-righteous man, but one who sincerely loved both his God and his people. The burden of Daniel's prayer was for his people, the city of Jerusalem, and most of all, the sanctuary.

Daniel 9:20-23: And whiles I was speaking, and praying, and confessing my sin and the sin of my people Israel, and presenting my supplication before the LORD my God for the holy mountain of my God; [21]Yea, whiles I was speaking in prayer, even the man Gabriel, whom I had seen in the vision at the begin-ning, being caused to fly swiftly, touched me about the time of the evening oblation. [22]And he informed me, and talked with me, and said, O Daniel, I am now come forth to give thee skill and understanding. [23]At the beginning of thy supplications the commandment came forth, and I am come to show thee; for thou art greatly beloved: therefore understand the matter, and consider the vision.

Gabriel, the angel of prophecy, needed to finish the explanation of the vision (Daniel 9:23). What vision? The vision of the 2,300 prophetic days which had overwhelmed Daniel. At the time of the evening sacrifice, Gabriel arrived to continue his explication of the vision. Even though the temple lay in ruins and the sacrifices were not now offered, Daniel still kept this time of prayer and supplication.

Daniel 9:24–27: Seventy weeks are determined upon thy people and upon thy holy city, to finish the transgression, and to make an end of sins, and to make reconciliation for iniquity, and to bring in everlasting righteousness, and to seal up the vision and prophecy, and to anoint the most Holy. ²⁵Know therefore and understand, that from the going forth of the commandment to restore and to build Jerusalem unto the Messiah the Prince shall be seven weeks, and threescore and two weeks: the street shall be built again, and the wall, even in troublous times. ²⁶And after threescore and two weeks shall Messiah be cut off, but not for himself: and the people of the prince that shall come shall destroy the city and the sanctuary; and the end thereof shall be with a flood, and unto the end of the war desolations are determined. ²⁷And he shall confirm the covenant with many for one week: and in the midst of the week he shall cause the sacrifice and the oblation to cease, and for the overspreading of abominations he shall make it desolate, even until the consummation, and that determined shall be poured upon the desolate.

In the mind of God's people in Daniel's time, Jerusalem represented the heart of the church. The city of Jerusalem encompassed the temple and all that it represented to them. Therefore in the book of Daniel, Jerusalem represents the church made desolate for all the sins committed in it. Now Gabriel gave Daniel hope for ruined Jerusalem and its desolated temple. Jerusalem would be rebuilt, but more importantly, the Hope of Israel was promised. More than 500 years in advance, God gave this remarkable prophecy in answer to His prophet's prayer.

This is one of the strongest evidences of the year-day principle. If the seventy weeks were literal, the Messiah would arrive in 455 B.C., just sixty-nine weeks from the decree to restore and rebuild Jerusalem in 457 B.C. This example alone clearly shows that one prophetic day equals one literal year.

The seventy-week prophecy with its exact dates that point out the Messiah was so compelling that in 1656, after a dispute between Jewish rabbis and the Catholics, the rabbis held a meeting and decided that from that time forward, any Jew who tried to understand this prophecy would be cursed.

Daniel 9:24: Seventy weeks are determined upon thy people and upon thy holy city, to finish the transgression, and to make an end of sins, and to make

reconciliation for iniquity, and to bring in everlasting righteousness, and to seal up the vision and prophecy, and to anoint the most Holy.

The seventy-week prophecy pertains to the Jewish people and covers a period of 490 years (70 weeks times 7 days in a week equals 490 years). In the book of Jeremiah, God had given His people seventy years to repent and follow Him. Now after Daniel prayed as he did, God gave them an additional 490 years to repent.

נֶחְתַּךְ (*nechtak*)

Nechtak, the Hebrew word for "determined," comes from the root word *chathak*. This word means "cut, divide, cut off, or amputated." In other words the seventy-week prophecy is cut off from the larger prophecy. The seventy weeks (490 literal years) are the first portion of the 2300-day prophecy.

When Daniel pleaded for understanding of the 2300-day prophecy, God sent Gabriel with the answer. Therefore the beginning date for the seventy-week prophecy was the starting point for the 2300-day prophecy. The seventy-week prophecy gave the good news of the Messiah's coming and His accomplishments during the seventieth week. This prophecy tells us about Jesus. When Peter asked Jesus how many times he should forgive someone, Jesus answered, "I do not say to you, up to seven times, but up to seventy times seven" (Matthew 18:22; NKJ). Thus He introduced Himself as the long-awaited Messiah. His long-suffering and forgiving love for His people would span 490 years of probation.

Adapted from Oxentenko, Daniel 9:24 lists the accomplishments of the seventy-week prophecy:[3]

1. **Finish the transgression**—During the 490 years of Jewish probation, they were to cease lawlessness and follow God.

2. **To make an end of sins**—Jesus' death on the cross saves us from our sins as we accept Him as our Lord and Savior.

3. **To make reconciliation for iniquity**—Jesus' death on the cross reconciles us to God when we accept Him as our substitute.

4. **To bring in everlasting righteousness**—Jesus bought the gift of everlasting righteousness for us at the cross.

5. **To seal up the vision and prophecy**—As Jesus fulfilled the seventy-week prophecy, He confirmed the accuracy of Daniel 8 and 9. Because the seventy-week portion of the 2,300 literal years was exactly fulfilled, God would also accomplish the rest of the 2300-year prophecy.

6. **To anoint the Most Holy**—Jesus, the holy One of God, was anointed in A.D. 27. Christ's anointing occurred on time at the beginning of the seventieth week.

---

[3] Oxentenko, 91-92.

Daniel 9:25: Know therefore and understand, that from the going forth of the commandment to restore and to build Jerusalem unto the Messiah the Prince shall be seven weeks, and threescore and two weeks: the street shall be built again, and the wall, even in troublous times.

The Three Decrees

The book of Ezra records three decrees written by three Persian kings: Cyrus, Darius, and Artaxerxes. The third decree was reaffirmed by Artaxerxes in the days of Nehemiah. This list is adapted from Oxentenko.[4]

- First decree issued by Cyrus in 538/537 B.C. (Ezra 1:1-4; 6:1-5)

- Second decree issued by Darius around 519 B.C. (Ezra 6:6-12)

- Third decree issued by Artaxerxes in 457 B.C., in his seventh year as king (Ezra 7:8, 11-26)

How do we know which decree marks the beginning of the seventy-week and 2300-day prophecies? Ford gives the historical background of these various decrees and how they relate to Bible prophecy:

History offers us four edicts concerned with the restoration of Israel. In 538/537, 519(?), 457, and 444 BC, decrees were issued by Cyrus, Darius Hystaspes, and Artaxerxes (two decrees) respectively. Therefore we must consider closely the requirements of the prophecy. "From the going forth of the word to restore and build Jerusalem" requires more than the first two edicts gave. The proclamations of Cyrus and Darius gave priority to the rebuilding of the temple rather than to the restoration of the civil state. Only the first decree of Artaxerxes in 457 BC gave the Jews full autonomy and provided for the building of the walls and gates of Jerusalem. The mandate given to Nehemiah in 444 BC had to do with the completion of the work provided for in the decree by Artaxerxes years earlier.[5]

Ezra 7:8 places the third decree in "the seventh year of the king." Four reliable sources allow scholars to establish 457 B.C. as the exact year of Artaxerxes' decree. The following list is adapted from Oxentenko.[6]

1. **Olympiad Dates**—records kept from 776 B.C. to A.D. 393.

2. **Ptolemy's Canon**—the reigns of kings from the seventh century B.C.

3. **Cuneiform Text**—Babylonian texts that give dates for kings from 626 B.C. to A.D. 75.

---

[4]   Ibid., 86.

[5]   Ford, 229.

[6]   Oxentenko, 86-88.

4. Elephantine Papyri—records of Jews on the island of Elephantine in southern Egypt. These dates use both the Persian-Babylonian lunar calendar and the Egyptian solar calendar.

The Three-Part Prophecy

1. 7 prophetic weeks which equal 49 literal years (Daniel 9:25)
2. 62 prophetic weeks which equal 434 literal years (Daniel 9:25)
3. 1 prophetic week which equals 7 literal years (Daniel 9:27) This last prophetic week is divided into two periods of 3 1/2 literal years.

7 Weeks

It took forty-nine years to rebuild the walls and the city during "the troublous times" as recorded in Ezra and Nehemiah. This work was completed in 408 B.C., fulfilling the prophecy.

62 Weeks

From 408 B.C. to A.D. 27 is exactly 434 years. Jesus was baptized and anointed with the Holy Spirit as the Messiah in A.D. 27. Luke's historical gospel places Christ's baptism "in the fifteenth year of the reign of Tiberius Caesar" (Luke 3:1) which was A.D. 27. Exactly at this time, Jesus proclaimed: "*The time is fulfilled*, and the kingdom of God is at hand. Repent, and believe in the gospel" (Mark 1:15; NKJ; emphasis mine). Thus Jesus announced that He was the fulfillment of Daniel's prophecy in chapter 9, the long awaited Messiah. With the baptism of Jesus, the seventieth week had begun.

One Last Week

During this week, the Most Holy Messiah would be anointed and carry out His mission of salvation, finishing transgression, making reconciliation for sin, and bringing in everlasting righteousness. The everlasting covenant of the Messiah would be confirmed: first through the work of the Messiah Himself during the three and a half years of His ministry, and then through the work of the apostles during the next three and a half years. After A.D. 27 the Messiah would be "cut off" in the middle of that last week of years and die as the Lamb depicted in Isaiah 53, ending sacrifices of the sanctuary service. The Jewish nation rejected both the work of the Messiah and the apostles, thus their probationary period of 490 years closed with the stoning of Stephen in A.D. 34.

Daniel 9:26 And after the sixty-two weeks Messiah shall be cut off, but not for Himself; And the people of the prince who is to come shall destroy the city and the sanctuary. The end of it shall be with a flood, and till the end of the war desolations are determined (NKJ).

The City and the Sanctuary Destroyed

The identity of these people is found within the text itself; they exist at the destruction of Jerusalem and continue until the end of time. Rome destroyed the city and the sanctuary, and another phase of Rome lasts until "the end."

Daniel 9:27: Then he shall confirm a covenant with many for one week; But in the middle of the week He shall bring an end to sacrifice and offering. And on the wing of abominations shall be one who makes desolate, Even until the consummation, which is determined, Is poured out on the desolate (NKJ).

At the end of 69 prophetic weeks in A.D. 27, the Holy Spirit in the form of a dove anointed Jesus as the Messiah. One week of prophetic time now remained in the prophecy. Verse 26 predicted that the Messiah would be cut off after A.D. 27, but Daniel 9:27 makes it even more clear: the Messiah would bring an end to the sacrifices in the middle of the last week. Adding 3 1/2 years to the fall of A.D. 27 brings us to the spring of A.D. 31, right at the time of the Passover.

At this very time, Jesus fulfilled Daniel's prophecy when He became our Passover Lamb (1 Corinthians 5:7). In A.D. 31, the fourteenth day of the first month fell on a Friday (Leviticus 23:5). During the fifteenth day of the first month, the day of unleavened bread, Jesus lay in the tomb (Leviticus 23:6). Just as unleavened bread does not rise, Jesus did not rise, but instead rested in the tomb on the Sabbath day. The day after the Sabbath was the sixteenth day of the first month when the wave sheaf offering of first fruits was waved before the Lord. Jesus arose from the grave on that day and became our first fruits offering to God. With marvellous accuracy, type met anti-type in Jesus Christ our Messiah.

The last week of the 490-year prophecy (the seventieth week) is as important to the whole as are the first 489 years. Right on time, in the middle of the last prophetic week of seven literal years, Jesus' death is one of the strongest proofs that He is the Messiah.

Even as Jesus confirmed the covenant during His three-and-a-half year ministry, the disciples continued to confirm this covenant for the last three and a half years of the seventy-week prophecy. This was all that remained of the probationary period for the Jews as God's chosen people. The 70-weeks prophecy ended in A.D. 34. History records that at this very time Stephen was stoned for preaching that Jesus was at the right hand of God. When Jesus was crucified, the Jews received permission from Rome to crucify Him. When Stephen died, the Sanhedrin did the stoning. According to Acts, Saul (later Paul) was present at Stephan's execution. Thus the 490 merciful years of probation came to an end for the Jewish people as a nation. Since A.D. 34 the Jewish people may still receive forgiveness individually just as anyone else. Paul said, "If you are Christ's, then you are Abraham's seed, and heirs according to the promise" (Galatians 3:29; NKJ). All who accept Christ as their substitute Lamb and submit to His Lordship have the assurance that His blood will cover their sins.

Two key points remain. At the end of the 490 years, Jesus established the Christian church. At the end of the 2,300 years He restored the divine purpose of the church in preparing God's people for His return. To visualize the 70-week prophecy, note the diagram below.

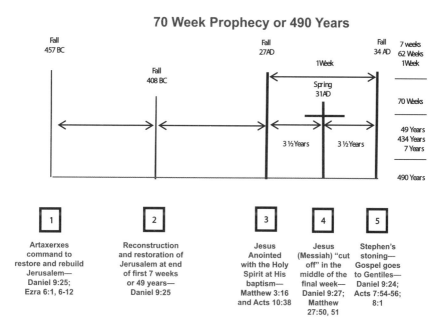

70 Week Prophecy or 490 Years

	1	2	3	4	5
	Artaxerxes command to restore and rebuild Jerusalem— Daniel 9:25; Ezra 6:1, 6-12	Reconstruction and restoration of Jerusalem at end of first 7 weeks or 49 years— Daniel 9:25	Jesus Anointed with the Holy Spirit at His baptism— Matthew 3:16 and Acts 10:38	Jesus (Messiah) "cut off" in the middle of the final week— Daniel 9:27; Matthew 27:50, 51	Stephen's stoning— Gospel goes to Gentiles— Daniel 9:24; Acts 7:54-56; 8:1

Summary

More than 500 years in advance, God's gift of prophecy in Daniel 9 provided undeniable proof of Jesus' claim to be the Messiah. The seventy-week prophecy is the key to understand the fulfillment of the spring feasts. Type met anti-type when Pentecost took place fifty days after the Sabbath of unleavened bread, fulfilling the ceremonial Feast of Weeks (Leviticus 23:15-16).

The 490 years began in 457 B.C. and ended in A.D. 34. Now the end of the 2300-day prophecy can be calculated (2,300 years minus 490 years equals 1810 years). Add 1,810 years to A.D. 34 and you come to the year 1844. This date must correlate with the unfulfilled holy days of the seventh month. The cleansing of the sanctuary or Day of Atonement came on the tenth day of the seventh month.

When type met anti-type, the 2300-day prophecy ended on October 22, 1844. At this time Christ entered His final stage of ministry in the most holy place in heaven. Before 1844, God's people were to prepare for judgment. Even as the Feast of Trumpets prepared ancient Israel for the Day of Atonement, a ten-year period announcing God's coming judgment came at just the right time. This judgment hour message was preached in all the corners of the earth, bringing attention to the great atypical Day of Atonement that would begin in 1844. The early Millerites also expected the Feast of Tabernacles would be fulfilled at this time. In light of the judgment which had begun, this remnant preached the soon coming of Christ which would fulfill the Feast of Tabernacles, but that time has not yet come. When met with disappointment, they turned again to the prophecies. Wrestling with the word of God, the church born out of the 1844 experience later came to a biblical understanding of all the fall holy days. Thus type met antitype in the great Advent Awakening of 1844.

CHAPTER TEN

Daniel 10

Introduction

A s a unit, Daniel 10 through 12 describes the final repeat and enlarge segment of Daniel. These prophecies point to the end of the 2,300 literal years: "the time of the end." The prophet carefully outlines the history of God's people from his day to the last days of earth's history.

Daniel 10:1-4: In the third year of Cyrus king of Persia a thing was revealed unto Daniel, whose name was called Belteshazzar; and the thing was true, but the time appointed was long: and he understood the thing, and had understanding of the vision. ²In those days I Daniel was mourning three full weeks. ³I ate no pleasant bread, neither came flesh nor wine in my mouth, neither did I anoint myself at all, till three whole weeks were fulfilled. ⁴And in the four and twentieth day of the first month, as I was by the side of the great river, which is Hiddekel;

Daniel placed this date in the third year of King Cyrus' rule while Ezra 1:1-3 gave the time as the first year of King Cyrus. How should the apparent discrepancy of these texts be solved? History explains that Cyrus was co-regent with his Uncle Darius during his first two years as king. Therefore the third year of his rule was actually the first year of his independent reign over the Persian Empire. In 536 B.C. Cyrus began his independent reign and the seventy years of captivity in Babylon came to an end. Fulfilling the prophecies of Isaiah and Jeremiah, Cyrus ended the captivity of God's people (Isaiah 39:6-7; Jeremiah 25:11-12). This laid the groundwork for the fulfillment of the seventy-week prophecy.

Daniel looked forward to the end of the seventy years of captivity even though he did not return to Jerusalem. Like Jesus who died before going to the New Jerusalem in heaven, Daniel died as well and awaits the time when all God's people will meet in that heavenly city. Like Jesus, Daniel prayed as an intercessor for his people, fasting and mourning for three full weeks. He understood the vision of chapter 9 (Daniel 10:1), but he continued to pray because of the distressing content of the vision.

Daniel 10:14 provides a clue to the reason for Daniel's mourning: "I am come to make thee understand what shall befall thy people in the latter days." Daniel's concern was the destiny of God's people in the "latter days" during the seventy-week prophecy and the extremely long period of 2,300 years.

Daniel 10:5-9: Then I lifted up mine eyes, and looked, and behold a certain man clothed in linen, whose loins were girded with fine gold of Uphaz: ⁶His body also was like the beryl, and his face as the appearance of lightning, and his eyes as lamps of fire, and his arms and his feet like in colour to polished brass, and the voice of his words like the voice of a multitude. ⁷And I Daniel alone saw the vision: for the men that were with me saw not the vision; but a great quaking fell upon them, so that they fled to hide themselves. ⁸Therefore I was left alone, and saw this great vision, and there remained no strength in me: for my comeliness was turned in me into corruption, and I retained no strength. ⁹Yet heard I the voice of his words: and when I heard the voice of his words, then was I in a deep sleep on my face, and my face toward the ground.

Note the similarity of Daniel's vision here and the description of John's vision in Revelation 1:12-17. John described Jesus; therefore Daniel must also have seen a vision of Him. Christ was just as active in the affairs of His people in Old Testament times as He was in John's day. As in days of old, Christ is still actively involved in His people's lives today.

Daniel alone sees the vision, not those who were with him, similar to the story of Paul's first vision in Acts 9:7. Daniel lost his strength and was in a deep sleep with his face to the ground, similar to John's experience.

Daniel 10:10–14: And, behold, an hand touched me, which set me upon my knees and upon the palms of my hands. ¹¹And he said unto me, O Daniel, a man greatly beloved, understand the words that I speak unto thee, and stand upright: for unto thee am I now sent. And when he had spoken this word unto me, I stood trembling. ¹²Then said he unto me, Fear not, Daniel: for from the first day that thou didst set thine heart to understand, and to chasten thyself before thy God, thy words were heard, and I am come for thy words. ¹³But the prince of the kingdom of Persia withstood me one and twenty days: but, lo, Michael, one of the chief princes, came to help me; and I remained there with the kings of Persia. ¹⁴Now I am come to make thee understand what shall befall thy people in the latter days: for yet the vision is for many days.

The hand that touched him was most likely Gabriel's as seen by the context. Daniel humbled himself and set his heart to understand. God responds to our heartfelt prayers.

The prince of the kingdom of Persia had withstood Gabriel for twenty-one days, the same number of days Daniel had been praying. This is not King Cyrus but rather the spiritual prince or ruler of Persia. When Jesus was here on earth,

He identified Satan as the prince of this present world (John 12:31; 14:30; 16:11). Judah's neighbors tried to influence the king of Persia to withdraw his help and retract his command to rebuild Jerusalem. These enemies were under the influence of Satan, the real prince of Persia. This is why King Cyrus resisted for three whole weeks. Finally, Christ Himself came to relieve Gabriel so he could come to enlighten Daniel.

Who is Michael? He is not an angel! The word Michael means "who is like God" or "the likeness of God." Michael is the archangel, meaning the one above the angels like an arch is above a door and yet not the door. Only the members of the Godhead are above the angels. The term Michael is always the name given Christ when in battle against Satan, and Michael is always victorious over Satan. Gabriel is never called the archangel, and the Bible never uses the name archangel to describe an order of angels. These false ideas come from extra-biblical sources or tradition.

"The vision refers to many days yet to come" (10:14; NKJ). This long prophecy had been on Daniel's mind: the 2300-day prophecy refers to the end times.

Daniel 10:15-17: And when he had spoken such words unto me, I set my face toward the ground, and I became dumb. ¹⁶And, behold, one like the similitude of the sons of men touched my lips: then I opened my mouth, and spake, and said unto him that stood before me, O my lord, by the vision my sorrows are turned upon me, and I have retained no strength. ¹⁷For how can the servant of this my lord talk with this my lord? for as for me, straightway there remained no strength in me, neither is there breath left in me.

Daniel was overwhelmed with the fact that the vision of the 2,300 literal years was far into the future. The significance of this vision took his breath away! Only the touch from a heavenly being could bring him back to reality.

Daniel 10:18-21: Then there came again and touched me one like the appearance of a man, and he strengthened me, ¹⁹And said, O man greatly beloved, fear not: peace be unto thee, be strong, yea, be strong. And when he had spoken unto me, I was strengthened, and said, Let my lord speak; for thou hast strengthened me. ²⁰Then said he, Knowest thou wherefore I come unto thee? and now will I return to fight with the prince of Persia: and when I am gone forth, lo, the prince of Grecia shall come. ²¹But I will show thee that which is noted in the Scripture of truth: and there is none that holdeth with me in these things, but Michael your prince.

Daniel was touched a third time by a heavenly being who was commissioned to share more details with him. This message was about the future, but after the angel gave his message, he must return to fight with the prince of Persia. The angel mentioned the coming of the prince of Greece, thus predicting the conqueror of the Persian kingdom. This angelic involvement in the affairs of kings, countries, and common folk shows heaven's deep compassion for mankind.

According to White, in the play and interplay of decisions that mold life's events, God's providence plays the leading role: "The history of nations speaks to us today. To every nation and to every individual God has assigned a place in His great plan. Today men and nations are being tested by the plummet in the hand of Him who makes no mistake. All are by their own choice deciding their destiny, and God is overruling all for the accomplishment of His purposes."[1] Bible prophecy has proven faithful in the past and points out the future with certainty. Will we believe God or men?

Summary

Daniel 10 shows heaven's close connection with God's people on earth. Just as God answered Daniel's fervent prayers to understand the prophecies concerning his people, so today heaven longs to answer the prayers of spiritual Israel. The key to all prophetic interpretation is prayer! God will answer your prayers and make known to you the future. This will give you a vision of the glory of God, His salvation, and ultimate victory by His power.

---

[1]   White, *Prophets and Kings*, 536.

CHAPTER ELEVEN

Daniel 11

Introduction

Daniel 11 repeats and enlarges the previous prophecies of Daniel, starting with Persia, the fourth kingdom from Egypt and the second after Babylon. Here the history from Darius the Mede through our own time and into the future is recorded. Details given aid us in understanding the broad strokes of history as they pertain to the salvation of God's people and His church. Chapter 11 reveals the life of God's people in relation to the life of Jesus.

The context must be followed in unfolding the broad strokes of the prophecy. The Hebrew language in this section of Daniel is not easy to follow, but let the prophecy unveil itself historically. It is better to admit ignorance rather than force an interpretation upon the text. Wait on God with patience and pray for more light like Daniel did.

Daniel 11:1-2: Also I in the first year of Darius the Mede, even I, stood to confirm and to strengthen him. ²And now will I show thee the truth. Behold, there shall stand up yet three kings in Persia; and the fourth shall be far richer than they all: and by his strength through his riches he shall stir up all against the realm of Grecia.

This chapter begins with Darius the Mede who was followed by three more kings in Persia. The fourth Persian king would be far richer than all of them and stir up the realm of Greece. After the death of King Cyrus who ruled Persia at the time of this vision, the first of the three kings of Persia was Cambyses (530 to 522 B.C.) Cambyses died on his way back to put down a revolt led by an impostor who claimed to be his brother Bardiya. Several provinces of the empire accepted this Bardiya impostor as the new ruler, the second of the three. The impostor bribed his subjects with a remission of taxes for three years. Cambyses died, possibly by his own hand, but more likely from an infection following an accidental sword wound. The third was Darius I, one of the princes of the Achaemenid family and a leading general in Cambyses' army. He headed home with troops to crush a rebellion and ruled as Darius I from 522 to 486 B.C. The fourth king to rule Persia was Xerxes, better known to Bible readers as Ahasuerus, the husband of Queen Esther. Ruling from 486 to 465 B.C., he stockpiled supplies and man-power for a military expedition against Greece, thus "stirring up" Alexander's country, as the Scripture records.

Daniel 11:3-4: And a mighty king shall stand up, that shall rule with great do-minion, and do according to his will. ⁴And when he shall stand up, his king-dom shall be broken, and shall be divided toward the four winds of heaven; and not to his posterity, nor according to his dominion which he ruled: for his kingdom shall be plucked up, even for others beside those.

The ensuing battle between Alexander the Great, "the mighty king," and King Xerxes resulted in one of the most astonishing battles in history. Alexander was only twenty years old when he ascended the throne in Macedonia. Following his father's plans to invade Persia in revenge for Xerxes' invasion of Greece, the first battle was fought in 334 B.C. at Granicus in Asia Minor, resulting in a Greek victory. During the second battle at Issus, Alexander defeated Darius' army of 600,000 men with an army estimated to be between 35,000 and 40,000 men. The final battle took place near Arbela in 331 B.C. Alexander captured Babylon and went as far as India, so he ruled a "great dominion." Just as Scripture recorded, "his kingdom shall be broken up and divided toward the four winds of heaven, but not among his posterity" (Daniel 11:4; NKJ). This great conqueror died at the age of 32 in 323 B.C. Fifteen years after his death, his entire family—his mother, his wives, brother, and sons—were all dead. His kingdom did not pass to his posterity, and the struggle between his generals continued for twenty-two years. At the Battle of Ipsus in 301 B.C., Seleucus, Ptolemy, Lysimachus, and Cassander defeated Antigonus and partitioned the world into four divisions in directions reckoned from the viewpoint of Palestine, the homeland of Daniel the prophet.

Daniel 11:5-10: And the king of the south shall be strong, and one of his princ-es; and he shall be strong above him, and have dominion; his dominion shall be a great dominion. ⁶And in the end of years they shall join themselves to-gether; for the king's daughter of the south shall come to the king of the north to make an agreement: but she shall not retain the power of the arm; neither shall he stand, nor his arm: but she shall be given up, and they that brought her, and he that begat her, and he that strengthened her in these times. ⁷But out of a branch of her roots shall one stand up in his estate, which shall come with an army, and shall enter into the fortress of the king of the north, and shall deal against them, and shall prevail: ⁸And shall also carry captives into Egypt their gods, with their princes, and with their precious vessels of silver and of gold; and he shall continue more years than the king of the north. ⁹So the king of the south shall come into his kingdom, and shall return into his own land. ¹⁰But his sons shall be stirred up, and shall assemble a multitude of great forces: and one shall certainly come, and overflow, and pass through: then shall he return, and be stirred up, even to his fortress.

Over time the four divisions of Greece merged into just two. The Seleucid kingdom absorbed the kingdoms of Cassander and Lysimachus, thus controlling Palestine and the northern regions. Ptolemy ruled all the areas south of Palestine. Thus the king of the north and king of the south first emerge. Relating history to prophecy, Maxwell recites this sad tale:

> Around 250 B.C., King Ptolemy Philadelphus of Egypt and King Antiochus Theos of Syria attempted to guarantee peace between their countries by having King Antiochus marry King Ptolemy's daughter, Berenice.
>
> Antiochus already had a wife, called Laodice. It was part of the deal that he divorce her.
>
> So the divorce was arranged, the new marriage was celebrated, and in due course a baby boy arrived who could someday be the next king. Unfortunately Antiochus soon found that he didn't like Berenice very well. He kept making comparisons between her and his first wife. And when Berenice's father, the king of Egypt, died, Antiochus divorced her and took Laodice back again.
>
> But Laodice had become bitter. She was afraid, too, of what her husband might do next. So using her royal powers in a manner all too common in those days, she had Antiochus, Berenice, and Berenice's attendants and little son all murdered.[1]

The historian Henry Williams, who wrote a twenty-five volume set on ancient history, tells the same story, but gives more detail:

> These troubles and commotions in the East made Antiochus Theos weary of his war with Ptolemy; a treaty of peace was therefore concluded on the following terms: that Antiochus should divorce his former wife Laodice, who was his own sister by the father, marry Berenice, the daughter of Ptolemy, and settle the crown upon the male issue of that marriage. Two years after this marriage Ptolemy Philadelphus died— an event which Antiochus Theos, his son-in-law, no sooner understood than he removed Berenice from his bed, and recalled Laodice with her children Seleucus Callinicus, and Antiochus Hierax; but Laodice being well acquainted with his fickle temper, and fearing lest he might again abandon her and receive Berenice, resolved to improve the present opportunity and secure the succession to her son, for by the late treaty with Ptolemy, her children were disinherited and the crown settled on the son of Berenice. To effect this design, she caused Antiochus to be

---

[1]   Maxwell, *God Cares*, 1:277.

poisoned; when she saw him expiring, she ordered him to be privately conveyed away, and one Artemon, who greatly resembled him, as well in features as in tone of his voice, to be placed in his bed. Artemon acted his part with great dexterity, and personating Antiochus, tenderly recommended his dear Laodice and her children to the lords that visited him. In the name of Antiochus, whom the people believed still alive, orders were issued, enjoining all his subjects to obey his beloved son Seleucus Callinicus, and acknowledge him as their lawful sovereign. The crown being by this infamous contrivance secured to Callinicus, the death of the king was publicly declared, and Callinicus without any opposition ascended the throne."[2]

Verse 7: As a result, Ptolemy Euergetes, the brother of Berenice, invaded the kingdom of Callinicus and Laodice to avenge the death of his sister and her infant son. He drove the Seleucids all the way to the Taurus Mountains beyond the Tigris River.

Verses 8-9: Ptolemy Euergetes took 40,000 talents of silver, along with other precious items of gold and silver worth $30,000,000, and thousands of graven images that had been originally taken from Egypt by Cambyses.

Verse 10: Seleucus had two sons: Cerannus and Magnus known as Antiochus III. Both were bent on revenge. Cerannus invaded Asia Minor, but was assassinated in 223 B.C. Antiochus III was more warlike and recovered Syria, Phoenicia, and Palestine. The recapture of Seleucia, his former capital, fulfilled the prophecy. His conquests went as far as the frontier fortress of Pelusium of Egypt.

Daniel 11:11-13: And the king of the south shall be moved with choler, and shall come forth and fight with him, even with the king of the north: and he shall set forth a great multitude; but the multitude shall be given into his hand. [12]And when he hath taken away the multitude, his heart shall be lifted up; and he shall cast down many ten thousands: but he shall not be strengthened by it. [13]For the king of the north shall return, and shall set forth a multitude greater than the former, and shall certainly come after certain years with a great army and with much riches.

Verse 11: Ptolemy Philopater raised up an army larger than that of Antiochus and thus defeated him, recapturing Palestine. A peace was struck between the two.

Verse 12: Ptolemy did not take advantage of his victory. Instead, he returned home and on his way stopped in at Jerusalem. When he attempted to enter the holy of holies in the temple, he was restrained from doing so. As a result he returned to Egypt and began a relentless persecution of the Jews, slaying between forty and sixty thousand. Thus he "cast down tens of thousands" out of anger.

---

2   Henry Smith Williams, *The Historians' History of the World* (New York: Encyclopedia Brittanica, 1907), 4:557.

When insurrection broke out, he had to revoke his decrees against the Jews and restore them to their former privileges. After this he gave himself over to a life of drinking and lasciviousness for the rest of his life.

Verse 13: This verse pictures the second invasion by Antiochus Magnus. After fourteen years of peace and the death of the Egyptian ruler Ptolemy Philopater, Antiochus attacked when Philopater's five-year-old son, Ptolemy Epiphanes, came to the throne. At this same time, a power was developing in the west that would become the Roman Empire.

Daniel 11:14-19: And in those times there shall many stand up against the king of the south: also the robbers of thy people shall exalt themselves to establish the vision; but they shall fall. ¹⁵So the king of the north shall come, and cast up a mount, and take the most fenced cities: and the arms of the south shall not withstand, neither his chosen people, neither shall there be any strength to withstand. ¹⁶But he that cometh against him shall do according to his own will, and none shall stand before him: and he shall stand in the glorious land, which by his hand shall be consumed. ¹⁷He shall also set his face to enter with the strength of his whole kingdom, and upright ones with him; thus shall he do: and he shall give him the daughter of women, corrupting her: but she shall not stand on his side, neither be for him. ¹⁸After this shall he turn his face unto the isles, and shall take many: but a prince for his own behalf shall cause the reproach offered by him to cease; without his own reproach he shall cause it to turn upon him. ¹⁹Then he shall turn his face toward the fort of his own land: but he shall stumble and fall, and not be found.

Verse 14: The guardians of young Ptolemy Epiphanes appealed to the Roman republic. At this point Rome starts to be a player in this drama. This fourth line of prophecy in Daniel repeats the former prophecies and enlarges on them. Daniel 2 establishes the four successive kingdoms: Babylon, Medo-Persia, Greece, and Rome which later fractured into ten kingdoms. Daniel 7 adds the little horn that comes up among the ten horns, uprooting three of them in the process. The little horn rose out of the shambles of the pagan Roman empire. In Daniel 8 Rome was shown as an emerging power from the rubble of the Grecian empire with the little horn growing out of those same divisions. In just a few short verses Daniel 11 speaks of the two warring powers that arise from the ashes of the Grecian empire and quickly moves on to the emerging Roman empire with the rise of its little horn power.

The violent men of Daniel's people were Jews that had been captured, taken to Egypt, and persecuted by Ptolemy. These Hebrews planned trouble for the king of the south. With a war from without and insurrection from within, the young child king appealed to the emerging power that would succeed the Grecian empire—Rome.

Marcus Lepidus went to Egypt to aid the child king and conferred upon Aristomenes, an Acarnanian, to carry out the duties of guardian. Maxwell points out the shaky situation in the leadership of Egypt: At fourteen years of age, "according to the usage of the country, he was entitled to take the administration of the kingdom into his own hands. The folly of investing a person so young with absolute power was in this instance made fully apparent. The youth who had been universally popular whilst under the direction of Aristomenes, was no sooner enthroned than he placed himself under the influence of worthless men by whose advice he was led to the adoption of measures through which great disorders were introduced into every branch of the government; and at length his former able and honest minister was put to death."[3]

Verse 15 pictures the last campaign of Antiochus Magnus, better known as Antiochus Epiphanes, into Egypt. The Romans had appointed Scopas with an army of troops from Etolia to defend Egypt. Antiochus defeated them and took nearly all of Egypt, except Alexandria, before Popillius Laenus came from Rome to rescue the Egyptians from Antiochus. Just before Antiochus came to lay siege to Alexandria, Popillius Laenas delivered the decree of the Roman Senate to Antiochus, asking him to refrain from attacking the allies of the Roman republic. When Antiochus asked to speak with his officers first, Popillius Laenas took his staff and drew a circle in the sand around Antiochus, demanding an answer before he left the circle. Thus Antiochus yielded to the ultimatum of this new power emerging in the west in 168 B.C., the date of the true beginning of the Roman empire. This ended the prophetic history of Grecian empire.

Daniel 11:16: But he who comes against him shall do according to his own will, and no one shall stand against him. He shall stand in the Glorious Land with destruction in his power.

The context shows the change from Greece to the Roman Empire, describing the conquests of Pompey which included the "glorious land" of Palestine. As Rome came to power, it carried out its own will wherever it went and conquered. During the time of the Roman Republic, Judea was conquered by Pompey in 63 B.C. In A.D. 6 Judea became a Roman province under the rulership of procurators.

Daniel 11:17: "He shall also set his face to enter with the strength of his whole kingdom, and upright ones with him; thus shall he do. And he shall give him the daughter of women to destroy it; but she shall not stand with him, or be for him."

The scene quickly moves from the Roman republic to the time of the Roman empire, established by Julius Caesar. He set his mind to "enter with the strength of his whole kingdom." The only part of the old Grecian empire that Julius Caesar did not occupy at that point was Egypt. With the help of 3,000 Jews, called "the upright ones," and Antipater from Idumea, Julius Caesar subjected Egypt to

---

3   Ibid., 4:573.

Rome. Ptolemy Auletes and his sister Cleopatra ruled Egypt under the guardianship of Pompey. A quarrel between Julius Caesar and Pompey initiated the Battle of Pharsalia, resulting in the defeat of Pompey. The defeated general fled to Egypt only to be murdered by Ptolemy. Julius Caesar himself came to Egypt and assumed the guardianship of Cleopatra and Ptolemy who were quarreling over the throne. When Caesar summoned them to appear before him to settle the issue, Ptolemy found himself to be a hostage in his own palace. Cleopatra used her charm and beauty to gain the favor of Julius Caesar. Her strategy worked, and Caesar began to champion her cause. Although he fell to some of her sophistries, he was careful not to fall into a trap, protecting himself from his unscrupulous enemies. The language indicates immoral behavior between Cleopatra and Julius Caesar, and the record of history indicates that the Scripture is entirely accurate.

Daniel 11:18-19: After this he shall turn his face to the coastlands, and shall take many. But a ruler shall bring the reproach against them to an end; and with the reproach removed, he shall turn back on him. [19]Then he shall turn his face toward the fortress of his own land; but he shall stumble and fall, and not be found.

Then Julius Caesar turned toward the coastlands. The last campaign of Julius Caesar was against the Pompeian or Senatorial Party on the coastlands of Africa and the Mediterranean Sea. He conquered Pharnaces, the king of Pontus, in just five days. At Thapsus he met and defeated the last of the republic's leaders—Scipio, Varus, Juba, and Cato—before becoming the lord of the Roman empire, thus ending the republican system of rule via the senators.

When Julius Caesar returned to Rome, Brutus conspired with those who wanted to return to the republic and rid Rome of the dictatorship of Caesar. At a dinner in the home of the newly appointed governor of Gaul, the guests discussed what kind of death was more desirable. Caesar declared that the best death was a sudden one. The next day, March 15, 44 B.C., as soon as Julius Caesar was seated on his throne next to the statue of Pompey, the conspirators crowded around him as if to ask a favor and then ran their concealed daggers into him at the signal. Caesar received twenty-three wounds along with his wish for a sudden death. Sixty men were involved in his assassination which was led by Gaius Cassius Longinus.

Mark Antony's infatuation for Cleopatra prevented him from succeeding Julius Caesar as ruler of Rome. She turned him against Rome, and he was then defeated by Octavian. Changing his name to Augustus Caesar, Octavian became the next emperor of Rome.

Daniel 11:20-28: Then shall stand up in his estate a raiser of taxes in the glory of the kingdom: but within few days he shall be destroyed, neither in anger, nor in battle. [21]And in his estate shall stand up a vile person, to whom they shall not give the honour of the kingdom: but he shall come in peaceably, and

obtain the kingdom by flatteries. ²²And with the arms of a flood shall they be overflown from before him, and shall be broken; yea, also the prince of the covenant. ²³And after the league made with him he shall work deceitfully: for he shall come up, and shall become strong with a small people. ²⁴He shall enter peaceably even upon the fattest places of the province; and he shall do that which his fathers have not done, nor his fathers' fathers; he shall scatter among them the prey, and spoil, and riches: yea, and he shall forecast his devices against the strong holds, even for a time. ²⁵And he shall stir up his power and his courage against the king of the south with a great army; and the king of the south shall be stirred up to battle with a very great and mighty army; but he shall not stand: for they shall forecast devices against him. ²⁶Yea, they that feed of the portion of his meat shall destroy him, and his army shall overflow: and many shall fall down slain. ²⁷And both these kings' hearts shall be to do mischief, and they shall speak lies at one table; but it shall not prosper: for yet the end shall be at the time appointed. ²⁸Then shall he return into his land with great riches; and his heart shall be against the holy covenant; and he shall do exploits, and return to his own land.

Augustus Caesar was the "one who imposes taxes on the glorious kingdom" (Daniel 11:20; NKJ). These taxes, which were evenly distributed and paid by everyone, brought Joseph and Mary to Bethlehem for the birth of Jesus (Luke 2:1). During Augustus' reign there was immense building of enterprise and peace in the Roman Empire for the first time in many years. After this reign of peace, he died a natural death. Although he ruled for forty-three years, the angel calls it a "few days."

The Romans were a small group of people, yet they were able to outwit all their enemies. This is also in harmony with the prediction in Daniel 8:24-25. Rome rewarded those who fought with them, giving them wealth and benefits that kept their loyalty tied to Rome. During Augustus' rule immense wealth came from Egypt to the coffers of Rome.

Tiberius Caesar was associated with Augustus for the last two years of his reign and took over at his death in A.D. 14. Tiberius was the son of Livia, the wife of Augustus, but he was treated as Augustus' own son. Since Augustus did not have his own child, the insistence and "flattery" of Livia ultimately led Augustus to give Tiberius the rulership of the Roman Empire.

Tiberius was that "vile" person who entered into the kingdom with flattery. He was so wicked and vile that the whole nation rejoiced at his death. When they thought he had died, he suddenly revived, but his attendants murdered him by suffocation. His death took place in A.D. 37. According to verse 22, even the Prince of the covenant would be broken through this power. During Tiberius' reign, Jesus died on the cross in A.D. 31, just as the prophecy predicted.

Typical to prophetic portions of Scripture, verse 28 returns to the rule of Augustus. Known also as Octavian, Augustus defeated Mark Antony and

Cleopatra at Actium. Mark Antony's forces had so many defectors that he could not return to Rome; he died in Egypt. At this time the riches of Egypt were taken to Rome, thus reducing Egypt to almost nothing. The defeat deflated the money of Egypt to half its value so provisions cost twice as much.

"His heart shall be moved against the holy covenant" (Daniel 11:28; NKJ). Rome fought against the holy covenant made to Abraham and the patriarchs when the innocents were slaughtered in Bethlehem, in the subjection of Judea and Jerusalem, and in the death of the Messiah and persecution of His apostolic church. Jesus died in A.D. 31 and the 490-year prophecy ended in 34 A.D. The death of Jesus brought an end to the symbolism of the daily sacrifices, then stoning of Stephen three and a half years later ended the 490 years of Jewish probation. At this time, Jesus' prophecy came true: "Your house is left unto you desolate" (Matthew 23:28). Jerusalem's probation had ended and its desolation was sure. The holy covenant is only for those who, like Abraham, accept the Messiah and His work: they are Abraham's true seed and "heirs according to the promise" (Galatians 3:29). Rome continued its war on the Christian church during the first three centuries A.D., beginning with Nero and ending with Diocletian. John Foxe lists ten major campaigns of persecution, the tenth being the worst.[4] During this time period, Christianity was outlawed and considered treason against the Roman Empire; many Christians died for their faith.

Daniel 11:29-35: At the time appointed he shall return, and come toward the south; but it shall not be as the former, or as the latter. [30]For the ships of Chittim shall come against him: therefore he shall be grieved, and return, and have indignation against the holy covenant: so shall he do; he shall even return, and have intelligence with them that forsake the holy covenant. [31]And arms shall stand on his part, and they shall pollute the sanctuary of strength, and shall take away the daily sacrifice, and they shall place the abomination that maketh desolate. [32]And such as do wickedly against the covenant shall he corrupt by flatteries: but the people that do know their God shall be strong, and do exploits. [33]And they that understand among the people shall instruct many: yet they shall fall by the sword, and by flame, by captivity, and by spoil, many days. [34]Now when they shall fall, they shall be holpen with a little help: but many shall cleave to them with flatteries. [35]And some of them of understanding shall fall, to try them, and to purge, and to make them white, even to the time of the end: because it is yet for a time appointed.

As verse 28 pertains to pagan Rome's persecution of the Christians, **verse 30** jumps in time to the appointed time, the end of pagan Roman. The dissolution of Rome began when the seat of power moved from Rome to Constantinople. Barbarians from the north began streaming into the weakened, old Roman

4   John Foxe, *Fox's Book of Martyrs*, ed. William Byron Forbush (Grand Rapids, MI: Zondervan, 1962), 5-33.

Empire, making way for "the ascendancy of Papal Rome" in A.D. 476, as described by Bunch.[5] This new Roman power gained supremacy as the church claimed authority over both spiritual and civil matters.

Taking away the daily or *tamiyd* refers to the continual mediatorial ministry of Jesus, our Passover Lamb. See Daniel 8:12. He was crucified at the time of the morning sacrifice and died at the time of the evening sacrifice (Mark 15:25, 34-37), thus fulfilling the daily sacrifice offering. However, the Messiah's sacrifice and ministry would be replaced by something that Daniel calls the "abomination of desolation" (Daniel 11:31; NKJ).

During His ministry on earth, Jesus told the disciples that this abomination of desolation was still in the future (Matthew 24:15; Mark 13:14) and that it would come through Rome's conquest of Jerusalem. Since the context points to the end of the Western Roman Empire, this is more than Titus' capture of Jerusalem with the desecration and destruction of the temple. Jesus had already said that He was the temple (John 2:19, 20) and if they destroyed it, in three days He would raise it up. The re-born Roman power would overshadow Jesus' ministry in the heavenly sanctuary and wickedly work against the covenant. The term "ark of the covenant" plainly shows that the covenant refers to the Ten Commandments. According to the new covenant promise, this law would be written on the hearts of God's people by the Holy Spirit. The abomination of desolation is new Rome's attempt to tamper with the sacrifice and ministry of the Messiah and the law of God, His covenant. These two issues are prime targets in Rome's fight against the Lord of the covenant.

Daniel 9:27 states that the Messiah would "bring an end to sacrifice and offering. And on the wing of **abominations** shall be one who makes desolate" (NKJ). Abominations is plural. Jesus referred to one of the desolations in Matthew 24:15: the destruction of Jerusalem and the temple. Another abomination came into the church in the fourth century after Constantine's conversion to Christianity: the transfer of the sacred worship of the Creator from Sabbath to Sunday, a day of pagan origin. Hislop records some of the pagan customs that entered the church: During the fourth century, "when the queen of heaven, under the name of Mary, was beginning to be worshipped in the Christian Church, this 'unbloody sacrifice' also was brought in. . . . It was a small thin, *round* wafer," made purposefully round in imitation of the sun.[6] Hence a new form of sun worship entered the church through paganism.

After his conversion in the sixth century (A.D. 496), Clovis of France pledged military support to papal Rome in A.D. 508. This marked the beginning of papal Rome's supremacy in both religious and civil matters and fulfilled the starting point for the 1290-year period of Daniel 12:11. Catholicism won

5   Bunch, *The Book of Daniel*, 180.

6   Alexander Hislop, *The Two Babylons: Papal Worship* (United States of America: Loizeaux Brothers, 1959), 159.

secular support and became the dominant force and power in Europe. Papal Rome received a deadly wound at the end of the 1,290 years in 1798 when the pope was taken captive by General Berthier of France and died in captivity (1798 – 508 = 1290 years).

Rome's abomination of desolation was twofold: first, it attempted to change God's; moral law of Ten Commandments; secondly, it replaced Christ's sanctuary ministry with the pagan-derived mass and an earthly priesthood which claimed to re-crucify Christ with every celebration of this mysterious worship. The Bible says Jesus' sacrifice was done "once for all" (Romans 6:10; Hebrews 7:27; 9:12; 10:10), but they have forsaken the covenant and crucified the Lord of glory afresh.

Daniel 11:31: And arms shall stand on his part, and they shall pollute the sanctuary of strength, and shall take away the daily sacrifice, and they shall place the abomination that maketh desolate.

The Mosaic sanctuary no longer existed when John wrote about the coming antichrist power in the Revelation. The book of Hebrews points believers to look up by faith to the ministry of Christ in the heavenly temple made without hands. Psalm 77:13 (NKJ) says: "Your way, O God, is in the sanctuary; Who is so great a God as our God?" This perfect way was polluted as the apostate church made their bishops into priests and led the people to look to sinful man for salvation. This counterfeit system covered up the heavenly administration of Jesus and profaned the sanctuary in heaven. We have a Great High Priest in the heavens: Jesus makes intercession for us as the only Mediator between God and man. Attempting to replace Jesus' ministry in the sanctuary in heaven is an "abomination that makes desolate." Thus papal Rome continued the work begun by pagan Rome.

Daniel 11:32: And such as do wickedly against the covenant shall he corrupt by flatteries: but the people that do know their God shall be strong, and do exploits.

Papal Rome hid under pretense of flattery. People were willing to compromise truth for wealth, position, and honor. This church-state renounced the supreme authority of the Scriptures by the decrees and decisions of its councils and made the Bible subject to church traditions. The magisterium freely placed man's interpretation above a "thus saith the Lord" so that the customs and rules of men might reign. On the other hand, some people would not be taken in by any of Rome's flatteries; they would remain true to their God no matter what the cost.

This apostasy was never universal. There were always the faithful few. In number they seemed almost insignificant, but in God's sight they were strong because they knew Him. The Waldenses, Albigenses, Hussites, Lollards, Lutherans, Anabaptists, and Huguenots fanned the flames of faith that led to the

Reformation. Although small at first, their influence grew larger and wider until the whole earth was lightened by the truths they preserved.

Daniel 11:33: And they that understand among the people shall instruct many: yet they shall fall by the sword, and by flame, by captivity, and by spoil, many days.

"Many days" describes the 1260 years of papal rule over the kings of the earth. Foxe's book devotes more than 250 pages to the papal persecutions of these centuries.[7] They burned people at the stake to maintain their claim that the church did not shed blood. Often papal Rome used the civil authorities to carry out the judgments made by the Inquisition. Various instruments of torture were used so that the most pain could be inflicted before death came to the suffering martyr. Some were caged and hung up on the city's wall until they starved to death. Because they practiced the biblical method of baptism, Anabaptists were often drowned, including women and children. Starting in 1681, Louis XIV reduced the Protestant population of his country by employing the dragonnades. Wealthy Huguenots were forced to house rowdy soldiers who were allowed to harass them and violate their rights. Whole cities and regions were depopulated. In 1686, Louis bragged that of nearly a million Huguenots, only a thousand remained. The rest had fled to Switzerland, Holland, England, Prussian, and other more tolerant lands.

Daniel 11:34: Now when they shall fall, they shall be holpen with a little help: but many shall cleave to them with flatteries.

This same imagery is used in Revelation 12:16: the "earth" came to the aid of the persecuted church. The meaning of "earth" includes the mountain hideaways of the Waldenses and the Protestant Reformation that took hold in the German areas of Europe. Countries that came to the aide of God's people also restrained the work of persecution carried on by the papacy. Sadly, even Protestantism became popular, and many embraced the reformed faith from unworthy motives. The followers of the Reformers also fell prey to flatteries.

Daniel 11:35: And some of them of understanding shall fall, to try them, and to purge, and to make them white, even to the time of the end: because it is yet for a time appointed.

When people thought they were safe from persecution, it broke out again. England had been under Protestant rule since the days of Henry VIII, but the Marian Persecutions broke out for five years when his daughter Mary I took the throne after the death of Henry's son Edward VI. Foxe gave Mary the nickname "Bloody Mary" because she burned nearly three hundred people at the stake, many of them leading citizens and royalty, in her effort to purge England of

---

[7]   Foxe, 43-298.

Protestantism.[8] In one sense, persecution has proved to be a blessing in disguise as those not deeply committed to following Jesus as Lord and Savior forsook the faith in the face of death, leaving the church stronger and more vibrant. In the same way, persecution and trials in life purify one's faith.

Daniel 11:36: And the king shall do according to his will; and he shall exalt himself, and magnify himself above every god, and shall speak marvellous things against the God of gods, and shall prosper till the indignation be accomplished: for that that is determined shall be done.

The article "the" defines the king as the previous power: the head of the papal church that magnifies himself above every god and speaks blasphemies against the God of gods. Papal infallibility and the blasphemous title "Vicar of the Son of God" have been claimed by no other man on earth.

In their accusations of Jesus, the Pharisees help us to understand the biblical definition of blasphemy. **Matthew 9:2-3** (NKJ) says: "They brought to Him a paralytic lying on a bed. When Jesus saw their faith, He said to the paralytic, 'Son, be of good cheer; your sins are forgiven you.' And at once some of the scribes said within themselves, 'This Man blasphemes!'" It is blasphemy for a man who is not God to claim the power to forgive sins. The popes, bishops, and priests have long contended that they have the power to forgive sin; therefore their adherents confess to a man rather than to God Himself.

The papacy will come to a "determined" end when Jesus returns in glory at the end of the world. Babylon will receive its punishment during the seven last plagues of Revelation.

Daniel 11:37: Neither shall he regard the God of his fathers, nor the desire of women, nor regard any god: for he shall magnify himself above all.

This little horn power is different from all other powers before it. This compromising power has its feet planted in both Christianity and paganism. The pope claims worship and honor that belong only to God, thus by his claims magnifying himself above all others. This fulfills Paul's prediction: "He opposes and exalts himself above all that is called God" (2 Thessalonians 2:4; NKJ).

וְעַל־חֶמְדַּת נָשִׁים **"Nor the desire of women"**

The Hebrew word נָשִׁים (*nashiym*) means "women." חֶמְדַּת (*chemdath*) means "delight" or "pleasure," as used in the phrase, "the pleasant land." Here the phrase refers to the pleasures of marriage, thus it could be paraphrased, he will "not allow the pleasure of being married to a woman." The papacy denies its priests and nuns the privilege of marriage, thus disregarding the fulfillment of a heaven-ordained desire. This is not natural, nor is it a law of creation.

Daniel 11:38: But in his estate shall he honour the God of forces: and a god whom his fathers knew not shall he honour with gold, and silver, and with precious stones, and pleasant things.

When traveling in countries dominated by the Roman Church, it is readily seen that the cathedrals are built like large fortresses with enough gold, silver, and precious stones to feed the poor begging on those very grounds. Compare this with the early church and its humble beginnings. The apostles lived simply and spent everything they had to care for the poor and propel the gospel to the far reaches of the earth.

Daniel 11:39: Thus shall he do in the most strong holds with a strange god, whom he shall acknowledge and increase with glory: and he shall cause them to rule over many, and shall divide the land for gain.

Could the foreign god he acknowledges and advances in glory be Mary or the little wafer called the host? Could it be the power of the popes who claim to change the immutable law of God by commanding worship on the venerable day of the sun?

Divide the land for gain: This has been the course of Rome. As pagan Rome divided the world into provinces that were ruled by favored generals, papal Rome has done the same thing. The whole world is divided up and organized under bishops, archbishops, and cardinals. From these divisions the wealth flows into the coffers of Rome. Revelation 18:13 pictures a whole commercial system that even traffics in the "souls of men." For example, the country of Argentina gives a portion of its income each year to the church.

Verse 40: And at the time of the end shall the king of the south push at him: and the king of the north shall come against him like a whirlwind, with chariots, and with horsemen, and with many ships; and he shall enter into the countries, and shall overflow and pass over.

This brings us down to the time of the end. The "he" in verses 40-45 must be defined by the "he" in verses 36-39 which always refers to papal Rome. These are the final scenes of this earth's history. The prophecies here have not yet unfolded. Some preachers in the past have made correct predictions of future events based on prophecy. Early in the Soviet Union's history, Louis Were predicted the demise of the atheistic Soviet Union using Daniel 11:40-44, but he died before the fall of Communism. Were linked the Soviet Union's atheistic nature with the king of the south. Like ancient Egypt, the Soviet Union also defied God.

In eighteenth-century France, atheism had its rebirth and grew into adolescence. The seeds of this rebellion against God were carried to the Soviet Union where atheism grew into adulthood. The godlessness of this communist state became an obstacle to Rome and needed to be eliminated. True to Revelation 13 the Roman church worked in union with the government of the United States.

This joint effort of President Reagan and Pope John Paul II was termed the "Holy Alliance" by *Time* magazine as their labors brought down the communist system in the former Soviet Union and many other communist countries.

Verse 41: He shall enter also into the glorious land, and many countries shall be overthrown: but these shall escape out of his hand, even Edom, and Moab, and the chief of the children of Ammon.

This is still future in its interpretation. The lands of Ammon, Edom, and Moab are now Muslim strongholds. Egypt also became a Muslim stronghold. Since Ethiopia expelled the Jesuits, Catholicism has never been able to gain a stronghold there. Forty-five to fifty percent of the population is Muslim, thirty-five to forty percent of the population is Ethiopian Orthodox Christian. Egypt is ninety percent Sunni Muslim and six percent Coptic Christian. Due to the nature of the Sunni Moslems, Egypt is not as radical against Christians as the Shiites and other Muslim groups. Although the papacy has entered the glorious land, Palestine and Jerusalem in particular, and established itself in "many countries," it has not been able to establish itself in Muslim strongholds. The common thread of venerating Mary may change that in the future as Muslims are willing to go to Catholic churches to see and hear apparitions of Mary.

Verses 42, 43: He shall stretch forth his hand also upon the countries: and the land of Egypt shall not escape. ⁴³But he shall have power over the treasures of gold and of silver, and over all the precious things of Egypt: and the Libyans and the Ethiopians shall be at his steps.

In the future the papacy along with its allies may gain some sort of foothold to have power over Egypt's treasures of gold and silver. This would mean some sort of footing in Libya and Ethiopia also will follow suit.

Verse 44: But tidings out of the east and out of the north shall trouble him: therefore he shall go forth with great fury to destroy, and utterly to make away many.

God's throne was on the north side in the holy place of the earthly sanctuary. The temple gate was on the sanctuary's east side. So in the heavenly sanctuary, Jesus comes from the eastern gate and moves to His throne in the north. In Ezekiel, the image of jealousy was set up in the north and east. Prophecies of the abominations done by God's so-called people accurately describe the papacy. In the end, the papacy receives disturbing and threatening news. His seat of power will be threatened, and he will go out with fury to destroy and annihilate many.

Verse 45: And he shall plant the tabernacles of his palace between the seas in the glorious holy mountain; yet he shall come to his end, and none shall help him.

Symbolically the seas symbolize "peoples, multitudes, nations, and tongues" according to Revelation 17:15. According to Isaiah 66:20, the glorious holy mountain is Jerusalem. In the symbolic language of Revelation, this represents the New Jerusalem where God's people will dwell. Joel 3:17 says Zion is God's holy mountain. The papacy will plant itself in the last days between God's people and the peoples of this earth. Because he attempts to destroy God's people, he will come to an end and no one will be able to help him.

Summary

Daniel 11 spans the history of Medo-Persia, Greece, and finally Rome in both its pagan and Christian phases. Through every difficulty and persecution, each person is called make a choice. Whom will we serve? Giving us advance warning, these prophecies point out the final outcomes of each choice. As it was in heaven and the Garden of Eden, each individual is given the freedom to choose for or against God. May we be true and faithful unto death like Daniel.

CHAPTER TWELVE

Daniel 12

Introduction

D aniel's last vision in chapter 12 is the final act and, at the same time, a summary of this prophetic drama. The king of the north, which represents the papacy, comes to its end. This chapter is fixed in the time of the end as Michael stands to defend God's people. All who are found written in the book are delivered. Daniel 12 pictures the resurrection of the righteous, and the angel tells Daniel that the book was to be sealed until the time of the end.

There is a progression in the use of Michael in the book of Daniel. First, He is "one of the chief princes" (10:13), then "your Prince" (10:21), and at the last "the great Prince" (12:1). In Jude 1:9 He is "the Archangel" or Leader of the angels. The last biblical reference in Revelation 12:7 says: "Michael and his angels fought against the dragon." In each of these cases, Michael victoriously contends with Satan. When Michael stands up to defend His people, Satan is vanquished and the saints are rewarded with eternal life, forever to be with their Lord, Savior, and Defender.

Daniel 12:1-4: And at that time shall Michael stand up, the great prince which standeth for the children of thy people: and there shall be a time of trouble, such as never was since there was a nation even to that same time: and at that time thy people shall be delivered, every one that shall be found written in the book. ²And many of them that sleep in the dust of the earth shall awake, some to everlasting life, and some to shame and everlasting contempt. ³And they that be wise shall shine as the brightness of the firmament; and they that turn many to righteousness as the stars for ever and ever. ⁴But thou, O Daniel, shut up the words, and seal the book, even to the time of the end: many shall run to and fro, and knowledge shall be increased.

Verse 2 describes a special resurrection: White pictures this glorious scene: "Graves are opened, and 'many of them that sleep in the dust of the earth . . . awake, some to everlasting life, and some to shame and everlasting contempt.' Daniel 12:2. All who have died in the faith of the third angel's message come forth from the tomb glorified, to hear God's covenant of peace with those who have kept His law. 'They also which pierced Him' (Revelation 1:7), those that mocked and derided Christ's dying agonies, and the most violent opposers of His truth and His people, are raised to behold Him in His glory and to see the honor placed upon the loyal and obedient."[1]

At that time: Jesus will stand up for His people, both the living and those that are asleep in death. At this time, they will all be given everlasting life. Those who are not His people and not found in the book of life will be faced with everlasting shame and contempt. Instead of everlasting life, they will suffer the consequences of their choice.

Many shall run to and fro: Pfandl's exegesis makes this phrase clearer: "This is a Hebrew idiom for *searching* (cf. Jeremiah 5:1; Amos 8:12; Zechariah 4:10, KJV). When God's Spirit would unseal the book of Daniel after the commencement of the time of the end, knowledge regarding the prophecies in the book of Daniel would increase. From history we know that this is indeed what happened in the nineteenth century, following the end of the 1260 years in 1798."[2]

The prophecies of Daniel would be sealed until the time of the end. Then knowledge of God's word would increase and many would run to and fro, searching for the meaning of the prophecies. The angel made it clear that the prophecies of Daniel would be understood in the end time. The book of Daniel is sealed no longer! Daniel's prophecies also tell us when the time of the end begins.

Daniel 2, 7, 8, 9 and 10-12 are parallel prophecies, covering the same ground with increasing detail. Every vision was followed by an explanation. In this brief outline, Gerhard Pfandl points this out as follows:[3]

1. Daniel 2: vision (verses 31-35), explanation (verses 36-46)

2. Daniel 7: vision (verses 1-14), explanation (verses 15-27)

3. Daniel 8, 9: vision (Daniel 8:1-12), explanation (verses 13-26; Daniel 9:24-27)

4. Daniel 10-12: vision (Daniel 11:2-12:4), explanation (Daniel 12:5-13)

In the following paragraphs, Pfandl demonstrates that the prophetic time periods are a part of the explanation following the visions:

While it is true that the vision in Daniel 11:2-12:4 is itself an explanation of the vision in Daniel 8, we must not overlook the fact that in Daniel 7, 8, and 10-12 the time prophecies are always situated within the explanation section, not in the visions themselves. In Daniel 7 the vision ends in verse 14, and the time prophecy appears in verse 25. Daniel 8 has the

---

[1] White, *The Great Controversy*, 637.

[2] Gerhard Pfandl, *Daniel: The Seer of Babylon* (Hagerstown, MD: Review and Herald, 2004), 117.

[3] Ibid., 111-112.

vision conclude in verse 12 and presents the time prophecy in verse 14. Finally, in Daniel 10-12 the vision ends in Daniel 12:4, and the time prophecies follow in verses 5-13. To interpret Daniel 12:5-13 as a new vision will destroy the literary structure. . . .

Furthermore, we find a strong thematic and linguistic connection between the texts in Daniel 7:25 and 12:7:

Daniel 7:25: "[He] shall persecute the saints of the Most High. . . . The saints shall be given into his hand for a time and times and half a time."

Daniel 12:7: "He swore . . . that it shall be for a time, times, and a half a time; and when the power of the holy people has been completely shattered, all these things shall be finished."

The shattering of the power of the holy people in Daniel 12:7 lasts for three and a half times and is the same as the persecution of the saints in Daniel 7:25 that also lasts for three and a half times, further evidence that the times in Daniel 12 refer not to the future but to the past.[4]

Time of the End

Daniel 12:5–13: Then I Daniel looked, and, behold, there stood other two, the one on this side of the bank of the river, and the other on that side of the bank of the river. ⁶And one said to the man clothed in linen, which was upon the waters of the river, How long shall it be to the end of these wonders? ⁷And I heard the man clothed in linen, which was upon the waters of the river, when he held up his right hand and his left hand unto heaven, and sware by him that liveth for ever that it shall be for a time, times, and an half; and when he shall have accomplished to scatter the power of the holy people, all these things shall be finished. ⁸And I heard, but I understood not: then said I, O my Lord, what shall be the end of these things? ⁹And he said, Go thy way, Daniel: for the words are closed up and sealed till the *time of the end*. ¹⁰Many shall be purified, and made white, and tried; but the wicked shall do wickedly: and none of the wicked shall understand; but the wise shall understand. ¹¹And from the time that the daily sacrifice shall be taken away, and the abomination that maketh desolate set up, there shall be a thousand two hundred and ninety days. ¹²Blessed is he that waiteth, and cometh to the thousand three hundred and five and thirty days. ¹³But go thou thy way till the end be: for thou shalt rest, and stand in thy lot at the end of the days.

When will Daniel be unsealed? The answer is in verse 7: after "a time, times, and half a time" or 1,260 literal years (see Daniel 7:25). The papal church

---

[4]   Ibid., 112-113.

persecuted God's people for 1,260 years until 1798 when Berthier took the pope captive. The angel said that the time of the end would come at the end of the 1,260 years. Thus the captivity of the papacy in 1798 marked the beginning of the time of the end. From this time, interest in the prophecies, especially the book of Daniel, increased, and people studied to understand the end-time issues. As their knowledge increased, they began to share the prophecies of Daniel with others. The Advent Awakening in the early 1800s reached its zenith in 1844, the end of the 2,300-day prophecy. The time of the end lasts until Jesus comes in glory as the grand culmination of all Daniel's prophecies.

The angel pointed out that the wicked will not understand, but the wise will. The wise are those who sincerely search for the truth and then share it, turning many to righteousness and obedience. God's people will be purified through trials during this period while they wait for the return of Christ.

The wicked do not understand because they do not love the truth (2 Thessalonians 2:10). This leaves them vulnerable to the lies of Satan as promulgated by the papacy. This is how the false church stands in the way, between its adherents and God's people, blocking the light of truth and filling the earth with the miasma of lawlessness. In these last days, when Bible knowledge is increasing and God's truth is free to all who earnestly search for Him, it is sad that many turn away from their Creator and Redeemer, the only One who is the Way, the Truth, and the Life. Michael will stand up for all who step out in faith, willing to do whatever God asks of them.

History is the key to understanding the three prophetic year-day prophecies of Daniel 12. God gave these prophecies to warn and prepare His people living in this time of the end.

1290 and 1335 Days

When the angel first answered the question, "How long?" he repeated the 1260-day prophecy that had been given earlier in Daniel 7:25. The time of the end will come when the persecuting power of the papacy comes to an end. In 1798, the prophecy came true. The leader of the church that had taken many captives was now a captive himself. "He that leadeth into captivity shall go into captivity" (Revelation 13:10).

Now two more prophecies are given by the angel to guide those living in the time of the end. The question comes a second time: "How long until the end?" The angel answers, "From the time that the continual ministry of Christ is taken away and the desolating abomination is set up, there will be 1290 days."

Daniel asked the angel about the "end of these things." The ending point is 1798, the time of the end. Just like the 1260-day prophecy, the 1290 days ended in 1798. The difference between the two is 30 years; thus the 1290 days began 30 years earlier than the 1260-day prophecy. As he speaks of the 1290 days, the angel speaks of setting up the abomination, the preparation needed to promote the little horn's false religious teachings that desolate Christendom.

In A.D. 508, at the beginning of the 1290 days, King Clovis of the Franks began his mission, wielding the sword to eradicate the Arian tribes on behalf of the papacy. This marked the start of uprooting of the three horns that stood in the ways of the papacy's control in spiritual matters and prepared the way for Catholicism to reign supreme in Europe. As power shifted into the hands of papal Rome, Christ as High Priest in the heavenly sanctuary was hidden from men for many centuries. Pfandl describes it succinctly: "The joining of the civil and the religious power (Franks and the Papacy) at that time was an important step in 'setting up the abomination of desolation,' which refers to the unscriptural teachings of the Papacy and their enforcement through the union of church and state."[5]

Who is Clovis? He converted to Christianity after marrying the Burgundian princess Clotilda. Since his new wife was Catholic, Clovis became a champion of the Roman Church. During his reign, Clovis united all the Franks under his rule and gained the support of the Gallic clergy. He established his capital and base of operations in Paris and extended his holdings into Germany, laying the foundation for the French monarchy.

In A.D. 507 Clovis routed the Visigoth army, pursued them all the way to their southernmost strongholds, and defeated them in A.D. 508. For this victory, Clovis received the title of consul and "The Eldest Son of the Church" from the pope, ensuring France a leading role in the advancement of the papacy. Ironically, the power of France set up the religious authority of papal Rome in A.D. 508, but the papacy was overthrown in 1798 by the French army led by Napoleon.

Thirty years later in A.D. 538, the 1260-day prophecy began as the papacy became the recognized ruler of Western Europe. With the decree of Justinian and the power of the armies of Rome to back it up, the papacy established its religio-political stronghold in the Western Roman Empire and received its seat of authority and throne from pagan Rome.

Answering the question, "When is the time of the end?" the 1260 and 1290-day prophecies are linked by their common end point, 1798. In a similar manner, the 1290- and 1335-day prophecies are linked by their common starting point: the abomination of desolation set up in A.D. 508 (Daniel 12:11, 12). Clovis passed a law that required forced participation in the mass in A.D. 508. This false system of the Roman Church redirected the believer's spiritual eyes from the heavenly sanctuary to an earthly substitute. In the heavenly sanctuary, there is forgiveness through the "daily" or continual ministry and intercession of our great High Priest Jesus. The papacy took away the Sabbath, turning man's eyes away from their Creator. He puts a pagan day in its place, promoting lawlessness and turning men away from righteousness. The 1335-day prophecy tells us that the truth is coming back to God's people! Look to heaven, to the Lawgiver, Creator, Priest, and King!

---

[5] Ibid., 119.

With the same starting point as the 1290 days, the 1335-day prophecy continues an additional 45 years to 1843. The unsealing of Daniel culminated in 1843, the end of the 1335-year prophecy, as thousands of people heard a clear message from the prophecies of Daniel. The angel pronounced a special blessing on those who would wait obediently for this day. As the Advent message was preached, true believers were unified. False churches cast them out, but they continued to share the good news from Daniel, "Unto 2,300 days, then the sanctuary will be cleansed!" The power of the Holy Spirit to convert and transform sinners was proof of the authentic spiritual nature of the Advent message. Pfandl notes: "The book of Daniel does not connect the 1335-day prophecy with the activity of the little-horn power. Rather it relates it to a special blessing for those who live at the end of that time period. Another blessing for the time of the end appears in Revelation 14:13."[6]

The significance is staggering! These prophecies pinpoint God's prophetic movement in the stream of time. Daniel foretold the book would be unsealed in 1798 and would culminate in a blessing just before 1844. These time lines can be diagrammed as follows:

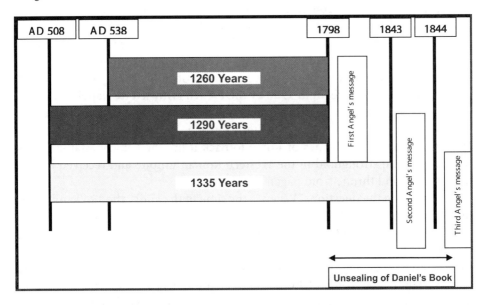

Verse 13: But go thou thy way till the end be: for thou shalt rest, and stand in thy lot at the end of the days.

Over 90 years of age, Daniel had fulfilled his purpose. His work was now complete. Time to rest had finally come after more than 70 years of faithful ministry in the courts of Babylon and Medo-Persia. Daniel must rest in the grave

---

6   Ibid.

until Jesus comes in the clouds to call him back to life. Soon everlasting life and immortality will be Daniel's inheritance! Will it be yours?

As the prophecies faithfully predicted events in the past, so they will prepare us for the future. God's faithful ones have the assurance that Michael will stand up for them and delivered them! "Even so, come, Lord Jesus" (Revelation 22:20).

Section Two

Introduction to

Revelation

Welcome to the study of "the revelation of Jesus Christ" (Revelation 1:1). Like Daniel, Revelation cannot stand alone or even be interpreted merely from the standpoint of the book of Daniel. As the books written before and after Daniel aid our interpretation and understanding, so the book of Revelation is the summary and final installment in the prophetic scheme of the Bible. All that was lost in Genesis is restored by the end of Revelation. As it reveals Christ, Revelation summarizes the plan of salvation. While Genesis is the book of beginnings, Revelation gives hope for the future in this uncertain world. Revelation reminds us that now is the time to prepare for the final events of earth's history. This preparation is not just some mental exercise, but a loving, trusting relationship with the Lion/Lamb of Revelation that leads to obedience and overcomes sin, Satan, and all the beastly powers of this earth.

יהוה in Genesis and Revelation

In Genesis His name is יהוה in Hebrew: Yahweh, the God of creation. In Revelation He is Jesus which means "Yahweh is salvation," signifying that our Creator is also our Redeemer. The first chapter begins as Genesis did with a progressive revelation of God. The Godhead is revealed through the Holy Spirit, symbolized by seven Spirits before His throne, and through Jesus Christ. Christ is the Alpha and Omega, the beginning and the end of all things. "Without Him nothing was made that was made" (John 1:3; NRV). Genesis begins with a perfect world falling under the curse, but Revelation ends with the curse of sin removed and the world restored to perfection. The tree of life in Genesis was lost, but Revelation pictures God's people eating of that tree again. In Genesis man walked and talked with God face to face; in Revelation God Himself will live with His people. Genesis introduces us to a personal, powerful God, and Revelation reveals that power unleashed in our salvation and re-creation.

Reaching the Churches

As Revelation begins, Jesus tells John to write to the seven churches in Asia Minor. These churches were in close proximity to each other. Ephesus, east of the

Isle of Patmos, received the first letter. Northwest of Ephesus is Smyrna, the second church. Leaving Smyrna, travel north to Pergamos, the third church, then go in a southeastern direction to Thyatira, the fourth church. Head southeast again for Sardis, the fifth church, and southeast again to Philadelphia, the sixth church. Again head southeast to Laodicea, the seventh church, which is just about as far eastward as Pergamos is northward. These seven neighboring cities formed a circuit of churches in Asia.

Authorship and Interpretation

Most scholars believe the book of Revelation was written during the reign of Domitian who ruled Rome from A.D. 81 to 96. This author trusts the biblical and extrabiblical evidence that points to John, the beloved disciple of Jesus, as the writer of Revelation. He also wrote the gospel of John and the three epistle of John. Early church fathers, circa A.D. 120, testify to John's authorship. Papias, a friend of Polycarp, listened to John and believed the Revelation was his book. John wrote the book of Revelation near A.D. 95 or 96 and died around A.D. 98.

As a historicist, this writer views Revelation as a symbolic portrait of the great controversy between Christ and Satan. Revelation also contains predictive prophecies of events, some of which have already taken place, but others are still in the future. Jesus reveals the future through Revelation: "Write **the things which you have seen, and the things which are,** *and the things which will take place after this*" (Revelation 1:19; NKJ). Revelation's prophetic clock had already started "for the time is near" (Revelation 1:3). In the scope of eternity, the end is but a short time. Today most of Revelation has been fulfilled. Only a moment of time, so to speak, remains between us and the coming of Christ.

There are two types of prophecy in the Bible: classical prophecy and apocalyptic prophecy. Classical prophecy is usually conditional upon certain things or incidents happening. Jonah's preaching in Ninevah is an example of classical prophecy. The apocalyptic prophecies of Daniel and Revelation explain when and why certain events will happen in the future, preparing God's people for the coming events and giving them hope and strength to reach the ultimate end safely.

Revelation begins and ends with a promise to those who read, hear, and act on the words of this book (Revelation 1:3; 22:14). Just as Jesus sat on the mount and pronounced blessings upon God's children, so He speaks to us again from the book of Revelation.

Sanctuary Imagery

The Hebrew word for sanctuary is קֹדֶשׁ (*qodesh*). The root meaning is "morally clean or holy." The holiness lost in Eden could be restored, but only by the blood of the Lamb. In the sanctuary service in ancient Israel, the priests wore a golden crown on their miter with the words "Holiness to Yahweh" inscribed upon it. All the ceremonies and sacrifices of this typical system pointed to our great High Priest and Savior who alone can restore us to holiness.

As the book of Hebrews reveals the ministry of Christ in heaven, so the setting for Revelation is the sanctuary in heaven. Therefore an understanding of the ceremonies and festivals of the sanctuary are a necessity for any student of Revelation.

The spring feasts and the ceremonies in the courtyard of the sanctuary were fulfilled during the first advent of Christ. He was baptized and anointed for His ministry, even as the priests were washed and anointed before serving in the sanctuary. On Friday, the fourteenth day of the first month, Christ our Passover Lamb was slain for us (1 Corinthians 5:7). After His resurrection, He presented the true first fruits offering before His Father on the sixteenth day of the month of Nisan. And the reality of Pentecost brought the power of the Holy Spirit upon the waiting church, enabling them to bring in a rich harvest of souls.

By the merit of His own blood, Christ inaugurated the heavenly sanctuary and has since served as our only Intercessor in His Father's presence. Hebrews and the book of Revelation speak of Christ's work in both the holy place and the most holy place, but Revelation and Leviticus 16 cover the latter in more detail. Revelation begins in the holy place with a vision of Jesus among the seven golden lamps. At a climactic point, the most holy place is opened to view with the ark of His covenant (Revelation 11:19). Though the Ten Commandments may be vilified on earth, they are a part of God's eternal throne in heaven.

Since the spring feast were fulfilled during the first advent of Christ, the fall feasts will also meet their antitypical fulfillment in Christ. Just as the spring festivals came at the culmination of the seventy-week prophecy, so we may expect the events leading up to the second advent of Christ to coincide with the conclusion of the 2300-day prophecy. As the ten-day Feast of Trumpets preceded the Day of Atonement, the warning was given to the world for ten years from 1834 to 1844. The Day of Atonement began as Christ entered a new phase of His ministry for us in the most holy place of the heavenly sanctuary. When He finishes this work, the pronouncement will be made: "He that is filthy, let him be filthy still: . . . and he that is holy, let him be holy still" (Revelation 22:11).

One more feast remains—the Feast of Tabernacles—when Christ will tabernacle with us once more. This will be fulfilled when Jesus returns to take us to His home. He promised to serve us at His banqueting table, and we will live and reign with Him in heaven for a thousand years!

After the final judgment is carried out upon the wicked, God will create a new heaven and a new earth. John "saw no temple therein: for the Lord God Almighty and the Lamb are the temple of it" (Revelation 21:22). The Greek word for temple is ναός (naos) which referred to the holy place and the holy of holies of the temple at Jerusalem. We do not need a ceremonial temple for we are then face to face with our God. Perfect communion and holiness have been restored. The New Jerusalem itself has a cubical shape like the most holy place in the sanctuary. Here is God's throne with real cherubim on either side. We will see Him high and lifted up on His throne. All the symbols are now replaced with heavenly realities as we praise Him for the miraculous, sacrificial, and completed plan of redemption.

The themes of the sanctuary are also the same themes covered in the books of Daniel and Revelation. Judgment was one aspect of the priestly ministry; God's judgments are revealed in Daniel and Revelation. As the sanctuary was the center of worship for ancient Israel, so worship is a life-and-death theme in both Daniel and Revelation. While the beast power craves worship he doesn't deserve, the Creator God calls His people back to true worship.

Literal Israel journeyed with the sanctuary as they left Egyptian bondage on their way to the earthly Canaan. The Revelation shows how we can journey with Jesus in the heavenly sanctuary as we come out of the bondage of spiritual Babylon on our way to the heavenly land of Canaan. The following chart shows the relationship between the feasts and their fulfillment in the life of Christ.

		Feast Day	Event	Time Fulfilled
Spring feasts – Fulfilled at time of Christ's death		Passover—Leviticus 23:5	Death of Christ—1 Corinthians 5:7	AD 31 – Slain between the two evenings of Nisan 14 (Passover) –went on the cross at the time of the morning sacrifice and died at the time of the evening sacrifice.—Mark 15:25, 33
		Sabbath of the feast of unleavened bread—Leviticus 23:6	Christ rested in the tomb over the Sabbath just as unleavened bread does not rise – He did not rise yet!—Luke 23:56	Nisan 15 – Sabbath became the memorial of redemption.—Hebrews 4:1-10—Desire of Ages, page 769
		Wave sheaf or first fruits offering—Leviticus 23:7,10,11	Christ's resurrection and appearance before the Father—John 20:17	Nisan 16—Took place on the very day the wave sheaf was offered—Christ became our first-fruits offering.—1 Corinthians 15:20
		Pentecost or Feast of Weeks—Leviticus 23:16	Outpouring of Holy Spirit on the Day of Pentecost—Acts 2:1-4	The Day of Pentecost—Acts 2:1
Fall Feasts – Fulfilled at time of the end		Feast of Trumpets Leviticus 23:24	Announcement 10 days before the Day of Atonement—giving 10 days to prepare.—Leviticus 23:24	AD 1834 – 1844 Millerite movement—Revelation 10
		Day of Atonement—Leviticus 23:27	Investigative judgment begins—Hebrews 9:24,25	Began on October 22, 1844 as predicted in Daniel 8
		Feast of Tabernacles—Leviticus 23:29	Rest in the New Jerusalem	Follows the completion of the investigative judgment.—Revelation 22

As in the book of Daniel, there are four lines of prophecy in Revelation. Note the chart below for a brief overview of the book of Revelation.

7 Churches	7 Seals	7 Trumpets	7 Last Plagues Call to Judgment Judgment on each aspect of the Beast Power
Ephesus Pure Infant Church	**White Horse** Pure Infant Church	**1st Trumpet** Gothic Invasion By Alaric in 410 AD	**1st Plague** Earth symbolic of dominion of beast. Sore: a kind of sore that even the miracle powers of Egypt were unable to heal. Falls on those that do not heed the 3 Angel's messages
Smyrna Persecuted Church	**Red Horse** Persecuted Church	**2nd Trumpet** Vandal Invasion by Genseric in circa 428-430 AD	**2nd Plague** Sea symbolizes peoples that give life to the beast. These are seen as they really are in God's sight when He judges them
Pergamos Church of the Dark Ages Errors brought into Church	**Black Horse** Church of the Dark Ages Errors brought into Church	**3rd Trumpet** Hum Invasion by Attila the Hun 451 AD	**3rd Plague** Like rivers are connected to the seas, so are those that deny God's law as leading to Jesus, the source of life
Thyatira Church of the Middle Ages Paganized Church persecutes faithful in the Church	**Pale Horse** Church of the Middle Ages Paganized Church persecutes faithful in the Church	**4th Trumpet** Heruli Invasion by Odoacer in 476 AD	**4th Plague** Sun is symbolic of Babylon's chief god. This Plague is directed at Sun Worship—the sign of rebellion
Sardis Church of the Reformation	**Souls under the Altar** Church of the Reformation	**5th Trumpet** Saracen Muslim Invasions starting in 632 AD	**5th Plague** Beast Power is under judgment and none can come to it's aid. Judgment comes to the very center of the Apostate power—ROME!
Philadelphia Church that loves so much it takes the WORD of God to the World. Bible Societies start	**Great Earthquake** Church that loves so much it takes the WORD of God to the World. Bible Societies start	**6th Trumpet** Ottoman Turk Invasions The Reformation develops while Papal Rome engaged in a conflict on another front with Islam	**6th Plague** Directed at the people that give Babylon her power. Sanctuary imagery used here. When the power of people is dried up, the way is prepared for the kings of the East

Considering all the symbolism of the sanctuary service and the yearly feasts, one can only come to one conclusion: the book of Revelation must be understood in symbolic language. Both the internal content and external evidence assure us of this. To move from symbolic to literal and back is incongruent with correct biblical hermeneutics.

CHAPTER THIRTEEN

Revelation 1

Introduction

Revelation 1:1-2: The Revelation of Jesus Christ, which God gave unto him, to show unto his servants things which must shortly come to pass; and he sent and signified it by his angel unto his servant John: ²Who bare record of the word of God, and of the testimony of Jesus Christ, and of all things that he saw.

Revelation clearly states its purpose and author. This book is the revelation of Jesus Christ. Both names are used for a reason. Jesus is a Greek form of Joshua, meaning "Yahweh is salvation." Christ is Greek for Messiah or "the anointed one." So Revelation reveals salvation through the anointed One.

The word "signified" means that the messages of Revelation are given in symbols. It is significant that John notes the symbolic nature of this book from Jesus in the very first verse.

This special revelation comes from God via an angel to John, His servant. As God's prophet, John bears witness and testimony only of what he sees and hears, nothing more and nothing less.

Revelation 1:3: Blessed is he that readeth, and they that hear the words of this prophecy, and keep those things which are written therein: for the time is at hand.

Revelation should be read publicly, and this book pronounces a blessing on both the reader and the hearers. From its beginning, Revelation was an unrestricted book to be read openly and for all to understand. Unlike Daniel, Revelation was never sealed. All who obey the things written in this book will be blessed.

For the time is at hand: This is a relevant, up-to-date book, both in John's day and our own. The wording shows that events recorded in Revelation were being fulfilled in John's time. The accuracy of this statement will be seen in the study of the seven churches.

Revelation 1:4-6: John to the seven churches which are in Asia: Grace be unto you, and peace, from him which is, and which was, and which is to come; and from the seven Spirits which are before his throne; ⁵And from Jesus Christ, who is the faithful witness, and the first begotten of the dead, and the prince of the kings of the earth. Unto him that loved us, and washed us from our sins in his own blood, ⁶And hath made us kings and priests unto God and his Father; to him be glory and dominion for ever and ever. Amen.

Verse 4: Again John states unequivocally that he is the author. No credible scholar denies this. He addresses his message to the seven churches in Asia Minor: "Grace be unto you, and peace." χάρις (charis) ὑμῖν (humin) **"Grace to you"** καί (kai) **"and"** εἰρήνη (eirene) **"peace."** This greeting of grace or peace was used throughout the New Testament. "Grace be unto you" is used by Paul, Peter, and John.

John alludes to the entire Godhead when he speaks of the one **"which is, and which was, and which is to come; and from the seven Spirits which are before his throne; and from Jesus Christ."** The One which is, was, and is to come is consistent with the biblical understanding of the Godhead. Then the two most important representatives of the Godhead to mankind are singled out: the Holy Spirit, symbolized by the seven spirits before the throne and Jesus Christ, the One revealed in Revelation.

Verses 5-6: John jumps to the end of the story, giving us a glimpse of what lies ahead in Revelation. John tells us what Jesus has done, is doing, and will be doing for us! Because Jesus loves us, He died for us to wash us from our sins with His own blood. The Revelation of Jesus Christ is our redemption guaranteed by His death on the cross.

What is Jesus doing for us now? Is there more than justification? The sanctuary service in Revelation begins with Jesus' death on the cross and leads to the final pronouncement in **Revelation 22:11**: "He that is unjust, let him be unjust still: and he which is filthy, let him be filthy still: and he that is righteous, let him be righteous still: and he that is holy, **let him be holy still.**" Even as the ancient sanctuary service restored righteous living and holiness to God's people, so today Christ in His heavenly sanctuary has the power to restore His holiness and obedience in us. The words "washed us from our sins" open before us the work of sanctification. "He shall save His people from their sins" (Matthew 1:21). Jesus' death provided the cleansing power to wash us from our sins.

He made us kings: In the Greek βασιλειαν (basileian) means "a kingdom of the people." Jesus wants us to share in His priestly work for all people. In the original language ἱερεῖς (hiereis) means priests or people who offer sacrifices and sacred rites for others. Christians washed by the blood of Jesus devote their life to Him and His service. As the Father sent Jesus to seek and save the lost, so He also gives this work to us. In our behavior, dressing, and deportment, remember that we are children of the kingdom. Priests wore special clothing so others would know and recognize their position. This same principle remains true today.

Although the future reward is important, God's people today should think about the joy of saving souls. Peter said to Jesus, "Lo, we have left all, and have followed thee." Jesus answered, "There is no man that hath left house, or brethren, or sisters, or father, or mother, or wife, or children, or lands, for my sake, and the gospel's, But he shall receive an hundredfold now in this time, houses, and brethren, and sisters, and mothers, and children, and lands, with persecutions; and in the world to come eternal life" (Mark 10:28-30). Now is the time to work for God's kingdom. While we look forward to the prize before us, nothing can compare to the joys of soul-winning on Jesus' team. The best of the Holy Spirit's power is available to us right now to share with others what Jesus has done for us. If we enter into that joy now, we will receive the promise at His second coming.

Revelation 1:7: Behold, he cometh with clouds; and every eye shall see him, and they also which pierced him: and all kindreds of the earth shall wail because of him. Even so, Amen.

Verse 7 confirms the special resurrection in Daniel 12:2. Verse 5 tells us that this is Jesus. A better translation reads "He is coming" because it is in the present tense within the context of future events. The future is certain in John's mind. He has already seen it in vision! In this introduction he shares the culmination of the vision. John also saw those who weren't ready for the King. These mourn at His coming because they lived their lives in darkness and lies, refusing the light of God's truth. John says: "Even so, Amen."

Every eye shall see him: All who are alive shall see Jesus when He returns. This is consistent with the rest of the Scripture. If someone speaks of a secret return, Jesus said, "Believe it not!" Christ is coming with the sound of the trumpet, the dead in Christ will arise from their graves, and He will come as King of kings in all of His splendor. The original language does not mean merely a spiritual eye or perception.

They also which pierced him: In addition to the living, those people who mocked and killed Jesus will also be resurrected to see Him coming. These have long since been laid to rest in their graves. Jesus Himself made reference to this special resurrection during His mock trial: "Hereafter shall ye see the Son of man sitting on the right hand of power, and coming in the clouds of heaven" (Matthew 26:64). This will be a terrifying experience for those who plotted Christ's death. According to Revelation 20:5, the rest of the wicked dead are not resurrected until the end of the thousand years.

Revelation 1:8: I am Alpha and Omega, the beginning and the ending, saith the Lord, which is, and which was, and which is to come, the Almighty.

Jesus is speaking here. This statement reminds us that the Lamb was slain in the past, but He is also the Lamb that has victory over death, both now and in the future. He is the beginning and the end, the first and last. From the beginning of the sanctuary service to the end, the focus is Jesus and what He does to save you. Christ's death on the cross means nothing if He does not keep His promise to come again. Revelation tells about Jesus keeping His promise. He will complete what He has started in our redemption.

Revelation 1:9: I John, who also am your brother, and companion in tribulation, and in the kingdom and patience of Jesus Christ, was in the isle that is called Patmos, for the word of God, and for the testimony of Jesus Christ.

John understood what it meant to suffer for his faith. He speaks as a brother to those who are reading and seeking to know God's will for their lives. God's kingdom is made up of those who call upon the name of Jesus and are willing to testify of their connection with Jesus, even if it means persecution.

In the isle that is called Patmos: John writes from Patmos, a desolate place where the Romans banished criminals. Tradition claims that John could not be killed, even when they put him in boiling oil, so he was banished to Patmos. Because he preached and shared the gospel of Jesus Christ, John was sentenced to Patmos. Tribulation is a part of the Christian life, but John reminds us to bear it with patience.

Revelation 1:10-11: I was in the Spirit on the Lord's day, and heard behind me a great voice, as of a trumpet, [11]Saying, I am Alpha and Omega, the first and the last: and, What thou seest, write in a book, and send it unto the seven churches which are in Asia; unto Ephesus, and unto Smyrna, and unto Pergamos, and unto Thyatira, and unto Sardis, and unto Philadelphia, and unto Laodicea.

Although banished to Patmos, he was not abandoned by God. Wherever we are, whether in a dungeon or cave, we are not alone if we are in Christ Jesus. God's eye was on His faithful servant. Instead of complaining, John was seeking fellowship with the Lord.

I was in the Spirit on the Lord's day: This is clear to Sabbath keepers because the Bible Sabbath has always been the Lord's day. God calls it "the holy of Yahweh" and "My holy day," so the holiness of God is linked to "the seventh day" which is "the Sabbath of the Lord your God" (Isaiah 58:13; Exodus 20:10-11). Jesus declared that He was the Lord of the Sabbath (Matthew 12:8). Therefore John specifically points out this day as different from any other.

Those who think it refers to Sunday have no internal or contextual evidence to verify such a conclusion. Go to the other books written by John to understand what he meant by the Lord's day. See how John's contemporaries understood the Lord's day. Don't rely on tradition because Jesus condemned it as a basis for belief. He reproved those who substituted tradition for the commandments of the Lord. The majority's belief does not constitute truth. In Scripture the majority viewpoint is called the "broad way" that leads to destruction (Matthew 7:13).

Matthew 12:8, Mark 2:27-28, and Luke 6:5 clarify the New Testament's understanding of the Lord's day. The seventh-day Sabbath has overwhelming evidence: in Genesis when the Sabbath was given, when God spoke the word "remember" in Exodus 20:12, and throughout both the Old and New Testament accounts. These words of God give meaning to John's statement, "the Lord's day."

Some believe that the "Lord's day" means the "gospel age" or an "eschatological age," but John is using simple language to give the setting for his book, telling us where he was, why he was there, what day of the week it was, and the things that he saw. To introduce a new paradigm would require more than two words. The context gives no room to jump to such conclusions. The Lord's day is the seventh-day Sabbath. As Paul and his friends gathered at the river to pray on the Sabbath in a place with no synagogue, so John is taking time on the Sabbath to be with his Lord.

The Greek phrase uses the word ἐν (en) which means "on, in, at, or with." No translations place this day as a gospel age or a yearly event, such as Easter Sunday. No evidence from the church of the first century exists for such an interpretation. While the apostles were still living, the faith of the early Christians remained pure, but heresies began to appear in the second century A.D. One hundred years after Christ's death, Sunday observance began to appear as a form of anti-Semitism due to the rebellion of the Jews against the Roman Empire.

In reality, the Christian church began as a sect of the Jewish faith, hence it is called the Judaeo-Christian church. Jesus was a Jew who came to reveal the Sabbath more fully during His ministry. Through Jesus, we can truly enter into the Sabbath rest. How fitting that John received his vision on the Sabbath! Jesus Himself said that salvation is of the Jews (John 4:22). In the plan of salvation through Christ, the Sabbath is a symbol of the divine rest of grace that is ours until Jesus comes again (see Hebrews 4). John had entered into the true Sabbath rest in Christ Jesus, and therefore the Lord chose to commune with him in this extraordinary way on His holy day!

And heard behind me a great voice, as of a trumpet: The voice of Jesus was glorified, unlike His manner of speaking while on earth. Now Jesus comes with the sound of the trumpet (Revelation 1:10; 1 Thessalonians 4:16).

I am Alpha and Omega, the first and the last: What fitting language to introduce who is speaking. This is, without any debate, Jesus Christ.

What thou seest, write in a book, and send it unto the seven churches which are in Asia; unto Ephesus, and unto Smyrna, and unto Pergamos, and unto Thyatira, and unto Sardis, and unto Philadelphia, and unto Laodicea: This great, trumpet-like voice commands John to write in a book what he sees and then send it to the seven churches in Asia. He names the towns and the churches to which the messages are primarily written.

Revelation 1:12-13: And I turned to see the voice that spake with me. And being turned, I saw seven golden candlesticks; ¹³And in the midst of the seven

candlesticks one like unto the Son of man, clothed with a garment down to the foot, and girt about the paps with a golden girdle.

Why does John mention the golden candlesticks or lampstand rather than Jesus first? Could it be that where Jesus stands is most significant? This scene begins with the holy place ministry of Jesus in the heavenly sanctuary service. The Greek word for candlesticks is λυχνία (luchnia), a singular word meaning lampstand or candelabra. Here Jesus is introduced in the midst of the lampstand.

Like unto the Son of man: Throughout the Bible, starting in the Pentateuch (Numbers 23:19), this term always refers to man in the normal sense of the word. In Ezekiel it signifies the prophet when God addresses him in comparison to God. In Daniel "Son of man" refers to Jesus coming in the clouds (Daniel 7:13). This same language is used in Revelation 1:13, so this must signify Jesus and His relation to man in the salvation process.

Clothed with a garment down to the foot: The language used here seems to signify regal clothing worn by someone of dignity or importance. It brings to mind sanctuary imagery because the clothing of the high priest on the Day of Atonement was white linen and not the magnificent garb mentioned in Exodus 28. When he went into the presence of the ark of the covenant in the most holy place, the high priest was to wear "the holy linen tunic and the linen trousers on his body; he shall be girded with a linen sash, and with the linen turban he shall be attired. These are holy garments" (Leviticus 16:4). Even His clothing represents His holiness.

Girt about the paps with a golden girdle: This is similar to Daniel 10:5. The golden girdle in Daniel is around His waist, but in Revelation it is upon his chest. This is similar to the placement of the golden breastplate on the high priest's regal attire. Another name for this is the "breastplate of judgment" (Exodus 28:15). Christ is coming in judgment, so this issue is close to the heart of Jesus.

Because the message of judgment is given in context with the lampstands, we need to view the judgment of Jesus as a part of the gospel light that Christ desires to share with the world. As we shine as lights for Jesus in this world, don't forget the message close to His heart.

The setting is the heavenly sanctuary and not the earthly one. Hebrews 8:1-2 tells about the sanctuary in heaven. The earthly temple had been destroyed in A.D. 70 during the destruction of Jerusalem, but the heavenly sanctuary remains.

Hebrews 8:1-2: "Now *this is* the main point of the things we are saying: We have such a High Priest, who is seated at the right hand of the throne of the Majesty **in the heavens**, a Minister of the sanctuary and of **the true tabernacle which the Lord erected, and not man**" (NKJ).

Revelation 1:14-16: His head and his hairs were white like wool, as white as snow; and his eyes were as a flame of fire; ¹⁵ And his feet like unto fine brass, as

if they burned in a furnace; and his voice as the sound of many waters. ¹⁶And he had in his right hand seven stars.

John attempted to explain in poor human language the glorious vision in verses 14 and 15. Human words are inadequate, but he does the best he can to graphically describe Jesus in His heavenly glory.

Revelation 1:17-18: And when I saw him, I fell at his feet as dead. And he laid his right hand upon me, saying unto me, Fear not; I am the first and the last: ¹⁸I am he that liveth, and was dead; and, behold, I am alive for evermore, Amen; and have the keys of hell and of death.

John beholds Christ in all of His glory and splendor, but this is more of Jesus than he has ever seen before. As John lays at His feet like a dead man, Jesus announces His power over death and the grave. When we see Jesus in all of His glory, we too will die to self. Then Jesus will lay His hand on us to raise us up to new life in Him.

Revelation 1:19: Write the things which thou hast seen, and the things which are, and the things which shall be hereafter.

The language indicates its prophetic importance. Revelation deals with the past, present, and future, no matter at what point in time it is read!

Revelation 1:20: The mystery of the seven stars which thou sawest in my right hand, and the seven golden candlesticks. The seven stars are the angels of the seven churches: and the seven candlesticks which thou sawest are the seven churches.

Verse 20 defines the seven stars as the angels (messengers or heralds) of the seven churches. The seven stars are angels or messengers or heralds to the seven churches. The question then comes to mind: "Which seven churches?" The next two chapters answer this question.

CHAPTER FOURTEEN

Revelation 2

Introduction

This chapter begins the messages to the seven churches. Each message contains a different description of Jesus and each church receives a specific exhortation. At the end of each message, Jesus gives a special promise to the overcomers.

Why are these seven churches singled out? There are many more churches of repute in Asia Minor than some of the seven mentioned, so it must not be that the particular church is of such great importance. Thus the message conveyed to each one should be of utmost importance. Since this is a revelation of Jesus and the final details in the plan of redemption, then the seven churches reveal what each church needs to know about their Savior. Taking a cue from Daniel, each vision retells the history of God's people from the prophet's day until the end of time. Thus the seven churches represent seven time periods from the cross to the return of Christ.

Christ's words to the seven churches are essential to understand the long time period from the cross to His second coming. Therefore chapters 2 and 3 of Revelation contain messages of extreme importance to us who are living in the last moments of earth's history.

As candlesticks give light, so these enlightening messages are given to us by the Holy Spirit. In John's vision, the candlesticks are linked to the seven spirits of God (Revelation 1:4, 10, 12; 3:1). Thus the Holy Spirit plays an important role in the work of Christ among the seven churches. This ties in with the holy place experience pictured by John in symbols. The work of the Holy Spirit in the life of the individual believer prepares him or her for the judgment. The Holy Spirit points to the body and the blood of the slain Lamb (Revelation 5:6), He lights up God's Word for the churches, and the Holy Spirit makes our prayers acceptable to God. All three of these functions are depicted in the table of showbread, the golden candlestick, and finally the altar of incense, also called the altar of prayer.

White summarizes the work of God's Spirit of truth: In the ministry of the holy place, the Holy Spirit "makes effectual what has been wrought out by the world's Redeemer."[1] As Jesus came to demonstrate the love of our heavenly Father for sinful man, so the Holy Spirit glorifies Christ "by revealing His grace to the world," declares White.[2] The holy place symbolically describes our new life and daily walk with Christ as the Holy Spirit prepares us for the final judgment.

The messages to the seven churches are also written as a unit. They were intended to be read by all the churches. In other words, the message to an individual church was not meant to be read only by that church. The construction of the letters make it clear that everyone should read all the messages of the book of Revelation. These admonitions and promises are for all peoples living in all ages from John's day to the end of time. The information in the letters gives us insight into what each church and city was like just as each congregation today has its own personality and characteristics. The Holy Spirit works to make these messages relevant to God's people, especially those living in the closing scenes of earth's history.

The progression in the messages depicts not only the history of God's people from the cross to the second coming, but also the salvation history of individual believers. The first love experience of new believers is linked to the message of the Ephesus church. The other churches are symbols of the problems faced by new believers as they struggle to overcome temptations and other obstacles in the Christian walk. In this sense, Jesus tells us what kinds of difficulties we will encounter, but He ties each problem to a specific promise of His grace that enables us to be victorious over sin, self, Satan, and the world. Keep this in mind while studying the details of Revelation 2 and 3. Remember your responsibility to hear and obey the counsel of Jesus as He works for the redemption of His churches.

Under each church, the setting will be given with a description of the city and God's people at that time. Although written in symbolic language, the Apocalypse prepares believers for the return of Jesus. Given first to the apostolic church and secondly to Christians of all ages, these messages portray the journey of God's people before they reach their Father's house.

I. Church of Ephesus

Revelation 2:1-7: "Unto the angel of the church of Ephesus write; These things saith he that holdeth the seven stars in his right hand, who walketh in the midst of the seven golden candlesticks; [2]I know thy works, and thy labour, and thy patience, and how thou canst not bear them which are evil: and thou hast tried them which say they are apostles, and are not, and hast found them liars: [3]And hast borne, and hast patience, and for my name's sake hast laboured, and hast not fainted. [4]Nevertheless I have *somewhat* against thee, because thou hast left thy first love. [5]Remember therefore from whence thou

---

[1]   Ellen G. White, *The Desire of Ages* (Mountain View, CA: Pacific Press, 1940), 671.

[2]   Ibid.

art fallen, and repent, and do the first works; or else I will come unto thee quickly, and will remove thy candlestick out of his place, except thou repent. ⁶But this thou hast, that thou hatest the deeds of the Nicolaitanes, which I also hate. ⁷He that hath an ear, let him hear what the Spirit saith unto the churches; To him that overcometh will I give to eat of the tree of life, which is in the midst of the paradise of God."

Ephesus means "first" or "desirable." The city was located in western Asia Minor at the mouth of the Cayster River in what is now known as modern Turkey. Although it is five to six miles inland due to the silt deposited by the river over the centuries, in John's day Ephesus was on the Mediterranean. Founded between 1500 and 1000 B.C. the population was about 500,000 by the time John wrote Revelation. This made Ephesus the largest Roman city in Asia Minor and one of the largest cities of its day.

Strategically located on the Great Sea, the Apostle Paul used Ephesus as his base of operations for a while. According to Acts 19:23-41, Paul's work there turned many away from idol worship.The silversmiths aroused a mob protest over this issue, but God's hand protected His people. Paul later wrote a letter to the Ephesians.

In the Bible, Ephesus is first mentioned in Acts 18:19. After Paul went to the synagogue and taught there, the Jews begged him to stay, but instead he left Priscilla and Aquila behind to carry on the work while he continued his journey. According to Acts 18:24, Apollos also came to Ephesus to preach the gospel; then Priscilla and Aquila taught him "more accurately" (Acts 18:26; NKJ).

Most scholars agree that Revelation was first read in Ephesus, then it was copied and sent on to the other six churches in the same order as they were given in the book, finishing with Laodicea. It makes sense that Ephesus received the messages of Revelation from John first since Ephesus is the closest city to Patmos.

John wrote apocalyptic messages to seven churches even as the apostle Paul wrote to seven churches, giving them admonitions with eternal consequences. Though these messages are symbolic, one senses their urgency and expectancy: Jesus waits eagerly for His churches to respond to Him. Interestingly, Ephesus was the only church that received a letter from both Paul and John.

Verse 2: I know thy works, and thy labour, and thy patience, and how thou canst not bear them which are evil: and thou hast tried them which say they are apostles, and are not, and hast found them liars: The Ephesian church not only professed Christ, but emulated those qualities that Christ expects from those who are truly committed to Him. The message is clear: God is calling His people to a higher standard than those around them. Unlike the political "correctness" of our day, they did not tolerate those who were evil. The Ephesian church was noted for its purity of faith. When someone came with a message to them, they discerned truth from error. Who did they find to be liars? This must refer to the Nicolaitans of verse 6.

Verse 3: And hast borne, and hast patience, and for my name's sake hast laboured, and hast not fainted. The church at Ephesus persevered with patience and did not become weary. They faithfully continued to labor for their Master, never tiring of sharing the love of Jesus with others.

Verses 4 and 5: Nevertheless I have *somewhat* against thee, because thou hast left thy first love. Remember therefore from whence thou art fallen. This message shows that even those diligent in God's service may lose their first love. White admits: "After a time the zeal of the believers began to wane, and their love for God and for one another grew less. Coldness crept into the church."[3] Rather than sharing their love for Christ with others, mere facts and doctrines took the place of loving zeal. They loved the doctrine more than the One who died for them. When we lose that first love, turning from sin becomes a burden instead of a joy. Compromise soon follows on the heels of cold doctrine.

The only solution for this is to remember the way He drew us to Himself and how Jesus transformed our lives. Think about those first days when your love for Christ was new. Remember the fire in your bones to tell others of Christ's ultimate sacrifice. As we invite Him back on the throne of our hearts, His love will reign from within. Words cannot explain the joy that is ours when we cannot get enough of Jesus. The word becomes paramount in our lives and we must share it with others.

Verse 5: and repent, and do the first works; or else I will come unto thee quickly, and will remove thy candlestick out of his place, except thou repent. Removal of the lampstand is understood in the context of the sanctuary. The golden lampstand symbolizes the Holy Spirit who lights the holy place. Unless we return to our first love, we will lose the light of the Holy Spirit in our hearts. Without Him, we can share nothing but darkness. The key word is "repent" which means regret, sorrow, remorse, or contrition for the wrongs we have done. True repentance is the work of the Holy Spirit (Acts 11:15-18). By God's grace we can turn from sin and never go back. If we repent and return to our first love, Jesus will not remove our lampstand from its place. Our prayer will be like David's: "Take not Thy Holy Spirit from me" (Psalm 51:11). As His goodness leads us to repentance, we too will be blessed by the power and light of the Holy Spirit.

Verse 6: But this thou hast, that thou hatest the deeds of the Nicolaitanes, which I also hate. Only Jesus can give a correct appraisal of the church. As the real author of Revelation, He gives this information to John for His people. In the letter to Ephesus, Jesus dislikes something so much that He uses the word "hate." Why does Jesus hate the deeds of the Nicolaitans? Not all scholars agree on who the Nicolaitans were, but all agree on one aspect—compromise! This has been the worst enemy of the church in all ages. The Nicolaitans allowed compromise to slide into the church under the guise of love. This misguided love

---

[3]   Ellen G. White, *Acts of the Apostles* (Mountain View, CA: Pacific Press, 1911), 580.

turned out to be indulgence rather than real love. To understand the character of the Nicolaitans, Maxwell turns to one of the church fathers: "Irenaeus, a second-century minister who grew up near Ephesus, referred to them in one of his writings. The Nicolaitans claimed to be Christians, he said, but they considered it 'a matter of indifference to practice adultery, and to eat things sacrificed to idols.'"[4] Haskell agrees: "The doctrine of the Nicolaitanes, as described under the church of Ephesus, was a mingling of the pure teachings of Christ with the philosophy of the Greeks."[5]

The danger of compromise arose within the church itself. We see the same thing today when people indulge the sins of others lest the evil of their own hearts be revealed. The Nicolaitans didn't feel the need of repentance because they were unwilling to give up their sins. Thus they distanced themselves from Jesus.

The Greek word for Nicolaitans gives us insight. Νικολαϊτῶν (*Nikolaitōn*) comes from the root word Νικολαΐτης (*Nikolaitēs*) which is made of two words. The first is Νικάω (*Nikaō*) which means "I conquer." The second half of the word is λαόσ (*laos*), which means "people or laity." Using the grammatical declension to determine the word's meaning, the Nicolaitans were "those who conquer the laity or people." In other words, the Nicolaitans were people within the church that worked through compromise to conquer the laity. The Ephesians kept this problem out of the church because they hated the work of the Nicolaitans.

Verse 7: He that hath an ear, let him hear what the Spirit saith unto the churches; To him that overcometh will I give to eat of the tree of life, which is in the midst of the paradise of God.

He that hath an ear: This phrase is used in each of the messages to the seven churches (Revelation 2:7, 11, 17, 29; 3:6, 13 and 22). It precedes a promise unique to that church except for the case of Thyatira in which the promise precedes the statement, "He that hath an ear."

"To him who overcomes I will give to eat from the tree of life, which is in the midst of the paradise of God" (Revelation 2:7; NKJ). Jesus promises to give the one who overcomes a restoration of what was first given to man in the garden of Eden—the right to eat from the tree of life!

The promises made to the seven churches move progressively, pointing out the steps in sanctification. Those who live by faith with Jesus in the holy place experience have already accepted Him as their sacrificial Lamb. The spiritual growth of a healthy Christian is revealed in the messages to the seven churches of Asia Minor.

The promise given to Ephesus is ours as we repent and return to our own first love experience with Jesus. Repentance is the first sign of conversion. When men come face to face with the beautiful Jesus and the law of God, they are

---

4   Maxwell, *God Cares*, 2:99.

5   Stephen N. Haskell, *The Story of the Seer of Patmos* (Nashville: Southern Publishing Association, 1905), 59.

convicted of their sinfulness. Then they feel remorse for their sins and desire to turn from them.

Every true Christian experiences the first love, but if this love is lost, compromise is sure to follow. Those who love Jesus supremely will test everything by the word of God. Note verse 2: the Ephesians tested those who claimed to be apostles and found them to be liars. The Bible as lit by the instruction of the Holy Spirit will enable you to discover who are the Nicolaitans, even if they have great credentials or claim to be apostles.

The first love experience is revealed in the love we show to others. "By this shall all men know that ye are My disciples, if ye have love one to another" (John 13:35). Cold Christians become critical, but those aglow with their first love for Jesus will persevere and have patience with others. Psalm 119:165 tells us: "Great peace have they which love Thy law: and nothing shall offend them." Steadfast in Christ, the "first love" Christian will not leave when tried by the offensive or erroneous statements of others.

Ephesus Period—The Time of the Apostles: A.D. 31 to 100

As we march in time through the sanctuary, the holy place is pictured as the messages of the seven churches, the seven seals, and the seven trumpets are given. When Revelation transitions from the holy place to the holy of holies, sacred prophecy moves in time to another phase of Christ's work. It is clear that certain attributes of the seventh church, seventh seal, and seventh trumpet take us into the holy of holies during the time of the judgment. For the churches, seals, and trumpets, the seventh represents that time right before Jesus comes back. The seventh church is the last church, as the seventh seal and trumpet point us to the events just before Christ's return. Thus the period of the seven churches carries us from John's day to the end of this world's history.

John was the last living apostle; therefore the time of the apostolic church ends with John. The Ephesus church covers the time period from A.D. 31 to 100, the latter date near the death of John the revelator. The time periods are only approximate as the characteristics of the churches tend to overlap one another.

The veil of the sanctuary symbolizes the flesh of Jesus (Hebrews 10:20). This veil was torn from top to bottom symbolizing that God opened up the most holy experience through the death of Christ. The way into the holy of holies is open to us through the blood of Jesus (Hebrews 9 and 10). There has been only one covenant from the beginning: the old covenant merely foreshadowed the new and living way through the blood of Christ, our holy Substitute and Sacrifice. The ceremonial animals are no longer needed because the true real Lamb of God has come.

Coming from the heavenly sanctuary, the messages of the churches, seals, and trumpets point us to Jesus the Lamb, our only hope of salvation. The sanctuary service teaches us that "without shedding of blood there is no remission.

Therefore it was necessary that the copies of the things in the heavens should be purified with these, but the heavenly things themselves with better sacrifices than these. For Christ has not entered the holy places made with hands, which are copies of the true, but into heaven itself, now to appear in the presence of God for us; not that He should offer Himself often, as the high priest enters the Most Holy Place every year with blood of another—He then would have had to suffer often since the foundation of the world; but now, once at the end of the ages, He has appeared to put away sin by the sacrifice of Himself. And as it is appointed for men to die once, but after this the judgment, so Christ was offered once to bear the sins of many. To those who eagerly wait for Him He will appear a second time, apart from sin, for salvation" (Hebrews 9:22-28; NKJ).

II. Church of Smyrna

Revelation 2:8-11: "And unto the angel of the church in Smyrna write; These things saith the first and the last, which was dead, and is alive; ⁹I know thy works, and tribulation, and poverty, (but thou art rich) and *I know* the blasphemy of them which say they are Jews, and are not, but *are* the synagogue of Satan. ¹⁰Fear none of those things which thou shalt suffer: behold, the devil shall cast *some* of you into prison, that ye may be tried; and ye shall have tribulation ten days: be thou faithful unto death, and I will give thee a crown of life. ¹¹He that hath an ear, let him hear what the Spirit saith unto the churches; He that overcometh shall not be hurt of the second death."

Smyrna was located at the mouth of the small river Hernus, a small river that empties at the end of a deep arm of the sea called the *Smyrnaeus Sinus*. This body of water reached far inland and allowed trading ships into the heart of Lydia. The word Smyrna means "myrrh" or "sweet scent." The many martyrs during the time of the Diocletian persecution show that this was a terrible time of earth's history, but in the sight of God, the death of His saints is precious (Psalm 116:15). The church of Smyrna was precious to God. Smyrna and Philadelphia were the only churches to which no reproof was given. The Christians at Smyrna gave all that they could to Jesus: their very lives were a living sacrifice. They followed their Jesus even to the grave for the gospel's sake. Because of this church, the Roman Empire discovered that they could not break or destroy Christianity. Even before the time period was over, both Galerius and Diocletian realized that they could not defeat the church of Christ through persecution.

Verse 8: These things saith the first and the last, which was dead, and is alive. Jesus' first message to Smyrna is comforting. Even as He died and is now alive again, those facing death would gain consolation from His victory over the grave. Bunch points out how Christ gave hope to the suffering church of Smyrna: "This introduction is well suited to a church that has passed through bitter persecution. To the church of martyrs was sent a message of good cheer from the One who had triumphed over death and the grave, and had the keys of the tomb in His keeping. By His death and resurrection triumph, Jesus had robbed death of its sting and the grave of its victory. In identifying Himself, Jesus uses the attributes that would bring courage and support to His people during persecution and martyrdom. If they would be 'faithful unto death,' they would be given 'a crown of life.'[6] The persecution which nearly crushed the church was really a blessing in disguise as it showed the world the beauty of both Christ and His purified church on this earth. Smith states: "Persecution is ever calculated to keep the church pure, and incite its members to piety and godliness."[7]

Smyrna was the home of Polycarp and also the place of his martyrdom in A.D. 168. Although the Turks tried to annihilate Christianity as did the Romans, Smyrna, now called Izmir, is the home of more Christians than any other city in the Muslim-controlled territories to this day. Many of the Christian missions have their headquarters in Izmir to reach out to this part of the world. Even though the Christians of Izmir were massacred in 1424 and again in 1922, the church still continues there. The Lord has promised them a crown of life if they are faithful unto death.

Verse 9: I know thy works, and tribulation, and poverty, (but thou art rich) and I know the blasphemy of them which say they are Jews, and are not, but are the synagogue of Satan. The Smyrna church was not like the church at Ephesus because the conditions of the church were different from that of Ephesus. Smyrna, although an important seaport, was not a trade center like Ephesus. The members of the church at Smyrna were no doubt poor, but in spite of the lack of wealth, they worked for the salvation of others. In the eyes of God, they were rich. The Smyrna church was threatened by teachers who claimed to be Jews, but were not. One's claim to be a Jew would not give more spiritual virtue because only those who belong to Christ are the true seed of Abraham and heirs according to the promise of Christ (Galatians 3:29).

Verse 10: Fear none of those things which thou shalt suffer: behold, the devil shall cast some of you into prison, that ye may be tried; and ye shall have tribulation ten days: be thou faithful unto death, and I will give thee a crown of life. This passage clearly shows that the messages to the churches cover successive periods in the history of God's people. A special prophecy is given to this church, predicting a time of persecution, **ten days** of tribulation. Here the book of Revelation shows the year-day principle as ten days of persecution would not be that notable or unbearable. History records the fact that these ten "days" were ten literal years from A.D. 303 to 313. Known as the Diocletian persecution, the emperor was convinced to issue the edict of persecution by a man named Galerius who also enforced this edict. When Diocletian abdicated in A.D. 305, Galerius continued the persecution until his death in A.D. 310. In spite of

---

6   Taylor G. Bunch, *The Seven Epistles of Christ* (Washington: Review and Herald Publishing Association, 1947), 131.

7   Smith, 372.

his death, Constantius I continued the policy of the two previous emperors for another three years. Thus the ten-year period of persecution ended in A.D. 313.

Before Diocletian abdicated, he unsuccessfully tried to stop the persecution because he realized it was an ineffective tool in the war against Christianity. The persecution ended during the reign of Constantine who embraced Christianity along with his paganism. Compromise with paganism became a more deadly tool against the Christian church than persecution. As the persecution ended, the church gained popularity under the reign of Constantine.

Verse 11: He that hath an ear, let him hear what the Spirit saith unto the churches. Jesus used this same language in Matthew 13:9; NKJ: **"He who has ears to hear, let him hear!"** The disciples asked Jesus, "Why do you speak to them in parables?" Jesus answered, **"Because it has been given to you to know the mysteries of the kingdom of heaven, but to them it has not been given. . . . But blessed are your eyes for they see, and your ears for they hear"** (Matthew 13:10-11; NKJ). The messages from Jesus may seem to be mysteries to us, but as we walk and talk with Jesus as the disciples did, we will find many things becoming clearer to us as we listen to Jesus through His word. The Bible is its own interpreter, and the student that spends time in the Scripture will find that there are many keys to understanding. **"For precept must *be* upon precept, precept upon precept, Line upon line, line upon line, Here a little, there a little"** (Isaiah 28:10).

Verse 11: He that overcometh shall not be hurt of the second death. The first death that comes from persecution is far less dangerous than the second death that comes as a result of succumbing to Satan's lies and wiles. The second death is the only death we should fear as this is reserved for Satan and those who are his.

The church at Smyrna, although far from perfect, could not be faulted because many gave their lives for Jesus. He promised that they shall not be hurt by the second death. Christians win the battle as they overcome by the blood of the Lamb. Smyrna was victorious, not by might, nor by power, but by the Holy Spirit (Zechariah 4:6). They left all in the hands of Jesus: some were permitted to live, while others were faithful even to death. Those that died for the faith did not do so in vain. "The blood of the martyrs" was "the seed of the church."[8] With amazement their persecutors witnessed the lack of fear on the face of those martyrs.

Smyrna Period—The Persecuted Church: A. D. 100 to 323

The historic period of persecution covered by the church of Smyrna began with the death of the apostles and continued to approximately A.D. 323.

---

[8]   Tertullian, *Apologeticus*, ch. 50.

III. Church of Pergamos

Revelation 2:12-17: And to the angel of the church in Pergamos write; These things saith he which hath the sharp sword with two edges; [13]I know thy works and where thou dwellest, even where Satan's seat is: and thou holdest fast my name, and hast not denied my faith, even in those days wherein Antipas was my faithful martyr, who was slain among you, where Satan dwelleth. [14]But I have a few things against thee, because thou hast there them that hold the doctrine of Balaam, who taught Balac to cast a stumblingblock before the children of Israel, to eat things sacrificed unto idols, and to commit fornication. [15]So hast thou also them that hold the doctrine of the Nicolaitanes, which thing I hate. [16]Repent; or else I will come unto thee quickly, and will fight against them with the sword of my mouth. [17]He that hath an ear, let him hear what the Spirit saith unto the churches; To him that overcometh will I give to eat of the hidden manna, and will give him a white stone, and in the stone a new name written, which no man knoweth saving he that receiveth it."

The word Pergamos means "elevation" or "exaltation." After Constantine came to the throne and claimed to be a convert to Christianity, the church gained prominence and appeared to prosper. The church compromised much of what it once believed in order to gain favor with the people. Although compromise yields short term popularity, the results are deadly for the church's spiritual life. Bunch writes: "Pliny called Pergamos the most illustrious city of Asia. It was the educational center of Western Asia. There Homer, one of the earliest poets, and Herodotus, 'the father of history,' studied and wrote, because of the great library, which according to Plutarch contained 200,000 volumes. It was second only to the world-famous library of Alexandria."[9]

Revelation 2:12; NKJ: And to the angel of the church in Pergamos write, "These things says He who has the sharp two-edged sword." Hebrews 4:12-13 speaks of this sword: "For the word of God is living and powerful, and sharper than any two-edged sword, piercing even to the division of soul and spirit, and of the joints and marrow, and is a discerner of the thoughts and intents of the heart. And there is no creature hidden from His sight, but all things are naked and open to the eyes of Him to whom we must give account."

As He speaks to Pergamos, Jesus wears His vesture of judgment and pronounces His findings. He knows the end from the beginning and can discern what is in someone's heart before they are aware of it themselves. God will show the intents of their hearts, so these must be words of importance.

Revelation 2:13; NKJ: I know your works, and where you dwell, where Satan's throne is. Weymouth's version translates it: "I know where you dwell. Satan's throne is there." Bunch describes the deities of Pergamos: "It was the

---

[9]   Bunch, *The Seven Epistles of Christ*, 145.

metropolis of heathen deities. Temples were built and dedicated to Jupiter, Zeus, Athena, Dionysius, and Aesculapius, the Greek god of medicine, and also called 'the god of Pergamum.'[10] Smith notes that "the city of Pergamos became the seat of ancient Babylonian sun worship."[11]

Verse 13; NKJ: And you hold fast to My name, and did not deny My faith even in the days in which Antipas was My faithful martyr, who was killed among you, where Satan dwells. In Pergamos a saint named Antipas was martyred for his faithfulness. This author believes Antipas was an actual person who would not compromise even when faced with death. He became a symbol to the early Christians of faithfulness. We are admonished to remain faithful by the example of this man's life and death.

Verse 14; NKJ: But I have a few things against you, because you have there those who hold the doctrine of Balaam, who taught Balak to put a stumbling block before the children of Israel, to eat things sacrificed to idols, and to commit sexual immorality. Jesus rebukes the church at Pergamos. As Israel neared the promised land, King Balak wanted to conquer the children of Israel. He summoned the prophet Balaam for assistance, and this false prophet became an infamous traitor to God's people. According to Bunch, historians confirm the historical data used symbolically in Revelation 3:14: "Josephus and Philo declare that Balaam showed Balac how to set a trap for the children of Israel so as to entice them into the twofold sin of idolatry and fornication, which always go hand in hand (Acts 15:20.)"[12]

Stott compares Balaam with the Nicolaitans: "What Balaam was to the old Israel the Nicolaitans were to the new. They were insinuating their vile doctrines into the camp of Israel of God. They dared to suggest that the liberty with which Christ has made us free was liberty to sin. 'Christ has redeemed us from the law', they argued. 'Therefore we are no longer under law but under grace. And so', their specious villainy continued, 'we may continue in sin that God's grace may continue to abound towards us in forgiveness.' This terrible travesty of the truth was to 'pervert the grace of our God into licentiousness and deny our only Master and Lord, Jesus Christ.' (Galatians 5:1; Rom 6:1; Jude 4)."[13]

Verse 15; NKJ: Thus you also have those who hold the doctrine of the Nicolaitans, which thing I hate. Unlike the Ephesians, the church at Pergamos did not hate the work of the Nicolaitans but rather embraced their evil works. Through compromise and the improper use of power and authority, the church officials exalted themselves over the regular member and ascribed to themselves

[10] Ibid., 148.

[11] Smith, 373.

[12] Bunch, *The Seven Epistles of Christ*, 153.

[13] John R. W. Stott, *What Christ Thinks of the Church*; in *Preaching for Today* (Grand Rapids, MI: Eerdmans, 1958), 59.

powers that were found only in the secular world. Instead of kingly tyrants, the church needs humble servants who obey the authority of God.

During the Pergamos period, the church compromised with worldly powers, uniting church and state. This is not the example that Christ gave to us. Jesus said: "Ye know that the princes of the Gentiles exercise dominion over them, and they that are great exercise authority upon them. But it shall not be so among you: but whosoever will be great among you, let him be your minister; and whosoever will be chief among you, let him be your servant" (Matthew 20:25-28). As the leaders of Pergamos exercised undue authority, compromises were made with the world and then adopted by some in the church. If the leaders fail in their duty to be faithful to the Scriptures, the members rarely rise above their low example. Something is wrong when spiritual leaders do not rebuke sexual immorality. This happened during the time period of the church at Pergamos.

Balaam, Balak, and the Nicolaitans have much in common. As Balaam and Balak led astray the children of Israel, so the Nicolaitans attempt to lead spiritual Israel into the paths of sin. May God help us to be pure and faithful, Abraham's seed according to the promise (Galatians 3:29).

Verse 16; NKJ: Repent, or else I will come to you quickly and will fight against them with the sword of My mouth. In the Greek "repent" is μετανοέω (*metanoeō*) which means "to have a change of mind or heart." Another translation is "to turn from." In other words, change your course or I will come quickly and fight against you with the sword of My mouth. Jesus speaks firmly to a church affected by apostasy within its ranks. This threat is aimed at those who had accepted and now taught false doctrines. Remember the context of Balaam: the angel held a drawn sword to turn Balaam from his plan to curse Israel. Jesus gives the same analogy to those who are a curse to the church of God. He will fight against "them" refers to the guilty ones in the plural. This infers that the faithful will repent, but the unfaithful will refuse to end their compromise with the world.

Verse 17; NKJ: He who has an ear, let him hear what the Spirit says to the churches. To him who overcomes I will give some of the hidden manna to eat. And I will give him a white stone, and on the stone a new name written which no one knows except him who receives *it*.

Bunch relates the pot of manna in the ancient sanctuary to these special gifts from Jesus: In His promise to Pergamos, "Christ offers access to the hidden manna and also a white stone containing the overcomer's divinely given new name describing his new character. A pot of manna was placed in the ark of the covenant in the most holy apartment of the earthly sanctuary as a pledge that all who obey the law will be fed. (Heb 9:3, 4.) This became known as the 'hidden manna,' because it was hidden from all except the high priest. Christ declared Himself to be the real manna or 'bread of life.' (John 6:26-63.) He said that only those who eat of the living Bread that came down from heaven can have eternal life."[14] See Revelation 2:11 for comments on the phrase "he who has an ear."

Pergamos Period—The Church Embraces Paganism: A.D. 323 to 538

During this era the church went from a persecuted minority to an elevated position because it united religion with the state. On the surface, Christianity appeared to have won its war with paganism, but in reality, paganism was infiltrating the church. The union of church and state culminated with Justinian's decree that gave the bishop at Rome not only religious authority, but also the power to enforce civil laws and muster an army, the armies of Rome. When Satan failed in the use of force, he turned to sophistry in his fight against the church. During this time, the transition from pagan Rome to papal Rome took place as Justinian's decrees made the popes successors to the caesars. While enlarging on papal Rome's expanding powers, Bunch demonstrates the relationship of this church-state power to pagan Rome:

> Pagan beliefs and practices were brought into the church, and Christianity was so changed by heathen influences that it virtually became "baptised paganism." During this time Isaiah 2:2, 3 was fulfilled, and the church was established in "the top of the mountains" or government of Rome, and "above the hills," or smaller states, where she dictated the laws of the land and became so popular that "all nations" flowed into it. The Bishop of Rome assumed the title of pope and became the supreme pontiff, or Pontifex Maximus, of the new semi-pagan religion, "controlling kings, dictating laws to ancient monarchies, and binding the souls of millions with a more perfect despotism than Oriental emperors ever sought or dreamed." John Lord, *Beacon Lights of History*, vol. 5, p.96.[15]

IV. Church of Thyatira

Revelation 2:18-29; NKJ: And to the angel of the church in Thyatira write, "These things says the Son of God, who has eyes like a flame of fire, and His feet like fine brass: [19]"I know your works, love, service, faith, and your patience; and *as* for your works, the last *are* more than the first. [20]Nevertheless I have a few things against you, because you allow that woman Jezebel, who calls herself a prophetess, to teach and seduce My servants to commit sexual immorality and eat things sacrificed to idols. [21]And I gave her time to repent of her sexual immorality, and she did not repent. [22]Indeed I will cast her into a sickbed, and those who commit adultery with her into great tribulation, unless they repent of their deeds. [23]I will kill her children with death, and all the churches shall know that I am He who searches the minds and hearts.

---

[14] Bunch, *The Seven Epistles of Christ*, 155-156.

[15] Ibid., 151-152.

And I will give to each one of you according to your works. ²⁴"Now to you I say, and to the rest in Thyatira, as many as do not have this doctrine, who have not known the depths of Satan, as they say, I will put on you no other burden. ²⁵But hold fast what you have till I come. ²⁶And he who overcomes, and keeps My works until the end, to him I will give power over the nations— ²⁷"He shall rule them with a rod of iron; They shall be dashed to pieces like the potter's vessels'—as I also have received from My Father; ²⁸and I will give him the morning star. ²⁹He who has an ear, let him hear what the Spirit says to the churches."

From the Son of God Himself, the message to Thyatira evidently needed to be longer than those written to the other churches. This is interesting, Stott writes, because "the city of Thyatira was certainly smaller and less significant than the previous three."[16] Thyatira was located southeast of Pergamos and according to Bunch, "was founded by Seleucus Nicator, one of the generals of Alexander. It was a garrison city built on the plains, with no natural fortifications, and was captured, destroyed, and rebuilt many times. On coins found in its ruins the city is represented by a horseman bearing a double-bladed battle-ax indicating that it was a cavalry post. The name is said to signify 'sweet savor of labor,' or 'sacrifice of contrition.' Sir William Ramsay says that the name indicates 'weakness made strong' (page 316), and other writers give the meaning as 'never weary of sacrifice.' The present population is about 12,000."[17]

Revelation 2:18; NKJ: And to the angel of the church in Thyatira write, "These things says the Son of God, who has eyes like a flame of fire, and His feet like fine brass." Jesus introduces Himself as the Son of God with eyes like a flame of fire and His feet like fine brass. Fire is a symbol of the all-seeing Holy Spirit. The Son of God sees in the church at Thyatira something that only God can see. From His holy place in heaven, the Son of God shines the spotlight of the Holy Spirit upon His earthly church. He knows where this church is going and what it will do. Not as "Son of Man" but as the "Son of God" He bears His divine witness of grave importance to the church in all ages as well as to the church of this time period.

Revelation 2:19; NKJ: I know your works, love, service, faith, and your patience; and *as* for your works, the last *are* more than the first. The last works of the church at Thyatira are more noted than those at the first. Thyatira was a church under fire, not only from without, but more so from within. This church was making progress in her walk with Jesus, and therefore it is said that her last works are more than the first. Some translate that verse to say that her last works are greater than her first works, so Thyatira is a church that makes steps of improvement in comparison to her early years. With the help of history, Stott records why this is so:

---

[16] Stott, 68-69.

[17] Bunch, *The Seven Epistles of Christ*, 160.

In view of this splendid record, it is tragic to read a little further and discover this church's moral compromise. In that fair field a poisonous weed was being allowed to luxuriate. In that healthy body a malignant cancer had begun to form. An enemy was being harboured in the midst of the fellowship. *But I have this against you*, the letter continues, *that you tolerate the woman Jezebel, who calls herself a prophetess and is teaching and beguiling my servants to practise immorality and to eat food sacrificed to idols* (v. 20). The church of Thyatira manifested love and faith, service and endurance, but holiness is not included among its qualities. Indeed, it is this which was missing. It permitted one of its members to teach outrageous licence and apparently made no attempt to restrain her. In this too the church of Thyatira was the opposite of the church of Ephesus. Ephesus could not bear evil, self-styled apostles but had no love (2:2, 4); Thyatira had love but tolerated an evil, self-styled prophetess.

Holiness of life, righteousness of character, is then another indispensable mark of the real Christian and of the true church.[18]

In the message to Thyatira, Jezebel claims to be a prophetess. A prophetess of what? we might well ask. According to the scriptural record, Jezebel was a heathen believer of Baal and a stumbling block to God's people. Married to King Ahab of Israel, she caused him to leave God and follow after Baal. She brought destruction to her own children. The end justified the means for Jezebel as she did whatever she could to procure that which was not hers, willing to murder to satiate her covetousness. She was sexually immoral as part of her religious customs and openly practiced what a follower of Christ would label compromise. God's judgment upon Jezebel was an example to those that would follow her course.

Thyatira is quite the opposite of the church at Ephesus. With their pure doctrines but lack of love, Ephesus appears legalistic in comparison to Thyatira's tolerance to sin within its ranks. However, the Son of God shows His great displeasure with Thyatira's whorish behavior.

Verse 24; NKJ: "Now to you I say, and to the rest in Thyatira, as many as do not have this doctrine, who have not known the depths of Satan, as they say, I will put on you no other burden. God's Son is pleased with the faithful ones in Thyatira that have not practiced any form of spiritual adultery. These have not let Satan affect their walk with Jesus. They remain faithful to Jesus while many others compromise, and Christ promises to put no other burden on them. They have fought a good fight and lived for the right no matter what the cost. This is a time of great spiritual darkness, but some in Thyatira see the light and fasten their minds and hearts on the the only true Light, Jesus. Stott makes this practical for Christians today:

---

[18]   Stott, 71.

An important lesson lurks in these phrases, which we shall do well to learn. It is this. A new immorality must not drive us into new asceticism. We may be surrounded by unchastity, but we are not to let an extreme of laxity around us stampede us to an extreme of rigidity in ourselves. Christ has no new burden for those living in an environment where standards are low. We are simply to hold fast what we already have, that is to say, what He has already given us in His written word. What is this? It is the balanced, joyful, exhilarating righteousness of the Bible, the glorious liberty of the royal law. It is the sane morality which regards the right use of sex as beautiful and sacred, and its wrong use as ugly and sordid. It is a teaching which says: "Let marriage be held in honour among all, and let the marriage bed be undefiled; for God will judge the immoral and adulterous" (Hebrews 13:4).[19]

Verse 25; NKJ: But hold fast what you have till I come. This simple but profound instruction is given for our admonition along with the believers in Thyatira. There are dark days also before us, and the divine Son of God reminds us to hold fast!

Verse 26; NKJ: And he who overcomes, and keeps My works until the end, to him I will give power over the nations. Stott differentiates between the free gift of justification and the power for victory over sin, another present from Jesus to His people:

This letter like all the others concludes with gracious promises to the conqueror. Indeed, in this case the conqueror is clearly defined. He is the one who obeys the moral law of Christ. *He who conquers* is, in the language of Christ here, the same as *he who keeps my works until the end* (v. 26). There are several references in this epistle to "works," the works by which we cannot be justified but by which we shall certainly be judged (v. 23). Works are never the ground or means of our salvation, but they are the evidence of it, and therefore they constitute an excellent basis for judgment. Christ speaks in this epistle of *your works* (vv. 19, 23), of *her works* (v. 22 A.V.), and of *my works* (v. 26). His desire is that our works shall ever be patterned after the example of Himself rather than of Jezebel and her tribe, so that we may be said to keep "His" rather than "her" works *until the end.*[20]

Verse 28: And I will give him the morning star. In these messages to the seven churches, the churches are depicted as lampstands. The angels or messengers to the churches are described as stars, but Christ is the bright morning Star. The Son of God is pledging Himself to the conqueror who overcomes in His name.

[19]   Ibid., 78-79.

[20]   Ibid., 80.

Verse 29; NKJ: He who has an ear, let him hear what the Spirit says to the churches. See comments for Revelation 2:7.

Thyatira Period—The Church of the Dark Ages: A.D. 538 to 1565

The Thyatiran period starts with the decree of Justinian in A.D. 538 and stretches to the time of the Reformation. A new day dawns for the Christian church as the Reformers boldly begin their work. The great tribulation refers to what Protestant writers of previous centuries termed the Dark Ages, while Middle Ages is the name preferred by Catholic writers and modern historians. Whatever you call it, this was a time of lawlessness. Ozment portrays the dismal picture of life during the Dark Ages:

> Western people walked through the valley of the shadow of death. The greatest famine of the Middle Ages struck in the second decade of the fourteenth century, and an estimated two-fifths of the overall population of Europe died when bubonic plague, or the Black Death, following trade routes, erupted in mid-century. The Hundred Years' War between England and France not only spanned the fourteenth and fifteenth centuries, but also introduced weaponry of modern warfare, in the form of gunpowder and heavy artillery, during its later stages. Great agrarian and urban revolts by the poor rent the social fabric in both town and countryside.[21]

For hundreds of years, Bunch notes, scholars have understood the major players of biblical prophecy: "It is interesting to note that the Reformation expositors were almost unanimous in their conclusions that imperial Rome fulfilled the prophecy of the fourth beast of Daniel 7, and that papal Rome met the specifications of the little horn of the same prophecy, the man of sin predicted by Paul, the beast of Revelation 13, the mystic Babylon of Revelation 17, and Jezebel the false prophetess of the Thyatiran letter."[22]

The letter to Thyatira describes the history of the church during the Dark or Middle Ages. This time period began when the Roman Church was given both religious and civil authority. At that point the papacy moved from being merely a religious power to being a religio-political power. No other religious system has taken upon itself the authority Rome claimed during the Dark Ages and still claims for herself to this day! With the start of the Reformation, a new period of church history begins.

---

[21] Steve Ozment, *The Age of Reform 1250-1550: An Intellectual and Religious History of Late Medieval and Reformation Europe* (New Haven: Yale University Press, 1980), 8; quoted in C. Mervyn Maxwell, *God Cares* (Boise, ID, Pacific Press, 1985), 2:125.

[22] Bunch, *The Seven Epistles of Christ*, 163.

CHAPTER FIFTEEN

Revelation 3

V. Church of Sardis

Revelation 3:1-6: And unto the angel of the church in Sardis write; These things saith he that hath the seven Spirits of God, and the seven stars; I know thy works, that thou hast a name that thou livest, and art dead. [2]Be watchful, and strengthen the things which remain, that are ready to die: for I have not found thy works perfect before God. [3]Remember therefore how thou hast received and heard, and hold fast, and repent. If therefore thou shalt not watch, I will come on thee as a thief, and thou shalt not know what hour I will come upon thee. [4]Thou hast a few names even in Sardis which have not defiled their garments; and they shall walk with me in white: for they are worthy. [5]He that overcometh, the same shall be clothed in white raiment; and I will not blot out his name out of the book of life, but I will confess his name before my Father, and before his angels. [6]He that hath an ear, let him hear what the Spirit saith unto the churches.

The exact meaning of Sardis seems to be in question as no two writers agree on its meaning. The message to Sardis indicates that the church starts out good, but its end is not as glorious. According to Stott: "Nothing is known of the origins of the church in Sardis, nor of its early growth, except what may be gathered from this epistle. It is interesting to note that one of its early bishops, toward the end of the second century, Melito by name, is the first known commentator on the Revelation."[1] Bunch gives the following background on Sardis:

> Sardis was founded in the twelfth century before Christ, and was one of the oldest and most important cities of Asia. It was located about thirty-five miles southeast of Thyatira. Until captured by Cyrus in 549 B.C., Sardis was the capital of the kingdom of Lydia, and became so again after the fall of the Roman power in Asia in A.D. 395. Lydia was one of the richest kingdoms of the ancient world. The Lydians are reputed to have been the inventors of coined money. . . .

---

[1]   Stott, 84.

The ancient city of Sardis was built on a plateau of crumbling rock rising 1,500 feet above the plain. The plateau was a part of Mount Tomolus, whose height was 6,700 feet. The walls of the elevation on which the city was built were almost perpendicular, and the city was inaccessible except by one narrow passage which was steep and easily fortified and guarded. At the base of the cliff flows the little Pactolus River, once famous for its golden sands. Sardis was considered an impregnable fortress. From Sardis, Cyrus marched against Artaxerxes, and at that place Xerxes gathered his mighty army before the expedition into Greece which ended in ignominious defeat at Marathon. In A.D. 1402, Tamerlane destroyed the city, and it was never rebuilt. A miserable little village near by still goes by the name of Sart. . . .

Sardis never fully recovered from the earthquake of A.D. 17, and was only partially rebuilt. When the epistle was written, the city was rapidly waning in prestige and glory, but its inhabitants were still boastful of the reputation and history of the past. Decay and death were inevitable, but the Sardians refused to recognize the fate of the city and continued to live on its ancient glory. The city had a name only, whereas in reality it was dead, or rapidly dying.[2]

With this historical background, one can see that the message to Sardis remains very practical and appropriate today.

Revelation 3:1-3: And unto the angel of the church in Sardis write; These things saith he that hath the seven Spirits of God, and the seven stars; I know thy works, that thou hast a name that thou livest, and art dead. [2]Be watchful, and strengthen the things which remain, that are ready to die: for I have not found thy works perfect before God [3]Remember therefore how thou hast received and heard, and hold fast, and repent. If therefore thou shalt not watch, I will come on thee as a thief, and thou shalt not know what hour I will come upon thee.

Although Sardis appeared to be alive and well, spiritually it was nearly dead. The works of this church were not perfect before God; they needed true repentance. The members of the Sardis church claimed the name of Christ, but the power of the gospel was not brought into their daily life. Christ calls upon them to cooperate with Him and be strengthened, for they are not yet dead. They were to hang on to the Son of God so that they would not die. Making it practical, Stott reminds us that only God can reveal what lies hidden in our hearts:

As Christians, we have indeed responsibilities to our fellowmen, but our chief responsibility is to God. It is unto Him that we live, before

---

[2] Bunch, *The Seven Epistles of Christ,* 177-178, 181.

Him that we stand, and to Him that one day we must give an account. Then let us not rate too highly the opinions of the world or even of the Church. Some Christians grow too depressed when criticized and too elated when flattered. We need to remember that "the LORD sees not as man sees; man looks on the outward appearance, but the LORD looks on the heart" (I Samuel 16:7). He looks beneath the surface. He can see how much reality there is behind our professions, how much life behind our façade.[3]

Verse 1: These things saith he that hath the seven Spirits of God, and the seven stars. This verse points back to chapter one and shows the connection between Jesus, the churches, and the work of the Holy Spirit (Revelation 1:4, 12, 13, 16, 20). The Son of God is filled with the Holy Spirit and promised to send the Spirit upon His people. Revelation shows the fulfillment of Christ's promise in John 16:7: "If I depart, I will send Him [the Holy Spirit] unto you."

Revelation 1:20 explains that the seven golden lampstands are the seven churches and the seven stars are the messengers of the seven churches. The symbol for the Holy Spirit, the seven Spirits of God, is inextricably linked to the work of the Son of God among the churches. From reading Christ's messages to each church, we can see that He expected growth, purification, and holiness in His people. Without this, the church will die. The message to Sardis plainly states that most of the members were not growing in Christ. This work of growth is called sanctification which simply means becoming more like Jesus. The Son of God longs to wake up this dying church and by His grace help them to grow in holiness through His Spirit. Only this will prepare His people to stand in the judgment.

The stars and the seven Spirits of God in the hand of Christ are a strong reminder to the leaders of Sardis. If only a few are wearing undefiled garments, then most of the members are defiled with sin. The remedy is in the hand of the Son of God; by the power of the Holy Spirit they must repent and return to spiritual strength, even as the first leaders of the Reformation stood firm against falsehoods in the face of death. Having the name isn't enough. Just because you call yourself a Lutheran, it doesn't mean that you have the courage of Luther. "Change your life, or change your name! Stop dishonoring Me," says the holy Son of God, "and return to your first love experience." This was the great need of the church of the Reformation: a return to primitive godliness, a return to Bible-based living, a return to the faith that would be true until death. White extends this idea:

> The Protestant churches of America,—and those of Europe as well,—so highly favored in receiving the blessings of the Reformation, failed to press forward in the path of reform. Though a few faithful men arose,

---

[3]   Stott, 85.

from time to time, to proclaim new truth and expose long-cherished error, **the majority**, like the Jews in Christ's day or the papists in the time of Luther, were content to believe as their fathers had believed and to live as they had lived. Therefore religion again **degenerated into formalism**; and errors and superstitions which would have been cast aside had the church continued to walk in the light of God's word, were retained and cherished. Thus the spirit inspired by the Reformation gradually died out, until there was almost as great need of reform in the Protestant churches as in the Roman Church in the time of Luther. There was the same worldliness and **spiritual stupor**, a similar reverence for the opinions of men, and substitution of human theories for the teachings of God's word (emphasis mine).[4]

"Stupor" is a nearly death-like state, a "completely suspended sense or feeling." The warning here is not only for the church of that period, but also for us today. We call ourselves Christians, but do we have a living faith or a stupified one? Is our faith genuine? Do all our outward actions reflect our inward beliefs? The Son of God through the Holy Spirit is looking deep into the heart. He knows that many are "playing church" so He warns that they are nearly dead. Rather than be judged as a hypocrite, become a living, growing Christian. Stott notes that hypocrite "is a Greek word in origin and meant literally to play a part on a stage, or to act in a drama. So hypocrisy is makebelieve, to assume a rôle which is not real. It is the 'let's pretend' of religion."[5]

This church needed to remember God's goodness, repent from sin, and watch. The Christians who watch and pray will avoid falling into temptation. Heed the message and watch. Don't sleep or His coming will be as a thief in the night. If the message of Jesus doesn't wake you up, beware! You must be nearly dead!

Revelation 3:4: Thou hast a few names even in Sardis which have not defiled their garments; and they shall walk with me in white: for they are worthy.

Just a few, a remnant in Sardis, did not defile their garments, but relied on Jesus' righteousness instead of outward show. Some in God's church maintained purity of doctrine and faithfulness in their daily walk with Jesus. Bunch summarizes the decline of the movement started by the Reformers: "Protestantism was founded on a protest against the doctrines and corrupt practices of Romanism. The name continues large with life and reputation, but it has largely lost its significance. The average Protestant is ignorant of the great truth of justification by faith and other doctrines on which Protestantism was founded. Lack of a

---

4   White, *The Great Controversy*, 297-298.

5   Stott, 87-88.

knowledge of the Scriptures has produced spiritual weakness and worldly conformity in many churches, and thus robbed most Protestants of their protest."[6]

Revelation 3:5-6: He that overcometh, the same shall be clothed in white raiment; and I will not blot out his name out of the book of life, but I will confess his name before my Father, and before his angels. [6]He that hath an ear, let him hear what the Spirit saith unto the churches.

For those that remain faithful and the ones who will awake from their spiritual stupor, there is a special promise. They will be clothed in the robe of Christ's righteousness. Because they confess Christ in every action of their life, He will confess them before His Father and all the holy angels. These who rely on the righteousness of Christ are not blotted out of the book of life. Jesus also warned us that the opposite holds true: "Whoever is ashamed of Me and My words, of him will the Son of man be ashamed when He comes in his own glory" (Luke 9:26; NKJ).

Sardis Period—The Reformation Church: 1565 to 1798

The Sardis period symbolizes the church of the Reformers: the birth and rise of the Protestant Reformation that occurred in the sixteenth, seventeenth, and much of the eighteenth century. This was a period when the church separated itself from the influence of the compromises symbolized by Balaam, the Nicolaitans, and Jezebel. The leaders of the Reformation were seeking after the pure faith given to the apostles. Although it was a time of doctrinal change, most of the people only went as far in their search for truth as the Reformer that they followed. Instead of following the Lamb, they followed man. The churches now had new doctrines, but not the Holy Spirit's power to sanctify the life of the church. Turner contrasts the inspiring start of the Reformation with its institutionalization:

> The Reformers began well, but many of their successors were not so consecrated as they and so their works were not found perfect before God. They had a name to live and yet were dead, and the life of vital godliness which sprang from the great doctrines of the Reformers, gradually degenerated into lifeless formalism, until at the time of John Wesley the conditions were such that many of the ministers of the Established Churches of Europe were drunkards and libertines and were among the lowest of the people. . . . Men like the Wesleys, Whitfield, the Puritans and the Pietists began to protest against these things with such earnestness and unction of the Spirit of God that they succeeded in bringing

---

[6]   Bunch, *The Seven Epistles of Christ*, 184.

about the modern revival and missionary period typified by the conditions at Philadelphia.[7]

Protestantism was founded upon a protest against the corruptness and falsehoods of the Roman system that had developed over the centuries, but soon became a victim of the same falsehoods. In both the old and new worlds, Protestantism became fashionable and many joined its ranks, but with popularity and increased numbers, the Protestant churches made many compromises and soon lost all their power. Sardis was devoid of the Holy Spirit. Cold formalism always seems to take over when the Spirit is lost. Sin was tolerated by the majority in the church, and as a result, only a few **"have not defiled their garments"** (Revelation 3:4).

The Reformation should have continued with the discovery of more light from the Scripture, but the Sardis period bears witness to the fact that it did not. Another church period would carry on its work. Historical evidence of this period points to a very good start followed by spiritual decline. It started well, but finished poorly. The heirs of the Reformation reverted to cold formalism and ceremony, devoid of the Spirit of Christ.

The message of Sardis warns the church today of the danger of starting strong and ending poorly. Bunch compares Sardis and Ephesus: "The similarity between the Ephesian and Sardis periods is striking. Both had a glorious beginning, with a corresponding spiritual decline to a condition of lukewarmness in affection and deadness in spiritual life. The Christians of both periods are therefore urged to remember the past and to repent and return to the love and faith and practice of their fathers. Because of the wonderful opportunities for advancement in knowledge and spiritual experience, the modern Sardians have no excuse for their backslidden state, and for them Christ has no praise or commendation."[8]

Because the Protestant churches ended up nearly as dead as the mother church, the Reformation's only boast soon became its long history, great past, and the leaders that once made it glorious. The great messages that their forefathers delivered have been forgotten by their children and fall on deaf ears. It is easy to recount the glories of a church's founding fathers, but it is another thing to talk about today's spiritual strengths, especially when there are none. Lasting from 1563 to 1798, the Sardis church received a stern censure from God. A revival is coming through the Philadelphian church.

VI. Church of Philadelphia

Revelation 3:7-13: And to the angel of the church in Philadelphia write; These things saith he that is holy, he that is true, he that hath the key of David, he

---

[7]   Samuel H. Turner, *Outline Studies in the Book of Revelation*, 13; quoted in Taylor G. Bunch, *The Seven Epistles of Christ* (Washington, DC: Review and Herald, 1947), 183-184.

[8]   Bunch, *The Seven Epistles of Christ*, 189-190.

that openeth, and no man shutteth; and shutteth, and no man openeth; [8]I know thy works: behold, I have set before thee an open door, and no man can shut it: for thou hast a little strength, and hast kept my word, and hast not denied my name. [9]Behold, I will make them of the synagogue of Satan, which say they are Jews, and are not, but do lie; behold, I will make them to come and worship before thy feet, and to know that I have loved thee. [10]Because thou hast kept the word of my patience, I also will keep thee from the hour of temptation, which shall come upon all the world, to try them that dwell upon the earth. [11]Behold, I come quickly: hold that fast which thou hast, that no man take thy crown. [12]Him that overcometh will I make a pillar in the temple of my God, and he shall go no more out: and I will write upon him the name of my God, and the name of the city of my God, *which is* new Jerusalem, which cometh down out of heaven from my God: and *I will write upon him my new name.* [13]He that hath an ear, let him hear what the Spirit saith unto the churches.

Philadelphia means the "city of brotherly love." In ancient Asia Minor, Philadelphia was a city of Lydia situated near the eastern base of Mount Timolus, about 28 miles southeast of Sardis. It was built on the banks of the Cogamus River that flowed into the Hermus River. The Pergamene king Attalus II Philadelphus founded the city and named it after himself. Philadephia came under Roman rule after the death of Attalus III Philometor in 133 B.C. Geography plays a role in understanding the message to Philadelphia, according to Bunch:

> Philadelphia guarded and commanded an important pass through the mountains between the Hermus and Meander valleys. It was thus the keeper of the *key* to the *door*, or gateway, to the eastern highlands, with the power to open and close according to the will of the officials. Through this portal passed the mail and trade commerce of the west to the wide regions of central and eastern Lydia. The introduction of Christ in His epistle therefore had a forceful meaning to the Philadelphians. He reminded them of other and more important doors, to which He alone holds the key, with the power and authority to open and shut.[9]

Unlike Sardis, Philadelphia received no censure from God. The whole letter speaks of God's commendation and approval. There had been some persecution at Philadelphia, yet the church faired well. They remained faithful and were rewarded for their faith.

Verses 7-8: And to the angel of the church in Philadelphia write; These things saith he that is holy, he that is true, he that hath the key of David, he that openeth, and no man shutteth; and shutteth, and no man openeth; I know thy works: behold, I have set before thee an open door, and no man can shut

---

9   Ibid., 195.

it: for thou hast a little strength, and hast kept my word, and hast not denied my name.

These verses provide the clue to Philadelphia's unique time period. What is this "open door" and what does it mean to the Philadelphian church? The contextual setting of the New Testament relates "open door" to an opportunity that opens the way for the gospel to be shared (1 Cor.16:9; 2 Corinthians 2:12; Col. 4:3). James 5:9 and Revelation 3:20 use the door symbol as a place for Judge Jesus to enter. Thus "open door" is the opportunity for the gospel of salvation to be preached. When the door is open, the opportunity is there. If the door is closed, knocking to gain entrance may yield another opportunity.

Jesus opens the door with the "key of David." What is this key? Go to the Old Testament Scriptures, Isaiah 22:20-22: **"And it shall come to pass in that day, that I will call my servant Eliakim the son of Hilkiah: And I will clothe him with thy robe, and strengthen him with thy girdle, and I will commit thy government into his hand: and he shall be a father to the inhabitants of Jerusalem, and to the house of Judah. And the *key of the house of David* will I lay upon his shoulder; so *he shall open, and none shall shut; and he shall shut, and none shall open.*"**

Obviously the language in Revelation 3:7-8 is lifted from Isaiah. The work of Eliakim prefigured the work of Jesus. As Eliahim was faithful over God's house, so is Christ.

Eliakim was the son of Hilkiah. Seven men in the Bible were named Hilkiah, but little is said about them. Hilkiah means "*Yah's part or share.*" Eliakim means "*God will establish, set up, or confirm.*" Taken together, these two names could mean "God will establish Yahweh as my portion." In other words, the key to the door is Jesus, our Provider of all good, the One established by God Himself.

This church period had very little strength of their own; therefore their strength must come from Jesus. This gave them brotherly love and total dependence upon Christ. The Philadelphian period produced powerful men of prayer and a great missionary movement driven by love for a world in need. Bible societies sprang up, and the gospel went to more parts of the world than any time before. Doors to many countries and many hearts opened like the door opened in heaven: the door of opportunity no one could shut.

Verses 9-10: Behold, I will make them of the synagogue of Satan, which say they are Jews, and are not, but do lie; behold, I will make them to come and worship before thy feet, and to know that I have loved thee. Because thou hast kept the word of my patience, I also will keep thee from the hour of temptation, which shall come upon all the world, to try them that dwell upon the earth.

Because they did not deny their faith and depended upon Christ, some were thrown out of worldly churches. Jesus promised to honor them in front of their enemies. Because Christ had opened the door of opportunity, many sinners from Satan's camp came to worship the true God as they saw the great things Jesus did for His church. Missionary stories from this time period tell of miraculous conversions due to the prayers of Moravian missionaries in the Americas and West Indies. This time period was less affected by the typical temptations we see today.

Verses 11-13: Behold, I come quickly: hold that fast which thou hast, that no man take thy crown. Him that overcometh will I make a pillar in the temple of my God, and he shall go no more out: and I will write upon him the name of my God, and the name of the city of my God, which is new Jerusalem, which cometh down out of heaven from my God: and I will write upon him my new name. He that hath an ear, let him hear what the Spirit saith unto the churches.

Jesus promises these overcomers that He will make them a pillar in the temple of God. They may have been thrown out of churches that did not love the truth, but Jesus will make them the supporting pillars of His church in the New Jerusalem. God's name and the name of His holy city will be written upon the faithful, and all will know that Jesus claims them for His very own. Then Jesus' words will come to pass: "Whoever confesses Me before men, him will I also confess before My Father who is in heaven" (Matthew 10:32; NKJ).

Philadelphian Period—The Loving Missionary Church: 1798 to 1844

On the heels of the Protestant Reformation came the period of brotherly love with the church of Philadelphia. A great revival among the Protestants during that time brought close bonds between the different bodies of believers. At this time, members adhered more closely to the dictates of Scripture than ever before or since. Bunch describes this revival movement:

The arrested Reformation was started again. Dead Christendom was mightily stirred by great spiritual revivals bringing renewed life and love and unity. The church entered upon a program of world evangelism to fulfill the great commission. May 31, 1792, William Carey preached his memorable sermon on foreign missions from Isaiah 54:2, 3. This date is reckoned as the birth of modern missions, and if an exact date can be chosen it may also mark the beginning of the Philadelphian period of the universal church.

The revival movement spread through all denominations and broke down many of the barriers that had hitherto separated the different religious sects. The Wesleys and Whitefield had an important part in this great movement that ushered in the era of brotherly love.[10]

---

[10] Ibid., 198-199.

The Moravians had a great impact on the Wesleys and inspired other bodies of Protestants to join in the great missionary movement in the new world. While the papacy lay wounded, a revival and reformation ignited, the effects of which are still seen in the world. This religious awakening brought in a purer ethic than the world had ever seen, sometimes called the Protestant ethic, but better yet, the ethic of Jesus.

With names and dates, Bunch recites the start of global evangelism: "In 1797 the first missionaries landed in Tahiti in the South Pacific. Robert Morrison went to China in 1807, and Robert Moffat to Africa in 1817. In the same year John Williams began the work of exploring and Christianizing the South Sea Island races. In 1840 David Livingstone began his missionary explorations of Africa. The British and Foreign Bible Society was organized in 1804, and the American Bible Society in 1816. The multiplication of Bibles in various languages was an essential part of the program of world evangelism that began with the Philadelphian era."[11]

The ground was prepared during this period for all churches to participate in the Great Advent Awakening. Just before 1798, events in the sun, moon, and stars aroused saints and sinners alike with a sense of urgency and a desire to prepare for the end of the world.

The study of Bible prophecies gave impetus to this revival, according to Bunch: "Church leaders around the world began the study of the prophetic word, and almost simultaneously came to the unanimous conclusion that the end of the reign of sin was near and that Jesus would soon return in fulfillment of His promise. In fact no other conclusion is possible from the study of Bible prophecy. This prophetic investigation centered on the books of Daniel and the Revelation, and the great sermon of Christ in answer to the question of the disciples, 'When shall these things be? and what shall be the sign of Thy coming, and of the end of the world?' as recorded in Matthew 24, Mark 13, and Luke 21."[12] Bunch enumerates the fulfilled end-time prophecies that startled even the ungodly:

On May 19, 1780, the sun was supernaturally darkened in fulfillment of prophecy, and the predicted shower of falling meteors followed on the night of November 13, 1833. Thousands of ministers of many denominations began to proclaim the message of the Second Advent, and all Christendom was stirred. Based on the 2300-year time prophecy of Daniel 8 and 9, many came to the conclusion that Christ would return in 1843, and, later, in 1844. There swept over the Christian world the greatest revival since Pentecost and early apostolic times. The believers in the Advent hope were brought into a state of brotherly love and unity and godliness such as had not been known since the beginning of the

---

[11]   Ibid., 200.

[12]   Ibid.

Christian Era. It has been suggested that the Philadelphian period began in 1798 with the close of the 1260 years of papal dominion, and reached to the close of the 2300-year time prophecy in 1844, when the investigative judgment began in heaven and the Laodicean state of the church was ushered in by the disappointment.[13]

VII. Church of Laodicea

Revelation 3:14-22; NKJ: And to the angel of the church of the Laodiceans write, "These things says the Amen, the Faithful and True Witness, the Beginning of the creation of God: [15]I know your works, that you are neither cold nor hot. I could wish you were cold or hot. [16]So then, because you are lukewarm, and neither cold nor hot, I will vomit you out of My mouth. [17]Because you say, 'I am rich, have become wealthy, and have need of nothing'—and do not know that you are wretched, miserable, poor, blind, and naked—[18]I counsel you to buy from Me gold refined in the fire, that you may be rich; and white garments, that you may be clothed, *that* the shame of your nakedness may not be revealed; and anoint your eyes with eye salve, that you may see. [19]As many as I love, I rebuke and chasten. Therefore be zealous and repent. [20]Behold, I stand at the door and knock. If anyone hears My voice and opens the door, I will come in to him and dine with him, and he with Me. [21]To him who overcomes I will grant to sit with Me on My throne, as I also overcame and sat down with My Father on His throne. [22]"He who has an ear, let him hear what the Spirit says to the churches."

Laodicea is made up of two Greek words: "people" and "judged" (or adjudged), so its meaning would be "a people judged." Thus their name itself signifies that during this time period, the people are judged. Stott enlarges on the message given by Jesus to the Laodiceans:

> In each of the letters Christ lays emphasis on a different mark which should characterize a true and living church. The Ephesian Christians are urged to return to their first, fresh love for Him, while the Christians at Smyrna are warned that if they do not compromise they will surely suffer. The church in Pergamum is to champion truth in the face of error, and the church of Thyatira is to follow righteousness in the midst of evil. In Sardis the need is for inward reality behind the church's outward show. Before the Philadelphian church the risen Lord has set an open door of opportunity for the spread of the gospel, and He bids them step boldly through it. The seventh letter is addressed to the church in Laodicea and combines with a fierce denunciation of complacency a tender appeal for wholeheartedness. . . .

---

[13]   Ibid., 200-201.

Whenever it had been founded, and however it may have prospered in its early history, the church in Laodicea had now fallen on evil days, and Jesus Christ sends to it the sternest of the seven letters, containing much censure and no praise. The church had not been infected with the poison of any special sin or error. We read neither of heretics nor of persecutors. But the Christians at Laodicea were *neither cold nor hot* (v. 15). They lacked wholeheartedness, so that the adjective "Laodicean" has passed into our language to describe somebody who is lukewarm in religion or politics and any other sphere.[14]

Laodicea was known for its rich farms and extensive banking system. When the city was destroyed by an earthquake in A.D. 60, the citizens refused help from the Roman government because they rebuilt it with their own money. This shows the self-sufficiency of the people of Laodicea. The difficulty with self-sufficiency is that one feels no need of Christ. How can Christians depend upon God when they think they are capable of handling everything by themselves? This is the problem with Laodicea.

World famous for its thermal springs, Laodicea attracted thousands of tourists who desired to bathe in its lukewarm, mineral-rich springs. The water was comfortable and relaxing for someone sitting in it, but if ingested, it would make you feel nauseated.

Today there is not one Christian in the area Laodicea occupied. The city has been deserted and most of the stones that made up the city have been removed to be used as building blocks for the nearby villages. Some ruins remain today as a reminder of the results of pride and arrogance.

It is tragic that the Philadelphian church of brotherly love was followed by Laodicea, the lukewarm church. Prosperous people don't feel the need for supernatural intervention. Riches give one a sense of self-righteousness; they must be doing well because God is blessing them above all others.

Laodicea is divided between the world and Christ. Bunch puts it this way: "It is too religious to entirely cast off the name of Christ, and too worldly to take a firm and united stand for Him. There is much pretension but little genuine Christianity. Works are plentiful, but faith is scarce; profession is abundant, but there is but little spiritual life to correspond."[15]

One commentary relates the merchandise of ancient Laodicea to the message given by Christ: "Lying in a country where great flocks of black sheep were raised, Laodicea became the trade center for glossy black wool and for black garments of local manufacture. Both the wool and the garments were exported to many countries. The city was also known as an export center for the famous Phrygian eye powder, and as a strong financial center, with several great banking houses that attracted much wealth. It obtained, furthermore, fame for being

---

[14]   Stott, 114-116.

[15]   Bunch, *The Seven Epistles of Christ*, 222.

near the Temple of Men Karou, where a well-known school of medicine was conducted."[16]

Laodiceans love to talk about love, but it is merely talk because Jesus is not enthroned in their hearts. The true Witness, the Amen, gives the final word of entreaty to Laodicea: Let Me in because you are desperately wretched, but you don't even realize it. White pictures Christ's self-sacrificing love and His reaction to our cold hearts:

> Christ left heaven and the bosom of His Father to come to a friendless, lost world to save those who would be saved. He exiled Himself from His Father and exchanged the pure companionship of angels for that of fallen humanity, all polluted with sin. With grief and amazement, Christ witnesses the coldness, the indifference and neglect, with which His professed followers . . . treat the light and the messages of warning and of love He has given them.[17]

Verse 14; NKJ: And to the angel of the church of the Laodiceans write, "These things says the Amen, the Faithful and True Witness, the Beginning of the creation of God." The city of Laodicea was named for Laodice, the wife (and sister) of the Seleucid King named Antiochus II Theos who ruled from 261 to 246 B.C. Thus the founder of the city and its namesake would be found wanting in the judgment. According to Leviticus 18:9, marriage with one's sister was forbidden by God. Jesus, the One through whom everything was created, is addressing the church at Laodicea and pronouncing His judgment. "Amen" in Hebrew signifies He is telling the truth.

Verses 15-17; NKJ: "I know your works, that you are neither cold nor hot. I could wish you were cold or hot. So then, because you are lukewarm, and neither cold nor hot, I will vomit you out of My mouth. Because you say, 'I am rich, have become wealthy, and have need of nothing'—and do not know that you are wretched, miserable, poor, blind, and naked." Jesus rebukes the very things that bring pride to the people of Laodicea. They were proud of their works, their lukewarm waters, and their wealth. All their "good" attributes were judged by Jesus as worthless.

Verses 18-19; NKJ: "I counsel you to buy from Me gold refined in the fire, that you may be rich; and white garments, that you may be clothed, that the shame of your nakedness may not be revealed; and anoint your eyes with eye salve, that you may see. As many as I love, I rebuke and chasten. Therefore be zealous and repent." One by one Jesus rebukes the spiritual deficits of Laodicea and offers His gifts of infinite value to replace their spiritually worthless goods. White describes how difficult it is to awaken those in Laodicea to see their need:

---

[16]   *The Seventh-day Adventist Commentary*, 7:101.

[17]   Ellen G. White, *Testimonies for the Church*, 9 vols. (Mountain View, CA: Pacific Press, 1948), 3:190.

The people slumber on in their sins. They continue to declare themselves rich and having need of nothing. Many inquire: Why are all these reproofs given? Why do the Testimonies continually charge us with backsliding and with grievous sins? We love the truth; we are prospering; we are in no need of these testimonies of warning and reproof. But let these murmurers see their hearts and compare their lives with the practical teachings of the Bible, let them humble their souls before God, let the grace of God illuminate the darkness, and the scales will fall from their eyes, and they will realize their true spiritual poverty and wretchedness. They will feel the necessity of buying gold, which is pure faith and love; white raiment, which is a spotless character made pure in the blood of their dear Redeemer; and eyesalve, which is the grace of God and which will give clear discernment of spiritual things and detect sin. These attainments are more precious than the gold of Ophir.

I have been shown that the greatest reason why the people of God are now found in this state of spiritual blindness is that they will not receive correction. Many have despised the reproofs and warnings given them. The True Witness condemns the lukewarm condition of the people of God, which gives Satan great power over them in this waiting, watching time. The selfish, the proud, and the lovers of sin are ever assailed with doubts.[18]

When all has been yielded to Jesus, Christ's robe of righteousness will replace our pride and spiritual eyesight will take the place of our blindness. Then we will realize that the heavenly kingdom is worth far more than anything this world has to offer. As we surrender, we begin to appreciate the benefits of God's rebukes and chastening. In repentance we will find real spiritual healing.

Spiritual wealth makes you rich in the kingdom of heaven, but material wealth will bring you nothing in the end. Spiritual riches come only from Jesus for He bought them for you at great cost. His free gift requires only the full surrender of your heart to Him.

The wealthy must let Jesus control all their worldly goods. Money and authority in our hands must be controlled by the Giver else we will misuse it. The poor person must surrender the desire to be rich or they will fall into covetousness. The adulterer must yield the lust of the flesh, those who hold the bitter fruits of hatred or animosity must drop them and yield to the forgiving love of Christ. Whatever prevents full surrender and total commitment must be given up to obtain the greatest wealth in Christ Jesus.

Verse 20; NKJ: Behold, I stand at the door and knock. If anyone hears My voice and opens the door, I will come in to him and dine with him, and he with Me. Interestingly, the church of Philadelphia had an open door that no one

[18] White, *Testimonies for the Church*, 3:254-255.

could shut, but the Laodiceans' door is closed. Since this door opens from the inside, Jesus asks His last church to give Him entrance. The Philadelphian church found the door to heaven wide open, but in the Laodicean church, people find it hard to open the door of their hearts to the Savior. These two churches show a wide contrast in spirituality.

Using imagery from the Song of Solomon, Doukhan paints an interesting word picture of this verse:

> God knocks passionately. . . . "Listen! My lover is knocking: 'Open to me my sister, my darling'" (S. of Sol. 5:2). In this context, the knocking is extremely violent. The Hebrew verb used here, *dafaq*, denotes heavy pounding. Scripture uses the same word of the shepherd who hurries his sheep along [See Genesis 33:13]. This text suggests that Yeshua is pounding on the door. His passion indicates the urgency and seriousness of the situation.[19]

Jesus is knocking on your heart's door. Let Him in, for He has the gifts you so desperately need. He made your heart, so let Him rule it. As we yield our will to Him, He will give us repentance and the power to obey His will. With Jesus ruling the throne of our heart, we will be ready to have a wonderful meal with our favorite Friend.

Verse 21; NKJ: To him who overcomes I will grant to sit with Me on My throne, as I also overcame and sat down with My Father on His throne. What a promise! We give Jesus the throne of our heart, and He promises to share His throne with us. Because Jesus overcame, we also may overcome through His power and gain the victory over every sin.

Verse 22: He who has an ear, let him hear what the Spirit says to the churches. Note that it reads: "Hear what the Spirit says to the *churches*." These seven messages should be read by all because the promises and admonitions are relevant to every age of the church. The progression of the messages through the life of an individual Christian can be seen as they move from the first love experience, through various trials, and end with sitting down on the throne with Christ. This theme provides the key to understanding the book of Revelation, especially the most misunderstood portion: the 144,000. Remember that apocalyptic prophecy, unlike classical prophecy, repeats and enlarges, giving more details until the whole picture emerges.

Laodicean Period—The Lukewarm Church: 1844 to Jesus' Second Coming

The messages to the seven churches will prepare God's people for the return of Jesus. The seventh and final message is a love letter, but not written with sentimental, indulgent love. Real love takes risks to save lives. In view of the coming

---

[19]   Jacques B. Doukhan, *Secrets of Revelation* (Hagerstown, MD: Review and Herald, 2002), 47.

judgments, Jesus urgently expresses His love for the self-deceived Laodiceans. Plainer words could not be given: You are wretched, miserable, poor, blind, and naked. God now commands all people everywhere to repent (Acts 17:30). Those who are honest at heart will accept this rebuke and repent because the truth is revealed and their blind, self-deceived state is proclaimed.

Laodicea is not a rejected church although rebuked harshly. He is standing at the door and knocking. Jesus' promise infers that some do open the door to Him. He keeps on knocking because He realizes the lukewarm condition of His people. When we are cold, we realize our need for warmth and would more easily open our door to Jesus. When we are hot, we are on fire for God, and Jesus is always near when there is Holy Fire! However, if you are lukewarm, you could sleep in spite of Christ's knocking at the door.

The worst of the seven churches is nearest the return of the Desire of all ages—Jesus! In spite of this, the reward for the seventh and last church is so much greater than the rewards of all the other churches combined. Why is this? Their great victory over this most deplorable state deserves a great reward. Bunch concurs:

> The promise is remarkable, not only because it reaches the very zenith, but also because the sin which the victim of deception and hypocrisy must overcome is almost insurmountable. The reward therefore should be commensurate to the victory gained. When we consider the abject bondage of the Laodiceans in their wretched, pitiable, poor, blind, and naked state, and the fact that they know it not, overcoming power is the more commendable and deserving of a rich recompense of reward. For a man in this condition to open his heart's door and invite the Saviour in is akin to stepping out of the miry pit to the throne.[20]

The time period from 1844 until the second coming of Jesus is an amazing story because it starts with such a bleak picture. The modern church has material prosperity, but compromise has made it nearly indistinguishable from the world. Protestantism has lost its understanding of justification by faith and forgotten the need for sanctification by faith, but Jesus is still offering His precious gifts. Yet even in this last time period, through those in the last church who open their hearts to Jesus, the Holy Spirit will work in a mighty way to awaken and prepare many for the coming of Christ.

---

[20] Bunch, *The Seven Epistles of Christ*, 251-252.

CHAPTER SIXTEEN

Revelation 4

Introduction

The first three chapters focus on the sanctuary symbol of the golden lampstand. Beginning with chapter four, the table of showbread in the holy place of the heavenly sanctuary becomes the next center of attention. This second prophetic section encompasses chapters 4 through 7 and includes at least the first verse of chapter 8. The seven seals are placed in the setting at the table of showbread which is the throne of God in the holy place.

Because Revelation reveals Jesus, it also unveils the nature of the sanctuary, the symbolized plan of salvation which moves through the history of this earth. To understand the imagery of chapter 4, study the first chapter of Ezekiel. The whirlwind judgment that comes out of the north refers to that portion of the sanctuary on the "sides of the north," the table of showbread (Ezekiel 1:4; Psalm 48:2). Thus the imagery of Ezekiel 1 and Revelation 4 complement one another. Zechariah also sheds light on the throne of God and the first four seals.

The prophecies have a two-fold purpose. First, they reveal Christ's actions in the heavenly sanctuary and second, they show the relationship of His heavenly actions to events on the earth. In the prophetic section covering the seven churches, Christ is pictured as our High Priest ministering in the heavenly sanctuary while the Holy Spirit makes Christ's work effectual for the church here on earth. In the seven seals, Jesus is portrayed in heaven as the slain sacrificial Lamb, while His blood ministers in behalf of His people on earth. Revelation shows us God's connection to His people, an inseparable bond between the Creator and all who give total allegiance to Him.

In summary, the first prophetic section in Revelation centers around the golden candlestick in the holy place of the heavenly sanctuary. These symbols show the connection between heaven and earth through the Holy Spirit, the One who brings Christ's messages, admonitions, and promises to His seven churches. In this second prophetic section of Revelation, the throne of God is represented by the table of showbread in the holy place of the sanctuary. From this throne on the sides of the north, God makes judgments in heaven that are carried out here on earth through the seven seals. Both of these prophetic sections, the seven churches and the seven seals, begin from the cross in A.D. 31 and continue until the time of the end and the hour of judgment.

The courtyard, the first area of the sanctuary, represented Christ's work on earth. He became our Passover Lamb and the Offering of the first fruits, fulfilling the spring feasts. The second part of the sanctuary is the holy place: here the daily, continual ministry of Christ in the holy place of the heavenly sanctuary comes to us by merit of His shed blood. He brings forgiveness, cleansing, and transformation to His people, but He also issues to the rebellious the covenant curses, the consequences of disobeying His holy law. Stephen saw Him in vision in the holy place in heaven, standing on the right hand of the Father, as the probation for the Jews ended in A.D. 34.

After the time of the end, the focus of Revelation changes from the holy to the most holy place, as the final judgment begins at the end of the 2300-day prophecy. The center of attention in the heavenly sanctuary is the ark of the covenant and the restoration of God's law to His people on earth. When all the decisions have been made, angels carry bowls full of God's wrath out of the most holy place. The final judgment made in heaven in favor of the saints will be carried out here on earth as Christ comes for the ones pronounced holy in His name, rescuing them from the filthy and unholy who seek their lives. The most holy place judgment is carried out against the wicked after the millennium as Satan and all his followers are destroyed.

All three sections of the sanctuary have their proper place in the plan of salvation that rids heaven, the earth, and God's people of sin and at the same time, punishes the guilty. The courtyard, the holy place, and the most holy place reveal not only the remedy for sin, but also the consequences and punishments of sin. In the courtyard, the cross revealed the antidote for sin and God's judgment against it as Christ suffered and died the "second death" for our sins (Revelation 20:14). The same is true of the prophetic sections from the holy place of the heavenly sanctuary. Within the messages to the seven churches, Christ's blessings are promised to those who overcome sin, but also His warnings and threatened punishments are given as well. Likewise God's judgments or curses play a role in the seven seals. While these are not the same as the final judgment, they point to that climactic event like a yellow caution light.

Revelation 4:1: After this I looked, and, behold, a door was opened in heaven: and the first voice which I heard was as it were of a trumpet talking with me; which said, Come up hither, and I will show thee things which must be hereafter.

After this I looked: The introduction indicates clearly this new and separate vision different from that of the seven churches. As Daniel 7 and 8 cover the same time period with two different visions, so the seven churches and seven seals cover the same time period as seen from two different viewpoints.

Daniel contains four parallel lines of prophecy with four different views of the same time frame. Each time the prophetic theme repeats and enlarges with ever increasing detail focusing on the time of the end. Revelation also has four parallel lines of prophecy that point forward to the final judgments of God. As the seven seals parallel the seven churches, this new vision will add details that help us understand even more about Christ's connection to earthly events.

Revelation is not organized chronologically, but repeats themes as deemed appropriate by the Author. In chapter 4, themes from the messages to the seven churches will be repeated. These help us to place each message within its correct time frame. The end of chapter 3 dealt with Laodicea, the people who are judged. This same context of judgment appears early in chapter 4 as the seven seals are introduced.

Behold, a door was opened in heaven: John did not see the door opening because it was already open. Davidson relates this imagery to the daily service in the holy place of the temple:

> The daily (*tāmîd*) setting of Revelation 1-8 is further substantiated as these chapters are compared with the order of daily services in the second Temple of the century in which John wrote. Recent studies have set forth the striking parallels between the order of sanctuary allusions in Revelation 1-8 and the description of the daily (*tāmîd*) services described in the Mishnah. We summarize as follows:

1. Trimming the lampstand (*m. Tāmîd* 3.9; cf. Revelation 1:12-20)

2. Great door open (*m. Tāmîd* 3.7; cf. Revelation 4:1)

3. Lamb slain (*m. Tāmîd* 3.7; 4:1-3, cf. Revelation 5:6)

4. Blood poured out at base of bronze altar (*m. Tāmîd* 4.1; cf. Revelation 6:9)

5. Incense offered at golden altar (*m. Tāmîd* 5.4; cf. Revelation 8:3, 4)

6. Break in the singing (*m. Tāmîd* 7.3; Revelation 8:1)

7. Trumpets blown to signal completion of sacrifice (*m. Tāmîd* 7.3; cf. 8:2-6)[1]

This vision correlates with the first chapter of Ezekiel which portrays heaven itself and the throne of God. It also reminds us of the golden lampstands with unlimited supplies of oil in Zechariah 4.

Revelation 4:2–11: And immediately I was in the spirit; and, behold, a throne was set in heaven, and one sat on the throne. ³And he that sat was to look upon like a jasper and a sardine stone: and there was a rainbow round about

---

[1] Richard M. Davidson, "Sanctuary Typology," in *Symposium on Revelation: Book 1*, Daniel and Revelation Committee Series, vol. 6 (Hagerstown, MD: Review and Herald, 1992), 113.

the throne, in sight like unto an emerald. ⁴And round about the throne were four and twenty seats: and upon the seats I saw four and twenty elders sitting, clothed in white raiment; and they had on their heads crowns of gold. ⁵And out of the throne proceeded lightnings and thunderings and voices: and there were seven lamps of fire burning before the throne, which are the seven Spirits of God. ⁶And before the throne there was a sea of glass like unto crystal: and in the midst of the throne, and round about the throne, were four beasts full of eyes before and behind. ⁷And the first beast was like a lion, and the second beast like a calf, and the third beast had a face as a man, and the fourth beast was like a flying eagle. ⁸And the four beasts had each of them six wings about him; and they were full of eyes within: and they rest not day and night, saying, Holy, holy, holy, Lord God Almighty, which was, and is, and is to come. ⁹And when those beasts give glory and honour and thanks to him that sat on the throne, who liveth for ever and ever, ¹⁰The four and twenty elders fall down before him that sat on the throne, and worship him that liveth for ever and ever, and cast their crowns before the throne, saying, ¹¹Thou art worthy, O Lord, to receive glory and honour and power: for thou hast created all things, and for thy pleasure they are and were created.

These verses must be taken as a whole to aid in understanding the meaning of this section that describes the throne room of God.

Verses 2: This throne is set in the heavenly sanctuary. The following verses indicate where the throne is set in the heavenly sanctuary.

Verse 3: Stephen saw Jesus standing at the right hand of His Father in A.D. 34 (Acts 7:56). In the message to the Laodiceans in the previous chapter, Jesus declared: "I also overcame, and am set down with my Father in his throne" (Revelation 3:21). Sanctuary language from Exodus 28:17-21 describes the One sitting on the throne. Jasper and sardius are the first and the last of the twelve stones set in the breastplate of the high priest. This description also reminds us of Ezekiel 1:4-28. "As the appearance of the bow that is in the cloud in the day of rain, so was the appearance of the brightness round about. This was the appearance of the likeness of the glory of the LORD. And when I saw it I fell upon my face, and I heard a voice of one that spake" (Ezekiel 1:28). In Revelation 4:3, the rainbow's color has the appearance of an emerald, the stone that represented the tribe of Judah. These details point out His identity as our High Priest: Christ, the First and the Last, and the Lion of the tribe of Judah.

Jesus has many dual roles: He is both Priest and King, both Judge and substitutionary Sacrifice, and amazingly, he is both Lawgiver and Forgiver! He lives and dies for man, and I could go on and on. Sometimes these paradoxes are the answer to our dilemma. Care must be taken in the interpretation of symbolism; jumping from symbolism to literalism yields mistaken views of prophecy.

Verse 4: To understand the holy place imagery, the 24 elders must be viewed in the context of the rest of the Old Testament. King David divided the priesthood into 24 courses. Each of these courses was under a leader chosen from the two sons of Aaron: Eleazer and Ithamar. Since Ithamar had fewer descendants, eight leaders were chosen from that family and sixteen were selected from the descendents of Eleazer. This added up to 24 leaders or elders.

The 24 elders wore white robes, the "daily garments" of the priests in the earthly tabernacle, so there must be a corresponding role in the heavenly sanctuary. In Revelation 5:8, the 24 elders offer incense, one of the holy place duties. This burning of incense represents "the prayers of the saints" (Revelation 5:8). The priests and elders occupied positions next to the king in the dedication of the earthly temple (1 Kings 8:1-3). Likewise in this apocalyptic vision the 24 elders are next to the King's throne; their white robes and crowns of gold symbolize their position and purity of life. Therefore this vision depicts a ceremony similar to that of Solomon's day. This holy place ministry continues until the change in Revelation 11:19 which introduces the ark of the covenant in the book of Revelation.

Verse 5: White links the earthly symbols to the heavenly realities which John saw:

> As in vision the apostle John was granted a view of the temple of God in heaven, he beheld there "seven lamps of fire burning before the throne." He saw an angel "having a golden censer; and there was given unto him much incense, that he should offer it with the prayers of all saints upon the golden altar which was before the throne." Revelation 4:5; 8:3. Here the prophet was permitted to behold the first apartment of the sanctuary in heaven; and he saw there the "seven lamps of fire" and the "golden altar" represented by the golden candlestick and the altar of incense in the sanctuary on earth.[2]

The holy place is pictured with candlestick imagery. "Lightnings and thunderings and voices" evoke images of Mount Sinai and its divine Lawgiver. This phrase also shows that Revelation's climax has not yet been reached in this sanctuary journey; that is reserved for Revelation 11:19 (cf. Revelation 4:5; 8:5; 11:19; 16:18).

Verses 6-8: The sea of glass before the throne harmonizes with Revelation 15:2: "And I saw as it were a sea of glass mingled with fire." The sea of glass "before" the throne could also be translated "over against," but not "in front of" as many would think. Its connection to the throne is emphasized here as it flows out from the throne itself. This again echoes the experience on Mount Sinai with the elders of Israel as described by Bunch:

> It is evident that the crystal sea represents the pavement of the throne room of the heavenly temple. When Nadab and Abihu and the seventy elders of Israel went up into Mount Sinai with Moses, "they saw the God

---

[2]   White, *Patriarchs and Prophets* (Mountain View, CA: Pacific Press), 356.

of Israel: and there was under his feet as it were a paved work of a sapphire stone, and as it were the body of heaven in his clearness." (Exodus 24:10). When Lucifer was the first of the anointed covering cherubs occupying the highest position in the government of God next to the members of the Godhead, he "walked up and down in the midst of the stones of fire." (Ezekiel 28:14). The glittering gems that compose the mosaic tile-work of the floor of the celestial court are well described as "stones of fire" or "glass mingled with fire."[3]

The water of the courtyard laver was not stable and any movement or wind destroyed its glassy surface. This pavement is stable and clear like crystal glass, like the heavens in its clarity. It is solid and calm.

John attempts to describe the heavenly throne with earthly language. Ezekiel had the same dilemma. Apparent discrepancies arise because this awesome sight has no earthly correlation. The standards of the twelve tribes found in Numbers 2 help explain the throne room imagery of the four living beings.

In the encampment of Israel, the families from the tribe of Levi closely surrounded the sanctuary on all sides. Aaron's family camped at the east gate, the Kohathites were south of the sanctuary, and the Gershonites and Merarites lived on the west and north sides respectively. The rest of the tribes were each given a particular location in relation to the sanctuary. On the east side the tribe of Judah guarded the entrance of the tabernacle; its standard was a lion. Issachar and Zebulun camped next to Judah. Reuben's standard on the south side had the face of a man. Simeon and Gad also camped on the south side. The west side flew Ephraim's standard which pictured an ox. Manasseh and Benjamin camped near Ephraim. Dan's standard of the eagle flew on the north side; the tribes of Asher and Naphtali camped there as well. These symbols on the banners relate to the visions of John and Ezekiel. While Ezekiel describes them as composite beings, John pictures them as separate creatures. Obviously the symbols are more important than an exact description. Similar language in Ezekiel 1 and 10, Daniel 7, and Psalm 18:10 clarify that these celestial beings are connected with the throne of God.

Bunch notes: "The man, ox, lion, and eagle represent the four most conspicuous forms of animal life. They rule in the realms of intellect, the field, the forest and the air."[4] In Ezekiel's account the right side of each of the living being featured the faces of a man and a lion; the left side of each living being had the faces of an ox and an eagle. These are characteristics of Jesus. He is the lion of the tribe of Judah and the Son of man on the right side, signifying His right to rule mankind. The ox and eagle banners reveal Him as our substitutionary

---

3   Taylor G. Bunch, "The Revelation," Typewritten manuscript, 1952, Center for Adventist Research, James White Library, Andrews University, Berrien Springs, MI, 10.

4   Ibid., 14

Sacrifice and our Judge. These symbols remind us that He has earned the right to take upon Himself our sins and credit us with His righteousness.

The following diagram from *Principles of Life* shows the arrangement of the tribes and standards around the sanctuary:[5]

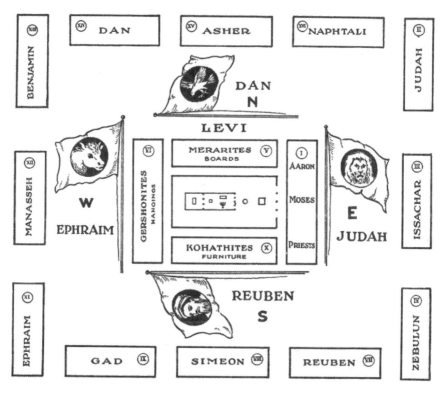

In Revelation 4:8, the four living beings cry out: "Holy, holy, holy, Lord God Almighty, which was, and is, and is to come." The 24 elders answer antiphonally in verse 11: "Thou art worthy, O Lord, to receive glory and honour and power: for thou hast created all things, and for thy pleasure they are and were created."

Verses 9 through 11: The four living beings and the 24 elders are two different groups. The four living creatures or beings describe God in eternal terms (which was, and is, and is to come), while the 24 elders are obviously those who have had the experience of redemption. All those who are redeemed from the earth will someday join the 24 elders, proclaiming the worthiness of the One who redeemed us by His blood.

5   E. E. Cossentine, ed., *Principles of Life From the Word of God* (Mountain View, CA: Pacific Press, 1952), 224 .

CHAPTER SEVENTEEN

Revelation 5

Introduction

This chapter continues the throne room scene of Revelation 4. The scroll with its seals is introduced immediately. The significance of this chapter is summarized by White: "The fifth chapter of Revelation needs to be closely studied. It is of great importance to those who shall act a part in the work of God for these last days."[1]

Revelation 5:1: And I saw in the right hand of him that sat on the throne a book written within and on the backside, sealed with seven seals.

This scroll is sealed not once, but seven times! The contents and messages of the scroll cannot be read until the seals are broken. The scroll is written on the inside with the seven seals on the outside or the backside. These seals must be broken before anything on the inside could be revealed. The seven seals are the only focus at first.

Revelation 5:2-4: And I saw a strong angel proclaiming with a loud voice, Who is worthy to open the book, and to loose the seals thereof? ³And no man in heaven, nor in earth, neither under the earth, was able to open the book, neither to look thereon. ⁴And I wept much, because no man was found worthy to open and to read the book, neither to look thereon.

With a loud voice, one mighty angel asks a fearful question in verse 2: **"Who is worthy to open the book, and to loose the seals thereof?"** Silence meets his question. **"And no man in heaven, nor in earth, neither under the earth, was able to open the book, neither to look thereon"** (Revelation 5:3). No one with the qualifications to open the seals is found. John wept when it appeared no one would meet the necessary requirements.

Revelation 5:5-6: And one of the elders saith unto me, Weep not: behold, the Lion of the tribe of Juda, the Root of David, hath prevailed to open the book, and to loose the seven seals thereof. ⁶And I beheld, and, lo, in the midst of the

---

throne and of the four beasts, and in the midst of the elders, stood a Lamb as it had been slain, having seven horns and seven eyes, which are the seven Spirits of God sent forth into all the earth.

One of the 24 elders had good news for John: the Lion of the tribe of Judah has prevailed. This lion symbol for Judah was first recorded in Jacob's last words to his sons (Genesis 49:9); the Root of David symbol comes from Isaiah 11:1.

Commenting on Christ's worthiness, Paulien writes: "The Lamb is the exalted Christ of Revelation 1-3, who is qualified to take the book, not only on account of what He had done (His death on the cross), but on account of who He is. Thus, implicit in the text is the full divinity and humanity that the Lamb had to embody in order to carry out the redemptive task. The Lamb's humanity is evident in that He was slain. His divinity is evident in that He is exalted to the throne of God to receive the worship of all creation."[2]

The Lamb is in the midst of the throne: He is divine. He is in the midst of the four living beings: He is Captain of the hosts of heaven. He is in the midst of the elders: He is not ashamed to call us His brothers and sisters. This Lamb is symbolic for no earthly lamb has seven horns and seven eyes. These represent the same symbol as the seven Spirits of God sent forth into all the earth. Again, as in the first three chapters, Christ's work is intimately connected with the work of the Holy Spirit. This Lamb is worthy because He overcame sin. Through His blood, we have forgiveness. Only by the merits of Christ may we enter the heavenly sanctuary by faith.

Revelation 5:7-8: And he came and took the book out of the right hand of him that sat upon the throne. [8]And when he had taken the book, the four beasts and four *and* twenty elders fell down before the Lamb, having every one of them harps, and golden vials full of odours, which are the prayers of saints.

By virtue of His unique merits and worthiness, the Lamb takes the scroll from the hand of His Father. The purpose of the Apocalypse is to reveal Christ as our Substitute, Lord, and King. In this vision we see the symbolism of Jesus, our Lamb, as the "One mediator between God and men, the man Christ Jesus" (1 Timothy 2:5).

Golden Vials: In Greek the word is φιάλη (*phialē*, pronounced fee-al'-ay). "According to Josephus, *phialai* of incense were placed on the showbread in the sanctuary (*Antiquities* iii. 6.6 [143])," the *Adventist Bible Commentary* states.[3] Vials of incense on the table of showbread provide another clue that the setting for the seven seals is the holy place.

2   Jon Paulien, "The Seven Seals," in *Symposium on Revelation: Book 1*, Daniel and Revelation Committee Series, vol. 6 (Hagerstown, MD: Review and Herald, 1992), 220.

3   *The Seventh-day Adventist Bible Commentary*, 7:772.

Note that the Lamb is in the midst of the throne. This refers to the God/man: His humanity and divinity. As the Lamb, He is linked with humanity. As Creator and Lord He is divine.

Revelation 5:9-10: And they sung a new song, saying, Thou art worthy to take the book, and to open the seals thereof: for thou wast slain, and hast redeemed us to God by thy blood out of every kindred, and tongue, and people, and nation; [10]And hast made us unto our God kings and priests: and we shall reign on the earth.

This song is sung by the redeemed, so the pronoun "they" in verse 9 refers to the 24 elders, who represent those who have been redeemed "out of every kindred, and tongue, and people, and nation." The crucifixion has a direct bearing upon the future events in the Apocalypse. His sinless life, substitutionary death, and resurrection gave Christ the right to take the scroll and to open its seals. Because we share in Jesus' victory, He makes us priests and kings unto God.

Revelation 5:11: And I beheld, and I heard the voice of many angels round about the throne and the beasts and the elders: and the number of them was ten thousand times ten thousand, and thousands of thousands;

Rather than the exact number of angels in heaven, this verse indicates the size of the heavenly sanctuary. Although they cannot share in the redemption through the blood of Jesus; they have cooperated with Christ in the salvation of mankind. All heaven works with Christ to restore fallen humanity to the image of God.

Revelation 5:12-14: Saying with a loud voice, Worthy is the Lamb that was slain to receive power, and riches, and wisdom, and strength, and honour, and glory, and blessing. [13]And every creature which is in heaven, and on the earth, and under the earth, and such as are in the sea, and all that are in them, heard I saying, Blessing, and honour, and glory, and power, *be* unto him that sitteth upon the throne, and unto the Lamb for ever and ever. [14]And the four beasts said, Amen. And the four *and* twenty elders fell down and worshipped him that liveth for ever and ever.

The slain Lamb invites us to share the throne with Him and worship Him throughout the ceaseless ages of eternity. The four living beings exclaim, "Amen!" as the 24 elders fall down and worship. "Amen" means "so be it," "assuredly," or "in verity." All the heavenly beings agree that assuredly the Lamb is worthy.

The seven seals could only be opened because of the worthy sacrifice of the Lamb. The working out of the plan of redemption could never start without the cross. The full benefits of salvation may now be freely offered to all because One was worthy to open the scroll. This brings assurance that in the end, God's righteous judgment will deliver His people and put an end to sin forever. Before Jesus appears as the Judge of all men, He is first revealed as their Savior and

Redeemer. The Father, the angelic hosts of heaven, and the redeemed all agree that He is worthy to be worshiped. The great controversy involves worship, and the grand throne room scene reminds us that only the Creator is rightly worshiped by His creatures. As self is forgotten and Jesus is given first place, real worship commences.

CHAPTER EIGHTEEN

Revelation 6

Introduction

Chapters 4 and 5 show that the seals are opened by the Lamb in the heavenly sanctuary, whereas the sixth chapter describes the events of the first six seals as they take place on the earth. Like the seven churches, the seven seals are seven successive time periods with the seventh seal signaling the end. Only Jesus' death could open the seven seals, so the events portrayed must begin *after* the death of Jesus in A.D. 31.

Like Daniel, the book of Revelation contains apocalyptic prophecy. In four parallel prophecies, events are repeated and enlarged, adding even more details to the big picture of prophecy. The Revelation focuses on the main characters in the spiritual drama of the great controversy, giving enought information to clearly identify them. This knowledge helps sustain and prepare God's people for the events that take place during their lifetime. Our loving Savior has not left us in the dark, but has given us the sure word of prophecy to light our path.

Jesus' death, burial, and resurrection gave Him title and right to open the seals of the future for us to understand. The setting for Christ's heavenly ministry is the daily and continual work in the holy place as represented by the bleeding Lamb. Revelation moves through the sanctuary from the lampstand to the table of showbread and on to the altar of incense, showing us the plan of salvation in symbols. The symbolism of the sanctuary reveals these prophetic themes. Bunch explains it this way:

> The seven seals do not present a new period of history from that of the seven letters, but again covers [sic] the Christian dispensation from another viewpoint. These symbols reveal a series of religious events between the first and second advents of Christ giving the changing conditions of the church. The letters make their special appeal to the ear, while the seals with their symbols make their impressions through the eye. These are the two best methods of imparting instruction. The four symbolic horses with their riders represent the church from its triumphant beginning, through the Dark Ages, and to the Reformation. The great apostasy or "falling away" in the church is especially emphasized. The

remaining seals present the revival and reformation for the restoration of the primitive faith through the testimony of the Two Witnesses, the sealing message, the second advent of Christ, and the glorious triumph of the church militant. The horse is symbolic of the church, its color represents her spiritual condition, and the rider her responsible leadership. As a rider guides and controls his horse, so the movements of the church are determined by the leading officials.[1]

Like Revelation 4 and 5, this chapter uses imagery of the throne of God within the heavenly sanctuary. According to Thiele, Zechariah aids our understanding of the four horses in the first four seals:

> In Zechariah there were four horses and chariots, which we are told were "the four spirits of the heavens, which go forth from standing before the Lord of all the earth." (Zechariah 6:5) "These are they whom the Lord hath sent to walk to and fro through the earth." (Zechariah 1:10). As in Revelation heavenly commands were issued to the horses, so also in Zechariah: "Get you hence, walk to and from through the earth. So they walked to and fro through the earth." (Zechariah 6:7) As these messengers were sent by Heaven they accomplish the purpose of Heaven: "Behold, these that go toward the north country have quieted my spirit in the north country." (Zechariah 6:8)[2]

The horses of Zechariah are given in the context of the four horns that scattered Jerusalem and Israel. These four horns or kingdoms are Babylon, Medo-Persia, Greece, and Rome. The visions in Zechariah are introduced with language that speaks of a forthcoming judgment: Israel is judged first, then the surrounding nations, and lastly the Messiah comes to set things right. As the seven seals are opened in the book of Revelation, there is an increasing longing for the judgment of God. In the Old Testament, judges were seen as deliverers and executors of justice, and it is in this context that God's people call for judgment in the fifth seal.

The Lamb opens the seven seals one at a time. The first four seals are announced by one of the living beings with the words "Come and see."

The living beings of Ezekiel and Revelation are the same. Note that the Septuagint, the Greek version of the Old Testament, uses the same word in Ezekiel as is found in Revelation. Thiele summarizes the Old Testament vision: "In Ezekiel there were also four wheels, one by each of the cherubim (Ezekiel 10:9). The wheels were under the direction and control of the living

---

[1]   Bunch, "The Revelation," 30.

[2]   Edwin R. Thiele, "Outline Studies in Revelation," Typewritten manuscript, 1952, Center for Adventist Research, James White Library, Andrews University, Berrien Springs, MI, 115-116.

creatures or cherubim (Ezekiel 1:19-21; 10:16, 17), and moved with the 'Spirit' (Ezekiel 1:12, 20; 10:17)."[3]

Each of the horses in the first four seals is under the direction of one of the living beings and each has a mission. The first is like a lion, the second like an ox, the third is a man, and the fourth an eagle. This symbols help us understand the first four seals.

I. First Seal

Revelation 6:1-2: And I saw when the Lamb opened one of the seals, and I heard, as it were the noise of thunder, one of the four beasts saying, Come and see. ²And I saw, and behold a white horse: and he that sat on him had a bow; and a crown was given unto him: and he went forth conquering, and to conquer.

With the crown and armed with a bow, the rider of the white horse went forth both conquering and to conquer. Using the order of the living beings of Revelation 4:7, the lion is linked to the first seal. The Lion of the tribe of Judah symbolizes Jesus Christ. The symbolism is clear; the rider of this white horse can be none other than Jesus Himself, the head of the Ephesian church in the first century. This pictures the purity of the church while the apostles were still alive.

Whenever a Roman general returned home after a victory, he rode on a white horse or in a chariot pulled by white horses. At that time, the strength of the army came from the archers on horseback. The color white shows the purity of the church, the bow symbolizes the gospel propelled swiftly, and the horse symbol means the speed with which the gospel conquered from A.D. 31 to 100.

The first seal covers the same time period as the church of Ephesus. During the lifetime of John the Revelator, the church was militant and successful in its victories. Bunch links Old Testament prophecies to the Revelation:

> This apocalyptic symbolism is not new, but is borrowed from the Old Testament. The prophet Habakkuk described the triumps [sic] of the gospel in symbols no less striking: "Thou didst ride upon thine horses and thy chariots of salvation. Thy bow was made quite naked . . . *even thy word* . . . The mountains saw thee, and they trembled: the overflowing of the waters passed by: the deep uttered his voice, and lifted up his hands on high. The sun and moon stood still in their habitation: at the light of thine arrows they went, and at the shining of thy glittering spear. Thou didst march through the land in indignation, thou didst thresh the hea-then in anger. Thou wentest forth for the salvation of thy people, even for salvation for[4] thine anointed; thou woundedst the head out of the house of the wicked." Habakkuk 3:8-13. In Psalm 45:2-7 Christ is pictured as

---

[3]   Ibid., 115.

[4]   "For" should read "with" per the King James translation.

a mounted archer whose messages pierce the hearts of His enemies like sharp arrows: "Thou art fairer than the children of men: grace is poured into thy lips: therefore God hath blessed thee forever. Gird thy sword upon thy thigh, O most mighty, with thy glory and thy majesty. And in thy majesty ride prosperously because of truth and meekness and righteousness; and thy right hand shall teach thee terrible things. Thine arrows are sharp in the heart of the king's enemies; whereby the people fall under thee. Thy throne, O God, is for ever and ever: the sceptre of thy kingdom is a right sceptre. Thou lovest righteousness, and hatest wickedness: therefore God, thy God, hath anointed thee with the oil of gladness above thy fellows." The Septuagint of verse four reads: "And in Thy majesty ride, and bend Thy bow, and prosper and reign, because of truth." "Success to you as you ride forth . . . Sharp are your arrows; nations shall fall before you, and the king's foes lose heart," (Moffat). In this passage the arrows imply the use of a bow, just as the bow in the apocalyptic vision indicates the use of arrows. The two are inseparable. That Christ is the royal Warrior of this prophecy is beyond the possibility of dispute. These Old Testament symbols interpret the meaning of the symbols of the first seal so that we can safely discard the many fanciful but unscriptural views that are extant.[5]

Time of the First Seal: A.D. 31 to 100

The color of the first horse is appropriate for the church of this time period. The purity of the first century church has never been challenged by anyone. During this period the church began the conquest of the then-known world. Within the first seventy years, the church had permeated every nook and cranny of the Roman Empire. The bow is also an appropriate symbol of the first century church as the gospel's arrows were shot everywhere. As a result, the apostle Paul could say: "First, I thank my God through Jesus Christ for you all, that your faith is spoken of throughout the whole world" (Romans 1:8).

Bunch contrasts the first seal with the next three: "Surely there is no room to question the application of the first seal to the gospel under the power of the Holy Spirit as it started out for the moral and spiritual conquest of this rebel world. But its work was hindered and finally brought to a virtual standstill by the 'falling away' that ended in the great apostasy of the Middle Ages as pictured in the three succeeding seals."[6]

Although the first seal coincides with the church of Ephesus, the parallel prophecies of the seals added information and fill in some missing components.

---

[5]   Bunch, "The Revelation," 32.

[6]   Ibid., 34.

II. Second Seal

Revelation 6:3-4: And when he had opened the second seal, I heard the second beast say, Come and see. ⁴And there went out another horse that was red: and power was given to him that sat thereon to take peace from the earth, and that they should kill one another: and there was given unto him a great sword.

As in the first seal, the invitation "come and see" is given. The horse represents the church, the color reveals its spiritual condition, and the rider symbolizes its responsible leadership. The living being that introduces the second seal is linked to the ox, noted for its strength. The church is still strong like an ox, but during this time the church endured periods of heavy persecution. The ox also symbolizes sacrifice; the bullocks of the ancient sanctuary service were killed to prefigure the death of Christ. Likewise, the martyrdom of God's people under the second seal reveals their ultimate sacrifice as they maintain steadfast loyalty to their Lord and Savior.

The church's spiritual condition is depicted as red. The first seal represented the early church as pure white so the red must represent a bloody church. The rider of this blood-red horse takes peace from the earth. He has a great sword, and people are killing one another. Basing his reasoning on the symbols of the second seal, Bunch relates other portions of Scripture to this next phase of church history:

In the period of church history represented by the red horse, the church has drifted away from the former state of purity of character and the affection that constrained the soldiers of the cross to go forth with the holy zeal that conquers. The church begins to adopt false doctrines and is corrupted by worldly influences. Red or scarlet is symbolic of sin, just as white is the symbol of righteousness. "Though your sins be as scarlet, they shall be as white as snow; though they be red like crimson, they shall be as wool." Isaiah 1:18. The color of the second horse shows its relation to the "red dragon," the "scarlet colored beast," and the woman "arrayed in purple and scarlet colour," called "Babylon the Great, the mother of harlots and abominations of the earth." See Revelation 12:3; 17:1-5. These symbolic representations are satanic in character and work. History attests that the predictions of Paul concerning an apostasy in the church were strikingly fulfilled during the period represented by the red horse. See Acts 20:28-30; 2 Thessalonians 2:3-7.[7]

Time of the Second Seal: A.D. 100 to 325

As the last of the apostles died, a struggle emerged over church authority. During the ten years of the Diocletian persecution from A.D. 303 to 313, many

---
[7]   Ibid., 34-35.

that feared for their lives forsook the faith. God ended that period of persecution, and now those who had fled the church wanted to return. Controversy arose over how to handle these deserters. Part of the church was willing to accept the apostates back into the church, while others wanted the leaders to reject them.

Before the apostles died, they did not appoint others to take their place as apostles, but the Bible is clear that the apostles had chosen bishops or elders to oversee each local church. As the persecution waned, these bishops began to exercise their influence over larger areas. The bishop of Rome felt that he should have more influence because he represented Rome, the capital of the empire.

There was no biblical foundation for the primacy of one of the bishops, neither was this a doctrine of the apostolic church. No one claimed that Peter was the rock upon which the church was built because the early Christians fully understood that the church was built on the Rock of Christ. Peter (*petros*) was merely a stone. God established His church on the Rock (*petra*) that led Israel in the wilderness, namely Christ Himself (1 Corinthians 10:4). These battles within the church started over influence, power, and authority. Ultimately, the majority followed the leadership of the bishop at Rome. He eventually gained power over the other bishops; thus began this unbiblical tradition.

The headship of one bishop led to a hierarchical system that took control of the leaders in the local churches. This led to a schism in the church. Then the church at Rome seized upon the right to grant or deny church membership, while the outlying areas did not take that same stand. As a result, the church under the influence of the pagan Roman Empire compromised with heathenism as it sought to gain converts. These internal struggles continued into the time of the next seal.

Under the red horse seal, pagan rites and ceremonies crept into the church as heathens joined the church, yet kept their superstitious beliefs. Those who objected to this were ostracized by the majority within the church. The philosophies of pagan Rome won within the church, leading to the transition between pagan Rome and the new papal Rome as the bishop of Rome gained power over all the bishops.

This period ended with Constantine's conversion. Rather than a victory for the church, this combination of paganism and Christianity became the Trojan horse that entered the heart of church and took the throne. Thus Satan gained a victory over the most influential bishopric in the empire.

The second seal began with the death of John the Revelator and ended with the conversion of Constantine. The second, third, and fourth centuries were a time of bloody struggles within the church. Unlike the pure church on a white horse that followed the words of Jesus in the first century, the church of this age was willing to use the sword in spiritual battles.

The time of the second seal coincides with the church of Smyrna, A.D. 100 to 325. The Christian church was persecuted by pagan Rome. When this strategy didn't work, Rome embraced the church. Thus began the paganization of the Christian church.

III. Third Seal

Revelation 6:5-6: And when he had opened the third seal, I heard the third beast say, Come and see. And I beheld, and lo a black horse; and he that sat on him had a pair of balances in his hand. ⁶And I heard a voice in the midst of the four beasts say, A measure of wheat for a penny, and three measures of barley for a penny; and *see* thou hurt not the oil and the wine.

The third horse is black, an appropriate color for the time period after the second seal. Note that the rider has balances in his hand. Black is the opposite of white, therefore the church during this time period is the opposite of pure. The paganization of the church is completely fulfilled. The bishopric of Rome gained full control of Western Europe just as he had ascended to primacy over all the other bishops. The black horse represents papal Rome. With imagery from Daniel, Bunch describes church leadership under the third seal:

> The rider of the black horse, representing the responsible leadership of the church, holds in his hand a pair of balances. This has always been, and still is, the emblem of judgment. It represents the authority to weigh evidence and make decisions. Ancient pagan religions recognized a god of scales who weighed the deeds of the dead to determine their reward. "Thou art weighed in the balances and art found wanting," was the message of doom written by the unseen hand on the palace wall of Belshazzar, king of Babylon. A hand holding a pair of balances is still the emblem of justice and judgment and is often engraved on the front of buildings devoted to the administering of justice.[8]

The riders symbolize church leadership; the horse's color shows its spiritual condition. The balances in the rider's hand reveal that the leaders of the church attempt to carry out a work that is not theirs. Only the God of heaven rightfully judges in spiritual issues and reads the heart; the church should determine church membership by upholding Bible standards. Since judgment is also in the hand of civil powers, this clue points to a mingling of church and state. Ultimately, the church uses the civil powers to enforce her judgments because the bishop at Rome claimed to be the sole ruler of heaven and earth. Bunch supports this change in the church with historical evidence:

> The bishop of Rome became the supreme judge and ruler of the world and from his decisions even kings had no appeal. The controversy between Henry IV of Germany, and Pope Gregory VII, which resulted in the humiliation and subjection of the king, is a notable illustration of the

---

[8]   Ibid., 39-40.

judicial power and authority of the church leaders of this period. In the latter part of the thirteenth century, Pope Boniface clothed himself in a cuirass, and with a helmet on his head and a sword in his right hand held aloft, cried out: "Am I not the sovereign pontiff? Is not this the chair of St. Peter? Cannot I protect the rights of the empire? I am a Caesar, I am the emperor," (Giesler, in *Ecclesiastical History*, Vol. 3, p. 140.)[9]

The living creature that introduces the third seal has the face of a man. This symbolizes the church that relies upon human wisdom instead of God's. During this time, human authority took the place of God's authority.

Verse 6: A measure of wheat for a penny, and three measures of barley for a penny; and *see* thou hurt not the oil and the wine. The three great feasts of the Jewish ceremonial system centered around the various harvests in Israel. Each feast reveals some aspect of Christ's work in the courtyard which represents this earth. The two pieces of furniture in the court were the brazen altar and the laver. The brazen altar symbolized the cross and is thus linked with the Passover. Paul says in 1 Corinthians 5:7: "Christ our Passover is sacrificed for us." The laver was full of water, a fitting symbol of the Holy Spirit which was poured out at Pentecost, also called the Feast of Weeks. These first two feasts were fulfilled at Christ's first advent in A.D. 31. The third feast, the Feast of Tabernacles, represents the final harvest of this earth which will take place at Christ's second advent.

Passover came at the beginning of the first harvest of spring barley. Two days after the Passover, the first fruits of grain were waved on the second day of the feast unleavened bread. After the wheat harvest was finished, Pentecost was celebrated. This feast was also called the Feast of Harvest because it took place after the last harvest of grain in the spring (Exodus 23:16). The last feast of the year was the Feast of Tabernacles or Feast of Ingathering which arrived at the conclusion of olive and grape harvests.

Therefore barley, wheat, olives, and grapes—the four dietary staples listed in Revelation 6:6— represent the foundation of the Jewish agricultural economy and feast system. Wheat is mentioned first because it was the most valuable grain. Since the prices for wheat and barley listed in this verse are exorbitant, this represents a time of famine. Barley and wheat were used to make bread, a symbol of the word of God which became a scarce commodity during this time period. The Bible was available, but scarcely used. "The days are coming—declares the Lord Yahweh—when I shall send a famine in the country; not a hunger for food, nor thirst for water, but famine for hearing Yahweh's word" (Amos 8:11; NJB).

Time of the Third Seal: A.D. 325 to 538

The Dark Ages began under the third seal. Treiyer writes about this time period: "The only representative religious power which rose up within the Christian church, in the very capital of the empire, once the Caesars of the Roman empire

---

9   Ibid.

fell, was the papal system. When the empire of imperial Rome fell, there were no more emperors in the millennial city. The only authority that then appears there is the bishop of Rome. He assumes, in the sixth century, not only spiritual prerogatives as the head of the Christian church, but also temporal power."[10]

During this time period, the church kept the common people in ignorance; the black horse is a fitting description of the the spiritual darkness of this time period. The symbol of balances points to the control of civil authority by the church leaders. According to Treiyer, this meant a time of gross spiritual darkness for Western Europe:

> When in the fourth and fifth centuries, the Christian church attained supremacy in the territories of the Roman Empire, Christians started to persecute the heathen, and to employ the weapons of warfare in order to impose their decrees. This is the way the Church of Rome acted even toward other centers of Christendom. In the sixth century, which is the starting point of the ascendancy of the Roman antichrist, temporal weapons are used, more and more, to convert the barbarian or Germanic tribes which had become established in different regions of Europe. . . .
>
> As has been recognized by historians, without Clovis, the king of the Francs, and Justinian, the Eastern emperor, a few years later, Europe would have not been converted to the Roman Catholic faith. What would then have happened to the history of our civilization? They affirm that Christendom would have been developed in a different direction, without having a pope in Rome as the head of the church to dispute his temporal predominance with the European kings. Neither would a king such as Charlemagne have appeared to convert the rest of the empire which was still pagan, into subjects of the Roman religion. Charlemagne employed the same horrific methods of extortion used by Clovis and all those who preceded him in the instauration of the papacy.[11]

The Roman Church, while claiming to be Christian, did not use Christian principles to enlarge its borders. The spirit of true Christianity was lost. Instead of the beauty of Christ in the simplicity of the gospel, the Roman Church used force and violence to gain converts. When force is used, the spirit and power of God is non-existent. Religion that places man's authority over God's becomes a dogmatic, persecuting power, and the beauty of the gospel is lost.

The time of the third seal coincides with the Pergamos period, A.D. 325 to 538, the beginning of the Dark Ages.

---

[10] Alberto Treiyer, *The Seals and the Trumpets* (Siloam Springs, AR: Distinctive Messages, 2005), 50.

[11] Ibid., 77-78.

IV. Fourth Seal

Revelation 6:7-8: And when he had opened the fourth seal, I heard the voice of the fourth beast say, Come and see. [8]And I looked, and behold a pale horse: and his name that sat on him was Death, and Hell followed with him. And power was given unto them over the fourth part of the earth, to kill with sword, and with hunger, and with death, and with the beasts of the earth.

A pale horse with its rider called Death and the Grave follow the black horse. "Hell" in this verse is *hades*, the place of the dead, so a better translation would be "the grave." This agrees with the meaning of *hades* in the rest of Revelation (1:18; 20:13, 14) and the New Testament (Acts 2:27, 31).

The last living creature symbolized by a flying eagle introduces the pale horse. Jesus spoke of the eagle in connection with His second coming: "For as the lightning cometh out of the east, and shineth even unto the west; so shall also the coming of the Son of man be. For wheresoever the carcase is, there will the eagles be gathered together" (Matthew 24:27, 28). Eagles have gathered to feast on the dead. The horse is pale, the color of death, reinforcing the fact that the rider's name is "Death and the Grave."

Spiritual death marks the time of the fourth seal. Truths once prominent in God's church had been lost. The Bible was outlawed during this period, so there was nothing to give life. The church now fought against the Sabbath and the true worship of the Creator. Idols and images became substitutes for the invisible God. The sanctuary and Christ's ministry as High Priest were thrown down and trampled upon by priests who practice baptized paganism. Apostasy was swift once the church lost sight of the Sabbath.

Persecution comes under the fourth seal. Thyatira had some faithful witnesses to the truths of God's word, but they were persecuted mercilessly. As the flying eagle acted as a vulture, so the church murdered Jews and Sabbath keepers, allowing the eagles to eat their flesh. Jesus prophesied that these evil-doers would become food for the eagles at the last great supper for the birds (Revelation 19:17-18).

Even in the bleakest hour, the seals opened by the Lamb remind us that heaven is still in control. Men may reject God's authority and think they can run their own life, but they have lost sight of reality. God permits evil to run its course; therefore prophecy is written in advance of the events so we may know that God foresaw the wicked consequences of defiant decisions. Men may reject God's mercy and warnings, but the seals also look forward to that time when sin comes to an end. His "strange act" will come upon those who hate God and "love death" (Isaiah 28:21; Proverbs 8:36).

This seal is a warning to the pompous church of this period. At the nadir of Israel's apostasy, Isaiah, Hosea, and Amos were sent by God to warn them of impending judgments. Under the fourth seal, the worst apostasy is recorded with the imagery of the pale horse. The attack against God and His people did not come from pagans, but from within the church itself. Rather than the self-sacrificing love of the Lamb, the church appears to be controlled by Satan, butchering those who follow the Bible. Popes and priests become the ministers of death themselves.

The Cathars were nearly exterminated. Because lies were disseminated about them, Kirsch declares: Cathars "were wrongly believed to prefer any kind of sexual activity that did not lead to conception."[12] Actually, the Cathars were a prolific people, proving the stereotype given them by the church to be false. Thus, many false accusations were made against those whom the church wished to liquidate. Like the Cathars, the Waldenses were also hunted like animals and killed.

One branch of the Cathars, know as the Albigenses or "the friends of God," was annihilated by the papal church for their faithfulness to God's word.[13] The Albigenses comprised no small group; according to Hamilton, "they numbered more than one million people in Europe."[14] The church spread rumors and falsehoods about this group of people in order to justify their destruction. Deception helped to accomplish Rome's deadly goal of eliminating supposed heretics.

Nearly all that is known of the Albigenses is gleaned from Catholic sources. Religious leaders destroyed all the records they could find of this people group, leaving only those manuscripts used in defending the actions of the church. Therefore much that is written about this group is suspect. The Roman Church labeled the Albigenses as "family destroyers," claiming "they condemned marriage" and "considered procreation as sin,"[15] according to Hamilton.

On the contrary, the Albigenses were quite prolific, growing to nearly a million in the area known today as southern France. From their own records, Albigenses only advised celibacy for those who were itinerant preachers as these men would not be home often. Rather than condemning marriage, this actually expresses their strong belief in family. Ironically, the Roman Church forced all married priests to separate from their wives when celibacy was imposed upon the priests in 1139.

The Albigenses were also accused of regarding the Scriptures as ridiculous and untruthful in all areas but the gospels, yet their own writings show that they encouraged the use of the whole Bible. Again the Catholic Church was guilty of the accusations they pinned upon others. In 1234 the church made possession of the Bible a criminal offense. The Albigenses were accused of anti-Trinitarianism; however, their writing expressed belief in the divinity of Christ and the need of

---

[12]   Jonathan Kirsch, *The Grand Inquisitor's Manual* (New York: HarperOne, 2008), 20.

[13]   Treiyer, *The Seals and the Trumpets*, 156.

[14]   Bernard Hamilton, *The Medieval Inquisition: Foundations of Medieval History* (New York: Holmes and Meier Publishing, 1981), 78.

[15]   Ibid.

receiving the Holy Spirit. As Jesus said, those who lead godly lives will suffer persecution. As Christ was accused of having a devil, so were His followers.

The year 1184 marked the beginning of the Inquisition. In 1252, this institution of religious torture and execution was then sanctioned by Pope Innocent IV in his papal bull *Ad exstirpanda*. This official document authorized torture as a legitimate means of investigating heresy. How ironic that the man named Innocent instituted the Inquisition that tortured the innocent followers of Christ!

Although the name of the Inquisition has been changed more than once over the last millennium, its purpose has remained the same. Pope John Paul II chose Cardinal Ratzinger in 1981 to be prefect of the Congregation of the Doctrine of the Faith, the modern name for the office of the Inquisition. Later Ratzinger was chosen as pope after John Paul's death, changing his name to Benedict XVI.

The Inquisition has never died. History books are filled with the inhumanities and executions that were carried out by the church in the name of God. With startling clarity, the agnostic historian Durant counts this period as the nadir of human history: "Compared with the persecution of heresy in Europe from 1227 to 1492, the persecution of Christians by the Romans in the first three centuries after Christ was a mild and humane procedure. Making every allowance required of an historian and permitted to a Christian, we must rank the Inquisition, . . . as among the darkest blots on the record of mankind, revealing a ferocity unknown in any beast."[16]

Under the fourth seal, power was given to the church over one-fourth of the earth to kill with sword, hunger, death, and beasts of the earth. The papacy ruled Europe, North Africa, and Western Asia, about one-fourth of the Old World's land area.

Time of the Fourth Seal: A.D. 538 to 1563

Although this period is called the Middle Ages by politically correct scholars, the darkness of the Dark Ages continued in this time period as well. The pagan heresies accepted by the church were now forced upon the people with edict and sword. In 1234, Bibles were banned and burned. The paganized church became the persecuting church. Those who disagreed with the pagan doctrines were killed. Smith summarizes the fourth seal: "The period during which this seal applies can hardly be mistaken. It must refer to the time in which the papacy bore its unrebuked, unrestrained, and persecuting rule, beginning about A.D. 538, and extending to the time when the Reformers began their work of exposing the corruptions of the papal system."[17]

16   Will Durant, *The Age of Faith*, vol. 2, *The Story of Civilization* (New York: Simon and Schuster, 1950), 784; quoted in Alberto R. Treiyer, *Apocalypse: Seals and Trumpets* (Siloam Springs, AR: Distinctive Messages, 2005), 122.

17   Smith, 431.

There is neither time nor space to write all the atrocities which were done in the name of God and Christianity during the period of the fourth seal. The church itself destroyed many of the records of those they called heretics. Papal Rome arose out of the ashes of the Roman Empire and exercised far more power and influence than that of its predecessor. The church claimed not only political power, but also spiritual power over the dictates of men's hearts.

The time of the fourth seal or the pale horse coincides with the Thyatira period, 538 to 1563, a time known as the worst in history because of the inhumanity of the so-called Christian church.

V. Fifth Seal

Revelation 6:9-11: And when he had opened the fifth seal, I saw under the altar the souls of them that were slain for the word of God, and for the testimony which they held: [10]And they cried with a loud voice, saying, How long, O Lord, holy and true, dost thou not judge and avenge our blood on them that dwell on the earth? [11]And white robes were given unto every one of them; and it was said unto them, that they should rest yet for a little season, until their fellowservants also and their brethren, that should be killed as they *were*, should be fulfilled.

The four living creatures announced the first four seals, but the fifth seal opens with the cries of the souls who were slain, tortured, and martyred for their faithfulness to the word of God. The blood of the Albigenses and Waldenses cry out from under the altar for vindication and vengeance. Their "speaking" is symbolic language, echoing the words used in Genesis 4:10: "And he said, What hast thou done? the voice of thy brother's blood crieth unto me from the ground." This language obviously symbolizes their blood begging for judgment and provides evidence that the time for the judgment must be near. From the perspective of the ancient temple, Bunch adds to the meaning of these verses:

> It is evident that the altar of the fifth seal must represent the earth on which the victims were slain and under which they are buried. In the typical temple there were two altars: the altar of incense in the holy place, and the altar of burnt offerings in the court where the victims were slain and the sacrifices offered. The blood of the sacrificial victims was poured out at the foot of the altar on which they were offered. See Leviticus 4:7. Under the altar of burnt offerings in Solomon's temple was a deep excavation in the solid rock into which the blood of the thousands of victims ran or was poured and from which it emptied into the Kedron. This is now in the middle of the Mosque of Omar and is covered with a marble slab. The Moslems call it "The Well of Spirits."[18]

---

[18]   Bunch, "The Revelation," 44.

Obviously this period follows the pale horse of death and the grave. One-fourth of the earth has endured papal persecution, and the blood of the martyrs cries out to God for justice. Some would like to use vengeance for the Greek word ἐκδικεῖς (pronounced ek-dik-eis) which more often means "to vindicate" than "to avenge." Bunch believes the answer to the cry from under the altar was the Reformation: "When Europe was awakened to the real nature of the papacy as the result of the Reformation, a cry for vengeance was the logical result of the change of attitude toward those who died as 'heretics' but were now being vener-ated as 'saints' and 'martyrs.'"[19]

The white robes given them symbolize the righteousness of Christ. White is a symbol of purity, thus these robes depict their faithfulness even to death. God will reward them for their loyalty in the face of persecution. However, there would still be a short time when more people would be martyred for their faith. The time for judgment has not yet come.

Time of the Fifth Seal: 1563 to 1798

The time depicted by the fifth seal was during the church of the Reformation, the dead church of the fifth church era. The dead souls under the altar in the fifth seal provide an interesting, yet ironic match with the dead church of Sardis. The church of the fifth seal isn't crying out for justice, but the dead slain before this time are more noted than God's church during this time period. The slain souls represent all who were killed under the previous four seals. It is estimated that more than fifty million were martyred for the sake of Christ from the time of the cross to the Reformation. Whole people groups were persecuted and de-stroyed for their unwillingness to compromise with Rome. Historians agree that the number of Christian martyrs is greater than those murdered by Hitler and Stalin combined. For these martyrs, the promise is sure: Be faithful unto death, and I will give you a crown of life (Revelation 2:10).[20]

The period covered by the fifth seal coincides with the Sardis period: 1563 to 1798, a time when the persecution was coming to an end. The Protestant Reformation opened way for the re-discovery of even more Bible truths during the next era.

VI. Sixth Seal

Revelation 6:12-17: And I beheld when he had opened the sixth seal, and, lo, there was a great earthquake; and the sun became black as sackcloth of hair, and the moon became as blood; [13]And the stars of heaven fell unto the earth, even as a fig tree casteth her untimely figs, when she is shaken of a mighty wind. [14]And the heaven departed as a scroll when it is rolled together; and

---

[19]   Ibid., 45.

[20]   For more information on this time period, see J. A. Wylie, *The History of the Waldenses* (London: Cassell and Co., 1860).

every mountain and island were moved out of their places. ¹⁵And the kings of the earth, and the great men, and the rich men, and the chief captains, and the mighty men, and every bondman, and every free man, hid themselves in the dens and in the rocks of the mountains; ¹⁶And said to the mountains and rocks, Fall on us, and hide us from the face of him that sitteth on the throne, and from the wrath of the Lamb: ¹⁷For the great day of his wrath is come; and who shall be able to stand?

Notice the language here. When the sixth seal is opened, the description is literal. These are real events that were predicted by Jesus in Matthew 24 and Luke 21. Smith clarifies the timing of these fulfillments of prophecy:

> The sixth seal does not bring us to the second advent of Christ, although it embraces events closely connected with that coming. It introduces the fearful commotions of the elements, described as the heavens rolling together as a scroll, the breaking up of the surface of the earth, and the confession by the wicked that the great day of God's wrath is come. They are doubtless in momentary expectation of seeing the King appear in glory. But the seal stops just short of that event. The personal appearing of Christ must therefore be allotted to the next seal.[21]

The sixth seal is introduced in the context of a "great earthquake" and continues with the signs Jesus gave to His disciples of the end of the world. Great earthquakes in different places would herald His second coming along with the three events mentioned in verse 12. In the time of the sixth seal, there would be (1) a great earthquake, (2) the sun as black as sackcloth, (3) the blood-red moon, and (4) the falling of the stars. All four herald the opening of the sixth seal and the time of the end.

The language here suggests that the sixth and seventh seals must be taken as one. Remember the context is the pre-advent judgment that determines before the coming of Christ those who are holy and those who are not. Now is the time to be prepared for the final judgment. The last two seals describe the signs that come just before the great day of the Lord, better understood as the final judgment.

In the previous seal, the martyrs called out for judgment; the sixth seal heralds the coming judgment and the coming King. The day of God's wrath is coming in answer to the call for vengeance by the blood of millions of martyrs. The letters to the seven churches and the seven seals give the approximate time of these events. The signs of the sixth seal announce the nearness of the judgment predicted by Daniel 7 and the surety of Jesus' soon coming. These events also prepare us for the seventh seal. Notice the dates for these four great events:

1. Great earthquake: Great Lisbon earthquake, November 1, 1755

---

[21] Smith, 473.

2. Sun darkened: Dark Day, May 19, 1780

3. Moon became like blood: after midnight on May 20, 1780

4. Stars of heaven fell to the earth: Falling of the stars, November 14, 1833

Great Lisbon Earthquake: November 1, 1755

The first sign of the sixth seal was the great earthquake. Jesus foretold in Luke 21:11, **"And great earthquakes shall be in divers places."** History records that the Lisbon earthquake was the first of the great modern earthquakes. Others may have had the same magnitude, but they did not have as profound effect on the Christian world as did the Lisbon earthquake which was felt over an area of four million square miles. Since that historic quake, there has been an intensifying of earthquakes. This is exactly what Jesus said would happen before He comes.

The Lisbon Earthquake was not the only great earthquake, but it was the defining earthquake of the sixth seal. This great earthquake impressed the minds of people who lived in the territory that was strongly influenced by the papal power. Therefore the great Lisbon Earthquake ushers in the sixth seal.

Sun Darkened and Moon turned to blood: May 19 and 20, 1780

This reached fulfillment in the Dark Day of May 19, 1780. History records a strange, deep darkness over New England that reached as far west as Albany, New York and as far east as Portland, Maine. At this time, the highest concentration of the American population was located in the New England states. Thus this Dark Day became a most remarkable sign to the inhabitants of this new nation, formed only four years earlier.

The darkness was so great that people in many places had to light candles at midday. The darkness remained until a while after midnight. The moon, although it was full at that time, gave no light. Many people believed that the "day of judgment" had come. No satisfactory scientific reason for this darkness has ever been given, except what we find in the words of Christ. The "dark day" and the "moon turned to blood" were to be signs that His coming was near.

White records this grand manifestation in the heavens: Shortly after midnight on the twentieth of May, "the darkness disappeared, and the moon, when first visible, had the appearance of blood."[22] This remarkable event fulfilled the prophecy.

Falling of the Stars: November 14, 1833

This spectacular display of falling stars in 1833 was witnessed by many, including White who was alive at this time. Her comments include many descriptions found in the newspapers of that day:

---

[22] White, *The Great Controversy*, 307.

John in the Revelation declared, as he beheld in vision the scenes that should herald the day of God: "The stars of heaven fell unto the earth, even as a fig tree casteth her untimely figs, when she is shaken of a mighty wind." Revelation 6:13. This prophecy received a striking and impressive fulfillment in the great meteoric shower of November 13, 1833. That was the most extensive and wonderful display of falling stars which has ever been recorded; "the whole firmament, over all the United States, being then, for hours, in fiery commotion! No celestial phenomenon has ever occurred in this country, since its first settlement, which was viewed with such intense admiration by one class in the community, or with so much dread and alarm by another." "Its sublimity and awful beauty still linger in many minds. . . . Never did rain fall much thicker than the meteors fell toward the earth; east, west, north, and south, it was the same. In a word, the whole heavens seemed in motion. . . . The display, as described in Professor Silliman's *Journal*, was seen all over North America. . . . From two o'clock until broad daylight, the sky being perfectly serene and cloudless, an incessant play of dazzlingly brilliant luminosities was kept up in the whole heavens."—R. M. Devens, *American Progress; or, The Great Events of the Greatest Century*, ch. 28, pars. 1-5.

"No language, indeed, can come up to the splendor of that magnificent display; . . . no one who did not witness it can form an adequate conception of its glory. It seemed as if the whole starry heavens had congregated at one point near the zenith, and were simultaneously shooting forth, with the velocity of lightning, to every part of the horizon; and yet they were not exhausted—thousands swiftly followed in the tracks of thousands, as if created for the occasion."—F. Reed, in the *Christian Advocate and Journal*, Dec. 13, 1833. "A more correct picture of a fig tree casting its figs when blown by a mighty wind, it was not possible to behold."— "The Old Countryman," in Portland *Evening Advertiser*, Nov. 26, 1833.

In the New York *Journal of Commerce* of November 14, 1833, appeared a long article regarding this wonderful phenomenon, containing this statement: "No philosopher or scholar has told or recorded an event, I suppose, like that of yesterday morning. A prophet eighteen hundred years ago foretold it exactly, if we will be at the trouble of understanding stars falling to mean falling stars, . . . in the only sense in which it is possible to be literally true."

Thus was displayed the last of those signs of His coming, concerning which Jesus bade His disciples: "When ye shall see all these things, *know* that it is near, even at the doors." Matthew 24:33. After these signs, John beheld, as the great event next impending, the heavens departing as a scroll, while the earth quaked, mountains and islands removed out of their places, and the wicked in terror sought to flee from the presence of the Son of man. Revelation 6:12-17.

Many who witnessed the falling of the stars, looked upon it as a herald of the coming judgment, "an awful type, a sure forerunner, a merciful sign, of that great and dreadful day."—"The Old Countryman," in Portland *Evening Advertiser,* Nov. 26, 1833. Thus the attention of the people was directed to the fulfillment of prophecy, and many were led to give heed to the warning of the second advent.[23]

Verses 14-16: And the heaven departed as a scroll when it is rolled together; and every mountain and island were moved out of their places. [15]And the kings of the earth, and the great men, and the rich men, and the chief captains, and the mighty men, and every bondman, and every free man, hid themselves in the dens and in the rocks of the mountains; [16]And said to the mountains and rocks, Fall on us, and hide us from the face of him that sitteth on the throne, and from the wrath of the Lamb: [17]For the great day of his wrath is come; and who shall be able to stand?

The language indicates a future event, the second coming of Christ, in connection with what has come before it. Verse 14 must be understood in light of verses 15 to 17, according to the *Adventist Bible Commentary*: "The picture here is of the sky being rolled up like a roll of parchment. In ancient cosmology the sky was considered to be a solid vault above the earth. The prophet now sees the sky rolled back, that the earth may stand unshielded before God. . . . This event is yet future and is closely connected with the actual appearance of the Son of man in the heavens."[24]

The climax of the ages is presented in graphic language. Verse 15 names every station in life from kings all the way down to bond servants. No one is left out here. Their reaction tells us that they are not ready to see the King of kings in peace. They have not heeded the warnings of the seven churches and seven seals. That is why they are not prepared for the return of the Lamb. This vision of His coming linked with the terror of those who are unprepared marks the urgency of this message in the sixth seal. The judgment is coming, and Jesus will return. Then there will be no place to hide. Today we may choose whose side we will take. Will you choose the Lamb? Without Him, you will fear the return of the Lord in judgment.

Verse 17: For the great day of his wrath is come; and who shall be able to stand? This rhetorical question is answered in the next chapter of Revelation.

---

[23]   Ibid., 333-334.

[24]   *The Seventh-day Adventist Bible Commentary,* 7:779.

Time of the Sixth Seal: 1798 to 1844

The time of the sixth seal begins in 1798 with the end of the 1260-day prophecy. Its message correlates with the church of Philadelphia. The church comes alive with the preaching of the return of Christ. They faithfully predicted the coming of the judgment as their understanding of the book of Daniel increased. Those who joined in the Advent Awakening believed that Jesus would return in 1844, and everyone would then face the judgment. They discovered that indeed the judgment had come, but in a way they had not expected.

Laodicea, the next church, would be the seventh and the last: the people of the judgment. The "seventh-month" movement of 1844 spread the message of the great antitypical Day of Atonement and gave birth to the final message for the end of the world. The seventh church and seventh seal and the seventh-month movement would also open the eyes of God's people to a long-forgotten commandment. With the opening of the heavenly ark of the covenant pictured in Revelation 11:19, they would rediscover this long-lost truth in the heart of the Ten Commandments.

CHAPTER NINETEEN

Revelation 7

Introduction

C hapter 7 answers the question of the sixth seal, and is, in that sense, a continuation of the sixth seal. With the vision of terrified people facing the return of the wrathful Lamb, the question arose in the last verse of the sixth chapter of Revelation: Who will be able to stand? This question needs to be answered.

The ones who are able to stand during the return of the Lamb are those who have been sealed with the seal of the living God. All those that do not have the seal of the living God will hide in the caves and secret places of this earth, but they cannot hide from the face of God.

The word in the original language is ἀριθμός (*ar-ith-mos'*) with the following definitions: (1) a fixed and definite number, or (2) an indefinite number, a multitude. John did not count the number of the 144,000; he heard the number (verse 4). Internal and external evidence point to the 144,000 as a symbolic number in Revelation, the symbolic book. Doukhan gives reasons to support this conclusion: "The style, language, and the numeric symbolism of the text all testify to the presence of all Israel. The 144,000 depict Israel marching as a whole. It is the 'all Israel' dreamed by the apostle Paul (Rom.11:26), the 'complete' number of the saved, as alluded to in the fifth seal (Revelation 6:11)."[1]

Nearly all Christian commentators agree that the 144,000 belong to *spiritual Israel*, not literal Israel. If those that make up the 144,000 are symbolic of *spiritual Israel*, then it would only make sense that the number has spiritual significance, rather than the importance of the number itself. The number itself is significant. Each of the twelve tribes is represented in this number by 12,000.

Are they 12,000 Jews from each tribe? After the Babylonian captivity, it was difficult in Ezra's day for Levites to prove their lineage (Ezra 2:61-63). Matters were even worse for the ten northern tribes who reverted to heathenism and intermarried with the surrounding nations. When John wrote the book of Revelation, tracing the geneology of the tribes became humanly impossible. Doukhan notes: "In Yohanan's [John's] time, however, the records of who belonged to most tribes

---

[1]   Doukhan, *Secrets of Revelation*, 73.

had disappeared with the destruction of the Temple."[2] Jesus did not give His promises only to ethnic Hebrews. The great commission of the Master included all nations, both Jews and Gentiles. Paul summarizes this fact: "If ye be Christ's, then are ye Abraham's seed, and heirs according to the promise" (Galatians 3:29).

Not ethnic heritage, but the *sealing* makes them a part of the 144,000. This means that people are not born into the 144,000. Therefore it is not a specific race or ethnic group. The 144,000 represent the lives of those who truly profess Jesus and overcome by the blood of the Lamb. Revelation moves in time through the sanctuary and through the experience of salvation. Let us hear the message of Revelation 7.

Revelation 7:1-3: And after these things I saw four angels standing on the four corners of the earth, holding the four winds of the earth, that the wind should not blow on the earth, nor on the sea, nor on any tree. ²And I saw another angel ascending from the east, having the seal of the living God: and he cried with a loud voice to the four angels, to whom it was given to hurt the earth and the sea, ³ Saying, Hurt not the earth, neither the sea, nor the trees, till we have sealed the servants of our God in their foreheads.

The angels standing at the four corners of the earth are symbolic of God's power to hold back worldwide strife. The world would have destroyed itself by now if it were not for the restraining power of the Master of the universe. The forces of violence and bloodshed are held back so that the sealing of God's people can be completed. This work is finished before the seventh seal is opened.

Sealing the Obedient

With angels holding back the world from destruction, this sealing process must be of vital importance. The Holy Spirit has a role in the sealing of the believers: "After that ye believed, ye were sealed with that Holy Spirit of promise" (Ephesians 1:13). When we accept Him by faith, not only as our Savior, but also as our Lord, we enter into the holy place experience of sanctification, a daily walk of obedience by His grace. Peter declares boldly to the Jewish leaders: "We are His witnesses of these things; and so is also the Holy Ghost, whom God hath given to them that **obey** Him" (Acts 5:32).

With Jesus as Lord of our life and the King on the throne of our hearts, we are spiritual Israel. Because we belong to Christ, we are Abraham's seed. Like Abraham, we demonstrate our love to God by obedience to His commands. The fourth commandment is called the "sign" or "seal" of sanctification: "Verily My Sabbaths ye shall keep: for it is a sign between Me and you throughout your generations; that ye may know that I am the LORD that doth sanctify you" (Exodus 31:13).

Those that are sealed are forgiven, purified, and sanctified. The sanctuary symbolized this experience. In the court of the sanctuary, the altar of burnt offering represented the cross. All who accept by faith the death, burial, and

2   Ibid., 71.

resurrection of Jesus are made just and right with God. The laver represented baptism and cleansing from sin. Then by faith we follow Jesus into the holy place experience. Eating His bread by the light of the lampstand symbolizes reading His word with the enlightenment of the Holy Spirit. His intercession and grace empower us to obey all that we learn from His word. "Sanctified by obeying His word," we become more like Jesus day by day.[3]

Another angel ascends from the east, the direction of the entrance to the sanctuary. God's sealed servants obey Him. Why are they sealed in their foreheads? Our frontal lobe, just behind our forehead, is where we make decisions and choices that form our character. By the grace of God, the sealing process transforms our character and makes us like Jesus. Before we see God face to face, Christ must be the Lord and King of our character.

Revelation 7:4-8: And I heard the number of them which were sealed: and there were sealed an hundred and forty and four thousand of all the tribes of the children of Israel. [5]Of the tribe of Juda were sealed twelve thousand. Of the tribe of Reuben were sealed twelve thousand. Of the tribe of Gad were sealed twelve thousand. [6]Of the tribe of Aser were sealed twelve thousand. Of the tribe of Nephthalim were sealed twelve thousand. Of the tribe of Manasses were sealed twelve thousand. [7]Of the tribe of Simeon were sealed twelve thousand. Of the tribe of Levi were sealed twelve thousand. Of the tribe of Issachar were sealed twelve thousand. [8]Of the tribe of Zabulon were sealed twelve thousand. Of the tribe of Joseph were sealed twelve thousand. Of the tribe of Benjamin were sealed twelve thousand.

This particular order given the tribes in Revelation 7 is not found anywhere else in the Bible and seems to have no rhyme nor reason. Genesis 29 to 30 gives the brothers' birth order.

In Genesis 49, Jacob groups the names, not according to birth order, but does something unusual. He lists all of Leah's children: Reuben, Simeon, Levi, Judah, Zebulun, and Issachar. Then comes Dan, the firstborn of Rachel's servant Bilhah, and Gad, the firstborn of Leah's servant Zilpah. Zilpah's second child, Asher, and Bilhah's second son, Naphtali, are then named. Lastly, Rachel's sons are given: Joseph and Benjamin. Jacob's blessings and curses give insight into the characters and behavior of his sons. Genesis 49 was written in the context of chapter 48: Jacob's blessing upon the sons of Joseph. Jacob intentionally gave the blessing of the firstborn to the youngest son and promised Joseph a double portion among the sons of Israel.

Jacob's purpose in Genesis 49 was to reveal future of each tribe in the last days. Using the prophetic messages in Genesis 49 and the meanings of the names given to each son in Genesis 30, a message of salvation emerges as we read the

---

[3]   Franklin E. Beldon, from the lyrics of his hymn "Cover with His Life," 1899.

character descriptions of Jacob's sons according to the tribal order given in Revelation 7. Notice the names of each tribe and their prophetic blessings.

1. Judah: **praise**
2. Reuben: **behold, a son!**
3. Gad: **a great company**
4. Asher: **blessed**
5. Naphtali: **wrestles and prevails**
6. Manasseh: **forgetting**
7. Simeon: **[the Lord] hears**
8. Levi: **joined [to the Lord]**
9. Issachar: **bought with a pri**ce
10. Zebulun: **[God] will dwell**
11. Joseph: **fruitful bough**
12. Benjamin: **son of the right hand** (signifies rulership)

These blessings and name meanings, when ordered according to Revelation 7, describe the Christian experience. Beginning with your first acceptance of Jesus as your Savior and Lord and ending with the heavenly promise, the last-day blessings of Jacob describe every true Christian and the 144,000.

When you realize what He has done, you **praise** God! You are now a **son** or daughter of God, along with **a great company** of fellow believers. You are **blessed** because you have **wrestled and prevailed** with God. Knowing your own weakness, you forgive yourself and others, **forgetting** the wrongs others have done. **The Lord hears** your plea to be **joined to the Lord** because you were **bought with a price**. **God will dwell** with you and make you a **fruitful bough**. You are now the **son of His right hand** of God and will reign with Him forever.

Character transformation tells the story of the gospel in the individual lives of the believers. Jacob, the heel-grabbing trickster, was transformed by the grace of God and renamed by his Lord. As the morning dawned in that famous wrestling match, God spoke to his repentant son, "Thy name shall be called no more Jacob, but Israel: for as a prince hast thou power with God and with men, and hast prevailed" (Genesis 32:28).

In Haskell's book *The Cross and Its Shadow*, pages 287 to 367 are devoted to the characteristics of each tribe, the transforming power of the gospel of Jesus, and the 144,000. "The Lord names individuals according to their character," Haskell asserts, and since the 144,000 are grouped according to the names of the twelve tribes of Israel, "there must be something in the character of Jacob's sons and of the twelve tribes of Israel worthy of careful study."[4]

---

4   Stephen N. Haskell, *The Cross and Its Shadow* (Nashville, TN: Southern Publishing Association, 1970), 287.

This transformation of character is most clearly seen in the life of Judah. You could say that his was a dysfunctional family, the kind that Hollywood loves to display. Chapters 38 and 39 of Genesis are strategically placed next to each other to highlight the difference between the impurity of Judah and the integrity of Joseph. And just as Joseph's future changed dramatically when he refused the advances of Pharaoh's wife, so Judah's life began to change when he admitted that he had wronged his daughter-in-law Tamar.

Judah's change of heart and character was clearly evident in his offer to pledge his life for Benjamin's safety (Genesis 43:3-10). In Egypt, Judah earnestly pleaded to be punished and imprisoned in place of Benjamin (Genesis 43:18-34). Haskell concludes: "By strict integrity to principle, Judah had won the confidence of his father and his brethren. The whole story is told in the blessing pronounced over Judah by his aged father, just before his death: 'Judah, thou art he whom thy brethren shall praise.'"[5]

Levi had given himself over to cruelty and murder, but by the blood of the Lamb, the tribe of Levi was the first to stand up for the Lord during the apostasy of the golden calf. Benjamin was transformed from a "ravening wolf" to one who would boldly stand in defense of God's people. One of the most notable members of the tribe of Benjamin was Saul of Tarsus. He rabidly persecuted the followers of Christ, but after he met Jesus and submitted to His Lordship, Saul became Paul, the noble defender of the faith. Every one who passes through those tribal gates of the New Jerusalem will have a story to tell. Regardless of their home environment or their inherited tendencies, each child of God has become an overcomer.

On the list in Revelation 7, one of the tribes is missing. There are twelve on the list: Joseph has his double portion of blessing, listed along with his son Manesseh. Why is one tribe missing? Before answering that question, look at the following list. When Israel left Egypt, they camped around the tabernacle in a specific order. As you can see, there were actually 13 tribes listed:

1. Levi—surrounding the tabernacle

2. Judah—east: flag of the lion

3. Issachar—east

4. Zebulun—east

5. Reuben—south: flag of the man

6. Simeon—south

7. Gad—south

8. Ephraim—west: flag of the ox

9. Manasseh—west

---

[5] Ibid., 307.

10. Benjamin—west

11. Dan—north: flag of the eagle

12. Asher—north

13. Naphtali—north

Although Joseph's name per se is missing from the camping list, he is actually doubly represented by his two sons, Ephraim and Manasseh. Again, Joseph received the double blessing promised by his father. Ephraim's standard was raised even though Manasseh was the oldest. This also speaks of Jacob's bestowal of the firstborn's blessing upon Ephraim, the youngest. These blessings were given under the direction and inspiration of God.

The Missing Tribe: Now let's look at the list in Revelation 7: only one of Jacob's sons is missing. Dan is replaced with Manasseh, the first born of Joseph. Why is Dan missing from the list of the sealed tribes of Israel? Listen to Jacob's prophecy about Dan in Genesis 49:16-18 and learn from the words inspired by the Holy Spirit: "Dan shall **judge** his people, as one of the tribes of Israel. Dan shall be a **serpent** by the way, an adder in the path, that biteth the horse heels, so that his rider shall fall backward. I have waited for thy salvation, O LORD."

Because Dan judges people, Jacob compares him to a poisonous snake. Like the devil, Dan is a critical thinker who induces others to fall spiritually. Those who are sealed for God's eternal kingdom will not "bite" or be judgmental and critical, causing others to fall away from Christ.

Manasseh replaces Dan in the list of Revelation 7 because his name means "forgetting." Manasseh was able to forget the wrongs of others even as his father Joseph "forgot" and forgave the cruel treatment from his brothers. Those who become like Jesus will forget the past mistakes of others. The message the missing tribe of Dan tells us that critical, judgmental people will not be a part of spiritual Israel. They cannot be sealed because they are not like Jesus. May we be forgiving like Manasseh and not critical like Dan!

The tribes listed as the 144,000 warn us of our need to prepare for the judgment. Because of the critical spirit cherished in his character, the missing tribe of Dan represents those Christians who claim the power of Christ, but do now allow Him to transform their lives. This chapter also calls us to a growing and life-transforming experience with Jesus. The message of the 144,000 answers the question, "Who is able to stand?" The answer comes through loud and clear: "Those who grow in their relationship with Jesus." This growth begins with justification at the cross and continues with sanctification, a life of loving obedience to the Lordship of Christ. The last step is glorification at the end of the final judgment. This is the sealing process.

The blood of the righteous cry out for God's judgment under the fifth seal. Eleven of Jacob's sons are worthy; one is not. All of these messages are set in *judgment language.* When the twelve tribes are sealed, they are ready for the fiercest storms to blow. When Christ returns, He knows who are His. Jesus is bringing His reward with Him, so the sealing process involves God's judgment before Jesus returns.

That reward is the fulfillment of God's covenant or agreement. Our acceptance of His mercy and promises is revealed through our relationship with Jesus and growth in obedience to His will. "If you love Me, keep My commandments" (John 14:15). When Jesus comes, He will give the final installment of His promise to all who are faithful and obedient to His word—"immortality," eternal life with our Savior. Yes, immortality or glorification is the final installment. This gift has not yet been bestowed, but it soon will be given to those who are obedient by His grace to the will of God.

Revelation 7:9-12: After this I beheld, and, lo, a great multitude, which no man could number, of all nations, and kindreds, and people, and tongues, stood before the throne, and before the Lamb, clothed with white robes, and palms in their hands; ¹⁰And cried with a loud voice, saying, Salvation to our God which sitteth upon the throne, and unto the Lamb. ¹¹And all the angels stood round about the throne, and *about* the elders and the four beasts, and fell before the throne on their faces, and worshipped God, ¹²Saying, Amen: Blessing, and glory, and wisdom, and thanksgiving, and honour, and power, and might, *be* unto our God for ever and ever. Amen.

The white robes and palms in their hands are symbols of the Feast of Tabernacles. The first fruits have already been gathered and the harvest completed. The Feast of Tabernacles also celebrated the end of Israel's wilderness wanderings and their entrance into the "promised land." Like Israel, this vast crowd has made it to the "promised land" triumphantly without tasting death.

The 144,000 and the great multitude correlate with the first fruits and the main harvest respectively. The whole harvest is represented by the great multitude that no one could number; the 144,000 represent the first fruits of the harvest. Their words are a simple, heart-felt cry full of gratitude for such a great salvation as they fall down and worship their Creator. This heavenly scene is a preview of what will happen after the final trumpet sounds and the final seal is opened.

Revelation 7:13-17: And one of the elders answered, saying unto me, What are these which are arrayed in white robes? and whence came they? ¹⁴And I said unto him, Sir, thou knowest. And he said to me, These are they which came out of great tribulation, and have washed their robes, and made them white in the blood of the Lamb. ¹⁵Therefore are they before the throne of God, and serve him day and night in his temple: and he that sitteth on the throne shall dwell among them. ¹⁶They shall hunger no more, neither thirst any more; neither shall the sun light on them, nor any heat. ¹⁷For the Lamb which is in the

midst of the throne shall feed them, and shall lead them unto living fountains of waters: and God shall wipe away all tears from their eyes.

These verses indicate clearly heavenly scenes that preview the future. John describes the people who will be able to stand when Jesus comes as he is pointed ahead to their final reward. Verse 17 clearly points to the time of Revelation 21:4, the consummation of the Revelation, when all tears will be wiped away. The sixth seal points forward to a time when all is finished. This is similar to the messages of the sixth church and sixth seal.

From 1798 to 1844, people expected Jesus to come in their lifetime and interpreted everything through that filter. From every church, people who believed the advent message prepared for the return of their Lord. Like the disciples before them, they thought that the judgment and the coming of Christ were one and the same event. They were right about the importance of 1844, but they did not understand the entire sanctuary message and the fulfillment of feasts. The Day of Atonement was not the end of the yearly feasts. Earth's final harvest and the fulfillment of the Feast of Tabernacles were still in the future. The next section parallels Israel's entry into the promised land with the prophecies that are yet to be fulfilled for God's people today.

Examples from the Exodus

The sufferings of God's great last-day multitude listed in Revelation 7:16—hunger, thirst, and heat—allude to the Exodus. Like ancient Israel, the spiritual Israelites of the last days go through a time of suffering. Before Moses led Israel out of Egypt, God's people were given a test: Would they keep the Sabbath or not? They obeyed, even though it brought more persecution upon them (Exodus 5:4-9). Spiritual Israel also passes the test of obedience in the last days. "Here are they that keep the commandments of God, and the faith of Jesus" (Revelation 14:12).

Ancient Israel was protected while the seven last plagues fell upon the unbelieving Egyptians. Those who were obedient put the mark of lamb's blood on their doorposts, and therefore the destroying angel passed over them. This is the origin of Passover. The same is true of these sealed tribes of spiritual Israel. The blood of the Lamb is on the doorposts of their hearts. As the seven last plagues are poured out on the wicked, God's obedient people are protected as He promised: "A thousand shall fall at thy side, and ten thousand at thy right hand; but it shall not come nigh thee. Only with thine eyes shalt thou behold and see the reward of the wicked" (Psalm 91:7-8).

As the seventh plague fell on the Egyptians, Israel of old escaped from their captors. So it will be in the last days. The seventh plague that is so devastating to the wicked brings deliverance to God's people as Jesus comes in the clouds to rescue His people. The saints in the last days have washed their robes and made them white in the blood of Christ, their Passover Lamb. Worthy is the Lamb that was slain!

CHAPTER TWENTY

Revelation 8

The Seventh Seal: The Feast of Tabernacles

Revelation 8:1: And when he had opened the seventh seal, there was silence in heaven about the space of half an hour.

A s the seventh seal is opened there is silence in heaven for a half hour. In prophetic time, this would be about one week. To calculate this, remember that one prophetic day equals one literal year. Because there are 24 hours in a day, you could substitute 24 hours for one day. Therefore one prophetic day (24 prophetic hours) equals one literal year. Since 24 prophetic hours equal one literal year, there would be 2 prophetic hours for each literal month. Hence half an hour of prophetic time would be about one week of literal time, or seven literal days.

In connection with the setting of the palm branches and white robes in chapter 7, these seven literal days would match the celebration of the Feast of Tabernacles. This last feast of the year began with a Sabbath, continued for six days, and then ended on another Sabbath (Leviticus 23:33-36). The Hebrew word *sukkot* is plural and refers to the temporary booths made of freshly cut tree branches that people lived in during this celebration.[1] It was also know as the Feast of Ingathering because it came after the last harvest.

In the fall, *Sukkot* celebrated the harvest with all the fruits gathered and safely stored. This rightly fits the end of the world when Jesus comes to harvest the earth and take His harvest home. In this fulfillment of *Sukkot* we will have two Sabbaths plus six days between them to "camp" with Jesus on our way to the city of God. The feast ends with the Sabbath rest.

There will be silence in heaven in heaven for seven days because we will take a leisurely trip back to heaven with Jesus. Describing her vision, White writes of this scene: "We all entered the cloud together, and were seven days ascending to

---

[1]   Genesis 33:12-17 tells the story of Jacob who traveled back home slowly with his family and flocks. Verse 17 is the first use of *sukkot* in the Scriptures.

the sea of glass."[2] These seven days come after the return of Jesus. Silence reigns in heaven because no heavenly being wants to miss this magnificent event! Jesus finally gathers His children home, taking a seven-day march through the universe before they return to sit down at the table for their first Sabbath in heaven.

The seventh seal and the silence in heaven represent the second advent of Jesus when all the holy angels return with Him to this earth to gather the harvest of souls. In context, those harvested are the first fruits and the great multitude symbolized in chapter 7 as participants in the Feast of Ingathering or *Sukkot*. This feast symbolizes of the return of Jesus and the emptying of heaven as the holy beings join Him for the final harvest of the faithful on the earth. When the faithful and all the angels return to heaven with Jesus, they celebrate the first Sabbath rest in heaven at the end of the fulfillment of *Sukkot*. What a time that will be! No more worry, no more fear, no more wondering of what tomorrow holds, no more anxiety. We are finally home in the place called the heavenly Canaan.

Prelude to the Trumpets

Revelation 8:2-5: And I saw the seven angels which stood before God; and to them were given seven trumpets. [3]And another angel came and stood at the altar, having a golden censer; and there was given unto him much incense, that he should offer *it* with the prayers of all saints upon the golden altar which was before the throne. [4]And the smoke of the incense, *which came* with the prayers of the saints, ascended up before God out of the angel's hand. [5]And the angel took the censer, and filled it with fire of the altar, and cast *it* into the earth: and there were voices, and thunderings, and lightnings, and an earthquake.

Verse 2: Smith comments: "This verse introduces a new and distinct series of events. In the seals we have had the history of the church from the cross to Christ's coming. In the seven trumpets now introduced we have the principal political and warlike events that occur during the same time."[3]

Verses 3-5: The censer, coals of fire, and altar of incense point to the holy place ministry of Christ. These events announce the coming of the seventh seal. The golden altar of incense is now the center of activity for the trumpets; thus moving from the table of showbread which was the center of the seals.

Trumpets are used in feast and sanctuary imagery to sound the warning: Judgment is coming! "Blow ye the trumpet in Zion, and sound and alarm in My holy mountain: let all the inhabitants of the land tremble: for the day of the LORD cometh, for it is nigh at hand" (Joel 2:1). Stefanovic relates Revelation's trumpets to the ceremonies of ancient Israel:

[2]   Ellen G. White, *Early Writings* (Washington, DC: Review and Herald, 1945), 16.

[3]   Smith, 474.

John observes **seven angels** standing before God with **seven trumpets**, prepared to herald a new series of woes to be sent to the earth and its inhabitants. Before the angels blow the trumpets, a new symbolic scene catches John's attention. This introductory scene of the blowing of the seven trumpets sets the tone for the series of the seven trumpet. . . . John sees another angel with a **golden censer** standing in close proximity to **the altar** of burnt offering. After receiving much **incense**, the angel administers the incense by offering it **with the prayers of all the saints on the golden altar** of incense before the throne. This scene is built on the Old Testament cultic system, in which the end of the daily sacrifice was announced by the blowing of trumpets. After the sacrificial lamb had been placed upon the altar of burnt offering and the blood of the sacrifice had been poured out at the base of the altar, the assigned priest would have taken the golden censor and offered incense upon the golden altar inside the temple. After offering the incense, the priest came out to bless the people who were waiting quietly in the court. At that moment, the seven priests blew their trumpets, marking the end of the daily sacrifice ceremony.[4]

In context with the fifth and sixth seals, God hears the prayers of the souls under the altar and those who are asking, "Who is able to stand?" Along with the trumpet's call, God's people have a work to do: "Turn ye even to Me with all your heart, and with fasting, and with weeping and with mourning: and rend your heart, and not your garments" (Joel 2:12-13). The altar of incense is also called the altar of prayer. Smith's description emphasizes the fulfillment of the ancient symbols of the sanctuary:

> The altar is the altar of incense, which in the earthly sanctuary was placed in the first apartment. Here then is another proof that there exists in heaven a sanctuary with its corresponding vessels of service, of which the earthly was a figure, and that we are taken into that sanctuary by the visions of John. A work of ministration for all the saints in the sanctuary above is thus brought to view. Doubtless the entire work of mediation for the people of God during the gospel era is here presented. This is apparent from the fact that the angel offers his incense with the prayers of *all* saints.[5]

The censer and the golden altar symbolize the rising of our prayers like incense into the presence of God, but that same altar kindles the fires of God's wrath. Judgments fall upon the earth kindled with fire from the altar of incense. Smith links Christ's heavenly work to His people on earth:

---

[4] Ranko Stefanovic, *Revelation of Jesus Christ* (Berrien Springs, MI: Andrews University Press, 2002), 285.

[5] Smith, 474-475.

But why are these verses inserted here? They are a message of hope and comfort for the church. The seven angels with their warlike trumpets had been introduced; terrible scenes were to take place when they should sound; but before they begin to blow, the people of God are directed to behold the work of mediation in their behalf in heaven, and to look to their source of help and strength during this time. Though they should be tossed upon the tumultuous waves of strife and war, they were to know that their great High Priest still ministered for them in the sanctuary in heaven. To that sacred place they could direct their prayers with the assurance that they would be offered with incense to their Father in heaven. Thus could they gain strength and support in all their tribulation.[6]

Revelation reveals Jesus and His plan of redemption. This includes the preparation that His people must make. God cares so much for us that He laid down His life in our place. He cannot bear the thought of losing one of us. With trumpet-like tones, He warns us of the final judgment so that we will not be caught unaware.

Revelation 8:6: And the seven angels which had the seven trumpets prepared themselves to sound.

Trumpets sound warnings and battle calls. "For if the trumpet give an uncertain sound, who shall prepare himself to the battle?" 1 Corinthians 14:8. The seven trumpets represent scourges that fall upon the nations that rejected the gospel given during each of the Christian time periods. The trumpets sound God's own assessment of the ungodly political decisions made by man. They sow the wind and reap the whirlwind. Commentators, such as Albert Barnes, of the last century see the first four trumpets as the four main invasions of Western Rome by the barbarians.

The seven trumpets sound God's judgment upon those both inside and outside the church who do not take God seriously. Bunch explains how the trumpets and seals parallel each other:

The vision of the seven trumpets is the third apocalyptic view of world history affecting the Christian era and covering the same period as the seven letters and seven seals. The letters and seals deal chiefly with religious events and conditions, while the trumpets picture political and military movements among the nations. All three visions terminate in the coming of Christ and the victory of the church militant. They are all similar in that all three have introductory visions of Christ and His priestly ministrations in the heavenly sanctuary while the predicted events are taking place on the earth. The latter two are similar in that

---
6   Ibid., 475.

between the sixth and seventh are parenthetical prophecies of God's final gospel message that prepares a people for the second advent of Christ. This proves that the trumpets must be parallel with the seals and therefore cannot follow them.[7]

The Trumpets: A Twofold Vision: As each trumpet is sounded in the heavenly sanctuary, a chain of events occur on earth. Showing the relationship between earth and heaven, Bunch comments:

This vision, like the two that precede it, is twofold. Before describing the events to transpire on earth, a view is given of Christ's mediatorial work in the heavenly sanctuary. The heavenly and earthly events run parallel and cover the Christian era. While God's judgments are being visited upon the nations of earth, Christ is on duty at the throne of grace where He ministers the sweet incense of His righteousness in behalf of repentant sinners and praying saints. Here is the secret of peace in the midst of a world of strife. Jesus said, "Think not that I am come to send peace on earth: I came not to send peace, but a sword." Matthew 10:34. He also said, "These things I have spoken unto you, that in Me ye might have peace." John 16:33. Accepting Christ brings peace; rejecting Him brings the sword.[8]

First Trumpet

Revelation 8:7: The first angel sounded, and there followed hail and fire mingled with blood, and they were cast upon the earth: and the third part of trees was burnt up, and all green grass was burnt up.

This symbolic language reminds us of the judgments that fell on ancient Israel. Treiyer clarifies: "This was also the way in which the divine punishment over the ten confederated tribes of Northern Israel was depicted, '*like a hailstorm and a destructive wind*' caused by the Assyrian attack. That divine punishment in the hand of the Assyrians, 'tramples underfoot' the pride of the kingdom of Samaria (Isaiah 28:2). The prophets predicted the fall of the oppressive empire of Assyria with similar terms, 'with raging anger and consuming fire, with cloudburst, thunderstorm and hail' (Isaiah 30:30; see Ezekiel 38:22)."[9]

The seven trumpets of the Christian era come in answer to the prayers of the saints that ascend from the altar of incense to the throne of God (Revelation 8:2-4). This first trumpet was aimed at the nation that first shed the blood of God's apostolic church, pagan Rome and its paganized church.

---

[7]   Bunch, "The Revelation," 72.

[8]   Ibid.

[9]   Treiyer, *The Seals and the Trumpets*, 265.

God bore long with the apostasy of the church. The perversion and paganization of the church prevented it from fulfilling its mission. The sinfulness of unbelievers is to be expected, but heaven will not overlook wickedness within the church of God. The judgments of God must be meted out. Bunch concurs:

"The moral degeneration of Rome had become indescribable. Seneca, the Roman historian, said: 'Vice no longer hides itself; it stalks abroad before all eyes; innocence is no longer rare, it has ceased to exist.' A Roman poet said: 'Ye who desire to live a godly life, depart from Rome; for, although all things are lawful there, yet to be godly is unlawful.'"[10] The time had come for God to act. Bunch describes the divine judgment of the first trumpet:

> The first trumpet is prophetic of the first successful invasion of Rome by the Gothic barbarians from the north under the leadership of Alaric. The "hail" fitly represents the northern origin of the invaders who came from the shores of the Baltic, and the "fire mingled with blood," indicates the awful slaughter and destruction inflicted by them. They overran Greece, Asia Minor, Italy, Spain, Southern France, and in A.D. 410 captured and sacked the city of Rome. Jerome declared that as the result of this invasion, "nothing was left except the sky and the earth."[11]

The hail symbol points to the fact that the northern barbarians usually made their assaults during the dead of winter. In this way, they crossed into Roman territory over the frozen ice. The barbarian Goths set Rome on fire and blood was shed over large sections of the city; this fulfilled the symbols of fire and blood.

Christians during this time period felt that this invasion was a punishment from God for the evils of the city of Rome and its paganism. The faithful followers of Christ at this time had a special code name for Rome: Babylon. Revelation uses that same terminology for a later manifestation of Rome: Babylon the Great.

A Third Part of the Earth: Treiyer makes a good point: "The Roman empire was divided into three capitals: Ravenna, Constantinople and Rome. Only a third part fell under Alaric, that is, Rome, by then the principal capital of the empire."[12]

Third of Trees and Green Grass: Trees symbolize power and authority as in the case of Nebuchadnezzar, wealth as seen in Solomon's vast forest of cedars, and protection and sustenance for animals and people. One-third of the wealth, security, and power belonging to Rome was gone.

Green grass: In the Bible, grass symbolizes people and their brief lives. Treiyer's comments link this symbolism to history: "After surrounding the Roman walls, Alaric required Rome to surrender. But the Senate tried to frighten him with the impressive number of people living within the city. The general of

[10] Bunch, "The Revelation," 78.

[11] Ibid., 76.

[12] Treiyer, *The Seals and the Trumpets*, 268.

the Goths, however, was not intimidated. He answered them: 'When the grass is denser, better is its harvest.'"[13]

Alaric did not destroy any Christian churches as he stated that his war was against Rome and not the "apostles of the Lord."[14] Through the first trumpet, God punished pagan Rome for its persecution of His faithful people.

Second Trumpet

Revelation 8:8-9: And the second angel sounded, and as it were a great mountain burning with fire was cast into the sea: and the third part of the sea became blood; [9]And the third part of the creatures which were in the sea, and had life, died; and the third part of the ships were destroyed.

As the first trumpet heralded the first attack on the Roman Empire, so the second trumpet announced the second significant attack on Rome. This is portrayed by the symbol of a "great mountain burning with fire" that is cast into the sea. A mountain symbolizes a kingdom according to Revelation 17:9-10. The great mountain would be Rome again, but this attack would come from the sea. Jeremiah called Babylon "O destroying mountain" in Jeremiah 51:25, matching the name given Rome by God's faithful people.

Genseric, the Vandal general from northern Africa, made his terrible attack upon Rome. coming from the south across the Mediterranean Sea. Treiyer compares and contrasts the first and second trumpets: "While the first trumpet falls upon the earth, the second falls into the sea. In both cases there is shedding of blood, but the location is different. That the second trumpet deals with naval confrontations is seen in the statement that 'a third of the ships were destroyed' (Revelation 8:9). Isaiah described a similar divine judgment which would fall upon 'every trading ship' (Isa 2:16). This is a good antecedent to think that we are here before a similar fact."[15]

This vandal general was a pirate of the first degree, feared by all in the Mediterranean. Genseric's navy could not be matched even by the great Roman Empire. He looted both seacoasts and ships. Finally the Rome Empire confronted this pirate with fleets from Rome and Constantinople, but Genseric defeated both fleets and set their ships on fire, a total loss for Rome. When attacking the seacoast, Genseric also took prisoners, sailed them out to sea, and beheaded them. In one of his attacks, he took 500 principal men of a city, turning the sea to the color of blood as he massacred them.

As an Arian Christian, Genseric felt the Catholics were pagans like the Romans. Because he was a renegade against the church, Rome counted this Arian pirate a heretic. Anyone who would not recognize the authority of the

---

[13] Ibid., 269.

[14] Ibid., 270.

[15] Ibid., 272.

Catholic Church was called a heretic even as all who were not Romans were considered to be barbarians.

According to Treiyer, the judgment brought through Genseric is supported by history and historians: "It is curious to note that instead of cold stones, the new invaders came from the hot lands of Africa, and fell upon the sea and its coasts 'like a huge mountain, all ablaze.' Also noteworthy is the fact that several historians, like the profane and incredulous Gibbon, have concluded the history of the Vandal general and of his effect on the downfall of the Roman Empire, in the following terms: 'Genseric, a name which, in the destruction of the Roman Empire, has deserved an equal rank with the names of Alaric and Attila.'"[16]

Third Trumpet

Revelation 8:10-11: And the third angel sounded, and there fell a great star from heaven, burning as it were a lamp, and it fell upon the third part of the rivers, and upon the fountains of waters; [11]And the name of the star is called Wormwood: and the third part of the waters became wormwood; and many men died of the waters, because they were made bitter.

The third trumpet refers to the third onslaught and invasion of Rome, that of Attila the Hun. Called "Han" by the Chinese, "Hun-yu" by the Turks, and "Hunni" in Latin, the Huns actually called themselves Magyars. Bunch writes of this great Magyar warrior:

> Attila termed himself the "The Scourge of God." He claimed that he was divinely directed to scourge the Roman Empire. The symbolic meteor representing the Huns "fell" and was not "cast" upon the empire, as were the Goths and Vandals. The Huns were not driven by another foe but came voluntarily except as they claimed supernatural guidance. The Huns were of Mongolian stock and were Asiatics rather than Europeans. They conquered China in 200 B.C. They began their movement westward from North China in the first century of the Christian era. They were a shepherd people whose movements were controlled largely by the abundance or scarcity of pasture. In the beginning of the fourth century they occupied the vast plains north of the Caspian Sea and came into contact with outposts of the Ostrogoths. In the latter part of the fourth century they again marched westward driving the Teutonic tribes before them, literally pushing or casting them upon the empire of the Romans. Early in the fifth century Attila established his seat of government on the plains east of the Danube, one of the boundary rivers of the empire, and forced the Goths across the river into Roman territory.[17]

---

[16]   Ibid., 274.

[17]   Bunch, "The Revelation," 82-83.

The term "the third part of the rivers" indicates Attila's method of attack (Revelation 8:10). Unlike previous invaders, the Magyar offensive centered on the Danube, one of the three main rivers important to the commerce of the Roman Empire, thus the third part. The Magyars occupied the Danube valley and all its tributaries. Bunch relates this historical fact to the third trumpet: "Gibbon says, 'The Huns were masters of the great river.' Thus the meteor fell upon one third of the rivers, or one of the three rivers upon which the life of the empire depended. Attila and the Huns carried on all of their military operations inland from the sea and in that part of Europe that abounds in streams and rivers."[18] Attila's battles are described by Bunch:

> Attila's first invasion was to the very walls of Constantinople. Gibbon says that he destroyed seventy cities in his progress and forced upon the emperor of the East an oppressive peace. In 451 he declared war on the Western Empire and with 500,000 men swept through Germany pillaging as he went. He invaded Gaul and sacked and burned most of the cities of France as far south as Orleans. On the battlefield of the Chalons on the Marne, the combined armies of the Romans and Visigoths met him in one of the bloodiest and most decisive battles of history. A million men were engaged in battle, 500,000 on each side. At the close of the day, 160,000 men lay dead on the field. One historian placed the number killed as high as 300,000. When darkness came, both armies retired from the field of battle utterly exhausted, neither knowing who was the victor. During the darkness of the night the Huns retreated unobserved. They then invaded Italy and destroyed the cities of northern Italy and reduced the country to the condition of a desert. Attila claimed that the grass never grew where his horses' feet had trod."[19]

"Wormwood" is understood as Attila falling on the rivers, using them powerfully to become a bitter curse upon the Roman Empire.

Fourth Trumpet

Revelation 8:12-13: And the fourth angel sounded, and the third part of the sun was smitten, and the third part of the moon, and the third part of the stars; so as the third part of them was darkened, and the day shone not for a third part of it, and the night likewise. [13] And I beheld, and heard an angel flying through the midst of heaven, saying with a loud voice, Woe, woe, woe, to the inhabiters of the earth by reason of the other voices of the trumpet of the three angels, which are yet to sound!

Another symbol from nature is used to describe the fourth attack on Rome. Treiyer adds to the understanding of the symbols used in this prophecy:

---

[18] Ibid., 83.

[19] Ibid., 83-84.

The *fourth trumpet* struck "a third of the sun," "of the moon, and . . . of the stars" (Revelation 8:12). There is an apparent contradiction, for a part of the stars is not hurt during a part of the day or of the night, but "a third part of them" which is darkened. Notwithstanding, it is affirmed that its effect is the lack of light on "a third of the day . . . and of the night." Since this never happens in nature, we cannot interpret this prophecy literally. The idea seems to be that a third of the intensity of light is lost during the day in the case of the sun, and during the night in the case of the moon and of the stars. The decline of the power of the stars is, doubtless, that which is brought out in the fourth trumpet.[20]

The Roman Empire ended in 476; the final blow came in the form of Odoacer of the Heruli, one of the northern Teutonic or Germanic tribes. Joined by many other Germanic tribes, Odoacer crushed all the last vestiges of the once grand Roman Empire. According to Bunch, the invasions of the barbarians not only marked the end of the Roman Empire, "it also introduced that long period of demoralization in Europe, known as 'The Dark Ages.'"[21]

This dark period of history was limited to what we know as Europe. The rest of the world prospered during this period of time. The strife and spiritual darkness of Western Europe were the result of its rejection of the pure gospel of Christ. Like pagan Rome, the church of Rome desired earthly power and authority rather than the humble life of Christ's faithful followers. What a contrast between the meek and lowly Jesus and the pomp and wealth of the Roman Church. The fourth trumpet marked the start of a long era of spiritual darkness. Treiyer writes of this dark period that began with the fall of Rome:

> The historicist interpreters of the fourth trumpet were right, then, when they saw the decline of the western emperor, in the darkening of the heavenly bodies. The emperor was represented by the sun, the consulate by the moon, and of the senate by the stars. Jerome, the famous translator of the Bible into Latin, who lived during the time when Alaric seized Rome, wrote about this invasion and anticipated the final consequence for Imperial Rome: *Clarissimum terrarum lumen extinctum est,* "the world's glorious sun has been extinguished." However, the other two centers of the empire—Ravenna and Constantinople—survived for a longer time. Only a third of the empire fell, namely Rome.[22]

The "angel flying" in the midst of heaven in Revelation 8:13 should be translated "eagle flying." The Greek word is ἀετοῦ (*aetou*) which means eagle. Symbolic of one of the four living beings around God's throne, the eagle was Dan's tribal

20   Treiyer, *The Seals and the Trumpets,* 280-281.

21   Bunch, "The Revelation," 84.

22   Treiyer, *The Seals and the Trumpets,* 282.

standard, alluding to vengeance and judgment. With these visions the fifth trumpet is introduced.

Conclusion

The first four trumpets brought God's judgments to Rome. These four successive attacks led to the decline and fall of the pagan Roman Empire.

With its bronze claws as symbolized by Daniel 7:19, the iron kingdom of Rome owes much to Greek culture. A true study of the Roman culture will find that there was very little that was unique about it. Its language was not original, its architecture was borrowed, its culture a hand-me-down. Nearly everything Roman had its birth in one of the previous kingdoms. Rome took the best of each culture, but it also borrowed false worship from of each of those predecessors, invoking the displeasure of God.

Although Rome was a civil state, its religion was entwined around every fiber of Roman life. Rome's religion was eclectic, including the worship of heavenly bodies and deities borrowed from all the conquered nations: Greece, Medo-Persia, Babylon, Assyria, and Egypt. Sun worship was important to Rome, thus in the fourth trumpet the sun, moon, and stars are smitten by God. Ultimately, Rome was punished for shedding the blood of the martyrs. As Jesus warned: "All they that take the sword shall perish with the sword" (Matthew 26:52).

CHAPTER TWENTY-ONE

Revelation 9

Introduction

Revelation 8:13 introduces the fifth trumpet with its eagle imagery of judgment and vengeance. The pagan Roman Empire has collapsed, and the Christian church at Rome has taken over what will become the Holy Roman Empire. Eventually every civil power would yield to the church as papal Rome gained the power to coronate kings. The Dark Ages continue and deepen.

As an aside, most of recorded history in Western Europe has been written from a Catholic prospective. This bias has continued into modern times as the church's slant pervades Wikipedia and other prominent sources of information on the Internet. Recently, some historians of the Reformation ethic have arisen, but their work is not easily accomplished. In summary, think about what biases have influenced the sources upon which you depend for information. The Bible is the only truly dependable resource.

The Three Woes Begin

With the invasion of the barbarian tribes, the first four trumpet judgments are aimed at the pagan Roman Empire. Each of the next three trumpets—five, six, and seven—come with an exclamation of woe: "Woe, woe, woe, to the inhabiters of the earth by reason of the other voices of the trumpet of the three angels, which are yet to sound!" (Revelation 8:13). The angels thus call the fifth trumpet the first woe, the sixth is the second woe, and so on. The final seventh trumpet is the third and last woe.

Beginning with the fifth trumpet, God's judgments fall upon the power that claims to be God's representative on earth. A new vengeful and judgmental power is introduced that fulfills the symbolism of the fifth and sixth trumpets.

Arab Involvement in Prophecy

Christians want to understand the role of the Arabs in prophecy. Let's look in the book of beginnings. Go back to the origin of the Arab people and read what the Bible reveals about this subject. What did God tell us about Ishmael, the father of the Arabs, and what would happen to his descendents?

Genesis 16:10-12: And the angel of the LORD said unto her, I will multiply thy seed exceedingly, that it shall not be numbered for multitude. ¹¹And the angel of the LORD said unto her, Behold, thou art with child, and shalt bear a son, and shalt call his name Ishmael; because the LORD hath heard thy affliction. ¹²And he will be a wild man; his hand will be against every man, and every man's hand against him; and he shall dwell in the presence of all his brethren.

Notice how other versions translate Genesis 6:12:

"He shall be a wild ass of a man, with his hand against everyone, and everyone's hand against him; and he shall live at odds with all his kin." NRS.

"And he shall be as a wild ass among men; his hand shall be against every man, and every man's hand against him; and he shall dwell over against all his brethren." ASV.

Judaism, Christianity, and Islam all claim Abraham as their father. Judaism is the oldest of these three world religions, leaving us the legacy of the writings of the Old Testament Scriptures. After the death and resurrection of Christ, the Christian church developed out of Judaism. At first the Christians met in synagogues as they were considered a Jewish sect called "the way" (Acts 9:2; 19:9, 23; 22:4; 24:14). Jesus and His disciples proclaimed His fulfillment of the Old Testament Messianic prophecies. When Christians could no longer meet in the synagogues, the Christian church as a separate entity came into being.

Six hundred years after Christ, a radical, militant religion arose. Mohammed and his followers gained power through ethnic cleansing and subjugation of all who would not submit to this new philosophy. Islam venerates Abraham as its father and Jesus as a prophet, but today we can observe what the Scriptures predicted about children of Ishmael: "His hand shall be against everyone, and everyone's hand against him; and he shall live at odds with all his kin."

Although Genesis 6:12 foresaw the future of Ishmael's descendants, nothing is said prophetically about the Arabs in the New Testament until the ninth chapter of Revelation. Here the fifth and sixth trumpets introduce the Arabs as the scourge of apostate Christianity. Treiyer gives some background on this:

The Arabs emerged into Western civilization abruptly in the seventh century. They came so dramatically and powerfully that Beatus, a Spaniard monk of the eighth century, came to the conclusion that the symbol of the locusts of the fifth trumpet perfectly fits the Saracen Arabs. The Muslim expansion had been able to cover, from that time, Northern Africa, the Near East, and Spain.

Many interpreters followed Beatus in this interpretation, even during the time of the Protestant Reformation (such as Luther, for example). Bullinger, by the second half of the sixteenth century, was able to make a clear distinction between the two great expansionist movements of the Muslims. He saw the Saracens and the Ottoman Turks in the fifth and sixth trumpets respectively. More than one hundred authors agreed with him over the years, causing this interpretation to become the classic Protestant interpretation until the nineteenth century."[1]

The Protestant church of the twenty-first century has nearly abandoned the historicist interpretation of prophecy, replacing it with either preterism or futurism, two anti-Reformation prophetic interpretations. Today, Treiyer concludes, Seventh-day Adventists are one of the few groups that remains classical *historicists*:

> Actually, Protestants left Rome because they saw in the harlot of Revelation 17 an unmistakable symbolic picture of the Roman Catholic Church. In an attempt to deflect the blow, two interpreters introduced the Preterist interpretation (J. Henten, 1547; Louis de Alcazar, Jesuit, 1614), and another championed the futurist interpretation (Francisco Rivera, Jesuit, 1590). Should we be astonished that Protestants, as well as Evangelicals, who were departing from historicism in the twentieth century, were also being assimilated, little by little, into Babylon the Great? This will be the lot of anyone who falls into the temptation of following those who have lost their way in prophetic matters.[2]

Fifth Trumpet: First Woe

Treiyer outlines the work of the fifth trumpet: "The judgments associated with the *fifth trumpet* fall more specifically upon the territories of the heirs of the Caesars, that is, upon that apostate Christianity where the antichrist sets his dominion. Christian Rome's persecution against the preachers of the Word of God, as we have already seen in our study of the seals, was clearly sketched in prophecy. We also noticed that this trumpet, which starts the series of three *trumpet-woes*, places us at the threshold of the great tribulation of 1260 years."[3]

Revelation 9:1-12: And the fifth angel sounded, and I saw a star fall from heaven unto the earth: and to him was given the key of the bottomless pit. [2]And he opened the bottomless pit; and there arose a smoke out of the pit, as the smoke of a great furnace; and the sun and the air were darkened by reason of the smoke of the pit. [3]And there came out of the smoke locusts upon the earth: and unto them was given power, as the scorpions of the earth have power. [4]And it was commanded them that they should not hurt the grass of the earth, neither any green thing, neither any tree; but only those men which have not the seal of God in their foreheads. [5]And to them it was given that

---

[1]   Treiyer, *The Seals and the Trumpets*, 286.

[2]   Ibid., 287.

[3]   Ibid., 288.

they should not kill them, but that they should be tormented five months: and their torment *was* as the torment of a scorpion, when he striketh a man. [6]And in those days shall men seek death, and shall not find it; and shall desire to die, and death shall flee from them. [7]And the shapes of the locusts *were* like unto horses prepared unto battle; and on their heads *were* as it were crowns like gold, and their faces *were* as the faces of men. [8]And they had hair as the hair of women, and their teeth were as *the teeth* of lions. [9]And they had breastplates, as it were breastplates of iron; and the sound of their wings *was* as the sound of chariots of many horses running to battle. [10]And they had tails like unto scorpions, and there were stings in their tails: and their power *was* to hurt men five months. [11]And they had a king over them, *which is* the angel of the bottomless pit, whose name in the Hebrew tongue *is* Abaddon, but in the Greek tongue hath *his* name Apollyon. [12]One woe is past; *and*, behold, there come two woes more hereafter.

The Fallen Star: The original Greek, καὶ εἶδον ἀστέρα ἐκ τοῦ οὐρανοῦ πεπτωκότα εἰς τὴν γῆν (*kai eidon astera ek tou ouranou peptokota eis tein gein*), would better be rendered "and I saw a star out of the heaven **having fallen** to the earth." With this translation, the star had already fallen when seen by the prophet. This correlates with Isaiah 14:12 which depicts Lucifer as having fallen from heaven. Revelation 12:4 agrees: "His tail drew the third part of the stars of heaven, and did cast them to the earth," signifying that Satan's rebellion took a third of the angels. This *fallen star* symbolizes Satan who opens the symbolic bottomless pit. The symbol of a pit is used here and in Revelation 20 which describes the fate of Satan during the millennium.

Satan, the fallen star, is given a key to the bottomless pit. This fallen angel does his work through human instrumentalities, thus the fallen star in a secondary sense symbolizes Mohammed, the instrumentality used by Satan to punish the apostate church. "The key" symbolizes the "holy writings" Mohammed claimed to receive from the angel Gabriel.

Mohammed had contact with the two great religions in that part of the world: Judaism and Christianity. His writings contain some elements of both with the added element of *jihad*. Mohammed claimed to be the prophet of God and alledgedly the Koran was given to him by inspiration. If the God of the Old and New Testaments is the same as the God of the Koran, then everything in the Koran should agree with the Bible. However, the character of God and the fruits of the Koran are quite different from those of the Bible. Unlike the Bible, the Koran has no time prophecies that can be verified. Treiyer makes some pointed remarks about the Koran:

> Muslims presume to be humble, because the Koran requires them to walk humbly upon the earth (Sura 31:17), and surrender constantly to Allah (Sura 6:70; 33:35; 40:68; 41:33; 46:14, etc). But the real question has to do with the kind of inspiration Mohammed received. He believed

himself to be and is believed by millions of loyal devotees to be an apostle and prophet inspired by God. However, his course has caused millions to turn astray from the true God as He is revealed in the only true revelation, the Bible. In view of this consideration, then, he cannot honestly be considered a man who came from heaven, but rather one who followed the great Deceiver who fell from heaven.[4]

In the original language, the word for pit is "φρέαρ" (freh'-ar) which means shaft or well. A better translation would be "the shaft or well of the abyss" rather than "the bottomless pit." Explaining the symbolism, Treiyer writes: "This symbol is easy to identify as a reference to Arabia with its wilderness, desolate lands, and uninhabited regions. It implies a double symbolism of the diabolical origin of its religion. Its sudden and unexpected appearance caused them to expand from nothing, that is, from the 'abyss,' and emerge as a conquering empire."[5]

Even as Ishmael and Isaac were separated because of family discord, thus antagonism has continued between their descendants. This feud, as well as the prophecy given about Ishmael's seed, explains the rapid expansion of Islam. Fertile ground for discord was built into the heart and fiber of the nation that emerged out of the loins of Ishmael.

Hitti, a scholar of Arab history, comments on the amazing growth and power of Islam: "If someone in the first third of the seventh Christian century had the audacity to prophesy that within a decade or so some unheralded, unforeseen power from the hitherto barbarous and little-known land of Arabia was to make its appearance, hurl itself against the only two world powers of the age, fall heir to the one (the Sasanid) and strip the other (the Byzantine) of its fairest provinces, he would undoubtedly have been declared a lunatic. Yet that was exactly what happened. After the death of the Prophet, sterile Arabia seems to have been converted as if by magic into a nursery of heroes the like of whom, both in number and quality, would be hard to find anywhere."[6]

Smoke: The smoke and darkness of Islam obscured the light of the gospel, the good news of the One who outshines the sun. In countries dominated by Islam, the gospel cannot be preached without fear of death. Smoke permeates everything around it, not only hurting the eyes and causing them to shut, but also stifling life. Ultimately, this smoke brings death unless its source of fire is found and extinguished.

The darkness of Islam does not allow its citizens freedom to compare or even consider the light of the gospel. Truth is not fearful of scrutiny. Only a weak philosophy is afraid of examination and close inspection. Like Roman Christianity

---

[4]   Ibid., 293.

[5]   Ibid.

[6]   Philip K. Hitti, *The Arabs: A Short History* (Washington, DC: Regnery Publishing, 1996), 56-57.

which it despises, Islam brings spiritual darkness upon its people. In both religions the leaders control the interpretation of their holy book, while the people are kept in smoke-filled darkness. It is fitting that God used darkness out of Arabia during the fifth trumpet to punish the darkness of apostate Christianity.

Locusts Like Horses: This symbol reminds us of the locusts that were brought upon the Egyptians for their stubborn obstinacy against the only true God (Exodus 10:12-20). The locusts came with an east wind—from the direction of Arabia—to Egypt. Thick, widespread locusts from Arabia have literally spilled over into neighboring countries in the past. This description well suits the Saracenic invasion from the south which blew in from the south like a destroying wind. Bunch explores the locust and horse symbols in this prophecy: "The Arabs were the most expert horsemen in the world and they lived and fought so much on their horses that the horse and rider were almost inseparable. With the swiftness of flying locusts they rode their famous Arabian horses into battle."[7]

Verse 7-8: On their heads *were* as it were crowns like gold, and their faces *were* as the faces of men. And they had hair as the hair of women, and their teeth were as *the teeth* of lions. These two verses give some paradoxes, yet accurately portray in symbols the Saracenic Muslims. The Saracens' turbans were greenish gold and their hair was long like women's tresses, yet they were heavily bearded so it was obvious that they were men. The symbol of their teeth as the teeth of lions represents the savagery in which they conquered and destroyed.

Verses 9-10: And they had breastplates, as it were breastplates of iron; and the sound of their wings *was* as the sound of chariots of many horses running to battle. [10]And they had tails like unto scorpions, and there were stings in their tails. This describes the weapons and armor that the Saracens used. Their leather breastplates were hard and as strong as iron, and their horses were also protected by armor. Their weapons included the sword, spear, bow, and arrows. These skillful archers could shoot arrows behind them over their horses' tails while in retreat. This is symbolized by the scorpion. The Arabian scorpion is not slow like those in other places on earth. Although the sting is not always fatal, it is painful. Like the poison of the scorpion's bite, the arrows of the Saracens were laced with poison.

Five months: Verses 5 and 10 say nothing about destroying! For five prophetic months, their mission was to cause pain and agony so fearsome that some preferred death rather than life. The Saracens wished to be world conquerors. Early Advent preachers believed that these 5 months were fulfilled before Deacozes ascended the throne (see explanation of verse 15 by Josiah Litch). One explanation is that this may be referring to the development of the Islamic Empires) Bunch states it this way: "The ambitions of the Saracens was to make Islam the religion of the world. After the conquest of Western Asia and Northern Africa, the plan was to overrun Europe, but Constantinople stood in their way.

---

[7]   Bunch, "The Revelation," 88-89.

The failure to capture this strategic stronghold compelled them to change their plan and enter Europe by way of the Strait of Gibraltar. They intended to complete their circuit of the Mediterranean, but were brought to a standstill in the famous and decisive battle of Tours in 732 A.D. when Charles Martel defeated them in a seven days' battle."[8]

The 150-Year Prophecy: A.D. 632 to 782 or A.D. 1299 to 1449?

Five months of prophetic time equal 150 literal years. The locusts only attacked during this five-month time period. God's symbols are significant and appropriate; His timing accurate. The period of the fifth trumpet covers the main portion of the Saracen's triumph. Bunch tells how he believed the prophecy was fulfilled:

> It must be evident that the 150 years begins with the time when the symbolic locusts are released from the pit by the angel with the key and "given power" as "the scorpions of the earth" to "hurt" and "torment" for five prophetic months. It is also evident that this tormenting would begin with the "command" on the part of their leader to torment. The tormenting covers a century and a half and begins with the time the Saracens are commanded to hurt some and not to hurt others. It seems that no other conclusion is possible. The predicted command was given by Abu-Bekr at the beginning of the invasion of Syria in the year 632 A.D. Mohammed died in the year 632 and Abu-Bekr succeeded him. No sooner had he taken command of the government than he dispatched a letter to the Arabian tribes calling upon them to rally to the standard of the dead prophet and by the sword make Islam the religion of the world. No sooner had the messengers returned than Saracen warriors began to flock to Medina for the conquest of Syria and the world. . . .
>
> Fortunately historians have recorded the very command mentioned in the prophecy. Before beginning the invasion of Syria in 632, Abu-Bekr thus addressed his generals: "This is to inform you that I intend to send an army of the faithful into Syria to deliver that country from the infidels, and I remind you that to fight for the true faith is to obey God. Treat your soldiers with kindness and consideration. Be just in all your dealings with them, and consult their feelings and opinions. Fight valiantly, and never turn your back upon the foe. When victorious, harm not the aged and protect women and children. Destroy not the palm tree or fruit trees of any kind. Waste not the corn fields with fire; nor kill any cattle except for food. Stand faithfully to every covenant and promise; respect all religious persons who live in hermitages or convents, and spare their edifices. But should you meet a class of unbelievers of a different kind,

---

[8]   Ibid., 90.

who go about with shaven crowns and belong to the synagogue of Satan, be sure you cleave their skulls unless they embrace the true faith or render tribute."—*History of the World*, Ridpath, Vol. 4, p. 462. The very things that literal locusts hurt or devour, the symbolic locusts are commanded not to hurt. This is conclusive proof that symbols are employed.[9]

Abu-Bekr's invasion of Syria began in 632. When the Muslims were stopped at Constantinople, they invaded Europe from western Africa, and gained ground in the Iberian Peninsula. From this point of conquest, the Muslims attacked as far north as France. By 782, they controlled most of the peninsula, the area of modern-day Portugal and Spain. Although the Muslim forces ceased their military advance, their influence and population continued to increase. Four hundred years later in the Iberian Peninsula, eighty percent of the population of seven million was still Muslim.

At this same time, the Muslim capital in Syria was moved to Baghdad. Ameer Ali Syed gives the results of this change: "The Syrians lose the monopoly of influence and power they had hitherto possessed; and the tide of progress is diverted from the west to the east. But the unity of the Caliphate was gone forever. . . . 'The reign of the first Abbassides,' says a distinguished French scholar and historian, 'was the era of the greatest splendor of the Eastern Saracens. The age of conquest had passed; that of civilisation had commenced.'"[10] Therefore, the time period ends around A.D. 782, thus preceding Deacozes ascension.

Litch came up with a different scenario for the fulfillment of the 150 years. He understood that verse 15 (391 years and 15 days) must immdediately follow the 5 months (150 years) of verse 10. He believed the 150 years started with the first Turkish attack on the Byzantine Empire at Bapheum on July 27, 1299. Adding 150 years to that date led him to July 27, 1449. With this reasoning he could reconcile the connection between the 150 year prophecy in the 5th Trumpet and the 391 year and 15 day prophecy of the 6th Trumpet.

Sixth Trumpet: Second Woe

The first woe is over; the second woe is coming. The greatest and most powerful Muslim empire would last more than half a millennium, the Ottoman Empire. More than five centuries after the Muslim expansion into Syria and Spain, the Ottoman Turks took power in eastern Europe, the Middle East, and Northern Africa. Under the fifth trumpet, the Saracens would *hurt* or *torment*, but in the sixth trumpet, the Ottoman Turks would *slay* and *kill*.

Revelation 9:13-21: And the sixth angel sounded, and I heard a voice from the four horns of the golden altar which is before God, ¹⁴Saying to the sixth angel which had the trumpet, Loose the four angels which are bound in the great

---

9   Ibid., 91-92.

10   Ameer Ali Syed, *Short History of the Saracens* (London: Macmillan, 1916), 208-209.

river Euphrates. ¹⁵And the four angels were loosed, which were prepared for an hour, and a day, and a month, and a year, for to slay the third part of men. ¹⁶And the number of the army of the horsemen *were* two hundred thousand thousand: and I heard the number of them. ¹⁷And thus I saw the horses in the vision, and them that sat on them, having breastplates of fire, and of jacinth, and brimstone: and the heads of the horses *were* as the heads of lions; and out of their mouths issued fire and smoke and brimstone. ¹⁸By these three was the third part of men killed, by the fire, and by the smoke, and by the brimstone, which issued out of their mouths. ¹⁹For their power is in their mouth, and in their tails: for their tails *were* like unto serpents, and had heads, and with them they do hurt. ²⁰And the rest of the men which were not killed by these plagues yet repented not of the works of their hands, that they should not worship devils, and idols of gold, and silver, and brass, and stone, and of wood: which neither can see, nor hear, nor walk: ²¹Neither repented they of their murders, nor of their sorceries, nor of their fornication, nor of their thefts.

Verse 13: The four horns of the golden altar which is before God. This is the golden altar of incense that is in front of the ark of the covenant. The setting of the trumpets centers around the golden altar from the beginning of chapter 8. Bunch links the sanctuary imagery to the message of the trumpets:

> The altar of incense was the place where the priests ministered the blood of the victims slain at the altar of burnt offering in the court. The horns of the golden altar received the blood that atoned for the sins of Israel. This was a part of the "daily" service. The golden altar was symbolic of the mediatorial work of Christ in the heavenly sanctuary. The voice from the golden altar is therefore the voice of Christ. This is the only one of the seven trumpet-angels given specific instruction by Christ. It proves that His priestly ministry was still in progress during the sounding of the trumpets and that they therefore cannot be identified with the seven last plagues. It also shows that during the first six trumpets the "daily" ministration of Christ was in progress and that He had not yet entered upon the last phase of His ministry represented by the yearly service in the most holy place. It was the failure of the church to recognize the priestly ministry of Christ in the heavenly sanctuary that brought the trumpet-woes upon the professed Christian world. The heavenly service was trampled under foot by Papal Rome through the institution of an earthly and counterfeit system, therefore the Turks were loosed against them.[11]

Verse 14: Loose the four angels which are bound in the great river Euphrates. The four angels had been restrained until now, but under the sixth trumpet they are loosed to *slay* and *kill.*

---

[11]   Ibid., 97.

When the Saracen Empire began to decline, it split up into four sultanies that governed at four locations: Aleppo, Iconium, Damascas, and Baghdad. The word *angels* means messengers or ministers. As the leader of the Saracens that *tormented* Rome was called *the angel of the bottomless pit,* so the four sultanies of that same empire are also *angels* or "ministers" of the empire. Beginning with the fifth trumpet, they were held in check only to *hurt* or *torment,* but now under the sixth trumpet, they are unleashed to *slay* and *kill.*

What does the River Euphrates have to do with all this symbolically? The Euphrates was the eastern boundary of the Saracen Empire, but after its decline, the Ottoman Turks came from central Asia, Bunch notes, "as the allies to the Seljukian Turks against the Mongols, and for their aid received a grant of lands from the Sultan of Iconium, in Asia Minor. Their leader, Othman, became the most powerful Emir in Western Asia. In the year 1300, he proclaimed himself Sultan. Thus was founded the Empire of the Osman or Ottoman Turks in Asia. Osman's successors, princes of great courage and enterprise, who were animated moreover by religious fanaticism, and a passion for military glory, raised it to the rank of the first military power in both Europe and Asia."[12] Thus the symbolism of the Euphrates was no longer a boundary for this empire.

Verse 15: For an hour, and a day, and a month, and a year, for to slay the third part of men: In apocalyptic prophecy, an hour would equal 15 days, a day would equal one year, a month would equal 30 years, a prophetic year would equal 360 literal years, for a total of 391 years and 15 days of literal time. This would be the time allotted for the Ottoman Turk Empire to carry on its aggression and killing. White shows how this amazing prophecy was explained by Litch before it was literally fulfilled:

> In the year 1840 another remarkable fulfillment of prophecy excited widespread interest. Two years before, Josiah Litch, one of the leading ministers preaching the second advent, published an exposition of Revelation 9, predicting the fall of the Ottoman Empire. According to his calculations, this power was to be overthrown "in A.D. 1840, sometime in the month of August;" and only a few days previous to its accomplishment he wrote: "Allowing the first period, 150 years, to have been exactly fulfilled before Deacozes ascended the throne by permission of the Turks, and that the 391 years, fifteen days, commenced at the close of the first period, it will end on the 11th of August, 1840, when the Ottoman power in Constantinople may be expected to be broken. And this, I believe, will be found to be the case."—Josiah Litch, in *Signs of the Times, and Expositor of Prophecy,* Aug. 1, 1840.

> At the very time specified, Turkey, through her ambassadors, accepted the protection of the allied powers of Europe, and thus placed herself

---

[12] Ibid., 98.

under the control of Christian nations. The event exactly fulfilled the prediction. . . . When it became known, multitudes were convinced of the correctness of the principles of prophetic interpretation adopted by Miller and his associates, and a wonderful impetus was given to the advent movement. Men of learning and position united with Miller, both in preaching and in publishing his views, and from 1840 to 1844 the work rapidly extended.[13]

Along with the events that took place surrounding the fulfillment of this prophecy, Treiyer explains how Litch calculated this amazing prediction:

Now, since Litch understood that "the hour" formed part of the chronology, he deduced from the day (symbol for one year), the proportion of one hour, and did the same in relation to the year, obtaining fifteen additional days. But, what specific date in 1449 would he choose as a starting point in order to obtain the exact day of expiration of the 391 remaining years of the sixth trumpet? Surprisingly, he did not choose January 6, but July 27, without any specific event from history. He offered this date by linking the dates he proposed for the fifth trumpet, with that indicated for the sixth trumpet. Thus, the first Turkish battle of Bapheum in July 27, 1299, marked for him the beginning of the 150 years of the fifth trumpet. This led him to July 27, 1449, as being the end of the five yearly months of the fifth trumpet, as well as the beginning of the 391 years and fifteen days of the sixth trumpet, ending in August 11, 1840.

What happened in August 11? Rifat Bay, the Turkish emissary, arrived to Alexandria with the conditions of the London Convention to establish the succession of Egypt and Syria which were vacant after the dead [sic] of sultan Mahmud II. Also on that day, the ambassadors of the four European powers who signed that treaty of London (Great Britain, Austria, Prussia, and Russia), received a communiqué from the sultan where he asked them about the measures to be taken in what touched his empire so much. He was told that "provision has been made," but that he could not know what it was. Litch interpreted these events as an acknowledgment of the Turkish government that his independent power had disappeared.[14]

Revelation 9:16: And the number of the army of the horsemen *were* two hundred thousand thousand: and I heard the number of them.

---

[13]   White, *The Great Controversy*, 334-335. The omitted words are "(See Appendix.)" This appended material may be found on page 691 of *The Great Controversy*.

[14]   Treiyer, *The Seals and Trumpets*, 333-334.

Two hundred thousand thousand is two hundred million. This symbolic number represents innumerable numbers of soldiers. For four hundred years, the Ottoman Empire collected not only taxes, but a tax of children. The conquered nations were required to give twenty percent of their young boys to the empire, to be trained as soldiers and administrators in government. These children, who were trained in Islam, were given favors that made them influential in their own countries in preserving the power of the Ottoman Empire.

Revelation 9:17-19: And thus I saw the horses in the vision, and them that sat on them, having breastplates of fire, and of jacinth, and brimstone: and the heads of the horses *were* as the heads of lions; and out of their mouths issued fire and smoke and brimstone. [18]By these three was the third part of men killed, by the fire, and by the smoke, and by the brimstone, which issued out of their mouths. [19]For their power is in their mouth, and in their tails: for their tails *were* like unto serpents, and had heads, and with them they do hurt.

Uniforms and Weapons: "Now in my vision this is how I saw the horses and their riders. They wore ***red, blue, and yellow breastplates***, and the horses' heads were like the heads of lions, and out of their mouths came fire, smoke, and sulfur" (Revelation 9:17, NAB). Bunch gives the history behind this description from Scripture:

> The Cambridge Bible declares that the uniforms were "fiery red, smoky blue and sulfurous yellow." It is a well-known fact that these were the prominent colors in the uniforms of the Turkish soldiers of that period. The prophet also saw the use of different weapons than those used by the Saracens. "Fire, smoke, and sulfur, leaped from their mouths." (Fenton) To the prophet in vision it looked as if the fire, smoke and brimstone came out of the mouths of the charging horses. It is a fact that the use of firearms in warfare had its origin during the wars of this period, and that the Turks were the first to use them. "The use of gunpowder in cannon and bombs appears as a familiar practice."—*Gibbon's Roman Empire*, Vol. 4, p. 370. Hand grenades and small firearms were also used. The use of heavy cannon was an important factor in the capture of Constantinople. Where the Saracens had failed with the sword, lance and arrows, the Turks succeeded with gunpowder and cannons.[15]

Third Part: If we are to be consistent with the understanding of one-third, this would have to mean one-third of the old Roman Empire. Although Constantinople withstood the Saracens under the fifth trumpet, it finally fell to the Ottoman Turks under the sixth trumpet in 1453. Constantinople, which was the richest and largest city of Europe, was now the capital of the Ottoman Turk Empire. The conquest of Constantinople allowed the Turks to continue

---

[15] Bunch, "The Revelation," 100.

their invasion of eastern Europe, pushing as far north as modern-day Poland and Austria.

Conclusion

What about Islam in prophecy in the last days? God used the Muslim nations under the fifth and sixth trumpets to punish apostate Christianity, but this is the last specific reference to Islam in the Revelation. As God allowed the Soviet Union to fall so that the gospel message could advance in eastern Europe and Asia, so He will find a way to reach out to the people in Islamic nations as well. Who would have thought in the 1980s that the great Soviet Union would succumb to the powers of the gospel? When the Iron Curtain fell, so did all the barriers to the good news of the Bible. This may also be the case for Muslim nations in the future.

CHAPTER TWENTY-TWO

Revelation 10

Introduction

Before the seventh trumpet sounds, Revelation chapter 10 through 11:13 gives a very important message of preparation. This is similar to Revelation 7, another precious message sandwiched between the sixth and seventh seals. In chapter 10, God pauses to tell His people, "You need this to be ready for what is ahead of you."

The words are similar to the language in chapter one's introduction to Jesus among the seven golden lampstands. Jesus is the Archangel, the Leader of the angels. This word comes from ἀρχ (arch) and ἄγγελος (angel). Ἀρχάγγελος (archangel) could be translated "chief" or "one in charge" of the messengers (angels). In terms of architecture, as the arch is above the door, therefore the archangel is "above" or "chief" in charge of the angels.

In 1 Thessalonians 4:16, we read: "The Lord Himself shall descend from heaven with a shout, with the voice *of the archangel*, and with the trump of God: and the dead in Christ shall rise first." Speaking to His persecutors, Jesus predicted: "Verily, verily, I say unto you, The hour is coming, and now is, when the dead shall hear the voice of the Son of God: and they that hear shall live. For as the Father hath life in himself; so hath he given to the Son to have life in himself; And hath given him authority to execute judgment also, because he is the Son of man. Marvel not at this: for the hour is coming, in the which all that are in the graves shall *hear his voice*" (John 5:25-28).

Jesus speaks of Himself in these verses; therefore Jesus' voice is the Archangel's voice, the only One who can wake the dead. He is Michael in all the apocalyptic passages where He is portrayed in conflict with Satan.

Revelation 10:1: And I saw another mighty angel come down from heaven, clothed with a cloud: and a rainbow was upon his head, and his face was as it were the sun, and his feet as pillars of fire.

Cloud: Bunch links this symbol to the presence of Christ in ancient Israel: "While leading ancient Israel through the wilderness Christ veiled His presence in a pillar of cloud by day. In a cloud He came down on Mount Sinai to proclaim

His law, and in a cloud the Lord visited the holy of holies in the tabernacle."[1] This imagery of the chariot throne of God is seen in Psalm 104:3 "Who layeth the beams of his chambers in the waters: who maketh the clouds his chariot: who walketh upon the wings of the wind." Likewise Revelation calls Jesus a mighty Angel; "**a rainbow was upon his head, and his face was as it were the sun, and his feet as pillars of fire.**" The sanctuary language and colors associated with the High Priest remind us of the very presence of God.

Shea gives reasons to link this angel with divinity:

> **Evidence for a Christlike figure.** In favor of the identification with Christ, we observe that the four main characteristics of this angel are most commonly connected with representations of God. This applies to the appearance of his feet as pillars of fire, to the cloudy garment wrapped around him, to the glory seen radiating from his face, and to the rainbow seen over his head. All four characteristics occur in connection with descriptions of God elsewhere in the Bible. None of them are used exclusively for angels. If this is only an angelic figure, he surely has been endowed with extensive divinelike characteristics.
>
> An additional point derives from a consideration of similar passages available for comparison. These are Revelation 1, Daniel 10 and 12, and Ezekiel 1. In these passages the main figure is divine. In Revelation 1 it is Christ. Ezekiel 1 identifies its central character as Yahweh. The figure present in Daniel 10 is certainly Godlike and more exalted than the angels present in the narrative.
>
> Since these comparisons come the closest to the description of the angel of Revelation 10, and since these Persons are divine, these comparisons suggest that the figure present in Revelation 10 is Christlike, and not just an angel.[2]

The evidences above reveal symbols of Jesus! This is not just an angel. Often Jesus is pictured in relation to the angels or messengers, so this symbolic messenger gives us a picture of Christ.

The rainbow: "And I saw another mighty angel coming down from heaven, wrapped in a cloud, with a **rainbow over his head**; his face was like the sun, and his legs like pillars of fire" (Revelation 10:1, NRS). "Then I saw another mighty angel come down from heaven wrapped in a cloud, with a halo **around his head**; his face was like the sun and his feet were like pillars of fire" (Revelation 10:1,

[1]   Bunch, "The Revelation," 106.

[2]   William H. Shea, "The Mighty Angel and His Message," in *Symposium on Revelation: Book 1*, Daniel and Revelation Committee Series, vol. 6 (Silver Spring, MD: Biblical Research Institute, 1992), 290-291.

NAB). The rainbow encircled His head. According to Revelation 4:3: "And he that sat was to look upon like a **jasper and a sardine stone**: and there was a **rainbow round about the throne,** in sight like unto an **emerald.**"

The rainbow encircling the throne of God is an emblem of divinity and eternity. This message comes from the throne of God, signifying its divine origin. The use of the rainbow also symbolizes a message of God's mercy and grace toward repentant sinners. As the first rainbow was a sign that God would not destroy the earth again by a flood, so God's merciful kindness is again revealed in the last days between the second and third woe.

Revelation 10:2-6: And he had in his hand a little book open: and he set his right foot upon the sea, and his left foot on the earth, ³And cried with a loud voice, as when a lion roareth: and when he had cried, seven thunders uttered their voices. ⁴And when the seven thunders had uttered their voices, I was about to write: and I heard a voice from heaven saying unto me, Seal up those things which the seven thunders uttered, and write them not. ⁵And the angel which I saw stand upon the sea and upon the earth lifted up his hand to heaven, ⁶And sware by him that liveth for ever and ever, who created heaven, and the things that therein are, and the earth, and the things that therein are, and the sea, and the things which are therein, that there should be time no longer."

The position of the angel signifies the worldwide scope of the message, but even mercy has its limits. The angel proclaims with a loud voice, **"There should be time no longer."** All the world must hear the message of this angel. Two symbols signify the importance of this message: the roar of a lion and the seven thunders. The lion's loud roar symbolizes the voice of Jesus, the "Lion of the tribe of Judah" (Revelation 5:5). The message of the seven thunders was sealed, but the little book, the focus of this passage, is here unsealed.

Little Book Opened

Previously the little book must have been closed. This points back to Daniel 12:4: **"But thou, O Daniel, shut up the words, and seal the book, even to the time of the end: many shall run to and fro, and knowledge shall be increased."** Since Daniel's book was to be closed until the time of the end, then this must be the book that is now opened. Revelation reveals these sealed messages as this is the only reference in the Bible to the opening of a sealed book. Hence with Revelation 10 the closed book of Daniel is finally opened. Smith enumerates the reasons behind this interpretation:

All that now remains on this point is to ascertain when the time of the end began, and the book of Daniel itself furnishes data from which this can be done. In Daniel 11:30, the papal power is brought to view. In verse 35 we read, "Some of them of understanding shall fall, to try them, and to purge, and to make them white, *even to the time of the end.*" Here is the period of the supremacy of the little horn, during which time the saints, times, and laws were to be given into his hand, and from him suffer fearful persecutions. This is declared to reach to the time of the end. This period ended in A.D. 1798, when the 1260 years of papal supremacy expired. There the time of the end began, and the book was opened. Since that time, many have run to and fro, and knowledge on these prophetic subjects has marvelously increased. . . .

The chronology of the events of Revelation 10 is further ascertained from the fact that this angel appears to be identical with the first angel of Revelation 14. The points of identity between them are easily seen: They both have a special message to proclaim. They both utter their proclamation with a loud voice. They both use similar language, referring to the Creator as the maker of heaven and earth, the sea, and the things that are therein. And they both proclaim time, one swearing that time should be no more, and the other proclaiming that the hour of God's judgment has come.

But the message of Revelation 14:6 is located this side of the beginning of the time of the end. It is a proclamation of the hour of God's judgment come, and hence must have its application in the last generation. Paul did not preach the hour of judgment come. Martin Luther and his coadjutors did not preach it. Paul reasoned of a judgment to come, indefinitely future, and Luther placed it at least three hundred years beyond his day. Moreover, Paul warns the church against preaching that the hour of God's judgment has come, until a certain time. He says: "Now we beseech you, brethren, by the coming of our Lord Jesus Christ, and by our gathering together unto Him, that ye be not soon shaken in mind, or be troubled, neither by spirit, nor by word, nor by letter as from us, as that the day of Christ is at hand. Let no man deceive you by any means: for that day shall not come, except there come a falling away first, and that *man of sin be revealed*." 2 Thessalonians 2:1-3. Here Paul introduces to our view the man of sin, the little horn, or the papacy, and covers with a caution the whole period of his supremacy, which, as already noticed, continued 1260 years, ending in 1798.

In 1798, therefore, the restriction against proclaiming the day of Christ at hand ceased. In 1798 the time of the end began, and the seal was taken from the little book.[3]

Seven thunders: The seven thunders were seven messages. John would have written them, but he was told not to do so! Most likely John thought these thun-

---

3   Smith, 520-521.

ders would reveal a series of events similar to the seven churches, seven seals, and seven trumpets. Thunder often plays a role in Revelation as associated with the sanctuary in heaven (Revelation 4:5; 8:3, 5; 11:19). The latter verse associates thundering with the ark of the covenant, the throne of judgment in the most holy place. In Revelation 16:17-18, thunderings again come from the throne of God. White comments on the seven thunders:

> After these seven thunders uttered their voices, the injunction comes to John as to Daniel in regard to the little book: "Seal up those things which the seven thunders uttered." These relate to future events which will be disclosed in their order. Daniel shall stand in his lot at the end of the days. John sees the little book unsealed. Then Daniel's prophecies have their proper place in the first, second, and third angels' messages to be given to the world. The unsealing of the little book was the message in relation to time.

> The books of Daniel and the Revelation are one. One is a prophecy, the other a revelation; one a book sealed, the other a book opened. John heard the mysteries which the thunders uttered, but he was commanded not to write them.

> The special light given to John which was expressed in the seven thunders was a delineation of events which would transpire under the first and second angels' messages. It was not best for the people to know these things, for their faith must necessarily be tested. In the order of God most wonderful and advanced truths would be proclaimed. The first and second angels' messages were to be proclaimed, but no further light was to be revealed before these messages had done their specific work. This is represented by the angel standing with one foot on the sea, proclaiming with a most solemn oath that time should be no longer.

> This time, which the angel declares with a solemn oath, is not the end of this world's history, neither of probationary time, but of prophetic time, which should precede the advent of our Lord. That is, the people will not have another message upon definite time. After this period of time, reaching from 1842 to 1844, there can be no definite tracing of the prophetic time. The longest reckoning reaches to the autumn of 1844.[4]

Revelation 10:7-9: But in the days of the voice of the seventh angel, when he shall begin to sound, the mystery of God should be finished, as he hath de-

---

[4] Ellen G. White, Manuscript 59, 1900; quoted in *The Seventh-day Adventist Bible Commentary*, ed. F. D. Nichol, 2d ed. (Washington, DC: Review and Herald, 1980), 7:971.

clared to his servants the prophets. **⁸And the voice which I heard from heaven spake unto me again, and said, Go and take the little book which is open in the hand of the angel which standeth upon the sea and upon the earth. ⁹And I went unto the angel, and said unto him, Give me the little book. And he said unto me, Take it, and eat it up; and it shall make thy belly bitter, but it shall be in thy mouth sweet as honey. ¹⁰And I took the little book out of the angel's hand, and ate it up; and it was in my mouth sweet as honey: and as soon as I had eaten it, my belly was bitter.**

Verse 7 gives insight on the seventh trumpet that will soon be revealed. **"The mystery of God should be finished"** just before the seventh trumpet is sounded. What is the mystery of God? In Ephesians 1:9-10 we find these words: "Having made known unto us the mystery of his will, according to his good pleasure which he hath purposed in himself: That in the dispensation of the fullness of times he might gather together in one all things in Christ, both which are in heaven, and which are on earth; even in Him." Again in Ephesians 6:19 Paul speaks of this mystery in his prayer request: "And for me, that utterance may be given unto me, that I may open my mouth boldly, to make known the *mystery of the gospel.*" The "gospel" is declared to be a mystery. Once more Paul tells us in Ephesians 3:3-6: "By revelation he made known unto me *the mystery*; (as I wrote afore in few words, whereby, when ye read, ye may understand my knowledge in the *mystery of Christ*) which in other ages was not made known unto the sons of men, as it is now revealed unto his holy apostles and prophets by the Spirit; that the Gentiles should be fellow heirs, and of the same body, and partakers of his promise in Christ by *the gospel.*" Thus the mystery of God is none other than the gospel of salvation in Christ Jesus: "Christ in you, the hope of glory" (Col. 1:27).

Verses 8-10: "**Go and take the little book which is open in the hand of the angel which standeth upon the sea and upon the earth. ⁹And I went unto the angel, and said unto him, Give me the little book. And he said unto me, Take it, and eat it up; and it shall make thy belly bitter, but it shall be in thy mouth sweet as honey. And I took the little book out of the angel's hand, and ate it up; and it was in my mouth sweet as honey: and as soon as I had eaten it, my belly was bitter.**"

The bitter-sweet book: The little book open in the angel's hand is the book of Daniel. In Daniel 12:4, the angel promised Daniel that his prophecies would be opened and understood in the last days. This commenced in 1798, the termination of the 1260- and 1290-day prophecies.

During the years between 1798 and 1844, knowledge of the precious prophecies of Daniel rapidly increased world-wide, and God's people ran to and fro sharing the sweet message of the Advent hope. They believed that the Day of Atonement would soon be fulfilled and that this cleansing of the sanctuary symbolized the end of the world. Earnest Bible students from many denominations in various countries around the world came to the conclusion that 1844 would be the end of the 2300-day prophecy, and they expected that the Lord would return to cleanse the world. The words of Daniel tasted like honey to the believers.

Those who waited for the special blessing of 1843, the termination of the 1335-day prophecy, went everywhere preaching the sweet message of the soon return of Jesus. They expected to see Him in 1844, the end of the 2300-day prophecy.

When the date passed and the Lord did not come, all their sweetness melted away. Those who shared the hope of the imminent coming of Jesus on October 22, 1844 felt the bitterness of disappointment. Many who were part of the Advent cause turned on their fellow believers, making their bitterness even worse. This experience was foretold in Revelation 10:9-10.

Paradoxically, their misinterpretation of the 2300-day prophecy resulted in the unsealing of the book of Daniel and a better understanding of the sanctuary message. As they again studied the Scriptures even more deeply, they now realized the importance of 1844. White who lived through the bitter disappointment of 1844 remembers the spiritual power behind the Advent message:

> Of all the great religious movements since the days of the apostles, none have been more free from human imperfection and the wiles of Satan than was that of the autumn of 1844. Even now, after the lapse of many years, all who shared in that movement and who have stood firm upon the platform of truth still feel the holy influence of that blessed work and bear witness that it was of God.

> At the call, "The Bridegroom cometh; go ye out to meet Him," the waiting ones "arose and trimmed their lamps;" they studied the word of God with an intensity of interest before unknown. Angels were sent from heaven to arouse those who had become discouraged and prepare them to receive the message. The work did not stand in the wisdom and learning of men, but in the power of God. It was not the most talented, but the most humble and devoted, who were the first to hear and obey the call. Farmers left their crops standing in the fields, mechanics laid down their tools, and with tears and rejoicing went out to give the warning. Those who had formerly led in the cause were among the last to join in this movement. The churches in general closed their doors against this message, and a large company of those who received it withdrew from their connection. In the providence of God this proclamation united with the second angel's message and gave power to that work.

> The message, "Behold, the Bridegroom cometh!" was not so much a matter of argument, though the Scripture proof was clear and conclusive. There went with it an impelling power that moved the soul. There

was no doubt, no questioning. Upon the occasion of Christ's triumphal entry into Jerusalem the people who were assembled from all parts of the land to keep the feast flocked to the Mount of Olives, and as they joined the throng that were escorting Jesus they caught the inspiration of the hour and helped to swell the shout: "Blessed is He that cometh in the name of the Lord!" Matthew 21:9. In like manner did unbelievers who flocked to the Adventist meetings—some from curiosity, some merely to ridicule—feel the convincing power attending the message: "Behold, the Bridegroom cometh!"

At that time there was faith that brought answers to prayer—faith that had respect to the recompense of reward. Like showers of rain upon the thirsty earth, the Spirit of grace descended upon the earnest seekers. Those who expected soon to stand face to face with their Redeemer felt a solemn joy that was unutterable. The softening, subduing power of the Holy Spirit melted the heart as His blessing was bestowed in rich measure upon the faithful, believing ones.[5]

The bitter disappointment of 1844 was similar to the disciples' experience when Jesus was crucified in A.D. 31. The fondest hopes of the disciples had been shattered, but with the knowledge of the resurrection of Christ, they went back to the Scriptures to understand how they had misinterpreted the Messianic prophecies. The scales of human interpretation fell from their eyes as they remembered that Jesus' words had all come to pass. Now they became even more convinced of the truths they had professed before the death of Christ. The bitter disappointment also relieved the church of all who were not seriously committed to the Lord Jesus Christ and His holy word of truth. Today God is calling for a solid remnant willing to put their belief into action. Through His people, God will fulfill His purpose of a world-wide movement to propel the gospel to the whole world.

Revelation 10:11: And he said unto me, Thou must prophesy again before many peoples, and nations, and tongues, and kings.

When Jesus did not come in 1844, how could the Advent believers "prophesy again" after their earnest hopes had led to bitter disappointment? As they searched the Scriptures, they discovered that the symbolic sanctuary service held the key to the 2300 days of Daniel 8:14. The discovery of the heavenly sanctuary linked with the book of Hebrews gave them a clearer view of the significance of 1844.

As they studied the prophecies again, they learned that the fulfillment of the Day of Atonement pointed to a new phase of Christ's ministry for them in the heavenly sanctuary. For over a thousand years, this precious truth had been

5   White, *The Great Controversy*, 401-3.

trampled to the ground by the little horn power. Now the Adventists realized that Jesus' ministry had shifted from the holy place to the most holy place ministry of the heavenly sanctuary in 1844. Before the Feast of Tabernacles could be realized in the second coming of Christ, the Day of Atonement would be fulfilled through the ministry their great High Priest, Jesus Christ, and the sacredness of His holy law in the ark of the covenant would be proclaimed.

Conclusion

Those who announced the second advent of Christ in the 1840s understood themselves to be the seventh-month movement, fulfilling the fall feasts of trumpets, atonement, and tabernacles. The Advent believers mistakenly thought that the Day of Atonement which began in 1844 would be the end of the world. Instead, their announcement of this important date for ten years (1834 to 1844) fulfilled the Feast of Trumpets that proclaimed the great antitypical Day of Atonement. The prophecies of the book of Daniel were preached when Bible students all over the world heard the trumpet-like call from God's word, summoning all nations to prepare for God's judgment and to understand the prophecies in light of the second coming of Christ. They did not realize that on October 22, 1844, Christ would enter His final phase of ministry in the most holy place in heaven. After completing His ministry in the most holy place, then the Feast of Tabernacles would be fulfilled by the second coming of Jesus. We will see that imagery when we study Revelation 19:15.

After learning more of Christ's priestly ministry, the small body of Advent believers understood that they were to prophesy until Jesus returns to take His people home. That blessed day will be the fulfillment of the final Feast of Tabernacles when we will eat together at that great banquet table in heaven—the wedding supper of the Lamb!

CHAPTER TWENTY-THREE

Revelation 11

Introduction

Verses 1 and 2 are a continuation of the bitter experience in chapter 10. After the sweet period of preaching the prophecies of Daniel, the bitter experience of the disappointment of 1844 led the believers search the Scriptures again. Revelation 10:11 to 11:2 pointed them to the fact that their task was not yet finished. New light was yet to shine from the sanctuary in heaven.

Out of their bitter disappointment came a biblical understanding of the cleansing of the heavenly sanctuary that began in 1844. As they compared Scripture with Scripture, the Advent believers realized that they had focused on the earth instead of the sanctuary in heaven. As they read Revelation 10:11, they listened to the angel's words: "Thou must prophesy again before many peoples, and nations, and tongues, and kings."

What were they to prophesy? The answer lies in Revelation 11:1-2: the sanctuary service must be linked to what happened in 1844. Just as Paul pointed to the heavenly High Priest in the book of Hebrews, so does the book of Revelation. The opening verses of chapter 11 point us to Christ's work in the heavenly sanctuary and unveil Satan's attempt to obscure this ministry of our Savior.

At the cross when Jesus died to pay the penalty for sin, this fulfilled the symbol of the altar of burnt offering in the sanctuary service. While on earth, Jesus fulfilled the courtyard services, but when He ascended into heaven, His work in the heavenly sanctuary would begin. Revelation 11:1-2 reminds us that we need to look up by faith to our heavenly High Priest. This is why the first vision of Jesus in Revelation 1 is not in the court, but in the holy place of the sanctuary in heaven.

The first two verses of Revelation 11 point out that those who would follow Jesus by faith move their eyes from the earthly court to the heavenly sanctuary for their answers. However, this same passage also warns us that this heavenly sanctuary ministry would be trampled upon for more than 1,260 years. False teachings crept into the church and supplanted the truth of Christ's heavenly ministry. For more than a millennium, many were directed to an earthy priesthood rather than the ministry of our heavenly High Priest. In this way, the holy city was trampled underfoot for forty-two months which is 1,260 years of literal time. This holy city includes the saints of God who have followed Jesus into the heavenly sanctuary by faith, worshiping Christ in spirit and in truth. Those who direct people toward earthly priests take the worship away from Jesus and trample underfoot those who look up to heaven for their salvation.

The 1260 years are the key to Revelation 11, therefore this important prophetic time period is repeated seven times in Daniel and Revelation. This repetition ties these two books together. The 1260 years point to more than one millennium of papal persecution and obfuscation of the truth, showing the dragon-like nature of the Roman Church.

Revelation 11:1-2: And there was given me a reed like unto a rod: and the angel stood, saying, Rise, and measure the temple of God, and the altar, and them that worship therein. ²But the court which is without the temple leave out, and measure it not; for it is given unto the Gentiles: and the holy city shall they tread under foot forty and two months.

The measuring reed: The Greek word for reed is κάλαμος (kal'-am-os) meaning a measuring reed or rod. The Greek word for measure, μετρέω (met-reh'-o), can be used metaphorically, meaning "to judge according to any rule or standard."

This measuring is done in the contextual setting of the sweet experience of understanding the 2300-day prophecy. In the light of the sanctuary service, measuring also applies to the Day of Atonement. After the bitter experience of the Advent believers, God's people were told to measure the temple of God, but leave out the court. The angel seems to be telling us, "Look up!" Through a deeper understanding of Christ's ministry in the sanctuary, the trampling work of the little horn power was to be undone. Christ's ample provision through the sanctuary would be glorified and proclaimed.

Leviticus 16 parallels Revelation 11 with one difference: unlike the earthly priesthood, Christ does not need to make atonement for Himself. These parallels symbolize what Jesus our High Priest is doing for us in the heavenly sanctuary. The measuring points to God's judgment, reminding His faithful ones to follow Jesus into the heavenly sanctuary and seek an understanding of Christ's work in their behalf.

After much Bible study, the Advent believers understood the message that they must prophesy "before many peoples, and nations, and tongues, and kings." The reason for their bitter disappointment became clear as by faith they looked up to Christ in His sanctuary. Their world-wide message would include the 2300-day prophecy, seventy-week prophecy, the 1260-, 1290- and 1335-day prophecies as well as the other prophecies of Daniel and Revelation. On October 22, 1844, Jesus began His final ministry in the holy of holies, also called the most holy place. Leaving human interpretations behind, the Advent believers gained a biblical understanding from the light that shone from the sanctuary. Now they must prophesy again "before many peoples, and nations, and tongues, and kings." The truth gained from their bitter disappointment would point to Christ and call the world to make preparation for the return of Jesus Christ, the King of kings and Lord of lords. The time to come to Him is now, while Jesus is still ministering in the most holy place.

Verse 3 connects the two witnesses to history and to the bitter experience of Revelation 10:9. From 1798 through 1844 the message was preached in its sweetness, but on that bitter night in 1844, Jesus did not return. The Advent people had to re-evaluate and re-examine their beliefs, bringing them back under the scrutiny and light of the Word of God. Those who looked by faith to the heavenly sanctuary discovered the two phases of Christ's heavenly ministry: the holy place ministry known as "the daily" and the final ministration during the Day of Atonement in the most holy place. The cleansing of the sanctuary was not the end of the world, but the beginning of the great antitypical Day of Atonement. The cleansing of the sanctuary in heaven had begun—the last phase of Christ's work as our High Priest.

The two witnesses testify of the 1,260-day prophecy and explain when the seventh trumpet's message will take place and what it means. The Scriptures with both the Old and the New Testaments are God's witnesses. Jesus said, "They testify of Me" (John 5:39). The prophecies of the Bible, especially those in Daniel and Revelation, foretold the trampling of the holy city and the holy sanctuary. These faithful witnesses also gave birth to the Advent movement that swept like wildfire through all denominations. Reverence for the Word of God was fostered by Protestantism; this is why the Advent message spread rapidly through the churches in the northeastern states of New England. During the sixth church of Philadelphia and under the sixth seal, the sixth trumpet gave birth to a church that loved to share the gospel and boldly endeavored to take it to the entire world. Carey from England, Adoniram Judson from the United States, and many others determined to spread the gospel to the world. In this setting the Advent movement was born.

Adoniram Judson was a Congregationalist when he was sent to Burma, but his study of the Scriptures led him to a deeper understanding of baptism. He became a Baptist on his way to the mission field. This Bible-based environment birthed the Advent movement. The Bible and the Bible alone became the final rule and authority for Advent Christians. Judson was influenced by pietism; the basis of his lifestyle choices like music, jewelry, and dress point to a respect and reverence for the Bible.

Revelation 11:3: And I will give power unto my two witnesses, and they shall prophesy a thousand two hundred and threescore days, clothed in sackcloth.

Smith comments on this verse: "During this time of 1260 years the witnesses are in a state of sackcloth, or obscurity, and God gives them power to endure and maintain their testimony through that dark and dismal period."[1] White enlarges on this same theme:

> During the greater part of this period, God's witnesses remained in a state of obscurity. The papal power sought to hide from the people the word of truth, and set before them false witnesses to contradict its testimony. When the Bible was proscribed by religious and secular authority; when its testimony was perverted, and every effort made that men and demons could invent to turn the minds of the people from it; when those who dared proclaim its sacred truths were hunted, betrayed, tortured, buried in dungeon cells, martyred for their faith, or compelled to flee to mountain fastnesses, and to dens and caves of the earth—then the faithful witnesses prophesied in sackcloth. Yet they continued their testimony throughout the entire period of 1260 years. In the darkest times there were faithful men who loved God's word and were jealous for His honor. To these loyal servants were given wisdom, power, and authority to declare His truth during the whole of this time.[2]

Revelation 11:4: These are the two olive trees, and the two candlesticks standing before the God of the earth.

Smith brings it home: "Evident allusion is here made to Zechariah 4:11-14, where it is implied that the two olive trees are taken to represent the word of God. David testifies, 'The entrance of Thy words giveth light;' and, 'Thy word is a lamp unto my feet, and a light unto my path.' Psalm 119:130, 105. Written testimony is stronger than oral. Jesus declared of the Old Testament Scriptures, 'They are they which testify of Me.' John 5:39."[3]

Bible students of the 1800s clearly understood the two witnesses to be the Old and New Testaments of the Bible. Smith concludes with these words: "These declarations and considerations are sufficient to sustain the conclusion that the Old and New Testaments are Christ's two witnesses."[4]

Bunch lists those who held this truth: "Primasius, Bede, Bishop Andrews, Melchior, Affelman, Croly, Wordsworth, Uriah Smith, and others declared that the two witnesses are the two Testaments from which the Christian church proclaims the gospel message."[5] In the book *The Great Controversy*, White comments:

---

[1]   Smith, 533-534.

[2]   White, *The Great Controversy*, 267-268.

[3]   Smith, 534.

[4]   Ibid.

[5]   Bunch, "The Revelation," 122.

Concerning the two witnesses the prophet declares further: "These are the two olive trees, and the two candlesticks standing before the God of the earth." "Thy word," said the psalmist, "is a lamp unto my feet, and a light unto my path." Revelation 11:4; Psalm 119:105. The two witnesses represent the Scriptures of the Old and the New Testament. Both are important testimonies to the origin and perpetuity of the law of God. Both are witnesses also to the plan of salvation. The types, sacrifices, and prophecies of the Old Testament point forward to a Saviour to come. The Gospels and Epistles of the New Testament tell of a Saviour who has come in the exact manner foretold by type and prophecy.[6]

Revelation 11:5: And if any man will hurt them, fire proceedeth out of their mouth, and devoureth their enemies: and if any man will hurt them, he must in this manner be killed.

Smith relates this to our lives today: "To hurt the word of God is to oppose, corrupt, or pervert its testimony, and turn people away from it. Against those who do this work, fire proceedeth out of their mouth to devour them, that is, judgment of fire is pronounced in that word against such. It declares that they will have their punishment in the lake that burns with fire and brimstone. (Malachi 4:1; Revelation 20:15; 22:18, 19.)"[7] This explains the symbolic language of fire from the mouth of the two witnesses.

White concurs: "Men cannot with impunity trample upon the word of God. The meaning of this fearful denunciation is set forth in the closing chapter of the Revelation: 'I testify unto every man that heareth the words of the prophecy of this book, If any man shall add unto these things, God shall add unto him the plagues that are written in this book: and if any man shall take away from the words of the book of this prophecy, God shall take away his part out of the book of life, and out of the holy city, and from the things which are written in this book.' Revelation 22:18, 19."[8]

Revelation 11:6: These have power to shut heaven, that it rain not in the days of their prophecy: and have power over waters to turn them to blood, and to smite the earth with all plagues, as often as they will.

This verse uses imagery of Elijah's ministry during the time of Ahab (1 Kings 17 and 18). At the word of the prophet, heaven was shut up and there was no rain, and the drought ended only when the prophet spoke. As the word of Elijah shut the heavens, and there was no rain, so also the word of Moses brought the plagues upon Egypt. The words of both prophets are written in

---

6   White, *The Great Controversy*, 267.

7   Smith, 534.

8   White, *The Great Controversy*, 268.

the two witnesses. The three and a half literal years of drought remind us of the three and a half prophetic years of drought caused by the little horn power (Revelation 11:3).

Revelation 11:7-9: And when they shall have finished their testimony, the beast that ascendeth out of the bottomless pit shall make war against them, and shall overcome them, and kill them. ⁸And their dead bodies shall lie in the street of the great city, which spiritually is called Sodom and Egypt, where also our Lord was crucified. ⁹And they of the people and kindreds and tongues and nations shall see their dead bodies three days and an half, and shall not suffer their dead bodies to be put in graves.

In 1798 the time of sackcloth ended. What power made war on God's Word at this time? A power that did not recognize God, like Sodom and Egypt. Pharaoh declared in Exodus 5:2: "Who is the LORD, that I should obey his voice to let Israel go? I know not the LORD, neither will I let Israel go." Here are the roots of atheism. Was there a kingdom that manifested this same type of a spirit in 1798?

In the year 1793, France abolished the gospel by an act of the legislature. The government declared that it no longer acknowledged God, and the Bible was outlawed in France. God's holy Word was thrown out in the streets and burned. On November 11, 1793, a festival was dedicated to "Reason and Truth," and at the cathedral of the Notre Dame, a pyramid was erected in the center of the church with this incription: "To Philosophy."

Verse 8: And their dead bodies shall lie in the street of the great city, which spiritually is called Sodom and Egypt, where also our Lord was crucified: The Bible describes "this great city" as spiritual "Egypt" and spiritual "Sodom." What characteristics would link Sodom to France? Like Sodom, France slid into sin and licentiousness over the course of many years. In the 1200s France destroyed nearly one million Albigenses under the influence of the Roman church. The year 1572 marked a plot to destroy all the Huguenots in France: the St. Bartholomew's Day Massacre. Fifty thousand were murdered in cold blood. In Paris the streets were literally flowing with blood. During the French Revolution, the watchword of the French infidels became the cry, "Crush the Wretch" meaning Christ. Truly Christ was crucified through the spirit of the French Revolution and in the person of His persecuted and slain saints.

Speaking of the French Revolution, Storrs relates these details: "The Goddess of Reason was set up, in the person of a vile woman, and publicly worshiped. Surely here is a power that exactly answers the prophecy."⁹ This prostitute rightly represented the vile acts committed by the Parisians. Open immorality and sodomy appeared to be the norm and arose out of the corruption of the church.

9   George Storrs, *Midnight Cry*, May 4, 1843, vol. 4, no. 5,6, p. 47; quoted in Uriah Smith, *The Prophecies of Daniel and the Revelation* (Washington, DC: Review and Herald, 1944), 538.

Much of the leadership in the Revolution was led by priests who shed the garb of religion.

Revelation 11:10: And they that dwell upon the earth shall rejoice over them, and make merry, and shall send gifts one to another; because these two prophets tormented them that dwelt on the earth.

Commenting on this verse, Storrs continues: "This denotes the joy those felt who hated the Bible, or were tormented by it. Great was the joy of infidels everywhere for awhile. But 'the triumphing of the wicked is short;' so was it in France, for their war on the Bible and Christianity had well-nigh swallowed them all up. They set out to destroy Christ's 'two witnesses,' but they filled France with blood and horror, so that they were horror-struck at the result of their wicked deeds, and were glad to remove their impious hands from the Bible."[10]

Verse 11: And after three days and an half the Spirit of life from God entered into them, and they stood upon their feet; and great fear fell upon them which saw them.

The historical background of this prophetic time period is supplied by Storrs:

In 1793, the decree passed the French Assembly suppressing the Bible. Just three years after, a resolution was introduced into the Assembly going to supersede the decree, and giving toleration to the Scriptures. That resolution lay on the table six months, when it was taken up, and passed without a dissenting vote. Thus, in just three years and a half, the witnesses "stood upon their feet, and great fear fell upon them which saw them." Nothing but the appalling results of the rejection of the Bible could have induced France to take her hands off these witnesses.[11]

Writing in 1838, Croly records these revisions in the laws of France that restored freedom of worship:

A.D. 1797. On the 17th of June, Camille Jourdan, in the "Council of Five Hundred," brought up the memorable report on the "Revision of the laws relative to religious worship." It consisted of a number of propositions, abolishing alike the Republican restrictions on Popish worship, and the Popish restrictions on Protestant.

1. That *all* citizens might buy or hire edifices for the *free* exercise of religious worship.

2. That *all* congregations might assemble by the sound of bells.

3. That *no test* or *promise* of any sort unrequired from other citizens should

---

[10] Ibid., 539

[11] Ibid.

be required of the ministers of those congregations.

4. That any individual attempting to impede, or in any way interrupt the public worship should be fined, up to 500 livres, and not less than 50; and that if the interruption proceeded from the constituted authorities, such authorities should be fined double the sum.

5. That entrance to assemblies for the purpose of religious worship should be free for all citizens.

6. That all other laws concerning religious worship should be repealed.

Those regulations, in comprehending the whole state of worship in France, were, in fact, a peculiar boon to Protestantism. Popery was already in sight of full restoration. But Protestantism, crushed under the burthen [sic] of the laws of Louis XIV, and unsupported by the popular belief, required the direct support of the state to exist with safety. The Report seems even to have had an especial view to its grievances; the old prohibitions to hold public worship, to possess places of worship, to have ingress, &c.

From that period Protestantism has been free in France, and it now numbers probably as large a population as before its fall. It is a striking coincidence, that, almost at the moment when this great measure was determined on, the French army under Bonaparte was invading and partitioning the Papal territory. The next year, 1798, saw it master of Rome, the Popedom a Republic, and the Pope a prisoner and an exile.

The Church and the Bible had been slain in France from November 1793 till June 1797. The *three years* and a *half* were now *exactly* expended, and the Bible, so long and so sternly repressed before, was placed in honour, and was openly the BOOK of free Christianity![12]

Revelation 11:12: And they heard a great voice from heaven saying unto them, Come up hither. And they ascended up to heaven in a cloud; and their enemies beheld them.

The Old and New "Witnesses" of the Bible were exalted shortly after this time. The British and American Bible Societies were born, and the Bible was printed in many languages, propelling God's word throughout the whole world. At the dissolution of the old Soviet Union, people who had never owned a Bible treated the Scriptures with such reverence and respect as if it had "ascended up to

---

[12] George Croly, *The Apocalypse of St. John* (London: Gilbert & Rivington, 1838), 143-144.

heaven." Proof that God's word remains forever in heaven is found in this same chapter (Revelation 11:19).

Their enemies beheld them: The enemies of the Bible saw that it was the word of God. Remember Eastern Europe at the time of the fall of communism. Not only did the common people revere the Bible, but communists who had warred against the Bible now came to accept it. These former enemies of the Bible became staunch believers and in themselves proved its validity through their own conversions. This author participated in meetings that led to the conversion of hundreds of communists. Included in that group were KGB officers with ranks as high as colonel. During one series of evangelistic meetings, a retired general in the Soviet army was converted. He gave my son his colonel uniform as a memento of what had been one of the most dreaded armies on the earth. In this man's life, the KGB was defeated through the witness of the word of God, the Bible.

Revelation 11:13: And the same hour was there a great earthquake, and the tenth part of the city fell, and in the earthquake were slain of men seven thousand: and the remnant were affrighted, and gave glory to the God of heaven.

The Great City: If France is only a tenth part of the city, the great "city" symbol means more than one single city. The other nine-tenths of this "city" would be larger than the one-tenth that is France. Looking back to Daniel 2, the fourth kingdom of Rome is followed by ten kingdoms that emerge out of pagan Rome. Thus France is one-tenth of the old Roman Empire. In Revelation 11:13, only one-tenth of the "city" falls, so the rest of the "city" would include the other nine-tenths: the rest of Christian Western Europe. Who rules over Christian Western Europe? The papacy controlled Western Europe for 1,260 years as foretold by prophecy. Therefore the city that embraces all of Western Europe is Rome; she is the mother. Western Europe and other Christian nations are considered the daughters of Rome, the mother city.

Great Earthquake: This symbolic language does not refer to a literal earthquake. What happened in France shook the world. Marxism and atheism were born in France. In the reprobate society of France, the highest of all arrogance arose and developed into what would haunt the world through communism, the epitome of atheism. This "great earthquake" with its epicenter in France crucified our Savior afresh in its streets during the French Revolution.

Verse 14: The second woe is past; and, behold, the third woe cometh quickly. The second woe ended with the sixth trumpet. Now the third woe introduces the seventh trumpet. The language used points out a parenthetical time period between the second and third woes which is between the sixth and seventh trumpets. The book of Daniel is opened and understanding comes to faithful Bible students. During this time the two witnesses of the Bible, both the Old and New Testaments, ascended to heaven to speak, bringing their message of light to a darkened world.

The Seventh Trumpet: The Third Woe

Verses 15-17: And the seventh angel sounded; and there were great voices in heaven, saying, The kingdoms of this world are become the kingdoms of our Lord, and of his Christ; and he shall reign for ever and ever. ¹⁶And the four and twenty elders, which sat before God on their seats, fell upon their faces, and worshipped God, ¹⁷ Saying, We give thee thanks, O Lord God Almighty, which art, and wast, and art to come; because thou hast taken to thee thy great power, and hast reigned.

The seventh trumpet begins in this verse; thus commences the third and last woe. Linking these verses with Daniel 7:26-27 and 8:14 give the starting point for this period of time: 1844. Events in this temporal world are not the issue. The book of Revelation, particularly the portion with the seven trumpets, centers on preparing people *spiritually* for the great day of the Lord. The seventh and last trumpet is to awaken a spiritually sleeping world, proclaiming that its God, Judge, and King is about to return, and He will require something of all peoples of the earth.

Smith notes that "although the seventh trumpet has begun to sound, it may not yet be a fact that the great voices in heaven have proclaimed that the kingdoms of this world are become the kingdoms of our Lord and of His Christ, unless it be in anticipation of the speedy accomplishment of this event. But the seventh trumpet, like the preceding six, covers a period of time, and the transfer of the kingdoms from earthly powers to Him whose right it is to reign, is the principal event to occur in the early years of its sounding. Hence this event, to the exclusion of all else, here engages the mind of the prophet."[13]

Revelation 11:18: And the nations were angry, and thy wrath is come, and the time of the dead, that they should be judged, and that thou shouldest give reward unto thy servants the prophets, and to the saints, and them that fear thy name, small and great; and shouldest destroy them which destroy the earth.

This verse covers in a nutshell all the events from the judgment which began in 1844 until the final destruction of the wicked after the millennium. Verse 19 points to the special work of Christ for His people before the wrath of God is poured out upon those who despise His mercy.

The nations were angry: The second woe leads to the third as the rebellion fomented in France extends to the rest of the world. Revolution and bloodshed mark the last half of the nineteenth century, but this is only a prelude to the globalization of warfare that begins in the 1900s. Jesus' words in Matthew 24:6 are fulfilled.

Thy wrath is come, and the time of the dead, that they should be judged: After the light of verse 19 shines upon the world, proclaimed loudly as foretold in Revelation 18, Jesus will blot out the sins of all who accept His ministry for

---

13   Smith, 543.

them in the most holy place. As in the typical Day of Atonement, all who do not confess and forsake their sins during this great judgment hour will be cut off from God's people.

After this work of investigation and judgment is done, then the wrath of God is poured out without mercy. According to Revelation 15:1, God's wrath will soon be completely poured out upon the wicked as the seven angels empty their seven golden bowls containing the seven last plagues. The judgment of the dead that follows the wrath of God refers to the millennial judgment upon the wicked. This prepares God's people for the final destruction of the wicked after the thousand years.

Smith considers the timing of events in Revelation 11:18: "Inasmuch as this judgment of the dead follows the wrath of God, or the seven last plagues, it would seem necessary to refer it to the one thousand years of judgment upon the wicked, above mentioned; for the investigative judgment takes place *before* the plagues are poured out."[14]

Thou shouldest give reward unto thy servants the prophets: Smith continues his comment on this reward: "These will enter upon their reward at the second coming of Christ, for He brings their reward with Him. (Matthew 16:27; Revelation 22:12.) The full reward of the saints, however, is not reached until they enter upon the possession of the new earth. (Matthew 25:34.)"[15]

Destroy them which destroy the earth: This verse has taken on new meaning since the discovery of nuclear weapons and the pervading pollution that affects the lives of both man and beast. Smith adds that this "refers to the time when all the wicked, who have literally devastated vast regions and wantonly destroyed human life, will be forever devoured by those purifying fires from God out of heaven. (2 Peter 3:7; Revelation 20:9.) Thus the seventh trumpet reaches to the end of the one thousand years. Momentous, startling, yet joyous thought! The trumpet now sounding sees the final destruction of the wicked, and the saints, clothed in a glorious immortality, safely located on the earth made new."[16]

The Ark of the Covenant in Heaven

"Testament" in Revelation 11:19 is the same word as "covenant." The ark of the testament is the ark of the covenant. This amazing covenant contained in the ark of the covenant is the Ten Commandments, written by the Lord's own finger. God Himself explains His covenant, ratified with the blood of Jesus, the Lamb of God: "This is the covenant that I will make with them after those days, saith the Lord, I will put my laws into their hearts and in their minds will I write them; and their sins and iniquities will I remember no more" (Hebrews 10:16-17). This

---

[14]   Ibid., 545.

[15]   Ibid.

[16]   Ibid., 546.

speaks of the grace of the mercy seat upon the ark of the covenant and the power of the Holy Spirit.

God's covenant is everlasting, and He invites His people to come into covenant relationship with Him. He promises to write His Ten Commandment law into our minds and hearts. Revelation 5:6, 9 declares the efficacy of the blood of the slain Lamb who died to redeem us from sin and to give us "boldness to enter into the holiest by the blood of Jesus" (Hebrews 10:19).

Revelation 11:19: And the temple of God was opened in heaven, and there was seen in his temple the ark of his testament: and there were lightnings, and voices, and thunderings, and an earthquake, and great hail.

The second apartment of the heavenly sanctuary opens on a most spectacular view. Sinai-like splendor marks the shift from the holy place to the holy of holies of the sanctuary in heaven, introducing the ark of the covenant in the book of Revelation. To our world adrift without a moral compass, God reveals His glory and reminds us that He has not changed. With angels humbly bowing on either side of His magnificent throne, His immutable law is the foundation of His perfect government, with the pure gold covering of the mercy seat.

This verse reveals the plan of salvation: God's great mercy in forgiving the repentent sinner, and the restoration of the divine image of God in man as the finger of God writes His law upon the hearts of His people through the Holy Spirit. Based on the prophetic writings of Jeremiah, the apostle Paul writes: "This is the covenant that I will make with the house of Israel after those days, saith the Lord; I will put my laws into their mind, and write them in their hearts" (Hebrews 8:10; cf. 10:16). At the first Pentecost, the Creator Himself wrote the Ten Commandments on tables of stone, but He wants to do even more for His people. The Lord wants His law to be written "with the Spirit of the living God; not in tables of stone, but in fleshy tables of the heart" (2 Corinthians 3:3). This is the new covenant in verity. Smith speaks of this fulfillment of the final phase of Christ's heavenly ministry:

> The temple is opened, and the second apartment of the sanctuary is entered. We know it is the holy of holies that is here opened, for the ark is seen; and in that apartment alone the ark was deposited. This took place at the end of the 2300 days, when the sanctuary was to be cleansed. (Daniel 8:14.) At that time the prophetic periods ended and the seventh angel began to sound. Since 1844, the people of God have seen by faith the open door in heaven, and the ark of God's testament within. They are endeavoring to keep every precept of the holy law written upon the tables deposited there. That the tables of the law are there, just as they were in the ark in the sanctuary erected by Moses, is evident from the

terms which John uses in describing the ark. He calls it the "*ark of His testament*" (emphasis mine).[17]

Revelation 11:19 marks the change in the focus of Revelation from the holy place to the most holy place. The judgment scene is in place, and all of the following events center around God's righteous judgments. The language in Revelation shifts to reflect the process of judgment. Verse 18 warns of the coming wrath of God and His destruction of those who destroy the earth, but verse 19 holds the key to preparing for that day. Through God's great mercy, His people will follow the light from God's holy law. They are empowered by "the Holy Ghost whom God hath given to them that obey Him" (Acts 5:32).

Conclusion

As the seventh trumpet sounds, a long-awaited announcement is made: the kingdoms of this earth belong to the Lord and His Messiah. The gospel work has ended and the two witnesses have fulfilled their work. When all of God's people are sealed, the angels of God cease to hold the winds of strife. Revelation 10:7 announces: "In the days of the voice of the seventh angel, when he shall begin to sound, the mystery of God should be finished, as he hath declared to his servants the prophets." The intercessory ministry of Christ is finished during the seventh and last trumpet. The last soul has been saved; all have decided whom they will worship and obey: the beast or their Best Friend. Bunch brings it home:

> Like the seven churches and the seven seals, the seven trumpets reach down to the close of Christ's mediatorial work in heaven and His gospel work on earth. The seals and trumpets both embrace the day of God's indignation and the triumph of the church militant. When the seventh seal is broken there will be silence in heaven. When the seventh trumpet sounds there will be anger among the nations of the earth and the utmost confusion as the spirits of demons gain full control for a short time before they meet their doom. Then the saints of the most High will enter upon their endless inheritance, the first thousand years being in heaven and the remainder of eternity on this earth restored to its primitive Edenic condition.[18]

The last verse in Revelation 11 lays the foundation for understanding God's covenant relationship with His people. It also sheds light on the difference between those who worship the Creator according to His covenant law and those who rebelliously worship the beast. God's people have His laws written in their minds and in their hearts through the sealing work of the Holy Spirit (2 Corinthians 3:3).

---

[17] Ibid., 546-547.

[18] Bunch, "The Revelation," 131.

God's everlasting covenant is ratified by the blood of the One who died to save us. John wept until he saw the Lamb in the throne room of God. The power, majesty, and victory of the bleeding Lamb is the focus of the book of Revelation. As our Creator and Redeemer, He is worthy of our praise, obedience, and worship. The next chapter tells of God's people who keep the Ten Commandments and overcome the Devil by the blood of the Lamb (Revelation 12:11, 17).

CHAPTER TWENTY-FOUR

Revelation 12

Introduction

The first eleven chapters cover the historical portion of Revelation; the rest of the book focuses specifically on the final events. Chapter 12 is an important parenthetical message that links the beginning of Revelation to the last events on this earth. More than that, the twelfth chapter ties the great rebellion that began in heaven to the persecution of God's people here on earth. This helps us to understand the great battle through the ages between Christ and Satan.

In the book of Revelation, the parenthetical portions provide vital preparatory messages. Between the sixth and seventh seals, the sealing message of Revelation 7 tells how God's people are enabled to stand for Him through the last days. Between the sixth and seventh trumpets, Revelation 10:1 to 11:13 details the experiences of God's people and directs their focus to Christ's ministry in the heavenly sanctuary. Likewise, Revelation 12 lays the foundation for the final conflict between Christ and Satan, distinctly revealing the difference between truth and error. Before the wrath of God is poured out in the seven last plagues, this chapter introduces the true church and the purity of its message. Revelation 11:19 directed our focus to the ark of God's covenant—His throne is built on the foundation of His unchangeable law. Now we will see God's true people who "keep the commandments of God and have the testimony of Jesus Christ" (Revelation 12:17).

With grand strokes, chapter 12 summarizes the history God's church for nearly 6,000 years. Bunch states: "This outline of history sketches Satan's varied activities against the government of God; it presents a panorama of the long war between Michael and Lucifer; it lifts the curtain on the great drama of life and death in one great act."[1] He continues by listing the various eras in the this earth's spiritual battle:

> This chapter pictures the war between Christ and Satan in five of its six phases. (1) The war in heaven where the controversy began. (2) The

---

[1] Bunch, "The Revelation," 132.

struggle between the church and the serpent from the gates of Eden to the first advent of Christ while both were waiting for His birth. (3) The conflict between Christ and Satan during the former's earthly visit. (4) Satan's attacks against and persecutions of the church during the apostolic church period and down through the middle ages. (5) His war on the remnant reaching to the second advent. The remainder of the Apocalypse completes the panorama, giving in detail the struggles between Satan and the church militant, especially in its remnant phase; the final triumph of the church and the defeat and punishment of Satan and his followers in the lake of fire; and the reward of the forces of righteousness in the earth restored to its primitive glory. The sixth and last phase of the long conflict will take place after the millennium and is not presented in the introductory vision.[2]

Revelation 12:1-6: And there appeared a great wonder in heaven; a woman clothed with the sun, and the moon under her feet, and upon her head a crown of twelve stars: [2]And she being with child cried, travailing in birth, and pained to be delivered. [3]And there appeared another wonder in heaven; and behold a great red dragon, having seven heads and ten horns, and seven crowns upon his heads. [4]And his tail drew the third part of the stars of heaven, and did cast them to the earth: and the dragon stood before the woman which was ready to be delivered, for to devour her child as soon as it was born. [5]And she brought forth a man child, who was to rule all nations with a rod of iron: and her child was caught up unto God, and *to* his throne. [6]And the woman fled into the wilderness, where she hath a place prepared of God, that they should feed her there a thousand two hundred *and* threescore days.

A great wonder in heaven: This is symbolic language. The word for wonder is σημεῖον (*semeion*) which means "a sign." Extending from Eden lost to Eden restored, this pure woman represents God's true church here on earth. In Jeremiah 6:2, God explains His use of this symbol: "I have likened the daughter of Zion to a comely and delicate woman."

In contrast to the pure woman which represents God's church, Revelation 17 uses the symbol of a whore to represent an impure church. The harlot daughters of this apostate church share the characteristics of their harlot mother. Isaiah, Jeremiah, Ezekiel, and Hosea also used this same symbol to describe the apostasy of Israel.

In the Old and New Testament prophecies, the harlot and the pure woman symbolize the apostate and pure churches respectively; thus the woman in Revelation 12 is not Mary, the mother of Jesus. Note also that Revelation 12:12-17 clearly tells how the dragon persecuted the woman for 1,260 literal years; this corresponds to the reign of her persecutor: the little horn power. Daniel 7:25 and

---

[2]   Ibid.

Revelation 12:6, 14 clearly link the 1,260 prophetic days to the phrase "time, and times, and half a time." During this time of persecution, Satan worked through the church-state power that inherited its seat and authority from Rome, the fourth kingdom of Daniel. The riddle in chapter 17 marks this as the seventh power that from the beginning of time persecuted God's people.

This wonderful sign is seen "in heaven" and denotes that she is no earthly woman but rather heaven's symbolism of the pure church. This church period extends from Eden lost to Eden restored. Note the symbols used to describe her: the sun, moon, and twelve stars. Bunch comments on the phrase **"clothed with the sun."**

> What is the robe or garment of the church or bride of Christ? Christians **"put on the armor of light"** when they put on **"the Lord Jesus Christ."** See Romans 13:12, 14; Galatians 3:27. To put on Christ is to be clothed with His character or righteousness which is the wedding garment of the church or bride of Christ. See Isaiah 52:1; 61:10; Revelation 19:7, 8. Only when the church is clothed with the righteousness of Christ is it **"the light of the world."** When the remnant of the church are **"illuminated"** by the glory of God in the latter rain so that the members are all "the children of light" then will the church of Christ appear **"fair as the moon, clear as the sun, and terrible as an army of banners"** (emphasis mine).[3]

The moon under her feet: The woman symbolizes the church in all ages; the moon under her feet represents the foundation upon which she rests. God Himself speaks in Psalm 89:35-37: "Once have I sworn by my holiness that I will not lie unto David. His seed shall endure for ever, and his throne as the sun before me. It shall be established for ever as the moon, and as a faithful witness in heaven." The moon symbolizes something that is enduring or permanent. As the moon shines with light from the sun, so the Scriptures receive their light from Christ. According to the writings of the prophets and apostles, the church of God has stood on the permanent foundation of Christ, the Rock of all ages. Jesus is also the Word, another symbol of the Scriptures. (See Isaiah 28:16; 1 Corinthians 3:10, 11; Ephesians 2:20-22).

Upon her head a crown of twelve stars: The number twelve has been symbolic of faithfulness from the time of the patriarchs. As God chose twelve patriarchs to symbolize leadership of the Old Testament church, so Jesus chose twelve apostles to lead the New Testament church. The twelve stars therefore symbolize both the patriarchs and apostles, the faithful leaders of the church, chosen by God. In a similar manner, the 144,000 who are loyal to the Lamb in the last days are divided into twelve tribes.

---

[3]   Ibid., 135.

This symbolic woman represents the church because she is the object of the dragon's wrath. Her flight into the wilderness and miraculous help from God for 1,260 prophetic years does not fit Mary, the mother of Jesus. The woman is symbolic of the faithful church of God here on earth, and the child is none other than Jesus Christ (Revelation 12:10-12).

The great red dragon: The Greek word for red is πυρρός (*poor-hros*) which means the color of fire or red. The same Greek word is used in Revelation 6:4 referring to the red horse. Elsewhere in Revelation the color red symbolizes lawlessness or rebellion against law. According to Smith, this appropriately represents Satan and his kingdom:

> Next to the eagle the dragon was the principal standard of the Roman legions. That dragon was painted red, as if in faithful response to the picture held up by the seer of Patmos they would exclaim to the world, We are the nation which that picture represents.
>
> Rome, as we have seen, attempted to destroy Jesus Christ through the fiendish plot of Herod. The child who was born to the waiting and watching church, was our adorable Redeemer, who is soon to rule the nations with a rod of iron. Herod could not destroy Him. The combined powers of earth and hell could not overcome Him. Though held for a time under the dominion of the grave, He rent its cruel bands, opened a way of life for mankind, and was caught up to God and His throne. He ascended to heaven in the sight of His disciples, leaving to them and us the promise that He would come again.[4]

Smith draws his conclusion from both internal and external historical evidence: "While the dragon primarily represents Satan, it is in a secondary sense, representative of pagan Rome."[5]

Revelation 12:7-12: And there was war in heaven: Michael and his angels fought against the dragon; and the dragon fought and his angels, [8]And prevailed not; neither was their place found any more in heaven. [9]And the great dragon was cast out, that old serpent, called the Devil, and Satan, which deceiveth the whole world: he was cast out into the earth, and his angels were cast out with him. [10]And I heard a loud voice saying in heaven, Now is come salvation, and strength, and the kingdom of our God, and the power of his Christ: for the accuser of our brethren is cast down, which accused them before our God day and night. [11]And they overcame him by the blood of the Lamb, and by the word of their testimony; and they loved not their lives unto the death. [12]Therefore rejoice, *ye* heavens, and ye that dwell in them. Woe to

---

4   Smith, 553.

5   Ibid., 557.

the inhabiters of the earth and of the sea! for the devil is come down unto you, having great wrath, because he knoweth that he hath but a short time.

Obviously the dragon is not merely an earthly beast or power. In heaven, he fought a battle against Michael, the One who is like God, and as a result, the dragon and his angels were cast out of heaven. The great red dragon is the devil or Satan, the deceiver of the whole world. Using a graphic word picture, John tells how the woman groans in labor as the dragon lurks nearby, ready to consume her child at birth. This contextual evidence reveals the kingdom through which Satan worked at the birth of Christ: the earthly kingdom of Rome attempted to destroy the male child of the woman before he could complete work of salvation foretold by the prophets. Only Jesus fits this description for He is the only One born on earth that **"was caught up unto God, and to his throne."**

Good news: A voice from heaven declared that Satan was cast down. As a result of Christ's victory over the dragon, His people also overcame the devil through the blood of the Lamb and the word of their testimony. Fixing their faith upon the Lamb of God, they chose Jesus even when threatened with death. This symbolizes that many of God's people would become martyrs for their faith.

Revelation 12:13-17: And when the dragon saw that he was cast unto the earth, he persecuted the woman which brought forth the man *child.* **¹⁴And to the woman were given two wings of a great eagle, that she might fly into the wilderness, into her place, where she is nourished for a time, and times, and half a time, from the face of the serpent. ¹⁵And the serpent cast out of his mouth water as a flood after the woman, that he might cause her to be carried away of the flood. ¹⁶And the earth helped the woman, and the earth opened her mouth, and swallowed up the flood which the dragon cast out of his mouth. ¹⁷And the dragon was wroth with the woman, and went to make war with the remnant of her seed, which keep the commandments of God, and have the testimony of Jesus Christ.**

Persecuted the woman: The woman, symbolizing God's pure church, fled into the wilderness for 1,260 years. Therefore the woman does not represent a single individual as no woman on earth lived for 1,260 literal years. God's church hid in the wilderness from A.D. 538 to 1798. This pure woman dresses quite differently from the harlot of Revelation 17. The pure church wears white; the harlot's garb is scarlet and purple. God-given illumination brightens the face of the pure woman, while gold, pearls, and gaudy adornment mark the whore's attire. Therefore, notes Smith, the pure church is not the Roman Church who "during all the Dark Ages trumpeted her lordly commands into the ears of listening Christendom, and flaunted her ostentatious banners before gaping crowds."[6]

The true church was hidden and protected by God while the little horn church fell deeper into apostasy, compromising Bible truths through the acceptance of

---

6   Ibid.

pagan practices. The caves and recesses of the Piedmont region and the valleys of southern France provided one of the wilderness hiding places for God's people. When the church at Rome sought to enforce pagan beliefs upon the people, the true followers of Jesus were forced to flee.

Eagles wings: This symbol represents how swiftly the true church had to find refuge and safety from the man of sin who came to power in Rome. As in the days when Israel fled from Pharaoh, eagles' wings symbolized divine deliverance from persecuting powers. Exodus 19:4 gives God's promise: "Ye have seen what I did unto the Egyptians, and how I bare you on eagles' wings, and brought you unto myself."

She is nourished for a time and times and half a time: Smith comments on this prophecy: "The mention of the period during which the woman is nourished in the wilderness as 'a time and times and half a time,' similar phraseology to that used in Daniel 7:25, furnishes a key for the explanation of the latter passage. The same period is called in Revelation 12:6, 'a thousand two hundred and threescore days.' This shows that a time is one year, 360 days; two 'times,' two years, or 720 days; and 'half a time,' half a year, or 180 days, making in all 1260 days. These days, being symbolic, signify 1260 literal years."[7]

Verses 15-16: And the serpent cast out of his mouth water as a flood after the woman, that he might cause her to be carried away of the flood. ¹⁶And the earth helped the woman, and the earth opened her mouth, and swallowed up the flood which the dragon cast out of his mouth.

The Roman Church unleashed a flood of persecution against those who remained faithful to the written word of God. Millions of true believers were killed for their faithfulness to the Bible. They died rather than deny the lordship of Jesus Christ in their lives. Millions sought safety from Rome in Germany, southern France, and the Piedmont valleys of Italy, but many died for their faithfulness. In spite of persecution, others willingly took their place and kept the faith alive; thus the wilderness church was not totally swallowed up. The words of Revelation 13:16 predict some relief for the church: "The earth helped the woman." The Protestant Reformation began its work, opening its mouth and swallowing up the flood of persecution. Soon the spell of Rome was broken as much of northern Europe became obedient to the word of God.

Commandment Keepers Persecuted

Satan has continued his war on the remnant who are faithful to God's covenant. The anger of the dragon is especially aroused by those who keep the commandments of God and have the testimony of Jesus Christ. Satan tried to make people believe that those who keep the commandments do not have the

7   Ibid., 558.

testimony of Jesus, but Scripture opposes his wiles. Note the close connection in Revelation between obedience to the commandments and the testimony of Jesus.

This text points to those who keep all ten commandments. This includes the Sabbath commandment: the only commandment that most Christians refuse to keep. James describes the law as "the law of liberty" and "the royal law," reminding us that we will be judged by the law (James 1:25; 2:8, 12). He also warns us that we are transgressors if we keep only nine commandments instead of ten (James 2:10-11). Thus the remnant can be recognized by their obedience to the Sabbath command which sets them apart from the norm.

Revelation 11:19 and 12:17 set the stage for Revelation 13. Before the beast and his dreaded mark are brought to view, God opens to us the sacred ark of His testimony which contains the covenant written by His own finger: His Ten Commandments. God's people are like Him. They keep the commandments of God and have the testimony of Jesus. And just as Satan hated and persecuted Jesus, so he is angry with God's people who obey the Ten Commandments. This anger will come to full expression as Revelation 13 reaches its fulfillment, but God's people will remain unchanged by the wrath of the dragon. "Here is the patience of the saints: here are they that keep the commandments of God and the faith of Jesus" (Revelation 14:12).

Conclusion

Chapter 12 reminds us of the remnant church concept that is found throughout the Old and New Testament Scriptures. The faithful followers of Jesus go through a wilderness experience for 1,260 years from A.D. 538 to 1798. Both before and after the wilderness experience, the church's identity is marked by two characteristics: (1) they keep the commandments of God, and (2) they have the testimony of Jesus. With these two identifying characteristics, we can arrive at a correct understanding of who compose the "remnant of her seed."

Pfandl comments on this last day church that has come out of the wilderness experience after 1,260 years of persecution: "John foresees a time when the commandments of God will be a sign by which the true followers of God will be recognized, because the rest of Christianity will have 'commandments of God' which do not correspond to the original. Already Daniel foresaw the time when God's law would be changed (Dan 7:25)."[8] He must have also foreseen man's attempt to change the Sabbath from the seventh day of the week to the first day of the week, a change that has no support from the Bible. Pfandl gives the characteristics of God's remnant:

The keeping of the commandments refers to the keeping of the original commandments given by God on Mount Sinai. In particular, the fourth

---

8   Gerhard Pfandl, "The Remnant Church and the Spirit of Prophecy," in *Symposium on Revelation: Book 2*, Daniel and Revelation Committee Series, vol. 6 (Silver Spring, MD: Biblical Research Institute, 1992), 303.

commandment is the distinctive sign since it has been altered by apostate Christianity.

The testimony of Jesus—Christ's witness—refers to the prophetic gift, which is also present in the remnant church. God promises that through the Spirit of prophecy—the Holy Spirit—He will again manifest Himself in a special way to the remnant church to keep and to guide them in the last days, when Satan will make special efforts to destroy them. . . . This identification . . . does not accord them an exclusive status with God. Salvation is not guaranteed through membership in a specific church. There exists an invisible church of God where all are members who have accepted Christ as their personal Saviour, regardless of church affiliation. Yet at the same time God has an organized and structured church in the world, commissioned to prepare this world and its inhabitants for the second coming of Christ. That means this church has been ordained to give a special message—the three angels' message—to the world.[1]

In Revelation 12, the controversy between Jesus and Satan is clearly brought in view, but Jesus' people who obey all the commandments are the focus of His love and the enemy's wrath. Chapter 14 lists the three special messages that this same remnant group is to give to all the world. However, before these announcements are described, Jesus reveals the enemy's last game plan in Revelation 13. As the pure remnant church came to view in Revelation 12, so the contrasting system that speaks like a dragon is identified in Revelation 13.

9   Ibid., 327.

CHAPTER TWENTY-FIVE

Revelation 13

Introduction

Above all the chapters in the Apocalypse or the Bible itself, Revelation 13 has been universally neglected and ignored by the Christian church as a whole. The reason is perhaps that this chapter points its finger at the compromises that unite almost all the Christian world, putting those who bear the name of Christ in an embarrassing position.

This chapter identifies the two final forces during the very last stage of the great conflict involving heaven and earth. These two forces usher in the final moments of this earth's history.

Like Daniel 7, Revelation 13 uses beasts to represent these two great powers. The first beast comes up from the sea of humanity in the setting of the Apocalypse within the confines of the pagan Roman Empire. In fact Revelation specifically states that this first beast has the characteristics of the three powers preceding Rome and that it received its power, seat, and great authority from the dragon. As noted in the previous chapter, the dragon is primarily Satan, but in a secondary sense, it is also the power on earth he uses to carry out his wishes. Through Satan's deceptive doctrines, many errors crept into the church through compromises with paganism. Thus with obvious clarity, this system received its power from the dragon: it is not from God.

In the description of the first beast of Revelation 13, its characteristics (beast, leopard, bear, lion) are given in reverse order as compared with Daniel 7 (lion, bear, leopard, beast). This links the fourth beast of Daniel 7 with the first beast described in Revelation 13. The reverse order also shows that Revelation 13 looks back historically to predictive prophecies of Daniel 7.

The Beast Out of the Sea

Revelation 13:1-2: And I stood upon the sand of the sea, and saw a beast rise up out of the sea, having seven heads and ten horns, and upon his horns ten crowns, and upon his heads the name of blasphemy. ²And the beast which I saw was like unto a leopard, and his feet were as *the feet* of a bear, and his

mouth as the mouth of a lion: and the dragon gave him his power, and his seat, and great authority.

The two beasts in chapter 13 are similar in that they work together to accomplish the purposes of the dragon. To determine their identities, one must examine their differences. The first beast rises "up out of the sea," whereas the second beast comes "up out of the earth." The first is a leopard-like beast; the second is lamb-like. The first beast is worshiped; the second beast enforces the worship of the first beast. The first beast matches the description of the little horn of Daniel and receives a deadly wound; the second beast promotes the first beast after this wound has been healed.

The meaning of "waters" is identified in Revelation 17:15: "The waters which thou sawest, where the whore sitteth, are peoples, and multitudes, and nations, and tongues." Seas symbolize the masses of humanity or an area that is more densely populated. This is in harmony with Isaiah and Jeremiah (Isaiah 8:7, 8; 28:2; Jeremiah 46:8; 47:2-3; 51:12-13). Like the four beasts of Daniel 7, the first beast of Revelation 13 came up from the sea of humanity. As these four beasts were caricatures of four empires in Daniel, so this sea beast in Revelation 13 is a caricature of a kingdom that resembles the four kingdoms of Daniel 7.

According to Revelation 13:2, the beast power that came up out of the sea had characteristics of the three kingdoms that preceded it. It is "like unto a leopard" (Greece), with "feet of a bear" (Medo-Persia), and "the mouth of a lion" (Babylon). Remember Daniel 7 looked forward in its prophecy, while Revelation 13 expands and opens the understanding of Daniel, using Daniel and other prophetic books to aid in interpreting these characteristics. Revelation 13 begins with the last power in Daniel 7, the fourth kingdom of Rome. This is confirmed by Revelation 12 as the dragon worked through the power of pagan Rome in an attempt to destroy the male child Jesus when He was born.

How was the sea beast like a leopard? In this small clue, God accurately described the Roman Empire as being like the Greek Empire. The architecture, culture, language, and gods of pagan Rome were adopted from Greece. Rome was merely a copy of its predecessor. Latin root words are similar to Greek with different endings and a changed structure. Rome copied what it believed to be the best from each of its predecessors. Rome also took the gods of the preceding kingdoms, thus God's judgments fell upon Rome as described in first four trumpets of Revelation 8. Pagan Rome was not taken through war, but by the intrigue of the Holy Roman Empire known today as the Holy See or the Roman Catholic Church.

Seven Heads and Ten Horns: Each of the four beasts in Daniel 7 are successive empires, but in Revelation 13 these animals are united into one nondescript beast power with the added dimension of seven heads and ten horns. God wants us to understand that the four beasts (lion, bear, leopard, and nondescript beast) are merely part of seven worldly powers that have ruled and will rule the world. This is further described in Revelation 17.

Revelation views Daniel in the contextual setting of Isaiah, Jeremiah, and Hosea. Babylon was the third in a succession of seven powers. The eighth power is revealed in its contextual setting of Revelation 17. The seven heads symbolize the foundation of this seventh power and how each was an integral part of its kingdom. Therefore the first beast of Revelation 13 is the all-encompassing system built on the ruins of the previous six powers: Egypt, Assyria, Babylon, Medo-Persia, Greece, and pagan Rome.

Bunch points out the relationship of the seven heads and ten horns: "It should be noticed that with the dragon the crowns were on the heads indicating that they represented kingdoms or imperial powers. But with the beast the crowns are on the ten horns, indicating that under the seventh phase of the dragon power the civil authority is chiefly in the ten kingdoms and that the ruling head is not strictly a kingdom or civil power. It is different from the other six because it rules over and dominates and works through a number of independent civil kingdoms rather than a single universal empire."[1]

Power, Seat, and Great Authority from the Dragon

The dragon primarily represents Satan and secondarily pagan Rome which gave its power, seat, and great authority to the papacy. After the Ostrogoths were defeated by Belisarius in A.D. 538, Justinian pledged to defend with the armies of Rome the authority of the Roman bishop over all Christendom and proclaimed Catholicism as the state religion. Contextual evidence in chapter 12 reveals that this power would persecute the true remnant church for 1,260 years. The only power in history that fulfills these requirements is papal Rome.

The sea beast describes the development of the papacy after it received its power, seat, and great authority. The end of the 1,260 years is described in Revelation 13:3, 10. The leopard-like beast received a deadly wound, but now this deadly blow has been healed. This is further described in Revelation 17.

Revelation 13:3-6: And I saw one of his heads as it were wounded to death; and his deadly wound was healed: and all the world wondered after the beast. [4]And they worshipped the dragon which gave power unto the beast: and they worshipped the beast, saying, Who *is* like unto the beast? who is able to make war with him? [5]And there was given unto him a mouth speaking great things and blasphemies; and power was given unto him to continue forty *and* two months. [6]And he opened his mouth in blasphemy against God, to blaspheme his name, and his tabernacle, and them that dwell in heaven.

Verse 3: One of its heads was wounded to death, but the deadly wound was healed. At the end of the 1,260-year period of papal domination, the one who

---

[1]   Bunch, "The Revelation," 160.

had led many into captivity was captured by General Berthier in 1798. The power of the papacy was broken, the pope died in captivity (Revelation 13:3, 5, 10), but Jesus foretold the healing of this deadly wound (Revelation 13:3, 12, 14). White comments on this wound and the restoration of power to the beast.

> The infliction of the deadly wound points to the downfall of the papacy in 1798. After this, says the prophet, "his deadly wound was healed: and all the world wondered after the beast." Paul states plainly that the "man of sin" will continue until the second advent. 2 Thessalonians 2:3-8. To the very close of time he will carry forward the work of deception. And the revelator declares, also referring to the papacy: "All that dwell upon the earth shall worship him, whose names are not written in the book of life." Revelation 13:8. In both the Old and the New World, the papacy will receive homage in the honor paid to the Sunday institution, that rests solely upon the authority of the Roman Church.[2]

After the deadly wound, Rome would gradually regain its power, seat, and great authority. In 1929, the papacy recovered its seat in Rome through the Lateran Treaty which also established Roman Catholicism as the state religion of Italy. Although religious in nature, the Vatican is also a sovereign nation. Since that time, papal Rome has steadily regained political and economic power. The church is urging the European Union, the United States of America, and other Christian nations to enact laws that would protect Sunday. Even now the papacy is preparing to exercise great authority over the whole world.

Blasphemy against God

Revelation 13:5-6: And there was given unto him a mouth speaking great things and *blasphemies*; and power was given unto him to continue forty *and* two months. And he opened his mouth in blasphemy against God, to blaspheme his name, and his tabernacle, and them that dwell in heaven"

Another important mark of identification of the sea beast is its blasphemous mouth. The New Testament defines blasphemy because Jesus faced that charge when He forgave sins and claimed to be the Son of God. Notice these verses:

1. ***Forgiveness of Sin*** (Matthew 9:1-6): And he entered into a ship, and passed over, and came into his own city. And, behold, they brought to him a man sick of the palsy, lying on a bed: and Jesus seeing their faith said unto the sick of the palsy; Son, be of good cheer; thy sins be forgiven thee. And, behold, certain of the scribes said within themselves, This man blasphemeth. And Jesus knowing their thoughts said, Wherefore think ye evil in your hearts? For whether is easier, to say, Thy sins be forgiven thee; or to say, Arise, and walk? But that ye may know that the Son of man hath power on earth to forgive sins, (then saith he to the sick of the palsy,)

---

2   White, *The Great Controversy*, 579.

Arise, take up thy bed, and go unto thine house.

2. *Claiming to be God or equal to God* (John 10:33): The Jews answered him, saying, For a good work we stone thee not; but for blasphemy; and because that thou, being a man, makest thyself God.

Smith comments on these two forms of blasphemy:

In the Gospels we find two indications of what constitutes blasphemy. In John 10:33 we read that the Jews falsely charged Jesus with blasphemy because, said they, "Thou, being a man, makest Thyself God." This in the case of the Saviour was untrue, because He *was* the Son of God. He was "Immanuel, God With Us." But for man to assume the prerogatives of God and to take the titles of deity—this is blasphemy.

Again, in Luke 5:21 we see the Pharisees endeavoring to catch Jesus in His words. "Who is this which speaketh blasphemies?" said they. "Who can forgive sins, but God alone?" Jesus could pardon transgressions, for He was the divine Saviour. But for man, mortal man, to claim such authority is blasphemy indeed.[3]

The papacy makes both of these claims, and both are blasphemous. Penitents are instructed to confess their sins to a priest who prescribes penance for them. This takes away from the ministry of Christ by whose blood we are forgiven. Leist describes the papacy's claim to be equal with God: "The infallibility of the pope is the infallibility of Jesus Christ Himself," and "whenever the pope thinks, it is God Himself, who is thinking in him."[4] This is also blasphemy. Antichrist can mean "against Christ," but more importantly, it means "in place of Christ." Putting himself in the place of Christ, the antichrist claims for himself powers that belong only to Jesus Christ.

In addition to its claims to be equal with God and to forgive sin, the papacy has other blasphemous practices. In the mass the priest calls God down to earth in transubstantiation, claiming that the bread and wine actually become the body and blood of Jesus. If this were true, it would be cannibalism. Drinking blood breaks another command in the Scriptures: "But flesh with the life thereof, which is the blood thereof, shall ye not eat" (Genesis 9:4). During the ceremony of the mass, the priest purports to have the power to call Jesus from His throne in the heavenly sanctuary to re-crucify Him in every celebration of the mass. This is blasphemy. Romans 6:10 declares of Christ: "He died unto sin once."

Revelation 13:7-10: And it was given unto him to make war with the saints, and to overcome them: and power was given him over all kindreds, and tongues, and nations. ⁸And all that dwell upon the earth shall worship him,

---

[3]   Smith, 569.

[4]   Fritz Leist, *Der Gefangene des Vatikans* (Munich: Kosch, 1971), 344.

whose names are not written in the book of life of the Lamb slain from the foundation of the world. ⁹If any man have an ear, let him hear. ¹⁰He that leadeth into captivity shall go into captivity: he that killeth with the sword must be killed with the sword. Here is the patience and the faith of the saints.

War with the saints: During the 1,260 years of persecution from A.D. 538 to 1798, history records the terrible atrocities that Rome carried out against the Waldenses, Albigenses, Anabaptists, and Huguenots. The Albigenses were totally annihilated by the church. The false accusations against this group are now being proven false through the writings of their persecutors. In the end, every lie will be exposed, and the truth from God's throne will shine with undimmed clarity.

The sea beast power that wars on the saints received its power, throne, and great authority from the dragon as represented through Satan's power on earth in John's day: the pagan Roman Empire. History records that Justinian gave the bishop of Rome his seat of authority in A.D. 538, and "power was given unto him to continue forty and two months" (Revelation 13:5). Forty-two months of prophetic time is 1,260 literal years. What power reigned, blasphemed, and persecuted for more than a millennium after receiving its power, seat, and authority from pagan Rome? Only the papacy fits the prophecy.

Rome is represented by two symbols in Revelation 12 and 13: the dragon in Revelation 12 and the leopard-like beast of Revelation 13. The first phase of Rome was pagan Rome; the second phase is the professedly Christian phase of Rome represented by the leopard-like beast with its feet like a bear and mouth like a lion. Revelation points out that the deadly wound occurred during the leopard or papal phase.

Smith tells the story of the beast's deadly wound: "It was inflicted when the pope was taken prisoner by Berthier, the French general, and the papal government was for a time abolished, in 1798. Stripped of his power, both civil and ecclesiastical, the captive pope, Pius VI, died in exile at Valence in France, August 29, 1799."[5] White ties history to Revelation 13:9: In 1798, "the pope was made captive by the French army, the papal power received its deadly wound, and the prediction was fulfilled, 'He that leadeth into captivity shall go into captivity.'"[6]

Not written in the Lamb's book of life: This is a fearsome message. The beast wars against God's people, but in reality, he is fighting against the Lamb Himself. While demanding that others worship him, the beast diverts nearly everyone from worshiping the Lamb slain from the foundation of the world. Like Satan, he wants this honor for himself, but captivity and the sword will be his end. He will be treated as he treated the obedient people of God.

Patient, faithful saints: In the midst of this awful description of the satanic beast power, one of the Lord's favorite themes arises like a sweet perfume. His

---

5   Smith, 567.

6   White, *The Great Controversy*, 439.

beloved people endure captivity and the sword out of love for Jesus who died for them (Revelation 13:10).

The Beast out of the Earth

Revelation 13:11: And I beheld another beast coming up out of the earth; and he had two horns like a lamb, and he spake as a dragon.

Explicit language describes the second beast. This creature comes up out of the earth instead of the sea of humanity. The earth symbolizes an unpopulated region from which the beast arises. This beast is like a lamb instead of a leopard. Lamb-like brings to mind a Christ-like nation, and its two horns are not crowned like other nations which are ruled by kings. However, it will speak like a dragon and promote the worship of the sea beast which had the deadly wound that healed miraculously. Smith expounds on the great systems of religion in prophecy:

> The dragon, pagan Rome, and the leopard beast, papal Rome, present before us great organizations standing as the representatives of two great systems of false religion. Analogy would seem to require that the remaining symbol, the two-horned beast, have a similar application, and find its fulfillment in some nation which is the representative of still another great system of religion. The only remaining system which is exercising a controlling influence in the world today is Protestantism. Abstractly considered, paganism embraces all heathen lands, containing more than half the population of the globe. Catholicism, which may perhaps be considered as including the religion of the Greek Orthodox Church, so nearly identical with it, belongs to nations which compose a large part of Christendom. A clear portrayal of Mohammedanism and its influence has been given in other prophecies. (See comments on Daniel 11 and Revelation 9.) But Protestantism is the religion of nations which constitute the vanguard of the world in liberty, enlightenment, progress, and power.[7]

The United States in Prophecy

This second beast of Revelation 13 represents a nation with lamb-like qualities, a Christ-like, Bible-based country that would not be ruled by pope or king. In the early history of this nation, the Protestant principles of religious freedom and liberty of conscience were embraced by the two-horned, lamb-like beast. Because it arose out of the "earth," this nation did not come from teeming seas of humanity which surround the Mediterranean: the populated regions of Europe, Asia, and Africa. The countries of Europe trace their origins to the old Roman Empire.

---

[7]   Smith, 571.

What Christ-like, Protestant country arose in an sparsely populated area near 1798, the time of the first beast's deadly wound? The only nation that fits all the characteristics of this lamb-like, two-horned beast is the United States of America. Smith adds historical details:

"Governor Pownal, an English statesmen, predicted in 1780, while the American Revolution was in progress, that this country would become independent; that a civilizing activity, beyond what Europe could ever know, would animate it; and that its commercial and naval power would be found in every quarter of the globe. He then speaks of the probable establishment of this country as a free sovereign power as 'a revolution that has stranger marks of *divine interposition*, superseding the ordinary course of human affairs, than any other event which this world has experienced.'"[8] Notice the words of the late George Alfred Townsend who compared the United States with the other governments in the Western hemisphere: "The history of the United States was separated by a beneficent Providence far from this wild and cruel history of the rest of the continent, and, like a silent seed, we grew into empire."[9]

Beast wounded while another rises: The rise of the United States in its prophetic role must coincide with the deadly wound to the leopard beast in 1798. Smith elaborates on this subject:

> Can anyone doubt what nation was actually "coming up" in 1798? Certainly it must be admitted that the United States of America is the *only* power that meets the specifications of the prophecy on this point of chronology.

> The struggle of the American colonies for independence began in 1775. In 1776, they declared themselves a free and independent nation. In 1777, delegates from the thirteen original States—New Hampshire, Massachusetts, Rhode Island, Connecticut, New York, New Jersey, Pennsylvania, Delaware, Maryland, Virginia, North Carolina, South Carolina, and Georgia—in Congress assembled, adopted Articles of Confederation. In 1783, the War of the Revolution closed with a treaty of peace with Great Britain, whereby the independence of the United States was acknowledged, and territory ceded to the extent of 815,615 square miles. In 1787, the Constitution was framed, and by July 26, 1788, it was ratified by eleven of the thirteen original States; and on the 1st of March 1789, it went into effect. The United States thus began with less than one million square miles of territory, and less than four million

---

[8]   Ibid., 572.

[9]   George Alfred Townsend, *The New World Compared With the Old* (Hartford, CT: S. M. Betts and Company, 1869), 635.

citizens. Thus we come to the year 1798, when this nation is introduced into prophecy.[10]

While the colonies were still under the control of England, John Wesley wrote in 1754 of the coming of the two-horned beast in his notes on Revelation 13:11. He then published these comments in 1755: "But he is not yet come, though he cannot be far off. For he is to appear at the end of the forty-two months of the first beast."[11]

Lamb-like horns with the dragon's voice: The two horns symbolize civil and religious liberty which are based on the republican form of democracy and Protestantism respectively. The United States government is unique in the Western hemisphere because its representative democracy ideally protects the rights of the minority. This is in opposition to direct democracy in which the rule of the majority may easily trample the freedoms of minority groups. For more than two hundred years, many have fled to the United States seeking religious and civil freedom. It is our national duty to guard the rights of all.

White outlines the special nature of the government of the United States of America: "The Constitution guarantees to the people the right of self-government, providing that representatives elected by the popular vote shall enact and administer the laws. Freedom of religious faith was also granted, every man being permitted to worship God according to the dictates of his conscience. Republicanism and Protestantism became the fundamental principles of the nation. These principles are the secret of its power and prosperity."[12]

However, according to this prophecy, the republican form of democracy will be repudiated some time in the future. Then the majority will determine what is tolerated and what is not. That time is drawing near as the United States already speaks like a dragon in the world and at home. With the demise of the old Soviet Union, the two beasts of Revelation 13 remain the world's superpowers: the papacy and the United States.

In Revelation 16:13; 19:20; and 20:10 the dragon and the beast are associated with "the false prophet." Since the false prophet in Revelation 20:10 does the same miracles as the lamb-like beast in Revelation 13, they represent the same power. These prophecies predict that in the future the United States will work diligently to promote the worship of the beast power: papal Rome. Because religious liberty is anathema to Catholicism, we can expect to see our freedoms eroded in the United States. White comments: "The same spirit which actuated

[10]   Smith, 573-574.

[11]   John Wesley, *Explanatory Notes Upon the New Testament* (New York: Lane and Scott, 1850), 704.

[12]   White, *The Great Controversy*, 441.

papists in ages past will lead Protestants to pursue a similar course toward those who will maintain their loyalty to God."[13]

Bunch describes the apostasy of Protestantism: "The false prophet had two horns of a lamb, but the voice of a dragon. His profession was Christian but his character was satanic. Jesus warned of the false prophets, which come unto you in sheep's clothing, but inwardly they are ravening wolves. Matthew 7:15. Protestantism, which was the mouthpiece of God during the Reformation, becomes the spokesman of the dragon and is dominated by the same dragon spirit that controls the first beast. . . . Satan has always ruled the nations of earth and persecuted the people of God through false religions. It is through his counterfeit church that the god of this world speaks to mankind and demands allegiance and worship."

Healing the Deadly Wound

Revelation 13:12: And he exerciseth all the power of the first beast before him, and causeth the earth and them which dwell therein to worship the first beast, whose deadly wound was healed.

The papacy regained its seat through Mussolini who signed a concordat in 1929. This treaty granted the pope full authority over the state known as Vatican City. This 108.7-acre tract on Vatican Hill lies fully within the confines of the city of Rome. The pope was now monarch of his own political kingdom and claimed to be the leader of the religious world as well. More than that, he has claimed for over a thousand years to be the vicar of Christ on earth.

Since 1929 the position, fame, and authority of the pope has gained strength. Truman's unsuccessful attempt to nominate an ambassador to the Vatican in October 1951 shows the strong stance against popery once held in the United States. Nearly every Protestant voice opposed that nomination. However, no opposition was heard in March 1984 as Reagan nominated William A. Wilson, the first United States ambassador to the Vatican, and won it by a vote of 81 to 13. Each passing decade has increased the pope's influence and brought us closer to the fulfillment of prophecy. Revelation 13:3 predicts the end result: "All the world wondered after the beast." The biblical evidence is clear.

Revelation 13:13-14: And he doeth great wonders, so that he maketh fire come down from heaven on the earth in the sight of men, [14]And deceiveth them that dwell on the earth by *the means of* those miracles which he had power to do in the sight of the beast; saying to them that dwell on the earth, that they should make an image to the beast, which had the wound by a sword, and did live.

Miracles that deceive: Miracles only enhance the deceptive power of the beast from the earth. Seemingly like the divine fire sent in answer to Elijah's prayer, these miracles appear to be coming from heaven, but Jesus reveals their

---

[13] White, *Testimonies for the Church*, 5:449.

satanic source. God has warned us that miracles alone do not prove that a prophet is blessed by heaven. The miracles wrought by the magicians in Egypt did not come from God, but from a different supernatural source. Revelation 16:17 speaks plainly: "They are the spirits of devils, working miracles, which go forth unto the kings of the earth and of the whole world, to gather them together to the battle of that great day of God Almighty.

Image to the beast: White comments on this prophecy: "When the leading churches of the United States, uniting upon such points of doctrine as are held by them in common, shall influence the state to enforce their decrees and to sustain their institutions, then Protestant America will have formed an image of the Roman hierarchy, and the infliction of civil penalties upon dissenters will inevitably result . . . The 'image to the beast' represents that form of apostate Protestantism which will be developed when the Protestant churches shall seek the aid of the civil power for the enforcement of their dogmas."[14]

Along similar lines, Bunch adds: "The image to the beast is the last phase of apostate Protestantism after it has united with the state. When the false prophet, which is apostate Protestantism, succeeds in being united with the state through religious legislation, the image of the beast is fully formed and the two become identical. It is for this reason that the image of the beast and the false prophet are used interchangeably in the following chapters of the Revelation."[15]

Through the influence of the ecumenical movement, the Protestant churches have conceded on doctrinal issues and have begun their return to mother Rome. Protestant pulpits no longer preach the prophecies about the beast power of Revelation 13. Once an important topic from the conservative pulpits of America, there is now a deafening silence on this subject. Revelation 13 describes the promotion of papal interests through Protestantism and the movement of the Protestant churches back toward mother Rome. This explains why most Protestants no longer protest the errors of Rome.

Revelation 13:15-17: And he had power to give life unto the image of the beast, that the image of the beast should both speak, and cause that as many as would not worship the image of the beast should be killed. [16]And he causeth all, both small and great, rich and poor, free and bond, to receive a mark in their right hand, or in their foreheads: [17]And that no man might buy or sell, save he that had the mark, or the name of the beast, or the number of his name.

The Bible clearly reveals the difference between true and false worship. David Asscherick has an interesting sermon entitled "How Not to Get the Mark of the

---

[14]   White, *The Great Controversy*, 445.

[15]   Bunch, "The Revelation," 182-183.

Beast."[16] Before we discuss the mark of the beast, let's think about the protecting seal of God as it is described in the Bible. Only those who receive the seal of God in their foreheads are kept from the fearful mark of the beast.

The Seal of the Creator and Lawgiver

Isaiah prophesied, "Bind up the testimony, seal the law among My disciples" (Isaiah 8:16). Revelation reveals a sealed people who honor God as the Lawgiver. The Father's name is written in their foreheads (Revelation 14:1). The temple of God in heaven is opened in Revelation 11:19; His Ten-Commandment law is revealed to all men. Just before the mark of the beast is explained, God describes His people in Revelation 12:17. They are like Him in character because they are like Jesus. He keeps His covenant, and they do too. Like Jesus, they "keep the commandments of God, and have the testimony of Jesus Christ" (Revelation 12:17).

Immediately after the mark of the beast is explained in chapter 13, God describes His people again in Revelation 14:12: "Here is the patience of the saints: here are they that keep the commandments of God, and the faith of Jesus." In His awesome, last-day message to all the people of the earth, the God of the universe sandwiches the fearful warning of the mark of the beast between two beautiful, positive views of His obedient, Christ-like people. He prophesies that His people in the last days will keep His Ten Commandments by the faith of Jesus.

The seal of God glorifies Him as the Creator. The only commandment that describes the Lawgiver is the fourth, declaring His dominion and His role as Creator. This is the only commandment that bears His sacred name three times.

The first two chapters of Genesis proclaim God as the Creator, Designer, and Sustainer of the universe. In these last days, He is inviting every nation, kindred, tongue, and people to "worship Him that made heaven, and earth, and the sea, and the fountains of waters" (Revelation 14:7). In this quote from His holy fourth commandment, the Creator-Lawgiver contrasts His worshipers with those who worship the beast. "Worship Me, the Creator!" He cries to all the nations. "Keep the Sabbath. . . . It is a sign between Me and the children of Israel forever: for in six days the LORD made heaven and earth, and on the seventh day He rested, and was refreshed" (Exodus 31:14-17). The seventh-day Sabbath commemorates God's creation of the heavens and the earth in six days. By observing the seventh-day Sabbath, we acknowledge God as our Creator and His authority over our lives.

Jesus the Messiah, the Lord of the Sabbath, is the living Word of God who that created the heavens and the earth by the power of His divine authority. "All things were made by Him; and without Him was not any thing made that was made" (John 1:3). God "formed man of the dust of the ground, and breathed into

---

16   David Asscherick, "How Not to Get the Mark of the Beast" [sermon on-line] (Discover Prophecy: A Bible Prophecy Seminar, seminar 19 of 24); available from http://video.google.com/videoplay?docid=-6229218635583238951#; Internet; accessed 18 October 2009.

his nostrils the breath of life; and man became a living a living soul" (Genesis 2:7). The Sabbath is the sign that reminds us of our Creator; it is the seal of His authority and Lordship over our lives. We are not an accident or evolutionary happenstance. Every week the Sabbath reminds man of his true origin: made in the image of God (Genesis 1:26-27).

The Sign of Faith and Sanctification

God's seal shows His power to make us holy. Before sin entered the world, the blessing of the Sabbath was given to Adam and Eve in their perfection. After the Fall, the Sabbath took on a new meaning: "Verily My Sabbaths ye shall keep for it is a sign between Me and you that I am the Lord that doth sanctify you" (Exodus 31:13). To sanctify means to make us holy. The Sabbath reminds us of our redemption from bondage (Deuteronomy 5:12-15). God's seal glorifies the power of Lamb of God to change our lives. The free gift of salvation transforms sinners into saints. "I delight to do Thy will, O my God; yea, Thy law is within my heart" (Psalm 40:8). Obedience to the law of Jehovah is evidence of the Holy Spirit's sanctifying work in the heart and mind (Acts 5:32).

Christ magnified the law in the Sermon on the Mount. He did not come to destroy the law or the prophets. After Jesus' victory on the cross, the Sabbath expanded to include the believers' rest by faith in His perfect sacrifice for their salvation. "There remaineth therefore a rest to the people of God" (Hebrews 4:9). By faith, we rest on the Sabbath, knowing that we are saved only by His grace.

In these final days, God wants to be closer to us than He was at Mount Sinai. There He was among them; today He wants to live in us. The Creator-Lawgiver wants to write His holy law in our hearts and minds by the power of the Holy Spirit (Hebrews 10:16; 2 Corinthians 3:3). This is what it means to be a new covenant Christian. His character is imprinted on our hearts and we are restored to the image of God. No wonder Jesus said, "If you love Me, keep My commandments" (John 14:15). Thus the Ten Commandments are a revelation of God's love in His people (Romans 13:10). This is the sanctification and faith revealed through God's end-time saints in Revelation 12:17 and 14:12.

The Mark of the Beast

Verse 15: Will we choose loyalty and obedience in honor of the commands given by our loving Savior and Creator or will we bow to economic sanctions and laws enforced by men in honor of the beast's worship practices and traditions? While some of God's people will live until the second coming of Christ (1 Thessalonians 4:17; Revelation 6:17), Revelation 13 clearly indicates that in the last days there will again arise a fierce persecution. Revelation 20:4 tells of those who were "beheaded for the witness of Jesus, and for the word of God, and which had not worshipped the beast, neither his image, neither had received his mark upon their foreheads, or in their hands." This is a clear reference to the death decree in Revelation 13:15. The fifth seal also alludes to the martyrs who will be slain in the last days (Revelation 6:9-11).

Worship is the issue, and death is the penalty for disobedience. Those who will not worship the beast and his image will be threatened, even with death. However, those who do worship the beast and his image will suffer the plagues of Revelation 16 and, in the end, death in the lake of fire. It is a showdown between worshiping the beast and worshiping the Creator.

God revealed a similar situation to the prophet Ezekiel. While a few remained faithful and mourned the apostasy in Israel, many practiced abominable forms of worship in Jerusalem during Zedekiah's reign: idolatry, heathen practices, and women weeping for Tammuz, a pagan god. Then Ezekiel saw the last and worst abomination: men turned their backs to the Lord's temple while they worshiped the sun (Ezekiel 8:15-16). History repeats itself. Revelation shows the same abominations. Many in the last days have turned their backs to Christ's ministry in the heavenly sanctuary and His holy law. Instead, they have chosen to worship according to their own will and ways.

Verse 16: The forehead symbolizes our thoughts and choices. Just as God's seal is placed on the forehead (Ezekiel 9:4; Revelation 7:3), so men may also choose the mark of the beast. God will not force our will. Moral decisions are made in the frontal lobe right behind the forehead, and the moral conscience is one of the differences between man and the animals.

As the forehead is symbolic of the decisions made in the frontal lobe, the right hand symbolizes our works. Ecclesiastes 9:10 says: "Whatsoever thy hand findeth to do, do it with thy might; for there is no work, nor device, nor knowledge, nor wisdom, in the grave, whither thou goest." With our hands we work and make a living. The fourth commandment deals with the work week: "Six days shalt thou labor and do all thy work, but the seventh day is the sabbath of the Lord thy God" (Exodus 20:9-10). The question arises: Will men obey God's authority in the area of work and worship or will they worship the beast and work on God's holy day?

After Ezekiel was shown the abominable practices and sun worship in Jerusalem, he saw men coming to destroy those false worshippers (Ezekiel 9:1-2). However, not everyone in Jerusalem was destroyed. The Lord commanded an angel to put "a mark on the foreheads" of all those who were sorry for these abominations (Ezekiel 9:4). All those who hated the abominations received the mark of God; the rest of the people, both old and young, were slain. There were only two groups: those that mourned and cried against the abominations and false worship and those who practiced these abominations and sun worship.

In these last days, there will again be two groups: those who mourn and cry over the abominations and broken law of God and those who are breaking God's law. Speaking of the "man of sin," Paul calls the abominations of the last days the "mystery of lawlessness" (2 Thessalonians 2:7 RSV). The "wicked one" in 2 Thessalonians 2:8 is literally "the [one] destitute of law" or "the violator of the law."[17] Thus the antichrist beast power and his followers will not keep God's holy law.

As we choose to follow Jesus in keeping God's law by His grace and power, the seal of God will be placed upon our foreheads. On the other hand, when we willfully break God's law and join the lawless power of the beast, we are preparing to receive the mark of the beast instead of the seal of God. These marks are not visible; writing upon the foreheads signifies our power of choice. Thus a mark on the forehead symbolizes our decision.

Notice that the second beast in Revelation 13, the "lamb-like beast," causes all to receive a mark in one of two places as it promotes the antichrist beast. With historical support, Bunch notes that Protestants promote the invention of the papacy rather than the fourth commandment:

> **Papal Institution.** And strange as it may seem, the religious institution that Protestants are attempting to cause the state to protect and enforce is of Catholic and not divine origin. The observance of Sunday as a holy day has no foundation whatever in the Scriptures, but rests wholly upon the authority of the Catholic Church. "The Catholic Church of its own infallible authority created Sunday a holy day to take the place of the Sabbath of the old law."—*Kansas City Catholic*, Feb. 9, 1893. "The Catholic Church over 1000 years before the existence of a Protestant; by virtue of her divine mission, changed the day from Saturday to Sunday. . . . The Christian Sabbath is, therefore, to this day the acknowledged offspring of the Catholic Church, without a word of remonstrance from the Protestant world. . . . Reason and common sense demand the acceptance of one or the other of these alternatives; either Protestantism and the keeping of Saturday, or Catholicity and the keeping of Sunday."—*Catholic Mirror*, Dec. 23, 1893.[18]

Just as in the days of Ezekiel, end-time worshipers will turn their backs on Christ and His holy law in the heavenly sanctuary and give honor to the day devoted to the worship of the sun. There is absolutely no scriptural evidence to support a change in the fourth commandment, and both Catholics and honest Protestants alike agree. According to the prophetic scheme, there will come a time when legislation will enforce the observance of Sunday, named after the sun-god.

Mark of Paganism: Listen to the plain testimony of Hiscox, a prominent Baptist minister and author, as he addressed fellow ministers during a Baptist conference held in New York City in 1893: "There is no Scriptural evidence of the change of the Sabbath institution from the seventh to the first day of the week. . . . Of course, I quite well know that Sunday did come into use in early

---

[17] *The Seventh-day Adventist Bible Commentary*, 7:273.

[18] Bunch, "The Revelation," 186.

Christian history as a religious day, as we learn from the Christian Fathers and other sources. But what a pity that it comes branded with the *mark of paganism* and christened with the *name of the sun-god*, when adopted and sanctioned by the papal apostasy, and bequeathed as a sacred legacy to Protestantism. There was and is a commandment to 'keep holy the Sabbath day,' but that Sabbath was not Sunday."[19]

The mystery of lawlessness has been at work for many years, but it is a special sign of the last days. Ezekiel saw abominations and sun worship practiced in the last days of Jerusalem (Ezekiel 8). Daniel foresaw that the antichrist power would "speak *great* words against the most High, . . . and **think to change times and laws**" (Daniel 7:25; emphasis mine). Jesus spoke of those who would be lost at His second coming: "I never knew you! Get away from Me, you workers of lawlessness" (Matthew 7:23 NWT). Paul also foretold the end-time antichrist power that would violate God's holy law (2 Thessalonians 2:7). And Jesus showed John the same abominable work in Revelation 13. With quotes from Catholic writers, Bunch reveals the sign of Rome's authority:

> **Mark of Papal Power.** "The church changed the Sabbath to Sunday, and all the world bows down and worships upon the day in silent obedience to the mandates of the Catholic Church. Is this not a living miracle—that those who hate us so bitterly, obey and acknowledge our power every week and do not know it?"—Report of a lecture by Father Enright, President of Redemptorist College of Kansas City, Missouri, and delivered in the opera house in Hartford, Kansas, and reported in the *Hartford Weekly Call*, Feb. 22, 1884. In reply to a letter inquiring if the Catholic church changed the Sabbath and considers the change as a mark of her authority in religious matters, Cardinal Gibbons replied through his official organ, *The Catholic Mirror*, of Sept. 23, 1893: "Of course, the Catholic church claims that the change was her act. It could not have been otherwise, as none in those days would have dreamed of doing anything in matters spiritual and religious without her, and the act is a **mark** of her ecclesiastical power and authority in religious matters." Statements from Catholic authorities can be multiplied to show that they point to the change of the Sabbath as the outstanding sign or mark of their power and authority (emphasis mine).[20]

Who gives power to the beast? Notice Revelation 13:4: "And they worshipped the dragon which gave power unto the beast: and they worshipped the beast." The enemy of souls, Satan, that old serpent and the dragon of Revelation, wants

---

19   Edward T. Hiscox, "Transference of the Sabbath;" quoted in Taylor G. Bunch, "The Revelation," Typewritten manuscript, 1952, Center for Adventist Research, James White Library, Andrews University, Berrien Springs, MI, 186.

20   Bunch, "The Revelation," 186-187.

worship for himself. This created, but fallen, cherub gains the worship of men as they turn from the Creator's commandments to worship the beast power. The Creator Himself declared the seventh day to be holy, but Satan has authored sun worship to divert mankind from the seventh-day Sabbath of the Lord our God. The decision to choose the mark of the beast or the seal of God involves whom we decide to worship: the beast with his day which promotes sun and creature worship or the Creator with His holy day, the seventh-day Sabbath of the Scriptures.

Revelation 13:4 tells us that the power of Satan and all his evil angels will push for the enforcement of the beast's day of worship. The power of the devil seems to capture the whole world: "All that dwell upon the earth shall worship him, whose names are not written in the book of life of the Lamb slain from the foundation of the world" (Revelation 13:8).

When is the mark of the beast enforced? Revelation 13 repeats the words "cause" three times (vss. 12, 15, 16) and "power" seven times (vss. 2, 4, 5, 7, 12, 14, 15). Forced worship on the beast's day will come in the future with economic sanctions and eventually the death penalty. Although much political work goes on behind closed doors, the beast's worship policy has not yet been enforced through the secular power of the lamb-like beast (vss. 12, 15, 16).

White enlarges on these verses: "The enforcement of Sundaykeeping on the part of Protestant churches is an enforcement of the worship of the papacy—of the beast. Those who, understanding the claims of the fourth commandment, choose to observe the false instead of the true Sabbath are thereby paying homage to that power by which alone it is commanded. But in the very act of enforcing a religious duty by secular power, the churches would themselves form an image to the beast; hence the enforcement of Sundaykeeping in the United States would be an enforcement of the worship of the beast and his image."[21]

This enforcement of beast worship is not limited to any one nation. Revelation 13:3 predicts that "all the world" will worship the beast. Based on Revelation 13:12-16, White foresees that the withdrawal of religious freedom from God's commandment-keeping people will not be limited to one country or place. "There will be in different lands, a simultaneous movement for their destruction."[22]

Revelation 13:15 will soon come to pass: "He had power to give life unto the image of the beast, that the image of the beast should both speak, and cause that as many as would not worship the image of the beast should be killed."

The Notorious Number: Six Hundred Sixty-six

Revelation 13:18: Here is wisdom. Let him that hath understanding count the number of the beast: for it is the number of a man; and his number *is* Six hundred threescore *and* six.

---

[21]   White, *The Great Controversy*, 448-449.

[22]   Ibid., 635.

Using the Bible, we have already clearly identified the antichrist power symbolized by the little horn of Daniel 7 and the beast of Revelation 13: it is the
Roman church-state power (see the chapter on Daniel 7). Arising from the ruins
of the Roman Empire, reigning for 1,260 years, enforcing worship, and persecuting God's commandment-keeping people, the beast power of the papal church
arose out of the sea of people as a civil and religious power with authority over
vast portions of the world. The Roman Church received the capital of Rome as
its inheritance and ruled from the seat of the caesars.

To identify the beast power more clearly, Jesus gave John the number of the
beast's name. Revelation 13:18 gives the number "six hundred sixty-six" as an
important identifying mark of the beast even though the power can be clearly
identified without this text. God gives a special message that is only understood
by those who trust in His wisdom. Satan has worked overtime to steer us away
from this notorious number with myriads of fantastic interpretations.

Count the number of the beast

The original language is clear here: ψηφίζω, (psephizo) which means "to
count with pebbles, to compute or calculate." Thus the number of the beast's
name must be counted or calculated. The Greek reads: "ἑξακόσιοι (six hundred)
ἑξήκοντα (sixty) ἕξ (six)" or "χξς." In the latter, chi (χ) has the numerical value
of six hundred, xi (ξ) is worth sixty, and the value of stigma (ς) is six. Thus the
correct translation is a numerical value: "six hundred sixty-six." Notice that both
the Greek words for the numerals and the value of the three Greek letters add
up to six hundred sixty-six. This gives an important clue in understanding this
identifying mark.

Triple 6 error: Note that it is not "6-6-6" (six-six-six). Many err by claiming
this symbolizes the number six as man's number, reasoning that man was created on the sixth day, or by twisting the meaning of the verse to equal three sixes,
thereby doing violence to the word of God. This example from Hughes show
the faulty reasoning of those who translate Revelation 13:18 according to these
fallacies: "On the basis of the threefold six may be understood as indicative of a
human or humanistic trinity."[23] Obviously Hughes has disregarded the numerical value of the original Greek words: "six hundred sixty-six" and the injunction
to "count the number of the beast" (Revelation 13:18).

His number is six hundred sixty-six: Hughes' "triple 6" argument may
sound reasonable to some, but it is not based on the word of God. The Greek
reads ἑξήκοντα ἕξ χξς (six hundred sixty six), but Hughes would change the
Greek to read ἕξ ἕξ ἕξ (six six six). Sevens explains that the error of using triple

---

[23] Philip E. Hughes, *The Book of Revelation* (Grand Rapids, MI: Eerdmans, 1990), 154-
155.

sixes would change the original Greek to ϛϛϛ (*stigma stigma stigma*).[24] It is dangerous to change the sacred Scriptures or wrest the meaning of the text. Men may talk of a trinity of sixes, but the original language of the Holy Bible is "six hundred sixty-six."

The name of the beast has numerical value. His name adds up to a real and exact number according to Revelation 13:17-18: "the number of his name" is "six hundred sixty-six." That is why we are commanded to calculate or "count the number of the beast" (Revelation 13:18).

The Number of His Name

For more than a thousand years, the papacy has considered itself to be the vicar of Christ, claiming the place, position, and power of the Savior on earth. Protestants and Catholics alike have long known the papal title of *Vicarius Filii Dei* which means "Vicar of the Son of God." The claim for this title was defended for centuries while the power of this claim brought the Romish church acquisitions of land and authority over civil rulers.

Rome, the fourth kingdom, was turned over to the head of the Roman Church in A.D. 538 just as predicted in prophecy. The official language of the Roman Catholic Church has been Latin from the beginning. All official documents are usually published in the Latin language and then translated into the languages of other countries.

Vicarius Filii Dei

Latin, papal Rome's official language, has numerical values attached to some of her letters. Today we call these "Roman numerals." Most of us learned these values in elementary school. Note that the letter U in Latin is written as a V and thus has the numerical value of 5. This diagram shows the calculation of *Vicarius Filii Dei*:

V	= 5	**F**	=0	**D**	=500
I	= 1	**I**	=1	**E**	=0
C	= 100	**L**	=50	**I**	=1
A	= 0	**I**	=1		
R	= 0	**I**	=1		
I	= 1				
U (V)	= 5				
S	= 0				
	112	**plus** 53		**plus** 501	**equals** 666

His number is six hundred sixty-six

---

24   Jerry A. Stevens, *Vicarius Filii Dei: An Annotated Timeline: Connecting Links Between Revelation 13:16-18, the Infamous Number 666, and the Papal Headdress* (Berrien Springs, MI: Adventists Affirm, 2009), 12-13.

How does *Vicarius Filii Dei* Fit the Biblical Criteria?

Why was this name chosen among all the other names of the papacy? Edwin de Kock's manuscript, "The Truth About 666," lists eight characteristics of the name of the beast as based on Revelation 13:17-18. The following list is adapted from de Kock's eight points:[25]

1. **The name must be a specific name or title applicable to a human entity** because "it is the number of a man" (Revelation 13:18).

2. **The name must refer to the papacy**.

3. **The name must be Latin in its original form**.

4. **The name must be a single name or title**. "Revelation 13 in its first verse mentions a plurality of names, but at the end the prophecy focuses on only one, which has the numerical value of 666."[26]

5. **The name must be a blasphemous name or title** because the beast had "upon his heads the name of blasphemy" (Revelation 13:1). Since all of the names of the beast are blasphemous, this special name also must be blasphemous.

6. **The name must endure for centuries**. As the beast endures for more than a millennium, so will his name.

7. **The name must be authenticated by history** as all Bible prophecies are proven when the events foretold come to pass. The Donation of Constantine, in which this name is first used, is "the very charter of papal power and authority. For importance and its impact on history, it easily rates alongside England's Magna Carta (1215) and the Constitution of the United States of America (1787)."[27]

8. **The name must theologically characterize the papacy**. According to Paul in 2 Thessalonians 2:4, the antichrist power would usurp the role of God Himself. *Filius Dei*, the holy name which means "the Son of God," is honored by Christians, but "*Vicarius Filii Dei*, however, is virtually synonymous with 'Antichrist.' Why? The prefext *anti-* in the Greek can signify not only 'against' but also 'instead, in the place of,' while the Latin *Vicarius*—originally an adjective—means 'a deputy,' somebody 'put in place of.'"[28] The antichrist stands in the place of God; this claim is the same as that of the papacy.

---

[25] Edwin de Kock, "The Truth About 666 and the Mediterranean Apostasy," 3 vols. Digital manuscript, July 20, 2009, 1:63-76.

[26] Ibid., 1:67.

[27] Ibid., 1:72.

[28] Ibid., 1:77.

Why was *Vicarius Filii Dei* chosen instead of *Vicarius Christi*? Two important reasons are pointed out by de Kock:

> First, *Vicarius Filii Dei* is an exclusively papal title, never applied by the Roman Church to any other person, ecclesiastical or secular. On the other hand, *Vicarius Christi* began as a designation that the emperor Constantine invented for himself. As twentieth-century canon lawyers have admitted, it was also used by other emperors as well as bishops, the pope being just one of these.

> Second, *Vicarius Filii Dei*—unlike *Vicarius Christi*—invariably stresses the idea of divinity.[29]

For these reasons, *Vicarius Filii Dei* is like no other name. It is exclusively used as a papal title that stresses the divine nature, not of God or His Son, but of the pope himself. Truly, "he as God sitteth in the temple of God, shewing himself that he is God" (2 Thessalonians 2:4).

The Charter of Papal Authority

The Donation of Constantine was originally discovered in the Pseudo-Isidorian Decretals sometime between 847 and 853. For more than a thousand years, the Donation of Constantine has been cited by popes and other ecclesiastical leaders of the Roman church. Although this document was in part based on one of the most famous forgeries in European history, portions of the Donation of Constantine were incorporated into most of the medieval collections of Catholic canon law. Quoted by no less than ten popes, the Donation of Constantine was used as proof of their civil authority and sovereignty over the city of Rome and the papal states which included a very large portion of Italy. In 1440 Laurentius Valla exposed the Donation's claims as false, proving it had been written several centuries *after* the death of Constantine in A.D. 337. The Vatican condemned Valla's scholarly work by listing it in the *Index Liborum Prohibitorum*, an index of books prohibited by the papacy in 1559. In other words, the church backed up the authority of the Donation of Constantine with her own power because it was the supposed proof of her own authority.

Pseudo-Isidorian Decretals

The Pseudo-Isidorian Decretals in which the Donation of Constantine was found are fictitious letters claimed to be from early popes such as Clement (A.D. 100) through Gregory the Great (A.D. 600). These were collected by Isidore Mercator in the ninth century. Later their authenticity was called into question as Valla exposed them as a pious fraud in 1440. After these letters were proven fraudulent, they became known as the *Pseudo-Isidorian Decretals* or *False*

---

[29] Ibid., 1:78.

Decretals. Nonetheless, as late as 1580 the official edition of the *Corpus Juris* translation claimed them to be genuine.

Catholics finally abandoned the defense of the authenticity of the Donation of Constantine shortly after 1592 when Cesare Baronius published his *Ecclesiastical Annals*, admitting the fraud. The Donation and title *Vicarius Filii Dei* continued to appear in canon law and other Catholic publications well into the nineteenth century, in spite of this admission.

Vicarius Filii Dei and the Donation of Constantine

For many centuries the Catholic Church claimed that the Donation of Constantine was a genuine document. This false letter was used by popes to support their claims of civil and religious authority. When the document was proven false in 1440 by Valla in his *Declamatio*, the church's first plan was defend the Donation.

However, Protestants began using *Vicarius Filii Dei* from the Donation of Constantine in their explanations of Revelation 13:17-18. Their study of biblical prophecy revealed the papacy as the antichrist. Only then did the Catholic Church decide to employ a new strategy. In the past, they denounced anyone who claimed the Donation was forged, but now the Roman Church joined their former enemies in proclaiming the Donation a forgery and its title a fabrication of the enemies of the papacy. In other words, "We didn't write it! Someone else must have done it!"

What a sudden reversal! These documents emerged from the church and the popes themselves and had been their tools to enlarge their power for centuries. For nearly one thousand years, the papacy claimed and maintained a spiritual dictatorship over the Christian churches—such as Antioch, Alexandria, Constantinople, and Jerusalem—based upon their own forged documents. This temporal control began to decline during the Reformation as the light of the Bible shone over the dark countries of Europe.

In 1870, the papacy finally lost the last of the papal states it had gained through the authority of the Donation of Constantine. However, the Vatican did not formally relinquish their temporal claim to these papal states until 1929 when they signed the Lateran Treaty which granted the papacy sovereignty over 109 acres of land known as Vatican City. This does not mean that the Roman Church only reigns over Vatican City. On the contrary, she claims the whole world for herself and her dominion. As the Roman Catholic (universal) Church, she has never relinquished her claims of spiritual authority over the whole Christian world and the vast areas of heathen nations who have never heard the name of Jesus.

In agreement with the Donation of Constantine, the head of the Roman Church still claims the title of Vicar of the Son of God. Note what Martin Luther wrote in a letter to a man named Spalatin on February 23, 1520, about four years before Raphael's painting of the Donation of Constantine was completed: "I have at hand Lorenzo Valla's proof that the Donation of Constantine is a forgery.

Good heavens, what darkness and wickedness is at Rome. You wonder at the judgment of God that such unauthentic, crass, imprudent lies not only lived, but prevailed for so many centuries, that they were incorporated in the canon law . . . and became as articles of faith. I am in such a passion that I scarcely doubt that the pope is the Antichrist expected by the world, so closely do their acts, lives, sayings, and laws agree."[30]

Raphael painted the Donation of Constantine in the 1500s, but it did not end there. The lie that lives on in the painting is living proof that the papacy claimed it as her own for many years after it was proven fraudulent. Even today she claims for her head the title "Vicar of the Son of God." The number of this blasphemous name is six hundred sixty-six.

Conclusion

The evidence is clear. Revelation 13 points out the main characters used by Satan in his battle against Christ's remnant: the revived papacy and the power of the United States backed by apostate Protestantism. Prophecy predicts economic sanctions and a death decree for those who do not worship the beast. The seal of God and the mark of the beast are clearly found in Scripture. While chapter 13 reveals the antithesis of the 144,000—those who worship the beast, God begins chapter 14 with another glimpse of the 144,000—those who worship and follow the Lamb. The Bible's answer is clear: Follow the Lamb, not the beast!

---

[30] Martin Luther, Letter to Spalatin, Feb. 23, 1520; quoted in Loren Partridge, *The Art of Renaissance Rome* (New York: Harry N. Abrams, Inc., 1996), 159.

CHAPTER TWENTY-SIX

Revelation 14

Introduction

The seventh chapter of Revelation answers the question, "Who is able to stand," with resounding affirmation, "The 144,000 and the great multitude are able to stand." In a similar manner, chapter 14 answers the question from chapter 13, "What will happen to those who do not worship the beast or his image?"

Rising from the roots of pagan Rome, the beast power obtained the kingdom by flatteries, using the sword of civil authorities to destroy its enemies. During the 1,260 years of papal supremacy, millions who were faithful to God's word were killed by the civil-religious authority of Rome, the worst persecuting power on earth. These martyrs were Christ's true church, faithful even to death and represented by the pure woman of Revelation 12. Satan, who claims the world as his, is symbolized by the great red dragon. He works through the beast from the sea and gave the beast his throne, power, and great authority.

The blasphemous beast power we met in Revelation 13 has characteristics like Rome, Greece, Medo-Persia, and Babylon. During the time of the end, the first beast from the sea receives help from a second beast that comes up from the earth. Although this second beast has lamb-like features, it is soon under the dragon-like spell of the sea beast. On the other hand, the small remnant of people that stand up against these beasts from the earth and sea seem to have no chance.

Chapter 14 answers the question: "Is there anyone who will survive the enmity of the dragon and the treachery of these two beasts?" The 144,000 are God's answer to Satan and his kingdom. Like the Lamb, the Father's name is written on the foreheads of the 144,000, a symbol of their allegiance to God.

In contrast to the 144,000, those who worship the beast will honor the day instituted by Rome as a mark of her ecclesiastical authority: Sunday, the first day of the week. Nearly the whole world will worship the beast, either by choice or through force via economic sanctions and threat of violence.

Worshiping the beast on his man-made day stands in direct opposition to the Lord's holy seventh-day Sabbath, the twenty-four hour period which begins every Friday at sundown. Set aside as a memorial to the Creator of the heavens and the earth, the Sabbath is a mark, sign, or seal of loyalty to God. The 144,000 are totally obedient to all God's commandments, including the seventh-day Sabbath. They rest in the sanctifying power of Christ, their Redeemer. Enduring until the end, the 144,000 are living proof that God is able to overcome the dragon, the beast from the sea, and the beast out of the earth. By God's grace, the 144,000 are victorious.

The 144,000

Revelation 14:1-5: And I looked, and, lo, a Lamb stood on the mount Sion, and with him an hundred forty *and* four thousand, having his Father's name written in their foreheads. ²And I heard a voice from heaven, as the voice of many waters, and as the voice of a great thunder: and I heard the voice of harpers harping with their harps: ³And they sung as it were a new song before the throne, and before the four beasts, and the elders: and no man could learn that song but the hundred *and* forty *and* four thousand, which were redeemed from the earth. ⁴These are they which were not defiled with women; for they are virgins. These are they which follow the Lamb whithersoever he goeth. These were redeemed from among men, *being* the firstfruits unto God and to the Lamb. ⁵And in their mouth was found no guile: for they are without fault before the throne of God.

Verse 1: A Lamb or the Lamb? According to the Greek text τὸ ἀρνίον (tah arnion) is literally translated "the lamb." Revelation 5:6 introduces the Lamb in the midst of the throne, the four living beings, and the twenty-four elders. Twenty-eight times in Revelation, Jesus is called the Lamb. He is the Lamb who was slain from the foundation of the earth. The Lamb is vitally linked to the 144,000 because they have His Father's name written "in" their foreheads. Just behind the forehead is the frontal lobe of the brain where we make choices and exercise our will. This symbolizes that the 144,000 have chosen by their own free will to follow Jesus the Lamb.

Father's name written in their foreheads: This reminds us of Revelation 7:3: "Hurt not the earth, neither the sea, nor the trees, till we have sealed the servants of our God in their foreheads." This seal is mentioned again in Revelation 9:4: "the seal of God in their foreheads." The word "in" is ἐπί (ep-ee') which means "upon, on, at, by, before or in." Therefore "the seal of God in their foreheads" and "His Father's name written in their foreheads" are two ways to say the same thing. These sealed people honor the Lord's holy day of worship every week. Like Jesus, they keep the seventh-day Sabbath, remembering the command of the One who made the heavens and the earth.

Revelation reveals our Creator and Redeemer who is worthy of our worship. As the Spirit of truth writes God's holy law upon the hearts and minds of those who love Jesus, the seal of the living God is symbolically imbedded in their frontal lobe (Hebrews 10:15-16). They choose to worship the Creator and keep all

His commandments, including the fourth, as a sign of allegiance to His creative and redemptive power (Revelation 14:7, 12). Loyalty to the Lord's seventh-day Sabbath sets this group apart from atheists, pagans, eastern religions, and most Christian denominations. The seventh-day Sabbath is therefore both a sign and a seal of their faithfulness to the only true God (John 3:33; Revelation 11:19).

When false worship will be enforced, all will make their final choice. As a mark of its ecclesiastical power, the beast will attempt to pressure and coerce first-day worship. Those who follow the beast and refuse to honor God's seventh-day Sabbath will reveal disloyalty to heaven, but the 144,000 will honor all God's commandments, even when faced with economic hardship and death threats.

Verses 2 and 3: Heavenly harps play as the 144,000 sing a song of their unique experience that no one else will ever know. The song tells of their miraculous redemption from the earth. They are the same group we saw in chapter 7 which alludes to their earthly struggle and how they overcame, but in chapter 14 the setting is much different. Their earthly battle is over and they have received their reward. Only the 144,000 can sing this song because they remained obedient to God and endured the wrath of the dragon, beast, and false prophet through the grace and power of Christ. The 144,000 faced the beast's cruel sanctions and death decree, yet lived to sing about their great Deliverer.

Verses 4 and 5: The 144,000 are pure in heart and action. They are without fault before the throne and in their mouths there is found no guile. The imagery pictures them in front of the throne of judgment because nothing has been found that would exclude them from eternity. They follow the Lamb wherever He goes; this reveals that Jesus is the Lord of their lives. The 144,000 do all His commands and fully rely on His guidance.

The symbol of defiling women points to the seventeenth chapter of Revelation which pictures the false church riding upon the blasphemous beast. As we studied in Revelation 12, a woman in prophecy symbolizes a church. A pure woman is a pure church; an impure woman symbolizes an impure or harlot church. The masses of the earth are influenced by the impure mother church and her equally impure daughters. The language of Revelation speaks for itself. Rome calls herself the mother church and her daughters the churches that came from her. Because the 144,000 have no part with the harlot or her daughters, they are called virgins for their pure doctrinal stance.

Walking with God like Enoch: The 144,000 have much in common with Enoch. "By faith Enoch was translated that he should not see death; and was not found, because God had translated him: for before his translation he had this testimony, that he pleased God" (Hebrews 11:5). Similarly, the 144,000 please God. Enoch's lifestyle is described Genesis 5:19: "And *Enoch walked with God*: and he *was* not; for God took him." Again, the 144,000 are like Enoch because they walk with the Lamb wherever He goes.

Like Enoch, the 144,000 please God and walk with Him continually, and like Enoch, they will be translated. This means that they will be alive when Jesus returns to the earth. Revelation 6:17 asks an important question: "The great day of His [the Lamb's] wrath is come; and who shall be able to stand?" Revelation 7 tells us that the 144,000 will be standing when that great day comes. "Redeemed from the earth" and "redeemed from among men" (Revelation 14:3, 4) also indicate the translation of the 144,000 from the earth without seeing death.

First Fruits to God: In the Jewish economy, that which remained at the end of the harvest was left for the gleaners; therefore the last fruits would be the gleanings. The 144,000, however, are called the "firstfruits." This plainly shows that the 144,000 are not the whole number that will be saved. Revelation 7 introduced the 144,000 and a numberless throng called the great multitude. God calls the 144,000 the first fruits because they are linked in a special way to Jesus. On the sixteenth of Nisan in A.D. 31, Jesus Christ became our firstfruits or wave sheaf offering; this symbolized would happen at Christ's second coming. Since Jesus' victory as our firstfruits was a promise of the harvest to come, so in the last days, the 144,000 are also the firstfruits which point to the salvation of the great multitude. Bunch tells how the Jews prepared for the sixteenth of Nisan:

> The grain was threshed and thoroughly winnowed and the sifted-out chaff burned. The grain was then parched, ground into meal, and anointed with incense. Then the fragrant meal was waved toward the four points of the compass as the firstfruits of the spring harvest. This typical service met its antitype when Jesus, the Lord of the harvest, carefully selected the twelve apostles "from among men." They were the best He could find to train for their special mission. Their preparation included a threshing process and a thorough sifting out of all sin and sinners. Judas, the traitor, was sifted out from among them. Their heart-searching experience during the trials and crucifixion of Jesus and in the upper room, completed the preparation for their special mission. They were anointed with the Holy Spirit and their lives made fragrant for Christ.[1]

Just as Jesus specially prepared His twelve disciples during His earthly mission as the firstfruits of a great harvest of souls in Jerusalem, so today the 144,000 who follow Jesus in the last days will be instrumental in gathering the last great multitude of souls (Revelation 7:9-17).

The First Angel's Message

Revelation 14:6-7: And I saw another angel fly in the midst of heaven, having the everlasting gospel to preach unto them that dwell on the earth, and to every nation, and kindred, and tongue, and people, [7]Saying with a loud voice, Fear God, and give glory to him; for the hour of his judgment is come: and worship him that made heaven, and earth, and the sea, and the fountains of waters.

---

[1]   Bunch, "The Revelation," 194-195.

This angel is the first in a series of three angels that give three messages of the greatest import to those who dwell on the earth in the last days. This world-wide message is given "**to every nation, and kindred, and tongue, and people.**" No one is to be left out; it is not a localized message limited to one town, state, or nation. As God worked through His people in ages past, so again His last-day church will take these messages to the whole world.

The three angels' messages are intricately connected to each other. Because verse 9 speaks of the "third angel," we know that the previous two angels must be the first and second angels respectively. The announcement of judgment and true worship are given in the first angel's message, the false worship system is revealed in the second message, and the results of following Babylon's false worship doctrines are clearly stated in the third message.

Preaching the Good News: The first angel gives the gospel to the whole earth. This symbolizes Christ's messengers who carry the gospel to the whole world, a work which is the responsibility of each and every disciple of Jesus. Before His ascension into heaven, Jesus charged His disciples: "Go ye into all the world, and preach the gospel to every creature" (Mark 16:15).

The first angel's message reveals that this gospel includes more than just telling people that Jesus loves them. In this setting, the gospel reveals more than just the good news of salvation. The first angel's message announces the arrival of God's judgment and reminds the entire world of the Lord's command to worship "Him that made heaven, and earth, and the sea, and the fountains of waters" (Revelation 14:7). Heaven knows that mankind has forgotten the fourth commandment of the Decalogue, so in love, God points out their sin so that they may change their wicked ways and avoid condemnation in the judgment. Stefanovic comments on the judgment:

> "The hour of his judgment" pointed to by the first angel refers to the judgment, the first phase of which takes place *before* the Second Coming and its second phase (the final judgment) *after* the millennium (Revelation 20). Revelation 14:14-20 indicates that the destiny of every person is to be decided before the Second Coming and the final judgment. Christ will come to bring his reward with him, in order to "give to each as his work is" (Revelation 22:12). The final judgment after the millennium (Revelation 20:11-15) is the executive judgment that carries into execution that which the pre-advent judgment has ascertained. All decisions with reference to those who are included in the Kingdom and those who are excluded from it are brought before the throne at the pre-advent judgment. Jesus makes it very clear that the faithful one does not have a part in the final judgment, having already received "eternal life, and does not come into judgment, but has passed out of death into life" (John 5:24).[2]

2   Stefanovic, 442.

In the time of the end, the world is not giving God His due honor and glory. Even the Christian world has refused to give the Lord acceptable worship because they do not recognizing Him as the Creator and Author of the fourth commandment. Genesis tells of our origin. Immediately after the creation of man, God ended His work and rested on the seventh day which He Himself proclaimed holy, thus ending the creation of this world.

Genesis 2:1-3 describes the first Sabbath of the newly created planet called earth. Mentioned three times in this passage, the seventh day was set apart from all the other days of the week. On the seventh day God ended His work. On the seventh day He rested, not because He needed to rest, but as a memorial to His great work of creation. God blessed the seventh day and made that particular day holy because the Sabbath represented His finished work.

If the world had kept holy the seventh day of the week, mankind would not have forgotten the Creator and the confusion about man's origin would not exist. Sadly, man substituted the first day, a work day, in place of the Sabbath. What a fitting symbol of man's works substituted for the finished work of Christ! The first angel's message points out this apostasy of the world. With a loud voice, that angel calls us to remember the fourth commandment in Exodus 20:8-11 and bids us to keep the seventh day holy. This is heaven's good news for the last days, a call to rediscover the Creator and the relationship He desires to have with us.

Worship the Creator: The first angel's message of judgment and Creator worship is a worldwide movement that takes up the challenge to reach every nation, tongue, and people. This first message must be correctly understood in order to make sense of the other two angels' messages.

White points out the purpose of this wake-up call to the world: "By the first angel, men are called upon to 'fear God, and give glory to Him' and to worship Him as the Creator of the heavens and the earth. In order to do this, they must obey His law. Says the wise man: 'Fear God, and keep His commandments: for this is the whole duty of man.' Ecclesiastes 12:13. Without obedience to His commandments no worship can be pleasing to God."[3]

Nearly everyone on earth has forgotten the fourth commandment of the Creator. Instead they worship themselves or the opinions of others. Honor is given to the day of the beast and Satan, "the venerable day of the sun," or some day other than the seventh-day Sabbath. Putting their authority above the Creator, they dishonor the Lord's true Sabbath. Bunch compares the beast's day of worship with the Sabbath:

> They are worshiping the creature which is idolatry. The dragon, the beast, and the false prophet are the objects of obedience and worship. The heaven-sent message is given to counteract the message of the false prophet which demands that the inhabitants of the earth worship the beast and his image instead of the Creator of the heavens and the earth.

---

[3]   White, *The Great Controversy*, 436.

Both are world messages, one exalting the creature and the other the Creator. The worship of the Creator must include the observance of the Sabbath which is the memorial of creation. This is indicated by the fact that a part of the fourth commandment is quoted in the first angel's message. God's power to create is an evidence of His power to redeem, and for this reason reference to His creative power has been an important part of all heaven-sent messages. . . . The Sabbath is the sign and mark of true worship, just as Sunday is the sign and mark of apostasy and idolatry, "the wild solar holiday of all pagan times." Regarding the institution of the Sabbath and its purpose in the plan of salvation, a leading Methodist writer said: "God's blessing and sanctifying the day meant that He separated it from a common to a religious use, to be a perpetual memorial or sign that all who thus observe it would show themselves to be worshipers of that God who made the world in six days and rested on the seventh."—*Binney's Theological Compend Improved*, pp. 169, 170.[4]

The Hour of His Judgment Is Come: God's judgment must be understood from the sanctuary setting and language. Linking Daniel 8:14 with 9:24-27, the starting point for this first angel's message is 1844, the end of the 2,300-day prophecy. At this time Christ began the closing phase of His work in the most holy place in heaven. While this last work of judgment takes place in the in the holy of holies in heaven, the results are felt here on the earth. Thus the judgment hour message points us heavenward to Jesus' final work for us in the heavenly sanctuary. Here Jesus pleads His blood for us before the ark of His testimony, the ark of His Ten Commandments, with its throne of mercy. All heaven watches anxiously while the last full-gospel message is preached here on earth by God's faithful messengers, members of His pure and obedient church.

The Second Angel's Message

Revelation 14:8: And there followed another angel, saying, Babylon is fallen, is fallen, that great city, because she made all nations drink of the wine of the wrath of her fornication.

"Babylon is fallen, is fallen, that great city." Babylon was built on the premise of rebellion against God. The Lord promised that He would never again destroy the earth by a flood. He put the rainbow in the sky as a reminder of His covenant with us, but man built the tower of Babel as an act of defiance. When they attempted to reach heaven by human effort, God scattered the people by confusing their languages. The city that grew up around the tower of Babel was called Babylon. Satan worked through the apostasy of Nimrod, the great-grandson of Noah, to build and establish the city of Babylon; thus Nimrod became its first king. White uses the analogy of the first Babylon to explain the last-day system of confusion:

---

4   Bunch, "The Revelation," 199.

In the professedly Christian world many turn away from the plain teachings of the Bible and build up a creed from human speculations and pleasing fables, and they point to their tower as a way to climb up to heaven. Men hang with admiration upon the lips of eloquence while it teaches that the transgressor shall not die, that salvation may be secured without obedience to the law of God. If the professed followers of Christ would accept God's standard, it would bring them into unity; but so long as human wisdom is exalted above His Holy Word, there will be divisions and dissension. The existing confusion of conflicting creeds and sects is fitly represented by the term "Babylon," which prophecy (Revelation 14:8; 18:2) applies to the world-loving churches of the last days.[5]

The Babylonian religious system was founded on nature or creature worship. Babylon's rebellion culminated with the blasphemous debauchery of Belshazzar's feast. On that same night in 539 B.C., the city fell to the Medes and Persians.

Is Fallen, Is Fallen: This mournful statement from Revelation 14:8 is discussed by Bunch:

> **Modern Babylon.** The same conditions prevail to a large extent in the modern world ruled by Babylon in its modern form. Is it any wonder that the second angel's message declares that the cause of the fall of Babylon is "the furious wine of her prostitution"? (Concordant). Why is the statement "is fallen" repeated? See also Revelation 18:2. Doubtless chiefly for the same reason that important statements and announcements are usually repeated, to give emphasis. Of the reason why the same dream was twice given to Pharaoh, king of Egypt, we read: "And for that the dream was doubled unto Pharaoh twice; it is because the thing is established by God, and God will shortly bring it to pass." Genesis 41:32. This is the best of reasons for this repetition in the second angel's message.[6]

The mother church of Babylon has already fallen. Now at the end of time the daughter churches are returning to mother Rome. Both mother and daughters have now fallen. White concurs: "The message of Revelation 14, announcing the *fall* of Babylon must apply to religious bodies that were once pure and have become corrupt. Since this message follows the warning of the judgment, it must be given in the last days; therefore it cannot refer to the Roman Church alone, for that church has been in a fallen condition for many centuries."[7]

"Babylon the great" which symbolizes the false religious system of the last days resembles ancient Babylon in all of its facets (Revelation 17:1-7). Because

5   White, *Patriarchs and Prophets*, 124.

6   Bunch, "The Revelation," 203.

7   White, *The Great Controversy*, 383.

of its compromises and apostasy, Babylon has fallen already. The second angel declares that those who are God's messengers should preach the fall of Babylon the great. This is part two of the world-wide message that follows the first angel's message of glory, true worship, and judgment.

The Wine of False Doctrines: The second angel describes Babylon as more than just disobedient. Her apostasy has led the whole world into error. Bunch details these connections with paganism:

> The chief god and goddess of the Babylonians, and in fact of all pagan nations, were in their human originals Nimrod and Semiramis, the first king and queen of Babylon. After their deaths they were deified and under various names have been worshiped by different pagan nations ever since. Nimrod was "the father of the gods" and was worshiped under the names Ninus, Tammuz, Anu, Bel, Baal, Ammon-Ra, Marduk, Nebo, Jupiter, etc. He was identified with the sun and was therefore the chief deity of all pagan times. Lesser gods were represented by the planets. Semiramis was the moon-goddess or "Queen of Heaven." She was called "The Great Mother" and "The mother of the gods." In Babylon her name was usually Ishtar, the "Ashtoreth" of the Bible. She was identified with both the moon and Venus. Because of the hot weather in the Euphrates Valley the moon-goddess was often more popular than the sun-god. The Babylonian religion was polytheistic; that is the people worshiped many gods. . . .

> After the death of Nimrod or Tammuz, Semiramis or Ishtar proclaimed a period of mourning which continued forty days and was engaged in mostly by women. They often shaved their heads and presented their tresses as offerings to their dead and deified hero. Degrading and revolting rites accompanied this period of mourning which was called "Weeping for Tammuz." (See Ezekiel 8:14). . . . She [Semiramis] originated the celibacy of the priesthood, the use of beads in counting prayers (the rosary), holy water, confession to priests, the feast on the 25th of December commemorating the birth of her son for whom she claimed divinity, the offering of cakes to the "Queen of Heaven," the ancestor of the Catholic wafer. The initial "T" was stamped on the Babylonian wafer just as a likeness of the cross is stamped on the Catholic wafer. The original cross was made in the shape of T.[8]

Other symbols used by ancient Babylon and pagan religions were the golden ring symbolizing the circle of the sun, worn on the finger known in Oriental martial arts as the heartstring. This pagan custom was perpetuated by nuns and priests as a symbol that they are married to Christ. The different colors used on the vestments of the priests are changed according to the church calendar which

---

[8]   Bunch, "The Book of Daniel," 18-19.

is tied to the Babylonian reckoning. It is curious that many books were written in the last century about the origins of these Christian symbols, but these books can no longer be found in libraries anywhere in what is known as the land of the brave and home of the free.

The substitution of tradition above the Scriptures is another doctrine that is contrary to the word of God and opens the door for other false doctrines such as the doctrine of the immortality of the soul. Smith explains the source of these errors: "This was also derived from the pagan world, and the 'Fathers of the church' became the foster-fathers of this pernicious doctrine as a part of divine truth. This error nullifies the two great Scripture doctrines of the resurrection and the general judgment, and furnishes an open door to modern spiritism. From it have sprung such other evil doctrines as the conscious state of the dead, saint worship, mariology, purgatory, reward at death, prayers and baptisms for the dead, eternal torment and universal salvation."[9]

Smith points out another false doctrine from paganism: "sprinkling instead of immersion, the latter being the only Scriptural mode of baptism, and a fitting memorial of the burial and resurrection of our Lord, for which purpose it was designed. By the corruption of this ordinance and its destruction as a memorial of the resurrection of Christ, the way was prepared for the substitution of something else for this purpose—the Sunday rest day."[10] White continues this train of thought:

> God has a controversy with the churches of today. They are fulfilling the prophecy of John. "All nations have drunk of the wine of the wrath of her fornication." They have divorced themselves from God by refusing to receive His sign. They have not the spirit of God's true commandment-keeping people. And the people of the world, in giving their sanction to a false sabbath, and in trampling under their feet the Sabbath of the Lord, have drunk of the wine of the wrath of her fornication.[11]

The Third Angel's Message

Revelation 14:9-11: And the third angel followed them, saying with a loud voice, If any man worship the beast and his image, and receive *his* mark in his forehead, or in his hand, [10]The same shall drink of the wine of the wrath of God, which is poured out without mixture into the cup of his indignation; and he shall be tormented with fire and brimstone in the presence of the holy angels, and in the presence of the Lamb: [11]And the smoke of their torment ascendeth up for ever and ever: and they have no rest day nor night,

---

[9] Smith, 650.

[10] Ibid., 651.

[11] Ellen G. White, Letter 98, 1900; quoted in *The Seventh-day Adventist Bible Commentary*, 7:979.

who worship the beast and his image, and whosoever receiveth the mark of his name.

According to Revelation 13:15, those who do not worship the image of the beast will face the death sentence. Those who follow Jesus do not need to be afraid of these threats. They trust Him, knowing that He will give them the crown of life if they are faithful unto death.

Much more fearsome than the threat of death from man is the wrath of God poured out with no mercy. In giving the third angel's message, God pronounces the death sentence upon Satan and all his followers with a proclamation to the beast, the image of the beast, and the false prophet. Here the façade is torn away from the beast and the false prophet. In that day of indignation, nothing will protect them from the wrath of God. "Without mixture" means that the time of mercy and grace has come to an end for those who have proven to be incorrigible. The beast power will not give God's people any grace and therefore receives the same treatment that it would have meted out on God's people had she not been checked. Bunch points out the importance of obedience to God:

> Through the exaltation of any of his human agents to the place of God, Satan himself is thereby deified and worshiped. Against this satanic spirit of creature worship the final heaven-sent message gives its warning, and over it God's people must gain complete victory. All who accept the three angels' messages receive the character of God of which the Sabbath is the outward sign or mark. Those who reject this warning receive the character of Satan, of which Sunday observance is the outward sign or mark. When the two characters are fully developed, the significance of the two marks will be more fully comprehended. Then the third angel's message will be given with compelling power.[12]

Today, mercy and grace are still pleading. The One who came to save us from our sins has the power to make us obedient and faithful. With love, the message of the third angel is calling every person in the world to leave the false system of confusion and disloyalty to God's commandments. Now is the time to stand up for Jesus and all His truths. Don't delay to obey the Creator and His commands.

When will people receive the mark of the beast? Deception and enforcement are two main themes of Revelation 13. "Cause," which alludes to force, is repeated three times. The second beast "causeth the earth and them which dwell therein to worship the first beast, whose deadly wound was healed" (Revelation 13:12). He will also "cause that as many as would not worship the image of the beast should be killed" (Revelation 13:15). "And he causeth all, both small and great, rich and poor, free and bond, to receive a mark in their right hand, or in their foreheads" (Revelation 13:16).

---

12 Bunch, "The Revelation," 207.

While the beast power works through deception and enforcement, the power of God will enlighten the world with the truth of Jesus and His authority as the great Creator and Lawgiver. The messages of the three angels show us that in the last days, a loud call from heaven invites the world to keep all the commandments the Lord. Enraged by the light of truth, the beast power and false prophet will legislate sanctions and death decrees upon those who remain faithful to God's holy law. White shows the timing of the mark of the beast as it relates to the enforcement of Sunday and the enlightening power of God's commandments in the world:

> When Sunday observance shall be enforced by law, and the world shall be enlightened concerning the obligation of the true Sabbath, then whoever shall transgress the command of God, to obey a precept which has no higher authority than that of Rome, will thereby honor popery above God. He is paying homage to Rome and to the power which enforces the institution ordained by Rome. He is worshiping the beast and his image. As men then reject the institution which God has declared to be the sign of His authority, and honor in its stead that which Rome has chosen as the token of her supremacy, they will thereby accept the sign of allegiance to Rome—"the mark of the beast." And it is not until the issue is thus plainly set before the people, and they are brought to choose between the commandments of God and the commandments of men, that those who continue in transgressions will receive "the mark of the beast."[13]

Patient, Commandment-Keeping Saints

Revelation 14:12: Here is the patience of the saints: here *are* they that keep the commandments of God, and the faith of Jesus.

After the fearful warning of the third angel's message, this verse is like peace in the midst of the storm. In contrast to those who follow the beast and receive his mark, we see God's view of those who patiently wait for Him to vindicate them. Unlike their forceful enemies, they are patient. God calls them saints, not because they are perfect or have certain saintly attributes, but because of their loyalty and obedience to the will of God. "I delight to to Thy will, O my God: yea, Thy law is within my heart" (Psalm 40:8).

The saints have the seal of God because they love Jesus who is the Truth. This is demonstrated by their patient obedience to all the commandments of God through the faith they have from Jesus Himself. The patience, faith, and obedience of the saints have been tested and tried, yet they stand victorious.

They are justified because they accept Jesus as their Savior and Substitute. He took the death they deserved, and God treats them as Jesus deserves. Through the Holy Spirit, they receive from Jesus the sanctifying power to overcome sin

---

13   White, *The Great Controversy*, 449.

in their lives. Just as Jesus kept His Father's commandments, they too, through the power of the indwelling Christ, keep the commandments of God. Justified by the death of Christ for their sins and "sanctified by obeying His word,"[14] they will receive the gift of immortality at the second coming of Jesus. Every phase of Christ's sanctuary ministry is fulfilled in them: justification through the cross as represented in the courtyard, sanctification through Christ's daily ministry in the holy place, and prepared for *glorification* through the most holy place experience, purifying themselves "even as He is pure" (1 John 3:3).

Revelation 14:13: And I heard a voice from heaven saying unto me, Write, Blessed *are* the dead which die in the Lord from henceforth: Yea, saith the Spirit, that they may rest from their labours; and their works do follow them.

The command to "*write*" is given twelve times in the book of Revelation (1:11, 19; 2:1, 8, 12, 18; 3:1, 7, 14; 14:13; 19:9; 21:5). After this command, an important message is recorded each time. Verse 13 gives comfort for those who face the choice between disobeying the will of God and certain death if they are obedient to Christ. Death as a martyr brings with it the promise of blessing and real rest in Jesus. No earthly benefit or gain can compare with the blessing of God; no friend or family can be valued above our Lord. The Comforter promises that their works will follow them even after death. White comments on this promise from Jesus: "So will the works of the pure and the holy and the good reflect their light when they no longer live to speak and act themselves. Their works, their words, their example will forever live. 'The righteous shall be in everlasting remembrance.'"[15]

Revelation 14:14-16: And I looked, and behold a white cloud, and upon the cloud *one* sat like unto the Son of man, having on his head a golden crown, and in his hand a sharp sickle. [15]And another angel came out of the temple, crying with a loud voice to him that sat on the cloud, Thrust in thy sickle, and reap: for the time is come for thee to reap; for the harvest of the earth is ripe. [16]And he that sat on the cloud thrust in his sickle on the earth; and the earth was reaped.

White Cloud: The white cloud symbol indicates that the three angels' messages are tied to the soon return of Jesus. When Jesus ascended to heaven, a cloud received Him out of their sight (Acts 1:9). As the disciples gazed into heaven, two angels dressed in white asked them why they remained there staring, then they promised that Jesus would come back in the same way as He left. Jesus left the earth in a cloud and He will return on a cloud. With a golden crown and sharp

---

[14] Franklin E. Beldon, from the lyrics of his hymn "Cover with His Life," 1899.

[15] Ellen G. White, *Testimonies to Ministers and Gospel Workers* (Mountain View, CA: Pacific Press, 1962), 429.

sickle, the Son of Man comes as our returning King to reap earth's harvest. He is the royal Reaper!

In addition to portraying the second coming, the imagery points to the Feast of Tabernacles, the last of the yearly festivals. Through an angel, God the Father announces the final harvest. Thus the three angels' messages in the first half of Revelation 14 represent the final warning given to the world before Jesus returns and the harvest is gathered. The finality of the message is a sobering thought. When Jesus comes, the results of our choices will place us into the first harvest of pure grain or the second harvest of bloody grapes. We will be on the Lord's side or on Satan's based on our response to God's last call through messages of the three angels.

Revelation 14:17-20: And another angel came out of the temple which is in heaven, he also having a sharp sickle. [18]And another angel came out from the altar, which had power over fire; and cried with a loud cry to him that had the sharp sickle, saying, Thrust in thy sharp sickle, and gather the clusters of the vine of the earth; for her grapes are fully ripe. [19]And the angel thrust in his sickle into the earth, and gathered the vine of the earth, and cast *it* into the great winepress of the wrath of God. [20]And the winepress was trodden without the city, and blood came out of the winepress, even unto the horse bridles, by the space of a thousand *and* six hundred furlongs.

Angels of the harvest: An angel announces the harvest of Jesus as He gathers His wheat into His garner (Revelation 14:15; Matthew 13:30). Another angel with a sharp sickle comes out of the temple where the records have been kept. This signifies the judgment of Revelation 14:7 which took place at God's most holy place throne, the ark of the covenant. Yet another angel with power over fire symbolizes the fires that will purify the earth. He commands the angel with a sharp sickle to reap the earth's grapes.

God's pre-advent judgment reveals the choices of every person on earth, for or against Jesus. "He that is unjust, let him be unjust still: and he which is filthy, let him be filthy still: and he that is righteous, let him be righteous still: and he that is holy, let him be holy still. And, behold, I come quickly: and My reward is with Me, to give every man according as his work shall be" (Revelation 22:11-12). After this pronouncement is made, Jesus quickly comes to give each one the reward that they have chosen: death or everlasting life through the Savior's gift.

Two harvests: Let's examine the differences between these two harvests. The first harvest is announced by an angel from the temple. Then Jesus, the Son of man, thrusts in His sickle and reaps the harvest from the earth. The second harvest is announced by another angel from the temple. He directs an angel with a sharp sickle to gather the grapes and throw them into the great winepress of the "wrath of God." The first harvest is reaped by Jesus, and at the same time, His sharp sickle has cut away all who were not part of His harvest (Matthew

13:30). Therefore the second harvest must involve those who were not harvested by Jesus. This second group receives the wrath of God.

The first harvest was ready for Jesus' return as verse 15 tells us "the harvest of the earth is ripe." The second harvest was ready in another sense. Although the vine clusters were fully ripe, their end is gory. The ripeness of verse 18 points to their cup of iniquity which is full and running over. The second harvest gathers both the vines and the fruit of the vine. These vines are obviously different from Christ, the perfect Vine. These wild vines have borne evil fruit. The sharp sickle signifies a complete harvest; nothing is left for the gleaners. John sees the second coming when Jesus Himself treads "the winepress of the fierceness and wrath of Almighty God" (Revelation 19:15).

Doukhan relates Revelation 14:14-20 to the judgment scene of Daniel 7 and agricultural practices in the days of Jesus:

> The Son of man comes first as a reaper, who separates and gathers His people to Himself. It is a positive judgment, one in favor of the accused (Daniel 7:22). The harvest brings a message of life. Scripture's word choice here is particularly significant. The Greek words used by our passage for a "harvest" (*therimos*) and for "reaping" (*therizo*) specifically allude to the gathering of the sheaves and not to their cutting. The sheaves are laden with grain. The image evokes the idea of storage, hence of security. . . .

> On the other hand, the gathering of the grapes represents the punishment of the wicked. This time the vision associates the reaper with fire (Revelation 14:18), which, as in Daniel 7, is the instrument of negative judgment (Daniel 7:11). Moreover, we see the angel who executes the judgment emerging from the altar of the martyrs.[16]

Treading the grapes was one of the last events before the Jews made their pilgrimage to Jerusalem for the Feast of Booths or Tabernacles. As the grapes were gathered into the great winepress before the Feast of Tabernacles in ancient Israel, so the grapes of the earth are harvested before the final fulfillment of the Feast of Tabernacles.

Before our trip to the heavenly Jerusalem and that great banquet in heaven, Jesus will tread the winepress of the wrath of God. The language of the final harvest, and the imagery of the blood up to the horses' bridles symbolize the finality of this event. It also comes in answer to the cries of the martyrs for God's vengeance: "How long, O Lord, holy and true, dost thou not judge and avenge our blood on them that dwell on the earth?" (Revelation 6:10). Now the time has come. The tables are turned on those who have thirsted for the blood of God's people as He gives them their own blood to drink. The second phrase of

---

[16] Doukhan, *Secrets of Revelation*, 136-137.

Revelation 13:10 comes to pass: "He that killeth with the sword must be killed with the sword" as Jesus treads "the winepress of the fierceness and wrath of Almight God" (Revelation 19:15). The graphic imagery is a suitable introduction to the seven last plagues in the next chapter.

Conclusion

Sandwiched between the final exaltation of God's obedient people (Revelation 14:1-5) and the two very different harvests that take place at the second coming of Christ (Revelation 14:14-20), we find the three last messages to the world, given in love by our gracious Lord (Revelation 14:6-13). These three messages promise blessing, rest, and a place in the Lamb's book of life for those who heed the warnings and render obedience to the Creator. On the other hand, the messages of the three angels seek to awaken and rescue those who are following the deceptions of Babylon. The wrath of God, destruction, and death will come to all who follow and worship the beast. The greatest choice in the history of the world hangs upon our response to these graphic warnings. "If ye be willing and obedient, ye shall eat the good of the land: but if ye refuse and rebel, ye shall be devoured with the sword: for the mouth of the Lord hath spoken it" (Isaiah 1:19-20).

In the light from heaven through these three angels, all the lies of the beast are unmasked. In 508 Clovis enforced the worship of Rome, making attendance at mass mandatory and aiding the ascendancy of the papacy over all Christendom. Then the papacy received its power, seat, and great authority in 538 from the crumbling empire of Rome.

Today the deadly wound given in 1798 is healing. Papal ascendancy will again threaten the God-given command to worship the Creator. How will it end? The three angels' messages promise a total reversal of the deceptions practiced during the last days of earth's history and during the 1260 and 1290-day prophecies.

At the end of the 1335-day prophecy, the messages of the three angels came to throw light on the darkness of this world. Living during this time period, White comments: "The first and second messages were given in 1843 and 1844, and we are now under the proclamation of the third; but all three of the messages are still to be proclaimed, . . . showing in the line of prophetic history the things that have been and the things that will be."[17]

The bleeding Lamb has borne all the sins of the world. For the last time, mercy pleads: "Fear God, and give glory to Him; for the hour of His judgment is come: and worship Him that made heaven, and earth, and the sea, and the fountains of waters" (Revelation 14:7). What will be your answer to Him?

---

[17] Ellen G. White, *Selected Messages*, 3 vols. (Washington, DC: Review & Herald), 2:104-105.

CHAPTER TWENTY-SEVEN

Revelation 15

Introduction

C hapter 15 may be the shortest, but it introduces the next five chapters of Revelation. Chapters 16 to 20 describe the judgments of God upon a rebel world. These fall upon the dragon, the beast, and the false prophet: the earthly, satanic trinity that dominates the world. This chapter functions as a prologue to the most terrible scenes of the Apocalypse, the final scenes that picture the wrath of God poured out without mixture. Nothing in history has ever matched these punishments and the results of such unmitigated vengeance.

Revelation 15:1: And I saw another sign in heaven, great and marvellous, seven angels having the seven last plagues; for in them is filled up the wrath of God.

The imagery of chapter 14 carries over into this chapter as well. Bunch notes this similarity.

> Just as angels in the previous chapter symbolized heaven-sent messages carried to the world by the people of God, so angels are used to represent the series of divine judgments that are to be visited upon those who reject the everlasting gospel in its application to the last days and the final crisis. The angels of wrath follow the angels of love and mercy. Offered mercy before threatened judgments has always been the divine program. That was true in regard to the judgments of God upon the antediluvian world, Sodom and Gomorrah, and Jerusalem and the Jewish nation. The final judgments are called "the seven *last* plagues" because there are no others to follow. They fill up and finish the wrath of God against sin.[1]

Like the last seven plagues that fell in Egypt, Revelation again speaks of the seven last plagues. Note that before the Exodus, the first three plagues fell on everyone. Hebrews and Egyptians alike experienced bloody water, too many frogs, and an awful plague of lice. However, the last seven were reserved only for the

---

[1] Bunch, "The Revelation," 217.

Egyptians. By a divine miracle, God's people were sheltered during the seven last plagues in Egypt

This truth is repeated in Revelation. Only the impenitent and rebellious receive the seven last plagues. Seven symbolizes completeness; thus the seven last plagues complete that apocalyptic judgment. The repeated theme of seven points to the forgotten seventh-day Sabbath of God's fourth commandment: seven golden lampstands, seven churches, seven seals, seven trumpets. These seven-fold messages were given in the holy place of the heavenly sanctuary, but beginning with Revelation 11:19, we are ushered into the holy of holies with the sacred ark of the covenant. Thus the seven last plagues were given in the context of the throne of judgment, the atypical Day of Atonement, and the messages of the three angels. Given just before the second coming of Christ and the two final harvests, these plagues represent the literal pouring out of the wrath of God upon those who refuse to heed the pleas and warnings in the three angels' messages.

Revelation 15:2-4: And I saw as it were a sea of glass mingled with fire: and them that had gotten the victory over the beast, and over his image, and over his mark, *and* over the number of his name, stand on the sea of glass, having the harps of God. ³And they sing the song of Moses the servant of God, and the song of the Lamb, saying, Great and marvellous *are* thy works, Lord God Almighty; just and true *are* thy ways, thou King of saints. ⁴Who shall not fear thee, O Lord, and glorify thy name? for *thou* only *art* holy: for all nations shall come and worship before thee; for thy judgments are made manifest.

As the Israelites sang the song of Moses after the defeat of the Egyptians, so the redeemed will sing the song of Moses and the Lamb in heaven after the second coming of Christ. This vision shows us the group that stood through the last days of earth's history, divinely protected by Jesus during the seven last plagues.

Bunch gives reasons for this heavenly preview: "Before proceeding to describe the seven last plagues, Christ, through the angel of prophecy, interjects a brief preliminary vision for the comfort and encouragement of the exiled prophet and especially for the Christian warriors who engage in the closing struggle. Before the terrible judgments are revealed and described, there comes another break in the apocalyptic gloom. The eyes of the prophet are uplifted to behold the final triumph of the church. The Bible contains many of these cheering vistas to brighten the hope of the soldiers of the cross. This is especially true of the last book of Scripture."[2]

As God's people live through the horrors of the last days of earth's history, they will need to keep their eyes on Christ. By faith, they know their deliverance is near and that soon Jesus will come to rescue them from their enemies. White adds to this line of thought: "In the darkest days of her long conflict with evil, the church of God has been given revelations of the eternal purpose of Jehovah. His

---

[2]   Ibid., 218.

people have been permitted to look beyond the trials of the present to the triumphs of the future, when, the warfare having been accomplished, the redeemed will enter into possession of the promised land. These visions of future glory, scenes pictured by the hand of God, should be dear to His church today, when the controversy of the ages is rapidly closing and the promised blessings are soon to be realized in all their fullness."[3]

Sea of Glass Mingled with Fire: This sea mingled with fire provides a symbol of God's presence. See Revelation 4:6 to understand the sea of glass. Fire represents the presence of God. The burning, yet unconsumed bush exemplified the divine presence to Moses. Daily He manifested His presence to Israel through the cloud by day and the pillar of fire by night.

Fire also symbolizes cleansing. The refiner's fire purifies the precious metal while it destroys all the impurities of the ore. This second meaning of fire shows us that God's people have been purified as they passed through the refining fires of trial and conflict.

Who stands on the sea of glass? Those who have gotten the victory over the beast, over his image, over his mark, and over his name. This group has gone through the final conflict. Since the image to the beast has not yet fully formed, you and I may strive to be in that group as we daily overcome sin by the blood of the Lamb. Time will reveal those overcomers who live and endure and remain faithful until Jesus comes.

Song of Moses and the song of the Lamb: These two songs are songs of victory. The song of Moses is found in Exodus 15:1-19, the song of freedom from bondage and victory over the Egyptians. The song of the Lamb will be similar to the song of Moses since both may be sung together and still blend. Bunch meditates on this thought: "Music is the language of thoughts that are too deep for words. Mere words are not adequate to express the joyful animations of hearts thrilled with the joys of eternal victory and everlasting life."[4]

Revelation 15:3 linked the song of Moses and the song of the Lamb because both share a common experience. The song of Moses speaks of deliverance from the Egyptians; the song of the Lamb tells of deliverance from sin. The Israelites were protected during the seven last plagues in Egypt, even as the 144,000 will be protected from the last seven plagues on earth. Both groups experience marvellous miracles and mighty deliverance. Only the 144,000 live to see the seven last plagues unleashed on the wicked in the last days of earth's history. All who refuse to obey the God of heaven and His Son Jesus Christ as Creator and Redeemer will be destroyed and outlived by that universally hated, but obedient remnant. This is why only those who live through the end-time crisis can sing the song of Moses and the Lamb! Bunch envisions that great day:

---

3   White, *Prophets and Kings*, 722.

4   Bunch, "The Revelation," 218.

In order to repeat the song of Moses, God's remnant people must go all the way through the antitype of their deliverance. They must live through the seven last plagues and escape them. They must also face the sentence of death with no human possibility of escape when suddenly they are gloriously delivered by divine intervention. Then "standing on the sea of glass," or "standing by the sea of glass" (R.V.), and "having the harps of God," they celebrate their triumph by singing the song of Moses, which ancient Israel sang beside the Red Sea to the accompaniment of timbrel music. Again all glory is given to God for deliverance from the sentence of death and redemption through the blood of the Lamb. "I will sing unto the Lord, for He hath triumphed gloriously" is the opening sentence of the song. With a few minor changes in names, place and method of punishment, the song of Moses will be just as appropriate for those who are delivered from the last great crisis. See Exodus 15:2, 6, 7, 9-13.[5]

Revelation 14:3 is tied to 15:3-4: "No man could learn that song but the hundred and forty and four thousand, which were redeemed from the earth." Only the 144,000 can sing both the song of Moses and the song of the Lamb because they are the only ones who lived through the last days of earth's sinful history. They experience victory, overcome sin by the blood of the Lamb, and face death when the entire wicked world mercilessly turns against them. All their praise is given to the Lamb for they have come safely through the last great conflict.

Revelation 15:5-8: And after that I looked, and, behold, the temple of the tabernacle of the testimony in heaven was opened: ⁶And the seven angels came out of the temple, having the seven plagues, clothed in pure and white linen, and having their breasts girded with golden girdles. ⁷And one of the four beasts gave unto the seven angels seven golden vials full of the wrath of God, who liveth for ever and ever. ⁸And the temple was filled with smoke from the glory of God, and from his power; and no man was able to enter into the temple, till the seven plagues of the seven angels were fulfilled.

Seven angels come out of the temple of the tabernacle of the testimony in heaven. The language points back to Revelation 11:19 when the ark of His covenant is opened in splendor and majesty. With the setting of the most holy place of the sanctuary in heaven, the Day of Atonement is brought to view. "No man was able to enter" signifies that the time of mercy has ended (Revelation 15:8; cf. Leviticus 16:17). Probation has closed and intercession has ceased. As in ancient Israel, those who have not joined Jesus by faith are now "cut off" from the congregation (Leviticus 23:29).

Clothed in pure, white linen, the seven angels come out of the most holy place. Like Jesus, these messengers wear golden belts (Revelation 1:13), but they carry no censors filled with incense for mediation because Christ has completed

5   Ibid., 220.

His priestly ministry. White summarizes: "The seal of the living God is upon His people"[6] and sin no longer has power over the saints of God! By faith they have claimed the blood of the Lamb; the final word of their testimony will soon be given.

Although Christ's mediation in the sanctuary is over, the saints are sustained by the Spirit of God. The abundant outpouring of the latter rain has strengthened them to give their testimony in the face of death and prepared them for the final test of their faith. They are covered with that perfect wedding garment, paid for by the blood of Jesus. The final, irrevocable choice of every person on earth is made and announced: "He that is filthy, let him be filthy still: and he that is righteous, let him be righteous still" (Revelation 22:11).

Now the whole universe is ready for the seven last plagues to fall. From the full cup of the wrath of God (Revelation 14:10), the angels' bowls are filled. All that could be done to save the lost has been accomplished. They have made their last wrong choice, but can give no excuse for their disloyalty and disobedience. Heaven has warned the earth of its terrible destruction for centuries. Those who refuse the message of grace will see those prophecies fulfilled on themselves as the seven last plagues begin to fall.

---

[6] White, *Testimonies for the Church*, 5:213.

CHAPTER TWENTY-EIGHT

Revelation 16

Introduction

Revelation's warning of the seven last plagues could be compared to seven red lights across the road to the future, saying, "Stop! Look! Listen! Pray! Obey!" Seven terrible scourges lie just ahead of us. Beware! All too often people misunderstand God's love. The Lord is loving, forgiving, caring, kind, patient, and gracious beyond description, but God sets limitations on wickedness. We need to understand this. Centuries ago ten devastating plagues fell upon Egypt. Sodom and Gomorrha spent their last lustful night before God's sudden destruction. He is about to draw the line again. Seven severe and terrible scourges will smite this earth and its people. Thank God there is a way of escape!

The plagues fall after the mark of the beast has been imposed on the inhabitants of the earth. The faithful 144,000 and those still alive that will be a part of the great multitude have been threatened with the death decree. In spite of this, they steadfastly refuse to receive the mark of the beast: the forced observance of the first day of the week. Like Daniel, these faithful ones have already purposed in their hearts that they will not be defiled with disobedience. All that they are and own belongs to Jesus. As they make their choice and exercise the frontal lobe of the brain just behind their forehead, they symbolically receive the seal of the living God as opposed to the mark of the beast.

In stark contrast to the faithful saints are those who have received the mark of the beast. All who oppose the seventh-day Sabbath deny this memorial to Christ as Creator and Lord. God's warnings of His coming wrath have fallen on their deaf ears. As the beast and his followers vent their wrath upon God's people, the merciless wrath of God will fall upon their own heads. As surely as Christ will soon come, those who despise His mercy will face the wrath of the Lamb in the seven last plagues.

In the contextual setting of the three angels' messages of Revelation 14, the plagues come after the third angel's message. First God's last call and warnings are given, then the final judgments are poured out on the rebellious. The first and second angels' messages have been proclaimed since 1844, but the third angel's message will deepen and strengthen as the beast regains its lost power. The enforcement of the beast's worship is yet future, but we have clearly seen how quickly laws can be enacted when governments fear an enemy. White speaks of this strengthening of the message of the third angel as the enforcement of worship draws nigh:

> Heretofore those who presented the truths of the third angel's message have often been regarded as mere alarmists. Their predictions that religious intolerance would gain control in the United States, that church and state would unite to persecute those who keep the commandments of God, have been pronounced groundless and absurd. It has been confidently declared that this land could never become other than what it has been—the defender of religious freedom. But as the question of enforcing Sunday observance is widely agitated, the event so long doubted and disbelieved is seen to be approaching, and the third message will produce an effect which it could not have had before.[1]

The three angels' messages are still being preached, and all have not yet made their stand for God's commandments. Because the worship of the beast is not yet enforced, we are living in the time before the seven last plagues. The fifth plague helps us to understand that these last plagues of judgment fall on a single generation of people living at the end of time: They "blasphemed the God of heaven because of their pains and *their sores*, and repented not of their deeds" (Revelation 16:11; emphasis mine). These sores came from the first plague of judgment, therefore they are meted out in succession. Many will suffer the results of all these plagues because not all will be killed or swept away by the first six bowls of God's wrath.

Revelation 16:1: And I heard a great voice out of the temple saying to the seven angels, Go your ways, and pour out the vials of the wrath of God upon the earth.

The sixteenth chapter of Revelation is written as a beacon of warning. John heard a voice from heaven commanding seven angels to go and pour out the vials of God's wrath on the earth. The word in Greek for vials or bowls is φιάλη (*phiale*), pronounced "fee-al'-ay." This means "a broad shallow bowl" or "a deep saucer." Poured out at the command of the Lord Himself, these seven bowls of God's wrath are directed at every aspect of the beast power. All confederate with the beast are affected by the bowls of God's judgment.

The First Plague

Revelation 16:2: And the first went, and poured out his vial upon the earth; and there fell a noisome and grievous sore upon the men which had the mark of the beast, and upon them which worshipped his image.

---

[1]   White, *The Great Controversy*, 605-606.

This sore falls on all those who do not heed the warnings of the three angels. The beast has claimed power to change the laws of God, but this plague proves that it is unable to change the judgments of God. Changing the Sabbath from the seventh day of the week to the first was Rome's mark of authority, but now she receives these sores or marks of disease. Her claim of ecclesiastical power and authority in religious matters is shown to be diseased as literal "marks" or sores revealing the disease of sin appear upon those with the mark of the beast. Note what Cardinal Gibbons said in 1893 in *The Catholic Mirror* dated September 23, 1893: "Of course, the Catholic Church claims that the change was her act. It could not have been made otherwise, as none in those days would have dreamed of doing anything in matters spiritual and religious without her, and the act is a **mark of her ecclesiastical power and authority** in religious matters" (emphasis mine).[2]

For her haughty claims, she and all who have partnered with her in the observance of the first day of the week instead of the seventh day are struck with a loathsome sore that cannot be cured by any means available to man. The symbols of the beast, mark of the beast, and image of the beast show that the first plague is aimed at all those who have not chosen obedience to the Creator.

Today God in His mercy and grace offers a way out of the dreadful consequences of our wrong choices. He doesn't want us to remain ignorant; therefore the warning comes through His prophets and His people. If God's message of mercy is unwelcome and unheeded, they receive the results of their own obstinacy. No one will be able to claim ignorance on this matter! No one has a reason to blame God because He has warned the entire world.

The first plague is similar to the sixth plague in Egypt (Exodus 9:8-12). White mentions this parallel: "The plagues upon Egypt when God was about to deliver Israel were similar in character to those more terrible and extensive judgments which are to fall upon the world just before the final deliverance of God's people."[3]

The Second Plague

Revelation 16:3: And the second angel poured out his vial upon the sea; and it became as the blood of a dead man: and every living soul died in the sea.

The second angel pours out his vial upon the sea. Without a doubt, the sea will turn to blood, but the sea also symbolizes the peoples, multitudes, nations, and tongues: the great sea of humanity over which the beast has authority. The sea supports the shipping lines and goods that the beast uses to increase her power over the peoples of the earth. The beast has withheld these goods from

---

[2]   James Gibbons, *The Catholic Mirror* (23 September 1893); quoted in Taylor G. Bunch, "The Revelation," Typewritten manuscript, 1952, Center for Adventist Research, James White Library, Andrews University, Berrien Springs, MI, 186.

[3]   White, *The Great Controversy*, 627-628.

God's people because they refuse to receive the mark of the beast. Now the beast receives economic sanctions under the wrath of God.

The second angel's vial of God's wrath lays the axe at the heart of all commerce and material gain that keeps Babylon in her lush lifestyle. As she refused to allow God's people to buy or sell, now she cannot buy or sell because the seas and waters have turned to blood. This is an appropriate response to such tyranny. This plague is similar to the first plague unleashed on Egypt (Exodus 7:14-25).

The Third Plague

Revelation 16:4-6: And the third angel poured out his vial upon the rivers and fountains of waters; and they became blood. ⁵And I heard the angel of the waters say, Thou art righteous, O Lord, which art, and wast, and shalt be, because thou hast judged thus. ⁶For they have shed the blood of saints and prophets, and thou hast given them blood to drink; for they are worthy.

The third angel pours out his vial on the remaining waters and they also become blood. Those that thirsted for the blood of God's people are given blood to drink from the Lord Himself. Now God is laying His axe even deeper into the heart of the beast power. She has claimed power and authority over heaven and hell and over life and death when it comes to spiritual matters. God challenges her to reverse these plagues, but she is unable to do so! After all, if she has such power, why is she unable to do anything about this?

The symbolism shows that as rivers are connected to the seas, so those that deny God's law as a school master to lead us to Jesus also deny Jesus, the Source of the river of life. They hate those who look directly to Christ as their source of life and condemn God's people to death for not looking to them for their source. As they have sought to cut off life support from God's people, now the same judgment will be meted out upon them.

Like the second plague, the third is also connected to the first plague in Egypt. Obviously there are survivors or the plagues would not need to continue. White points this out: "These plagues are not universal, or the inhabitants of the earth would be wholly cut off."[4]

Revelation 16:7: And I heard another out of the altar say, Even so, Lord God Almighty, true and righteous are thy judgments.

Through all these judgments a voice is heard out of the altar confessing that God's judgments are righteous and just. Yes, this is a reminder that God had for centuries given warnings, yet the inhabitants of the earth refused to hear His entreaties of mercy and grace. Year after year, century after century, man has had ample time to hear God's warning to prepare for the end. It is not God's fault for He has done everything that He could. The Father sent His own Son to die on Calvary's cross to gain our attention.

---

[4]   Ibid., 628-629.

The Fourth Plague

Revelation 16:8-9: And the fourth angel poured out his vial upon the sun; and power was given unto him to scorch men with fire. ⁹And men were scorched with great heat, and blasphemed the name of God, which hath power over these plagues: and they repented not to give him glory.

The fourth vial is poured on the sun, giving it power to scorch the wicked. What a fitting judgment in the overall picture of the Apocalypse. Repeatedly Revelation calls us to worship the Creator God, but men have chosen the idolatry of sun worship. God's people were not allowed to buy or sell because they would not keep the "venerable day of the sun," but now their enemies are burned by their object of worship. The very day that is dedicated to sun worship becomes the reason they are scorched with fire. Notice the attitude of these individuals: they do not repent or recognize God and give Him the glory due His name.

Smith puts it this way: "It is worthy of notice that every succeeding plague tends to augment the calamity of the previous ones and to heighten the anguish of the guilty sufferers. We have now a noisome and grievous sore preying upon men, inflaming their blood, and pouring its feverish influence through their veins. In addition to this, they have only blood to allay their burning thirst. As if to crown all, power is given unto the sun, and it pours upon them a flood of fire, and they are scorched with great heat. Here, as the record runs, their woe first seeks utterance in fearful blasphemy."[5]

This plague is poured out on the sun, the symbol of Babylon's chief god. Thus with this judgment God directs His wrath at the very sign of rebellion.

The Fifth Plague

Revelation 16:10-11: And the fifth angel poured out his vial upon the seat of the beast; and his kingdom was full of darkness; and they gnawed their tongues for pain, ¹¹And blasphemed the God of heaven because of their pains and their sores, and repented not of their deeds.

The fifth vial is poured upon the seat of the beast: the papacy and the Vatican. His kingdom includes all who subject themselves to mother Rome, whether governments, individuals, or the daughter churches that return to Rome in theology and allegiance. All those daughter churches were once a part of the Reformation, but they have turned their backs on the reformers and their messages. They refused to follow the Scriptures alone and instead relied upon traditions that have no biblical authority. This is revealed by their allegiance to Sunday worship and their disobedience to the proclamation of the holy Sabbath of the Lord. They reason that others have kept Sunday for centuries; therefore it must be right.

---

[5] Smith, 690.

Those who receive the fifth plague also suffer from the previous four plagues. Revelation 16:11 mentions that they are still suffering from the results of the first plague. Bunch relates their sufferings to their murderous character:

> The results of the previous plagues are mental anguish as well as physical suffering. These verses show that all of the plagues fall upon the worshipers of the beast and with special force upon the officials of the beast power. So great is their bodily and mental anguish that they gnaw "their tongues for pain." The throne of Satan's earthly kingdom under the seventh head is at the Vatican in Rome. The headquarters of the papal kingdom that had so long kept millions in spiritual darkness will be visited with darkness so dense and terrible that it will painfully felt, as was the darkness during one of the plagues in Egypt [ninth plague: Exodus 10:21-23]. The same power that caused unnumbered millions of martyrs to gnaw their tongues for pain on the rack and the stake, now receive the terrible penalty meted out by the eternal law of justice and retribution. They are judged as they judged. What they gave to others comes back upon their own heads. . . .
>
> The tongues of the papal leaders have spoken blasphemies against God, His name, His sanctuary, and His truth, and now because of physical and mental anguish they punish their own tongues. They gnaw their tongues for pain and remorse. The fifth vial falls with telling force upon the ruling class of the papal power and especially on the pretended successor of the apostles who rules in royal splendor and extravagance in his kingly palace on the banks of the Tiber. Rome, the center of the world's intrigue, duplicity, pride, pretense, arrogance, craft, and hypocrisy, will have filled to her double the cup of suffering and sorrow she had filled for others to drink. The robber and despoiler of nations will be robbed of her glory and despoiled. The question, "Who is able to make war with him?" [Revelation 13:4] will then be fully answered. "And great Babylon came in remembrance before God, to give unto her the cup of the wine of the fierceness of his wrath." [Revelation 16:19]. Those who worshiped the beast will find that the beast cannot protect them, for the very object of their worship is also smitten. We must not forget that the purpose of the seven last plagues, like those of Egypt, is to expose the sin of creature worship and to prove to all that the Creator is the true and only God. The plagues will cause every knee to bow and every tongue to confess the true God whom the persecuted saints have worshiped "even unto death."[6]

---

6   Bunch, "The Revelation," 227.

The Sixth Plague

Revelation 16:12-16: And the sixth angel poured out his vial upon the great river Euphrates; and the water thereof was dried up, that the way of the kings of the east might be prepared. ¹³And I saw three unclean spirits like frogs *come* out of the mouth of the dragon, and out of the mouth of the beast, and out of the mouth of the false prophet. ¹⁴For they are the spirits of devils, working miracles, *which* go forth unto the kings of the earth and of the whole world, to gather them to the battle of that great day of God Almighty. ¹⁵Behold, I come as a thief. Blessed *is* he that watcheth, and keepeth his garments, lest he walk naked, and they see his shame. ¹⁶And he gathered them together into a place called in the Hebrew tongue Armageddon.

The sixth angel pours his vial or bowl upon the great river Euphrates. What does this river Euphrates symbolize? To understand this symbol, look back to the fall of Babylon in ancient times. For seventy years, God's people were held captive in Babylon. Those who studied Jeremiah's prophecy knew their release was near.

Isaiah foretold this great deliverance, giving the name of Cyrus before he was born and describing how Babylon would be taken by the Medes and Persians. As prophesied, Cyrus diverted the Euphrates River with the help of God and then gained access to the city through the river gates that had been left unlocked due to divine providence.

The Lord "saith to the deep, Be dry, and I will dry up thy rivers: That saith of Cyrus, He is My shepherd, and shall perform all My pleasure: even saying to Jerusalem, Thou shalt be built; and to the temple, Thy foundation shall be laid. Thus saith the Lord to His anointed, to Cyrus, whose right hand I have holden, to subdue nations before him; and I will loose the loins of kings, to open before him the two leaved gates; and the gates shall not be shut" (Isaiah 44:27-45:1).

The conquest of Cyrus marked the liberation of the Jews from Babylon and his decree allowed them to return to Jerusalem. This ancient providence in the marvellous deliverance of historical Israel parallels the imminent rescue of God's last day people from the wrath of Babylon the great. The wrath of God in the sixth plague strikes terror in the heart of His enemies, but it brings deliverance to His patient and obedient saints.

As the life-giving protection of the Euphrates was diverted from the ancient city of Babylon before its fall, so also the symbolic drying the Euphrates in the last day points to the drying up of the streams that give life to the papacy. Euphrates means "that which makes fruitful," therefore that which has made the papacy fruitful will be dried up. The sixth plague is directed at the many waters upon which the woman sits, the nations which give her power (Revelation 17:1, 15). When the wrath of God dries up this support from the kings of the earth, the way for the kings of the east is made ready.

Who are the kings of the east? As Cyrus, who delivered the Jews from Babylon, came from the east, so also will the "Sun of righteousness" arise from the east to deliver those who fear His name (Malachi 4:2). "As the lightning cometh out of the east, and shineth even unto the west; so shall also the coming of the Son of man be" (Matthew 24:27). As the dawning sun rises out of the east, so Zacharias prophesied of Christ's coming: "The dayspring from on high hath visited us" (Luke 1:78). And the wise men proclaimed, "We have seen His star in the east!" (Matthew 2:2).

The Greek word for the east is ἀνατολή (an-at-ol-ay) which means "the rising of the sun or the east, the direction of the dawning day." When He was born, Jesus entered the world as the King from the east. He died on the cross as symbolized by the altar of burnt offering. After He left this earth, He entered heaven's sanctuary, beginning His ministry in the holy place and completing His work the most holy place. In all these movements through His earthly and heavenly ministry, Jesus came from the east and moved to the west, just as we see in the structure of the book of Revelation.

The conflict of the ages is not just an earthly battle! Christ the King of heaven will fight the final battle of Armageddon against Satan and all his followers—the beast, the false prophet, and the kings of the earth. As three unclean spirits come out of the mouth of the dragon, the beast, and the false prophet, the forces of evil are united by this same spirit to war against the King of kings. "Tidings out of the east" provoke the three unclean spirits like frogs to gather the earthly kings to the battle of the great day of God Almighty (Daniel 11:44; Revelation 16:13-14).

The satanic trinity gathers the kings of the earth together to the place called Armegeddon in Hebrew language. Armageddon means Mount of Megiddo. The root of the name in Hebrew means "to cut off" or "slay." In other words, the battle of Armageddon will cut off or slay those who are the enemies of God. This spiritual battle is a life and death matter, so Jesus warns us: "Behold, I come as a thief. Blessed is he that watcheth, and keepeth his garments, lest he walk naked, and they see his shame" (Revelation 16:15).

Who is coming? Jesus is coming unexpectedly. Don't be caught unaware when the close of probation occurs. Christ and His legions of angels are the kings of the east who stand in opposition to the dragon, the beast, the false prophet, and the kings of the earth. The battle of all ages has never been an earthly battle! This battle involves all the earth and heaven as Christ and Satan meet at Armageddon.

All those who unite with Jesus will join Him in this battle against the dragon, the beast, the false prophet, and the kings of the earth. This spiritual battle takes place just before the coming of Christ. Verse 15 pronounces a blessing on those that watch and keep their garments. The group of the pure and blessed is contrasted with those who walk naked and ashamed. Jesus pronounces the blessing and the curse. The battlefield is over the soul of every man, woman, and child on the face of the earth. This question begs to be answered: Where will you stand in that great battle of that great day of God Almighty?

The Seventh Plague

Revelation 16:17-21: And the seventh angel poured out his vial into the air; and there came a great voice out of the temple of heaven, from the throne, saying, It is done. ¹⁸And there were voices, and thunders, and lightnings; and there was a great earthquake, such as was not since men were upon the earth, so mighty an earthquake, *and* so great. ¹⁹And the great city was divided into three parts, and the cities of the nations fell: and great Babylon came in remembrance before God, to give unto her the cup of the wine of the fierceness of his wrath. ²⁰And every island fled away, and the mountains were not found. ²¹And there fell upon men a great hail out of heaven, *every stone* about the weight of a talent: and men blasphemed God because of the plague of the hail; for the plague thereof was exceeding great.

The final angel pours his vial in the air, symbolizing the universality of the seventh and last plague! Bunch comments on the import of this scene: "At three different times the pronouncement, 'It is done,' goes forth from the throne of God. The first is when probation closes and the work of salvation is completed. The second is when the seventh plague is poured out which finishes or fill up the wrath of God against sin and sinners. The third and last is after the wicked have been destroyed and the earth renewed to its Edenic glory and God's eternal purpose for the earth and man is finally realized after the long delay caused by the reign of sin. See Revelation 21:5."[7]

Great earthquake: It is the voice of God thundering that seems to be symbolized here. It thunders and causes an earthquake of such magnitude that it is described as "such as was not since men were upon the earth, so mighty an earthquake, and so great." (Revelation 16:18).

Great city divided into three: In the seventh plague there is a great earthquake and gigantic hail falls upon man as Babylon's three-fold alliance of *religion, politics, and economics* is divided. All is seen for what it really is and nothing is hidden from view. White relates this final plague to the destruction of ancient Israel's enemies: "When the heathen Amorites had set themselves to resist His purposes, God interposed, casting down 'great stones from heaven' upon the enemies of Israel. We are told of a greater battle to take place in the closing scenes of earth's history, when 'Jehovah hath opened His armory, and hath brought forth the weapons of His indignation' Jeremiah 50:25."[8]

Hail the weight of a talent: Smith enlarges on magnitude and finality of the seventh plague:

Every hailstone is said to be 'about the weight of a talent.' According to various authorities, a talent as a weight is about fifty-seven pounds avoirdupois. What could withstand the force of stones of such an enormous

7   Bunch, "The Revelation," 233.

8   White, *Patriarchs and Prophets*, 509.

weight falling from heaven? But mankind, at this time, will have no shel-
ter. The cities have fallen in a mighty earthquake, the islands have fled
away, and the mountains are not found. Again the wicked give vent to
their woe in blasphemy, for the plague of the hail is "exceeding great."...

"There came a great voice out of the temple of heaven, from the throne,
saying: It is done!" Thus all is finished. The cup of human guilt has been
filled up. The last soul has availed itself of the plan of salvation. The
books are closed. The number of the saved is completed. The final period
is placed to this world's history. The vials of God's wrath are poured out
upon a corrupt generation. The wicked have drunk them to the dregs,
and sunk into the realm of death for a thousand years. Reader, where
do you wish to be found after that great decision?[9]

---

[9]   Smith, 703-705.

CHAPTER TWENTY-NINE

Revelation 17

Introduction

Revelation 17 announces the judgment of Babylon the great, the mother of harlots. She is unmasked, identified, judged, condemned, and ready for her final destruction as described in Revelation 18. One of the angels that bears the seven last plagues reveals this impure woman to John. Watch as God exactly identifies Babylon the great. Thiele notes four judgments in this chapter:[1]

- Judgment of the harlot (17:1, 16)
- Judgment of the beast (17:8, 11)
- Judgment of the seven heads (17:10)
- Judgment of the ten horns (17:14)

Babylon the Great, Mother of Harlots

Revelation 17:1-6: And there came one of the seven angels which had the seven vials, and talked with me, saying unto me, Come hither; I will show unto thee the judgment of the great whore that sitteth upon many waters: [2]With whom the kings of the earth have committed fornication, and the inhabitants of the earth have been made drunk with the wine of her fornication. [3]So he carried me away in the spirit into the wilderness: and I saw a woman sit upon a scarlet coloured beast, full of names of blasphemy, having seven heads and ten horns. [4]And the woman was arrayed in purple and scarlet colour, and decked with gold and precious stones and pearls, having a golden cup in her hand full of abominations and filthiness of her fornication: [5]And upon her forehead _was_ a name written, MYSTERY, BABYLON THE GREAT, THE MOTHER OF HARLOTS AND ABOMINATIONS OF THE EARTH. [6]And I saw the woman drunken with the blood of the saints, and with the blood of the martyrs of Jesus: and when I saw her, I wondered with great admiration.

---

[1] Thiele, 253.

Verse 1: God introduces the judgment of Babylon in the contextual setting of the seven last plagues. An angel who carried a plague bowl talks with John about the judgment of the *great whore* that sits on many waters, defined as peoples, multitudes, nations, and tongues (Revelation 17:15).

Verse 2: Graphic language shows the filthiness of this woman who rules over the world. Multitudes fall under her influence, drunk with the wine of her fornication. This wine symbolizes her evil and sinful influence over them. As civil governments of the earth have cooperated with her, separation between the church and the state has ceased to exist. This infers the loss of religious freedom as chapter 13 clearly foretells.

Verse 3: Carried away by the Spirit to the wilderness, John sees the harlot riding a seven-headed, ten-horned scarlet beast full of blasphemous names. The wilderness symbol helps us understand that this woman does not have Jesus as her husband or else she would not be in the wilderness. The Greek word for wilderness is ἔρημος (er'-ay-mos), "a solitary, lonely, desolate, uninhabited place or a desert, wilderness." This word describes literal deserted places or lonely regions, but it may also have a more abstract meaning: "deprived of protection of others, especially of friends, acquaintances, and kindred." Lastly, and maybe the most fitting in this case, *eremos* may mean "a women neglected by her husband, from whom the husband withholds himself." This definition best fits the contextual setting of the great whore full of blasphemy.

In the Bible, a woman symbolizes a church. Obviously a pure woman symbolizes a pure church and an impure woman represents an apostate church divorced from the Lord. The whore dwells in the wilderness, similar to the scapegoat's destination. This whore, once the church of Christ, has left Him for another husband, one who lives in the wilderness like Satan. With wilderness imagery, verse 3 points us to the scapegoat and the millennium, Satan's housing on death row.

Using the same symbols as Revelation 13, this woman rides a beast with seven heads and ten horns. We learned in both Daniel 7 and Revelation 13 that the seven heads were symbolic of the seven kingdoms that are world kingdoms:

- Egypt
- Assyria
- Babylon
- Medo-Persia
- Greece
- Pagan Rome
- Christian or Papal Rome

We also learned that the ten horns symbolize ten kingdoms that come out of the pagan Rome as depicted in Daniel 2. With the understanding of Daniel coupled with Revelation, obviously the ten horns are spiritually ruled by the beast power. This beast full of blasphemous names provides a ride for the great harlot. Through this symbol, God reveals how Satan works through political powers throughout the ages as depicted by the seven heads and ten horns.

Purple and Scarlet

Verse 4: Graphic language describes her dress of "**purple and scarlet colour, and decked with gold and precious stones and pearls, having a golden cup in her hand full of abominations and filthiness of her fornication.**" This chapter clearly indicates that this woman and the beast she sits upon are world-embracing, global symbols. Her sins are not merely her own, but includes Satan's reign of sin over the whole world. This unrighteous rulership involves world leaders and all the inhabitants of the world. Bunch discusses the colors connected with this fallen woman:

> Purple was at that time the royal color worn by kings and queens, and scarlet was until in recent years the identifying raiment of harlots. Scarlet is the Biblical symbol of sin and rebellion. See Isaiah 1:18. It is therefore the color of the symbols of Satan's kingdom. See Revelation 12:3; 17:3. It is appropriate that a scarlet robe be the wedding garment of Satan's wife or bride. It indicates her sinful character in contrast with the white robe of Christ's righteousness which clothes the bride of Christ. It is a significant fact that both purple and scarlet are the most prominent colors in the official robes and caps of the popes, cardinals, and other officials of the Roman Catholic Church. The pope's wardrobe is estimated to be worth $100,000,000. It contains the costumes of many of the popes. Among them are a few white garments but most of them are scarlet and purple representing a combination of royalty and harlotry. The shoes of the popes are decked with pearls. There is a collection of fourteen crowns for various occasions, the smallest being worth about $1,000,000. The triple crown is one of the most valuable ever made. It is literally "decked with gold and precious stones and pearls," of almost inestimable value.[2]

The Golden Cup

Bunch writes: The harlot's cup "contains the wine of error which makes all the nations drunk. 'The nations have drunken of her wine; therefore the nations are mad.' (Jeremiah 51:7). The golden cup with its poisonous wine represents a beautiful exterior or ritual with inward error and corruption. Gold is the symbol of truth but intoxicating wine is the symbol of falsehood. The pretense is

---

[2]   Bunch, "The Revelation," 244-245.

Christian, but the character is satanic."[3] Seiss enlarges on the symbolism of the harlot's cup:

> The cup held out is *golden*. To the sensual and carnal heart and imagination the world's religion and progress is something bright and glorious, the glittering fullness of good and blessing. But in that shining cup is only abomination and uncleanness—spiritual prostitution—nothing but spiritual prostitution.

> The cup is *one*; and in all the varied systems of false faith and false worship which taint our world there is held out and received but one and the same essence, and that essence is the harlotry of old Babylon. It is most direct in Paganism; but it is in Mohammedanism, in Papalism, in the degenerate Catholicism of the Eastern churches, and in all the heretical isms, infidelities, and mere goodishnesses which afflict our Protestant Christianity as well. So true is it that Great Babylon, the mother of the harlots and of the abominations of the earth, hath made the inhabitants of the earth drunk with the wine of her fornication.[4]

Revelation speaks of two women diametrically opposed to each other: the pure bride of Christ in chapter 12 and the mother of harlots in Revelation 17. Only one of these women rides a beast.Chapter 13 introduced the beast that works against Christ and His true church. Here in chapter 17 the apostate woman rides the beast which represents both Satan and his kingdoms that have spanned the history of the world as depicted by the seven heads and ten horns. This impure church certainly cannot be the bride for whom Christ is coming! She has prostituted herself with the kings of the earth and the leaders of the nations, bringing them under her control.

Christ and His arch-rival Satan have visible churches here on earth. Chapter 12 introduced the pure woman robed in light and founded on the faith of the twelve patriarchs and twelve apostles. In stark contrast, the garish whore of Revelation 17 bases her authority on this world, the kingdoms of this world, and her wealth and prosperity. Her fallen condition is revealed by her dress, her filthy golden cup, and her violent behavior toward the saints.

Verse 5: And upon her forehead *was* a name written, MYSTERY, BABYLON THE GREAT, THE MOTHER OF HARLOTS AND ABOMINATIONS OF THE EARTH.

---

3   Ibid., 245.

4   Joseph A. Seiss, *The Apocalypse: An Exposition of the Book of Revelation* (New York: Charles C. Cook, 1900; reprint, Grand Rapids, MI: Kregel Publications, 1987), 390 (page citations are to the reprint edition).

Using Old Testament allusions, Seiss fills out the abominable portrait of the great whore:

> One of the most characteristic features of this Woman is her *harlotry*. The Angel calls her "The Great Harlot," and she wears upon her forehead as her name, "The mother of the harlots, and of the abominations of the earth." Harlotry is the standing symbol in the word of God for a debauched worship, idolatry, and false devotion. When people worship for God what is not God, or give their hearts to idols, or institute systems, doctrines, rites, or administrations, to take the place of what God has revealed and appointed, the Scriptures call it whoredom, adultery, fornication. (Jeremiah 3:6, 8, 9; Ez. 16:32; Hosea 1 and 2; Revelation 2:22.) The reasons are obvious. The breaking down of the divine laws and ordinances necessarily carries with it the dishonour of the marriage institution, and hence all supports of godly chastity and pureness. Accordingly all false religions are ever attended with lewdness, even in connection with their most honoured rites. The sacredness of marriage has no place in them. Besides, the very essence of the divine law is, that we love God our Lord with all the heart, mind, soul, and strength. This is Jehovah's due and requirement of all that live. Hence the bestowal of worshipful affection on any other object, or putting of anything whatever in the place of the true God, is, in the very nature of the case, a great spiritual harlotry; for it is the turning of the soul from the only legitimate object of its adoration, to take into its embrace what has no right to such room and place. And as this Woman is a *harlot*, "the great Harlot," and "the mother of the harlots and the abominations of the earth," she must needs be the great embodiment, source, and representative of all idolatry, false worship, and perversion of the word and institutes of God.[5]

She is the mother of harlots; therefore harlotry occupies her daughters as well. Like their mother, the daughters of Babylon also compromise and fornicate. They too possess the filthy insignia of Babylon. Note carefully the immodest colors and adornment of Babylon and her daughters. Unlike the pure woman of Revelation 12, the great harlot and her daughters bring into the church a connection with the world in dress, deportment in worship, and adornment. Instead of looking like a bride in white, the women in chapter 17 appear like women of the night. The true church of God here on earth will not have the same trappings of gold, showy apparel, and worldly habits and addictions. In contrast, those who are not connected spiritually with Christ would rebel against such modest behavior and consider it restrictive.

Verse 6: This harlot woman gets drunk from the blood of the saints and martyrs. These graphic symbols clearly point to a persecuting power. In fact, Babylon

---

[5]   Seiss, *The Apocalypse*, 387.

finds delight in the destruction of those who, by virtue of their holy lives, draw her ire. Enraged by their obedient witness and their refusal to idolize her, the great whore eliminates those who remind her of her whoredoms. The pages of history fairly drip with the blood of her slain during the 1,260 years of papal supremacy. To this very day historians are uncovering the atrocities of the Roman Church through the ages. Babylon the great points to more than papal Rome because neither papal Rome nor any of the powers that ruled the world killed the prophets. Since the beginning of time, atrocities have been committed by those apostates who claimed to be God's chosen. The symbolism here is amazing.

Revelation 17:7-18: And the angel said unto me, Wherefore didst thou marvel? I will tell thee the mystery of the woman, and of the beast that carrieth her, which hath the seven heads and ten horns. ⁸The beast that thou sawest was, and is not; and shall ascend out of the bottomless pit, and go into perdition: and they that dwell on the earth shall wonder, whose names were not written in the book of life from the foundation of the world, when they behold the beast that was, and is not, and yet is. ⁹And here *is* the mind which hath wisdom. The seven heads are seven mountains, on which the woman sitteth. ¹⁰And there are seven kings: five are fallen, and one is, *and* the other is not yet come; and when he cometh, he must continue a short space. ¹¹And the beast that was, and is not, even he is the eighth, and is of the seven, and goeth into perdition. ¹²And the ten horns which thou sawest are ten kings, which have received no kingdom as yet; but receive power as kings one hour with the beast. ¹³These have one mind, and shall give their power and strength unto the beast. ¹⁴These shall make war with the Lamb, and the Lamb shall overcome them: for he is Lord of lords, and King of kings: and they that are with him *are* called, and chosen, and faithful. ¹⁵And he saith unto me, The waters which thou sawest, where the whore sitteth, are peoples, and multitudes, and nations, and tongues. ¹⁶And the ten horns which thou sawest upon the beast, these shall hate the whore, and shall make her desolate and naked, and shall eat her flesh, and burn her with fire. ¹⁷For God hath put in their hearts to fulfil his will, and to agree, and give their kingdom unto the beast, until the words of God shall be fulfilled. ¹⁸And the woman which thou sawest is that great city, which reigneth over the kings of the earth.

Verse 7: The angel says to John, "**Wherefore didst thou marvel?**" This sort of language implies that enough evidence has been given. There should be no reason for amazement. God anticipates a generation of people on the earth so steeped in the sins of Babylon that John cannot believe so many have been taken in by the whoredoms of Babylon the great. God has plainly exposed the sins Babylon the great. How can she still have so much power over the majority of the world? This is "the mystery of iniquity" (2 Thessalonians 2:7).

Next John is told: "**I will tell thee the mystery of the woman, and of the beast that carrieth her, which hath the seven heads and ten horns.**" What comes next should answer the question, "Who is this woman and what do the seven heads and ten horns represent?"

Verse 8: "was, and is not, and yet is." This language can only be understood in the light of Revelation 13:3: "I saw one of his heads as though it were wounded to death." Later this deadly wound on one of the beast's heads is healed. This can only mean the seventh head since history records the deadly wound of the papacy at the end of her 1,260-year reign. This deadly wound of the papacy and its subsequent healing are found in the words: **"Was, and is not, and yet is."** This refers also to verses 10 and 11.

Verses 9 and 10: "Here *is* the mind which hath wisdom. The seven heads are seven mountains, on which the woman sitteth. And there are seven kings: five are fallen, and one is, *and* the other is not yet come; and when he cometh, he must continue a short space." The clue to understanding this woman's identity is found in the seven mountains on which she sits. The seven mountains cannot be the seven hills of Rome or else five of the hills would have already fallen. John writes in symbols, and therefore his words must be understood as symbolic. The key to this verse lies in the five that have fallen and the one that *is*. Seiss shows why these must be viewed as symbols: "The seven *hills* of the city of Rome, to begin with, are not *mountains*, as every one who has been there can testify; and if they were, they are not more characteristic of the situation of Rome than the seven hills are characteristic of Jerusalem. But the taking of them as literal hills or mountains at all is founded upon a total misreading of the angel's words."[6]

Verse 10: "And there are seven kings: five are fallen, and one is, *and* the other is not yet come; and when he cometh, he must continue a short space." Understanding this verse is rather simple. Here we have the key: five have fallen, and John is living in the time of the sixth power. That sixth power can be understood only as that of Rome, and therefore the five that have fallen are Egypt, Assyria, Babylon, Medo-Persia, and Greece. Rome was the sixth. Seiss comments:

> What regal mountain, then, was in power at the time John wrote? There can be no question on that point; it was the Roman empire. Thus, then, we ascertain and identify the sixth in the list, which shows what sort of *kings* the angel meant. Of the same class with this, and belonging to the same category, there are five others—five which had then already run their courses and passed away. But what five imperial mountains like Rome had been and gone, up to that time? Is history so obscure as not to tell us with unmistakable certainty? Preceding Rome the world had but five great names or nationalities answering to imperial Rome, and those scarce a schoolboy ought to miss. They are Greece, Persia, Babylon, Assyria, and Egypt; no more, and no less. And these all were imperial powers like Rome. Here, then, are six of these regal mountains;

---

6   Ibid., 391.

the seventh is not yet come. When it comes it is to endure but a short time. This implies that each of the others continues a long time; and so, again, could not mean the dictators, decemvirs, and military tribunes of the early history of Rome, for some of them lasted but a year or two. Thus, then, by the clearest, most direct, and most natural signification of the words of the record, we are brought to the identification of these seven mountain kings as the seven great world-powers, which stretch from the beginning of our present world to the end of it. Daniel makes the number less; but he started with his own times, and looked only down the stream. Here the account looks backward as well as forward. That which is first in Daniel is the third here, and that which is the sixth here is the fourth in Daniel. Only in the commencing point is there any difference. The visions of Daniel and the visions of John are from the same Divine mind, and they perfectly harmonize, only that the latest are the amplest.[7]

Thus the five that have fallen are [1]Egypt, [2]Assyria, [3]Babylon, [4]Medo-Persia, and [5]Greece. The one that is—[6]Rome. Living in the twenty-first century, we know that pagan Rome gave its "power, seat and great authority" over to Christian Rome or what is known as [7]papal Rome.

Verse 11: The beast **"was, and is not, is himself also the eighth."** Verse 8 said: **"was, and is not, and yet is."** This refers to the beast of Revelation 13:3 which receives a deadly wound that is healed. Here the Revelator tells us that the eighth power really came from the first seven. Therefore the simple understanding is found in the healing of the deadly wound. Thus the eighth is the rebirth of the seventh power which we know to be papal Rome.

Verse 12: The ten horns are linked to the beast. When John wrote the book of Revelation, the ten toes of Daniel had not yet come into being. These ten toes are the same as the ten horns of Revelation. They are the ten divisions of Europe, originally known as ten Christian kingdoms.

One hour: The kings receive authority for "one hour," the time period linked to the destruction of the beast. Their power continues only a short period of time. In prophetic time one hour is merely two literal weeks. After that very short time period, the beast is destroyed.

Verse 13: The ten horns or kingdoms are of one mind and give their power and strength to the beast! See Daniel 7:7 for an explanation of the ten horns since these are the same as the ten toes of Daniel 2. According to verse 12, these ten horns receive their power for one hour. In Greek it reads: μίαν ὥραν (*mian horan*). *Mia* means "one." *Hora* can mean: (1) a certain definite time or season, (2) the daytime (bounded by the rising and setting of the sun), a day, (3) a twelfth part of the daytime, an hour, (4) any definite time, point of time, moment. The context determines the meaning. Greek scholars translate μίαν ὥραν

(*mian horan*) to mean "in the same time or era." Therefore we should understand that the ten horns are in the same era or existing at the same time as the beast. This language refers to a time when the ten kingdoms are in total support of the Papacy. However, in the future these ten kingdoms will have a change of heart and turn against the beast.

Verse 14: Soon the ten horns will make war with the Lamb. Smith elaborates: "Here we are carried into the future, to the time of the great and final battle, for at this time the Lamb bears the title of King of kings and Lord of lords, a title which He assumes when He ceases His intercessory priesthood at the close of probation. (Revelation 19:11-16.)"[8]

Verse 15: This verse defines the symbolic meaning of waters: the populated parts of the earth in the contextual setting of Europe and the pagan Roman Empire. "Waters" symbolizes the ten kingdoms that formed the nations of Europe after the demise of the Roman Empire.

Verse 16: The ten horns that once supported papal Rome will turn against her. This is the judgment of the great harlot. Also, the great harlot is identified without a shadow of a doubt here as papal Rome. Babylon is the great city that rules over the kings of the earth. History is rife with examples of the authority Rome has exercised over rulers in Europe. When kings chose not obey her wishes, their lives were threatened as the church used her power over the populace to control monarchs. The next chapter reveals the destiny of Babylon the great and her harlot daughters.

---

[8]   Smith, 712.

CHAPTER THIRTY

Revelation 18

Introduction

C overing the destruction of Babylon the great, chapter 18 is divided into three main sections: (1) heaven's last call to come out of Babylon for it will be destroyed (18:1-8), (2) the reaction of the earthly kingdoms to her destruction (18:9-19), and (3) heaven's reaction to the destruction of Babylon (18:20-24). Babylon is destroyed because she has filled her cup of iniquity and spurned the warnings of God for so long that there is no remedy.

Chapter eighteen warns God's people to get out of spiritual Babylon. This final call out of Babylon amplifies the second angel's message of Revelation 14:8. Given since 1844, God's plea to leave Babylon strengthens and grows louder as the time of mercy grows shorter. This is not a short call with very little warning. On the contrary, God has pleaded with His people for years just as Noah preached the same sermon for 120 years before the Flood destroyed the earth.

After this loud repetition of God's call, there is nothing more that can be done for all that remain in Babylon. They have refused to leave their fallen churches and stubbornly hang on to tradition, clinging to the false doctrines of Babylon. The final message also presumes that there are some who used to belong to God's people, but made the mistake of drinking of the wine of her fornications. They can no longer discern between truth and error. Some who were once part of God's true church will drink of that wine and succumb to her intoxication. Who are these people? Take a cursory look at the description of Babylon the great in Revelation 17: her dress, her deportment, the wine, and everything about her. God is calling His faithful away from these worldly allurements. We must cut all ties with Babylon *before* the seven last plagues begin to fall on her and her adherents.

Heaven's Last Call before Babylon's Destruction

Revelation 18:1-8: And after these things I saw another angel come down from heaven, having great power; and the earth was lightened with his glory. ²And he cried mightily with a strong voice, saying, Babylon the great is fallen, is fallen, and is become the habitation of devils, and the hold of every foul spirit,

and a cage of every unclean and hateful bird. ³For all nations have drunk of the wine of the wrath of her fornication, and the kings of the earth have committed fornication with her, and the merchants of the earth are waxed rich through the abundance of her delicacies. ⁴And I heard another voice from heaven, saying, Come out of her, my people, that ye be not partakers of her sins, and that ye receive not of her plagues. ⁵For her sins have reached unto heaven, and God hath remembered her iniquities. ⁶Reward her even as she rewarded you, and double unto her double according to her works: in the cup which she hath filled fill to her double. ⁷How much she hath glorified herself, and lived deliciously, so much torment and sorrow give her: for she saith in her heart, I sit a queen, and am no widow, and shall see no sorrow. ⁸Therefore shall her plagues come in one day, death, and mourning, and famine; and she shall be utterly burned with fire: for strong is the Lord God who judgeth her.

The last angel's call (18:1-3): Another angel came down from heaven having great power and the earth was lightened with his glory. This glory and the darkness of Babylon stand in sharp contrast to each other. The heavenly light brings God's good news of truth: *the gospel of salvation*. Babylon's intoxicating counterfeit worship keeps its followers in the darkness of sin and error.

The glory of the gospel of salvation enlightens us and proclaims our redemption and deliverance from sin. All in Babylon are bound by Satan, but we cannot free ourselves from the sin's shackles. Only the blood of the Lamb liberates us from the Babylon's bondage of ignorance, false worship, and tradition.

Babylon influences the entire spiritual world. The battle is for the souls of the men and women of the earth. This false religious system will keep her grip upon all by every means imaginable. Through compromise, materialism, possessions, pride, works, religious practice, Babylon will do whatever it takes to keep the souls of men caught in her web of deceit.

Christ's Final Call

"Come out of her, My people, that ye be not partakers of her sins, and that ye receive not of her plagues" (Revelation 18:4). Angels and human messengers have sounded warning after warning, but now Jesus Himself gives the last warning call, "Come out of Babylon and her influences." This message comes before the plagues because God is still mercifully calling His people out of Babylon.

The language of Revelation 18:4-8 repeats several aspects of the messages of the three angels (Revelation 14:6-13). The angel comes from heaven, bringing glory to the earth, and calls with a loud voice (Revelation14:6-7). His message repeats and adds to the second angel's message (Revelation 14:8). Then the voice of God Himself calls His people out of Babylon, warning them to flee the seven last plagues prepared for Babylon, the final outpouring of the "wrath of God" (Revelation 14:10). Those who listen to His voice will obey His call. Thus God's gracious power helps them to obey and exempts them from the plagues that are directed at Babylon.

Each one of the seven last plagues is aimed at some aspect of Babylon's power over the peoples and kingdoms of the earth. Each plague strips Babylon of her control as the people she has deluded realize that their fateful choice has brought the judgments of God upon them. Too late they realize that they have heaped scorn upon heaven's merciful calls to come out of Babylon.

The sins of Babylon have reached all the way to heaven, and God remembers all her iniquities (Revelation 18:5). Babylon stands in stark contrast to those who follow the Lamb Jesus Christ. Happily those who accept the gospel of Jesus are protected from the plagues that ravage Babylon. Their sins and iniquities are forgiven and no longer remembered.

God prophesies that Babylon will be rewarded or punished according to her works. She boasts of her own works as she says in her heart: "**I sit a queen, and am no widow, and shall see no sorrow**" (Revelation 18:7).

These plagues will come in "a day" (Revelation 18:8). This surely cannot mean that they will come in one literal day. Smith relates the day-year principle in Isaiah to the judgments meted out by God on Israel's foes: "The plain inference from the language of this verse in connection with Isaiah 34:8, is that a year will be occupied in that terrible visitation."[1] In the next chapter, Isaiah adds this encouragement: "Be strong, fear not: behold, your God will come with vengeance, even God with a recompence; He will come and save you" (Isaiah 35:4). When we see these plagues, we may know that the coming of Jesus is very near.

Earthly Kings React to Babylon's Destruction

Revelation 18:9-19: And the kings of the earth, who have committed fornication and lived deliciously with her, shall bewail her, and lament for her, when they shall see the smoke of her burning, [10]Standing afar off for the fear of her torment, saying, Alas, alas that great city Babylon, that mighty city! for in one hour is thy judgment come. [11]And the merchants of the earth shall weep and mourn over her; for no man buyeth their merchandise any more: [12]The merchandise of gold, and silver, and precious stones, and of pearls, and fine linen, and purple, and silk, and scarlet, and all thyine wood, and all manner vessels of ivory, and all manner vessels of most precious wood, and of brass, and iron, and marble, [13]And cinnamon, and odours, and ointments, and frankincense, and wine, and oil, and fine flour, and wheat, and beasts, and sheep, and horses, and chariots, and slaves, and souls of men. [14]And the fruits that thy soul lusted after are departed from thee, and all things which were dainty and goodly are departed from thee, and thou shalt find them no more at all. [15]The merchants of these things, which were made rich by her, shall stand afar off for the fear of her torment, weeping and wailing, [16]And saying, Alas, alas, that great city, that was clothed in fine linen, and purple, and scarlet, and decked with gold, and precious stones, and pearls! [17]For in

---

[1]   Smith, 726.

one hour so great riches is come to nought. And every shipmaster, and all the company in ships, and sailors, and as many as trade by sea, stood afar off, ¹⁸And cried when they saw the smoke of her burning, saying, What city is like unto this great city! ¹⁹And they cast dust on their heads, and cried, weeping and wailing, saying, Alas, alas, that great city, wherein were made rich all that had ships in the sea by reason of her costliness! for in one hour is she made desolate.

Verses 9-11: The kings of the earth stand afar off weeping and lamenting for Babylon when they see the burning of the city. The spiritual fornication they have committed with spiritual Babylon is now seen as it really is and was! They lament not only for Babylon, but for themselves. Through Babylon they obtained influence, power, and material gain as they received the mark of the beast. Now they realize that they have lost out on that which is worth more than all the political advantage, power, and riches of the whole earth. Their temporal riches are now destroyed, but they have no spiritual wealth. They have given their time to the great whore and missed out on an eternity with Jesus. They ignored the One who owns the cattle on a thousand hills. They now find that Solomon was right; all earthly pursuits are vanity.

Allusion to the first plague: All who wail have received the mark of Babylon's ecclesiastical authority upon them, that of Sunday observance. They worshiped the beast and rejected the Sabbath, the sign of allegiance to the Creator of the universe. Now they face the reality of the awful judgments reserved for this day.

Allusion to the second and third plagues: verses 12 and 13: Smith writes: "In these verses we have an enumeration of great Babylon's merchandise, which includes everything pertaining to luxurious living, pomp, and worldly display. All kinds of mercantile traffic are brought to view. The declaration concerning 'slaves and souls of men' may pertain more particularly to the spiritual domain, and have reference to slavery of conscience by the creeds of these bodies, which in some cases is more oppressive than physical bondage."[2] The people's support dries up and nothing is bought. Babylon no longer has the spiritual power she once had over men. She can no longer sell her false spiritual goods.

Allusion to the fourth plague: verse 14: This points to the delicacies of Babylon that are cut off as a result of a famine which results from the fourth plague.

Allusion to the fifth and sixth plagues: verses 15-19: The throne of the beast is affected as everything that made Babylon great is taken and she is left desolate. No longer does she have influence over the whole world, but all stand off in amazement to watch as she loses everything that made her a queen. This alludes to the fifth and sixth plagues which prepare the way for the final and last plague (Revelation 18:20-24).

One hour: This is the same amount of time found in Revelation 17:12. Babylon the great and her destruction are linked here with the same "*one hour*"

---

2   Ibid., 728.

time period. All who are not God's people mourn her demise. Heaven's inhabitants, however, have different feelings about this great destruction.

Heaven Reacts to Babylon's Destruction

Revelation 18:20-24: Rejoice over her, thou heaven, and ye holy apostles and prophets; for God hath avenged you on her. ²¹And a mighty angel took up a stone like a great millstone, and cast it into the sea, saying, Thus with violence shall that great city Babylon be thrown down, and shall be found no more at all. ²²And the voice of harpers, and musicians, and of pipers, and trumpeters, shall be heard no more at all in thee; and no craftsman, of whatsoever craft he be, shall be found any more in thee; and the sound of a millstone shall be heard no more at all in thee; ²³And the light of a candle shall shine no more at all in thee; and the voice of the bridegroom and of the bride shall be heard no more at all in thee: for thy merchants were the great men of the earth; for by thy sorceries were all nations deceived. ²⁴And in her was found the blood of prophets, and of saints, and of all that were slain upon the earth.

Allusion to the seventh plague: verse 20: This is a prelude to heaven's response in Revelation 19:1-16. All heaven rejoices as Babylon's final fall is brought to view.

Verses 21-24: The finality of Babylon's destruction is described by Smith: "Like a great millstone dropped into the sea, Babylon sinks to rise no more. The various arts and crafts that have been employed in her midst, and have ministered to her desires, shall be practiced no more. The pompous music that has been heard in her imposing but formal and lifeless service, dies away forever. The scenes of festivity and gladness, when the bridegroom and the bride have been led before her altars, shall be witnessed no more."[3]

Conclusion

The final words in this chapter tell of the blood of prophets and saints which are laid at Babylon's door. Persecution of the honest, faithful, and obedient has always been the spirit of Babylon. Revelation 18 describes spiritual Babylon in all of its forms—the mother church and her daughters who found their pleasure in worldly things. Those who love the world hate God and persecute the faithful in the church throughout the ages. Even the reformed churches and some who claim to be of God's remnant church have practiced the same lordship over others who remained faithful to Christ. In the end, some who have claimed to be Christ's followers will discover that in reality, they are aligned with Babylon.

In contrast, nothing but purity is associated with God's true church in the last days. In Revelation 18, heaven's messengers and God Himself give the last call to His people to come out of Babylon. Her destruction is imminent, and they will be destroyed with her if they do not flee her false religious system.

---

[3]   Ibid., 729.

Revelation 18 calls all who are honest in heart to yield their allegiance totally to Christ the King.

Chapter 18 also reveals that Babylon's followers have put their hopes in her instead of in Christ. They mourn the loss of the most wicked power in the history of the Christian church. While the wicked weep and wail, all heaven rejoices. Judgment has finally come to the woman drunk with the blood of the saints.

CHAPTER THIRTY-ONE

Revelation 19

Introduction

The heavenly rejoicing over the destruction of Babylon in Revelation 18 spills over into this chapter. John the Revelator hears the song of triumph of the great multitude of the saved. Their song seems like the sound of many waters and mighty thunderings. In the past, these words have been applied only to God, but now the redeemed are so linked with God and their number is so great that they sound like their heavenly Father! They are one with Him! What an amazing picture!

The prophecies of Daniel and Revelation follow the principle of repeat and enlarge. Chapter 19 repeats what has already been said, but more details are added. Like a high-powered microscope, Revelation 19 expands on the period of the seventh trumpet of Revelation 11:15-19 and the seventh plague of Revelation 16:17-21.

Most importantly, the wedding supper is announced with great rejoicing, while the armies of heaven prepare to join Jesus as they go to bring the guests who have accepted this supreme invitation. The King of kings and Lord of lords victoriously defeats all the hellish powers of earth. After gathering His people, only the slain of the Lord remain. Those who refused Christ's wedding invitation have become themselves the other supper, the banquet of the vultures.

Revelation 19:1-3: And after these things I heard a great voice of much people in heaven, saying, Alleluia; Salvation, and glory, and honour, and power, unto the Lord our God: ² For true and righteous are his judgments: for he hath judged the great whore, which did corrupt the earth with her fornication, and hath avenged the blood of his servants at her hand. ³And again they said, Alleluia. And her smoke rose up for ever and ever.

This language is similar to that of Daniel 7:8 and onward as it describes the "little horn" that comes out of Rome. This little horn arose after the ten horns, then it uprooted three of the ten horns, leaving only seven. Since the little horn is not one of seven remaining horns, it is sometimes called "the eighth." The language of Daniel 7 and Revelation 17 proves accurate. Every honest Bible student may discover who Babylon is and the judgment she deserves. As all heaven declares the righteousness and justice of God's judgments, the time has come for Jesus to rescue His people.

Verses 1 and 2: After these things refers to the vision we have just considered in Revelation 18. We are ushered into the heavenly scene and hear praise to our Lord God for His just and righteous judgment of Babylon. The universe has followed God's judgment process and agrees with the verdict of final destruction for Babylon. Heaven's praise for the well-deserved destruction of Babylon comes right before the return of Jesus to this earth. Vengeance has finally come to the evil kingdom of Babylon that has so long ruled the affairs of the world. Confirmation, approval, and praise fill every heavenly being as with one accord they lift up the name of the Almighty and the Lamb.

Verse 3: And her smoke rose up for ever and ever. This points to the fulfillment of the third angel's message of Revelation 14:11: "And the smoke of their torment ascendeth up for ever and ever: and they have no rest day nor night, who worship the beast and his image, and whosoever receiveth the mark of his name." The warning given in the third angel's message has come to pass. Destruction and death are the sure results of rejecting the messages from heaven.

Revelation 19:4-8: And the four and twenty elders and the four beasts fell down and worshipped God that sat on the throne, saying, Amen; Alleluia. 5And a voice came out of the throne, saying, Praise our God, all ye his servants, and ye that fear him, both small and great. 6And I heard as it were the voice of a great multitude, and as the voice of many waters, and as the voice of mighty thunderings, saying, Alleluia: for the Lord God omnipotent reigneth. 7Let us be glad and rejoice, and give honour to him: for the marriage of the Lamb is come, and his wife hath made herself ready. 8And to her was granted that she should be arrayed in fine linen, clean and white: for the fine linen is the righteousness of saints.

This imagery reminds us of Revelation 11:15-19 as the twenty-four elders and the four beasts fell down and worshiped God on His throne. The scene moved from the holy place to the most holy as the ark of His testimony was opened. As this final judgment scene draws to a close, the marriage of the Lamb will take place!

Christ's bride is given the symbol of fine linen, clean and white which represents the righteousness of the saints. Not of works, this righteousness is a gift from the Lamb to cover their nakedness. The church, which is Christ's bride, has made herself ready by receiving this spotless garment and keeping it clean by His grace. In practical terms, receiving the gift of Christ's righteousness is our readiness for heaven. Through the righteousness of Christ, we are made pure through His blood and given His power to live a victorious life. As we yield our whole heart over to Jesus to live out His life in us, we are not saved by our righteous deeds or works, but by the mercy and grace of God.

If we don't believe that Jesus can help us overcome sin in our present life, we deny Him the power He is waiting to bestow on us. The only thing that shackles us to our besetting sins is our unwillingness to turn over our wills to Him and trust Him to know what is best for us. Our lack of faith restrains the real power that the Lord desires to unleash in our lives. That power becomes real to us as we lift up Jesus in sharing the gospel with others and asking them to rely upon the power of Christ to strengthen their faith. As we see this miraculous power of God in action, we dare to ask for more of it ourselves. This is the power of the gospel to transform lives. The righteousness of Christ prepares the church of God to be His pure bride.

The Lamb's Wedding Supper

Revelation 19:9-10: And he saith unto me, Write, Blessed are they which are called unto the marriage supper of the Lamb. And he saith unto me, These are the true sayings of God. ¹⁰And I fell at his feet to worship him. And he said unto me, See thou do it not: I am thy fellowservant, and of thy brethren that have the testimony of Jesus: worship God: for the testimony of Jesus is the spirit of prophecy.

Verse 9: Called unto the marriage supper of the Lamb. The imagery here points to the Feast of Tabernacles, a time to rejoice in deliverance from bondage and the celebration after the final harvest. The supper comes at the end of the Feast of Tabernacles just as the marriage supper comes after the wedding. The marriage supper of the Lamb takes place after Christ returns to this earth to claim His bride, the church.

Revelation 19:11-16 describes the most amazing bridal rescue ever attempted. The Groom is victorious because He is the King of kings and the Lord of lords! On the way back to His Father's house, Jesus takes a seven-day journey with His people, showing them around the universe. This parallels the week of the Feast of Tabernacles with its closing banquet. Then at the end of the week-long journey, we sit down for the marriage supper of the Lamb in heaven. This begins the thousand years known as the millennium.

Verse 10: John starts to worship the messenger, but the angel straightens him out, admonishing him to worship God, the Creator, and not a created being. This is quite the opposite of Babylon the great who desires, demands, and dictates worship of herself. True messengers of God are unwilling to accept such worship. They have seen the results of Satan's inexcusable thirst for worship and the rebellion that ensued with all the pain and suffering in this world and the universe.

Blood-stained Warrior on a White Steed

Revelation 19:11-16: And I saw heaven opened, and behold a white horse; and he that sat upon him was called Faithful and True, and in righteousness he doth judge and make war. ¹²His eyes were as a flame of fire, and on his head were many crowns; and he had a name written, that no man knew, but he

himself. ¹³**And he was clothed with a vesture dipped in blood: and his name is called The Word of God. ¹⁴And the armies which were in heaven followed him upon white horses, clothed in fine linen, white and clean. ¹⁵And out of his mouth goeth a sharp sword, that with it he should smite the nations: and he shall rule them with a rod of iron: and he treadeth the winepress of the fierceness and wrath of Almighty God. ¹⁶And he hath on his vesture and on his thigh a name written, KING OF KINGS, AND LORD OF LORDS.**

Smith describes the biblical coming of Christ as Deliverer and Warrior to rescue His chosen bride:

> A new scene is introduced. We are here carried back to the second coming of Christ, this time under the symbol of a warrior riding forth to battle. Why is He represented thus?—Because He is going forth to war, to meet the "kings of the earth and their armies," and this would be the only proper character in which to represent Him on such a mission. His vesture is dipped in blood. (See a description of the same scene in Isaiah 63:1-4.) The armies of heaven, the angels of God, follow Him. Verse 15 shows how He rules the nations with a rod of iron when they are given Him for an inheritance, as recorded in the second Psalm, which popular theology interprets to mean the conversion of the world.

> But would such an expression as "treadeth the winepress of the fierceness and wrath of Almighty God," be a very singular description of a work of grace upon the hearts of the heathen for their conversion? The great and final display of the "winepress of God's wrath," and also of "the lake of fire," occurs at the end of the thousand years, as described in Revelation 20; and to that it would seem that the full and formal description of Revelation 14:18-20 must apply. But the destruction of the living wicked at the second coming of Christ, at the beginning of the thousand years, furnishes a scene on a smaller scale, similar in both these respects to what takes place at the close of that period. Hence in the verses before us we have this mention of both the winepress of wrath and the lake of fire.

> Christ has at this time closed His mediatorial work, and laid off His priestly robes for kingly attire; for He has on His vesture and on His thigh a name written, King of kings and Lord of lords. This is in harmony with the character in which He here appears, for it was the custom of warriors anciently to have some kind of title inscribed upon their vesture. (Verse 16.)[1]

---

[1]   Smith, 735-736.

Faithful and True: Christ leads the armies of heaven to earth to make war on those who are now threatening the life of His bride, the church. He comes as the King of kings and Lord of lords completing on this earth the battle that started in heaven so long ago. For thousands of years, Satan has attacked God's people, but the last onslaught of the forces of evil is merciless. In this setting the war of Armageddon is fought. The outlook for God's people appears hopeless as the whole world turns on them and sentences them to death. Armed with his hot anger, Satan's last war against God's people has united nearly the whole world against them. Thus the end of the sixth plague leads to the battle of Armageddon: this initiates the seventh and final plague.

Verse 12: His eyes were as a flame of fire: Nothing escapes the eyes of Jesus. This emphasizes the intensity of His gaze. In John's first vision of Jesus, he saw that same fiery gaze (Revelation 1:14). These fire-filled eyes reveal love to those who return His love (Song of Sol. 8:6), but how can the disobedient meet His flaming eyes?

On his head were many crowns: The original language reads διαδήματα πολλα (*diademata polla*); this means "many diadems." Diadem refers to a kingly crown. The saints who overcome by the blood of the Lamb wear the victor's crown or wreath. The saints' crowns come from a different Greek word, Στέφανος (*stefanos*), which means a "wreath of honor or victory." Note that He is not merely wearing one diadem, understood in ancient times as a blue band marked with white which Persian kings used to bind on the turban or tiara they wore. King Jesus wears many diadems and it appears that one of them had a name of which only He knew its meaning.

An ancient tradition says that if a man knows the name of a deity, he has power over that god. As if to lay any doubts to rest, Jesus has a special name that no one knows. No one can have power over Jesus Christ because He has a name that no one else knows. In the Bible, a new name refers to an experience or change in character. Since Christ's character has always remained the same, His new name refers to the fact that He has experienced what no other living being ever has or ever will experience. He is the only One who took the second death for all humanity's sins and then came back from the dead. He is the only hope of His waiting people. This special, secret name is added to the many names already ascribed to Him.

Verse 13: Clothes dipped in blood: Immediately after His secret name is mentioned, Jesus' clothing is described: **"He was clothed with a vesture dipped in blood: and His name is called The Word of God."** The prophet Isaiah foretells a similar picture: "I have trodden the winepress alone; and of the people there was none with me: for I will tread them in mine anger, and trample them in my fury; and their blood shall be sprinkled upon my garments, and I will stain all my raiment" (Isaiah 63:3). His secret name is related to this experience: He walked this path alone, and no one else can understand that name or experience.

All His other names may be understood by reading the Word of God, but we will never be able to say to Jesus, "I understand what You felt on that cross."

His clothes are not stained with the blood of the wicked, for He is traveling from heaven to the earth to trample the winepress of His wrath. This blood must be what He shed on Calvary for us! Therefore the striking similarity between Isaiah 63:1-6 and Revelation 19:13 point to the fulfillment of Isaiah 63.

Verse 14: Armies of heaven: These armies must refer to the angels and other heavenly beings. Jesus promised that He would return "in the glory of His Father with all the holy angels" (Mark 8:38). "Then He shall reward every man according to his works" (Matthew 6:27). Since Christ has not returned to the earth and the dead in Christ have not yet risen, these truly are "the armies of heaven" (Revelation 19:14).

Verses 15 and 16: Sharp Sword from His Mouth: The word of God symbolizes who He is and what He says. "For the word of God *is* living and powerful, and sharper than any two-edged sword, piercing even to the division of soul and spirit, and of joints and marrow, and is a discerner of the thoughts and intents of the heart" (Hebrews 4:12). Ephesians 6:17 backs this up: "And take the helmet of salvation, and the sword of the Spirit, which is the word of God." Again these symbols point out the same Jesus whom John saw in his first vision: "Out of His mouth went a sharp twoedged sword" (Revelation 1:16).

The Vulture's Supper

Revelation 19:17-21: And I saw an angel standing in the sun; and he cried with a loud voice, saying to all the fowls that fly in the midst of heaven, Come and gather yourselves together unto the supper of the great God; [18]That ye may eat the flesh of kings, and the flesh of captains, and the flesh of mighty men, and the flesh of horses, and of them that sit on them, and the flesh of all men, both free and bond, both small and great. [19]And I saw the beast, and the kings of the earth, and their armies, gathered together to make war against him that sat on the horse, and against his army. [20]And the beast was taken, and with him the false prophet that wrought miracles before him, with which he deceived them that had received the mark of the beast, and them that worshipped his image. These both were cast alive into a lake of fire burning with brimstone. [21]And the remnant were slain with the sword of him that sat upon the horse, which sword proceeded out of his mouth: and all the fowls were filled with their flesh.

Verses 17: "The sun" refers to sanctuary imagery of God's shekinah glory. One commentary notes: "Perhaps the blinding light of the sun is here descriptive of the glorious light of the divine presence (cf. 2 Thessalonians 2:8, 9; Revelation 6:15-17). Thus the angel who issues the challenge of ch. 19:17 would be standing next to Christ, as in ancient combat an armorbearer would be near his lord."[2]

---

[2]   *The Seventh-day Adventist Bible Commentary*, 7:875.

Before the wedding supper of the Lamb, heaven invites us to come. In like manner, before the destruction of the wicked, the birds are invited to feast upon the corpses of the wicked. Rank and status do not save the wicked in the day of God's wrath. "Both small and great" are slain at His coming and become the banquet for the birds (Revelation 19:18).

Supper of the Great God: Two choices are given: you can eat good food or be food for the birds. The invitation to the "marriage supper of the Lamb" is given to all the inhabitants of the world. Our Savior also provides us with the only clothing suitable for this wedding supper (Matthew 22:11-12; cf. Revelation 3:18). In Matthew 22:1-14, Jesus tells a parable about the marriage supper for the king's son. The invitation was extended to all, but sadly, those who gave the invitation to others were ridiculed or killed. The king sent his armies and "destroyed those murderers" (Matthew 22:7).

God is not inviting us to the "supper of the great God" (Revelation 19:17). Only the birds are invited, but all those who refuse the heavenly invitation to the supper of the Lamb will become the menu for the birds' supper. Our choice determines which supper we attend. Let's accept the gracious invitation to the supper of the Lamb and the free gift—His pure white robe of righteousness. The terrible alternative to *eating the supper* of the Lamb is *to be the supper* of the fowls of heaven. We would be much wiser to accept the invitation of the King of the universe to the marriage supper of the Lamb. Let's not spurn His invitation. No one in his right mind would choose to be food for the vultures.

The Battle of Armegeddon

Verse 19: And I saw the beast, and the kings of the earth, and their armies, gathered together to make war against him that sat on the horse, and against his army.

These words point to the setting of the sixth plague: "For they are the spirits of devils, working miracles, which go forth unto the kings of the earth and of the whole world, to gather them to the battle of that great day of God Almighty. . . . And he gathered them together into a place called in the Hebrew tongue Armageddon" (Revelation 16:14, 16).

Verse 20: The beast and the false prophet are both cast into the lake of fire. As was stated in Revelation 17:3, the beast symbolizes the persecuting church-state power. Satan has worked through political powers throughout the ages as depicted by the seven heads and ten horns who have submitted to his control. The nature and description of this beast remind us that from the time of Egypt, the first of the seven heads, to that of papal Rome, religio-civil powers have always persecuted God's faithful.

The false prophet refers to apostate Protestantism, the harlot daughters of Rome that follow in the footsteps of the mother church. Through the crafty deceptions of Satan, these churches have been deluded by him. They then become his puppets as they cooperate and submit to Satan's control. Like the beast, the false prophet also mixes religion with the state. All the apostate churches join the Roman Church in the enforcement of Sunday observance. Rejecting heaven's call to keep the commandments of God leads to rendering obedience to this enforcement of papal worship. Obedience to the beast's enforced worship constitutes the mark of the beast.

Verse 21: This remnant is different than the one we saw in Revelation 12:17. Only the disobedient are slain by the armies of heaven. Thus the slain remnant refers to the rest of earth's wicked inhabitants who have survived the first six plagues. They have refused life through Christ and are killed by the Word of God. In other words, the Scriptures will testify against and reveal their disobedience to the Word of God. They are killed by "the brightness of His coming" (2 Thessalonians 2:8). The return of Jesus Christ to this earth brings deliverance to His people, but death to all His enemies. This constitutes the seventh and last plague upon the wicked.

Conclusion

Revelation 19 gives a prophetic picture of the last days of earth's history. After all heaven praises the righteous judgments of God, heaven opens up and Jesus descends with all the armies of heaven. He comes to claim His rightful subjects and destroy those who wish to slay His people. This is the culmination of the judgment which began in 1844 and ends with the final judgment of Babylon, the beast, and the false prophet. The seventh plague, so terrible to the wicked, means deliverance and rescue for God's obedient people. All those who refused to come out of Babylon are destroyed. The warnings of God have now become reality. The reign of the beast has ended. Satan, the accuser of the brethren, no longer taunts and threatens God's people. "Where I am, there ye may be also" has finally come true (John 14:3). This ushers in the thousand-year period known as the millennium, the main subject of chapter 20.

CHAPTER THIRTY-TWO

Revelation 20

Introduction

Revelation 20 continues to move in time through the sanctuary service. The seven lampstands provided the setting for the seven churches. Imagery from the table of showbread illustrated the seven seals. The events of the seven trumpets revolved around the altar of incense. In the final scenes of Revelation, the ark of the covenant is the center of attention. From this viewpoint, God's last messages of instruction and warning prepare His people to come out of Babylon, and then the seven last plagues of judgment are poured out unmingled with mercy upon those who despise the commandments of the Lamb.

In the earthly sanctuary, the high priest would cast lots on two goats near the end of the services on the Day of Atonement. One goat was for the Lord and the other for the scapegoat. The Lord's goat was killed and its blood was sprinkled on the mercy seat of the ark of the covenant. This symbolically cleansed the sanctuary.

Then the priest came into the court and laid his hands on the scapegoat, symbolically transferring to the goat the confessed sins of God's people that had accumulated in the sanctuary throughout the year. A "fit man" took the goat out into the wilderness and left it there (Leviticus 16:21). Every trace of the sins of God's people was removed from the sanctuary. This ceremony constituted the cleansing of the sanctuary. Five days later the Feast of Tabernacles was celebrated. Both the Day of Atonement and the Feast of Tabernacles help us to understand Revelation 20.

As the scapegoat was taken out into the wilderness at the end of the Day of Atonement, so Satan is pointed out as the instigator of all the sins of God's people. During the millennium, the father of sin and rebellion is left with no one to tempt as he waits on death row. Thus the scapegoat ritual symbolizes the final end of Satan.

At the end of the thousand-year period, the white throne judgment is pictured. After a last-ditch effort to dethrone the rightful Ruler of the universe, Satan is destroyed along with all his followers. All sin and sinners are eradicated from both heaven and earth! Even death itself is thrown into the lake of fire.

Revelation 20:1-3: And I saw an angel come down from heaven, having the key of the bottomless pit and a great chain in his hand. ²And he laid hold on the dragon, that old serpent, which is the Devil, and Satan, and bound him a thousand years, ³And cast him into the bottomless pit, and shut him up, and set a seal upon him, that he should deceive the nations no more, till the thousand years should be fulfilled: and after that he must be loosed a little season.

Verse 1: An Angel: Who is this "angel" that corresponds to the "fit man" of Leviticus 16:22? The answer again lies in the ritual of the scapegoat. Smith relates this question to the book of Hebrews: In the ceremony of the Lord's goat, we see "the great offering for the world made on Calvary. The sins of all those who avail themselves of the merits of Christ's shed blood by faith in Him, are borne by the ministration of Christ into the new-covenant sanctuary. After Christ, the minister of the true tabernacle (Hebrews 8:2), has finished His ministration, He will remove the sins of His people from the sanctuary, and lay them upon the head of their author, the antitypical scapegoat, the devil. The devil will be sent away, bearing them into a land not inhabited."[1]

Whalley adds his comments: "Let us contemplate that scene at Christ's return to earth. The Church has been judged; Israel has been judged; the Gentile nations have also been judged. . . . Now it is Satan's turn to be judged also; and our High Priest is seen 'putting' the moral blame to where it rightly belongs; judging the great corruptor and banishing him to a place of separation from the affairs of men."[2]

In conclusion, according to the ritual in Leviticus 16:21, a fit or timely man must deal with the scapegoat. No one is more fit than Christ Jesus, our High Priest, Savior, and King. Jesus told a parable about binding a strong man. In order to do this, "a stronger than he" would come (Luke 11:21, cf. Matthew 12:29). Satan at one time was the covering cherub and leader of the angels. Only One is stronger than he, thus it is only Jesus who can bind Satan to this earth.

The symbolic chain: The context of this symbolic chain reveals a chain of circumstances that leaves Satan and his evil angels with no one left to torment or tempt. The key, chain, seal, and binding (Revelation 20:1-3) are explained by verse 3: Satan is situated so that **"he should deceive the nations no more"** until the thousand years are over.

The symbol of the bottomless pit: The Greek word for bottomless pit is ἄβυσσος (*abussos*) which means "abyss." This pit symbolizes a very deep gulf or chasm in the lowest parts of the earth used as the common receptacle of the dead and especially as the abode of demons. This is a fitting symbol of the earth after Satan's rebellion has brought utter desolation and the seven last plagues have

[1]   Smith, 741.

[2]   Albert Whalley, *The Red Letter Days of Israel* (London: Marshall Bros., 1926), 125; quoted in Uriah Smith, *The Prophecies of Daniel and Revelation* (Nashville, TN: Southern Publishing Association, 1944), 741.

wreaked havoc on the earth. The bottomless pit is Satan's prison of circumstances for a thousand years. The one who wreaked havoc upon the inhabitants of the world for thousands of years spends his last days surrounded by the results of his rebellion.

Living and reigning with Christ: Revelation 20:4, 6 describes the contrasting situation of the saints. While Satan has nothing but the wreck of this world, the saints are in heaven, living and reigning with Christ. The persecutor is chained, while those he chained on earth have been set free by Jesus. They now live where he once lived—in the glorious place called heaven.

As described in Revelation 19:11-21, the return of Christ before the millennium marks this great change. All the wicked were destroyed at His coming (2 Thessalonians 1:8; 2:8). This ended the death threat to God's people in a startling manner! At the second coming of Christ, all the righteous dead awoke at the voice of the archangel and the trump of God so that all His people could be "caught up together" and "meet the Lord in the air" (1 Thessalonians 4:16-17).

On death row: With all the righteous now in heaven and all the wicked dead or slain, Satan and all of his evil angels will be here alone to contemplate what they have done. One thousand years is a long time to think, but God saw the need for this time period.

At the end of the thousand years, Satan will be loosed again. His symbolic "chains" are gone because the wicked dead come back to life at the end of the thousand years (Revelation 20:5). Then he will resume his deceptions and control the nations for a short time (Revelation 20:7-8). Satan's vast army of fallen angels and the wicked of all ages surround the holy city and attempt to take it for themselves. This brings God's final judgment as total destruction comes to Satan and all his followers (Revelation 20: 9-10, 13-15).

The symbol of Azazel: As the Lord's goat, Jesus took upon Himself the penalty for all our sins. Satan as symbolized by the scapegoat dies at end of the millennium. As God's word warned, "The wages of sin is death" (Romans 6:23). Because Satan's deceptions crept into nearly all the churches in the last days, most modern-day commentators don't mention Satan's connection with the scapegoat. However, this has been common knowledge in commentaries from the nineteenth century. Smith in his book *Daniel and Revelation* connected the scapegoat or Azazel with the millennium. White concurs in her book *The Great Controversy*:

> In the typical service the high priest, having made the atonement for Israel, came forth and blessed the congregation. So Christ, at the close of His work as mediator, will appear, "without sin unto salvation" (Hebrews 9:28), to bless His waiting people with eternal life. As the priest, in removing the sins from the sanctuary, confessed them upon the head of the scapegoat, **so Christ will place all these sins upon Satan, the originator and instigator of sin.** The scapegoat, bearing the sins of Israel, was

sent away "unto a land not inhabited" (Leviticus 16:22); so Satan, bearing the guilt of all the sins which he has caused God's people to commit, will be for a thousand years confined to the earth, which will then be desolate, without inhabitant, and he will at last suffer the full penalty of sin in the fires that shall destroy all the wicked. Thus the great plan of redemption will reach its accomplishment in the final eradication of sin and the deliverance of all who have been willing to renounce evil (emphasis mine).[3]

Three main points link Satan with the scapegoat. First, Leviticus 16:8 says "one lot for the Lord and the other for scapegoat." Obviously the scapegoat is not the Lord's goat, nor can the scapegoat be a figure of Jesus because it is not sacrificed. The Bible says clearly, "Without shedding of blood [there] is no remission" of sin (Hebrews 9:22; cf. Leviticus 17:11). Therefore Azazel the scapegoat cannot represent Christ.

Secondly, during the Day of Atonement ceremony, the scapegoat played no role inside the temple or holy tent. The lot for the scapegoat was cast in the courtyard which represents the earth. The scapegoat's release into the wilderness, away from any human contact, clearly shows the chain of circumstances faced by Satan during the millennium. When God's final act of judgment comes at the end of the millennium, Satan will receive his just reward for introducing sin into the world.

Lastly, the scapegoat has no role in the cleansing ceremonies of the Day of Atonement. The blame for Israel's sins fall upon the scapegoat **after** the sanctuary has been cleansed. Thus Azazel plays no part in eradicating sin from the lives of God's people. Jesus paid it all with His precious blood!

Satan claims to be like the Most High or, in other words, like Jesus. In this ritual God shows the difference. Satan wants to take over the place of Christ, but he could not pay the penalty for our sins. He is not only unwilling, but also unqualified to do so. In the end he will receive his just reward as the originator of sin. The death penalty will come to him and to all those who reject the blood of the Lamb of God.

The Millennium

Revelation 20 is known as the millennium chapter. This is the only place in the Bible that speaks of the millennium ushered in at Christ's second coming. Millennium is made up of the two Latin words of *mille* and *annum*. *Mille* means one thousand and *annum* means years; thus one thousand years.

The Holy Spirit revealed two resurrections to the prophet Daniel: "Many of them that sleep in the dust of the earth shall awake, some to everlasting life, and some to shame and everlasting contempt" (Daniel 12:2).

Jesus also clearly taught that there would be two resurrections: the resurrection of life and the resurrection of damnation (John 5:28-29). Both Jesus and

---

[3]   White, *The Great Controversy*, 485-486.

Paul revealed the timing of the first resurrection; the righteous will wake up from the sleep of death when Jesus returns with power and great glory. "I will come again, and receive you unto Myself; that where I am, there ye may be also" (John 14:3). "For the Lord Himself shall descend from heaven with a shout, with the voice of the archangel and with the trump of God: and the dead in Christ shall rise first" (1 Thessalonians 4:16). Revelation 20 gives the timing for both resurrections based on events before and after the millennium.

The Resurrection of Life

Revelation 20:4-10: And I saw thrones, and they sat upon them, and judgment was given unto them: and *I saw* the souls of them that were beheaded for the witness of Jesus, and for the word of God, and which had not worshipped the beast, neither his image, neither had received *his* mark upon their foreheads, or in their hands; and they lived and reigned with Christ a thousand years. ⁵But the rest of the dead lived not again until the thousand years were finished. This *is* the first resurrection. ⁶Blessed and holy *is* he that hath part in the first resurrection: on such the second death hath no power, but they shall be priests of God and of Christ, and shall reign with him a thousand years.

The millennium begins: The second coming of Christ and the first resurrection occur at the beginning of the millennium. Jesus comes to receive to Himself all those who are "blessed and holy" (Revelation 20:6). All those who have died in Christ will come back to life "and reign with Him a thousand years" (Revelation 20:6). The second death has no power over them (Revelation 20:6). John is so excited about this resurrection that he repeats the message twice: God's people are the ones who live and reign "with Christ a thousand years" (Revelation 20:4). The people in this first resurrection "awake to everlasting life," (Daniel 12:2) so this must refer to the "resurrection of life" as foretold by Christ, Paul, John, and His prophet Daniel (John 5:29).

The millennium is like a thousand-year vacation in heaven with Jesus, but the saints will not be idle. John sees the redeemed sitting on thrones as they reign with Christ. They are given a work of judgment. Paul explains this work: "Do you not know that the saints shall judge the world? and if the world shall be judged by you, are ye unworthy to judge the smallest matters? Know ye not that we shall judge angels? how much more things that pertain to this life?" (1 Corinthians 6:2, 3). Jesus also will give a special work of judgment to His disciples: "Ye which have followed Me, in the regeneration when the Son of man shall sit in the throne of His glory, ye also shall sit upon twelve thrones, judging the twelve tribes of Israel" (Matthew 19:28).

John mentions another special group: those who "were beheaded for the witness of Jesus, and for the word of God, and which had not worshipped the beast, neither his image, neither had received his mark upon their foreheads, or in their hands" (Revelation 20:4). Thrones are placed for those who have not worshiped the beast or his image. These have kept all the commandments of God, including the fourth: the special Sabbath sign. Filled with the Holy Spirit, they have stood for the truth of Jesus while all the world, filled with the spirit of Satan, raged against them, filled with the spirit of Satan.

White notes the character of those who gain eternal life: "Those who have belonged to the family of God here below, who have striven to honor His name, have gained an experience that will make them as kings and priests unto God; and they will be accepted as faithful servants. To them the words will be spoken, "Well done, good and faithful servant: . . . enter thou into the joy of thy Lord."[4]

All the righteous receive the blessing of eternal life, but best of all, they shall be forever with their Lord and Savior. All their questions will be answered. During their work of judgment, the books of heaven will be opened to their examination. Every inquiry will be investigated, and they will join the angels in proclaiming the justice and righteousness of God's judgments. "Great and marvellous are Thy works, Lord God Almighty; just and true are Thy ways, O King of saints" (Revelation 15:3).

The Resurrection of Damnation

Revelation 20:7-10: And when the thousand years are expired, Satan shall be loosed out of his prison, [8]And shall go out to deceive the nations which are in the four quarters of the earth, Gog and Magog, to gather them together to battle: the number of whom *is* as the sand of the sea. [9]And they went up on the breadth of the earth, and compassed the camp of the saints about, and the beloved city: and fire came down from God out of heaven, and devoured them. [10]And the devil that deceived them was cast into the lake of fire and brimstone, where the beast and the false prophet *are*, and shall be tormented day and night for ever and ever.

At the end of the millennium: The rest of the dead do not live again until the thousand years are ended. This clearly shows that the resurrection of damnation does not take place until the end of the millennium. This description does not portray a joyful scene. All those who have compromised with sin, all those who have idolized self, all who have followed Babylon the great in rejecting the Sabbath as a memorial to the Creator have rejected Jesus. They thought they could choose their own day of worship instead of the seventh day which God sanctified, blessed, and made holy. They have trampled God's holy law by using the holy Sabbath day as a common day of work. Professed Christians will rise in the resurrection of damnation. Unbeknownst to themselves, they have given their allegiance over to Satan because they have failed to be obedient to the Scriptures.

Jesus speaks of this group who considered themselves to be Christians: "Not everyone that saith unto Me, Lord, Lord, shall enter into the kingdom of heaven;

4   Ellen G. White, *Counsels on Stewardship* (Washington, DC: Review & Herald, 1940), 129.

but he that doeth the will of My Father which is in heaven. Many will say to Me in that day, Lord, Lord, have we not prophesied in Thy name? and in Thy name have cast out devils? and in Thy name done many wonderful works? And then will I profess unto them, I never knew you: depart from Me, ye that work iniquity" (Matthew 7:21-23). The Greek word for "iniquity" is *anomia* which means "lawlessness." The Father's will is revealed in His law. They wanted Christ's salvation and power, but not His law written in their hearts by the Holy Spirit. They wanted Him as Savior, but not as Lord. Jesus does not recognize these lawless ones as His own.

Satan loosed: "The rest of the dead lived not again until the thousand years were finished" (Revelation 20:5). When the millennium comes to an end, the Devil and his wicked angels will have something to do again because once more they will again have someone to deceive. Christ brings the wicked back to life so they can face the final judgment. This resurrection is different than the first: the wicked do not receive the gift of immortal life or incorruptible bodies. Jesus called this "the resurrection of damnation" (John 5:29). They come up with the same rebellious attitude.

The New Jerusalem descends from heaven: Satan gives his battle plan to these hordes of unrighteous people. They surround the "camp of the saints" and "the beloved city," planning to take it for themselves (Revelation 20:9). How did the New Jerusalem come down upon the earth? John explains this in the next chapter. The vision given to him by God has so many last day events that he cannot write them all down at the same time! "I John saw the holy city, new Jerusalem, coming down from God out of heaven, prepared as a bride adorned for her husband" (Revelation 21:2). One of the angels showed John "that great city, the holy Jerusalem, descending out of heaven from God" (Revelation 21:10). This is the "beloved city" which is surrounded by Satan and the armies of the damned.

As the first two chapters of Genesis tell the same story, but add different details, so Revelation 20 twice tells about the resurrection of damnation and the end of the wicked, giving different details both times. Revelation 20:7-10 speaks of their last rebellion and fiery demise. Verses 11 to 15 describe the final great white throne judgment which comes before the end of Satan and all sinners.

The Great White Throne Judgment

Revelation 20:11-15: And I saw a great white throne, and him that sat on it, from whose face the earth and the heaven fled away; and there was found no place for them. ¹²And I saw the dead, small and great, stand before God; and the books were opened: and another book was opened, which is *the book* of life: and the dead were judged out of those things which were written in the books, according to their works. ¹³And the sea gave up the dead which were in it; and death and hell delivered up the dead which were in them: and they were judged every man according to their works. ¹⁴And death and hell were

cast into the lake of fire. This is the second death. ¹⁵And whosoever was not found written in the book of life was cast into the lake of fire.

Satan and the wicked of all ages have surrounded the beautiful city that came down out of heaven. White speaks of his final deception: "With fiendish exultation he points to the unnumbered millions who have been raised from the dead and declares that as their leader he is well able to overthrow the city and regain his throne and his kingdom."[5] This assault brings the final showdown between the forces of evil and the God of the universe.

The wiley schemes of Satan's host are interrupted by God Himself as all eyes focus on His "great white throne" (Revelation 20:11). Heaven's books are opened while each one in the Devil's throng, and even Satan himself, face the reality and results of their wrong choices. Isaiah prophesied of this moment: "Unto Me every knee shall bow, . . . All that are incensed against Him shall be ashamed" (Isaiah 45:23-24). Paul uses the same Old Testament reference to describe the judgment of God: "As I live, saith the Lord, every knee shall bow to Me, and every tongue shall confess to God" (Romans 14:11). Even Satan himself bows in recognition of the goodness of God that he has despised.

All the wicked, including the beast and its followers, acknowledge their guilt as well as the mercy and justice of God's sentence. They have not accepted Christ as the Lord of their lives. Many felt that Jesus could be just their Savior, but they dismissed His commands, saying, "We will not have this Man to reign over us" (Luke 19:14). Desiring salvation is not enough; Jesus is the King of kings and the Lord of lords. All those who did not make Jesus the King and Lord of their lives have unfitted themselves for His kingdom. God plainly says, "All they that hate Me, love death" (Proverbs 8:36).

The hatred we need: The first Messianic promise, given in Eden, included "enmity" or hatred: "I will put enmity between thee [the serpent] and the woman" (Genesis 3:15). This promise enabled Joseph to flee from Potiphar's wife. Naturally sinners, we need the supernatural power of God to give us a hatred for sin and all Satan's deceptions. As we choose Jesus as the Lord, Lawgiver, and King of our lives, we will experience real victory over sin and sinning. We sing, "Victory in Jesus,"[6] but do we believe that He will save His people from their sins? (Matthew 1:21). Turn your life over to Jesus, trust Him, and take Him at His word. Acknowledge Jesus as the all-powerful God and Creator and believe that He enables you to overcome sin in right here on earth. Yield your life to Him, and He will re-create you in His likeness. Jesus promised to create a hatred for sin in your heart (Genesis 3:15), and by His grace, you will express your love to Him in obedience to all His commands (John 14:15).

Verses 11 and 12: God's final sentencing of the wicked comes from "the great white throne" of judgment. While the righteous watch from the safety of

---

5   White, *Great Controversy*, 663.

6   "Victory in Jesus," words and music by E. M. Bartlett, 1939.

the holy city, Satan and his vast army receive the awful sentence of condemnation and death. "The books were opened: and another book was opened, which is the book of life" (Revelation 20:12). These heavenly books contain the works of all who have lived on the earth and record the deeds of those who do not have their name written in the book of life (Psalm 56:8; cf. Matthew 12:37). All the records are compared with the book of life.

Jesus told His disciples: "Rejoice, because your names are written in heaven" (Luke 10:20). Revelation contains **seven** references to the book of life, more than any other book of the Bible. The faithful, patient saints who overcome sin are in the book of life and in the New Jerusalem (Revelation 3:5; 21:27). Those who worship the beast are not in the book of life (Revelation 13:8; 17:8). God warns us of two reasons why our names may be removed from of the book of life. Those who do not overcome sin will be removed from the book of life, as well as those who attempt to add or take away from God's words (Revelation 3:5; 22:18-19).

Verses 14 and 15: Finally, all those who are not found in the book of life are cast into the lake of fire (Revelation 20:12-15). Death itself and the grave[7] are also thrown into the lake of fire. Only those who have their names written in the book of life have no fear of the second death. No wonder Jesus emphasized the importance of this book in Revelation!

Before God's presence on the great white throne, the heavens and the earth flee away so that no place is found for the wicked. Peter's prophecy comes to pass as the consuming fire of God devours the ungodly. Even the "elements shall melt with fervent heat" (2 Peter 3:12). Smith speaks of the final destruction of Satan and all who have opposed the will of God:

> Here is the final epitaph of all the forces from first to last that have risen up to oppose the will and work of the Lord. Satan originated and led out in this nefarious [evil, despicable, immoral] work. A part of heaven's angels joined him in his false position and murderous work, and for him and them the everlasting fire was prepared. (Matthew 25:41.) Men become involved only because they join him in his rebellion. But here the controversy closes. The fire is to them everlasting because it allows of no escape, and of no cessation until they are consumed. The second death is their punishment, and it is "everlasting punishment" (Matthew 25:46) because they never find release from its dread embrace. "The wages of sin is *death*," not punishing forever. Romans 6:23.[8]

Conclusion: Revelation 20 reveals the timing of the two resurrections and the differences between the rewards of the saved and the lost. When Jesus comes with all His holy angels to gather His saints from the earth, the righteous dead

---

[7] In Revelation 20:13-14, the Greek word *hades* is translated "hell" in the King James Version. However, *hades* simply means "the grave" (cf. 1 Corinthians 15:55).

[8] Smith, 753.

are resurrected. Those who live until Christ's coming join the resurrected ones as Jesus takes them home to His Father's house. This "resurrection of life" takes place at the beginning of the millennium (John 5:29).

With all the wicked slain at the coming of the Lord, Satan has no one left to tempt. He is bound to the earth by this chain of circumstances and given a thousand years to think of the awful results of his rebellion. The righteous live and reign in heaven with Christ during the millennium, giving them ample time to ask questions and examine the record books in heaven.

When the thousand years are finished, the resurrection of damnation gives Satan a vast throng of followers whom he deceives yet again. After the New Jerusalem descends from heaven to the earth, Satan inspires the wicked to surround the city and attack it. Their plans are aborted as God speaks from His great white throne. Conscious of their guilt and their neglect of God's gracious gift of salvation, every knee bows to the Creator, including Satan's. God's judgment executes the fatal choice of the wicked. Satan, along with death, the grave, and the wicked, are cast into the lake of fire. This brings the second and final death. Notice how the following chart puts each verse in its right perspective:

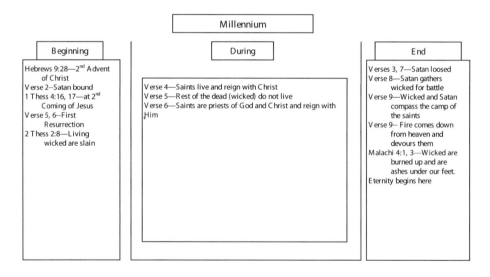

Dear friend, is your name written in the Lamb's book of life? I beg you to invite Jesus into your life. Take Him completely, not only as your Savior, but as the Lord and Lawgiver of your life. Trust His word and rely on Him to overcome the besetting sins in your life. This is impossible in your own strength, but with His divine grace and power, He will enable you to overcome all iniquity. Then you will give glory to God, and your tongue will confess His miraculous power at work in your life.

CHAPTER THIRTY-THREE

Revelation 21

Introduction

The final phase of judgment begins in chapter 17 with the punishment of Babylon the great and continues through chapter 20 which describes the destruction of Satan and all who belonged to him. Satan, sinners, death, and the grave are thrown into the lake of fire and totally annihilated. The final phase of the judgment is now complete. With chapter 21, we are introduced to a new scene—John's marvellous vision of the new heaven, the new earth, and the new capital on this earth made new: the New Jerusalem.

The language John uses to describe the new earth seems familiar to us because it is rooted in the prophecies of the Old Testament. As the description of God's throne in Revelation 4 has similarities with Ezekiel's vision, so here in chapter 21, we hear phrases similar to Ezekiel, Isaiah, and Zechariah.

Enjoy as God unfolds to our imaginations the wonderful rewards He has prepared for us! These visions encourage us to remain faithful to Jesus and obedient to His word. They strengthen us to trust God's ability to carry us through to the end! Watch as God unfolds the glorious future awaiting the redeemed.

Setting of the vision: John's vision of the New Jerusalem begins in Revelation 21:1 and ends with Revelation 22:5. The first eight verses of this chapter are the culmination of the eschtological events described in Revelation 19:11 to 20:15. Therefore Revelation 21:1-8 is both the climatic ending to all the events surrounding the millennium and the official starting point of the new earth with no more pain, death, or sorrow. Revelation 21:1-8 provides the key to understanding Revelation 20:9-12, but these verses are also connected to the vision of the New Jerusalem by both content and imagery. The holy city descends, sin and sinners are destroyed, the earth is made new, and there are no more tears. Thus the joys of God's people in the New Jerusalem on the new earth are contrasted with Babylon's destruction and the pointlessness of sin and rebellion.

The End of the First Earth

Revelation 21:1: And I saw a new heaven and a new earth: for the first heaven and the first earth were passed away; and there was no more sea.

The curtain rises on a new view in the final prophetic drama of the apocalyptic story. In the previous chapter, we witnessed the terminal scenes of the judgment of Satan and all who followed him. In Revelation 21:1, 8, John emphasizes the end of the earth as we know it now. Before the new heaven and the new earth come into existence, the first heaven and the first earth must be destroyed.

As the wicked suffer the second death in the lake of fire, their demise concludes their existence. "What do ye imagine against the Lord? He will make an utter end: affliction shall not rise up the second time. . . . They shall be devoured as stubble fully dry" (Nahum 1:9-10). Satan himself also comes to an end: "Therefore will I bring forth a fire from the midst of thee, it shall devour thee, and I will bring thee to ashes upon the earth. . . , and never shalt thou be any more" (Ezekiel 28:18-19). White adds:

> The fire that consumes the wicked purifies the earth. Every trace of the curse is swept away. No eternally burning hell will keep before the ransomed the fearful consequences of sin.
>
> One reminder alone remains: Our Redeemer will ever bear the marks of His crucifixion. Upon His wounded head, upon His side, His hands and feet, are the only traces of the cruel work that sin has wrought. Says the prophet, beholding Christ in His glory: "He had bright beams coming out of His side: and there was the hiding of His power." Habakkuk 3:4, margin.[1]

God gives us glimpses of the most glorious experience. The redeemed who loved and obeyed their Creator will witness the re-creation of a new heaven and a new earth. "There was no more sea" to separate friends and family from each other, even as John was exiled on an island surrounded by the sea (Revelation 21:1). The new heaven and the new earth are just as real as the first. The drama of Christ's new creation gives us a preview of what the new earth will be like when the first heaven and earth pass away.

God's New Address

Revelation 21:2-6: And I John saw the holy city, new Jerusalem, coming down from God out of heaven, prepared as a bride adorned for her husband. ³And I heard a great voice out of heaven saying, Behold, the tabernacle of God *is* with men, and he will dwell with them, and they shall be his people, and God himself shall be with them, *and be* their God. ⁴And God shall wipe away all tears from their eyes; and there shall be no more death, neither sorrow, nor crying, neither shall there be any more pain: for the former things are passed away. ⁵And he that sat upon the throne said, Behold, I make all things new. And he said unto me, Write: for these words are true and faithful. ⁶And he

---

[1]   White, *The Great Controversy*, 674.

said unto me, It is done. I am Alpha and Omega, the beginning and the end. I will give unto him that is athirst of the fountain of the water of life freely.

At the end of the millennium, God moves from heaven to this earth. Instead of a moving van to take His furniture to a new house, He brings His entire heavenly city down to this world! The New Jerusalem descends in all her glory.

Revelation 20:9 briefly mentions Satan's attack against God's city, but the focus in Revelation 21 is not God's last battle against sinners. Rather these verses assure us of God's everlasting presence, living with His people on the earth made new. After the fires of destruction are past, He takes time to dry their tears. His promise is sure: "The former things are passed away" (Revelation 21:4).

This is probably the most amazing passage in the Bible! In the evening, Adam and Eve walked with God in the Garden of Eden, then Jesus came to live on this earth as a man for thirty-three years, but now "the tabernacle of God is with men, and He will dwell with them, and they shall be His people, and God Himself shall be with them, and be their God" (Revelation 21:3).

The Lord uses beautiful language to illustrate this point: God Himself lives with His "peoples" (Revelation 21:3). The Greek word λαοὶ (pronounced la-oi) is plural rather than the singular λαός (pronounced la-os). This signifies peoples redeemed from all the nations of the earth rather than a certain ethnic group of people. The New Jerusalem is clothed with splendor, but that pales in light of the fact that God Himself will live with us! This city becomes the dwelling place of both man and God. Oh, praise God for His matchless love!

With sin and suffering ended forevermore, there are no tears, no death, and no pain because God's presence makes things all new. "The inhabitant shall not say, I am sick; the people that dwell therein shall be forgiven their iniquity" (Isaiah 33:24). We see in the New Jerusalem a gloriously different way to live! Sinners justified by Christ's death and "sanctified by obeying His word"[2] have now come to the last step of their salvation: glorification. The glory we have waited for is found in the presence of God.

"He that sits upon the throne" is the same One who commands John to write in the book of Revelation (Revelation 21:5). The One on the throne is "Alpha and Omega, the beginning and the end," the same One who said, "I come quickly" (Revelation 21:6; 22:13). These are obvious references to Christ, the Source of living water. Jesus is the One mentioned on the great white throne of Revelation 20:11, 12. "The Father judgeth no man, but hath committed all judgment unto the Son" (John 5:22). The same One, the Word of God, who made "all things" in the beginning of this earth's history will "make all things new" in the end (John 1:3; Revelation 21:5).

Smith notes this distinction: Jesus says, "I make all things new." He did *not* say, "I make all new things." Smith continues his comments: "All things are made over new. Let us rejoice that these words are true. When this is accomplished,

2   Franklin E. Beldon, from the lyrics of his hymn "Cover with His Life," 1899.

all will be ready for the utterance of that sublime sentence, 'It is done.' The dark shadow of sin has then forever vanished. The wicked, root and branch (Malachi 4:1), are destroyed out of the land of the living, and the universal anthem of praise and thanksgiving (Revelation 5:13) goes up from a redeemed world and a clean universe to a covenant-keeping God."[3] "The Lord is our Judge, the Lord is our Lawgiver, the Lord is our King; He will save us" (Isaiah 33:22). All will recognize that God has kept all the promises made long ago in His covenant.

Promises and Warnings

Revelation 21:7-8: He that overcometh shall inherit all things; and I will be his God, and he shall be my son. [8]But the fearful, and unbelieving, and the abominable, and murderers, and whoremongers, and sorcerers, and idolaters, and all liars, shall have their part in the lake which burneth with fire and brimstone: which is the second death.

Revelation 21:2-6 gives God's promise to live with us in His holy capital where all the meek will "inherit the earth" (Matthew 5:5). Verses 7 and 8 contrast those who accept His invitation with those who do not.

Verse 7: Those who overcome are promised the greatest inheritance settlement in the history of the universe. What do they overcome? The original Greek for "overcometh" is νικάω (pronounced nik-ah'-o) meaning "to conquer or to come off victorious." The ones who are victorious are contrasted with the group in verse 8. Thus the context shouts the answer, "The overcomers are victorious over sin!" They will "inherit all things" because God is their inheritance. He personally belongs to them, and they are the children of God. David exclaimed: "The Lord is the portion of mine inheritance" (Psalm 16:5; cf. Numbers 18:20). What an awesome inheritance!

Verse 8: Not all will receive this promised inheritance. "No whoremonger, nor unclean person, nor covetous man, who is an idolater, hath any inheritance in the kingdom of Christ and of God" (Ephesians 5:5). This fearful warning is repeated in Revelation 21:8 to those who have not overcome sin. The list is rather comprehensive: fearful, unbelieving, abominable, murderers, whoremongers, sorcerers, idolaters, and liars. All of these are burned up in the lake of fire which is the second death. "Whoremongers" comes from the Greek word πόρνος (*pornos*) meaning "a man who prostitutes his body to another's lust for hire; a male prostitute; a man who indulges in unlawful sexual intercourse, a fornicator."

The "fearful" referred to in Revelation 21:8 are afraid of ridicule and opposition. The Greek word δειλός (pronounced day-loss) means "timid and fearful." For fear of what others may think, they will yield to compromise and disobedience. This type of fear is related to unbelief and is therefore placed on the list.

Sincere Christians may have had times of fear; thus they might be concerned that they could be counted with the unfaithful. For these loyal and obedient

---

[3]   Smith, 759.

Christians, Psalm 56:3 contains a precious promise: "Whenever I am afraid, I will trust in Thee." By God's grace, the sincere Christian will not yield to external pressures. Because they believe in God with all their heart, they maintain their love and loyalty to the Creator under the most adverse circumstances. This trusting relationship is described in verse 7: He will be our God, and we will be His children.

The Holy Jerusalem

Revelation 21:9-14: And there came unto me one of the seven angels which had the seven vials full of the seven last plagues, and talked with me, saying, Come hither, I will shew thee the bride, the Lamb's wife. [10]And he carried me away in the spirit to a great and high mountain, and showed me that great city, the holy Jerusalem, descending out of heaven from God, [11]Having the glory of God: and her light *was* like unto a stone most precious, even like a jasper stone, clear as crystal; [12]And had a wall great and high, *and* had twelve gates, and at the gates twelve angels, and names written thereon, which are *the names* of the twelve tribes of the children of Israel: [13]On the east three gates; on the north three gates; on the south three gates; and on the west three gates. [14]And the wall of the city had twelve foundations, and in them the names of the twelve apostles of the Lamb.

Verse 9: What a precious description of the New Jerusalem! Revelation is a book of contrasts: Babylon the great harlot versus the holy Jerusalem. Unlike Babylon and her inhabitants, the New Jerusalem is pure and holy. Christ's bride, symbolized by God's holy city, is His pure church. White spells it out: "The church is the bride, the Lamb's wife. Every true believer is a part of the body of Christ."[4] The holy Jerusalem consists of His saints who have been purified by the blood of the Lamb.

One of the angels who carried a vial during the seven last plagues speaks with excitement as he shows John the Lamb's bride. This view is strikingly different from the plagues so recently poured out upon the great whore of Babylon. The language contrasts the love of the Lamb for His bride with the idolatrous worship earthly rulers have given to fallen Babylon.

Verse 10 and 11: John is taken in the spirit to a great and high mountain and shown the New Jerusalem as it descends to this earth from heaven. With human words, he attempts to explain the glory of God's great city. Bunch enlarges on this vision:

> The Oriental jasper is of a beautiful sea-green color and the finest quality is very clear like the diamond or rock-crystal. Green is the predominating color in nature. It is the most restful and agreeable color to the

---

4   White, Letter 39, 1902; quoted in *The Seventh-day Adventist Bible Commentary*, 7:985-986.

eyes and to which they are best adapted. Other colors often fatigue and sometimes injure the eyesight. The lighting system of the New Jerusalem is not that of the bright, glaring white light with which our modern cities are illuminated, but a soft and mellow-green light, which will harmonize with the peaceful and restful spirit of the city and its inhabitants. The promise is: "And my people shall dwell in a peaceable habitation, and in sure dwellings, and in quiet resting places." Isaiah 32:18. How appealing this should be to the weary pilgrims of earth who "have no abiding city here" where life is filled with the stress and strain that must be expected in a world cursed by sin and in rebellion against God.[5]

Twelve Gates and Twelve Foundations

Verses 12 and 13: These verses tell more than what first meets our eyes. The high wall surrounding the city has twelve gates, and each is inscribed with one of the names of the twelve tribes of Israel. Like the twelve tribal stones carried next to the heart of the high priest, so everyone who enters this city has been grafted into the family of God. They are carried on the heart of Jesus Christ, our great High Priest: "If ye be Christ's then are ye Abraham's seed, and heirs according to the promise" (Galatians 3:29).

Verse 13 speaks of the twelve foundations, one for each of the apostles. *The Adventist Bible Commentary* compares the description of the temple in Ezekiel 48:30-34 to the New Jerusalem: "Ezekiel describes the city that might have been; John, the one that will be. The figure of the nation of Israel, constituting God's people and divided into 12 tribes, is carried through the Bible story. The New Jerusalem, whose inhabitants are redeemed from every nation, kindred, tongue, and people, is shown with the names of the 12 tribes inscribed upon its gates. In Bible figure the redeemed, no matter of what race, are represented as being assigned a place among one of the 12 tribes (Romans 9-11; Galatians 3:29)."[6]

The contextual imagery of Ezekiel and Revelation are similar. Both ancient Israel and spiritual Israel have been delivered from Babylon. Ezekiel tells of deliverance from historic Babylon; in Revelation, spiritual Israel is rescued from spiritual Babylon the great. The final reward for all Israel is not just a new dwelling place, but God Himself will be our portion and inheritance.

Verse 14: Jesus promised the disciples that they would "sit upon twelve thrones, judging the twelve tribes of Israel" (Matthew 19:28). As the names of the twelve tribes of Israel are written on the gates of the New Jerusalem, so the foundations of the holy city are inscribed with the apostles' names. God's church is "built upon the foundation of the apostles and the prophets, Jesus Christ Himself being the chief corner stone" (Eph 2:20). Through Christ, both Jews and Gentiles

---

5   Bunch, "The Revelation," 284.

6   *The Seventh-day Adventist Bible Commentary*, 4:739.

are made members of "the commonwealth of Israel" and reconciled "unto God in one body by the cross" (Ephesians 2:12, 16).

Jesus Christ is the Hope of Israel, the Consolation of Israel, and the King of Israel (Acts 28:20; Luke 2:25; John 1:49). He clearly told the woman at the well, "We know what we worship, for salvation is of the Jews" (John 4:22). By faith in Christ, we are grafted into "the Israel of God" (Galatians 6:16; cf. Romans 11:17, 24). The new covenant, ratified by the blood of Jesus, is made "with the house of Israel" (Heb 8:8,10). "So then all Israel shall be saved" as they believe on the Lord Jesus Christ (Romans 11:26).

Revelation continues this theme. Jesus warns that some in the church will say they are Jews, but they are not (Revelation 2:9; 3:9). The "children of Israel" symbolize God's people who follow the Lamb wherever He goes (Revelation 7:4, 21:12). Before Christ came into the world, His obedient people sacrificed lambs, demonstrating their faith in the coming Messiah. After the cross, we look up by faith to the bleeding Lamb in the heavenly sanctuary. Our Savior shed His blood to save His people from their sins. The true Israel of God—all who look to Jesus by faith—will finally live together in the New Jerusalem.

The City's Colossal Dimensions

Revelation 21:15-18: And he that talked with me had a golden reed to measure the city, and the gates thereof, and the wall thereof. ¹⁶And the city lieth foursquare, and the length is as large as the breadth: and he measured the city with the reed, twelve thousand furlongs. The length and the breadth and the height of it are equal. ¹⁷And he measured the wall thereof, an hundred *and* forty *and* four cubits, *according to* the measure of a man, that is, of the angel. ¹⁸And the building of the wall of it was *of* jasper: and the city *was* pure gold, like unto clear glass.

Verses 15 to 17: The size of the holy city is immense. A furlong is about one-eighth mile. Therefore the perimeter of the city would be at least 1,500 miles, and some commentators believe each side would be 1,500 miles long. Taking the latter view, Joseph A. Seiss, one of the most popular and powerful Lutheran preachers of the nineteenth century, explains how large the New Jerusalem would be in modern geographical terms:

> This city is a solid cube of golden constructions, 1,500 miles every way. The base of it would stretch from furthest Maine to the furthest Florida, and from the shore of the Atlantic to Colorado. It would cover all Britain, Ireland, France, Spain, Italy, Germany, Austria, Prussia, European Turkey, and half of European Russia, taken together! Great was the City of Nineveh, so great that Jonah had only *begun* to enter it after a day's journey. How long then would it take a man to explore this city of gold, whose every street is one-fifth the length of the diameter of

the earth, and the number of whose main avenues, though a mile above each other, and a mile apart, would not be less than eight millions![7]

Smith defends the perimeter viewpoint: "Twelve thousand furlongs, eight furlongs to the mile, equal fifteen hundred miles. It may be understood that this measure is the measure of the whole circumference of the city, not merely of one side. This appears, from Kitto, to have been the ancient method of measuring cities. The whole circumference was taken, and that was said to be the measure of the city. According to this rule, the New Jerusalem will be three hundred and seventy-five miles in length on each side. The length, breadth, and height of it are equal."[8]

Stefanovic's study of the city concurs with Smith: "The new Jerusalem appears to John as lying *foursquare*. Each side is *12,000 stadia* in length. The measurements of the new Jerusalem reflect the description of ancient Babylon by Herodotus; according to this ancient historian, Babylon was built in the form of a square. However, the measurements reveal that the actual shape of the new Jerusalem is a perfect cube; its *length and width and height are equal.* It may be noted that a cube consists of twelve edges. Each edge of the new Jerusalem is 12,000 stadia long, equaling 144,000 stadia for the entire city."[9]

No matter which viewpoint the reader accepts, this is a colossal city. The smallest estimation would be about the size of the state of Oregon, large enough to house every person who has ever lived upon the earth. The largest calculation would be about one-fifth the size of the world. Surely this city has room enough for everyone!

The numbers used to describe the city are twelves or multiples of twelve. Revelation 21:12 speaks of twelve gates, twelve angels, and twelve tribes. Verse 14 describes twelve foundations with the names of the twelve apostles. In verse 16 the city measures 12,000 stadia or furlongs. Revelation 21:17 gives the measurement of the wall: 144 cubits. Verses 19 to 20 list twelve precious stones which comprise the foundations of the wall. The twelve gates are made of twelve pearls (Revelation 21:21). Lastly, the tree of life described in Revelation 22:2 furnishes twelve kinds of fruit.

Notice Revelation 21:16: "**The length and the breadth and the height of it are equal.**" This is the shape of a cube. Using the sanctuary imagery of Revelation and Ezekiel, this shape points to the most holy place of the sanctuary where God dwelt between the cherubim. Therefore the most holy place was a type of God's holy city, the New Jerusalem. Expressing the hope of ancient Israel, the prophecies of Isaiah and Ezekiel can be linked to their fulfillment in the realities of the New Testament.

[7]   Seiss, *The Apocalypse*, 498.

[8]   Smith, 763.

[9]   Stefanovic, 588.

Verse 17: The measurement of the walls is not easy to understand because we do not know which dimension of the wall is being measured. Stefanovic believes this refers to the thickness of the walls:

> The text does not indicate whether it is the height or the thickness of the wall that is *144 cubits*. However, John has already mentioned that the city wall was "great and high" (v. 12). In addition, he specifies the height of the city as being 12,000 stadia. It is natural, therefore, to understand the 144 cubits to refer to the wall's thickness. The new Jerusalem certainly does not need walls to protect it against enemies. This figuratively thick wall of the city affirms the security of the new Jerusalem. "'For I,' declares the Lord, 'will be a wall of fire around her, and I will be the glory in her midst'" (Zechariah 2:5). Whatever the purpose of describing the measurements of the city might be, John provides his readers with an assurance that the capital of the new earth, according to both *human* and *angelic* standards of *measurement*, is an ideal place, protected and safe to inhabit.[10]

Verse 18: Jasper walls are strong, according to Bunch: "The Oriental jasper is very hard and almost indestructible. Jasper pillars have been preserved for thousands of years with but little evidence of erosion. Although we are not told, this jasper is doubtless also transparent so that the walls will not hide the glory of the city. The city itself is constructed principally of gold far more pure and precious than the famed gold of Ophir. It is so pure that it is like 'clear glass.' In verse 21 we are told that 'the street of the city was pure gold, as it were transparent glass.'"[11]

Priceless Construction

Revelation 21:19-21: And the foundations of the wall of the city were garnished with all manner of precious stones. The first foundation was jasper; the second, sapphire; the third, a chalcedony; the fourth, an emerald; ²⁰The fifth, sardonyx; the sixth, sardius; the seventh, chrysolyte; the eighth, beryl; the ninth, a topaz; the tenth, a chrysoprasus; the eleventh, a jacinth; the twelfth, an amethyst. ²¹And the twelve gates were twelve pearls; every several gate was of one pearl: and the street of the city was pure gold, as it were transparent glass.

Abraham looked for this city "which hath foundations, whose builder and maker is God" (Hebrews 11:10). We also have been invited to share this glorious city with our Savior and King. The twelve stones listed each represent one of the foundations of the New Jerusalem as well as one of apostles.

---

10   Ibid., 588-589.

11   Bunch, "The Revelation," 285.

1. Jasper—sea-green.

2. Sapphire—clear azure blue. Much is said about sapphire in the Old Testament.

3. Chalcedony—green carbonate of copper found in the mines of Chalcedon.

4. Emerald—bright green.

5. Sardonyx or onyx—dark color of the agate variety.

6. Sardius—blood-red color. It was first found in Sardis.

7. Chrysolyte—dusky green with a cast of yellow, sometimes called the "gold stone."

8. Beryl—bluish-green variety of emerald.

9. Topaz—pale green-colored stone with a mixture of yellow.

10. Chrysoprasus—golden leek-green or yellowish pale-green hue.

11. Jacinth—reddish-brown stone with a mixture of yellow.

12. Amethyst—purple or violet color composed of strong blue and deep red.

Revelation 21:22: And I saw no temple therein: for the Lord God Almighty and the Lamb are the temple of it.

No temple therein: The Greek sentence Καὶ ναὸν οὐκ εἶδον ἐν αὐτῇ (*kai naon ouk eidon en autei*) can be literally translated: "And a temple I did not see in it." In John's mind, the sanctuary contained the courtyard as well as the holy and most holy places, but there is no temple like this in the New Jerusalem.

Revelation begins with sanctuary language, but the court is omitted. During the life of Jesus on this earth, the courtyard services were fulfilled, climaxing at the cross. Therefore Revelation follows Christ's heavenly ministry, beginning with imagery from the holy place in John's first vision of Jesus. Revelation 11:1-2 reminds us to follow Jesus by faith into the holy place in the heavenly sanctuary. Jesus moves from the holy place experience of the seven churches, seven seals, and seven trumpets to the ark of the covenant, the most holy place experience (Revelation 11:19).

The rest of the book of Revelation focuses on Christ's ministry in the holy of holies, so imagery from the holy place is omitted as the judgment begins. The temple, as John once knew it, is gone. All that remains is the fulfillment of the most holy place of the earthly sanctuary. In the New Jerusalem, God Himself dwells with man. Exodus 25:8 has reached complete fulfillment in the holy city itself. **"The Lord God Almighty and the Lamb are the temple of it."** Type has met anti-type!

Revelation 21:23-26: And the city had no need of the sun, neither of the moon, to shine in it: for the glory of God did lighten it, and the Lamb *is* the light thereof. ²⁴And the nations of them which are saved shall walk in the light of it: and the kings of the earth do bring their glory and honour into it. ²⁵And the gates of it shall not be shut at all by day: for there shall be no night there. ²⁶And they shall bring the glory and honour of the nations into it.

"No need" is the emphasis of verse 23. It does not say the sun and moon no longer exist; John simply states that the light of the sun and moon will be outshone by the light of the glory of God. The Light of this city is the Lamb. In Jerusalem of old, the light of God's presence was limited to the most holy place of the sanctuary as sinners would be consumed by His brightness.

In the holy city, Jesus will not need to veil His glory. The bright and fiery presence of the Lord lights the entire city of God. His glory graces this most holy place on the new earth. With its cubic dimensions, the vast holy city replaces the symbolic room-sized holy of holies in the earthly sanctuary as type meets reality.

What a glorious experience! The seraphims' song will be a note higher for truly now "the whole earth is full of His glory" (Isaiah 6:3). As long as the earth remains, Genesis 8:22 and Isaiah 66:23 prophesy the continuance of the daily, weekly, and monthly cycles as well as the seasons of earth, but we still cannot imagine all that the Lord has in store for us. Isaiah 30:26 predicts that the natural lights of the earth, the sun and moon, will shine more brightly than ever before. The new heaven and the new earth promise an entirely different environment, more glorious than ever before.

The kings who bring honor and glory into the holy city did not live in opposition to God. Like the wise men of old, they have honored God in their lives here on earth. These kings proclaim the King of kings "that shall rule My people Israel" (Matthew 2:6). The imagery includes His saints who live and reign with Jesus as kings and queens.

Revelation 21:27: "And there shall in no wise enter into it any thing that defileth, neither whatsoever worketh abomination, or maketh a lie: but they which are written in the Lamb's book of life."

This verse clearly delineates who would not qualify as a citizen of this city. Those who would defile the holy Jerusalem, treating it as a common city, are excluded. Jerusalem of old was defiled by the sins of its people, but this will never occur in the city of God.

The Greek word for "defile" is κοινόω (koy-no'-o) which means "to make common or to make (levitically) unclean, render unhallowed, one that works abomination." In the New King James Version, "causes an abomination" is the Greek phrase ποιῶν βδέλυγμα (poy-eh'-own bdel'-oog-mah) which literally means "making an abomination." The word βδέλυγμα (bdel'-oog-mah) means "a foul thing, a detestable thing of idols, and things pertaining to idolatry." In simple language, no one will be there who would treat the New Jerusalem as a common or unholy place. Those who cling to idolatry in any of its forms cannot live there.

Lastly, liars will not be there. Satan "is a liar, and the father of it" (John 8:44). In this generation, lies are the norm. Most people do not want to hear the truths of God's word, but in the New Jerusalem, people will be different than the generation from which they came. They do not seek honor for themselves or for their accomplishments. Instead, they give their honor, loyalty, obedience, and glory to the Lamb.

They have one distinguishing mark—all are written in the Lamb's book of life. In God's city, the only ones who qualify as citizens are those who have chosen to take the Jesus, the Lamb of God, as their substitute. As His blood was applied to their lives, their names were recorded in the Lamb's book of life. There is no greater honor.

CHAPTER THIRTY-FOUR

Revelation 22

Introduction

With imagery from Pentecost and the Feast of Tabernacles, the first five verses of chapter 22 continue the vision of the holy city from the previous chapter. All that was lost in the first three chapters of Genesis is restored in the last three chapters of Revelation. The curse is gone, and the tree of life is restored. The great harvest is over, and God dwells with His people.

From verse 6 and onward, the theme of the benedictory chapter of the Bible is the soon coming of Christ. In this last chapter, Jesus gives three last calls, and each time, He says, "I am coming soon!" Each urgent call from Jesus is followed by a blessing that teaches us how to be ready for His coming. The last three invitations, "Come to Jesus, the living Water!" are given by the church, the Holy Spirit, those who act on the words of Revelation, and Jesus Christ Himself. The last three warnings of danger are given to the world: decide for Jesus now, don't love sin, and don't change God's word. Like a pastor giving his final altar call, Christ the divine Shepherd pleads for the last time. As the drama of the ages nears its close, we see Jesus as our only hope, our only safety, our only God.

Revelation 22:1: And he showed me a pure river of water of life, clear as crystal, proceeding out of the throne of God and of the Lamb.

Two Streams: John continues his description of the New Jerusalem from the previous chapter. The pure river of life, clear as crystal, flows from two sources: the throne and the Lamb. This word picture points to John 19:34, 35: "One of the soldiers with a spear pierced his side, and forthwith came there out *blood and water*. And he that saw it bare record, and his record is true: and he knoweth that he saith true, that ye might believe." The blood and the water from Christ's wounded side are symbolized in the two streams that flow from the throne and the Lamb.

Every year at the Feast of Tabernacles, the priests performed a ceremony that pointed forward to the double stream that would flow from Jesus's side. Edersheim describes the Feast of Tabernacles in Jesus' day:

When the Temple-procession had reached the Pool of Siloam, the Priest filled his golden pitcher from its waters. Then they went back to the Temple, so timing it, that they should arrive just as they were laying the pieces of the sacrifice on the great Altar of Burnt-offering, towards the close of the ordinary Morning-Sacrifice service. A threefold blast of the Priests' trumpets welcomed the arrival of the Priest, as he entered through the 'Water-gate,' which obtained its name from this ceremony, and passed straight into the Court of the Priests. Here he was joined by another Priest, who carried the wine for the drink-offering. The two Priests ascended 'the rise' of the altar, and turned to the left. There were two silver funnels here, with narrow openings, leading down to the base of the altar. Into that at the east, which was somewhat wider, the wine was poured, and, at the same time, the water into the western and narrower opening, the people shouting to the Priest to raise his hand, so as to make sure that he poured the water into the funnel. . . .

We can have little difficulty in determining at what part of the services of the 'last, the Great Day of the Feast,' Jesus stood and cried, 'If any one thirst, let him come unto Me and drink!'[1]

In his gospel, John recorded Jesus' words at the Feast of Tabernacles and testified of the water and the blood flowing from Jesus' side (John 7:37-39; 19:34-37). In Revelation 22 all three accounts come together in the symbolic language of living water flowing from God's throne.

During His last earthly Feast of Tabernacles before His crucifixion, Jesus joined the throngs in Jerusalem as the priests ceremoniously poured both wine and water which flowed into the Kidron River. Then He called out, "If any man thirst, let him come unto Me and drink. He that believeth on Me, as the scripture hath said, out of his belly shall flow rivers of living water" (John 7:37-38). White points to Christ's fulfillment of this ceremony: "Christ's words were the water of life. There in the presence of the assembled multitude He set Himself apart to be smitten, that the water of life might flow to the world."[2]

After His crucifixion at Passover in A.D. 31, the outpouring of the Holy Spirit would bring a great harvest of souls at Pentecost, but "the Holy Ghost was not yet given; because that Jesus was not yet glorified" (John 7:39). White writes: After Christ ascended to His Father's throne, "the Pentecostal outpouring was Heaven's communication that the Redeemer's inauguration was accomplished."[3]

---

[1] Alfred Edersheim, *The Life and Times of Jesus the Messiah* (New York: Longmans, Green, and Company, 1883), 2:158, 160.

[2] White, *The Desire of Ages*, 454.

[3] White, *The Acts of the Apostles*, 39.

The Throne of God

The imagery of God's throne also points back to the first Pentecost in Exodus 24:10-12: "And they saw the God of Israel: and there was under his feet as it were a paved work of a sapphire stone, and as it were the body of heaven in his clearness. And upon the nobles of the children of Israel he laid not his hand: also they saw God, and did eat and drink. And the LORD said unto Moses, Come up to me into the mount, and be there: and I will give thee tables of stone, and a law, and commandments which I have written; that thou mayest teach them."

After their amazing deliverance from Egypt, the children of Israel celebrated their first Pentecost at Mount Sinai. God Himself ate a mountain-top meal with the seventy elders, Moses, Aaron, and Aaron's two sons, Nadab and Abihu (Exodus 24:9-11). As the first harvest of Pentecost pointed forward to the promise of the final harvest, so this Pentecostal meal on Mount Sinai pointed forward to the fulfillment of final harvest celebration, the Feast of Tabernacles, when God would live and eat with His people on Mount Zion in the New Jerusalem.

At Sinai, the foundation or pavement of God's throne was the precious, blue sapphire stone (Exodus 24:10). This harmonizes with the blue water flowing from God's throne in Revelation 22:1. Blue is the color of obedience. To remind them of God's commandments, and especially the Sabbath, God instructed the children of Israel to wear a ribbon of blue on the edges of their garments (Numbers 15:38). This rule was given immediately after one of the Israelites was stoned for breaking the Sabbath (Numbers 15:32-36). The blue of obedience is clearly stated in Exodus 24:10: "There was under his feet as it were a paved work of a sapphire stone, and as it were the body of heaven in his clearness." John uses similar language in describing God's throne in Revelation 4.

The Tables of the Stone

In the following section, the author is indebted to Michael Oxentenko for "The Blue Stone" chapter of his unpublished manuscript "Daniel and Revelation."[4]

In Exodus 24:12, the Hebrew reads אֶת־לֻחֹת הָאֶבֶן (*'eth-luhoth ha'eben*), "the tables of the stone." This literal translation would render the verse: "And the LORD said unto Moses, Come up to me into the mount, and be there: and *I will give thee the tables of the stone*, and a law, and commandments which I have written; that thou mayest teach them" (Exodus 24:12; emphasis mine).

What stone? The context refers to the blue sapphire stone of the throne of God. The two tables of God's law are blue like the water of life. Galatians 3:24 says: "Wherefore the law was our schoolmaster to bring us unto Christ, that we might be justified by faith." The law, made from the stone of God's throne, reminds us that we need the Rock of Jesus. "For they drank of that spiritual Rock that followed them: and that Rock was Christ." (1 Corinthians 10:4). The Rock that followed the children of Israel in the wilderness was their constant source

---

4   Oxentenko, 18-26.

of water, like the throne of God in the holy city. Thus the symbolic throne of the most holy place, the ark of the covenant, contained the Ten Commandments. Written by God's finger on beautiful, blue sapphire from His real throne, God's law is a transcript of His character and the basis for both the old and new covenants (Hebrews 8:7-10).

The Tree of Life

Revelation 22:2-5: In the midst of the street of it, and on either side of the river, was there the tree of life, which bare twelve manner of fruits, and yielded her fruit every month: and the leaves of the tree were for the healing of the nations. ³And there shall be no more curse: but the throne of God and of the Lamb shall be in it; and his servants shall serve him: ⁴And they shall see his face; and his name shall be in their foreheads. ⁵And there shall be no night there; and they need no candle, neither light of the sun; for the Lord God giveth them light: and they shall reign for ever and ever.

Genesis 2:9 tells of the tree of life in the middle of the Garden of Eden, but access to the tree was guarded by angels after the fall of Adam and Eve (Genesis 3:24). In Revelation, Jesus promises that Eden will be restored, and John sees the tree of life growing by the river of life in the New Jerusalem. Although it is call "the tree," somehow it grows on both sides of the river and in the middle of the street of the New Jerusalem. Perhaps the trunks unite at the top to form one tree. The source of the living water is God's throne for He is Life. In Him all living beings exist and from Him we receive eternal life.

Twelve Manner of Fruit: The tree of life yields fruit monthly. The Greek phrase κατὰ μῆνα ἕκαστον (*kata mēna hekaston*) means "according to each month." This clarifies Isaiah 66:23: "And it shall come to pass, that from one new moon to another, and from one sabbath to another, shall all flesh come to worship before me, saith the LORD." Sabbath by Sabbath and month by month, all the inhabitants of the new earth will come together to enjoy this life-giving fruit from the tree of life. All living beings, trees, and plants are nourished by the waters that flow from the throne of God and the Lamb. Human words fail to describe the gloriousness of John's vision of this amazing holy city.

Healing of the nations: The imagery points back to Ezekiel 47:1-12 with two rivers flowing from the temple. These rivers flow into the sea and it is healed. Remember that the harlot sat upon the waters, and the plagues were sent upon the waters where she sat. Ezekiel's prophecy shows the healing of the seas from the two rivers of water flowing from the throne of God. In Ezekiel, the rivers flow out of the temple; Revelation has no temple because the Lord Himself is the temple. The tent or temple symbol no longer in exists in the New Jerusalem, so the river of life flows from the throne of God, from the One who is the real temple. Wherever those waters flow there is life and healing.

The two streams that flow from the throne and the Lamb bring healing to the nations. The leaves of the tree symbolize the healing of the life-giving waters.

The first sign of a sick tree is the dead leaves, but a healthy tree has green, healing leaves. David compares the righteous to this tree: "He shall be like a tree planted by the rivers of water, that bringeth forth his fruit in his season; his leaf also shall not wither; and whatsoever he doeth shall prosper" (Psalm 1:3). To understand how to begin eating from that tree of life now, study Proverbs 3:13-18, 11:30; 13:12; 15:4.

No more curse: Because Christ bore the curse for our sins on the cross, no trace of the curse remains except for the marks of His cruel crucifixion (Zechariah 13:6). White adds: "Jesus will lead us beside the living stream flowing from the throne of God and will explain to us the dark providences through which on this earth He brought us in order to perfect our characters."[5] The earth and God's people have been redeemed from the curse of sin. The results of the fall are reversed as Eden blossoms on earth once more.

His name in their foreheads: John saw the fulfillment of Revelation 14:1 as the "Lamb stood on the mount Sion, and with him an hundred forty and four thousand, having *his Father's name written in their foreheads* (emphasis mine)." White summarizes: "From the first intimation of hope in the sentence pronounced in Eden to that last glorious promise of the Revelation, 'They shall see His face; and His name shall be in their foreheads,' . . . the burden of every book and every passage of the Bible is the unfolding of this wondrous theme,— man's uplifting,—the power of God, 'which giveth us the victory through our Lord Jesus Christ.'"[6] (1 Corinthians 15:57).

The description of the New Jerusalem ends with verse 5. Now Revelation gives us the last words from Jesus to His children. These final warnings and last urgent pleas to prepare for Christ's soon coming resonate in the closing words of the book of Revelation. Please read these invitations and exhortations carefully for Jesus Himself is speaking to you.

I Am Coming Soon!

Now Lord Jesus Christ speaks personally to each reader. He cannot bear to lose even one of those for whom He died. Revelation began with John telling us about the second coming of Christ (Revelation 1:4, 7, 8), but these last three calls from come Jesus Himself. Revelation ends with His urgent pleas, His blessings, and His warnings.

Revelation 22:6-10: And he said unto me, These sayings are faithful and true: and the Lord God of the holy prophets sent his angel to show unto his servants the things which must shortly be done. ⁷Behold, I come quickly: blessed is he that keepeth the sayings of the prophecy of this book. ⁸And I John saw these things, and heard them. And when I had heard and seen, I fell down to worship before the feet of the angel which showed me these things. ⁹Then

---

5   White, *Testimonies for the Church*, 8:254.

6   White, *Education*, 125-126.

saith he unto me, See thou do it not: for I am thy fellowservant, and of thy brethren the prophets, and of them which keep the sayings of this book: worship God. ¹⁰And he saith unto me, Seal not the sayings of the prophecy of this book: for the time is at hand.

God's word promises that these sayings are faithful and true; John tells us that all the prophecies of Revelation will come to pass soon. Even as angels were sent long ago to the prophets of ancient Israel, so today God has given us the testimony of John, the words from holy angels, but best of all, the direct testimony of His Son Jesus Christ. They tell us what will come in the future so that God's people can prepare for His return. Most of Revelation's prophecies have already come to pass, assuring us that all will soon be fulfilled.

I come quickly! Jesus exclaims this phrase three times in Revelation's last chapter (22:7, 12, 20). How can we ignore His calls? Each urgent cry from Jesus is followed by His benediction on the obedient reader.

Blessed as we share Jesus' prophecies: "Blessed is he that keepeth the sayings of this book" (Revelation 22:7). To "keep" His words, we must cherish them, share them, and watch for the fulfillment of these prophecies. Both the blessings and the prophecies of Revelation come from Jesus. How we need to treasure and guard His predictions and benedictions! We must tell others of the treasure we have found in Christ's words. Only a selfish heart tries to hoard its blessings.

"I am coming soon! You will be blessed if you do what Revelation says." Jesus tells us that it is not enough just to read or even to understand the book of Revelation. To receive His blessing, we must put the words of Revelation into practice. We must let Jesus into our hearts daily. We must allow the Holy Spirit to write His laws upon our minds and hearts. We must share the alarming messages of the three angels of Revelation 14. And we must tell others that Jesus is coming soon!

Worship God: John was so overwhelmed by the glory of the heavenly messenger that he fell down to worship him. The angel's warning echoes the message of the first angel in Revelation 14:6-7: "Fear God, and give glory to Him; for the hour of His judgment is come: and *worship Him* that made heaven, and earth, and the sea, and the fountains of waters." The warnings in Revelation are given to prepare us for the second coming of Jesus. Only the Creator God may rightly be worshiped and adored. The angel gave John the clear, unadulterated truth: "Do not worship any created being." This points out again the issue of worship in the prophetic books of Daniel and Revelation.

Unlike Daniel, the prophecies of Revelation have never been sealed. This precious words from Jesus have revealed God's plan from the moment they were written. The events of Revelation follow the church of Christ from the cross to the crown, from John's day until the New Jerusalem. In Revelation, the clearest picture of the character of Christ has been revealed. The dangers and deceptions of the enemy are exposed, while the marvellous and awesome goodness of our Creator is brought to light. God revealed the future in symbols to guide His faithful ones, protect them from Satan's snares, and prepare them for their Lord's return.

The Danger of Indecision

Revelation 22:11: He that is unjust, let him be unjust still: and he which is filthy, let him be filthy still: and he that is righteous, let him be righteous still: and he that is holy, let him be holy still.

As taught through the symbolic ceremonies of the Day of Atonement, the time for mercy will soon come to an end. All those who have not confessed their sins and humbled themselves before God are cut off from His people. Some believe in riding the fence, a "wait and see" attitude, but this is most dangerous. "Now is the accepted time; behold, now is the day of salvation" (2 Corinthians 6:2). Choose Christ as the Lord of your life today. You cannot afford to delay. All who do not come fully on the side of the Lord will be cut off with the unbelievers.

Smith refers to this cut-off point: "The declaration of verse 11 marks the close of probation, which is the close of Christ's work as mediator. But we are taught by the subject of the sanctuary that this work closes with the examination of the cases of the living in the investigative judgment. When this is accomplished, the irrevocable fiat can be pronounced."[7] There is no court of appeals for this final and solemn judgment because this irrevocable decision will come down from the highest court of the universe, from the righteous Judge Himself.

I Am Coming Soon!

Revelation 22:12-14: And, behold, I come quickly; and my reward is with me, to give every man according as his work shall be. [13] I am Alpha and Omega, the beginning and the end, the first and the last. [14]Blessed are they that do his commandments, that they may have right to the tree of life, and may enter in through the gates into the city.

Again Jesus cries, "I am coming quickly!" This urgent call enlarges to include the rewards He brings with Him. What will your reward be? Do your actions and words reveal the faith you claim to have? We need the faith of Jesus. By His grace, He calls us to be "doers of the word, and not hearers only" (James 1:22). "Faith without works is dead;" James reminds us that we will be judged by the royal law, the law of liberty (James 2:20, 8, 12).

Blessed as we keep Jesus' commandments: This is the seventh and last blessing in Revelation. Revelation's series of sevens, repetition of the fourth commandment, and descriptions of God's commandment-keeping people clearly point to God's Ten Commandments. Written by the Lord's own finger twice on Sinai and treasured in the ark of His testimony in the most holy place of the heavenly sanctuary, the Ten Commandments outline our love relationship with

---

[7]   Smith, 775.

Jesus and our fellow human beings. Jesus Himself pronounces a blessing upon all who keep His commandments.

This last special blessing from Jesus matches His message about His rewards: Those who "do His commandments" will receive the reward of eternal life from Jesus (Revelation 22:14). Commandment keepers have the right to eat from the tree of life and free entry into the holy city. How can poor sinners keep His holy law? Jesus backs up His commands with who He is—Alpha and Omega, the beginning and the end, the first and the last. Look to Him! He has the power to begin His good work in you, and He will enable you to walk in His ways (John 1:12). "The revelation of Jesus Christ" points to Him as the only Source of cleansing, power, and victory (Revelation 1:1).

Instead of "do His commandments," some manuscripts read "blessed are they that wash their robes." Smith demurs: "There seems to be good evidence that the first is the original, from which the latter is a variation through transcription errors. Thus the Syriac New Testament, one of the very earliest translations from the original Greek, reads according to the Authorized Version. And Cyprian, whose writings antedate any extant Greek manuscript, quotes the text as reading, 'Blessed are they that do His commandments.' We may therefore safely consider this as the genuine reading."[8]

Contextually, the message from Jesus in verse 12 fits commandment keeping better than robe washing. In harmony with verse 15, the lawless are contrasted with the obedient. Those who love to break God's commandments are excluded from heaven, On the other hand, those who love Jesus and keep His commandments have right to the tree of life because His grace and power have saved them from sin.

The Danger of Loving Sin

Revelation 22:15: For without are dogs, and sorcerers, and whoremongers, and murderers, and idolaters, and whosoever loveth and maketh a lie.

If we love sin, we are God's enemies. The good news is that Jesus loves His enemies; hence the Holy Spirit, God's church, and all who believe the messages of Revelation will cooperate with Jesus in saving the lost. The apostle Paul himself and some of his church members used to be on this list of sinners, but they were washed in the blood of the Lamb! Jesus calls us to love Him more than sin, but if we cling to our sins instead of Jesus, we will be excluded from the New Jerusalem. (See comments on Revelation 21:8, 27.)

Come! Come! Come to Jesus!

Jesus can forgive any sin. Nothing is too hard for Him! Verse 17 gives three final invitations calling sinners to come to Jesus and accept His gift of everlasting life (John 4:14).

---

[8]   Ibid., 776.

Revelation 22:16-17: I Jesus have sent mine angel to testify unto you these things in the churches. I am the root and the offspring of David, and the bright and morning star. ¹⁷And the Spirit and the bride say, Come. And let him that heareth say, Come. And let him that is athirst come. And whosoever will, let him take the water of life freely.

Smith uplifts Christ's testimony: "Jesus testifies these things in the churches, showing that the entire book of Revelation is given to the seven churches, which is another incidental proof that the seven churches are representatives of the church through the entire gospel age. Christ is the offspring of David, in that He appeared on earth in the line of David's descendents. He is the root of David, inasmuch as He is the great prototype of David, and the maker and upholder of all things."[9] Christ exalted, praised, and honored must remain the theme of our song.

Bright and morning star: After the darkness of night, the morning star presents a welcome sight. As each dawn brings light and a new day, so God's mercies are "new every morning" (Lam. 3:23). The darkest midnight of earth's history will arrive soon, but Jesus is coming quickly! He promised to give "the morning star" to those who overcome sin's dark night (Revelation 2:8). Jesus Himself is the "bright and morning star," our shield and infinitely priceless reward (Revelation 22:16; Genesis 15:1).

The three-fold invitation: The Holy Spirit and the church are calling sinners to come to Jesus. Those who cherish the prophecies in Revelation are sharing them with sinners and calling them to Christ. White adds: "Everyone who hears is to repeat the invitation. Whatever one's calling in life, his first interest should be to win souls for Christ."[10]

All are invited to come by Jesus Himself, a personal invitation from the King of kings. His gifts are offered freely. What greater incentives could He give? This is the *last invitation*. What will your answer be?

The Danger of Changing God's Word

Revelation 22:18-19: For I testify unto every man that heareth the words of the prophecy of this book, If any man shall add unto these things, God shall add unto him the plagues that are written in this book: ¹⁹And if any man shall take away from the words of the book of this prophecy, God shall take away his part out of the book of life, and out of the holy city, and from the things which are written in this book.

The language of Jesus points back to Deuteronomy which gives a special warning to those who would tamper with the word of God: "Ye shall not add unto the word which I command you, neither shall ye diminish ought from it,

---

[9]   Ibid.

[10]   White, *Desire of Ages*, 822.

that ye may keep the commandments of the Lord your God which I command you" (Deuteronomy 4:2; cf. 12:32). Jesus reminds us: "I am the Lord; I change not" (Malachi 3:6).

This warning especially applies to all who have followed the church/state power of the beast which was represented in Daniel as the little horn power: "He will think to change times and laws" (Daniel 7:25). When we put our traditions, opinions, customs, culture, and convenience above the word of God, we make ourself into a god and break the first commandment. White enlarges on these solemn curses given by God Himself:

> Such are the warnings which God has given to guard men against chang-ing in any manner that which He has revealed or commanded. These solemn denunciations apply to all who by their influence lead men to re-gard lightly the law of God. They should cause those to fear and tremble who flippantly declare it a matter of little consequence whether we obey God's law or not. All who exalt their own opinions above divine revela-tion, all who would change the plain meaning of Scripture to suit their own convenience, or for the sake of conforming to the world, are taking upon themselves a fearful responsibility. The written word, the law of God, will measure the character of every man and condemn all whom this unerring test shall declare wanting.[11]

I Am Coming Soon!

Revelation 22:20-21: He which testifieth these things saith, Surely I come quickly. Amen. Even so, come, Lord Jesus. ²¹The grace of our Lord Jesus Christ be with you all. Amen.

For the last time, Jesus Himself tells us that He is coming quickly. These final words are quite brief, as if He is making haste to come back as quickly as possible. "Testifies"—symbolizes the nature of the promise. He has already testified with His blood the surety of the promise of eternal life. With that same assurance we may trust Him at His word that He will come quickly.

John finishes with this blessing as the whole chapter has been a benedictory closing to the drama of the ages. The last verse of Revelation ends where the plan of salvation began—with the grace of our Lord Jesus Christ. This final benedic-tion is also a promise that has kept Christians as they wait for the soon coming of Jesus. Through the grace of Jesus alone we have all been saved. Through the grace of Jesus we have received the gift of eternal life. Through the grace of Jesus the whole plan of salvation has been displayed in all of its glory in the book of Revelation. Because of the grace of Jesus, someday we will look back and see that all that every prophecy was fulfilled just as promised. After John's last benedic-tory prayer for God's people, Revelation ends with his "Amen!"

---

[11] White, *The Great Controversy*, 268.

Conclusion

The last chapter of Revelation completes the vision of the holy Jerusalem. Then the last three announcements of His soon coming are spoken by Jesus Himself. The final blessings and warnings are written in God's last book. All those who choose Jesus join His bride and the Holy Spirit in making the very last urgent prayers and pleadings for lost sinners to come to Him before it is too late.

Now is the time to join Jesus, the angels, and His church in proclaiming these last-day messages to the world. Daniel stood firm as he witnessed for God before the greatest kings of his day. As he fasted and prayed to understand the Scriptures, God gave him visions and dreams, laying the foundation of Old Testament prophecy. The beloved disciple John spoke fearlessly of Jesus and shared the good news about His soon return. Then on one special Sabbath of his exile on Patmos, Jesus gave John the greatest revelation of Himself, the grand finale of all biblical prophecies.

Soon this same Jesus will come, and everything in Revelation will be fulfilled. Most of the world and even professed Christians treat His last precious messages coldly and indifferently. Don't let the lukewarmness of this world cool your love for Him. Jesus longs to fill us with His presence and power as He did in the days of Daniel and John.

Let's join those who overcome the wicked one by the blood of the Lamb and the word of their testimony. Let's determine like Daniel and John to be faithful even unto death. Christ's promise of eternal life is sure. He longs to see us, and those for whom we've labored, face to face. Meet me at the northeastern gate!

Appendix

The following material written by Taylor G. Bunch supports this book's chapter on Daniel 7. Bunch no longer lives, but through his pen, he is still speaking. Because the material in this appendix is taken directly from Bunch's typewritten syllabus, "The Book of Daniel," I have placed it in the back of my book because the historical material is difficult to obtain elsewhere.

In his syllabus, Bunch lists sixteen characteristics that identify the little horn as the papacy. Of these scriptural and historical proofs, Bunch declares: "The chain of evidence is so complete that not one link is missing."[1] The rest of the appendix, including the paragraph below and sixteen extensive characteristics of the papacy, is quoted directly from pages 98 to 109 of Bunch's "Book of Daniel."

Bunch Identifies the Little Horn Power

The evidence of fulfilled prophecy proves papal Rome guilty as the lawless and persecuting anti-Christian power pictured in Daniel as the eleventh horn of the fourth beast. No other organization in human history fits the prophetic mold. Examine these identifying marks to see if any other power meets the tests of prophetic revelation and historic investigation.

1. **Small Beginning.** The power represented in our prophecy comes up as a "little horn" and then gradually grows into an ecclesiastical kingdom that rules the kingdoms of Europe and dominates the earth. See Daniel 8:9-12. The Papacy had a small and humble beginning. Paul declared that this religious despotism had begun to appear in his day. The first step in the establishment of the Papal hierarchy was the "falling away" or apostasy from the true faith. This was accomplished by the exaltation of man. The bishops were exalted above the elders in rank. Then followed a long and bitter rivalry between the bishops of the leading churches, Antioch, Jerusalem, Alexandria, Constantinople and Rome. Finally the Bishop at Rome gained the supremacy and the Papacy was established.

---

[1]   Bunch, "The Book of Daniel," 96.

2. **Another Kingdom.** "Another horn" indicates that the eleventh horn is a kingdom or monarchy as were the ten. This power would claim civil and kingly authority as well as ecclesiastical authority. It would be a religio-political organization. That the rulers of the Papacy claim kingly power and authority is well established by historical evidence as well as the confessions of Catholics. The Pope claims to be "father of princes and kings" and "ruler of the world." He assumes the titles of "Sovereign of the State of Vatican City, Gloriously Reigning," and "King of kings and Lord of lords." During the celebration in honor of the signing of the Concordat on Feb. 11, 1929, hundreds of priests cried out: "Long live the Pope-King."

3. **Diverse or Different.** While this power is symbolized by a horn and was thus a kingdom, it was declared to be "diverse" from the others. "So different from all the rest."—Moffatt. This new empire claimed dominion over the spirits and souls of men as well as their bodies. It exercised its sovereign authority through popes instead of kings; through bishops instead of princes. The Pope maintains a royal court where nations must be represented by ambassadors and ministers of state just as other earthly governments. There has been nothing else like it in all human history.

4. **Among the Ten.** The eleventh horn came up among the ten, and thus the Papacy would make its appearance in the territory of Imperial Rome and among the nations of divided Rome. The little horn came up out of the beast symbolizing Pagan Rome and is therefore a continuation of the Roman religion and dominion. It occupies the same capital and is indeed and in reality a Roman power. Barnes in his *General History*, p. 321, declares that for centuries the Papacy kept gaining strength until finally "a new Rome rose from the ashes of the old, far mightier than the vanquished empire, for it claimed dominion over the spirits of men." A recent Catholic writer said: "Long ages ago, when Rome through the neglect of the Western Emperors was left to the mercy of the barbarous hordes, the Romans turned to one figure for aid and protection, and asked him to rule them; and thus, in this simple manner the best title of all to kingly right, commenced the temporal sovereignty of the popes. And meekly stepping to the throne of Caesar, the vicar of Christ took up the scepter to which the emperors and kings of Europe were to bow in reverence through so many ages."—James P. Conroy, in the *American Quarterly Review* of April, 1911. The papacy designates herself "The Holy Roman Church," and "The Roman Catholic Church."

5. **After the Ten.** The eleventh horn did not appear until after the ten were established. The Papacy would not reach the position of kingly power until after Rome was divided into the ten divisions, although it had been

quietly developing since apostolic days. By the close of the fifth century the breaking up of Rome was complete. All during the overthrow of Imperial Rome and the establishment of the ten kingdoms the Papacy was growing up "in the midst of them."—Douay. It was among them but not of them. Papal supremacy as a religio-political kingdom began in the sixth century and continued for twelve hundred years. The ten were established before the prophet saw the eleventh uproot the three and began its persecuting and blasphemous career.

6.   **Uproots Three.** "He shall subdue three kings," is the prediction, or "before whom three fell." The three were "plucked up by the roots," indicating complete destruction. It was "three of the *first* horns" that were uprooted or subdued. In the fourth century, Arius, a priest of Alexandria, began teaching that Christ was the first created being and was therefore inferior to the Father. The Council of Nicea, called by Constantine in 325 A.D., condemned Arius as a heretic and his teachings as heresy. Arianism, however, continued to grow until four of the ten kingdoms were Arian in belief. Three of these were the Heruli, the Vandals, and Ostrogoths. Through war and diplomacy the Papacy, which clung to the Nicene Creed, endeavored to destroy these heretical nations. It was three of the first that were uprooted and destroyed.

   (1) **The Heruli.** "The first kingdom established by the barbarians in Italy was that of the Heruli."—Ridpath. The historian gives the date of the overthrow of the Heruli as 493 A.D. They were overthrown by the Goths under Theodoric by what he called a divine commission from Zeno, the emperor of Eastern Rome. The fact that the Heruli and Ostrogoths were both Arian in belief did not restrain the scheming pontiff from using the one to destroy the other when the outcome resulted in his advancement in power. See *History of the World*, by Ridpath, Vol. 4, chap. 74, and Gibbon's *Roman Empire*, chapters 39 and 40. The destruction of this Arian nation was complete. "After the middle of the sixth century, however, their name completely disappears."—*Encyclopedia Britannia* [sic], Vol. XIII, p. 403, art. "Heruli." "After this their name disappears from history."—*Standard Encyclopedia of World Knowledge*, Vol. XIII, p. 334. See also the *New Standard Encyclopedia*, art. "Heruli." The kingdom was so completely uprooted that no trace is left, and no modern nation or province bears the name or can be identified with the Heruli.

   (2) **The Vandals.** The Vandals crossed into Northern Africa and took possession of Carthage in 431 A.D. They accepted the Arian doctrine and were therefore marked for destruction. Ridpath

gives the date of their destruction as 534. "Their power was at its height when Genseric died (477). In his time the Vandals became Christians, but they were Arians, and fiercely persecuted orthodox believers and other heretics. In 533 the Byzantine general Belisarius, landed in Africa. The Vandals were several times defeated, and Carthage was entered on Sept. 15, 533; and in November of the same year they were routed in the decisive battle of Tricamaron. In the next year Africa, Sardinia, and Porsica [Corsica] were restored to the Roman Empire. As a nation, the Vandals soon ceased to exist."—*Nelson's Encyclopedia*, Vol. XII, art. "Vandals."

Further Evidence. "Being Arian Christians, the Vandals persecuted with furious zeal the Orthodox party, the followers of Athanasius. Moved by the entreaties of the African Catholics, Justinian, the Eastern emperor, sent his general Belisarius to drive the barbarians from Africa. The expedition was successful. . . . The Vandals remaining in the country were gradually absorbed by the old Roman population, and after a few generations no certain trace of the barbarian invaders could be detected. . . . The Vandal nation had disappeared; the name alone remained."—*A History of Rome*, by Myers, p. 193.

Race Exterminated. "The Arian heresy (of the Vandals) was proscribed, and the race of these remarkable conquerors was in a short time exterminated. A single generation sufficed to confound their women and children in the mass of the Roman inhabitants of the province, and their very name was soon totally forgotten. There are few instances in history of a nation disappearing so rapidly and so completely as the Vandals of Africa."—*History of Greece*, George Finlay, Vol. 1, p. 232. "It is reckoned that during the reign of Justinian, Africa lost five millions of its inhabitants; thus Arianism was extinguished in that region, not by any enforcement of conformity, but by the extermination of the race which had introduced and professed it."—*History of the Christian Church*, J. C. Robertson, Vol. 1, p. 521.

(3) **The Ostrogoths.** Ridpath dates the establishment of the Ostrogothic nation in 493, and its overthrow in 538, and its total destruction in 554. The following is from Ridpath's *History of the World*, Vol. IV, pp. 408-417: "Bishop Wulfila, or Ulfilas, labored for forty years among the Goths, and saw as the fruits of his labors the conversion of the entire people to the Arian branch of Christianity. . . . The Ostrogoths had grown to be first in influence among the barbarian states. . . . In religious faith Theodoric, like his people, was an Arian. This fact opened a chasm be-

tween the Goths and the Italians, the latter accepting the Nicene creed. . . . Certain it is that Justinian, who had now succeeded to power at Constantinople, resolved to purge the church of heresy as well in the West as in his paternal dominions." The agent of the emperor in the extermination of heresy was Belisarius who had destroyed the Vandal nation.

The Nation Destroyed. "Nearly the whole Gothic nation gathered around the Eternal City, but Belisarius held out until reinforcements arrived from the East, and after a siege of a year and nine days' duration, Rome was delivered from the clutch of her assailants. Vitiges (the Ostrogothic leader) was obliged to burn his tents and retreat (538) before his pursuing antagonist to Ravenna. . . . It was evident that the kingdom of the Goths was in the hour and article of death." Speaking of the final defeat of the Goths in his book, Ridpath says that there was "inflicted on the barbarians a defeat so decisive as to refix the status of Italy. The greater part of the Gothic army perished either by sword or in attempting to cross the river. . . . As for the Goths, they either retired to their native seats beyond the mountains or were absorbed by the Italians."—Id. In chapter 41 of Gibbon's *Roman Empire* is a graphic description of the campaigns of Belisarius against the Vandals and Ostrogoths resulting in their defeat and overthrow. Thus the three Arian nations who refused to renounce their heretical faith were uprooted or subdued and the other Arian peoples turned orthodox leaving the bishop of Rome the undisputed ruler of nations and the corrector of heretics. How completely the prophecy was fulfilled.

Not the Lombards. An attempt is being made to substitute the Lombards for the Heruli in enumerating the three nations destroyed. It is true that the Lombards accepted the Arian faith but they later renounced it and returned to the Catholic fold. Then too they were never destroyed as a nation. In the twelfth century they were the leading maritime nation of the world, and when Napoleon conquered Italy he crowned himself with the crown of the Lombards. Lombardy is to this day one of the most important provinces of Northern Italy. The Lombard kingdom does not fit the specifications of the prophecy regarding one of the three uprooted horns and must therefore be eliminated. It is really the ancestor of the modern Italian kingdom.

7. **Human Eyes.** Daniel 7:7, 8, 20. "Eyes like human eyes."—Fenton. Eyes are symbolic of both vision and wisdom. In Revelation 5:6 Christ is symbolized as a lamb with seven horns and seven eyes to indicate that He is omnipotent in power and omniscient in wisdom. The cherubim are symbolized in the same apocalyptic vision as "living creatures full of

eyes before and behind." Revelation 4:6. The Power symbolized by the little horn is noted for its far-seeing vision, sagacity and diplomacy. The cunning foresight, subtlety, and secret diplomacy of the Papacy and especially of the Jesuits is a well known fact. For centuries the Vatican has been the center of the world's intrigue and diplomacy. During the World War it was called "the listening post of Europe." See Daniel 8:25. "The masterpiece of the world's wisdom."—*Christ's Object Lessons*, p. 78.

Historian's Testimony. Dr. John Lord in his *Beacon Lights of History* says of the Papacy, "It has proved to be the most wonderful fabric of what we call worldly wisdom that our world has seen,—controlling kings, dictating laws to ancient monarchies, and binding the souls of millions with a more perfect despotism than Oriental emperors ever sought or dreamed." "Was there ever such a mystery, so occult are its arts, so subtile its policy, so plausible its pretensions, so certain its shafts?"—Vol. 3, pp. 96, 99. The pope terms himself the "Overseer of overseers." He claims more than human wisdom and foresight and there can be no doubt but his cunning policies and almost uncanny vision are inspired by that mighty angel who before his fall was declared to be "full of wisdom." See Revelation 13:2.

8. **Haughty Expression.** "His look was more stout than his fellows." "Whose expression was more haughty than its companions."—Fenton. See Daniel 8:23. "Fierce expression."—Fenton. This represents a bold, arrogant, pompous and pretentious attitude. The arrogancy of the popes, cardinals, bishops and priests in their dealings with kings and civil governments is a well authenticated characteristic. Claiming to be the vicegerent of Christ on earth and therefore the "King of kings and Lord of lords," popes have compelled kings to hold their stirrups when they mounted their horses, serve them at table, and prostrate themselves before them as slaves before their masters. The way Pope Gregory VII humiliated Henry IV of Germany at the fortress of Canossa in the Alps is an example of the haughty arrogance of papal rulers. The king was compelled to wait three days before the pope would grant him an audience and then he fell prostrate before the pontiff who placed his foot on his neck indicating complete submission as the only road to a restoration to his favor.

9. **A Speaking Mouth.** The horn had "a mouth speaking great things," or "very great things." "A mouth full of proud words."—Moffatt. *Verse 25.* "The word *against* has the meaning of *to the side of*, meaning self-exaltation to a place alongside of God."—*Pulpit Commentary*.Jerome quotes Symmachus as translating this text: "He shall speak as if he were God." Who can fulfill this prediction but the one and only ruler who claims to

be God on earth? Other prophecies of this same power emphasize this same characteristic. Daniel 11:36; Revelation 13:6, 2; Thessalonians 2:3, 4. "Setting himself forth as God."—R.V. Here is a boasting and blasphemous power that would claim unlimited jurisdiction on earth and even assume power and authority that belong alone to God. The decree of the Vatican Council in 1870 enunciating the dogma of papal infallibility, together with the blasphemous titles assumed by and claimed for the pope clearly identifies the speaking horn. It fits no other earthly power but the papacy.

Historical Evidence. To the Emperor Leo, Pope Gregory II said: "All they of the West have their eyes bent on our humility; they regard us as a god on earth."—*History of the Popes*, Ranke, p. 9. Pope Boniface VIII said: "The Pope alone is called most holy, . . . divine monarch, and supreme emperor and king of kings. . . . The Pope is of so great dignity and power that he constitutes one and the same tribunal with Christ, so that whatsoever the Pope does seems to proceed from the mouth of God. . . . The Pope is God on earth."—quoted by Guinness in *Romanism and the Reformation*. Cardinal Bellarmine declared: "All names which in the Scriptures are applied to Christ, by virtue of which it is established that He is over the church, all the same names are applied to the Pope."—*On the Authority of the Councils*, Vol. II, page 17. "The decision of the Pope and the decision of God constitute one decision. . . . Since, therefore, an appeal is always taken from an inferior judge to a superior, as no one is greater than himself, so no appeal holds when made from the Pope to God, because there is one consistory of the Pope himself and of God himself, of which consistory the Pope himself is the key bearer and door-keeper. Therefore no one can appeal from the Pope to God. . . . There is one decision and one curia of God and of the Pope."—Augustinus de Ancona, "On an Appeal from a Decision of the Pope." (From a Latin copy of the writings of Augustinus, in the British Museum.)

Catholic Claims. The following extracts are taken from Ferraris' *Ecclesiastical Dictionary* (Roman Catholic), article, "The Pope":

"The Pope is of so great dignity and so exalted that he is not a mere man, but as it were God, and the vicar of God."

"The Pope is as it were God on earth, sole sovereign of the faithful of Christ, chief king of kings, having plenitude of power, to whom has been entrusted by the omnipotent God direction not only of the earthly but also of the heavenly kingdom."

The following is taken from a papal letter: "We hold on this earth the place of God Almighty."—Pope Leo XIII, in an encyclical letter dated June 20, 1894, "The Great Encyclical Letters of Leo XIII," p. 304.

10. **A Persecuting Power.** Verses 21, 25. "He shall crush the saints of the Most High."—Douay. See Daniel 8:24; 11:33; Matthew 24:21, 22; Revelation 13:7; 17:6. In a standard Catholic work published in 1911 it is boldly claimed that the church has the divine right to "confiscate the property of heretics, imprison their persons, and condemn them to the flames. . . . In our age the right to inflict the severest penalties, even death, belongs to the church. . . . Since experience teaches us that there is no other remedy, . . . the last recourse is the death penalty. . . . There is no graver offense than heresy, . . . and therefore it must be rooted out with fire and sword. It is a Catholic tenet which must be faithfully held, that the extreme penalty not only may, but must be inflicted on obstinate heretics."—*Institutes of Public Ecclesiastical Law.*

Chief Persecutions. "After the signal of open martyrdom had been given in the Canons of Orleans, there followed the extirpation of the Albigenses under the form of a crusade, the establishment of the Inquisition, the cruel attempts to extinguish the Waldenses, the martyrdoms of the Lollards, the cruel wars to exterminate the Bohemians, the burning of Huss and Jerome, and multitudes of other confessors, before the Reformation; and afterwards, the ferocious cruelties practiced in the Netherlands, the martyrdoms of Queen Mary's reign, the extinction by fire and sword of the Reformation in Spain and Italy, by fraud and open persecution in Poland, the Massacre of Bartholomew, the persecution of the Huguenots by the League, the extirpation of the Vaudois, and all the cruelties and prejudices connected with the revocation of the Edict of Nantes. These are the more open and conspicuous facts which explain the prophecy, besides the slow and secret murders of the holy tribunal of the Inquisition."—*The First Two Visions of Daniel*, Revelation T. R. Birks, M. A., London, 1845, pp. 248, 249.

Acknowledge Persecutions. "Our heroes are the Duke of Alva and Catherine de Medici. They knew the Huguenots, and they drove them off the continent. You cannot excite any pity in our souls by whining accounts of Catholic atrocities in the 17th century. We have never written a line in extenuation or palliation of the Inquisition. We never thought it needed a defense."—*Western Watchman*, (Catholic) Nov. 21, 1912. "The church has persecuted. Only a tyro in church history will deny that. . . . One hundred and fifty years after Constantine the Donatists were persecuted, and sometimes put to death. . . . Protestants were persecuted in France and Spain with the full approval of the church authorities. We have always defended the persecution of the Huguenots, and the Spanish Inquisition. Wherever and whenever there is honest Catholicity, there will be a clear distinction drawn between truth and error, and Catholicity and all forms of heresy. When she thinks it good to use physical force, she will use it. . . . But will the Catholic Church give bond that she will not persecute at all? Will she guarantee absolute freedom and equality of all churches and all faiths? The Catholic Church gives no bonds for her good behavior."—*The Western Watchman* (R.C.) Dec. 24, 1908.

"There can be no doubt, therefore, that the church claimed the right to use physical coercion against formal apostates. . . . She adapts her discipline to the times and circumstances in order that it may fulfill its salutary purpose. Her own children are not punished by fines, imprisonment, or other temporal punishments, but by spiritual pains and penalties, and heretics are treated as she treated pagans."—*The Catholic Encyclopedia*, Vol. XI, p. 703, art., "Persecution."

11. **A Lawless Power.** Verse 25 "The times and the law."—R.V. "He shall plan to alter the sacred seasons and the law."—Moffatt. Hebrew students declare that "the time of the law" would be a correct translation. The only part of the law of God that deals with time is the fourth commandment, and that is the commandment that the Papacy has especially altered. "He shall think himself able" is the Douay Version. No power is really able to change God's eternal and unchangeable law. "The man of sin" in 2 Thessalonians 2:3, is translated "the lawless one" by Moffatt, and "the mystery of iniquity" in verse 7 is translated "the mystery of lawlessness" in the Revised Version. Commenting on 2 Thessalonians 2:2-7 the *Catholic Encyclopedia* says: "After studying the picture of Antichrist in St. Paul's epistle to the Thessalonians one easily recognizes the 'man of sin' in Daniel 7:8, 11, 20, 21, where the prophet describes the 'little horn.'"—Vol. 1, p. 560.

Papal Claims: "The pope is of such great authority and power that he can modify, explain, or interpret even divine laws. The pope can modify divine law since his power is not of man but of God, and he acts as vicegerent of God upon the earth with most ample power of binding and loosing his sheep."—*Ecclesiastical Dictionary* (Catholic), by Ferraris, art.: "Pope." "For he can dispense with the law, he can turn injustice into justice by correcting and changing the law, and he has the fullness of power."—*Decretals of Gregory*, book 1, title 7, chapter 3.

"Christ intrusted his office to the chief Pontiff; . . . therefore the chief Pontiff, who is his vicar, will have this power."—Gloss on "Extravagantes Communes," or *Roman Canon Law*, book 1, chap. 1. The papacy changed the Sabbath from the seventh to the first day of the week and boasts of the same. Many other Christian institutions were changed or paganized.

Authority of Pope. Croley quotes Pope Gregory VII as saying: "The Roman Pontiff alone is by right universal. In him alone is the right of making laws. Let all kings kiss the feet of the Pope. His name alone shall be heard in the churches. It is the only name in the world. It is his right to depose kings. His word is not to be repealed by any one. It is to be repealed by himself alone. He is to be judged by none. The church of Rome has never erred; and the Scriptures testify, it shall never err." He also quotes from the bull of Pope Pius against Queen Elizabeth: "This one he (God) hath constituted Prince over all nations, and all kingdoms, that he might pluck up, destroy, dissipate, overturn, plant, and build."

12. **Dominion for 1260 years.** Verse 25. "For three years and a half the saints shall be handed over to him."—Moffatt. Both the law and the saints of the Most High are given into the power of the papacy for three and a half prophetic years or 1260 literal years. "A day for a year" is the rule of prophetic time. Ezekiel 4:6. That the papacy was the most potent ruler of the world for more than twelve centuries is abundantly proved. "From the date of the imperial epistle of Justinian to Pope John, in March, 533, the saints, and times, and laws of the church, may therefore be considered to have been formally delivered into the hands of the Papacy, and this is consequently the true era of the 1260 years." "A Dissertation on the Seals and Trumpets of the Apocalypse," William Cuninghame, pp. 185, 186.

Another Writer. "In A.D. 533 came the memorable letter, or decree, of Justinian recognizing the supremacy of the Pope, and in A.D. 538 came the stroke with the sword at Rome cleaving the way, and setting on the papal throne the first of the new order of popes,—the kingly rulers of the state. The prophecy assigned a period of 1260 years to this supremacy. At the end of that period came equally significant and epoch-making events, advertising to the world the end of the prophetic period. Just 1260 years from the decree of A.D. 533 in favor of the papacy, came a decree in 1793, aimed at the papacy; just 1260 years from that stroke of the sword at Rome against the papacy."—*The Hand of God in History*, W.A. Spicer, page 110.

[**Author's note:** Just as in A.D. 533 the decree was made, and in 538, the sword was given in defense of the decree; so, in 1793 the decree was made, but not followed through until 1798, when General Berthier took the Bishop at Rome captive and he died in captivity.]

Decree of Justinian. "Justinian, pious, fortunate, renowned, triumphant, Emperor, consul etc., to John the most holy Archbishop of our city of Rome, and patriarch. Rendering honor to the apostolic chair, and to your holiness, as has been always and is our wish, and honoring your blessedness as a father; we have hastened to bring to the knowledge of your holiness all matters relating to the state of the churches. It having been at all times our great desire to preserve the unity of your apostolic chair, and the constitution of the holy churches of God which has obtained hitherto, and still obtains.

"Therefore we have made no delay in subjecting and uniting to your holiness all the priests of the whole east. For this reason we have thought fit to bring to your notice the present matters of disturbance; though they are manifest and unquestionable, and always firmly held and declared by the whole priesthood, according to the doctrine of your apostolic chair. For we cannot suffer that anything which relates to the state of the church, however manifest and unquestionable, should be moved without the knowledge of your holiness, who are the head of all the holy churches, for in all things, as we have already declared, we are anxious to increase the honor and authority of your apostolic chair."

Ended Controversy. This decree of the Emperor Justinian brought to a close a long and bitter struggle between the bishops of several cities as to who was the greatest. This contest was especially severe between the bishops of Constantinople and Rome. On March 25th of the same year the emperor wrote to the Archbishop of Constantinople, acknowledging the letter to the Archbishop of Rome as his, and maintaining that "he is the true and effective corrector of heretics." In his "Norville," published in 534, Justinian decreed further: "We therefore decree that the most holy Pope of the elder Rome, is the first of all the priesthood, and the most blessed archbishop of Constantinople, the New Rome, shall hold second rank, after the holy apostolic chair of the elder Rome."—131st on Eccl. titles and privileges,—Croley.

13. **The Judgment.** Verse 26. "Then the court of justice shall sit and his dominion shall be taken away, to be destroyed and ended for all time."—Moffatt. An important part of the work of the judgment is to deal with the papal power represented by the little horn. The judgment is pictured in verses 9 and 10. The time of this scene is placed between the close of the 1260 years and the coming of Christ which is pictured in verses 11-14. In the eighth chapter the exact time of the beginning of the judgment is given. Daniel was watching the little horn when his attention was attracted to this scene in heaven; the tribunal that would bring an end to the dominion and career of the papal power. "I watched until an Assize (court) was held, when a primaeval Being sat on the throne of justice."—Moffatt.

The Supreme Court. The court here described has a jury or a number of judges besides the Chief Justice. "Thrones were placed."—R. V. "Thrones as here used means not so much a royal throne as the seat of a judge."—Behrmann. The same tribunal is pictured in Revelation 4 and the number of thrones given is 24 which are in a circle around the throne of God. "It is the grand inquest of eternity now set for the awarding of doom and destiny upon these beasts, especially the last, blasphemous eleventh horn." *Voices from Babylon*, Seiss, p. 186. It is a chariot or movable throne that is described with "wheels as burning fire." The description is similar to that of Ezekiel 1 and 10. It is doubtless the cherubim chariot of living creatures or angels described in Psalm 104:3; 68:17, 18; 18:10. The scene is indescribably glorious. "A swift stream of fire issued forth from before Him."—Douay. "A stream of fire poured from His presence; millions of angels were at His service and myriads attended Him. The court was held and the records were opened."

Dominion Destroyed. A faithful record of the words and deeds of the little horn has been kept and from this record the lawless and anti-Christian papal power is tried and found wanting by the Supreme Court of the Universe. The first act of the tribunal is to bring to an end the absolute dominion of the papacy. Verse 26 evidently refers to the gradual loss of papal spiritual dominion "over the spirits of men." This is a far worse dominion than temporal sovereignty. The wounding of the papal power by the sword of the Spirit during the great Reformation and the final stroke by the sword of Napoleon in 1798, paved the way for the gradual decreasing of spiritual authority as God's final message gains headway in the earth. With the beginning of the judgment in heaven began the judgment-hour message on earth which is a warning against the dominion of the papacy over the souls of earth's inhabitants. See Revelation 14:6-14. An important part of this message is to reveal to mankind the mediatorial work of Christ in the heavenly sanctuary in contrast to the false and counterfeit papal system by which her priests bind human souls "with a more perfect despotism than Oriental emperors ever sought or dreamed."

A World Message. The message that destroys the spiritual dominion of the papacy is world-wide. It lightens the whole earth with its glory. As this heaven-sent message increases in scope and power, the dominion of the papal monarchy over men's souls will decrease "to consume and to destroy it unto the end." It may gain headway in a temporal and political sense, but its spiritual dominion decreases. Under the latter rain the whole earth will be brought to an intelligent decision between the true and false priestly and mediatorial systems. The papacy will be completely unveiled before the world and every honest hearted soul will obey the call: "Come out of her My people."

14. **Warfare Continues.** Verses 21, 22. As God's message increases in extent and power His spiritual dominion over the souls of men is extended until finally the earth itself is given to the saints. But during the final struggle for the supremacy of the earth the papal power will continue its warfare to the very end. The struggle of the ages has been over the dominion of the earth and its temporal sovereignty depends upon its spiritual rulership. In the final struggle God's remnant people will again be persecuted. Revelation 12:17. Many are to be purged and made white by persecution "even in the time of the end." Daniel 11:35. "Throughout the land the papacy is piling up her lofty and massive structures, in the secret recesses of which her former persecutions are to be repeated." [*Testimonies for the Church*] (Vol. 5, p. 449).

15. **Final Destruction.** Verses 11, 12. The dreadful symbolic beast represents all earthly kingdoms including the papacy from the downfall of imperial Rome to the coming of Christ. All are destroyed because of their relation to the blasphemous papal power. The little horn dominates the world to the end and the whole world must share its doom. See Revelation 18. The "burning flame" that destroys the beast is first, that which proceeds from the glory of Christ at His second advent; and second, the final lake of fire. 2 Thessalonians 2:8; Revelation 19:20. Verse 12 is doubtless a parenthetical statement to show the contrast between the downfall of the nations represented by the first three beasts and the Roman beast and especially Papal Rome. Babylon, Medo-Persia, and Grecia lost their dominion when they were overthrown although they continued to live as a part of the state that supplanted them. Not so with the papacy.

16. **Kingdom of God.** The little horn power is supplanted by the kingdom of God. Verses 13, 14. Christ is the commander-in-chief of the forces that wins back the dominion and kingdom of this earth for the Father. He is the "Lord strong and mighty, the Lord mighty in battle."—Psalm 24:8. To Christ the Victor comes the "first dominion" that He might restore it to the redeemed family of Adam. See Micah 4:8. Christ wins back the lost dominion that He might return it to the saints of the Most High. Daniel 7:18, 22, 27. Those against whom the little horn had made war and prevailed for ages will then rule over the very dominion held by their enemy and in which they were so long pilgrims and strangers. Their rule is not to be temporary but they will "take the kingdom, and possess the kingdom for ever, even for ever and ever."

Effect on Daniel. Verse 28. "My thoughts greatly alarmed me: I lost color, but kept everything in mind."—Moffatt. When the vision was first given, Daniel was grieved and troubled. Verse 15. The explanation of Gabriel regarding the career of the little horn left him still more puzzled and grieved. Another vision was necessary to further clear up the mystery of the little horn power and it was given two years later. Then Daniel fainted and was sick for some time before he could care for the duties of his office. With such a picture of cruel bondage and persecution before him Daniel could not rejoice, even with the prospect of the coming kingdom of glory, so far in the future. We can now rejoice that the long period of papal supremacy is in the past and that the kingdom of heaven is at hand.

Worse than Savages. "And yet what crimes and abominations have not been committed in the name of the church? . . . Ah, interrogate the Albigenses, the Waldenses, the shades of Jerome of Prague, of Huss, of Savonarola, of Cranmer, of Coligny, of Galileo; interrogate the martyrs of the Thirty Years War, and those who were slain by the dragonnades of Louis XIV, those who fell by the hand of Alva and Charles IX; go to Smithfield, and Paris on Saint Bartholomew; think of gunpowder plots and inquisitions, and intrigues and tortures, all vigorously carried on under the cloak of Religion—barbarities worse than those of savages, inflicted at the command of the ministers of a gospel of love! . . . Whether exaggerated or not, they were more disgraceful than the persecutions of Christians by Roman emperors."—*Beacon Lights of History*, Dr. John Lord, Vol. 3, pp. 100, 101.

Bibliography

Asscherick, David. "How Not to Get the Mark of the Beast." Sermon on-line. Discover Prophecy: A Bible Seminar, seminar 19 of 24. Available from http://video.google.com/videoplay?docid=-6229218635583238951#. Internet; accessed 18 October 2009.

Bunch, Taylor G. "The Book of Daniel." Typewritten manuscript, 1950. Department of Archives and Special Collections, Del Webb Memorial Library, Loma Linda University, Loma Linda, CA.

____. "The Revelation." Typewritten manuscript, 1952. Center for Adventist Research, James White Library, Andrews University, Berrien Springs, MI.

____. *The Seven Epistles of Christ*. Washington, DC: Review and Herald, 1947.

Cossentine, E. E., ed. *Principles of Life From the Word of God*. Mountain View, CA: Pacific Press Publishing Association, 1952.

Croly, George. *The Apocalypse of St. John*. London: Gilbert and Rivington, 1838.

Davidson, Richard M. "Sanctuary Typology." In *Symposium on Revelation: Book 1*, 99-130. Daniel and Revelation Committee Series. Vol. 6. Hagerstown, MD: Review and Herald, 1992.

de Kock, Edwin. *Christ and Antichrist in Prophecy and History*. Edinburg, TX: Diadone Enterprises, 2001.

____. "The Truth About 666 and the Mediterranean Apostasy." 3 vols. Digital manuscript. July 20, 2009.

Doukhan, Jacques B. *Secrets of Daniel*. Hagerstown, MD: Review and Herald, 2000.

____. *Secrets of Revelation*. Hagerstown, MD: Review and Herald, 2002

Durant, Will. *The Age of Faith*. Vol. 2. *The Story of Civilization*. New York: Simon and Schuster, 1950, 784. Quoted in Alberto R. Treiyer, *Apocalypse: Seals and Trumpets*, 122. Siloam Springs, AR: Distinctive Messages, 2005.

Edersheim, Alfred. *The Life and Times of Jesus the Messiah*. 2 vols. New York: Longmans, Green, and Company, 1883.

Ford, Desmond. *Daniel*. Nashville, TN: Southern Publishing Association, 1978.

Fox, John. *Fox's Book of Martyrs*. Ed. William Byron Forbush. Grand Rapids, MI: Zondervan, 1962.

Gibbons, James. *The Catholic Mirror*. 23 September 1893. Quoted in Taylor G. Bunch, "The Revelation," 186. Typewritten manuscript, Center for Adventist Research, James White Library, Andrews University, Berrien Springs, MI, 1952.

Hamilton, Bernard. *The Medieval Inquisition: Foundations of Medieval History*. New York: Holmes and Meier Publishing, 1981.

Haskell, Stephen N. *The Cross and Its Shadow*. Nashville, TN: Southern Publishing Association, 1970.

____. *The Story of the Seer of Patmos*. Nashville, TN: Southern Publishing Association, 1905.

Hiscox, Edward T. "Transference of the Sabbath." Quoted in Taylor G. Bunch, "The Revelation," 186. Typewritten manuscript, Center for Adventist Research, James White Library, Andrews University, Berrien Springs, MI, 1952.

Hislop, Alexander. *The Two Babylons: Papal Worship*. United States of America: Loizeaux Brothers, 1959.

Hitti, Phillip K. *The Arabs: A Short History*. Washington, DC: Regnery Publishing, 1996.

Hughes, Philip E. *The Book of Revelation*. Grand Rapids, MI: Eerdmans, 1990.

Kirsch, Jonathan. *The Grand Inquisitor's Manual*. New York: HarperOne, 2008.

Knox, Ronald Arbuthnot. *The Holy Bible: A translation from the Latin Vulgate in the light of the Hebrew and Greek Originals*. New York: Sheed and Ward, 1950.

Leist, Fritz. *Der Gefangene des Vatikans*. Munich: Kosch, 1971.

Luther, Martin. Letter to Spalatin. Feb. 23, 1520. Quoted in Loren Partridge, *The Art of Renaissance Rome*, 159. New York: Harry N. Abrams, Inc., 1996.

Maxwell, Mervyn C. *God Cares.* 2 vols. Nampa, ID: Pacific Press, 1981.

Oxentenko, Michael. "Daniel and Revelation." Typewritten manuscript, 1995, Center for Adventist Research, James White Library, Andrews University, Berrien Springs, MI.

Ozment, Steve. *The Age of Reform 1250-1550: An Intellectual and Religious History of Late Medieval and Reformation Europe.* New Haven: Yale University Press, 1980, 8. Quoted in C. Mervyn Maxwell, *God Cares.* 2:125. Boise, ID, Pacific Press, 1985.

Paulien, Jon. " The Seven Seals." In *Symposium on Revelation: Book 1*, 199-243. Daniel and Revelation Committee Series. Vol. 6. Hagerstown, MD: Review and Herald, 1992.

Pfandl, Gerhard. *Daniel: The Seer of Babylon.* Hagerstown, MD: Review and Herald, 2004.

____. "The Remnant Church and the Spirit of Prophecy." In *Symposium on Revelation: Book 2*, 295-333. Daniel and Revelation Committee Series. Vol. 7. Hagerstown, MD: Review and Herald, 1992.

Ridpath, John Clarke. *History of the World.* Vol. 3. Cincinnati, OH: The Jones Bros. Publishing Co., 1894.

Seiss, Joseph A. *The Apocalypse: An Exposition of the Book of Revelation.* New York: Charles C. Cook, 1900. Reprint, Grand Rapids, MI: Kregel Publications, 1987.

____. *Voices from Babylon.* Philadelphia, PA: Porter and Coates, 1879.

The Seventh-day Adventist Commentary. Ed.F. D. Nichol. 2d ed. 7 vols. Washington, DC: Review and Herald, 1957.

Shea, William H. *Daniel: A Reader's Guide.* Nampa, ID: Pacific Press, 2005.

____. "The Mighty Angel and His Message." In *Symposium on Revelation: Book 1*, 279-325. Daniel and Revelation Committee Series. Vol. 6. Hagerstown, MD: Review and Herald, 1992.

____. *Selected Studies on Prophetic Interpretation.* Daniel and Revelation Committee Series. Vol. 1. Hagerstown, MD: Review and Herald, 1992.

____. "Unity of Daniel." In *Symposium on Daniel*, 165-255. Daniel and Revelation Committee Series, Vol. 2. Hagerstown, MD: Review and Herald, 1986.

____. "The Year-Day Principle: Part 1." In *Selected Studies on Prophetic Interpretation.* 67-104. Daniel and Revelation Committee Series. Vol. 1. Hagerstown, MD: Review and Herald, 1992.

Smith, Uriah. *The Prophecies of Daniel and Revelation*. Nashville, TN: Southern Publishing Association, 1944.

Stefanovic, Ranko. *Revelation of Jesus Christ: Commentary on the Book of Revelation*. Berrien Springs, MI: Andrews University Press, 2002.

Stevens, Jerry A. *VICARIUS FILII DEI: An Annotated Timeline;Connecting Links Between Revelation 13:16-18, the Infamous Number 666, and the Papal Headdress*. Berrien Springs, MI: Adventists Affirm, 2009.

Storrs, George. *Midnight Cry*. May 4, 1843. Vol. 4, No. 5, 6, p. 47. Quoted in Uriah Smith, *The Prophecies of Daniel and the Revelation*, 538-539. Washington, DC: Review and Herald, 1944.

Stott, John R. W. *What Christ Thinks of the Church*. In *Preaching for Today*. Grand Rapids, MI: Eerdmans, 1958.

Swain, Joseph Ward. *The Ancient World*. 2 vols. New York: Harper & Row, 1950, 2:40-42. Quoted in Mervyn C. Maxwell, *God Cares*. 1:111. Boise, ID, Pacific Press, 1985.

Syed, Ameer Ali. *Short History of the Saracens*. London: Macmillan, 1916.

Thiele, Edwin R. "Outline Studies in Revelation." Typewritten manuscript, 1949. Center for Adventist Research, James White Library, Andrews University, Berrien Springs, MI.

Thomson, W. H. *The Great Argument*. London: Sampson Low, Marston, Searle, and Rivington, 1884.

Townsend, George Alfred. *The New World Compared with the Old*. Hartford, CT: S. M. Betts and Company, 1869.

Treiyer, Albert. *The Day of Atonement and the Heavenly Judgment: From the Pentateuch to Revelation*. Siloam Springs, AR: Creation Enterprises International, 1992.

____. *The Seals and the Trumpets*. Siloam Springs, AR: Distinctive Messages, 2005.

Turner, Samuel H. *Outline Studies in the Book of Revelation*, 13. Quoted in Taylor G. Bunch, *The Seven Epistles of Christ*, 183-184. Washington, DC: Review and Herald, 1947.

Wesley, John. *Explanatory Notes Upon the New Testament*. New York: Lane and Scott, 1850.

White, Ellen G. *Acts of the Apostles*. Mountain View, CA: Pacific Press, 1911.

____. *Counsels on Health*. Mountain View, CA: Pacific Press, 1951.

____. *Counsels on Stewardship.* Washington, DC: Review and Herald, 1940.

____. *The Desire of Ages.* Mountain View, CA: Pacific Press, 1940.

____. *Early Writings.* Washington, DC: Review and Herald, 1945.

____. *Education.* Mountain View, CA: Pacific Press, 1952.

____. *The Great Controversy Between Christ and Satan.* Mountain View, CA: Pacific Press, 1950.

____. Letter 98, 1900. Quoted in *The Seventh-day Adventist Bible Commentary,* ed. F. D. Nichol, 2d ed. 7:979. Washington, DC: Review and Herald, 1980.

____. Letter 39, 1902. Quoted in *The Seventh-day Adventist Bible Commentary,* ed. F. D. Nichol, 2d ed. 7:985-986. Washington, DC: Review and Herald, 1980.

____. Manuscript 59, 1900. Quoted in *The Seventh-day Adventist Bible Commentary,* ed. F. D. Nichol, 2d ed. 7:971. Washington, DC: Review and Herald, 1980.

____. *Patriarchs and Prophets.* Mountain View, CA: Pacific Press, 1958.

____. *Prophets and Kings.* Mountain View, CA: Pacific Press, 1943.

____. *Selected Messages.* 3 vols. Washington, DC: Review and Herald, 1958.

____. *Testimonies for the Church.* 9 vols. Mountain View, CA: Pacific Press, 1948.

____. *Testimonies to Ministers and Gospel Workers.* Mountain View, CA: Pacific Press, 1962.

Whalley, Albert. *The Red Letter Days of Israel,* 125, London: Marshall Bros., 1926. Quoted in Uriah Smith, *The Prophecies of Daniel and Revelation,* 741. Nashville, TN: Southern Publishing Association, 1944.

Williams, Henry Smith. *The Historians' History of the World.* Vol. 4. New York: Encyclopedia Brittanica, 1907.

Wright, C. H. H. *Daniel and His Prophecies.* London: 1906, 168. Quoted in Taylor G. Bunch, "The Book of Daniel," 98. Typewritten manuscript, Department of Archives and Special Collections, Del Webb Memorial Library, Loma Linda University, Loma Linda, CA, 1950.

Wylie, J. A. *The History of the Waldenses.* London: Cassell and Co., 1860.